The First Three Books of the West Baden Murders Series

REAPER

RETRIBUTION

SINS OF THE FATHER

Patrick J. O'Brian

PUBLISHED BY FIDELI PUBLISHING INC.

ISBN: 978-1-60414-775-9

This manuscript is dedicated to firefighters,
police officers, emergency medical technicians and paramedics
everywhere who put their lives on the line every day.

Acknowledgements

I owe many thanks to Troy Smith, John Leach, Erica Cosgrove, Joey Oliver, and especially Troy Lobosky, because without their help, this book would not have the degree of accuracy I wanted it to. Additional thanks to Brad Wiemer and Korby Sommers.

Thanks also to Jim Lenox, Jennifer Sorrells, Troy Lobosky, Richard Cranor, and Rick Shellabarger for their time. And to Chris Mangas for use of his scythe for creative purposes.

As always, thanks to Kendrick at KLS for making a spectacular cover. Check out KLS Digital at www.klsdigital.com

Also check out the author's website at

www.pjobooks.com

to see the latest works by Patrick J. O'Brian,
a history of the West Baden Springs Hotel,
and where to purchase his books.

Other novels by
Patrick J. O'Brian include:

The Fallen

The Brotherhood

Retribution: Book Two of the West Baden Murders Series

Sins of the Father: Book Three of the West Baden Murders Series

Snowbound: Book Four of the West Baden Murders Series

Ghosts of West Baden: Book Five of the West Baden Murders Series

The Doomsday Clock: Book Six of the West Baden Murders Series

Stolen Time

Six Days

Dysfunction

The Sleeping Phoenix

Sawmill Road

Red Rain

Sin Killer

Non-fiction projects by Patrick J. O'Brian include:
Risen from the Ashes: The History of the West Baden Springs Hotel

www.pjobooks.com

REAPER

Book One of the West Baden Murders Series

This story takes place circa 1998 to keep pace with the true historical events at the West Baden Springs Hotel.

Chapter 1

A stiff breeze darted across the open porch of a white Indiana farmhouse as a bare foot stepped gingerly onto the cold wooden planks.

Leaves from several bushes along the house shivered, rustling as though a thunderstorm was coming, while the last flickers of a dying candle burned inside a jack-o-lantern.

Halloween night neared its end.

Angela Clouse plucked the lid off the gutted vegetable, putting an end to the candle's fading existence with a quick puff of breath. Her nose took in the unpleasant combination of burnt wax and decaying pumpkin innards. For a moment, she stared at the single crooked tooth in the pumpkin her son had insisted on carving himself with the grin of a proud parent. Replacing the top, she suddenly felt uneasy standing in the cold.

In the middle of nowhere.

Looking across the spacious yard she could find nothing out of the ordinary. During daylight hours, Angie could view what she called God's paintbrush, with all the leaves changing colors before their seesaw descent toward the ground.

Familiar smells of freshly-cut wood, horse manure, and apple cider from neighboring houses let her know she had escaped the confines of nearby Bloomington and the Indiana University campus. At thirty-one years of age, it was time for her to start living for herself.

Her car sat in front of the old barn, and the dogs were quietly within sight, reassuring her the property was safe. A chill ran from the bottom of her feet, into her bloodstream, telling her it was time to return to the warmth of the house.

A white paper ghost swinging freely from the top of the porch nearly struck her head as she turned around. Angie stepped inside, locking the doorknob and deadbolt immediately.

Trick-or-treat time was definitely over.

As midnight drew near, the selection of movies on television would be worse than the horror sections in the local video stores. Taking a seat in her comfortable plush chair, Angie flipped through the channels until she found the beginning of *Night of the Living Dead* on a local station.

She loved how the flickers and the black and white footage added to the dreary effect of the movie. A familiar vehicle pulled into the cemetery as the opening credits rolled, and she knew what happened next. Johnny would always tease, then unwittingly die at the hands of the first zombie.

"They're coming to get you, Barbara," Angie said in her best Vincent Price voice as she stood and darted to the kitchen, wanting some popcorn before the movie got to the good parts. She had the entire weekend to sleep in if she stayed up too late.

As she opened the bag of popcorn, one of the dogs barked from the backyard, catching her attention. Angie peered out the window, finding nothing out of the ordinary, and dismissed Spot, her husband's Dalmatian, as paranoid schizophrenic.

"That dog barks at everything," she commented to herself, surprised he hadn't barked at her when she stepped outside.

She stuck the bag in the microwave, set the timer, and took a seat as the cordless phone rang beside her.

"Hello?" she answered, eyes glued to the screen as Barbara and Johnny emerged from their car, ready to place flowers on the gravesite after a grueling drive.

"Hey, Ang, it's Margo," one of her friends said from the other end. "I figured you'd still be up."

"Are you tricked out too?"

"I spent half the night keeping the kids out of the candy and the other half getting them to bed. They wanted to watch some scary movie-thon on satellite."

"Oh, I know," Angie replied. "It took forever to get Zach to bed. We were out until eight-thirty, then I had kids coming out here until almost ten."

"It must be rough living in total isolation. At least you don't have neighbor kids screaming, crying, and hitting softballs through your window," Margo teased. "How is it alone these days?"

Angie stood to fetch her popcorn.

"I'm getting by. With Zach at preschool, I'm getting a lot more done with the business, and a lot of clients have called about my new software. Referrals are my best friends lately."

"I thought I was your best friend."

"You are, but you don't pay my bills."

Opening the microwave, Angie took out the bag, opened it, and let the steam filter out as she took a diet cola from the refrigerator. She took a moment to look in the mirror, noticing how much better her dark hair looked without a failed perm. Puffy hair always seemed to accent her already small nose, and most of her do-it-yourself hair jobs made her look like a rocker from the Eighties.

She agreed with her mother that her hair looked much better without winding curls, which brought out the natural beauty her husband always said she had.

"Another couple of days and I'll be out with another software upgrade for returning clients, which will make them very happy," Angie said, sitting down to find Johnny and the zombie struggle as Barbara watched in horror.

"You still haven't really answered my question."

"What's that?"

"Has anything changed between you and Paul lately?"

Angie visualized a time when she could cuddle with her husband in front of a warm fire on cool nights like this. She missed the companionship, but things had changed between them recently.

"Nothing new between us. He's been busy with both jobs and I-"

A thumping noise from upstairs diverted her attention from both the movie and her conversation. She missed whatever question Margo had asked.

"Ang? You there?"

"Sorry. I just heard something from upstairs."

"Probably Zach feeling the effects of too much candy."

"Maybe," Angie said, standing up. "Let me go check on him and I'll call you right—"

A few abrupt clicks came over the phone line, cutting her sentence short as a dead silence took the place of what normally might have been a dial tone.

"You there?" Angie asked, getting no response.

Her phone was completely dead.

Sounds of thunder in the distance offset the notion that it was anything but a storm downing the phone lines. Still, it was supposed to be a light rain, if anything, that evening.

Setting the phone on the coffee table, Angie looked up at the ceiling where the noise had originated. The spot above her was neither Zach's room, nor the bathroom. Her son had no reason to be rummaging through the spare bedroom, and after a full night in town, any four-year-old would probably be asleep soon after his head hit the pillow.

Darkness encumbered the den as she walked through it, sidestepping furniture on her way to the stairs. Since her husband had moved out Angie seldom used the room, or the large fireplace inside it. It once served as a place where they worked and played as a family. Now the house was segmented into seldom-used rooms, each with a particular purpose.

Angie paused, taking a moment to look outside one of the windows. There were no new vehicles in the driveway, and nothing else seemed different than a few minutes before when she stepped onto the porch.

Once again, she heard a thump, then a few footsteps. Zach was too small to make footsteps heard so easily. Now she was spooked, but her son was up there.

Like everything else in her life, the furniture in the den was very orderly and easily avoided. She reached the bottom of the stairs, took hold of the solid oak railing and looked up, seeing only a slight flicker of light from above, off to the right.

A glow illuminated the lower half of the hallway wall, though the light was quite dim.

There were no candles upstairs, and Zach had no nightlight, leaving her curious where such an illumination might come from. Flipping the light switch beside her, Angie took in a cautious breath when the light above failed to come on. Strangely, it worked just fine when she tucked her son into bed earlier, leaving her very apprehensive about investigating the noises from above.

Cautiously, she ascended the stairs, keeping her eyes focused on the flickers. Her son's bedroom door on the left appeared closed. The light source had to originate from the hallway, the bathroom, or the spare bedroom, where the noise apparently came from.

Something strange was going on, and she knew Zach would not play Halloween tricks at his age. He was too young to understand anything about the holiday aside from costumes and candy.

Still, it was the witching holiday and she felt uneasy about what awaited her atop the stairs.

Feeling reasonably certain she had kept every door locked while she was out with Zach, Angie could not fathom how anyone might enter the residence without a key. An uneasy feeling Zach was not awake nagged at her, and none of the protective dogs were in the house. She had to check on her son and know everything was safe before returning Margo's call.

Assuming, of course, the phone still worked.

Clutching the handrail, Angie reached the top of the stairs, slowly peering to the right where the eerie orange glow appeared the most intense. Her eyes widened, taking in the horror at the end of the hall where the flicker of a candle's flame peered through the carved portions of a jack-o-lantern with a single, crooked tooth. Thinking it impossible, she looked closer to see if it was the one from the front porch.

One in the same.

Low light was not the reason visibility was so bad, but rather a large clump eclipsing the Halloween decoration. Squinting to see better, Angie was drawn to the object, focusing intently as she walked along the hallway floor, realizing, much to her horror, the object was a body and this was no prank.

Her eyes had adjusted enough to the darkness that she could make out shapes, even from the dim orange glow. On either side of the clump, she could see tiny hands, rigidly contorted into a half fist. One leg appeared buckled at the knee, sticking upward, leaving little doubt about exactly what she was viewing.

She dared not look at the head, feeling the evidence before her was compelling enough to warrant the numbing sensation creeping through her body.

Drawing her hand to her mouth in a gasp, Angie shrank away from the sight, feeling nothing but utter shock that someone had violated her home, and harmed the most precious thing in her life.

Her child.

Instinctively, Angie reached for the door behind her, where Zach had gone to bed just hours before, wanting to check on him to make certain she wasn't falling victim to a Halloween prank. After swiping at, and missing the knob, she turned to look for it, but heard a noise from the bathroom at the far end of the hall. The light from the jack-o-lantern was momentarily blocked, distracting her from Zach's room.

She turned to see a figure streak across the hallway toward her, then felt a sharp pain in her right shoulder as a sharp object gleamed in the low light before penetrating her skin.

Leaving her no time to react, or assess the danger she was in, the blade swung back, then toward her again. Barely ducking from the deadly swing, Angie darted down the stairs, blood dripping from her wound as the attacker yanked his weapon from the wall, taking chase.

As quickly as she descended the stairs, he seemed equally nimble. She reached the bottom of the staircase, cutting right as the blade struck the wall behind her, forcing an involuntary shriek from her mouth.

Her attacker spent a moment freeing his weapon, giving her an opportunity to reach the kitchen and the freedom of the backdoor. So many times the solid wooden door had given her a welcome retreat to the beauty and clean air of the country outside. Now it could provide freedom from certain death if she could just get it open.

Unlocking the doorknob, she tugged on the door, but it would not budge.

"Deadbolt," she stammered, nervously turning the lock.

Finally swinging the door open, she started for the porch, but felt a sharp, painful sensation rip through her back, as the breath was knocked from her body.

Paralyzed with pain and terror, Angie looked down at her chest, seeing the blade of a sickle or scythe, covered in her own blood, piercing her upper torso from behind.

Before she could contemplate escape, or the nature of her wound, the killer yanked the weapon, and her with it, back into the house. Her muffled screams went unheard through the vacant countryside as the killer went to work with his curved, deadly weapon.

Chapter 2

A single brown cowboy boot with a gold tip on the toe stepped across the red *DANGER DO NOT ENTER* tape, followed by its counterpart as their owner stood a moment, hands firmly cupped on his waist, admiring his work. A photo of him at that moment would have mimicked any 20th century inventor beside his life's greatest accomplishment.

Naturally, the construction of the West Baden Springs Hotel was not Paul Clouse's own work, but he was a crucial part of the crew working on the restoration of the hotel to its previous glory. And to think, it was partly by accident he was working on one of the most interesting buildings in the world, right in his home state.

Standing at one of the four major entrances in the hotel's atrium, Clouse looked like the busy construction workers around him, wearing a hard hat as he stared at the glass dome 200 feet above him. Sunlight could stream downward much of the day, and the chandelier served as more of a centerpiece than a source of light during the evening hours. The thought of such a large, self-supported dome still awed him, considering it was built during an era when domes were rare, particularly in the States.

Before the National Preservation Society stepped in, the hotel had fallen to ruins, and one entire wall had literally fallen, prompting the group's action to begin funding the reconstruction of the nationally accredited landmark.

Clouse recalled his early graduate work at Indiana University, majoring in architecture. He created a comprehensive blueprint of the hotel as part of the final project for one of his more challenging courses. At the time, the hotel lay in ruins with overgrown weeds and bushes, and Clouse had one of his friends on the county police department sneak him inside.

Beyond the faded paint, dust, and cobwebs, Clouse had found the beauty that drew visitors from around the world during the hotel's heyday. He took photos of various rooms, learned the layout, and discovered what held the hotel together.

That was the easy part.

Drawing six stories of floors in the building's unusual shape, complete with glass dome, proved much tougher. It took him another month and three more visits to complete a detailed blueprint.

He got an 'A' on the project, but memories of the blueprint and his studies in architecture faded after his appointment to the Bloomington Fire Department.

After a year-and-a-half on the fire department, he considered finishing work on his master's degree because it was so close to completion, but found an intriguing article in the newspaper about the restoration of the hotel, so he pursued a different avenue. His love for historical landmarks, and an opportunity to see parts of the hotel few others could, prompted him to show his blueprints to David Landamere, the project leader, and the creative foreman for Kieffer Construction, the team contracted to remodel the hotel.

In a way, it was the perfect arrangement. Landamere hired Clouse as a part-time consultant, mostly for the use of his blueprints to save valuable time. It turned out the two had similar ideas, and knew how to save both time and money in the construction process. Clouse was getting paid for something he already loved.

"Morning, Paul," Landamere said from behind, patting Clouse on the back.

"Hey, Dave," Clouse replied, rubbing his chin, then the thick mustache above the smirk on his lips. "Ready to walk the grounds?"

Every week on Wednesday or Thursday, depending on his schedule at the fire department, Clouse met Landamere for a tour of the hotel grounds to see what areas needed immediate attention, and which areas took priority in the restoration.

"It's a little nippy out there, Paul," Landamere commented. "They say it might snow today."

"This whole winter's supposed to be bad."

For a moment, both looked at the atrium where guests had once relaxed, danced, and viewed lavish entertainment night after night. Intricate, detailed murals stood in sharp green, gold, and red colors along every wall and pillar. Every wall, ceiling, and floor displayed crafted designs that were beyond traditional American vision or make. Almost every square inch was completed with fresh paint, looking exactly as they had been when the hotel was renovated and updated in 1917.

Looking across the atrium was like staring at the opposite end of a football field. People could not simply walk across it without gazing at the designs above them in amazement. Without the benefit of furnishings, it echoed whenever people walked across the marble floor or spoke out loud.

To Clouse, it was like stepping into a marvelous classic church, only more vast.

Marble parquet, a form of beautiful, shiny tiles joined to form intricate leaf and various Indian designs now covered less than half the floor. Part of it was being replaced by new carpet of similar designs in the next few months. The move was neither cost-effective, nor practical in keeping the hotel historically accurate, but it was necessary. Like several other items in the hotel, the marble tile had been imported almost a century prior, and could not be replicated cheaply or identically. Carpet was the only realistic alternative in replacing the damaged areas.

Above him, Clouse could see five more floors before the beginning of the dome and the two dozen metallic ribs that kept it towering above guests and rooms alike for years. Several rooms had small balconies where guests would be able to step out and see the activities in the atrium below. Along the walls of the round atrium were detailed paintings that matched the floor in both color and design.

After every third room stood a mammoth eggshell-colored pillar that almost gave the firefighter the impression he was back in church as a kid, with columns reaching for the sky and paintings of the Virgin Mary looking down on him. Of course, the hotel's artwork wasn't biblical in nature as the Greco-Roman theme continued to dominate the walls.

Church scared Clouse to death during his childhood, but the atrium provided a calming effect whenever he stepped inside.

Restoration would give the hotel back its original look, hopefully attracting buyers who would finish the multi-million-dollar job. More than anything, Clouse wanted to see that dream become a reality and be around for the completion. Every day off from his city job he spent visiting the landmark to find something new on the grounds, or inside. He could envision the final product, and strangely enough, had an idea of how to make it happen.

"You know how much cheaper it would have been just to tear it down and build a new one?" Landamere asked, looking from the grand fireplace to his right, back to his designer.

"But then it's not restoration, is it?" Clouse replied with a grin, knowing exactly what specifications the NPS had laid before them.

Both men walked through the open entrance to the hotel lobby. Unlike the atrium they had just come from, the hallway was gutted and barren of decor. Much of the hotel was still skeletal in appearance, leaving only plasterboard, wood, and drywall framing on the upper floors where guest rooms once housed hundreds of visitors at a time. Only the atrium and selected primary rooms were being redone for the time being.

"So how are things going with you and the wife?" Landamere asked, knowing his favorite consultant appeared glum lately. "I haven't seen you together since the ball last month."

Landamere referred to a fund-raising ball held in mid-October. Tours and special events were a way to raise money for, what local residents hoped, would be a full restoration of the property. The ball was the last time Angie had agreed to be publically seen with Clouse before their separation. Both had remained quiet about their parting, and neither seemed to understand why they felt no more happy, or miserable, than they had together.

"It's been busy," Clouse replied as they entered Landamere's office, hating the truth of the situation.

He unzipped his brown leather jacket with its forest-green collar, hanging it behind the door. Now several years old, the jacket was probably out of style, but it remained his favorite. Clouse looked out the window, spying several leaves caught by the breeze as they fell from nearby trees. He took a seat beside Landamere's desk, virtually slumping into the padded chair.

Clouse wore a sweatshirt bearing his department's emblem on the front, and comfortable blue jeans. The sweatshirt hid his broad shoulders and powerful arms, which served him at work, and on the farm where he once resided until a few weeks prior. He currently found little use for a solid body in the one-bedroom apartment he paid too much for in Bloomington.

Things had been going so well with their marriage that it seemed a shame to cut everything off. Angie was a beautiful businesswoman with a prospering self-made career, working out of their home. Clouse was a dedicated, handsome firefighter who had plenty of time at home for family before he started work at the hotel. In many ways, he seemed the ideal husband and family man by mainstream standards.

Angie's notion of ideal differed from his definition. She wanted a husband home most of the time, helping her take care of their son. With him working two jobs, she felt saddled with responsibility, raising their son while supporting their family just as much as he did.

Working on the West Baden Springs Hotel was not the problem in his marriage, however, as Clouse's blue eyes, his smirk, and the nature of his career got him in trouble several times before their separation. Angie knew certain women adored firemen, and despite complete love and devotion from her husband, she always had a suspicious nature about his whereabouts, predominantly spawned by rumors she heard, most of which he easily disproved.

To say the least, Clouse's feelings were hurt. He hated that his wife didn't trust him when he provided no cause for her actions. While he refused to throw in the towel regarding their marriage, he hoped Angie meant the words she spoke, saying she simply needed some time to think things over.

In his early thirties, Clouse had the best of both worlds if only his marriage had worked. He was well on his way to some excellent jobs in architecture with Landamere, while under the protective umbrella of a city job and its benefit package.

"You haven't missed much this week," Landamere commented, sitting behind his desk, looking around the bland office. Both the filing cabinet and desk were buried beneath blueprints and shuffled papers. "They found some more of the statues we thought were lost during the Jesuit era, and it appears one of the grave sites was disturbed last night," the foreman added, slowly shaking his head.

"Security didn't see anything?"

"No, it probably happened before they got here last night. Someone took a body out of there and it hasn't turned up yet."

Clouse disliked the thought of Jesuit priests being dug up from the cemetery less than a quarter mile from the hotel. During an era after World War II, Jesuit priests had control of the hotel and buried their dead in the nearby site. Some kids probably got their kicks by digging up the body for a Halloween prank, failing to realize the severity of their crime in the material and divine worlds.

After owning the grounds several decades, the Jesuits were entitled to bury their dead on the hill, but no one else received such special treatment. Clouse realized the historical significance of the dead buried there, but the priests had done so much to decimate the traditional appearance of the hotel, that he resented them in part. Of course, if they hadn't resided on the grounds the better part of three decades, a vacant hotel might have crumbled from a lack of upkeep.

After the Second World War, the priests bought the grounds to use as a seminary, doing away with many of the statues, the decorative trim atop the hotel, and imported art Clouse and Landamere fought daily to recover. Through newspaper ads, radio, and even word of mouth, their construction company desperately sought anyone possessing the hotel's old treasures.

"If I find any of the boys dug it up for kicks I'll fire 'em," Landamere scoffed, speaking of the missing body. "That's plain unprofessional."

"I doubt any of them would," Clouse stated, kicking the corner of the desk with one of his boots.

Angie always hated him wearing them. She believed anything that didn't look upper class, including her husband, hurt her chances of landing better clients.

"It's pointless to dig up a body with security here after hours," Clouse commented, finishing his thought. "And what the hell would you do with it?"

Landamere looked at his watch, seeing it was just past nine. The morning was wasting away, and they still had an inspection of the grounds to conduct.

"Take it on tour?" Landamere commented sarcastically, putting on his reading glasses to peruse the plans atop his desk.

Most of his hair had bypassed the gray state, turning a smoky color of white. With his glasses on he reminded Clouse of his grandfather, who lived on a farm when he was a boy.

He was nearing retirement age, but appeared nowhere near it, despite the hair. Landamere could work all day, just like his crew, if necessary. A born leader, it showed whenever the man spoke or picked up a hammer.

"Well, grab your coat and let's get this started," he ordered Clouse.

As the two walked into the lobby toward the stained glass front doors, Clouse looked around the lobby area, taking note of the lights and decor, thinking how incredibly good it looked in comparison to the start of the project. Back then, the floors were covered in puddles of water from the leaky ceilings, and the walls were either faded or deteriorated from the elements. Clouse had seen buildings slated for demolition in better condition than the hotel when it stood in neglect.

Ordinarily tourists poured through the doors after ten o'clock with their preservationist volunteer tour guides in awe of the hotel's appearance. Some only made the trip once a year, and what a difference a year made in the reconstruction process. Clouse, like many of the construction workers, stayed clear of the tourist groups, though many would snap pictures of the workers in action.

Clouse thought someday the photos might be historically significant, and didn't mind being the subject of a photo every now and then when he and Landamere toured the grounds. Occasionally, since he was more regularly dressed than the construction workers, he would eavesdrop on a tour to hear what tourists said about the hotel and how gorgeous it looked.

As they stepped outside, and down a long row of concrete steps, Clouse looked behind him at the looming hotel. From ground level, he could see the covered veranda before his eyes traced the yellow walls with stark white trim up their six stories, where the great rustic-red dome capped off its magnificence. Now four new towers, which did little more than beautify the landmark, had replaced the originals removed during the Jesuit era. They nearly matched the height of the dome, adding to the complexity and mystery of the West Baden Springs Hotel.

"Any ideas what we should do with the storage barn yet?" Landamere asked as they crossed the sunken garden and the now-active water fountain, which displayed stone frogs propped in the center spitting streams of water toward their turtle counterparts, sitting just above the waterline closer to the outer edge.

"We're obviously not wanting anything too permanent," Clouse said, knowing the building was a billiards hall and bowling alley combination in its day. "It's the right shape to house an indoor pool. But it's a little far from the hotel to be trudging barefoot with a towel. We could make it a bowling alley again, or just clean it out and leave it to the buyer's imagination."

"Maybe clean it, paint it a neutral color, and leave it," Landamere thought aloud.

To Clouse, Landamere was almost like an uncle. He was older, wiser, and always willing to see the good in people. He held no respect for laziness or what he called 'boneheaded' mistakes. His crew knew better than to cross him, and they worked hard or they wouldn't be employed very long.

Landamere had a distinguished air about him that set him apart from his men. He seldom did manual labor himself, but no one, Clouse included, doubted his labor skills. More than once Clouse had witnessed him work wonders with a hammer or any number of saws in an instant. The man had nothing to prove around his crew.

Like Clouse, Landamere dressed better than the crew, which let tourists and volunteer workers know he was someone with clout. Though not arrogant,

Landamere wanted people to know who he was, and he often wore his personality outright.

Clouse looked up at the overcast sky as they walked through the sunken garden, then toward the storage building and the disturbed cemetery. It looked as though snow could spit from the sky at any moment, but it seemed far too soon for winter's arrival. Southern Indiana usually had a brief, mild winter after the holiday season, but rumor had it this year would be different.

"We need to get those fountains shut off and drained pretty soon if it's going to be this cold," Clouse noted aloud.

"Good point," Landamere replied as they walked up a small embankment toward the plain gray slabs serving as grave markers, and the single white cross behind them, nearly obscured by thick trees on the hillside.

A concrete stairway curved up the hill, surrounded on either side by impassible shrubs to the small cemetery where two dozen graves sat to the left, another dozen to the right, and one single grave above those on the right side, completely cut off from the others by shrubs and the stairway.

There was no lack of space from what Clouse could ever see, since the graves were extremely close in proximity. He seemed to remember hearing a reason for the grave set by itself, but failed to recall the details of the legend at that moment.

It was that single grave on the right that appeared disturbed with small mounds of dirt on either side. In the cover of darkness, and with trees looming in every direction, Clouse figured it would be easy to dig up the grave undetected.

But why?

"Well, isn't this precious?" Landamere asked sarcastically, looking into the greatly deteriorated wooden box that once held a body.

Shreds of cloth and what Clouse hoped weren't pieces of skin tissue littered the casket. He could see dark tufts of hair at one end, and an eerie feeling shot through his body. They looked brittle, as though they might disintegrate to the touch. The stiff, frail nature of the hair reminded him of something familiar, but he could not recall exactly what.

"How long was that body in here?" he asked.

"I'm pretty sure it was Jesuit," Landamere replied. "The local library has some literature on these graves if you want to play detective."

Clouse shook his head.

"It's not that. It just seems quite preserved for being here four decades."

"It's a shady, cool spot. Strange things happen six feet under."

"More like three," Clouse said, noting how shallow the grave appeared.

"The priests had better things to do than dig graves all day."

"Yeah, it seems like they dug enough of them," Clouse replied, counting about three-dozen stones. "Did they import their dead or what?"

Landamere chuckled, leading Clouse away from the grave, down the brick steps. He gave his designer another hearty pat on the back, reinforcing the uncle relationship Clouse rather enjoyed. Not that he and Landamere usually saw much of one another outside of work, but he liked knowing he was wanted, and there would always be a stable secondary income for him.

Most firefighters around him had second jobs, but most didn't like their work, or it was mandatory. To Clouse, working on the hotel was not necessary for income, or to fill his time. He simply enjoyed doing work that put his degree to use. A number of colleagues envied him for being so happy with both occupations.

As the two neared the bottom of the steps, two men in suits came into view from across the grounds. While Clouse figured they were businessmen wanting information about the hotel, Landamere guessed they were police detectives, there to look at the grave robbery he had phoned in that morning.

He was partly correct.

When they neared the two hotel restorers the men took out identification in the form of badges and presented them.

"Detectives Kendle and Daniels, Bloomington Police Department," the first said, indicating he was Kendle. "Are you Paul Clouse?" he asked, looking directly at the younger of the two.

"I am," Clouse answered, unsure of what to expect since the two were from Bloomington.

"I'm afraid we have some bad news for you, sir."

Chapter 3

Even as he sat inside an interview room alone, Clouse had any number of things to ponder. The news of Angie's death had shocked him, and he felt any number of emotions coursing through his body, changing by the minute.

He was between interviews, and knew little, as they were asking him all the questions and leaking few details. Clouse knew his son was alive since Zach was the one who called 911 after finding his mother lying on the kitchen floor. They promised a reunion with Zach after the interviews, which irritated him.

He never imagined all the time spent teaching his son about distress calls would be used in such a way.

Stuck in a plain brown room that smelled faintly of smoke with nothing but three chairs, a small table, and an unconvincing two-way mirror, Clouse was alone with his thoughts. Unfortunately, his thoughts were the worst possible companions he could have at the moment.

Both detectives found it difficult to believe he had heard nothing of his wife's death, considering he was working in Bloomington the night before. Angie's murder happened too late for the local newspaper to cover, and no one at the fire station had the television on that morning, so he had no way of knowing.

Refusing to mourn until he was alone, Clouse kept his irritation at the police, his grief over Angie's death, and his desperation to see his son to himself. He was outraged about being the prime suspect in Angie's death, and there were certainly more important things to worry about than clearing his name for a crime he would never dream of committing.

Clouse was horrified Zach had found his mother murdered, but relieved his son was fine. From what he understood, Zach had seen and heard nothing during the night. This neither hurt nor helped Clouse in clearing his name. The detectives seemed bent on extracting any piece of incriminating evidence from him, despite the firefighter already providing what he considered an airtight alibi. He spent the night at a firehouse with half a dozen firefighters, making him wonder how one could provide a more solid alibi.

He understood the importance in finding the killer, and eliminating suspects, but Clouse wanted to speak with friends and family, especially his son, before dealing with the law. Minutes seemed like hours until the door finally opened and Detective Larry Kendle stepped in.

"Just a few more questions for you, Mr. Clouse," he said, standing over the table and Clouse. It was an empowering trick investigators used for leverage over interviewees, but Clouse was in no mood for games. "Rumor has it you and the missis were separated."

"We were," Clouse replied.

"She apparently made little secret of it from what her friends tell us," Kendle noted. "You, on the other hand, weren't very open about it. Even when your boss asked you this morning, you dodged the question of your relationship with your wife."

Clouse said nothing, simply looking at the detective.

Kendle reminded him of a bulldog, and not just because of the wrinkles beginning to outline his face. His graying brown hair gave Clouse the idea he was nearing retirement age. He tended to show his teeth, whether in a sneering smile or with a curved lip to show his displeasure at how the interview went. His tie was perfectly straight, and his long-sleeved shirt was pressed, with no wrinkles. Kendle wore his firearm traditionally at his side, giving Clouse every indication he was of military background, and very regimented.

Clouse was somewhat surprised the detectives had interviewed so many people so quickly, but he knew most murder cases were solved within the first forty-eight hours or they often went unsolved. Many a night was spent watching the Discovery Channel at the firehouse.

Legwork was a must for any investigator in Indiana because forensic analysis had such a long turnaround time. Kendle knew he would have to put together a solid case with his own evidence, or risk losing a conviction if he made an arrest. Often it took months, even half a year, to receive results from the Indiana State

Police lab, unless a case was considered a major priority. Clouse, too, had knowledge of such things from his friends in police work.

"Were you simply too proud to admit your wife left you, Mr. Clouse? Or were you planning something much bigger, where public knowledge of your separation might hurt your chances of success?"

Clouse sighed aloud.

"Pressing my buttons won't get you any closer to solving this case, detective," he said. "You know full well I worked at Station 2 last night and any of the guys I worked with will tell you I never left the station."

"We'll be talking to them later, sir. Usually firefighters turn in early, don't they? I mean the murder occurred around midnight or later. And your house really isn't that far from the station."

"I see where this is going," Clouse said, notably disgusted. "Unless you're going to formally charge me with murder I want to see my son, and I would like to speak with my family about arrangements. I'd also like to get inside my house this afternoon and see for myself, since you people refuse to tell me any details about what happened last night."

"We were hoping you might tell us."

"No," Clouse said, standing from his chair, snatching his jacket from the table. "You were hoping for an easy way out."

Opening the door, Clouse stomped into the hallway, turning around after a few steps. "You really don't know a thing about me, detective!" he said angrily, edging dangerously close to the man. "I'm the kind of guy who enjoys boating, fishing, my family, occasionally going to church, and working my ass off to get where I want to be in life. I'm no murderer."

Daniels stepped from the viewing room area to join his partner, afraid Clouse's agitation might lead to violence.

"Where is my son?" he demanded of Kendle.

"Kelli Summers picked him up this morning after we questioned him," Daniels answered before his partner could say something irrational.

Just great, Clouse thought as he stormed out of the police station. His son had been subjected to the same inconsiderate detectives, and he was in the care of Angie's sister. Things were not improving in the least.

He understood why investigators might consider him the prime suspect, because no one else stood to gain what he did. To Clouse, the marriage was never irreconcilable and he could never consider taking such a drastic measure for financial gain. Still, he could think of no one else with a motive to kill Angie.

Perhaps that was how the detectives thought.

Climbing into his Chevy pickup, he let his emotions take over. He shut the door, feeling tears well in his eyes. Away from the detectives and the family he would soon have to confront, he let uncontrollable sobs run free for nearly ten minutes before starting the engine.

Clouse felt selfish for hoping the blame would not wrongfully fall on him, but longed for the opportunity to finish living the life he and Angie always wanted together. For six years, everything in their lives aimed toward one dream, and just as it had all come together, their relationship seemed to fall apart.

Angie finally saw profit in her business, they had a child, owned gorgeous property with everything they'd ever dreamed of, just outside of Bloomington, and Clouse had gotten a second job that finally made him happy while using his degree.

Perhaps it was his own happiness that caused the problems. Throughout their marriage, both had sacrificed, and both had conformed for one another. Clouse always thought he gave up more than she did, but never really minded. When they separated, he enjoyed the personal freedom, feeling more like his old self again. He grew tired of living for Angie sometimes, and perhaps she felt the same.

It was such a simple dilemma, yet so complex. Now it would never be resolved.

His tears settled as he saw the driveway full of cars only a block ahead. The notion of facing Angie's family alone distressed him, but he needed to see Zach. He expected mixed reactions from everyone there, hoping most knew him well enough to believe he was incapable of cold-blooded murder.

Pasty flakes of snow splattered on his truck's windshield as he pulled beside the drive, seeing a variety of family members inside the house, several shooting disparaging looks when they saw his truck. He felt like the devil arriving to fulfill their prophecy.

Even before he reached the side door, it opened, revealing Kelli Summers, his sister-in-law. She, more than most of the family, knew Clouse. He stared into a face of sadness, but found assurance that she believed he was unable to commit such an act on her sister.

Unlike her sister, Kelli kept her hair cut short. Her usually bright hazel eyes appeared misted, surrounded by flush skin from tears. Her petite figure attracted men every time she went out with Clouse or Angie, but somehow she remained single.

"Zach's been asking for you all morning," she said, pulling the door nearly shut behind her as they stood in the cold.

"How is everyone?" he asked.

"Holding up," she replied before looking to the ground. "The police haven't said much. They just asked us all a lot of questions. Mostly about you."

"No surprise there," Clouse noted with a hint of agitation. "Can I see Zach a minute?" he asked, not wanting to intrude.

"Sure," she replied with no hesitation. "Let me get him."

When Zach came to the door, Clouse could see the close resemblance his son held to him, more than ever. From the chocolate-brown hair to the piercing blue eyes, Zach always looked more like Clouse than he did his mother. It was another thing that always seemed to irritate Angie when people saw their son.

"Daddy," he said, embracing Clouse, who was thrilled his son had not suffered so much as a scratch from the night before.

"How are you holding up, kid?" he asked, holding his son in front of him in a secure grip by the shoulders after planting a kiss on his forehead.

"Everyone keeps crying and telling me Mommy's gone," Zach said with youthful innocence and ignorance of the situation. "Why isn't she coming back?"

Clouse fought back a tear, pulling Zach into another hug.

"She just isn't, Zach," he said. "Mommy's in a better place now, and someday you'll see her again."

"But I want to see her now," Zach insisted, pushing against his father's broad shoulders, seeing the hurt in Clouse's eyes. For his son's sake, he fought back the urge to cry. "What's wrong, Daddy?"

"Everything will be okay, son," Clouse explained. "I'll be back for you later."

"But—"

"I know," Clouse cut Zach off with a foreboding finger. "I need you to stay with Aunt Kelli for a while longer. I'll be back tonight. Okay?"

"Okay," Zach reluctantly agreed.

"Roger wants to see you a second," Kelli said before taking Zach into the house.

Roger Summers, Angie's brother and a fellow firefighter on the department, had always been close to Angie and Clouse. He was the one person Clouse knew was incapable of murdering Angie, but he would also be one of the most distraught by her death.

At a time when Clouse was unsure of whether or not to approach Kieffer Construction about using his blueprints, it was Summers who insisted he talk to one of the general managers.

"Paul," he said coming to the door with a greeting nod. His eyes were puffy and red, displaying the hardship he shared with his family.

Dressed in sweat pants and a sweatshirt bearing fire department emblems, it was obvious Summers had been at work when the news came. He was barefoot, holding a steaming cup of coffee in his right hand as he stepped outside. His thicket of black hair appeared strewn like a wheat field after a thunderstorm.

"Rodge, how are you holding up?" Clouse asked uneasily.

"Doing okay, considering the police won't give us any details. My understanding is it'll probably be a closed casket service."

"Oh, God," Clouse said under his breath, only imagining how horrific the murder must have been.

"I got the news as I was getting off work this morning," Summers said with an involuntary sniffle. "Everyone's here helping with the arrangements."

"I'm sorry, Rodge," Clouse said, trying to excuse himself from the awkward situation. "I'll be back later to pick up Zach, but I can't imagine I'm going to be welcome here."

Summers thought a moment, then realized what his brother-in-law meant.

"Did the police question you?"

"They took it a step beyond that," Clouse replied. "I seem to be the extent of their search for suspects."

"That's not right!" Summers objected aloud, immediately realizing he could be heard inside. "You couldn't do anything like that, Paul. I know you'd never hurt Angie."

"Thanks, Rodge," Clouse said sincerely. "I'm glad someone thinks that."

"If you need *anything,* just call me. There's no sense in you going through this alone."

"Thanks. I'll be back later," Clouse said, drawing away from the house. "There are a few things I need to go check on with the police."

"Take care, Paul," Summers said, retreating to the warmth of the house and the comfort of loved ones.

Taking the lonely walk to his truck, Clouse opened the door, picking up the cellular phone from its charger as he climbed in. At the time he needed friends and allies the most, he was finding few, and one of his last chances to quickly find answers might lie in an old high school buddy.

He started the truck and pressed a button to automatically dial his friend's number on the cellular phone.

Chapter 4

After contacting the only person who might help him find answers, Clouse stopped for a light lunch, then drove to his house, only to find a Bloomington officer guarding the end of his driveway. Seated in his patrol car, the officer worked diligently on a crossword puzzle. An unmarked car sat nearby, belonging to the officers conducting forensic tests inside.

Though the officer refused to give out much information, Clouse took a good look at the house and the yellow tape surrounding it. He could see what appeared to be blood spatters on the porch, but little else of significance. It would be the next day before he could get inside.

Now he pulled into the only place he felt comfortable. Even with dark clouds looming overhead, the hotel looked incredible to him. He was in no mood to speak with the crew, or even Landamere, but knew it would be impossible to simply brood alone on the grounds. Besides, Ken Kaiser, his old high school pal, would be dropping by shortly. Clouse hoped to find out anything about the murder from the Orange County police officer.

Both had graduated from Bloomington North High School the same year, then went separate ways soon thereafter. While Clouse attended Indiana University, Kaiser immediately pursued various law enforcement channels, first joining the Orleans Police Department in a small town several miles north of the hotel. When an opportunity to join the county police came, Kaiser jumped at the chance for a pay raise and a take home car with his first child on the way.

Fate brought the friends together again, when Clouse began his design work and Kaiser was one of three officers able to snatch up some part-time security work on the grounds after operating hours. He was the one person Clouse knew who seemed to have contacts with every department in Southern Indiana. He could possibly shed some light on Clouse's unfortunate situation if he was privy to the information.

He would be granted no time alone as he stepped from his truck, only to be met by Rusty Cranor, Landamere's chief assistant on the project.

A working foreman, Rusty wore a yellow hard hat, and blue jeans tattered with dirt and a few minor tears. Nearly fifty-years-old, Rusty kept a red beard peppered with gray hairs. A year-round tan and several wrinkles under his eyes were the results of a career working outdoor labor in the worst of conditions.

"Hi, Paul," he said with his usual easy smile, obviously not knowing the bad news yet.

"Hey, Rusty. How goes the project?"

"That's what I wanted to ask you about," Rusty said, the smile fading. "Dave left this morning shortly after you did, and left me in charge. He hasn't come back yet."

"Everything's okay, isn't it?" Clouse asked, walking with the foreman toward the hotel's main entrance.

"Well, yeah, but I thought he was supposed to be right back. Do you know what he wanted us to do in the basement today?"

The basement held most of the tools, lumber, roofing supplies, and whatever else its gigantic locked door could keep behind it. It housed several divided rooms within one large area, and an ideal spot to cut wood planks, hide from a foreman, or relax. Clouse often walked the basement to check the stability of the hotel, and create ideas, working from the ground up.

"I think he wanted some of the supplies moved from the first room to the roof," Clouse answered. "We need to get that trim work done before winter."

"I'll get down there and see what needs moving," Rusty said, beginning to walk away. He turned around after a few steps. "You know where Dave went?"

Clouse shrugged. "No. I'm sure he'll be back soon."

As Rusty walked into the hotel, Clouse spied a county police car pulling through the gigantic yellow gates of the hotel, then up the brick walkway, parking next to several of the workers' vehicles.

"Good timing," Clouse said to himself, anxious to see his longtime friend.

"I'm so sorry about Angie," Ken Kaiser told Clouse as the two met on the walkway, quickly shaking hands before Kaiser pulled him in for a quick hug.

His friend was dressed for the weather, a nylon police jacket covering his uniform shirt, complete with clip-on tie.

Kaiser was one of the very few people Clouse had talked to about his marital problems. The officer was simply biding time, doing security several nights a week, and turned out to be a good listener.

"It wasn't pretty," the officer said, walking with Clouse toward the front balcony area of the hotel. "The detective I talked to said there was blood everywhere in the kitchen, and multiple puncture wounds on the body."

"God," Clouse said, wiping beads of sweat from his forehead. All morning his body felt overly warm as he expelled nervous energy. All of the tension was wearing him down, possibly toward a sickened state.

"They know it was a bladed weapon, but they won't know what until the autopsy is conducted. It occurred around midnight, and they're checking your house for every kind of DNA sample they can find."

Clouse noticed his friend had decided to shave his face clean again. He could never make up his mind how he wanted to look. This week, it seemed, he wanted the younger, former military look of the cops he worked with. His black hair was buzzed nearly to the point that his scalp was entirely visible. And just in time for winter, Clouse thought sarcastically.

To say Kaiser was impulsive or rash never quite covered it. He often bought items on the spur of the moment, and sometimes returned them the same day when his wife found out. Lately, the cop had an itching for a Harley-Davidson motorcycle, which Clouse's sensible advice had kept him from buying, at least to this point.

Clouse was amazed his high school buddy remained married with the stunts he pulled.

"Who would want to see Angie dead?" Clouse pondered aloud, stumped for an answer.

"The Bloomington Police think they know," Kaiser noted, shaking his head.

"That they do," Clouse replied. "And if they're looking at me, they're not looking for the right person, and he'll get away with it."

Both walked the front steps of the hotel up to the balcony, not saying a word. Taking a right turn atop the stairs, they stood on intricately designed concrete, surrounded by pillars along the hotel walls, and potted plants and trees on the outer rim of the walkway. Tourists were forbidden to walk this area for fear they might separate from their groups and take a personal tour of the hotel's off-limit rooms.

A terrible liability case if any accidents ever happened.

"I know you worked last night, Paul," Kaiser said in a hushed voice, making certain no construction workers overheard. "Is your alibi airtight?"

"It won't be, considering most of the guys went to bed fairly early last night," Clouse confided, speaking of his fellow firefighters. "They won't be able to vouch for certain whether or not I was there at the time of the murder."

Clouse and his fellow firefighters shared a common bunk area. If no one had awoken around midnight with insomnia, or to take a bathroom break, he had no sure alibi. No calls took them out of the station until closer to dawn.

"How is Zach?"

"Confused. He doesn't really understand what's going on, and I know Angie's family is going to try keeping him from me."

"Do they think you did it?"

"Some do, I'm sure," Clouse replied. "Her parents turned on me when we separated. I think Roger and Kelli know me better than that." He sighed. "But it could get ugly."

Kaiser leaned against the balcony railing, feeling the wind whip around the circular walkway. He folded his arms, looking out to the grounds of the hotel, still littered with machinery and supplies, waiting their turn to contribute to the monumental project. Like Clouse, Kaiser shared a love for the hotel that went beyond working there. He knew the history of the land as well as any tour guide, sometimes noting quirky facts that annoyed his co-workers, sick of hearing him ramble about West Baden Springs.

"Just remember, Paul, they need concrete proof you were at the house to make a case. The DNA tests should lead them away from you as a suspect."

"But you know they're going to find my hair and skin samples in there, Ken," Clouse retorted. "It hasn't been that long since I lived there, remember?"

"I guess it hasn't," Kaiser concurred. "Then it can't hurt your case, either."

"But it won't help," Clouse said, trying to rub away the beginning of a headache from his forehead.

"There's no murder weapon," Kaiser said, recounting the facts. "There aren't any witnesses, and there are a ton of people Angie was in contact with."

Clouse let out a controlled chuckle. "You going to be my lawyer, Ken?"

"No, but I know what it takes to get a case to court, and they're not even close. Don't sweat it, Paul. We've got plenty of time to prove your innocence and get things back to normal."

"Normal? Here we are talking about my wife like she's a name on the eight o'clock news, and how to clear me, when I didn't do anything."

"It's not fair," Kaiser noted. "You're not supposed to worry about shit like that when your wife is, well, you know."

"Yeah, I know."

Clouse wondered what the 'normal' Kaiser spoke of would be from now on. It certainly made things clearer for him without Angie around, but he would now be a single parent. Almost an entire family would never dismiss his involvement in Angie's death because he stood the most to gain from her demise.

Life insurance was substantial on both he and Angie, and there was the property, the house, the boat, and everything else they worked so hard to own. Only now did Clouse realize how much he had sacrificed to get them there, and how nothing could ever be the same again. His situation was by no means good before, but he would take it over the mess he confronted now.

"You can't stay here and work," Kaiser said. "Take the day off. Go grab some coffee or something."

"I don't really have anywhere to go," Clouse confessed. "They've condemned my house, I'd go stir crazy in the apartment, and I can't pick up Zach until tonight. That is, if the family lets me have him."

"They can't deny you your son," Kaiser said vehemently.

"If they want to, they'll find a way."

Clouse was about to suggest they head inside when Rusty came out the front door, frantically looking in every direction until he spotted the two men talking on the balcony.

"Paul!" he called. "Paul! You've got to see what's downstairs! It's the damnedest thing I've ever seen."

Without saying a word, Clouse and Kaiser followed Rusty through the hotel, down to the basement where the first door stood open, its contents easily seen from a distance. To Clouse, nothing looked out of the usual, with various tiles, lumber, and boxes lining the room. As he drew closer, however, it became clear what the foreman was upset about.

Next to a sealed box, a mass of bone, decomposed dried skin, and small tufts of hair comprised what Clouse could only assume was the missing body from the cemetery on the hill. Most of the bones were still attached, but the body lay in a heap, as though thrown there. Small pieces of the dried skin and hair sat on the dirty concrete floor beside the body, thrown loose from the impact.

By no means did the body look peaceful with the jaw wide open, and the hands curved, as though he had died defending himself. Most of the bone was fully exposed, and dark gray in color. It seemed short and shriveled compared to how Clouse thought a decomposed body would look.

In no way did it appear at rest.

"Do you want the police?" Rusty asked of Clouse.

Rather than answer, the firefighter shot Rusty a questioning stare, then looked to Kaiser as an answer.

"Who has keys to this area?" Kaiser asked, taking control of the situation.

His friend and the foreman glanced at one another, then Clouse answered.

"We both do, and Dave Landamere."

Kaiser shook his head, knowing he could not be partial in such a bizarre affair.

"Yeah, you better call the police," he instructed Rusty.

Chapter 5

Clouds still covered the skies as a stiff wind crossed the hotel grounds, causing various leaves to fall around Clouse, adding to the untended blanket along the landscape. He watched as Kaiser argued with a state trooper and the Bloomington detectives, who had shown up to possibly accuse him of more wrongdoings.

Regardless, Clouse knew everyone's curiosity would be triggered, and rumors would spread like wildfire. He was not the least bit interested in being part of a media circus. Performing either of his jobs would be difficult if the local papers got wind of his potential involvement in Angie's death, or the exhumation of Jesuit bodies.

He understood his friend's position, and there was little Kaiser could do to help him. Clouse would never ask him to lie, and there was nothing the county officer could do to provide an alibi. At this point, he needed witnesses to confirm his exact whereabouts from the night before to convince the detectives of his innocence, and they weren't forthcoming.

Because there were none.

Staring at his friend and the two police cars next to Kaiser's, he realized what a scene this had to be at the normally tranquil hotel. He looked behind him, taking notice of over a dozen eyes surveying the activity, avoiding their work a moment. Clouse could order them to return to work, but he was not their foreman, and Landamere was not around to back his authority.

After a few minutes, Kaiser returned to his friend, apparently unhappy with the result of his chat with fellow officers.

"Well?" Clouse asked.

"This body doesn't help your situation," Kaiser replied. "Their forensics people went through your house, and found skin and bone tissue upstairs near a jack-o-lantern. By the looks of the fragments found at the house, there's reason to believe the body back there is the same tissue."

"This is insane!" Clouse fired back, realizing too late that others were listening.

"They also found some other things that don't help. There was no forced entry to the house, and the locks were all secured, except for the kitchen deadbolt, where the killer apparently left. Also, one of Angie's friends reported talking to her around midnight, and your firefighter buddies said you left your truck parked outside last night. They also said you often leave it inside."

Clouse looked away from his friend, slowing shaking his head, knowing the entire story looked bleak, and he could disprove none of it.

If he had parked his truck inside the firehouse garage, starting it, or opening the bay doors to leave, would certainly have awoken at least one of his colleagues. It would certainly appear he left it outside with intent.

"They want to check your truck bed for traces of the DNA, Paul," Kaiser said in a tone that hinted it might not be in his friend's best interest.

Clouse agreed, but knew if he declined, the situation looked worse, and DNA lingered long periods of time wherever it settled. His choice was basically made for him, even if someone was going to great lengths to frame him.

"Let them."

Kaiser gave a questioning look, providing an opportunity to back out.

"No, do it," Clouse confirmed. "I've got nothing to hide, and nothing to lose at this point."

Kaiser looked as though he had just warranted his best friend to death as he dragged himself back to the officers. Clouse could not read exactly where his friend stood, or if Kaiser truly believed him, but it was in the hands of forensic science now.

He felt powerless, knowing everyone figured him guilty, with no way to prove otherwise. There was little he could do because even he had no idea who might want Angie dead. If he lost Kaiser's support, he would have no one to confide in, or ascertain answers from in a police perspective.

Clouse decided waiting around would do him no good, and decided to look for answers himself. As he walked toward the sunken garden, then the cemetery area, an officer with a bag carrying the exhumed body passed him. It was that body

Clouse wanted to start with. If it was connected in any way to Angie's murder, which he suspected it was, he needed to know its significance.

Heading up the hill for the second time that day, Clouse paid closer attention to the white slabs atop the graves. He took notice of how each had a name and date, much like any ordinary marker, except for the open grave. It simply held the name "Ernest" inscribed on its cold, hard stone.

"No dates, no nothing," Clouse commented to himself. Suddenly the grave had a bit of meaning, or at least a distinct difference from the others.

He looked into the hole for anything overlooked, but saw nothing aside from the splinters of the casket, and pieces of the body. Picking up a bone fragment, Clouse could see the same dark patterns the entire body seemed to have. Thinking it looked dark, almost charred, he smelled it, but found no distinctive odor. After several decades of lying in the ground, he expected little else.

Landamere mentioned the library having historical materials concerning the hotel. Though he doubted much about the Jesuits or the cemetery would be documented, it would be worth a try if it meant possibly clearing his name.

"You seem to have a morbid curiosity about that grave," a voice said from behind the firefighter.

"Detective Kendle," Clouse replied, standing to face the man he least wanted to see.

"Your friend says we have your blessing to check the back your truck?"

"Be my guest. I'm sure you'll come up with something to aid your narrowly-focused search."

Clouse started walking the brick steps down to the garden. The detective immediately followed, keeping a step behind.

"Do you have any guesses who might want your wife dead?"

"No," Clouse simply answered. "But I assure you, this is not the way I would do it."

"Oh, come on," the detective said with a light tone. "Blood everywhere, the body hacked to shreds, the boy left untouched? This has crime of passion written all over it."

Clouse stopped walking, turning to point a finger at the detective.

"*Now* you tell me this shit," he said angrily. "This morning you were all too vague because I was supposed to provide your clues, and now you're singing like a canary. Well, I don't have your answers, detective, and I am not capable of cold-blooded murder, much less dissecting a human body."

He started to walk off once more, but turned after another thought crossed his mind.

"Now I feel obligated to do your job for you, because you're looking at no one but me. For every minute you spend checking up on me, you're letting other leads drop. This is all I have to say to you."

Clouse stormed off, leaving Kendle to ponder the words a moment before he returned to his fellow officers.

***

"You want some ice cream, sport?" Clouse asked Zach from across his apartment that evening.

"No, Daddy."

After only a month of rental, the apartment truly looked like a bachelor pad. Sight alone could not determine whether the clothes hanging over various pieces of furniture were clean, or the cereal inside several boxes left on the counter would prove delicious or stale. The refrigerator held only a few staple goods, and even the freshness of those was in question.

A moderate one-bedroom apartment, it was enough for the fireman who spent much of his life at work. He was anxious to clean the house and move back, knowing full well it would only make his character look worse. If Zach were staying with him, he would not keep them trapped inside an apartment, even if it meant moving back to a house that would haunt them both. Houses could be sold, and to an extent, the past left behind.

It was nearing both of their bedtimes, but neither was going to sleep. Clouse wanted his son to tire after the exhausting day and possibly sleep some of the emotional pain away. His personal agony went far deeper because six years of his life were wiped out in one night.

Kelli was the only person Clouse saw when he picked Zach up. He sensed his presence was unwanted, but there was no objection to him keeping the four-year-old. Zach was the one thing keeping him sane through this whole ordeal, but only childhood ignorance kept his son from accusing him of murder as well.

"I'm just being paranoid," Clouse told himself as he pulled a bag of peanuts from the kitchen cupboard above the refrigerator.

"Do you miss Mommy?" Zach asked as Clouse entered the living room. He was lying on the couch, head heavily on a pair of pillows, watching an adventure on the Sci-Fi Channel with sleepy eyelids.

"Of course I do. Don't let anyone tell you any different, Zach."

"Are you going to leave me too?"

"No," Clouse said with more assurance than he felt. He could only hope the samples vacuumed from the bed of his truck would provide no further incriminating evidence against him. "You know I'd never leave you, son. And Mommy didn't want to leave either."

No answer.

Clouse took a blanket from the one chair inside his living room and flipped it out, covering his son with it. Assured Zach was snug and warm, he checked the thermostat and went to bed, leaving his door open in case Zach awoke and didn't want to be alone. For both, tomorrow would be a new day.

A day in which to start over.

Chapter 6

"I can't believe you don't think he did it," Larry Kendle said to his partner, who calmly toyed with an unlit cigarette, feet propped on his desk in the detectives' division office.

"What does he really have to gain, Larry?" Mark Daniels asked rhetorically, staring at the ceiling as he replied. "I mean they didn't have the house, the boat, or even their vehicles fully paid off, so there's not much property or financial gain. And if you're going to bump off the wife, why do it like that?"

"He was on his way to divorce. This way he gets the kid, keeps everything, and moves on with his life before she gets the chance to ruin it."

"I don't know about you, partner," Daniels said, fingering his tie. It was one of several nervous habits he couldn't break.

Daniels came from a different mold than his partner.

After earning a two-year degree from a local college in law enforcement, he had tested for the state police, and several local departments, before getting hired by the Bloomington Police Department. Most people on the department barely had their high school diplomas, much less any further schooling outside of their work.

Taller than his partner, Daniels had a naturally strong upper body, but he constantly worried more about his mind than his body. One common factor the partners shared was their obsession with neatness. Daniels wore his shirt wrinkle-free, and the tie he tied himself centered in just the right spot so the strongest gale wind couldn't budge it.

His dirty-blond hair was cut short, though never buzzed like the younger officers on his department preferred theirs. Never much of a conformist, Daniels acted and looked as he pleased. He wore shined shoes, pressed pants, and a look that showed he was constantly thinking of something, though no one else ever knew exactly what.

Unless, of course, he chose to fill them in.

Kendle picked a file up from his desk, waving it at his partner.

"This right here is the first step in putting Paul Clouse behind bars. Come on, there was no forced entry, there's a connection to this body at the hotel, and he has plenty of motive. He's the *only* one with motive."

Daniels put the cigarette back in the hard pack within his shirt pocket, not sold on his partner's analysis. He looked outside the window to the parking lot below. The morning view, covered by fog, reminded him of how his brain felt after countless cups of coffee two nights before when a new major case came along.

"If I'm going to kill someone, I don't go through the trouble of digging up a body, I don't risk my career by getting caught skipping out of work, and I certainly wouldn't make a gigantic mess in my own house when a simple application of poison, or an overdose, would be difficult to detect and attract less attention."

Kendle slumped into his chair across from Daniels, settling in for a battle of words. It was the most effective way the partners established links and clues in their cases. By arguing, they brought up various viewpoints and scenarios. Kendle naturally argued often, and did not particularly like being partnered with the rookie detective, which sometimes made him almost unbearable for Daniels.

"But it's a crime of passion," the older detective said, defending his view. "He couldn't help himself in mutilating her body once he started. He sneaks out of work, ten-minute drive home, ten minutes to kill her, ten minutes to drive back. There weren't any fire dispatches recorded until almost five in the morning, so his risk paid off. He fakes some grief, sells the house, and moves on."

Daniels chuckled a few seconds at the notion.

"You speak of thirty minutes total, when it's probably closer to three hours."

"How so?" Kendle questioned.

"The evidence points toward the body being dug up last night *after* the staff all went home at the hotel and before security noticed in the overnight. So he sneaks out of the station, drives south, digs up the body, and sets up this whole sick scenario upstairs and lies in wait until she comes upstairs, all when he's pressed for time?"

"Exactly!" Kendle said, as though his partner had fully solved the case. "It's pitch dark. The wife can't see what the body is, thinks it might be her kid, gets freaked out and distracted, so he's able to catch her off-guard and get in the first blow. And there's no pinpointed time for that body being dug up at the hotel. It could've happened a day earlier for all we know."

"Bullshit," Daniels countered, not giving in. "Regardless of the body, if you're that pressed for time, you don't set all that up. He'd have to be clinically insane to do that, and even *you* would agree he's not."

"But he's bright," Kendle noted. "The man has a degree, knows where he's going, and no one's going to keep him from getting there."

"Oh, like the wife who just gave him his freedom?" Daniels asked sarcastically.

Daniels could irritate Kendle to no end. He was younger than his partner, and certainly less experienced, but he always seemed to have answers, or at least thought he did. After only three years on the force, he was placed in the investigative division for a reason.

Though Kendle thought that reason was simply to agitate him, Daniels brought new perspectives to a clan of detectives long since stuck in their methods and beliefs.

Kendle hated the way his partner contradicted him, appearing unconcerned about whether he was correct or not. Daniels always spoke in a soft, mild-mannered voice that many mistook for arrogance rather than his usual nature. He believed police officers needed to raise their voices only when necessary, and wasn't afraid to show people his true self.

"You know, kid, you're going to be wrong on this one," Kendle warned with a grin.

"We'll see. I just don't see a strong motive, and there are a lot of other people and places we can check out."

"You want to split up on this one?" Kendle asked, suggesting a tactic they sometimes used where each would investigate certain facets of a case, then compare facts on a daily basis.

Since the two were obligated to work together during regular hours, the split often meant additional work outside their regular shift, which irritated Daniels, because he enjoyed time with his family. Still, he liked proving Kendle wrong, and loved challenges.

"Yeah, you can dog Clouse all you want, but I think there's more to it. I'm not saying he's necessarily innocent, but if he did it, I don't think he was the one wielding the blade."

"Well, here's to violating Paul Clouse's civil rights," Kendle said as the two shook hands on the agreement, playing on his partner's words.

Daniels looked at the file a moment, somewhat puzzled. Attached to it was a plastic evidence bag. Holding it up, he looked at its contents, then to his partner.

"This shred of black cloth, Larry. What do you make of it?"

"It's silk, like a Halloween costume. Maybe one of those killer outfits from the slasher movies, or a witch's outfit," he guessed, attempting to explain the black coloration. "The kid might have worn it out that night."

"No," Daniels replied. "The kid went as an alien. Green costume. This snagged on a nail at the top of the staircase, but there wasn't any blood. And no respectable boy dresses as a witch by the way."

Kendle grinned inwardly. They both knew blood testing for DNA would make for an open and shut case if the suspect's DNA was found in a database. Murder cases never came that easy for them. He stood, stretched, and walked toward the door.

"Where are you going?" Daniels asked.

"I've got civil liberties to violate, partner."

***

In the numbing chairs near the magazine section of Indiana University's extensive library, four friends gathered on a quiet Sunday morning, talking amongst themselves, studying, and reading recent events in the Bloomington newspaper.

"Hey, did you read this story in the paper?" Tina Kindrick asked her friends after glancing through the local news.

"What?" Andy Smith asked, putting down his English homework.

As her three friends listened attentively, Tina paraphrased the article.

"It says here the body of a Jesuit priest at the West Baden Springs Hotel was dug up and removed from its plot yesterday," she began. "Little information is being released about the body or why it may have been exhumed, but police did say the marker simply read 'Ernest' and that the grave was some distance away from the others on the hill where the priests were buried."

Her friends simply stared at her, wondering how this was the least bit important.

"Don't you guys remember Professor Zanchas' story?" she probed. "The one about the mad priest at the hotel?"

Eli Zanchas was from the Middle East where legends of pharaohs and pyramids were not uncommon. Yet, he found a local legend in Southern Indiana most intriguing, and shared it with his class one day.

"Wasn't it something about the hotel being bought by the priests after the Depression, and one of them going mad?" Nicole Brinkman asked.

"It went a lot further than that," Tina recalled, going into a story telling mode. "The hotel burned at the turn of the last century, and Father Ernest claimed to his fellow priests the dead spoke to him, though there were no reported deaths from the fire."

She paused a moment, trying to remember the details.

"Ernest was incensed that no one would listen to him, much less believe him. He slowly fell into his own world of darkness, trapped with the spirits some said, but alone nonetheless. Some said he went about preaching to anyone who would listen, when visiting the hotel, but what he preached seemed insane, and perhaps too dark for the others."

Tina could see the looks her friends gave as they recalled the story, but they failed to be equally captured in its meaning. Undaunted, she continued.

"The priests kept Father Ernest locked in a safe room most of the day when guests came to the hotel, telling no one about the maddened priest they harbored. Growing more disillusioned, Ernest began believing he was a reaper of souls as the dead told him, and believed in his power, telling those around him how he chose life or death, heaven or hell, for the souls he claimed. They say he dressed in dark attire and robes constantly, just to shadow himself from society and remain in his own world."

"Is this nearing the end?" Nicole asked, trying not so subtly to drop a hint.

"Yes," Tina assured her. "They say in his final days Ernest went completely mad, ranting and raving in his tormented state, locked inside his room. One night he managed to find his way to the basement, where the priests stored the old statues they had removed from the hotel lobby and center court. The sight of these objects reminded Ernest of souls trapped without release, and it was there he took his own life, setting himself ablaze, dead before anyone could find his charred corpse."

"Touching," Smith noted. "So you think that's the same grave?"

"Why else would anyone dig it up?" Tina wondered aloud. "That is so cool that someone dug up the very same grave Professor Zanchas talked about. I would love to go see that place sometime," she said, sincerely excited about the idea.

"You've got a vivid imagination," Nicole said. "Maybe we can take you there sometime and give you your own padded room."

"Thanks," Tina replied with the same sarcastic tone her friends used. "It's nice to know I'm loved," she added before flipping through more of the paper.

"That story is such bullshit," Smith commented with a chuckle. "It's just an urban legend that gets bigger every year when someone else tells it."

Though her story had failed to impress her friends, it caught the attention of the man seated behind them, reading some materials of his own, ironically related to the same topic.

Clouse could not help but overhear the story as he sifted through history books concerning the hotel, and the story gave him a faint glimmer of hope that perhaps the grave did hold some connection to the murder of his wife. His search could now be broadened.

He recalled the legend, but not the name associated with it. Now he realized why the grave would be apart from the others, with so little description. Somehow, the idea of an insane priest setting himself on fire didn't seem realistic, but legends tended to deviate over time. He wondered if and how the tale might tie into his situation.

Most of the books he read held little information about the Jesuit era of the hotel. The priests spent most of their era hidden away from a public that tormented them for decimating their favorite historical landmark. After all, most of the statues were sold or hidden, and the baths removed from all rooms on the inner ring of the hotel's circular form, which Clouse himself now had the overwhelming task of restoring. Many of the changes during the Jesuit era posed the greatest challenges to the construction company throughout the reconstruction.

Few people entered the walls of the hotel during that era, much less documented the visits. The only noteworthy mass gathering of West Baden residents occurred during the funeral of Ed Ballard, the hotel's former owner, who had, in essence, handed his great property over to the Jesuits for no more than one dollar. It was one of the rare occasions when outsiders were allowed onto the grounds, and for that reason the Ernest legend could never be disproved or verified.

Clouse knew asking the police for a peek at the body would be a complete waste of time, but he wanted another look at it, just to see if it was indeed charred. Perhaps Kaiser could pull one last string for him.

With the advent of computerized library checkouts, Clouse had no idea who had read the books before him. Only dates were stamped on the slips of paper tucked in the back. His brain scrambled for a way to trace who might have perused the materials in recent weeks or months, but nothing came to mind.

Such information was confidential, hidden behind the help desks, but he was determined there had to be a way. If computers were the keepers of information, he knew access to them would be helpful, but he was no hacker, and knew few people with skill enough to dig into the files from an outside line.

He would save that thought for more desperate times.

In the meantime, there was a full day ahead of him that began with picking up his son from his parents' house and searching for answers at the hotel. On a Sunday, no one else would be there, and he held a master key, which strangely enough, the police could use against him. Clouse put the detectives out of his mind, ready to confront the truth.

No matter where it took him.

Chapter 7

Before Clouse could visit the hotel, he needed to stop by the house to feed the animals. With a reluctant blessing from the Bloomington Police Department, the house was his again. He assumed every bit of vacuuming and photography possible had been done the day before, sent off to forensic labs for analysis.

Wasting little time, he phoned the cleaners, and despite being a Sunday, managed to get in touch with one for a Monday appointment. One more night in the apartment for Zach and himself would help them heal. They'd be away from Angie's family and the house where so many good memories were now covered in blood.

"You want to feed the cows?" Clouse asked his son as they stepped down from the truck.

"Sure," Zach said with little more than a shrug.

To Clouse his son seemed apathetic to nearly everything he suggested. Zach needed time to recover from the loss of his mother, or perhaps the gravity of the situation had yet to hit home for the child. Clouse was patient enough to deal with that. He understood children dealt with pain differently, though Angie had always been more willing to wait than he was. Clouse had always wanted results from his job, his life, and his child much faster.

What he wanted came at a heavy price.

With Angie gone, there was little choice but to wait for Zach to recover at his own pace.

While Zach went into the barn where he had helped feed livestock the past several months, Clouse retrieved some dog food from a shed behind the house, walked out to his two dogs, tied up at their small dog houses, untangled their chains, and fed them. There was little time to pet them today. He would make it up to them when he and Zach settled back into the house.

Walking back from the doghouses, kept behind the house at the edge of one field, Clouse surveyed his land. Three sides of his property were open fields, giving his horse and two cows plenty of roaming room. Across from the house stood a full barn, partly converted into garage space, and beside it, a lean-to of equal size, which sheltered sparsely-used farm equipment, hay, and occasionally, his truck.

Another such building stood at the beginning of the drive for a small tractor and several more pieces of farm equipment owned by his father until the end of every summer when Clouse would suddenly be given custody of them because only he had room enough to store the lot.

Stepping slowly up to the porch, Clouse felt a sense of apprehension before walking into the house, knowing what to expect, but not the extent. Scuffing his boots along the porch's wooden floor, he paced a moment, drawing deep breaths. Lifting the yellow tape after a minute, he stepped inside his house, instantly feeling like an intruder.

"My God," Clouse stammered, seeing dried pools of blood across the kitchen floor, the largest nearly the size of his favorite recliner at the fire station. In certain spots, it almost looked like water color paint atop the linoleum floor, but there was quite a difference.

As a first responder, he grew accustomed to seeing bodies and blood several times a year, but this numbed him. Someone did this to his wife, the woman he vowed to protect and care for through thick and thin. Now he was never going to see her walk through the front door again, or ask him how his day went. When they separated, he never dreamed of something this permanent taking her away from him.

Walking into the family room, he noticed how empty and boring it looked without the usual family photos and furniture inside. Angie wasted little time in casting out his property once he left the house. Perhaps she had vented some frustration, or put him out of her mind by covering up his belongings. A few pieces remained, covered by sheets or tarps like ghosts left to remind him of the not so distant past.

Clouse walked through the room to the bottom of the stairs, looking at the drips of blood, which fell along each step during Angie's escape attempt. He knelt a moment, running his finger along one of the red spots, at the base of the stairs, finding it completely dry. Slowly lifting his head, he saw the darkness of the hallway above, wondering what horrors had unfolded upstairs. He stood, hesitating a moment.

Clouse flipped on a light switch, illuminating the upstairs before he walked up. The light revealed more blood spots, and a notable gash in the wall at the bottom of the stairway. Clouse could already see a similar splintered area of the wall upstairs, but only damage and signs of death lingered.

Any traces of the jack-o-lantern and the crumpled body were gone, probably housed within police labs. In all, Clouse had inherited a house with bloodstains, bad memories, and a spirit that could haunt him for eternity. He realized nothing good would come of his present situation.

He returned to the downstairs, anxiously heading outside to check on Zach, thankful his son hadn't come inside the house.

"Zach?" he called.

No answer.

"Zach?" he called again, more anxious this time. "Where are you?"

In the next few seconds, he ran toward the barn, throwing open the large sliding door where his boat was stored for the winter. Its white frame loomed overhead, set upon the self-launching boat trailer Clouse had spent good money on when he had a family life.

"Zach, where are you?" Clouse yelled, pushing his way past the boat, towards the door leading to the stalls.

He threw open the door, finding a startled Zach staring up at him. Clouse dropped to one knee, putting his hands on Zach's shoulders.

"Thank God," he muttered to himself. "Why didn't you answer?"

"I didn't hear you, Daddy," Zach answered quietly. "I was thinking about Mommy."

Clouse pulled his son into a hug, knowing it would do little to ebb the pain. The least he could do was let Zach know he was there, and that he would never leave him.

At least he prayed that thought held true.

"Did you feed the cows?" Clouse asked, outwardly flashing a smile, dying a little more on the inside.

"Yeah, and Bucky too," Zach replied, making reference to the family horse.

Clouse hated the idea of anyone but himself feeding the horse with its unpredictable nature, but he said nothing for the moment, spying the horse grazing in the open field. It was part of the reason he was concerned for Zach's safety.

On several occasions, Bucky had attempted to bite or kick Clouse, and he knew that beast would think nothing of performing the same acts on a child. For some reason Zach was fond of the horse, which was part of the reason it remained on the property.

He looked quickly to see if Zach had actually carried out the chores, which he had. Clouse needed to make certain the animals wouldn't go hungry.

Taking his son's hand, Clouse led him back to the truck, intentionally keeping a distance from the house. Zach made no comment about going inside, but simply climbed into the truck's cab, ready to go wherever his father decided next. He was too numb inside and confused to care. Clouse realized this, knowing how much more devotion and attention he needed to give his son. Zach was very susceptible to what other people said, and to wandering off for no reason.

Clouse started the truck, ready for over an hour's drive to West Baden. Today was his one chance to investigate without others around, and without the fear of being closely watched by police detectives. He planned to make every second count.

***

Heavy white I-beams intersected like railroad tracks overhead as the construction worker walked the outer level of the hotel on the sixth floor. Each of the bolts holding the beams steadily in place left small rust spots on the otherwise spotless metal.

The beams gave the West Baden Springs Hotel enough structural integrity to bring the walls and floors up to code, preventing them from eventually caving in. Nearing a century in age, the building needed several improvements. The beams were one of the first necessary restoration areas started on the hotel. Connected to brick and concrete supports, the beams were now part of the hotel's framework, ensuring no part of it would collapse again.

Though brick and concrete kept the building upright, its primary internal makeup was a homely combination of plasterboard, tattered wallpaper, and the remains of oil-based paint that had long since faded and chipped. The unique blend of elements covering the walls probably gave any visitor to the gutted rooms the notion they were inside a condemned building.

Whistling to himself, the construction worker imagined he was a trolley following the tracks overhead, toward his destination. He wore tennis shoes, jeans, and a flannel shirt, indicative of what one might wear on his day off.

Brian Mathis was simply thankful to be inside the building, considering there was no work today and security was tight under ordinary circumstances.

With the strange events surrounding the exhumation of the Jesuit priest, work would be more trying the next several weeks. Luckily, the state trooper patrolling the outskirts of the hotel found sympathy in his plight, and unlocked the lobby door long enough for Mathis to get what he came for.

Walking into a numberless room, Mathis touched the doorframe, finding it naked like every other room in the hotel. The rooms were gutted of plumbing, doors, and divider walls. Without doors, the hallway and vacant rooms seemed to mesh as one complete open space. Only skeletal wooden frames served as any sort of division between the old rooms. Occasionally the rooms contained tubs or sink fixtures, depending on where they were located.

Rooms on the outside ring were mostly bare of any content, while the inner rooms sometimes held remnants of furniture, or perhaps a mirror. They were considered more important, holding priority because of the better view. They faced the atrium, which was nearly complete in the restoration. From the atrium floor, the rooms usually appeared with a single light bulb inside, providing a hint to how empty they truly were.

Mathis pulled a plasterboard sheet from a wall where it appeared to have a perfect fit. It was the ideal hiding place for several of his smaller tools. Lugging them down five flights of stairs, or waiting for a turn on the elevator annoyed him, so he simply hid his tools where his co-workers would never look. Until remodeling began upstairs, he would have a useful secret, because some of his colleagues were not as trustworthy as himself.

For the past two weeks, his wife had nagged at him to do some repairs around the house, including the eaves along the roof, and several divider walls she wanted installed in the closets. For such jobs, Mathis needed his cordless drill, which he usually left at work.

He was lucky the state trooper had let him in. The workers seldom had trouble getting into the building with any officers. After all, it was their job to be at the hotel too. Knowing no one was in the building, Mathis promised the trooper he would get his tools and be right back.

Pulling a loaded tool belt from the wall, Mathis snatched up what he needed, and replaced the belt, reaching for his drill case. Soon he would be putting it to use on his only day off. Working on his house would definitely pay off in the long run. Mathis and his wife were expecting their third child in a few months, which meant his current living situation would get crowded.

For the past two years Mathis had fought to make improvements on the roof, the interior, and the basement, raising the market value so he could sell it for far more than he paid. When that happened, he and his family could move into the country to build their dream home, and he could look forward to retirement once the loan was paid in full. Of course his occupation allowed him to buy materials and do labor himself for fractions of contractor costs.

Before he finished assembling his collection for transport, a tapping noise from the hallway startled him.

"Who's there?" he called, thinking it sounded like a rock skipping off the concrete floor.

No answer came, and Mathis carefully set his tools in a pile before stepping outside the barren room to look. His range of vision was limited by the curvature of the hallway. He saw very little either way because the hallway disappeared around the bend about twenty feet in either direction. He was ready to dismiss the noise when the tap came again to his right, just out of sight.

Cautiously, Mathis stepped to his right, cocking his head for a better view before he rounded the corner. The hallway came into sight, revealing nothing. He passed the first door to his right, seeing nothing inside. An eerie darkness encompassed the rooms, because the hazy day allowed little light to peer through the plastic sheets covering the windows on the other side of the hall from the outside.

Mathis wondered if the trooper had put someone up to playing a prank on him. Any of his co-workers would happily give the construction worker a scare if they happened to be on the grounds. Even on days they worked, most had fun at the expense of others, several times per shift.

Drawing near the second door, Mathis glanced outside, seeing little but treetops and the gray sky that seemed a permanent fixture the entire fall season. He turned his head back too late as the scythe was already coming toward him.

He drew back as the weapon cut into his abdomen, immediately drawing blood as it pierced several organs. Mathis grunted as his back hit the wall, but he was not mortally wounded. Grabbing the wooden handle of the scythe, he shoved it out and away from his body, taking flight down the hallway, stumbling as he went.

A quick loss of blood and the gash in his stomach forced him to clutch his lower torso as he ran, dripping blood along the dusty concrete floor. He stood little chance, unless the elevator was open and ready to go. Mathis would need to fight off the killer long enough to shut the large door and take the elevator car down to safety if he hoped to survive.

His faceless killer, donning a black cloak, took chase, walking briskly behind his damaged victim. Mathis felt the warmth on his side, sensing his life ebb a bit further with every desperate step. Survival instincts took over, leaving him no choice but to run, because he was incapable of defending himself in a lengthy confrontation.

Feeling a great loss of energy and warmth, Mathis slumped against the wall for support, still stumbling toward the elevator. He was unaware of how slow he had become, or that this was now a game of cat and mouse.

When the elevator drew near, Mathis made one final push toward it, only to have his legs tripped up by the killer's scythe. The construction worker collapsed to the ground, his shins lacerated and his side still dripping blood. Rolling himself over slowly, in pain, he could only lie still and breathe, waiting for the killer to decide his fate as he looked up in a semiconscious haze.

Helplessly on the ground, leaking blood into a pool beside him, Mathis watched as the killer stared at him from above, as though deciding exactly what to do. Behind the hood, cold eyes stared through a mask of pure black, revealing none of the killer's features from behind the shroud of death he wore.

In fact, the costume was that of the grim reaper. He held the scythe above Mathis in judgment, studying his victim before he decided what fate to place on the construction worker. Mathis could only groan slightly as his fingers twitched, displaying what little mobility he now possessed.

Mathis actually wondered in his disoriented state if death itself had come for him. He felt positive the next world awaited him as his consciousness wavered. As the killer grabbed hold of his foot, dragging him toward the elevator, Mathis knew his final destiny awaited, wherever this reaper decided.

***

In Landamere's office downstairs, Clouse shuffled several papers together, placing them in a folder. Earlier that morning Rusty Cranor had phoned him, informing him that Landamere was nowhere to be found, and he could not be reached. The assistant foreman had orders from Dr. Martin Smith, the hotel's current owner and driving force behind the restoration, to place Clouse in charge of the project if he was willing and able, with all the turbulent events occurring in his life.

Clouse looked around the office, making certain he had the essentials to take over the project he had reluctantly agreed to. Though Rusty knew far more about construction than Clouse, the man refused to take a true leadership position over the men he worked side by side with every day. Clouse didn't mind overseeing the construction, because he and Landamere shared similar taste and ideas. Besides, unbeknownst to the workers, the next month's work was fully planned.

"You ready, Zach?" Clouse asked, taking one final look around.

"Sure."

Things were getting no better for the firefighter as his wife's calling hours took place the following day, and it would look worse with him taking time off at the fire department only to work at the hotel. Of course, their chief had actually requested both he and Roger Summers take at least one week off.

Clouse cared less about how others thought, but wondered if keeping his emotions held in, and missing so much time with family at a time when he needed others, might lead him to a breakdown. Eventually everything would catch up to him, emotionally and physically, if he continued to work nonstop.

As he and Zach stepped from the office, Clouse locked the door, hearing a noise from down the hall. From the loud metallic thud, he assumed the elevator had reached the bottom floor. The officer outside had informed him Brian Mathis was upstairs, and ordinarily Clouse would have stepped over to say hello.

But not today.

Taking Zach by the hand, and he headed for the lobby door, anxious to get home before anything else bad happened in his life. He worried about Landamere's whereabouts, realizing a number of strange occurrences were taking place around him the past few days. How everything went from being nearly picture perfect to completely disastrous was beyond him. Clouse could only take life one day at a time and put the shattered pieces back in a dysfunctional jigsaw puzzle.

He walked outside, giving a wave goodbye and a forced grin to the uniformed trooper before helping Zach into the truck, leaving the hotel with the hope Landamere might return to handle the affairs by Monday morning. Clouse needed personal space before his emotions exploded. His truck pulled through the arched entrance gate as he gave the great structure one last glance, hoping his luck improved by the next time he visited.

***

Nearly an hour passed before trooper Jason Brinkman noticed Mathis' truck parked along the brick path that led to the hotel entrance. He had walked the grounds both outside and along the first floor of the structure, losing track of time, assuming the construction worker was long since finished retrieving his tools.

"Damn it," Brinkman said under his breath, followed by a sigh.

A dark sky rumbled overhead as clouds shuffled into position for a thunderstorm. To the officer, the weather seemed too cold for anything but snow, but distant thunder and blackening clouds made him a believer.

He was in no mood to search for Mathis, but standing outside with the cold and wind was about his only other option. The only lighting inside on a Sunday would be auxiliary lights, usually atop posts, or mounted to walls. Brinkman knew turning on additional lights was impossible, because there were none until the electricians rewired the building.

Removing his flashlight from his gun belt, the trooper unlocked the front door, stepping inside from the unfavorable weather. The sound of the glass door closing behind him echoed throughout the ground level as he turned the flashlight on, heading for the elevator.

He knew Mathis and his group were working on the sixth floor, gutting several rooms and redoing plumbing fixtures. Brinkman also knew the sixth floor had absolutely no lighting, or power, unless extension cords were present from the lower levels. He wondered what would keep Mathis so long, praying no accident had occurred.

He could see the word "liability" hung over his neck like an albatross, after losing his job, if anything happened to the laborer. No one except the foremen were technically allowed to enter the hotel on the off days, but security officers were usually kind enough to let police colleagues look around, or construction workers fetch their belongings. For his sake, he hoped his kindness hadn't forsaken him.

During the elevator ride up, Brinkman shined his flashlight around the metallic box, finding nothing except white paint, peppered rust, and what, at first, he considered to be more rust spots on the gray floor plate. Kneeling down, he found what appeared to be partially dried specks of blood, possibly from a small wound. He imagined cuts were common for construction workers in their line of work.

When the elevator drew to a stop, the trooper opened the solid door, greeted by a large puddle of blood pooling atop the concrete floor. Shining his light, he saw a red trail leading around a corner along the hallway wall.

"Holy mother of God," he stammered, knowing all too well this was no prank.

Carefully stepping forward, away from the reddish trail, the trooper shined his light around the corner, the beam shimmering off the liquid.

Finally, it led into the fifth room where Brinkman shined the light inside with his left hand while the other clasped the Beretta nine-millimeter at his side, his thumb undoing the holster latch. The blood went further than this room, but he noticed a prominent pool outside this particular door.

Carefully stepping around the blood, Brinkman slid around the doorway, finding nothing but an arranged pile of tools in the corner, ready for transport, but lacking an owner. The lightning flashed outside the window, startling the trooper, while highlighting just how much blood was on the floor outside the room.

"Oh, shit," the trooper said, plucking the Motorola radio from his duty belt. He needed backup immediately.

Chapter 8

Brinkman waited outside the hotel, wearing a rain slicker as the thunderstorm unleashed its fury on the town of West Baden. His Smokey the Bear hat, covered in protective plastic, was not enough to keep his head dry as rain ricocheted from his shoulders, soaking him thoroughly down his shirt collar.

When red and blue lights pierced the dense rainfall at the edge of the drive, the trooper breathed a sigh of relief to see Ken Kaiser's patrol car. Kaiser often spent his Sunday afternoons watching the hotel, but a schedule change kept him on patrol this week.

"What's the matter?" Kaiser asked, stepping from the car, protected only by his departmental jacket. Wearing no hat, the county officer was drenched by the freezing rain within seconds of stepping from the vehicle. "You sounded spooked on the radio."

Brinkman's hands were animated as he answered.

"Ken, there's a huge puddle of blood upstairs and the construction worker I let in to get his tools has been gone over an hour."

Remaining calm, Kaiser took the lead toward the hotel.

"There has to be some explanation," he stated. "Maybe the guy cut himself getting at his things. It's dark up there, you know."

When the elevator reached the sixth floor, Kaiser's expression matched that of Brinkman's initial response.

"That's some cut," the county cop said in awe, staring at the trail of blood illuminated by his flashlight.

"It leads back to a room where I found some tools. I think they're his," Brinkman said, referring to Mathis. He took a moment to show Kaiser the specks of blood along the elevator's bare floor.

Kaiser walked alongside the trail to its sudden end where he found a large spatter of red on the wall, along with a hole that looked carved by a bladed object. Now he knew where the blood began, but not where it ended.

"Well?" Brinkman almost demanded the older officer's opinion.

"He made it to the elevator, but I don't know where he went from there."

"It could be any floor," Brinkman hypothesized.

"I don't think so," Kaiser said with some thought. "If he was bleeding that bad, he didn't get very far on his own. Someone probably dragged him into that elevator, possibly using a sheet or a tarp. There isn't much blood in the elevator itself."

"Would they take him to a different floor?"

"Hard telling, especially without any light around here."

Kaiser led the way back to the elevator, formulating a plan. He considered calling more officers on the radio, but coverage in Orange County was thin and Kaiser didn't want to look a fool if this was some elaborate prank.

"Let's check the ground floor first, then work our way back up if necessary."

Several flashes of lightning greeted the officers when the elevator door opened on the ground floor. Kaiser ignored the power of Mother Nature, shining his flashlight beam toward the tile floor, kneeling for a closer look. If Mathis was placed on plastic, as he suspected, drops of blood would occasionally trickle off, but they would be scarce, and difficult to spot.

"Anything?" Brinkman asked.

"Not yet," Kaiser replied, straining to see any variances in the dark patterns along the floor. The tile had its own shimmering effect, making detection of blood drops highly difficult.

Rubbing his hand along the tile, the county officer felt a slight wetness graze one of his fingers. Unsure if it was the water they had tracked in, or more blood, he shined his light beam over his palm, finding traces of red.

"Oh, no," he said, realizing the direction of the thin trail led toward a back entrance.

Brinkman noted the blood under the light as well, looking down the dark hallway. There were only a few ways Mathis could have been dragged. The most likely would have been out the rear door, which led to a nearby path visitors might want to travel along the hotel grounds.

Kaiser threw open the backdoor, unhappy about being in the pouring rain again. The trooper followed a pace behind, like a puppy anxious to learn a new trick. He was nervous and excited at the same time. Brinkman was new enough to have never seen a dead body, and his curiosity got the better of his professionalism.

Once both stepped across the back lawn, consisting of mowed grass and clumps of dirt awaiting a use, Kaiser pointed to his right.

"Check over there around the truck entrance," he ordered.

While Brinkman investigated the secondary entrance, Kaiser looked around the lawn, finding nothing out of place, and no dead body as he'd expected. He looked up the hill where flowerbeds would be planted in the spring, seeing little through the thickets of trees that encumbered the hillside.

He trudged up the hill, collecting mud on his treaded boots with every step. The trees seemed to amplify the amount of precipitation hammering him from above as he walked along the hill, looking for any disturbances in the muddy embankment. Shining the light to his left, the deputy thought he spied a glimpse of color in the otherwise dark terrain.

Drawing closer to the object, he could see a blur that looked like flesh, then a leg emerging from the murky ground. His jaw dropped when he saw ripped blue jeans gripping the leg of a person he assumed to be Brian Mathis. Before approaching the body, he yelled urgently through the rainfall for Brinkman, hoping the trooper would hear.

He was about to radio the trooper when he whirled to confront a crunching noise behind him. Kaiser let out a sigh of relief when he found Brinkman had already arrived.

"Up here," Kaiser led the way, wondering what remained of Mathis.

Both stared into a makeshift grave which left an arm and a leg of its victim lying out, the dirt barely covering most the head and torso. Half afraid to touch the body, fearing evidence contamination, Kaiser could only stare, noticing several areas along the muddy grave where a plastic painter's tarp pierced the soil. He heard distinct tapping sounds as the rain drops smacked its synthetic edges.

Crouching beside the horrific grave, Kaiser stared up to the dark sky, allowing the moisture to strike him squarely in the face. He wondered what possessed someone to murder a family man, simply at the hotel a few minutes to gather some tools.

Standing up, he plucked his radio from the left side of his gun belt, ready to call for the necessary authorities to investigate a homicide when he saw Brinkman look more intently at the grave, as though something possessed his attention.

"I think he's still breathing," the trooper said in awe, staring for further evidence to support his claim. It came a few seconds later with a heave of Mathis' barely exposed abdomen where blood seemed to encompass the man's skin and clothing.

"You sure?" Kaiser asked almost defiantly as the trooper began to claw dirt away from the construction worker, convinced what he witnessed was true.

"Yes, now help me get him out of here!" Brinkman yelled, still pawing dirt behind him like a crazed dog getting close to his prized bone.

Reluctantly, Kaiser knelt down, helping the trooper, hoping Brinkman was right, praying they weren't disturbing evidence of a homicide. He knew of few quicker or more severe ways to be reprimanded by any police department than tampering with evidence at a crime scene.

***

"He's damn lucky to be alive," a doctor told the two officers standing across the hall from the room Mathis was resting in. "He lost a tremendous amount of blood."

"Has he said anything?" Kaiser inquired.

"He hasn't regained consciousness yet, but he keeps muttering something about a reaper, like a grim reaper, and gets agitated when he sleeps. The next forty-eight hours will determine whether or not he makes it."

Kaiser nearly missed the last of what the doctor stated, realizing the reaper statement from Mathis fit the coroner's findings of a curved blade used to kill Angie Clouse. He wondered how well a farm tool served as a murder weapon, and if someone was using a grim reaper gimmick to kill in serial fashion. It sounded preposterous, like something out of a teen slasher flick.

As the doctor entered Mathis' room, Kaiser stared down the hall at Larry Kendle. The detective read a Sunday paper, sitting patiently on a cushioned bench, waiting for a crack at either officer, or Brian Mathis, if he regained consciousness.

Kaiser felt for the man's family, who paced the Bloomington Hospital surgical waiting room, hoping for good news that might never come. The officer had written Mathis off, but whoever buried the construction worker packed dirt tightly over the tarp covering Mathis' wound. This act put just enough pressure on the gouge to prevent fatal bleeding, whether it was intentional or not.

To Kaiser, Kendle lived up to his reputation of being a bulldog, fighting and tearing his way toward answers, but the deputy felt the detective was barking up the wrong tree. He knew Kendle wanted to pin Angie's murder on his friend, but he knew there wasn't much evidence supporting Clouse either.

Taking a look at the clock down the hall, Kaiser found midnight a lot closer than he expected. Mathis' surgery took over nine hours with several surgeons working in shifts. Shock had kept him alive through cold rain and a partial burial, but he had yet to awaken from the ordeal. Now two hours removed from the cutting table, time would tell.

While Kaiser waited patiently at the hospital, Brinkman had finished his shift at the hotel, gone home, and changed clothes before making the trip to Bloomington. Kaiser had comforted Mathis' family while the trooper gathered what information he could from surgeons as they left the operating room. Until now, the two had barely spoken a word to one another since finding Mathis behind the hotel.

"Was anyone else there this morning?" Kaiser asked Brinkman in a hushed voice, staring down at Kendle, who perused the sports section.

Taking notice of the stare, the trooper turned Kaiser away from the detective before answering, knowing how his answer would impact the county officer.

"Your buddy Paul Clouse stopped by with his son for a few minutes just after Mathis went inside," the trooper replied.

Kaiser closed his eyes dejectedly. He rubbed his cheeks and chin with both hands, nervously searching for any positive thoughts that might separate Clouse from this tragedy. It seemed ridiculous that the firefighter was around every time blood was spilled, or bodies popped up, but even he could not overlook the coincidence.

"How long was he there?"

"About ten minutes or so," Brinkman replied, trying to clearly recall. "He came out carrying a briefcase, acting normal as could be."

"And Zach?"

The trooper shot a questioning look.

"His son," Kaiser clarified.

"Oh, he acted pretty down, but certainly not worried or scared."

Kaiser considered the attempted murder situation momentarily, realizing no one could commit such an act and leave the scene without some trace evidence on him. Blood, dirt, or DNA would have to be present on Clouse's clothes, or in his truck. The plastic would be checked for prints, which he imagined would turn up nothing, indicating the killer had used gloves.

Given the circumstances, Kaiser seriously doubted his friend would have time to settle Zach, don gloves, go up the elevator, commit murder, partially bury Mathis, dispose of evidence properly, and leave the scene while he and Zach acted perfectly calm and collected. He wanted Kendle to immediately check his friend for evidence, but shared Clouse's fear.

Someone could be setting him up.

"Did Dave Landamere show up today?" Kaiser asked curiously.

"No," Brinkman answered. "Why?"

"Nothing, really. He's been gone since Friday when all of this mess started."

"You think something's up with him?"

"Hard telling," Kaiser said, feeling more restless with each passing second. He wanted to get home and hug his entire family more than anything. "This whole weekend has been one big shitball. I'd probably take off too."

He started down the hall, needing to find Clouse before the police did, even if it was getting late.

"Where are you going?" Brinkman called.

"To see a friend," the deputy replied without breaking stride. "You can fill Detective Kendle in on everything," he added, shooting the detective a cold stare as he passed the bench.

***

Two hours ago Clouse had been ready to return to his apartment. That was before Zach fell asleep on Kelli Summers' couch and Clouse found all sorts of topics to discuss with Kelli about the next day's calling hours, memories with Angie, and several secrets he never knew.

"So Angie didn't plan to get back with me," he replied more to himself than Kelli, who had led into such an unfortunate statement with several others that softened the blow.

"She still loved you very much, Paul, but Angie saw how much you both flourished when you were apart."

"That doesn't sound like her and that's not how I looked at it," Clouse stated calmly, carefully adjusting how he sat on the loveseat in the dimly lit living room. He looked at his son sleeping peacefully beside him; head nestled atop his lap, oblivious to the adult conversation filling the room. "It was always rewarding when I got home to see this little one and Ang waiting for me."

Kelli took a sip from her sweetened tea, looking at the nephew she always enjoyed caring for. While Angie found love early, her younger sister waited patiently for the right partner, learning from her sister's trials and tribulations in marriage.

"He sleeps so soundly," Kelli noted, quickly changing subjects. "Most kids fuss, or they toss and turn, but Zach always goes right to sleep."

"This has been so rough on him. I think sleep is his only escape right now."

"And you?"

"Work," Clouse answered. "It's the only thing that keeps me going."

"You need time off to be with him, Paul," Kelli advised. "Zach needs you more than ever right now."

"I know, but I'm not left with any choice. The head foreman at the hotel took a hiatus without telling anyone. I'm the only one who can fill in."

Kelli threw her arms up in disgust.

"Screw the hotel, Paul. It can wait, or they can rebuild it without you. You've got yourself and your son to worry about. This was part of the reason Ang was always pissed at you. You always made work your number one priority and got to family matters when you had time."

Such a statement could have angered Clouse, but it was too true for him to argue against.

"I know." He took a drink from the warm beer can beside him. It was only his second of the night. There was no arguing the point. As happy as his family life appeared, and actually was, the joyous moments seemed scattered over six years of marriage, never consistent. "So I won't cause any waves at the calling hours tomorrow?"

Kelli thought several seconds, taking note of a police car turning onto her street a block away.

"Mom and Dad aren't thrilled about you being there, but they don't have a choice, and I don't think anyone here yesterday truly considered you capable of murder. Hard as this has been, I know in my heart you would never hurt my sister, Paul."

"Thanks," he said with a sincere nod of appreciation. "You're about the only one who thinks that."

"Roger's been your biggest advocate," Kelli admitted. "He told everyone to leave you alone the next few days, and that the breakup with Angie didn't mean a thing."

It meant a great deal to Clouse, now more than ever. He had no idea she intended their separation to be so permanent, or that her personal ambition had made him an obstacle. If what Kelli said was true, Angie still loved him, but lost use for him as part of her life. Being used and discarded did not suit Clouse, and now a serious emotional dilemma haunted him.

Roger Summers, his brother-in-law, had been as much of a close friend as anyone the last several years. Summers was a groomsman at his wedding, helped him land his job at the fire department, and often took Clouse boating with him on Lake Monroe during the summer. Strangely, he took Clouse's side in the separation, telling his sister she was insane for even considering parting ways.

In some ways he was like the older brother Clouse never had.

Before he could wallow further into the implications of a dissolving marriage, or the notion that he permanently solved his problems through murder, a knock came at the front door, which failed to stir Zach from using his father's leg as a pillow.

"I'll get it," Kelli said, opening the door to find Ken Kaiser standing outside, a look of concern across his face.

"Ken," Clouse said with an air of surprise. Carefully replacing his leg with a real pillow, Clouse let Zach slumber as he stepped past Kelli. "I'll be back in a minute," he told her, closing the door behind him, leaving the two friends in the cold silence of the night.

"Were you at the hotel today?" Kaiser asked before Clouse could inquire how his friend had learned his current whereabouts.

"Yeah. Why?"

"Someone tried to kill Brian Mathis, and they still might have."

"What?" Clouse asked, genuinely shocked.

"He got cut up pretty good, dragged to the elevator, went six floors down, then the prick buried him in a shallow grave out back," Kaiser abridged the story. "You arrived a few minutes after he did and left a few minutes later."

"Ken, I couldn't have-"

"I know. Kendle's going to have a field day when he finds out you were there. He'll want to check your truck and your clothes for DNA again."

"Let him."

"That's what I say. We've got to get some evidence in your favor, Paul. Sometimes a lack of evidence can be just as good as an alibi."

"Damn it," Clouse said, caressing his forehead, angered that someone dared attack an employee at the hotel. "Is someone setting me up, Ken? I mean this whole thing is going too far."

"You still wearing the same clothes you were this morning?" Kaiser asked, ready to help however he could, but avoiding his friend's question.

Clouse looked at his jeans and shirt, then to the tan, lizard-skin cowboy boots. Everything was the same. He nodded an affirmative to Kaiser.

"Let's go to the hospital, have Brinkman identify what you're wearing, and get this over with so Kendle can't bitch that you're evading him," the county officer suggested.

"Okay," Clouse agreed, thinking of something he'd prefer to give Kendle, like a broken jaw. "Let me tell Kelli what's going on, so she can keep Zach tonight."

Kaiser stared at the frost forming on the lawn in the quiet Bloomington neighborhood, as Clouse walked inside. He wondered if his efforts would be enough to keep Kendle from crucifying the firefighter, as he had so many others. The detective had a reputation for tenaciously pursuing suspects, sometimes ignoring important facts. Several cases had been overturned in appeals with evidence Kendle never presented to the court. The detective had been accused of creating his own verdict and leaving no room for opinion inside court hearings.

Kaiser respected Kendle's abilities, but not his methods. He understood most homicide cases were open and shut with obvious motive or overwhelming evidence, but sometimes the easiest solution was not the most accurate. Kaiser regretted having to protect his friend's name by playing a pretrial game with the detective. He hoped Kendle was open to all possibilities, but he would push the envelope to make certain the detective remained impartial.

Clouse returned in a moment with a look on his face Kaiser could not read. He looked worn, almost defeated, yet hopeful deep down that this could be resolved. He had never seen his friend so dejected, so Kaiser felt more certain than ever Clouse was innocent.

"Ready?" he asked.

"Let's do it," Clouse answered as they walked toward his truck.

Chapter 9

Monday morning and afternoon came and went quickly for Clouse. Landamere failed to show up for work at the hotel again, but Clouse left Rusty in charge, taking a full day off for the calling hours and time with his son.

Rusty informed him Landamere's wife had considered involving the police by listing her husband as a missing person. Strangely, no sign of the man's car, wallet, or anything he left the hotel with on Friday had turned up. Clouse found it odd the project manager would up and leave without notice, but imagined it might simply be a self-made vacation. With all the strange events surrounding the hotel and his life, he hoped that was all it might be.

Under ordinary circumstances Landamere's wife, Joan, probably would have involved the police, but Clouse knew from what Rusty told him that theirs was a marriage of convenience where either partner could leave at any time and sleep around as they pleased. Clouse found the situation odd, but he knew this was not the first time Landamere had taken unexpected time off. It was the first time he had left without informing his crew though.

As he drove toward the funeral home, Zach in the passenger seat beside him, Clouse thought of how much he had learned for such an inactive day. Keeping an eye on the red taillights in front of his truck, he let his memory wander.

Kaiser's helpful idea turned out to be less useful than Clouse expected. For every piece of evidence the county officer told Kendle he needed, the detective came up with a counter of how Clouse might have hidden or discarded it.

No trace of the Jesuit priest's remains turned up in the bed of the fireman's truck, but Kendle noted a large plastic sack or trunk of some sort could have been used for transporting the body. Kaiser insisted a hair or dried flesh sample would have appeared somewhere, but Kendle would not hear of it.

From the partial autopsy done on Angie's body, it was determined a scythe was indeed the murder weapon, and that it was several years old. Tiny rustic flakes were found in the body, but the weapon's exact age could not be determined. Though Clouse had never owned a scythe, or needed to, Kendle decided it might have come from anywhere, such as a neighbor's farm, or a friend who had lent it.

Kendle's reasoning for Clouse taking so little time in the hotel was that he could have attempted murder on Mathis, left the body a few minutes, and returned in the back where security would probably not have seen him, to bury the construction worker in the shallow grave.

"What about the muddy footprints we found around the grave?" Kaiser had questioned, knowing they would not match Clouse's cowboy boots.

Kendle countered, saying Clouse could have easily changed to a more practical treaded construction boot for burying the body, then replaced it, possibly in the hotel, where no one might think to look. A careful change of footwear before reentering the hotel would have prevented any muddy tracks on the tile floors inside. The detective went on to criticize Kaiser for treading on the crime scene himself, despite saving a life.

Kaiser countered by asking how Clouse could pull off any kind of attack with Zach present, but Kendle explained how easily children were amused, and that Zach, in a state of mild shock from his mother's death, likely sat in the office for a few minutes without question.

Clouse left halfway through the discussion, disgusted at Kendle's lack of effort on the case. Kaiser later filled him in on the missing details, including the fact it was verified the Jesuit body was indeed in the upstairs of his house. There was no reason Clouse could imagine why it would be placed up there, unless to implicate him. Even so, it seemed highly unlikely, and hardly feasible, that he would risk taking nearly three hours to leave the fire station, dig up a body, kill Angie, then hide the Jesuit body until morning.

Firefighters were never allowed to individually leave the station unless they ran an errand assigned by an officer, or special circumstances took precedence. Getting caught in such a situation out of the station typically provided a stiff punishment from the chief's office. In this scenario, the move would have certainly implicated Clouse in the murder if he were caught doing so. To Clouse, it made little sense that someone might set him up that way.

He wondered if Kendle realized there was nothing but circumstantial evidence on him. Otherwise, the detective would charge him with murder, Clouse decided. He realized the evidence was weak, if not too bizarre for him to have killed Angie. He wished the police would begin drawing some of the same conclusions.

"You okay, sport?" he asked Zach as the truck pulled into the funeral home parking lot.

"I'm okay."

Clouse noticed the cars of his in-laws, Roger Summers, and Kelli already there. The calling hours would have an open casket because the funeral home director announced he was able to create a presentable look for Angie once the coroner's office was done.

Both he and Zach dressed in gray suits, and Clouse made a point of wearing shined black shoes, which he typically wore only when working at the fire station. He felt the knots tying inside his stomach as he stepped from the truck, knowing his discomfort would either intensify or lessen once he dealt with Angie's parents.

Clouse hoped the open casket would help Zach put some closure on his mother's death. He debated the entire morning about the effects on Zach if he attended, but Kelli talked him into bringing the boy. She agreed with Clouse that actually seeing his mother dead would hurt tremendously in the beginning, but make the healing process smoother in the long run.

Four-years-old was too young to lose a loved one, Clouse thought, especially a parent. In the past, he had played the reverse scenario in his head, knowing it was always possible he might go into a fire and never come out. He always thought Zach would be protected, and taken care of financially, but never truly considered the emotional scars. Now, being Zach's only parent, Clouse needed to change his outlook at work, and his reasons for making it home after every shift.

Stepping through the front door, Clouse drew the attention of everyone present, including Angie's parents. He said an uncomfortable hello to Ralph and Susan Summers, then to Kelli and Roger, suspecting it would be a long two hours.

It turned out he was right.

Clouse spent the calling hours accepting condolences from his fellow firefighters, most having no knowledge of his separation. A good number of Angie's family avoided him, while his own family steadfastly stayed by his side. It was the first time Clouse had truly seen his own parents in over a week. He barely found time to speak with his mother about Angie's incident the morning he found out.

"You okay?" Ken Kaiser asked toward the end of the ceremony, walking up to Clouse with Tim Niemeyer, another close friend from high school.

A thick man with conditioned arms and a waistline as robust as his chest, Niemeyer had played football, and run around with both the cop and the firefighter during their teenage years. Eventually he went his own way after high school, working construction for other people, while drawing a steady paycheck, but feeling something was missing from his life.

He realized how much better he could do working for himself, finally having time for his own family, if he removed some of life's obstacles. Each year as a business owner he saw less of his friends, but made himself available when Kaiser informed him of Clouse's trouble.

"I'm getting by," Clouse said to Kaiser's inquiry. "Good to see you, Tim," he said, finding himself pulled into a solid hug from Niemeyer.

"I'm sorry, Paul. Truly I am."

"Thanks."

"Anything we can do?" Kaiser asked.

Clouse hesitated. He wanted to tell them not to leave, or to make things right again, but asking the impossible did no good. His friends would think him crazy if he suddenly became dependent on them, or asked them for a night on the town to forget his troubles.

That would be selfish.

In truth, he wanted to be alone and have the people he cared about all around him at the same time. A river of emotions traveled through his body, changing by the second, leaving him emotionally torn.

"Thanks, guys, but I just need time alone," he finally answered the appropriate response.

After his friends moved on, every passing second felt more uncomfortable and the urge to leave intensified. When it drew to a close, Clouse barely recalled who was there or what words transpired between everyone. Guilt overwhelmed him and he could not help but think of the investigation against him and how his life was turned upside down.

To some, the funeral was closure, but Clouse considered it just another step in piecing his life together. He needed to know who killed his wife, or he would never live comfortably again.

As the last few guests walked out the front door, Clouse approached his parents. Before he could say a word, his mother's arms were around him with unsaid reassurance. Helen Clouse wanted to be with her son much more, but his schedule made it nearly impossible.

"How are you doing?" she asked.

"Fine, Mom," he replied, choking back tears now that the majority of people were departing. "I guess the worst of it's over."

"Are you getting the third degree?" John Clouse asked his son, looking in the direction of Angie's family.

"It could be worse."

He paused, afraid to ask a favor after neglecting his parents for so long, even if it could not be helped.

"Can you two keep Zach for the night? I could use some time alone."

Helen saw the pain in his face as he said those words. Even the strong-willed needed to mourn in their own way. She knew from personal experience he needed the evening to himself. Zach would feel the same, regardless of where he went. Her son, however, was too strong to show emotion in public. He would deal with Angie's death his own way and move on.

"We'll keep him," she replied. "You do what you have to."

***

When Clouse opened his front door, he was already partly undressed, barely holding back the flood of emotions knocking at his mental dam. He pulled the dangling tie from around his neck, flinging it over the apartment's kitchen table. Undoing the last few buttons on his dress shirt, he tossed it as well. He felt tears well up in his eyes as the night's events flashed before him, accompanied by all the good times he realized were gone, never to be relived with Angie.

He slumped against a wall, his bare back sliding down until he was seated on the carpet, tears of mourning once again slipping through. He quit fighting his emotion, letting it run free as he remembered his honeymoon with Angie in Florida.

Clouse recalled them running on the beach, carefree of life or anything in Bloomington. He envisioned himself grasping the gritty sand atop the beach as they made love every evening for two weeks at sunset. He could hear the waves caressing the sand while they lay across the beach, staring at the stars, their feet massaged by the tide. Occasionally they would giggle for no apparent reason, and he rather enjoyed Angie letting go of her serious nature, if even just for a little while.

After the memories of Florida, his mind ventured to visions of the wedding day itself. Clouse remembered the photos before the wedding, how uncomfortable the tux was, and how he disliked breaking the tradition of seeing the bride before the ceremony.

Her practical nature won him over, and they were able to attend the reception immediately following, instead of putting it off for pictures. It was the first of many concessions he recalled making for Angie. At that point, it was the happiest day of his life.

His memory turned to riding horses at her parents' farm during summers past, Angie's hair blowing gently in the wind. She smiled so much then, and so little toward the end. He remembered her laughing just for fun as they rode through open fields and tamed woods. One year they went through the effort of having a picnic at her favorite clearing, and she talked of her adventures growing up on the farm. He felt so close to her, hearing such personal details of her childhood that she never shared with anyone else.

As he sniffled, the memories of boating at Lake Monroe returned. Many of these were with Zach and other family members, but there were several nights when he and Angie escaped the world together, cruising until they found a secluded area of the lake. After setting anchor, they would talk or frolic before sleeping under the stars. He savored the evenings they had alone because so many obstacles kept them apart during the daytime.

Clouse rubbed his eyes, realizing how much they hurt from crying. Despite keeping his emotions checked in public, he could no longer hold back the pain. Nor could he let Zach see him mourn. It would only add to his son's confusion and compound the loss. He realized he could not keep pawning Zach off on others, or he risked losing the thing he held dear.

Standing up, Clouse kicked off his shoes and undid his belt before a knock came to the apartment door. Rubbing the moisture from his eyes, he quickly located the shirt and answered the door after putting it back on, surprised at who was visiting him.

"Kelli?"

"I'm sorry, Paul," Kelli Summers said, gently holding her hands at her waist.

She looked beautiful in the navy blue dress covering her slender form. With her hair down Kelli looked similar to Angie when Clouse first met her. In some ways, she was like a younger sister to him. Clouse often gave her advice on her house, or ran errands for her when a truck was necessary. In the dress, she looked young and innocent, like he felt a younger sister should.

He realized he was standing in complete darkness and flipped on a light.

"Were you going to bed?" she asked, as though interrupting something.

"No," he answered quickly. "Come on in."

Kelli stepped inside, surveying the apartment and its bachelor-like qualities. He knew she had seen the redness of his eyes and probably assumed she could help him through the loss. Clouse wondered how she was so strong through the entire ordeal.

"It's not easy, is it?" she asked.

"No."

"I did all of my crying the morning I found out," Kelli admitted, as though knowing his thoughts. "Tomorrow will be tough when they-"

"I know," Clouse nodded in understanding, fully aware that Angie would be buried in the morning.

He planned to attend unceremoniously, since her parents made all the arrangements. Clouse actually preferred it that way, letting them have a sense of finality with Angie's death, knowing they came as close to her final wishes as possible.

"My parents don't really hate you like you think," she said as he led her to the small living room.

"They don't?" he asked skeptically, taking a seat on the couch as she picked the recliner.

"This hasn't been easy on anyone," Kelli noted, "but they just want whoever did this to pay."

"And I do too," Clouse said, wondering what his sister-in-law was getting at.

"I would like to go through Angie's things with you, Paul, if I could. Maybe if we get into her computer files something will pop up."

"Maybe," he said reluctantly, wondering about the sincerity of the offer. He became more paranoid about people incriminating him further with each passing day. Clouse had to suspect everyone else to keep his objective perfectly clear. "Your family has just as much right as I do to sort through her things. I just can't bring myself to that point yet."

"Me neither. I just wanted you to know, and to see if you needed anything."

"I appreciate it," Clouse replied. "I pawned Zach off on my parents so he wouldn't see me like this."

Kelli shifted her seated position.

"Roger has his family and my parents have each other. I was just on my way home when I thought of you being alone, too."

Clouse forced a grin.

"I'm good. Really."

"I'll leave you alone," Kelli said, apparently realizing they both needed time to themselves as she stood.

He walked her to the door, unable to say much more. His mind felt numb, and he felt saying nothing would prove better than uttering something regrettable.

"See you tomorrow, Paul," she said, giving him a kiss on the cheek.

"Good night, Kelli," he replied before shutting the door, suddenly feeling awkward about the entire evening.

He headed for the bedroom, figuring sleep might do him more good than he realized, or at least give him a temporary escape from reality.

Chapter 10

Most of the funeral was like Clouse envisioned it would be. Again, he numbly waited it out, letting the images of the casket and its descent into the ground burn into his mind. He could not believe it was over, but the book of his life as he knew it closed.

While he traveled to the hotel for a routine inspection of the grounds he left Zach with Kelli, promising she could go to the house with him afterward to look through Angie's belongings. The cleaners had called Monday afternoon to inform him the house was cleaned and, what he assumed was a sizable receipt, had been left on the table. He put it on the credit card, unconcerned with the cost because whether he stayed or sold the house it needed to look presentable.

Looking over the grounds, Clouse noticed most of the workers steadily carrying items or hammering on various areas of the hotel. From the front, one could see and hear nearly everything going on. He was disappointed in Landamere for failing to show another day, refusing to believe it was anything but the manager dodging the circumstances surrounding the priest's body, or the Mathis incident. If the man's wife wasn't concerned enough to report him missing, Clouse decided to adopt a similar attitude.

An unannounced vacation was still a feasible possibility, but Landamere informed no one of his intentions, leaving the outside possibility foul play might be involved in his disappearance.

"You hear about Mathis?" Rusty Cranor asked, approaching the firefighter from behind.

"What about him?"

"Died this morning. It's been all over the radio. Now everyone's going to think this place is spooked."

Clouse's eyes widened.

"You mean they let the public know about the attack here?"

"Yeah," the foreman replied. "It's absolutely everywhere, Paul. That, and the priest's body isn't going to help our publicity campaign in the least."

Funded primarily by local residents, Dr. Martin Smith, and the occasional anonymous donation, the hotel needed community support and tourism to flourish in the remodel. If police cluttered the grounds more rumors would fly, and charitable dollars would certainly dwindle. People might balk at helping restore a historical site notorious for murders and strange hauntings. Clouse foresaw immeasurable peril if the media made a circus out of the latest events.

"We've already had police around here this morning looking for any clues they missed, I suppose," Rusty added.

"I'm sure the hired help won't get any boost in morale when they see a blood-soaked floor up there, or that grave out back," Clouse said.

Rusty drew close to Landamere's designer, looking around cautiously.

"I heard you were here that day."

"I was," Clouse replied. "Just to get some papers. I've already talked to the police and cleared everything up."

"Maybe you were lucky."

"How so?"

"Here you were that close to the killer and walked out. It could have been you if you'd gone upstairs," the foreman noted.

Somehow, Clouse doubted that. If he was being set up for these murders, it made no sense to harm him. He could not imagine being caught off-guard enough to allow a scythe to slice him open anyhow. Lately he was on edge wherever he walked.

Walking toward the sunken garden, Clouse took note of the fountains. Water still spat from the frog statues, reminding him of what winter weather could do to them. Though today was moderately warm, he knew a cold snap might hit Indiana and remain there through the entire winter.

"Rusty, please make sure those fountains are shut off and drained by tomorrow," he told the foreman. "The last thing we need is for those to freeze up and bust."

"Sure thing, Paul."

From the garden, Clouse spied activity on the graveyard hill. The old grounds keeper, known only as Vern, dug the barren grave even deeper to prevent further mishap. Beside him lay the bagged, bony remains of what everyone claimed was Father Ernest.

The police were done with the corpse, but Clouse felt an undying urge to know if the body was actually burned or not. He put little stock in the legend of Father Ernest's fiery death, or the notion that a priest considered himself some dark angel, without knowing the truth about the body. He needed to speak with Kaiser about any forensic findings.

Clouse disliked the grounds keeper. He considered Vern more of a local drunk, given a job out of sympathy because of his past hardships. The man's job was basically to clean up after the construction workers and keep the hotel property from looking messy.

I want to see that body, Clouse thought to himself, wishing the old stubborn man would leave his post a moment to sneak a drink. Before he realized it, he had stepped several paces toward the cemetery, away from Rusty. He was drawn to the body, becoming obsessed with the truth.

"Paul?" Rusty called.

"Yeah?"

"You okay?"

Clouse turned around, finding the foreman busily studying the layout of the garden, but attentive enough to monitor him. It seemed a lot of people were looking out for him lately.

"I'm fine," Clouse said, realizing he would not receive a chance to examine the body as Vern began shoveling dirt atop the newly deeper grave.

"Good. Let's get back inside," Rusty said, shooting a suspicious look back toward the grounds keeper, as though Vern's work efforts didn't meet his specifications.

Walking with Rusty toward the hotel, Clouse thought of lengths he might need to go to find the truth. He could not picture himself digging up bodies at midnight to disprove local legends, or combing through his house for samples he had no chance of analyzing. He could, however, begin rummaging through Angie's belongings and her computer for clues about who might have a grudge against her, or Clouse himself, for that matter.

Nearing the hotel, Clouse looked to the top of the towering building, despite the rare appearance by the sun nearly blinding him. He could see several workers walking without fear along the top of the dome, even as dark clouds moved closer, threatening to unleash a storm. Despite his work as a firefighter, he maintained a controlled reverence for heights.

Some of the workers could walk all day six stories above solid ground and take it for granted the materials beneath their feet would never collapse, or that an accident would never send them tumbling off the side. Clouse took no such thing for granted.

As his eyes panned down the hotel, something on the third floor caught his attention, keeping his eyes focused on the windows of the gutted rooms. He nearly dismissed it as glare from the sun when a dark streak crossed one window, then another. As Rusty started up the stairs toward the main lobby, Clouse stared, this time seeing more clearly a dark-cloaked figure scurrying along the floor where he knew several workers were clearing the remains of the gutted rooms for disposal.

"Oh, shit," he said to himself, rushing up the stairs past Rusty.

"Paul, what's wrong?"

"Get to the third floor as quick as you can," he ordered the foreman, darting up the remainder of the exterior steps, Rusty following several paces behind.

Avoiding the elevator, Clouse took a direct route of stairs up to the third floor. He barely heard the clopping of his boots against the old concrete landings, or the echoes they produced in the hotel's open spaces. He soon found himself standing at the third floor doorway, looking to the sawdust atop the floor before cautiously stepping into the hallway. He had lost Rusty a few floors back as the older foreman grew winded.

Walking quickly along the bare, exposed hall, the firefighter peered in each room as he passed it, finding nothing out of the ordinary.

Door after door passed without incident. When he neared a bend in the hallway Clouse heard Rusty reach the top of the stairs behind him. He turned to look without breaking stride, and hit a solid object as he rounded the bend in the hallway.

Startled, Clouse stumbled back, finding one of the workers in front of him, wearing dark clothes as he carried several worn boards, probably for disposal.

"Stevens," he said the man's last name, catching his breath. He was thankful to run into a live human being. "Who's up here with you?"

"It's just me and Felding, Mr. Clouse. Did you need something?" he asked as Rusty approached Clouse from behind.

"You haven't seen anyone else?" Clouse asked for clarification.

"Nope. We've been the only two people up here all morning."

"Thanks," Clouse said, turning away, ignoring the shocked look on the foreman's face.

Rusty waited until they were several steps away from Stevens to rip into Clouse's strange behavior.

"What in the hell was that about?"

"I thought I saw someone up here that didn't belong."

Rusty shot a puzzled look.

"You drag my old ass up three flights of stairs for that? You may be the boss right now, but I'm worried about your state of mind, Paul."

"I'm starting to worry, too," Clouse replied, wondering if his imagination and the recent talk of scythes and reapers were getting to him.

"Take the rest of the day off, Paul," Rusty suggested. "I can handle it."

Clouse gave a weak grin, knowing how the foreman must have felt about his erratic actions. He could accomplish more at home than the hotel anyhow.

"You win, Rusty. I'll probably see you tomorrow."

As Clouse walked down the hallway to leave, the foreman wondered just what demons ran through the mind of Paul Clouse, and if they would ever be exorcized.

***

Atop an electric pole behind the hotel, Robert Bennett put the finishing touches on the new wiring that would bring the facility into the current decade. Part of the reason so few lights were on could be blamed on old, faulty wiring, which Bennett was subcontracted to correct. Owning his own company, he was thankful for the business, and the notoriety that went with helping restore one of the greatest historical monuments in the country.

After checking the transformer sitting atop the ground behind the hotel, Bennett realized his problem stood a bit further back in the wiring connected to the nearest pole. The closest power company workers were often more than an hour away, and seldom did they rush to check component connections.

He knew from experience they usually sat around drinking coffee unless something urgent, like a downed power line, or a sparking transformer, was called in.

Bennett decided it would be in his best interest to climb the pole and probe around to save time.

Supported only by a line belt and correct placement of his feet, Bennett finished securing the wire to its connection points, checked it and the brackets holding it in place, and began his descent. As he slowly climbed down, the electrician looked over to the grand dome, loving the view from such a high vantage point.

He would see more of it in the coming weeks once he set to work on the backup generators in the basement and installed new wiring along each floor. Several relatives had nagged him for photos of the hotel's interior. Diehard fans of the West Baden Springs Hotel always wanted to see what the inaccessible rooms looked like. He promised to take pictures of whatever he could, hoping his traditionally poor photography skills might be enough to get some decent pictures.

From above the grounds, he had taken some shots using his telephoto lens the week before. Outdoor shots were easy, but without a good flash for his old Canon camera, photos inside might prove more difficult.

He had received the camera in high school as a gift when he took a photography class just to get into a newspaper class the next semester. It was top-of-the-line then, and he had refused to upgrade since. Little had his parents known his interest in journalism was merely to be around his girlfriend in a few more classes.

Eventually he married her; eventually they divorced, and in between had a daughter who was now going on eight years.

Owning a business kept Bennett too busy to see his daughter more than once or twice a month. He made it a point to schedule time in for her because he could work every waking day if he wished. Electrical work was always plentiful, but his employees also needed time for their families, so he carefully planned blocks of days off for them.

Bennett removed the spurs from the underside of his boots when his feet touched the unfinished landscape behind the hotel. He then took off his tool belt, setting his equipment on the soil while he peeled the front of his sweaty shirt away from his chest.

Dirt clumps and piles were everywhere, and would be until the layout of the hotel's lavish grounds was complete. He didn't care about it. After all, his work would be above the grounds, or in the hotel basement below.

Whistling to himself, Bennett carried his gear over to the white van with his business name painted along both sides in red lettering. He swung the back door open, tossing his gear inside. The gleam of his Canon camera caught his attention from behind some wire bales. Taking up the object, he removed the telephoto lens, replacing it with a regular lens. He had time for a few shots inside the hotel before returning to the shop.

He checked the counter, reassuring himself there was film still inside. He saw a high number of shots left, so he set it on a rapid shot setting, hoping for some artistic shots along the balcony as he walked it. Holding it up, he looked through the viewfinder, seeing nothing but pitch black inside the van.

Bennett lowered the camera, turned around, and saw a dark streak hurl toward him as his insides ripped apart. Pain jolted through all of his nerves simultaneously, causing his finger to lodge on the camera's shooting button.

A scythe remained lodged in his abdomen while someone covered in a black robe, with no visible face, pushed him back with the object against his van. The camera dropped from Bennett's hand, shooting off two more pictures before it, and its automatic winding system, fell to the ground just behind the dying electrician, under the bumper.

Bennett groaned as the killer propped a foot against his van's rear bumper, using it for leverage as he freed the sharp instrument of death from the mass of pink innards bulging from the electrician's abdomen. It tangled on part of his large intestine, pulling the stringy organ halfway out before the blade gave release. The scythe dripped blood as the killer stood a moment, watching Bennett slumped against his own vehicle, clutching his stomach. The mortally wounded man could only look at the killer with blank eyes, as though to ask 'Why?'

Picking Bennett up by his belt, the killer propped him against the van, watching him suffer, leaking blood a moment more. The electrician could only watch helplessly in his weakened state as the killer drew the scythe back and let it swing toward his throat, finishing the job as red droplets splattered across the white van.

Taking a quick glance around him, the killer was relieved to see no one had seen his deed, and no one would probably miss a utility man on the renovation project. He loaded the body of Robert Bennett into the van, scuffling dirt over the blood pools and specks around the scene. His load intact, the killer climbed into the driver's seat, heading out the back entrance where no one would see him. He had plans for the body and the van, so he needed to be extra careful.

Leaving a trail of gravel dust behind it, the van headed for the rear entrance after turning around in the narrow road. Its tires barely missed several blood specks on a tiny dirt mound beside a partly obscured camera, hidden beneath a thin layer of fresh dust.

Chapter 11

Steam rose from the pot atop Clouse's stove as he and Zach stared down at the noodles in the boiling water. Macaroni and cheese was not the father's idea of a hearty supper, but Angie had left little in her cupboards aside from boxed items and health dishes. The refrigerator and freezer held surprisingly less.

Signs of a happy homecoming were scarce.

Thanks to the firehouse, Clouse's cooking skills were above average. The food he found available was inadequate to test his ability. Angie often preferred to eat out when they were together as a family. This upset Clouse because he never wanted Zach to believe eating out was healthy, or economically sound.

"You want peanut butter and jelly or bologna?" Clouse offered Zach the only two choices available.

"Jelly," Zach answered, climbing down from the chair that gave him a vantage point into the boiling pot.

He walked to the kitchen window, staring at the field past the backyard, illuminated by intense orange light from the late afternoon sun. Clouse looked at his son while draining the water from the pot, noting how well Zach took to being in the house again, despite the tragedy only days prior.

Zach's reaction to his mother lying in a coffin was less animated than Clouse expected. True, the boy cried, but he was by no means hysterical. Perhaps getting over Angie's death wouldn't prove as hard as Clouse anticipated for Zach. He felt certain he was kidding himself with such a thought though.

Clouse quickly finished his son's late lunch and placed it on the table as Kelli pulled into the driveway in her small beige Toyota. He was thankful for the company to sort through Angie's belongings, but felt a need to check everything himself, just to be certain nothing was overlooked or misplaced.

Zach continued to nibble on his food while Clouse walked outside, greeting Kelli as she stepped from her car.

"Hello," he said, giving her a hug as she approached. "I appreciate you doing this."

"I'm happy to help," Kelli replied, refusing to release her end of the hug just yet. "I want to know who did this as much as you do."

"The police went through everything," Clouse said, having already glanced over the boxes. "We probably know more than they do about Angie's stuff, so maybe we'll find something they missed."

"Have you checked out her office?"

"I started with the cabinets. The desk and computer will probably give the most clues, so I'm saving them for last."

As they entered the kitchen, Clouse noticed Zach barely touching any of his lunch.

"Is it that bad, Zach?" he asked.

"I'm not hungry."

"It's okay. You want to play outside with the dogs awhile?"

"Yeah," Zach answered, hopping down from the chair. He darted out the front door, ready to enjoy one of the last decent afternoons before winter cold fronts moved in.

"No playing with Bucky!" Clouse called.

Kelli smiled as Clouse turned to face her.

"You're so lucky, Paul," she said, looking out to Zach who was now running circles around the dogs.

"I know. He's been a real trooper through all of this."

Clouse led the way to the family room where a line of boxes awaited them. To the right, he had Angie's office open with all of the lights turned on. Both the boxes and office were a mess after police had sifted through them a full day, apparently finding little or nothing of use.

"I'm going to start with the cabinets in there," Clouse said, nodding toward the office. "The boxes have a lot of personal stuff Ang stored away. Some of it will be wedding stuff, her old business books, and whatever else."

"Okay," Kelli said, digging into the first boxes of papers and tiny bins.

Clouse opened the large storage cabinet in Angie's office, finding little but manuals, software boxes with instructions, and a few tax books. As he expected, it was organized specifically for her business.

As he sifted through the desk, he found little more of use. Several pictures had been put away, most with him in them. She had several personal letters from out-of-state friends in the second drawer. He set them aside for reading later. He also set aside an address book that contained both personal friends and business associates.

Little else besides envelopes, a change pouch, and other staple items a desk required could be found inside the drawers. As Clouse finished his search he turned the computer on, suspecting it might hold more answers than anything else. He left one desk drawer for searching once he finished with the computer.

Angie worked quite a bit over the internet and kept most of her business dealings in her computer's hard drive. She once told him it was the heart and soul of her business. Clouse hoped an autopsy might reveal everything it held to him.

"You finding anything?" he called to Kelli.

"Nothing helpful," she replied. "I've been looking at some of your wedding photos."

Clouse rolled his eyes, but he knew he would probably do the same thing if he were looking through the boxes. In fact, he would probably have Zach look through them with him, so his son realized he would not let Angie's memory fade.

As he looked over the top of the desk, an envelope caught his attention next to the stack of important books and documents he planned to review later. Clouse picked up the envelope, recognizing the Florida address in the top left corner. He pulled out the letter from the already opened envelope, saw it was dated three weeks prior, and read it.

Dear Paul & Angie,

We're looking forward to having you down to the ranch after the holidays. Our company just expanded in St. Louis and Kansas City so we've been busy traveling. I still love keeping my hands in the business.

Just put out six new albums and printed over a dozen books last month. The online business has been phenomenal and we're looking at expanding there too. Maybe we can get Angie to help us develop our website.

> Concerning the hotel property in West Baden you sent me information on, Paul, it looks very promising for some projects I've got in mind, and I'll be talking it over with my partners at our next meeting. I'll be in touch with you once I have some more information. If you're working on the restoration, I'm certain it will be a major success.
>
> We'll be talking to you both soon.
>
> Michael Hathaway

Clouse put the letter and envelope on the desk, contemplating what opportunity he might have missed by not seeing it three weeks prior. The Hathaways were a couple he and Angie had met in Florida during their honeymoon. Michael Hathaway owned Trident Enterprises, a company that worked in music and print media. A shrewd businessman, Hathaway had made an impact with his books and music labels years before, then dabbled in business properties for sport.

About a month before he and Angie separated, Clouse had sent Hathaway a packet of information concerning his work on the hotel and what solid potential the hotel had if the businessman was interested. He explained the renovation was partial, and that the new owner would have limited creative control over the project's completion.

Clouse wondered if Hathaway had called during the separation. The invitation was to the couple's ranch in Texas where they spent part of the year. Angie certainly would have turned them down, and possibly explained the circumstances surrounding the separation. If she hadn't, Clouse felt obligated to decline the offer to vacation with them when he spoke with them again.

Clouse hoped the man was seriously considering buying the property. He easily had the financial resources and a genuine love for historic properties. Though persuasive writing was not his forte, Clouse had tried to sell Hathaway on the idea of buying the property as best he could. If Hathaway passed, the hotel might not sell for years, or the restoration might come to a standstill. Clouse also liked the idea of having a free pass to the property at any time, which he felt sure the businessman would give him.

Martin Smith technically owned the property, but wanted to sell to a worthy buyer who would not tarnish everything they had worked so hard to restore.

Smith merely bought the property to expedite the repairs, teaming with preservationists to save the hotel before it degenerated further.

Easily valued in the millions, Hathaway would get the West Baden Springs Hotel at a bargain if he generated the funds with his partners. The only conditions the National Preservation Society made clear to potential buyers were that the property would need its renovation finished, and that no major changes could be made, keeping the original design of the historical building intact.

Of course, certain updates were necessary to keep the building within modern code, but the remaining visible portions of the building were required to appear as they did when the hotel opened a century earlier.

Using the mouse beside the computer, Clouse clicked on a business program where Angie often kept her financial records, as well as information about her clients. While the program loaded, he checked the last desk drawer, finding telephone statements, carbon copies of her business checks, and several other opened envelopes. He set them on the desk with the other items he wanted to examine more closely later.

Clouse clicked on the client information box, calling up a list of Angie's software buyers from the time she began her business to the present. He skimmed the list of names and addresses, finding a high number of people in her life he knew nothing about. Most of the clients lived within Indiana, but Clouse knew only a handful of the names.

He printed a copy of the list to place with the stack atop the desk. Clouse then called up Angie's internet server and found her user name in place, but the program called for a password before he could log on to look for anything.

"I'll be damned," he said to himself, typing in several notions of what her password might be with no success.

He tried simple words like Zach's name, various animal names on his property, her friends' names, and even a nickname he gave her when they were first married. Nothing worked, then he recalled a message the server sometimes gave when he logged off his own computer about creating a password with a mixture of letters and numbers to prevent unwanted entry. Angie was quite practical, and that was something she would certainly do to keep Clouse and Zach away from her business files.

"I'll never get in there like that," he told himself. He needed to gain access to her online information, but it would take someone who knew how to hack passwords.

Clouse had someone in mind.

"I'm not finding anything in these boxes," Kelli called from the family room. "You having any luck?"

"Not much. I've got a lot of papers to look through later."

Clouse suddenly thought of something concerning Hathaway's letter. Whatever Kelli said from the next room went ignored as he picked the letter up, looking at its date.

"Damn her," he said under his breath.

After the separation, Angie had agreed to make one last appearance with Clouse, knowing how important the fund-raising ball was to his work with Landamere. The ball raised thousands for the restoration of the hotel, while providing a setting for many of the financial elite in Southern Indiana to meet. Clouse would not have missed the event for anything, and virtually pleaded with Angie to get her to attend.

From the date on the letter, it was in Angie's possession, and more than likely opened, before the ball took place. Throughout the entire party, they gave the appearance of a perfectly happy couple. Angie never strayed one moment from her charade, even to tell him about the letter. She looked beautiful in her dark blue dress, cut low around the neck so that her diamond necklace glistened in the various lighting. Angie bought it for herself after she landed her first corporate client to celebrate the occasion.

Clouse remembered disliking his rented tuxedo, even though it gave him a distinguished look he seldom got to enjoy. Angie's perfume reminded him of a subtle lilac scent that only drew Clouse to her all the more. Everything about his wife that evening caused his thoughts to wander.

Perhaps things were going so well she forgot about the letter, or meant to tell him later. Perhaps Angie saw Clouse in his glory, living out the notion they were still happily married. To him there never was a problem, but now he wondered just what Angie might have hidden from him.

Did she intentionally keep the letter's contents from him, perhaps for personal gain?

"Did you hear me?" Kelli asked, standing at the door of the office.

"Sorry, Kelli. I was just thinking."

He stood from the chair, suddenly uncomfortable being in the office.

"I've got to go. Roger wants the family over for drinks while everyone's in town. He said you were invited."

"I can't," Clouse refused softly, looking out toward Zach, still playing with the dogs. "If you and Roger get a chance to drop by later, we'd love the company."

Before turning to leave, Kelli dropped an unexpected kiss on Clouse's lips, surprising him, though it came and went in the blink of an eye. He wondered if she had missed her mark, but it was over so quickly he couldn't react.

"Take care, Paul," Kelli said without any lingering, or comment on the kiss, as she turned to go. "We'll be by later."

It wasn't uncommon for Kelli to kiss him before she left, but usually they were pecks on the cheek. Clouse often thought of her as his little sister, certain the feeling was mutual. Perhaps the kiss was innocent, but emotions were running high in the family lately, and he certainly didn't want a replacement for Angie, even in the form of her sister.

Still shocked by Kelli's kiss placement, Clouse slowly turned to the desk. He looked over the stack of papers atop the desk, shook his head, and walked into the family room. Several boxes of photos, both wedding, and Zach's early childhood, caught his attention. It was time to call Zach inside and recall some better days.

Chapter 12

Most of the afternoon built up to one large thunderstorm in West Baden until the dark clouds cut loose at dusk.

Even the hotel's elegant lampposts were barely visible through the downpour of rain as thunder rolled in the distance. Occasionally, lightning struck behind the huge, rounded hotel, making it appear like a castle, daring would-be travelers to step inside for shelter.

Sean Timmons threw back a clump of hard dirt with a vengeance before thrusting his shovel into the ground once more. It was bad enough digging the grave of an alleged nutcase, but doing so in the middle of the pouring rain seemed even more absurd.

"You know, you could have avoided this by getting here a little sooner," Vern, the grounds keeper, said from behind Timmons, startling the teenager.

"There is such a thing as school, you know," Timmons retorted.

"Not that I'd imagine you attend much," Vern fired back, keeping himself dry beneath an old umbrella as he took a swig from his flask.

His raspy sentences, often framed with audible exhaling, sent shivers through Timmons' body whenever he heard the man speak.

"I can think of worse fates than digging that hole, boy."

"I can't."

"It beats me reporting you for firing your little gun on the hotel grounds, doesn't it?"

Timmons merely grumbled to himself as the grounds keeper walked away, whistling cheerfully as he went, probably to distract the security guard.

Only the day before, his life had seemed much better, never having met the grounds keeper. Timmons always made it a point to carefully check around before firing the gun. Either Vern had outsmarted him or happened to be lucky enough to hear him this time.

Unfortunately, after several months of using the woods behind the hotel for a target practice area, Timmons was caught by the snoopy Vern.

He had only fired his .22 pistol on the grounds because there were no other areas available, but the keeper refused to hear his testimony. Instead, he set the young man to doing his dirty work. Though he hated the notion of being blackmailed, the teen had little choice but to comply, or his parents would surely ground him and take away his firearm. Any action such as taking away his gun would certainly be out of spite, and not stemming from concern for his wellbeing. His parents spent most of their time arguing about how much booze was stocked in their cabinets, or when Timmons' father planned to sell one of the dozen cars in the yard that didn't run. Often his whereabouts and school grades took a backseat to the trivial matters in their lives.

Timmons simply bided his time until he was able to move away, whether he found a trade school somewhere, or a job offer came along that took him far away from Orange County. In just under two years, high school graduation would provide him some freedom to live on his own and escape the hell his parents created around him.

Vern had not dug the grave deep enough to suit Rusty Cranor that morning. The foreman wanted to ensure no one else could disturb Father Ernest's resting place, and caught the grounds keeper just before his shift ended, stating he wanted the job done before the construction crew arrived the next day.

Timmons dug a few more minutes before his arms began to ache. The rain pounded his head and back as he threw the heavy, soaked chunks of dirt up behind him. Sighing aloud, he wiped a combination of sweat and cool rain from his forehead, pulling himself out from the grave.

His arm brushed against the canvas bag containing the bony remains of Ernest. A hand grayed with age, still containing traces of flaky skin, emerged from the open end of the bag, its fingers curled as though summoning someone to it.

Timmons made a disgusted noise to himself, jerking his arm back as he stood beside the grave a moment.

Leaving the shovel beside the open hole, he wandered down the hill in search of where Vern might have gone. He called the man's name several times through the dense rain, seeing and hearing nothing.

"Damn," he said, turning to the brick path beside him to ascend the stairs toward the grave.

His parents would begin to wonder exactly where he was on a school night. His driver's license was less than a month old and easily taken away if they suspected he was out doing no good. They helped him obtain his license simply to find relief from the burden, as they called it, of driving him places.

When he returned to the gravesite, Timmons noticed the shovel missing. He searched wildly around the area, knowing he was gone only a moment. Even in the dense rain, the light gray of the tombstones along the hill left them highly visible. The thought of being on a hill filled with corpses, completely alone, without a shovel, frightened him.

Desperately looking around for Vern, the teenager stepped back a few feet. As the rain impaired his vision and hearing, Timmons never saw the blade of a scythe rise from the hole he had just added depth to a few minutes earlier.

He cried out as the curved blade lodged its sharp end into the back of his leg's calve muscle, tripping him as it yanked back.

Timmons hit the ground face-first, clawing at the dirt for an escape as the killer attempted to pull him back, using the weapon as a pulley. Several seconds into the process the scythe slipped out, forcing the killer to rise from the grave, cloaked in black, as the teen scrambled to regain his footing.

Unable to escape very quickly on the slick ground, Timmons opted to pull his .22 pistol from beneath his jacket, flipping to his backside for a better aim at the reaper stalking him. Attempting to distance himself from the killer first, Timmons began backpedaling his way down the hill like a fiddler crab. The slick grass and fresh mud kept tripping up his hands, nearly dislodging the gun from his right hand.

He finally stopped to nervously raise and fire the gun into the chest of the reaper who loomed above him on the high ground.

No damage.

Not even a flinch.

He fired again and again into the chest, seeing no reaction from the killer as he walked ominously toward his victim. Frozen in terror, his gun empty, Timmons could only stare upward as the killer towered over him.

With one swift action, the reaper swung the weapon like an axe, lodging it in the teenager's thigh muscle, causing another scream, this one longer due to the intense pain coursing through his leg.

"No! Please!" Timmons pleaded as the killer dragged him toward the grave, screaming, and kicking with his free leg, clawing at the liquefying soil for any way possible to slow or stop the killer from finishing the job.

Using the scythe for leverage, the killer swung Timmons into the grave, letting the weapon's blade release with an upward jerk. As the teenager fell hard into the rectangular opening, the reaper reached for the shovel hidden behind the dirt pile, scooping dirt into the occupied grave.

Refusing to be buried alive, Timmons leaped to his feet, despite the agony of his crippled leg, clasping the killer by his ankle, tripping him up. As the reaper lost his footing, Timmons began to scale the other side of the large opening, attempting an escape.

Before he could raise his second leg over the ledge, he felt something tug him back. The killer had entered the grave to stop him. After pulling him back, the killer whirled Timmons around, allowing the teenager to claw at his mask.

Timmons' attempt to unmask the killer only resulted in him receiving a swift knife to, and through, his abdomen, as it stuck in the dirt wall behind him. He felt the hollow void death would soon leave within the confines of his stomach, as the knife twisted around his guts, knocking part of the soil behind him loose.

Groaning his last few sounds, the teenager smelled the stench of stomach acid and the remainder of his lunch intertwined as his intestines split open, assuring his death would come momentarily. He slumped to the ground, tasting a few drops of rain as they belted his lips, becoming the last things he would feel in life.

***

As Zach lie asleep on the couch, Clouse looked through the last of the papers from the desk. If there was crucial information in any of the documentation he would never have recognized it. Angie's clients stretched from coast to coast, and most were probably contacts established through her online accounts.

Clouse felt helpless, knowing her business life never included him. She was independent in her business, constantly working alone. Many of the people and businesses listed in her manifests sounded powerful and well-established.

He wondered if Angie had intentionally hidden the letter from him, trying to locate her own buyer for the hotel her husband worked so hard to rebuild. That would be downright hateful, and he never pictured her acting that way. He wasn't sure any of her clients possessed money or influence enough to make a legitimate bid for the hotel anyway.

Clouse never imagined Angie being so bitter. She would never be that vengeful toward him, or undermine his work, he decided. After all, *she* was the one who wanted the separation.

Then why did she not tell him about the letter?

Clouse picked up an album full of wedding photos taken by friends and relatives, remembering it as his favorite. Some of the pictures were a tad embarrassing after the alcohol wore off, and the honeymoon was over, but he didn't mind. He figured receptions were meant to be fun, and he certainly enjoyed himself, though most of the night's events were hazy in retrospect.

Brief thunderstorms gave way to a cool, overcast evening surrounding the house. As a blaze finally grew in the fireplace, Clouse turned on a floor lamp, opened the photo album, and peered at the memories he once held dear.

A thousand or more photos had been snapped that day. One of his favorite had been taken by Roger Summers. It showed the newly married couple taking their first dance at the reception. He'd got them to smile once the professional photographer had taken his shots.

It was at that moment Clouse remembered being the happiest he had ever felt. At that point, everything seemed perfect.

Zach had looked through several albums with him, but lost interest and grew sleepy from his adventures outside. Clouse was happy his son could be a kid again, and begin moving on. The happier Zach became the easier being a father would be for Clouse. Much of his reason for moving back to the house was to provide his son with some familiar surroundings.

Before he could get too far into the album, headlights flooded the window in the office, catching his attention. Clouse walked to the kitchen, opening the door to greet his guests without waking Zach.

"Hey," he said happily after stepping outside, seeing Roger Summers approach, Kelli a few steps behind.

Kelli gave a smile that left him uneasy. He could not help but wonder what her kiss that afternoon meant, if anything. Clouse focused on Summers as Kelli stepped past him into the house.

"Get some clothes on," Summers ordered in a tone of voice indicating he had something mischievous in mind.

"Why?" Clouse asked, perfectly content with a pair of sweat pants.

"We're going out."

"Out?"

"The family had its time together, so I figure its time you get your mind off things. Even if it's just tonight."

Clouse shot a suspicious look.

"Where are we going?"

"Get dressed," Summers said. "You'll see."

"And my kid?"

"Kelli volunteered to stay with him as long as we need," Clouse's brother-in-law replied. "We're covered, so get ready."

Reluctant, but with nothing else to do, Clouse stepped inside to get dressed.

***

Two hours later, the two sat inside the Sport's Fanatic, a sports bar just outside the Bloomington city limits. From his bar stool beside Summers, Clouse took in the sights. Several cardboard cutouts of racecar drivers and country singers stood along different walls. Three pool tables were active around the corner, while the bar's jukebox blared out a Clint Black song.

A smoky smell carried through the bar, equaled only by the odor of onion rings, steaks, and seasoned fries. Dim lights provided obscurity for everyone in the bar, making it difficult to be recognized, or find someone suitable to take home. Three television sets were mounted above the bar at even intervals. Each carried a different sports program via satellite, but Clouse did not find the college basketball game above him the least bit interesting.

In the back corner, a band took down their equipment after playing several sets. Clouse considered it odd that a band would play any night before the weekend, quickly discarding the thought as he tipped the beer bottle to his lips. It was his seventh, and he felt better than he had all day.

"You okay, Paul?" Summers asked, noticing how much Clouse took in the view, his eyes possibly a bit more glazed than he realized.

"Fine."

Clouse found a growing number of people paying cover charge, filling the bar. He usually felt uncomfortable around large groups of complete strangers. This place was loud, and potentially hostile, based on what he overheard at some of the pool tables. Only the numbing effects of the alcohol kept him calm.

"Kelli said you guys looked through Angie's things this afternoon?"

"Didn't get far. We kept getting stuck on old pictures."

"Understandable," Summers said, finishing his beer with a deep gulp. He motioned to the female bartender for another, leaving another sizable tip on the bar when the bottle arrived.

He seemed to know her pretty well from the way both had acted when the two firemen entered the bar.

Summers flirted with the bartender for several minutes, making it obvious to Clouse he was a regular at the bar. Clouse knew it was unusual for his brother-in-law to be openly coy in public. Since Angie's death, Summers had acted strangely, trying to channel his emotions toward other people.

"Is Dierker pretty good with computers?" Clouse asked, quickly moving on once the bartender left.

"Tony? Yeah, he's always getting into city files he shouldn't be. The dumb son-of-a-bitch is going to get caught one of these days," Summers said with a laugh. "Why you asking?"

"Angie's online files are password protected and I can't break it. I'm hoping Tony can get me by the code."

Tony Dierker worked with both men on the fire department, often bringing a laptop computer into work. He spent most of his downtime creating small programs, or improving his computer's configurations. Clouse seemed to recall the man once challenging him to create a password, only for Dierker's self-made program to crack it within ten minutes.

"What else are you thinking, brother?" Summers inquired, motioning to the bartender to bring Clouse another drink. Summers often referred to Clouse as his brother; with everything the two had been through, it seemed fitting.

"I keep wondering how I'm going to raise Zach myself."

"You'll do okay," Summers encouraged him, obviously feeling better after several drinks. "You keeping the house?"

"I don't think I can," Clouse admitted. "But it'll be awhile before I can think about looking for another place. Zach doesn't seem to mind, and it's stupid to live anywhere else with all of our stuff there."

He looked to the back of the bar where the four members of the Paradise Band continued packing their equipment. Never heard of them, Clouse thought as he started on the new beer.

"So how are *you* holding up?" he asked Summers.

"Okay. It's actually tough being around the family like this. I needed to get away from them, and I felt so bad for you, Paul. You don't have anyone to talk to."

"My parents want to help, but with the police involvement I hate dragging them into it."

Summers stared at the basketball game on the television screen above the bar. As the station went to commercial he took a swig from his beer bottle, then slapped Clouse on the shoulder as he stood from his bar stool.

"Let's go throw some darts."

Questioning his brother-in-law's sobriety, Clouse gave a brief stare, then stood, grabbing his leather jacket and beer bottle. He followed Summers through a sea of people who danced, or simply crossed the wooden dance floor like themselves.

Clouse favored the bar stools to the dart boards, which he considered dangerously close to the pool tables where several bikers were arguing about who won which game. They were obviously more affected by alcohol than he and Summers, and showed little regard for whoever knew it.

While Summers fed the electronic dartboard a few quarters, bringing it to life, Clouse set his beer on a ledge and his jacket on a nearby stool, as far from the pool tables as possible. All night he had been fighting the urge to tell Summers about Kelli's sudden kiss. He was extremely curious why Kelli would plant a kiss on him like that, but decided against talking about it. Summers had enough on his mind without hearing about his other sister.

"You go first," Summers said, dumping the darts into Clouse's hands.

Taking relatively careful aim, Clouse hit the eighteen-point mark twice, then missed the board completely on his third shot.

"You a bit tipsy, Paul?" Summers teased.

"Not at all," Clouse said, placing a hand against the wall for support while his brother firefighter shot.

After barely being bested, Clouse took up the darts again, trying to find the right spot to stand. He suddenly felt cognizant about the angle of his darts, realizing the beers were thinking for him. Ordinarily, he could care less about bar sports, but Summers had accomplished his mission. Clouse was thinking about everything except Angie.

Whether he backed into the man, or the biker shooting pool behind him shifted for better position, Clouse would never know, but their bodies connected. Clouse felt an elbow or a pool stick jab his back, causing him to jerk forward, turning around as he did.

"You ruined my shot, asshole!" the man verbally charged Clouse, gaining the attention of the entire bar.

The biker smelled of cigar smoke and hard liquor with a build somewhat larger and bulkier than Clouse's.

Clouse attempted a quick apology, but a fist striking his jaw prevented the words from forming. Summers quickly stepped in, as Clouse toppled backwards to the floor. His brother-in-law said something he could not make out, but it sounded defensive. With blood dripping from his lip, Clouse felt anything but sympathetic when he wiped the red liquid away with his thumb, a coppery taste reaching his taste buds.

In a flash Clouse regained his footing, elbowed Summers aside, and threw a thunderous right hand that floored the biker, rendering him unconscious, or close to it. Regaining his composure, Summers quickly directed Clouse toward the front door. He grabbed their belongings as he nudged Clouse in the right direction.

"Let's get out of here before you do any more damage, slugger," he said.

"Did I knock him out?" Clouse asked with glassy eyes as they reached the front door, attempting to shove his arm down his jacket sleeve with a degree of trouble.

Summers looked back, seeing several people on the floor beside the semiconscious biker, who would surely be unruly when he came to.

"I think you had an assist from the fifth of Vodka he downed earlier, brother."

"Can I drive?" Clouse asked, finding the last sleeve in his jacket, pulling it up as the two stepped outside.

The cold air hit them both like a midnight lake swim.

"I think I better drive, Mike Tyson. We need to get back in one piece."

Both climbed into Summers' truck, shut the doors, and stared back at the bar. Apparently, no one took too much exception to Clouse clocking a loudmouth biker. It was the first time the fireman had struck anyone since junior high when he won a parking lot fistfight with a high school bully.

Both chuckled momentarily at the trouble they nearly found themselves in, despite the terrible week now behind them. Summers waited a few minutes to test whether or not he was capable of driving them both home. Satisfied he could drive them a few miles without incident, he started his truck and pulled away from the gravel parking lot.

Nearly a mile away from Clouse's house, Summers turned to ask a question, finding Clouse passed out beside him. He hated carrying his own kids into the house, much less a family member who weighed as much as himself.

"Good thing you didn't drive," Summers said more to himself than the unconscious Clouse as he pulled into the driveway.

Chapter 13

Daylight broke over the garden of the West Baden Springs Hotel as Rusty Cranor walked along the veranda outside the main lobby, parallel to the first floor of the building. He was up early, checking the grounds for necessary winter preparation, figuring neither Clouse, nor Landamere, would show up for work.

He hated being in command.

Usually Landamere or another manager was there to give creative direction while Rusty oversaw the work of the men. Now he had to do both, and it was frustrating to plan upcoming stages of renovation while keeping an eye on the workers. He knew additional breaks would be snuck past him, or the work might go slower than he hoped, but it was to be expected.

None of the construction workers were at the hotel yet, and some were probably still in bed. It wasn't uncommon for many to come in and work until dark, especially with winter weather arriving early. Rusty had any number of rooms, buildings, and garden areas that needed securing or protecting from frigid weather.

As the foreman admired some of the stained glass windows along the building's side, he failed to notice someone approaching along the balcony behind him.

"You the man in charge?" Mark Daniels asked, startling the foreman.

"Holy shit," Rusty replied, catching his breath as his left hand clasped his chest. "I'm the only one left, so don't scare me like that." He looked the detective over, recognizing him. "You're the one who interviewed everyone the day we found that body."

"Sorry," the detective replied in a rather quiet tone, causing Rusty to question his sincerity. "Mark Daniels," he said, extending his hand.

"Rusty Cranor," the foreman replied, shaking it. "Awful early to be out here, isn't it, detective?"

"I wanted to get a look around the grounds after I ask you a few questions. You know, before the workers arrive."

"I think your partner did most the talking the last time you were here," Rusty recalled.

Daniels grinned.

"He usually does. I wanted to talk to you about several issues that have come up concerning the murder of Angela Clouse, and the body you found here."

Rusty's look explained his confusion, but he needed to ask.

"Are the body and the murder related?"

"I think so," Daniels replied. "Before we get into this, can you call Paul Clouse and have him come down here? I think he's going to want to hear some of what I've got to say."

"I can certainly try. It's tough getting anyone in charge out here these days."

***

On the third ring, Clouse finally heard his phone, groaned, and rolled over to answer it, impeded by a warm body. Stretching over the body, his mind not thinking clearly, he picked up the cordless phone from a nightstand. He pressed the talk button, falling back into his sleeping area.

"Hello?"

"Paul, this is Rusty. I've got Detective Mark Daniels here at the hotel. He wants to talk to you."

"What time is it, Rusty?" Clouse asked, his head throbbing with pain in every direction from a hangover.

"A little after six."

"You're at the hotel this early?"

"Someone has to be. So, you coming down?"

"I'll be there as soon as I can."

"He's going to look around the grounds after he's done with me, so don't drive like a maniac or anything."

"I won't," Clouse said, pressing the button to hang up.

He swung his feet out to assume a seated position on the bed, trying to set the phone on the nearby nightstand and missing as it clunked against the floor.

For a moment his mind had lapsed into the past, thinking Angie was in bed beside him. He let the phone fall from his hand to the floor, barely able to think past the pain inside his head. Vague images of the night before came and went through his mind, and the last thing he recalled was being shoved during a game of darts.

His eyes twitched open as he turned to see who was sleeping beside him.

"Shit!" he said, clambering away from the bed, standing up to see Kelli lying there.

"What?" she asked from the under the covers, covered by a bathrobe from what he could see.

Clouse tried to recall the prior evening with every ounce of mental power he could muster, but the bookmark stood at the bar in the story of his life. All the makings of a good hangover loomed inside his skull, adding to the already awkward start of his day.

"Did we?" he left the question open, hoping his fun was limited to the bar.

"No, Paul," Kelli answered defensively. "Rodge carried you in when you guys got back. I helped him tuck you in."

"I was pretty far gone. Wasn't I?"

"I'd say," Kelli said, sitting up with a smile. "Knocking out a biker isn't part of your usual routine."

"My God," Clouse said, suddenly remembering the incident. "I did do it," he added, putting his hand against his aching forehead. "It wasn't a dream."

"I stayed to keep Zach company. Zach wanted to sleep on the couch and I wasn't about to sleep upstairs alone. Roger's going to pick me up later."

Clouse picked up the phone from the floor, realizing underwear was the only thing keeping Kelli from seeing all of him. He instantly felt uneasy.

"I've got to talk to a detective at the hotel. Can you keep Zach until I get back?"

"No problem," Kelli answered, pulling the covers over her chest. "You weren't hoping we'd fooled around, were you?" she kidded.

Clouse simply grunted, walking to the bathroom for a shower and some aspirin.

***

"So you believe Paul is innocent?" Rusty asked the detective as they walked around the grounds.

Daniels drew on a cigarette, looking at the ground as he walked alongside the foreman.

"I just find this whole thing kind of bizarre. There was no reason for him to come over here, dig up a body, and leave it in the upstairs of his house."

"But you said you've pieced together a likely scenario of what happened," Rusty urged for information.

Stopping at the edge of the brick path where the dirt-covered back entrance began, the detective took a final drag from his cigarette before crushing it under his shoe. He exhaled upward, staring pensively at the clear sky beyond the hotel grounds.

"I have a scenario, but that's what I want to talk to Clouse about. In the meantime, I want you to tell me everything you know about the weird events happening *here* lately."

Rusty thought a moment, trying to think of where it all began.

"First thing I remember is Dave Landamere coming to work on Friday, bitching about the empty grave on the hill and how he'd fire any of us who dug it up. The boys have some strange ways of having fun, but I doubt any of them would ever do that."

"I doubt any of them did," Daniels commented.

"So anyway, we found the body later that day around the same time Dave disappeared."

"That's part of what I wanted to talk with you about. Dave Landamere hasn't been seen or heard from since Friday?"

Rusty chuckled with a crooked grin, indicating he knew something about Landamere others would not.

"Dave doesn't much care for the press, and he probably feared a media swarm around this place after that body popped up. He left me in charge, said he would be back, but never said when. I just assumed he meant later that day."

"But he didn't tell Clouse, didn't tell his wife, and there's no trace of the man."

"That's the thing about Dave, detective, is he'll sometimes take a break from it all without telling a soul. It's not against his contract with Kieffer Construction, and he could care less if his wife knew or not."

Daniels smirked.

"Marriage of convenience?"

"Anymore, yes it is," the foreman said, a strange look crossing his face as he patted himself down.

"Lose something?"

"I'm always setting my damn keys down and forgetting them," Rusty replied, not finding them in his pockets, or hanging from his belt loop.

Taking a few steps to his right, Rusty looked along the balcony, spying his key ring shimmering atop the railing, close to the main entrance. While examining some of the windows earlier, he had set them down to use a tape measure.

Daniels wondered how often Rusty misplaced his keys, and if anyone else had access to them while they were missing. A copy of one certain key might give the wrong people access to the hotel. No one had mentioned Rusty's forgetfulness in earlier interviews, either because they found it irrelevant or wanted to protect him.

Deciding not to press the issue, Daniels viewed the hotel's exterior, noting how the golden beige walls with white trim looked similar to the scheme used on Mexican villas he saw on the Discovery Channel. He wondered what inspired such a look at the turn of the last century when the hotel was built.

"So what do you know of Brian Mathis?" he asked Rusty.

"Good worker, good kid," the foreman summed it up. "He was one of the few I trusted to get a job done quick. One of the first in, usually the last to leave. Was a real shame what happened to him for his family and all."

"Did he have anyone who didn't like him?"

"No. He was always quiet, but he'd joke around with the guys. Everyone here liked him."

"What about Paul Clouse?"

"I'm not sure they really knew each other," Rusty replied with a thoughtful look. "How does his death tie into all of this?"

"He was killed with the same weapon that murdered Angela Clouse," Daniels revealed, figuring it would be public knowledge soon enough. "I'm trying to figure out how all of this ties in myself. There's not even a remote link between the two killings, the priest's body, and Landamere's disappearance."

"Well, I already told you my view on Dave's disappearance, but there might be a little something between the murders."

"How so?" Daniels asked, fishing in his shirt breast pocket for another cigarette.

"Someone told me Mathis was mumbling something about a reaper before he died. This true?" The detective nodded affirmatively before lighting up. "Do you know whose body was dug up?"

"Father Ernest. No last name given," Daniels said slowly, making certain he remembered correctly.

"And that doesn't ring a bell for you?" Rusty asked, forgetting how young the detective was in relevance to what he asked.

"Not particularly."

"You never heard the legend of Father Ernest, the one all the Jesuits kept locked up because he went mad, believing he was the taker of souls?"

Daniels' face showed his amazement as the connection hit him.

"The one who dressed in dark robes and eventually set himself on fire?"

"The one," Rusty confirmed.

"But that's just a myth I heard as a kid. It's not true, is it?"

Rusty shrugged his shoulders, unable to prove or disprove the myth.

"So someone could be using the legend as a cover-up for these murders," the detective told himself. "But what's the motive? And why two completely different settings?"

Daniels found an entirely new set of circumstances to ponder. He berated himself for not realizing the connection earlier, but felt assured new answers would come from this information. He knew the central figure in the entire mess was Paul Clouse, but refused to believe the man was foolhardy enough to intentionally become the central figure in the murders.

But if he wasn't behind the killings, who was? And why?

"Care if I take a walk around the grounds?" Daniels asked Rusty, who was anxious to finish his rounds.

"Go right ahead. I'll be around if you need anything."

Smoking as he walked the brick walkways surrounding the building, Daniels felt an eerie calm around him. For so long the hotel had stood vacated, and in the morning, before construction workers filed in, everything about the building appeared tranquil, as though the hotel was meant to remain this way. A fog that materialized in the Springs Valley that morning now retreated up the hill behind the structure as though a living creature wanting to avoid being spotted.

The detective wondered what the fate of the great building would ultimately be, and if it was destined to have human companionship again.

He found it odd that a foreman would misplace his keys on a regular basis. It would give someone ample opportunity to copy important keys if Rusty left them in the open. From what he gathered, the foreman knew his business, but seemed oblivious to most everything else. Perhaps he was one of the chosen few whose work was his life.

Daniels knew the feeling, wondering why he was working before most of his fellow detectives even heard the shrill of their alarm clocks.

A free trip across the grounds would have meant more to him if not for the bizarre circumstances drawing him in. He sensed the connection between Angie Clouse's death and that of Brian Mathis, and possibly the disappearance of Dave Landamere.

Several newspapers were beginning to surmise the theory of a Father Ernest tie-in, which angered the detective. Local murders were not fair game for sensationalism in his eyes. He also felt irritated they had seen the connection to the legend before he had.

Such notions probably played into the hands of the killer, raising public attention to the possibility of supernatural involvement. He knew if they fell for the ruse panic would grow in the West Baden community if more murders occurred. It seemed an easy way to place a dark cloud over the hotel and keep people away, but for what purpose?

His mind raced in a thousand directions, seeking answers from every piece of information or physical evidence he knew about. Daniels took pride in the fact that he sought more than one solution, unlike his partner, but chided himself for not finding anything more concrete than Kendle.

Daniels found himself in the back of the building, about to turn back when he decided to explore, knowing that Mathis was dragged through the grass and buried in back. The construction entrance was also an area where people might be able to come and go without attention. He felt the integrity of the gate would be worth checking, if nothing else.

As he crossed the grounds, Daniels noticed the morning fog dissipating more quickly as the sun showed itself. He heard several birds from nearby trees as the stiff, cold breeze lessened in intensity.

A thick chain and padlock kept the back gate closed, not surprising him. It was adequate security in the evening, but he wondered how secure it was during the day. Few trucks came in and out of the gate during work hours, so he wondered if it was locked, and who had access to it.

Whoever was responsible for the murders probably had access to the hotel grounds, and the number of people involved with the restoration was more than met the eye. He knew over two dozen people stepped onto the grounds most days due to their position in a historical group, the restoration crew, or hotel ownership.

Growing frustrated with the thought of investigating so many people, Daniels kicked a small clump of dirt on his return to the formal walking path.

"Damn it," he said, looking to see how much dust his shoe collected from the kick. He hated polishing them more than necessary, and cursed himself for losing his temper.

His eyes caught a glimmer from something different than the black leather of his shoes as the sun reflected off an object several feet ahead of him. His face twisted to a puzzled stare as the detective walked toward a fallen camera, half buried, and plucked it from its resting spot.

A quick examination showed nothing wrong with the piece. Daniels was familiar with all sorts of photography equipment from various surveillance details.

Kneeling down, he found nothing else around the camera except several dried, darkened spots atop the dirt, which he dismissed as remnants of the morning dew fallen from trees overhead. He stood a moment later, dusting off the camera, hoping Rusty Cranor agreed with his philosophy of finders-keepers.

Chapter 14

Clouse drove up the hotel's lengthy driveway to find Mark Daniels and Rusty outside, talking on the staircase that led to the hotel's secondary entrance beyond the lobby doors. He parked in front of the hotel, feeling it was allowed since the helm was his to command.

When he ascended the stairs, it looked as though he might have interrupted a discussion between the two men, but Daniels nodded to Rusty, allowing the foreman to return to his work.

"Thanks," Daniels said as the foreman climbed the stairs, holding the camera over his head.

Daniels sauntered down the steps toward Clouse, carefully placing the camera's strap around his neck where it rested upon his sport coat's collar.

"Rusty showering you with gifts?" Clouse asked.

"Not quite. Found this out back. Said I could have it if the film didn't reveal who the owner was."

Clouse stared at it a moment, noting the dusty coating.

"Yours?" Daniels inquired, thinking he knew something about it.

"Nope. So what brings you here, detective?"

Both descended the stairs, walking toward the open garden area.

"It's unusual for someone in my position to speak openly with the primary suspect in a murder case, but that's what I'm here for."

"So you believe I'm innocent?"

"I can't say with any certainty, but that's my gut feeling."

Daniels led the way along the garden paths where dying flowers shriveled beside the red brick walkway.

"I've been doing some investigation of my own," Clouse remarked.

"Getting anywhere?"

"Nothing concrete, but once I break the code to Angie's computer it might give me more information about her clients and contacts."

"It doesn't look good for you, living in the house and all," Daniels noted.

"I don't have much choice. My son is *not* spending another day without me, and we're not going to be crammed in some apartment. Once everything settles down, I'll sell and move on. Zach is young enough to put this behind him."

Clouse felt his eyes mist a bit, thinking of the painful week still freshly behind him. He wiped a wet formation from the corner of his eye before the detective noticed.

Daniels stopped in front of the fountain, staring at the cemetery atop the hill, some distance away.

"I've got a little one of my own," the detective confessed. "They become your whole world the day they're born."

Clouse grinned, agreeing fully, but knowing his entire world was rocked by Angie's death. Every day following came just a bit easier, despite the murderer label hanging around his neck like an albatross.

"So what can I do to help you?" he asked, drawing Daniels' attention from the graves.

"Tell me who might have motive to kill your wife."

"I don't know," Clouse answered emphatically. "But the more I think about it, the more it occurs to me that Angie might not be the focus of this whole ordeal."

"You're talking about the hotel, and the dead priest?"

"I did some research at the library and checked out that story, and it all ties in. Father Ernest apparently thought he was some sort of soul reaper toward the end, and burned himself alive, which created the legend we all heard growing up."

"It may be nothing more than legend," Daniels supposed aloud. "Someone could be using that angle for the murders, but what purpose would it serve?"

"I'm not sure. It would scare away the local population, or at least tarnish their memories of this landmark, but it's not exactly under sole ownership, so there wouldn't be financial gain, except maybe lowering the selling price."

"And even at that, there's lots of work to be done, correct?"

"Yeah," Clouse said, pointing to the upper floors. "All those rooms are completely gutted to concrete, plaster, and steel. You're talking millions more in work."

Daniels sighed.

"I can check into potential buyers," he said, pulling a notepad from his coat pocket to write himself a reminder. "Oh, can you take me to Landamere's office?"

As they walked inside the hotel a moment later, Clouse finished explaining how he had contacted a potential buyer for the hotel and never received an answer, until finding a letter from Michael Hathaway among Angie's things.

"And she never told you?"

"No," Clouse replied. "And she had an opportunity at the ball. Maybe things just slipped her mind or she was going to surprise me with the news later."

Clouse unlocked the door to Landamere's office, flipping on the fluorescent lights before either entered.

Instantly the room sprang to life as a floor to ceiling bookcase loomed behind Landamere's desk, filled with family photos, clipboards, several notepads, and a miniature model of the hotel and its grounds.

As Daniels took a seat in the swivel chair, surveying the mildly cluttered area around the desk, Clouse looked at the filing cabinet in one corner and several folding chairs set randomly in areas of the room, often used for impromptu meetings with foremen or various renovation leaders.

"Care if I take a look?" Daniels asked, pointing to the desk.

Clouse turned his head toward the door, as though expecting Landamere to catch them in his office any second, then thought more rationally.

"Go ahead."

While the detective rummaged through several drawers, Clouse walked to the restroom down the hall. He loved the way both restrooms were done to match the rest of the hotel's interior. Beautiful gold and green tile covered both the walls and floor of each room.

In the men's room, stalls and urinal dividers were painted a dark, rich green to accent the trim on the wall tiles. It was a touch of class compared to the closet-sized rooms he and the construction workers were forced to use when the project first began.

"Feel better?" Daniels asked when Clouse returned to the office.

"Much."

"I don't suppose your boss informed you about this?" the detective asked, holding up a letter, which Clouse took and unfolded.

He skimmed the contents, learning that Michael Hathaway had sent a letter of inquiry to Dr. Smith and copies to Landamere and several other project board members. From the look on Clouse's face, Daniels knew the answer.

"Landamere didn't tell you about this?"

"He didn't," Clouse replied.

"I get the impression several people were keeping it from you for a reason."

"If they were trying to surprise me, it wouldn't exactly have shocked me. Unless Michael wanted to tell me himself."

Daniels replaced the letter, closing the desk drawers. The two men left the room, Clouse locking the door behind him.

"Has your friend contacted you about his interest in the property?"

"I haven't exactly been home the last month," Clouse admitted. "Knowing him, he probably wants to surprise me if he buys it."

"My main reason for coming here was to share my theory about your wife's murder with you," the detective said as they walked outside the hotel.

"And?"

"Unlike my partner, I don't think you had the time to pull it off. That doesn't mean you didn't have motive, but it seems odd that you would dig up a body *here*, transport it almost an hour away, and leave it upstairs for your wife to find."

"Why the body at all?"

"It's small enough that in the darkness, Angela may have thought it was your son and panicked, leading her right to the killer. We found your upstairs light bulb unscrewed, so it wouldn't have come on when she flipped the switch."

"Did someone choose that body with reason?"

"Probably the Father Ernest connection. Using a scythe to kill? Come on, it fits perfectly," Daniels said. "Every killer wants an angle. Whoever's doing this is carrying out some fantasy, but killing with a deeper intent than just random selection. The hotel is definitely tied in somehow."

As Clouse walked Daniels to his car, the detective found few encouraging words in parting.

"If you aren't responsible for any of this, someone close to you probably is," Daniels advised him. "It's awfully convenient that every time something bad happens around here, you're nearby," he added, opening the door to his Honda.

Though several years old, it was a car much like him — practical and efficient. With one child, and another on the way, Daniels watched every penny and worked every bit of overtime he could to save for his future and that of his family.

"If I were you, Mr. Clouse, I would keep a close eye on my friends, my family, and everyone at this place," Daniels said, waving a hand across the span of the hotel grounds. "And if it turns out you're in any way responsible for all this, damn me for believing you."

"Don't worry, you've got me pegged correctly," Clouse assured him.

"I hope so," Daniels said, climbing into his car.

"Can you do me a favor during the course of your investigation?"

"What would that be?"

"I'd like you to check out the gardener here. His name is Vern, but I don't know much more than that. He's just kind of an odd guy."

"No harm in checking," Daniels said with a shrug. "Watch your back."

Clouse watched as the maroon car rolled down the brick drive toward the town of West Baden.

A long day awaited him, and a good breakfast might do him good. Rusty would be around until he got back.

***

Larry Kendle's morning had consisted of little more than reviewing photos and evidence from the Angela Clouse murder. The wedge between he and Daniels grew because of their varying opinions.

Though he would never admit it, he liked having a partner who thought differently, but he wanted to bring Daniels along slowly. The man was new to the investigative division, and needed to be completely objective, letting the evidence guide him rather than relying upon his opinions and wild theories. Without evidence, opinions were useless in court.

Despite his reputation, Kendle played by the rules. He followed the evidence trail like a bloodhound, sniffing for the clues of his predetermined quarry.

He was concerned about Daniels' train of thought, and how he strayed from his veteran partner. Kendle had kept their temporary separation from his sergeant. Things would have to get completely out of hand before Kendle would say anything to their division leader, because the investigators prided themselves on being independent and capable.

Things had been much harder when he started investigating years before. The advances in forensic science made a world of difference, but Kendle knew the aspects of an investigation driven by detectives themselves made all the difference.

He could interview with the best, do surveillance, and comb a crime scene for evidence most officers missed, or stepped on. Kendle wanted to pass the torch to Daniels, but he feared the young detective might be too rash, and easily influenced, to be effective.

Daniels would need to learn self-control before he gained the respect of his fellow investigators. He had much more to learn than he realized.

But time was on his side.

One of only two detectives seated in the office, Kendle scooped up the phone on its first ring, hoping for something to distract him from the case for a few minutes.

"Detectives," he answered in short.

"Larry Kendle or Mark Daniels, please," the voice said.

"This is Kendle."

"Hi, Larry. This is Ed Miller from the state police."

Kendle remembered the state trooper from several cases they had worked together. Miller was now the second-in-command of the Bloomington post.

"Hello, Ed. What can I do for you?"

"Actually, I might have something for you. A conservation officer found a car at Mounds Park in Anderson. He ran the plates, and they came back registered to one David Landamere, whom I understand you wish to speak with."

"Word travels fast."

"Your case is all over the news," Miller added. "They haven't touched the car yet. You want a crack at it?"

"Definitely," Kendle said immediately. "Can you have one of your technicians meet me at the park in two hours?" he asked, knowing it would take that long to reach the city of Anderson.

"You got it."

"Thanks, Ed. I owe you one."

***

Everything in the town of West Baden seemed to have a historical ring to it, which nearly drove Clouse insane. He grew tired of seeing 'Historical Landmark' posted on every other building, and inside many others. He considered himself a visitor, and wondered if residents simply ignored the signs defacing their buildings, or if they were raised to love them.

When Clouse walked into the B.B. Café, few heads turned. He was as close to a regular customer as the small restaurant could get. It was also the only place relatively close to the hotel that served all three meals. Many of the construction workers took their lunch breaks at the café or stopped in for morning coffee.

The restaurant's ownership would see no decline in sales for at least a year while the construction continued.

Sliding into a stool at the bar, Clouse took up the menu he had practically memorized, scanning it for what sounded the most appetizing. He figured an order of eggs and bacon would cure his grumbling stomach, and informed Kayla, the waitress, of such.

While he waited for his meal, the waitress brought him some buttered toast as an attractive woman with notably long, brown hair slid onto the stool beside him. Her light complexion and soft skin, along with her attire, gave him the impression she was not a regular to the eatery, or the small town of West Baden.

Seated among a pool of truckers and construction workers, she added color to the otherwise bleak setting.

Dressed in dark slacks and a light blouse that accented her shapely figure, the woman reminded Clouse of Angie in several ways. She was pretty, appeared intelligent and self-assured, and commanded the attention of everyone in the building, himself included.

"Don't I know you?" she asked, returning Clouse's unintentional stare.

"Sorry," he quickly apologized, turning to the less exciting view of bottles behind the bar.

"No," she said with a laugh. "I meant don't I recognize you from the hotel?"

Clouse gave a curious stare, wondering what this lady of evident importance had to do with the hotel.

"I give tours there once or twice a week," she explained, unable to break the perplexed look from Clouse. "My mother lives down here, and I visit from Bloomington."

"Paul Clouse," he said, extending his hand after finally gaining some understanding of the situation.

"Jane Brooks," she replied, gently shaking it. "I see you at the hotel fairly often, so I gather you're part of the renovation?"

"I'm a designer for Dave Landamere, the project manager, when I'm not working for the City of Bloomington," Clouse explained.

"City job?"

"I'm a firefighter."

Jane smiled, apparently understanding why he wasn't visible on a daily basis.

"I run the Northway Medical Clinic in Bloomington," she informed Clouse.

"Doctor?" Clouse asked, raising an eyebrow. "And you share a love for the hotel with the rest of us?"

She laughed easily, not uptight like Angie. Clouse already enjoyed company who took the time to smile without thought.

"My mother brought me up to love the hotel. I can't count how many times she told me stories about the Jesuits, the college era, and how she and my father would sneak into the grounds when it was abandoned, just for a peek. I guess I'm just a sap for it now, so I volunteer on my days off."

"I'll bet your mother is proud."

"Oh, yes," Jane said with a grin. "She occasionally surprises me by showing up in one of my tours."

Clouse turned his attention briefly to the plate of scrambled eggs and crispy bacon laid before him as Jane placed her order for orange juice and wheat toast.

"So, do I get a mention in your tours now?" Clouse asked, chuckling.

"Only if you happen to be outside," she said, appearing serious. "You'd be surprised how many people want to know every little aspect of the grounds, including the people working on them."

For the next fifteen minutes, the two talked about their lives away from work, and what they enjoyed most about the West Baden Springs Hotel. Clouse finished his meal, left money for the bill, and a tip, and stood.

"I guess I'll see you on some of your tours today," he told Jane. "We'll be working on some details inside the atrium."

"Would you like to talk some more during lunch?" Jane asked. "I'll have breaks at eleven and two."

"I'd like that," Clouse answered with a friendly nod. "I'm easy to find."

"We'll talk later then," Jane confirmed.

Clouse gave partial wave before leaving the café for a full day's work.

***

At noon, Clouse found himself seated in a lawn chair beside Jane. They were behind the hotel where several other employees and tour guides ate lunch. Several large trees provided shade over several picnic tables and folding chairs. Most everyone brought their own lunch since the town had very few fast food or carry-out restaurants.

The day grew uncommonly warm, allowing everyone to eat outside one last time before the next cold front arrived, bringing the onset of winter.

"I keep noticing your wedding band," Jane commented between sips of iced tea. "Are you the one who-?"

"My wife was killed last week," Clouse said, finishing the sentence rather flatly. "And you shouldn't believe too much about what the papers are saying."

"I don't put much stock in them."

"So what's your status?"

"Divorced with a daughter of my own," Jane answered. "It's not been easy, but we all cope."

Clouse took a bite of his ham sandwich.

"You probably wonder why I'm working here so soon after Angie's death."

"It's not uncommon. Lots of people throw themselves into their work to avoid mourning a loved one."

Staring at his wedding band, Clouse wondered if and when the grief would end. He hadn't given up hope while she was alive concerning their relationship, making it tougher to put the ring away.

"I feel bad, like I'm not dealing with this right. My son is confused, and I feel powerless to explain this to him, or even console him," Clouse said, staring above the tree line toward the clear sky. "It's tough to even be around him right now, and it's not fair to Zach."

"You're being too hard on yourself, Paul. You need time and space. Everyone does. With everything going on around this place, I'm surprised you can keep your sanity."

Clouse forced a grin.

"Are you referring to the Father Ernest stories in the papers?"

"Was it really his body?" Jane asked with a squeamish look.

"Unfortunately, yes."

Several people turned to see a county police car pulling near the break area. Clouse recognized the driver as Kaiser.

"Looks like I've got to run," he said, standing.

Jane jotted something on a piece of paper, handing it to him.

"A few of my friends are meeting me at this pub later. If you want to stop by and talk, I promise to be a good listener."

"I appreciate that," Clouse said with a smile. "I'm probably going to spend some time with Zach tonight, though. If I can squeeze it in, maybe I'll stop in before I pick him up."

"If not, I know where to find you," Jane replied.

"It's my life," Clouse stated, looking up the hotel's six story walls. "Take care."

Tossing the remains of his lunch into a nearby trashcan, Clouse approached his friend, who wore a grim expression. Kaiser was out of uniform, meaning he made a personal trip to the hotel, which he seldom did.

"What's the matter, Ken?"

"It seems we've had a disappearance, and it might be related to this place," the county officer stated, steering Clouse away from the workers on break.

"What happened?"

"Robert Bennett, an electrician who owns his own business, was subcontracted to do some electrical work out here," Kaiser explained. "A couple days ago he came out to do some wiring, was seen heading out the back gate around dark, and hasn't been heard from since."

Clouse remembered who he was. He and Landamere had given the man a brief tour of the grounds so the electrician knew where to start. He kept talking to Clouse about unions and how they helped the workingman, so Clouse quickly made an excuse to leave Bennett in Landamere's hands. Already belonging to a fire union, Clouse didn't need to hear about the benefits, or waste valuable work time to idle chit-chat.

"But he left the grounds?" Clouse inquired, finding it hard to believe the man simply disappeared.

"His van was seen leaving, but no one could positively ID him as the driver."

"Not good," Clouse said. "No one's heard from him?"

"No. Two of his employees said he didn't show up for work yesterday or today. They claim it's extremely out of character for him to miss work, and if he does, they say he always calls."

"Are you handling it?"

Kaiser's expression soured.

"No, and my captain doesn't want me out here in any official capacity until this thing gets resolved. He doesn't want me around you either, because the department might get some bad publicity, or some bullshit like that. *And* he doesn't want me to do security detail here either, but he can't really stop me from that."

Clouse led his friend further from the others, toward the main steps.

"You say that electrician left around dark?"

Kaiser nodded.

"I was here until dark the other night, Ken."

"So?"

"Doesn't it seem a little coincidental that every single time something goes wrong around here I seem to be near it?"

"I suppose," Kaiser answered slowly, treading carefully around his friend's line of questioning.

"Maybe I need to stay away from this place."

"But if you're being set up, we won't be able to catch whoever's doing it."

"But maybe no one else will die or disappear," Clouse deduced aloud.

"I can help you nab whoever's doing this if we play our cards right," Kaiser suggested.

"You said it yourself. Your captain doesn't want you near here or me. Somehow I'm going to have to handle this myself."

"Running from it isn't the answer," Kaiser said emphatically. "I've never known you to back down from a challenge."

"Lives are at stake, Ken. I can't risk the killer framing me for all of this. I've got a son to look out for. Besides, if I leave maybe all this will end."

Kaiser shook his head negatively.

"You're being rash, Paul. I hope you aren't thinking of resigning your position over this?"

"Maybe I am, Ken. If that's what it takes, maybe I am."

The county officer made certain no one else was within earshot before handing out his next batch of bad news.

"There's a kid named Timmons who disappeared, too," Kaiser almost whispered to his friend.

"A kid?"

"Teenager. Not exactly your model citizen, but he was an okay kid."

"Surely that's not related."

"Might be nothing," Kaiser said with a shrug. "Wouldn't really surprise me if he ran away from home. Kind of the mischievous type, if you get my drift. I pulled him over a few times for—"

"I hate all this," Clouse interrupted. "Life used to be so much easier."

"It might be again if you let me help you figure out who's behind all this."

"I may not have much choice, Ken. But at the same time I don't want to see you walk into a trap, either."

Kaiser grinned.

"It'll take more than this guy to knock me off, buddy. Just hang in there," the cop said, walking toward his car. "I'll call you later."

Clouse gave a weak wave before turning to see almost two dozen eyes quickly disperse in every direction but his.

Life was not getting any easier.

***

When Kendle stepped from his unmarked car alone, he found a conservation officer and a forensics expert waiting for him beside a white Cadillac parked awkwardly at the edge of a small parking lot. A line of trees behind the lot led into the denser woods that comprised much of the state park. Several trees displayed yellow and orange coloration, but the overall view paled in comparison to what the detective's home area offered.

The lot, used exclusively for one particular exhibit, had only two other vehicles parked on it, leading Kendle to believe the car could have sat for a day or two without really being noticed. The Department of Natural Resources employees seldom checked such a small parking lot.

Snapping a latex glove over each hand, Kendle walked carefully around the car, looking for damage or anything unusual. He saw tufts of grass stuck to the tires and in between the fiberglass and chrome areas of the fenders. Around the front, he saw the driver's side of the windshield spider-webbed with speckles of blood where something might have hit it.

Amazingly, the keys were in the ignition and the doors unlocked. Both the state police technician and the officer stood by while Kendle silently went about his initial investigation. He looked at the door handle for traces of blood or stains, but found none.

"Start dusting here, please," he said to the technician. "I'm going to get inside and see if there's anything useful."

Kendle got inside, finding no rips or tears along the seats, and nothing unusual on the floor mats, but his flashlight helped him spot several dark stains along the driver's seat, near the head and shoulder area for most drivers. He asked the technician to swab the seat, and the cotton swab picked up relatively fresh blood from the surface.

Knowing how slow state police labs could be, usually due to an extensive back-log, the detective asked for a second swab to send to a friend at Indiana University in Bloomington. If he obtained a DNA sample from David Landamere, they could determine whether or not this was his blood on the seat.

"I can comb the vehicle for fingerprints, and vacuum for hair and fiber samples," the technician said when he assumed Kendle was finished, nearly half an hour later.

By this time the conservation officer had received another call, leaving Kendle and the technician alone. His agency found the vehicle, but found no reason to claim it or watch over it with members from two other departments present.

"Go ahead," Kendle answered in regards to a thorough inspection of the car. "I'll see about getting some comparison samples for you."

The technician pulled a card out from one of his pockets, handing it over to the investigator. Kendle did the same.

"Let me know if you find anything," Kendle urged. "It concerns several ongoing homicide investigations, and we don't have any thorough leads yet."

The technician grimaced.

"I'll put a rush on it, but you know how things go in the lab."

"I know, but I'd appreciate any help," Kendle said before getting into his car.

He wondered if his list of murder suspects was narrowing, or expanding. Kendle started the car and prepared for his two-hour trip home. A trip in which he could think about the new evidence he might land.

Evidence that might put him closer to the truth.

***

Most of the workers pulled away from the hotel grounds as the sun began to set in the late afternoon. Rusty had a tendency to send people home early, especially when he felt nervous about something.

Lately he had plenty to be nervous about.

As the foreman spoke with one of the workers about the hotel's winter preparation, Clouse walked to the back of the hotel where he spotted several clusters of construction workers talking or joking before heading out for the day. He was finishing up an exterior inspection of the hotel before heading home to Bloomington.

His body felt exhausted from walking all day, but his mind felt worse. The more he pondered the situation, the more he felt resigning his position would be for the best. If it saved lives, he had no reservations about leaving.

He also thought about what Mark Daniels had said concerning who the killer might be. Who around him could possibly be a murderer? Clouse chose his friends carefully, and felt no one in his family was capable of murder, much less framing him for it.

Motive seemed to be the missing element. He wondered what hidden motive someone had for linking several deaths and disappearances to the hotel. It had to be there, just not openly. Clouse felt helpless, knowing he was the only person who could help himself out of this predicament.

What Kaiser said was true, in that Clouse did not back away from challenges, but this appeared to be a no-win situation if he stuck by the status quo. There was no way to find the killer by himself at the hotel, and maybe if he took the time to carefully search Angie's things and crack her computer code he could find more answers.

Finishing his rounds, the temporary project manager looked to the brick road behind the hotel where several workers continued talking before they headed out. He crossed the lawn between them and the hotel, looking up at the great structure, seeing something unusual streak across a third story window.

Clouse stopped, looking for it again.

"No," he murmured, seeing a darkly clothed figure cross another window.

Sprinting directly toward the hotel's main entrance, Clouse passed Rusty, calling the foreman's name. After gaining Rusty's attention, he continued toward the entrance, unsure if the older man would follow this time.

***

On the third floor, Scott Beaman finished caulking the last of the windows on the building's west side. It had taken most of the day, but his side of the hotel would be ready for winter. Now he knelt, putting his equipment in a box for another crew to use the next day.

Most everyone else was out of the building, leaving him alone. He hated working by himself to begin with, and the strange occurrences around the hotel left him feeling more insecure. Beaman just wanted to pack up and get out.

An eerie calm overtook the hotel, and for a moment, Beaman heard no one talking outside, or any vehicles starting. A sensation he was completely alone spooked him enough that he walked to a window for a look outside. Seeing several men talking amongst themselves, he realized he was overreacting and went back to his equipment.

"Calm down, Scott," he told himself, thinking the barren walls of the hotel might close in on him at any moment.

He needed the money, or he would have left in search of another job, which sometimes took days or weeks to find. His employers didn't seem overly concerned with the safety of their men, which surprised him. Construction companies hated liability, and here they were leaving an inexperienced designer and a foreman with little backbone in charge.

The men respected Rusty Cranor, but he wasn't a tested general like David Landamere. He could not bark out orders, or stay on top of everything well enough to keep the project moving along as it had been.

Exhaling deeply to calm himself, Beaman packed up the caulk gun, the remaining tubes, and several hand tools before closing the box he knelt beside.

Quickly standing to leave, Beaman turned around, hearing a swoosh sound as a large curved blade tore through his abdomen, piercing his backside, cracking the window behind him.

Workers below heard the noise of the splintered glass, much like the sound in an automobile accident, looking up to the window where a spider web formed in the glass from the impact, highlighted in red mist. They saw Beaman's back against the stained window, knowing instantly what they viewed was no joke.

Mortally wounded, the construction worker could not defend himself as the killer pried the scythe from his body, throwing it to the floor. The killer took hold of his flannel shirt collar, pulling him away from the window slightly before launching him out the already weakened glass. Shattered glass rained on the ground three stories below, followed by Beaman's body, which landed backside first, accompanied by cracking and popping sounds as nature finished the job the killer had begun.

"No!" Clouse screamed from a gutted room's frame, too far away to have prevented Beaman's death, but able to see the events transpire through the skeletal framework almost two rooms away.

Taking up the weapon, the killer darted off in the opposite direction. Clouse delayed the chase just a few seconds to peer out a nearby window, seeing Beaman's mangled body on the ground, while several workers noticed his stare. Much like in the fire service, his concern for a colleague had initially overtaken a desire to catch the killer, but one look at Beaman's mangled body gave Clouse the green light to commence his hunt.

"Fuck!" the fireman said as he broke himself away from the gruesome view, pursuing the killer through the rooms devoid of any walls. He carefully leapt over structural frames, boxes, and piles of rubble as he gave chase.

Any number of staircases were available to the killer, and the two nearby elevators were in working order, meaning he could take them, or lead Clouse to think he had. Clouse rounded a corner, pulling to a stop before he looked down the staircase, finding nothing except winding flights of stairs. He stood, intently listening, hearing only the commotion in the backyard where Beaman had landed.

"Damn," he said to himself, continuing down the same hall, allowing the killer to slip from behind a partial wall once he was in the clear, and descend the stairs for a clean escape.

Walking along the hallway, Clouse knew the sound of his boots would give him away, but he refused to stop looking. He could also not afford to walk in socks with so many potential hazards on the floor just waiting to puncture human flesh. He approached a bend in the hallway and picked up his pace.

Clouse let out a yell as he impacted with another person around the bend. He stepped back, realizing the foreman had followed him upstairs again.

"I saw you from the stairs, Paul," Rusty said quickly. "I know you didn't do it."

"But whoever did got away," Clouse replied angrily, upset with himself for not stopping the killer, or finding him afterwards.

"There was nothing you could have done, Paul," the foreman said, clutching Clouse's arm, trying to settle him down. "Let's go call the police before you go and get yourself killed."

Clouse took a few deep breaths, realizing how out of hand things had become. No one would want to be around the hotel, or him for that matter. A sense of responsibility overtook his sense of reason, even if he had no direct hand in the murders.

"Okay, let's call the police," Clouse finally said, ready to put the matter where it belonged.

Chapter 15

Both Clouse and Zach sat on the couch watching television as the boy flipped through several channels, finding little of interest to watch.

Clouse didn't really care what was on. His mind stuck on the events almost four hours prior, and how Detective Larry Kendle refused to believe he was innocent of the murders at the hotel, and the one inside his own house.

Rusty's testimony of seeing Clouse too far from the murder spot failed to convince Kendle, because Rusty never actually saw the murderer from his vantage point. Even Daniels, who struggled to be impartial, asked why it was only Clouse who saw this dark figure on the upper floors twice.

Clouse had to question why they were so far out of their jurisdiction, working on a case two counties away from their own, probably sounding more defensive than he recalled. They said the killer had used the same weapon in all of the murders, tying the hotel murders in with Angie's, thus leaving him, or someone around him, a prime suspect.

Kendle went so far as to imply Clouse had a partner, and set up the scenario to prove his innocence to the police. There seemed to be nothing the firefighter could do to convince Kendle otherwise. He grew tired of the accusations and the senseless death surrounding him, yet Rusty's testimony seemed to shed some light on his innocence to those who would listen.

"This okay?" Zach asked permission, stopping on a movie of the week.

"Sure," Clouse answered before picking up another of Angie's printouts, studying it for any names or addresses that might seem suspicious.

He had gone through her papers several times, finding little of significance. It now seemed more logical that someone who knew the hotel well, and knew

Clouse's habits, was setting him up. He needed to look closer to home, or perhaps his workplace.

Still, he arranged for Tony Dierker to come over and look at Angie's computer. If anyone could bypass the code, it would be him. Dierker had the next day off from the fire department, and Clouse took advantage of it. He knew the man could not resist a challenge, so he invited him over to break the password.

While Zach watched the movie, Clouse pondered the day's events, wishing his life wasn't such a disaster. Things were so peaceful when he and Angie were married.

He remembered when there was time for days away from it all, just taking Zach to the park, or working around the house. It seemed they had become too busy for one another as a couple and drifted apart. Before Clouse could reconcile the differences, however, his life was changed forever.

Damned, perhaps.

As though he wasn't spooked enough by the week's events, Clouse heard a bump from outside the house, as though something had hit the siding. He sprang from the couch, looking back to see if Zach had noticed.

He hadn't.

With his son engrossed in the movie, Clouse stepped outside to see where the noise had come from, and whether it warranted further investigation.

It had come from the corner of the house, away from the porch. As he drew closer to the corner, the light from behind him grew fainter, leaving almost no visibility when he neared the origin of the noise.

He cautiously approached the area, looking around as he saw a large rock lying beside the foundation. No sounds emerged from the darkness, and no one could be seen in the shadows. None of his dogs had barked, leading him to believe maybe the rock had been there quite some time, and the noise was just a fluke.

Clouse returned to the house to find Zach calmly watching the movie. He wondered if his son sensed any of the danger that plagued him. As much as he tried to shield his concern, he felt certain some of it leaked through the facade.

He had just sat down again when something different caught his attention from the outside.

Headlights beamed through the family room window, and Clouse found it odd for a visit after dark. Expecting no one in particular, he arched his neck for a better look, not recognizing the BMW as anyone's he knew.

"Who is it, Dad?" Zach asked, probably hoping for company to break the monotony of his recent routine.

"Stay here, Zach," Clouse said, rising to answer the door.

He opened it to a totally unexpected visitor in the form of Dr. Martin Smith, the hotel's current owner, though Smith openly disliked the title.

He preferred to be labeled the hotel's caretaker or benefactor, though he paid the money to take it over, and much more in restoring it. Clouse knew the man was worth more than two billion dollars after his years of medical research paid off and his company made millions in pharmaceutical products used daily in hospitals nationwide.

"Dr. Smith," Clouse said with open surprise, forgetting momentarily to invite the older man inside. "What brings you out here?"

"I have some grave concerns about the hotel and what's been happening out there," the doctor replied.

In his sixties, Smith had more health than most men half his age, but the recent events had apparently taken a toll on him. A pale, ragged look took hold of his face instead of the usual easy smile and beaming green eyes. His gray hair appeared unkempt, as though a man of his stature held little value in his personal upkeep, or other matters took priority.

"Come in," Clouse said, finally waving the doctor inside the kitchen.

Smith looked suspiciously around, obviously aware that Clouse's wife had met her demise in the very room where he stood. It seemed he was aware of all of the recent events surrounding his hotel and its employees.

Zach came into the kitchen for a look, saw the doctor, stared a moment, then retreated to the family room for the empty comfort of television.

"So what can I do for you, doc?" Clouse asked, walking into the vacant living room, turning on the overhead light before offering the doctor a seat.

"I talked to Rusty Cranor after the incident today, and I'm growing worried about the situation at the hotel," Smith confessed after occupying a cushy chair. "We need to stop work on the grounds immediately," he continued with distress in his voice.

Clouse could tell it deeply hurt the man to stop work on the property he personally invested so much time and money into.

"Are you sure that's the answer?" Clouse asked.

"It has to be. If there's no one there to kill, the murders will have to cease."

"I was considering leaving the project anyway," Clouse admitted. "This whole ordeal seems to hinge around me, but I don't know why," he added, shaking his head.

"Some sick bastard is getting his jollies, that's why," Smith said angrily. "And why someone would want to desecrate that beautiful landmark is beyond me."

Clouse settled uneasily in his own chair.

"What are you going to do now? You were so close to getting the renovation complete."

Smith looked up to the ceiling, and perhaps beyond, for the strength to say what he planned to carry out.

"I may sell the property, Paul."

"What?" Clouse said in shock. "You could be playing into the hands of whoever's doing this."

"How are you so sure this isn't a plot against *you*?" Smith retorted.

"If they really wanted me framed for this, they could have planted evidence several times over. I think the killer just wants everyone terrified of the hotel. That Father Ernest story has a *lot* of people spooked, especially so soon after Halloween."

"Regardless of whether I sell it or not, tomorrow is the last day for construction. No one else should die needlessly for the sake of a building. I would like you and Rusty to inform everyone tomorrow that they will be given a paid leave," Smith said, getting up to make his way toward the door.

"Who would you sell to?" Clouse asked a moment later, walking the doctor to the door.

"There are a few potential buyers," Smith revealed. "I'm having my lawyer check out their reputations to see who would be a good match. If I don't find a buyer soon, everyone may get frightened away."

"Do you really think getting rid of the property will solve matters?"

"If it prevents more people from being murdered, I'll do it in a heartbeat," Smith answered, as though defeated in every other possibility. "Good night, Paul," he said, walking away as Clouse closed his front door.

"Good night indeed."

***

While most people readied themselves for bed, two teenagers snuck toward the West Baden Springs Hotel's back entrance, making their way to the cargo door.

Pressing their backs against the building, the two silently surveyed the sunken garden around the side of the building. They spied a flashlight beam bouncing further and further away from the hotel toward the storage buildings and the Jesuit cemetery.

"You sure you want to see this?" Dustin Thomas asked his girlfriend as she reached into her jeans pocket for a set of keys.

"Of course, silly," Melissa Cranor replied. "It isn't every day you get to see a murder scene firsthand."

Both stared at the yellow tape surrounding the ground where the body had fallen three stories. Getting a closer look put them at risk of being spotted by the security guard. Besides, the real story began inside, where the murder took place.

"How'd you get your dad's keys?" Dustin asked in a hushed voice.

"My dad always leaves them lying around. I made myself a copy one night so I can get in here whenever I want to," Melissa replied, putting the key in the lock, pulling the door open before she turned the key. "That's funny," she commented, staring at the door.

Usually every door in the building was locked down with the guard stationed in a room between the two main entrances, able to see anything coming from the outside.

Unless, of course, he was on rounds.

Over the years, Melissa had grown to know the people her father worked with, and felt comfortable around them.

The hotel held a special interest to her because it was near her hometown, and such a historical landmark. Something about it drew her to the grounds rather often, usually to visit her father. Even most of the security officers knew her on a first name basis.

Once inside, Melissa turned to look at the door once more. She had snuck onto the hotel grounds before, but the truck entrance was always locked. The guard had no need to unlock it, and it created more of a security risk if he did.

"What's the matter, babe?" Dustin whispered.

"That door is always locked," she replied.

"Maybe they forgot it in all the confusion. It's no big deal."

Melissa led her boyfriend through the darkened hotel, knowing her way around it well enough to navigate in almost complete darkness. Luckily, the moon peered through several clouds, down through the atrium's glass dome enough that she could see the outlines of statues and doorways along the first floor.

"Stay close," she warned Dustin, knowing the guard was the only danger to their presence.

With everything the local papers had to say about the murders and the speculation around them, it was all the pair could do to wait so late before entering the grounds to snoop. Her father had arrived home, anxious to tell the tale of the day's murder, but unhappy about the hotel's grim outlook, knowing Smith never took pressure well.

Between the articles and community speculation, people were losing sympathy for the great monument, and respect for Smith. Her father feared Smith might sell the hotel hastily, rather than sacrifice his pride.

Smith had little to worry about since he was not responsible for the murders, but he would feel the public somehow blamed him, and be rid of the troublesome publicity as quickly as possible.

"You think that fireman killed his wife and the people here?" Dustin inquired as they walked the first floor hallway to a set of stairs where Melissa could verify the whereabouts of the guard.

"My father swears he's innocent now," she replied, "but he wasn't so sure before today."

"I think he did it," Dustin commented as they rounded a corner. "Bam, sickle through the heart. Bam, slice and dice her insides. Gotta admit the guy's creative."

Melissa shushed him as they drew near the stairs, seeing something out of the ordinary ahead. Drawing to a stop, she peered ahead to a supervisor's office, seeing a flashlight beam dance across the inside through the frosted glass. Her body grew tense, positive the guard had heard them talking.

Creeping closer to the door, Melissa saw another beam of light outside, meaning the person inside the room was *not* the guard.

Meaning he or she did not belong there either.

It explained why the door was unlocked, but not who the person was. Melissa suddenly felt defensive about her father's work at the hotel, and wondered if the murderer had come back to cover his tracks.

She had to know.

"Dustin, we have to get help," she whispered quickly. "Whoever's in there isn't the guard, and it might be the killer."

"If we get the guard, we get busted," her boyfriend warned adamantly.

"Fine. I'll go see who it is myself."

"Melissa, wait!" he demanded in as hushed a voice as he could muster, but it was too late. His girlfriend was heading for the room, unconcerned about the ramifications of trespassing and getting caught, much less possessing illegal copies of her father's keys.

Dustin could not stand by and watch Melissa confront an adult, any adult, alone. It was partly his idea to break into the hotel. He followed, watching his girlfriend cautiously approach the room, monitoring the flashlight beam intently.

Drawing near the door, both watched the beam go out as quickly as it had moved through the air a moment before. Stopping dead in their tracks beside the door, both knew there was nothing to do but wait.

If the person was done snooping, he or she would venture out any second and see them. There was nowhere to run and remain undetected, and the only chance of hiding was the room across the hall, if it was unlocked.

Deciding not to chance it, Melissa pointed to a nearby stairwell where the two could hide behind limited cover until the snoop left. Darting across the hall, Dustin was painfully aware of his tennis shoes squeaking, but made his way safely into the stairwell as a man with no identifying traits emerged from the room. The economical dim lighting made it near impossible to get a good look at the man before he walked calmly down the hallway toward the back entrance.

Melissa strained to see any features before the man disappeared down the hall, doing her best to remain behind the staircase. After the man disappeared from view, she heard footsteps all the way down the hall until the sound of a door opening and closing reached her ears. Convinced they were alone at last, she gave Dustin a nudge, urging him toward the room.

Strangely, the man had left the room unlocked, and Melissa recalled it being Dave Landamere's office, which made the break-in more peculiar. She looked for the guard's flashlight, seeing it out toward the farther reaches of the sunken garden.

Breathing a sigh of relief, she stepped into the room, throwing the light switch, anxious to see if there were any traces of what the man might have been looking for.

"What was he looking for?" Dustin inquired.

"I don't know, but take a look around and see if you find anything unusual before that guard gets back. He'll see this light if we take too long."

Spending the next few minutes searching through the desk and shelves, the two were surprised when a person suddenly stepped into the room, staring at them.

"Oh, my God! You scared me!" Melissa said, recognizing the man as one she'd seen around the hotel. "We saw someone snooping in here and thought we'd see if he stole anything," she tried to explain.

Saying nothing, the person simply stood, staring.

"But we'll be on our way now," Dustin quickly chimed in, clasping Melissa's elbow as he headed toward the door.

Shaking his head in a foreboding manner, the man blocking the door closed it halfway, revealing a modified scythe behind the hinged object. Though the tool possessed the curvature of a scythe's blade, it was handheld like a sickle, having been modified for a different sort of reaping. As both teenagers looked in horror, he reached behind him to take up the weapon, never removing his cold eyes from the two intruders.

"Oh, come on," Dustin pleaded, moving in front of Melissa to protect her as the killer stepped slowly forward. "We didn't mean anything by-"

Before the young man could react the scythe moved with lightning-quick speed, its point launching upward, lodging itself crookedly in his right eye socket, penetrating several inches into his brain.

For a moment, Dustin's dying body shivered and twitched, refusing to fall, leaving just a gurgle to emit from his throat before the corpse slumped downward.

His body struck the desk, freeing the weapon from his head as Melissa shrunk back, possessed entirely by terror.

Like a timid puppy, she cowered along the other side of the desk, then bumped into it, causing her to dart frantically around it, using it as a shield from the man whose eyes seemed to know only one purpose.

Putting an end to her existence.

"No, please," she begged, seeing no remorse or emotion in the man's eyes.

To him, she was merely an object in the way of his ambitions. An object that needed to be disposed of permanently.

Melissa tried circling the desk but the killer blocked her path, forcing her back to a defensive position, where she had no hope. Tired of cat and mouse games, the killer knocked the large desk over, opening a clear path between himself and the last victim who might identify him.

"You can't do this," she pleaded, backing away from him and the weapon that dripped her boyfriend's blood. "Please," she urged one last time, stumbling into an unseen chair from behind that momentarily threw her off balance.

As she regained her balance, the killer found time to raise the weapon, letting the sharpened blade take flight toward her exposed neck, cutting off her piercing scream suddenly. Melissa's head tumbled from the body, landing neck-first squarely on the floor with a thud and a splat, like a dropped piece of moist liver. Her body slumped against the desk before landing limply on the ground near Dustin's.

No time remained for the killer to clean up the mess, and he was almost certain the scream had fallen on a pair of ears outside the hotel. Taking hold of the scythe, the killer shut off the lights and left the room, closing the door behind him.

***

"What the hell?" trooper Jason Brinkman asked himself as the scream reached his ears halfway across the sunken garden.

Working security at the hotel was more than he had ever bargained for, and he was determined to get another part-time job when an opportunity arose. He understood the risk of patrolling Indiana roads, but never expected a security job to be dangerous, or as irritating as this had proven to be.

He was sick of people sneaking into the grounds, wanting a look for themselves at the hotel. Access to the upper floors was forbidden on the guided tours, but it was hardly worth sneaking a peek he thought as he raced toward the front entrance.

His heartbeat and the creak of his leather gun belt were the only two sounds he heard during his run.

Whoever was trespassing was in deep trouble if he got his hands on them because he suspected someone was playing a sick prank on him.

Drawing his nine-millimeter, Brinkman raced up the main stairs toward the entrance, seeing nothing but several bulbs beyond the door that added to the hotel's decor, but did little to light the inside hallway. They were always on, but served only a cosmetic purpose.

Brinkman would be running blindly into the building, unsure of where to check first. Two sets of double doors made of thick clear glass stood between him and some answers.

Violently swinging the first glass door open, Brinkman stepped inside the building, throwing open the next right-hand door leading to the lobby. Though the doors added elegance to the hotel, they were sometimes a weighty hindrance.

Brinkman stepped inside, instantly lurching forward as the sharp end of a scythe carved through his abdomen. His gun hit the floor with a clack as the state trooper breathed in heaves, never given a chance to defend himself.

The trooper's attacker had hidden to the side of the glass in the hotel lobby, where lighting was scarce, and he was invisible behind a thick partition until the time to strike arrived.

Hunched over, Brinkman looked like an old-fashioned well pump as blood dripped from his mouth, bubbling up from his throat. The warm droplets hit the floor, creating a red pool from his injury.

Leaving the weapon where it was, the killer shoved the dying Brinkman back through both sets of glass doors, leaving blood streaks on all of the panels, until the brisk night air added a chill to the already eerie scene.

Standing along the edge of the balcony, with two flights of concrete stairs leading down directly behind the slumped officer, the killer began prying the weapon slowly from Brinkman's insides, listening to the agonized, barely audible cries from the trooper.

Both the weapon and victim trickled blood on the decorative concrete, staining it permanently as it pooled over the permanent carvings done decades before.

Tossing the weapon to the ground, the killer stood Brinkman up to his own level, grasping his uniform collar, looking into the trooper's fading eyes. Blood trickled from Brinkman's mouth as he coughed involuntarily, the red substance forming a foamy mist as it forcibly spewed from his mouth.

Brinkman's end drew near.

"You son-of-a-bitch," the trooper gasped between breaths. "You shouldn't be-"

Shoving forward with both arms, the killer launched Brinkman down the nearly three dozen steps that led to the front entrance, watching as the body tumbled end over end until it reached the bottom, rolling near the cop's own patrol car. Standing a moment, the killer watched for any movement from the resilient trooper.

Once the killer turned to head inside, Brinkman, determined to use his last few breaths of life for the betterment of man, reached for the radio transmitter clipped to his collar. Holding the button with a trembling thumb, he called the incident into his post.

"Officer down...officer...down," he said between gasps. "My...twenty...is... West Baden...Springs...Hotel," he added painfully, feeling blood trickles on his lip and cheek. "Send backup...officer...down," Brinkman added with his dying breath, falling limp after the last word.

What the trooper could not have known during his heroic attempt to stop the killer was that his radio unit was shattered, much like several of his bones during his tumble down the hotel's grand stairs.

Like its owner, it lay devoid of life on the concrete walkway, overshadowed by the domed structure and its new legacy.

Chapter 16

Clouse found the hotel grounds in shambles the next morning when he and Zach arrived. Between the crime scene tape along the yard and an empty state police cruiser sitting awkwardly along the brick drive, the hotel didn't look prim and proper as usual.

At such an early hour, Clouse could not find any family members to take his son, and there would be little need to supervise the workers because their workday would consist of placing tools and supplies in storage once he and Rusty broke the news.

He imagined most of the workers were frightened about coming into work anyhow after one of their colleagues was murdered; possibly by someone they all knew. While no one else was present, Clouse wanted to evaluate what needed to be accomplished before the hotel could be closed down.

It still seemed odd that tomorrow there would be no activity within the mammoth walls, and that he'd have nothing to do on his days off from the fire department. Both he and his brother-in-law were given an additional week off by their chief to settle any family affairs that might linger.

Clouse figured it was the chief's way of wiping his hands clean of any potential criminal investigations within his department, particularly aimed toward Clouse himself. It would certainly look bad to have Clouse working while the city police investigated him, but the front office, like any other, kept Summers from working as well, so it didn't look as though they were only targeting Clouse.

Clouse knew, and understood, but their reaction served only to further annoy him.

Thanks to the unrelenting press, most of the Bloomington area seemed to know Clouse was the prime suspect in Angie's murder. It worried him, not being able to prove otherwise, or speak out against the allegations.

Stopping beside the state police cruiser, Clouse stepped from his truck, surveying the car and wondering why Jason Brinkman would still be at the hotel.

Usually, whoever worked midnight security would be gone by morning, locking all of the entrances and gates around the hotel before heading out. He might have thought little about it, except for the pool of dried blood beside the patrol car.

"Oh, no," he told himself, fearing the worst if he went inside.

Along the last several steps, he could see chips of black plastic and more blood droplets. Signs of a turbulent fall were evident.

"Stay in the truck, Zach," he ordered his son, "and lock it."

Clouse walked the seemingly endless stained path up the steps, finding the front doors unlocked as he stepped inside. Cautiously walking into the unlit lobby, Clouse stepped in a pool of blood, still wet on the designer tile, which would cost a small fortune to replace.

"Shit," he said to himself, looking at the bottom of his boot, knowing he had already contaminated evidence.

Still, he could not help but see what horrors awaited him further inside. The firefighter observed the floor, finding nothing except a heavy flashlight, still sending a beam of light across the lobby. Resisting the urge to pick up the light, Clouse felt shivers up and down his spine as his heart began to beat faster. Now he wondered where its owner might be.

Clouse checked the atrium, barely illuminated by the dawn's hazy light from the glass dome above. Nothing inside was disturbed, so he took to the hallway and the nearby offices. Immediately he found more blood drippings near Landamere's office, and the door kicked in, but no one inside. He spied several blood smudges, worked into the floor in a circular motion, as though someone had tried to wipe them away.

He walked to his own office, finding the door kicked in, but nothing disturbed. The pristine condition of his office left him wondering if it was a decoy, or perhaps some other clever device to place blame on his shoulders. Of course, there was no official evidence of more murder.

Yet.

"What are you doing here?" a voice called from behind Clouse, startling him.

"Damn it, Rusty," Clouse reprimanded the foreman. "I'm surrounded by pools of blood and you find it necessary to sneak up on me?"

"What am I supposed to do? You've got your kid locked in the truck out there and there's no one else here yet. I thought maybe that sicko got you."

"You'd better phone the police," Clouse said.

"Already have. I came in early to look for Missy."

Clouse gave a puzzled look.

"She must have snuck out with that creep boyfriend of hers last night, and never made it home. Thought she might have come out here, so I came in early."

"What makes you think that?"

"Oh, they like to find places they can make out," Rusty said with a wave of his hand, obviously remembering his days as a teenager. "Movie theaters, parking lots, old hotels."

"Thankfully I haven't seen her," Clouse said, referring to the implications of being on the wrong end of the bloody mess around them. "I haven't found anything besides blood, and I kind of hope it stays that way."

"Any sign of that trooper?"

"Not yet. And I'm not looking through the entire hotel by myself."

"Good point. Let's wait for the police."

Carefully walking outside, around the blood this time, Clouse looked across the grounds before walking down the stairs, watching the morning fog lift as the sun rose over the horizon. Even this close to winter, the sunken garden looked like one large, intricate work of art, and Clouse wondered how it could be marred with blood, and by whom.

"Well, our last day here is off to a fine start," Rusty commented as the two walked down the stairs.

"And it might get worse, Rusty," Clouse replied, seeing the first county police car pull into the hotel's drive. "It just might."

***

Taking a sip of coffee from an irreversibly stained mug, Mark Daniels skimmed the local newspaper, finding little of interest.

He enjoyed a few minutes at home every morning before he hurried to work, but they seemed to go fast. If his wife worked, he rushed their daughter to the appropriate sitter before heading to the office, and if Cindy stayed home, he spent what time he could with her before heading off to the police station, knowing she would be working the afternoon shift when he got home.

Life with children was tough, especially with their second child on the way. He was hoping for a son, and suspected Cindy was, too. In another five months, they would find out for certain. Though the ultrasound had already revealed the baby's sex to doctors, the two were somewhat old-fashioned, choosing to be surprised when the time came.

Cindy supported her husband the best she could, but there were many aspects of his new investigative position he simply could not, or would not tell her. She knew the chief wanted some fresh blood in his division to attain better results, but Daniels never told her about the pressure he felt working around veteran detectives.

Many resented him for having so little time on the force and making the grade. Some disliked him working mornings when it took most officers considerably longer to get out of the midnight or afternoon shifts. Things that seemed trivial to Daniels and other young officers were the best issues veterans could come up with to bitch about.

Of any detective on his shift, Daniels worked the hardest. This also bothered the veterans, being upstaged by a youngster in their division. Regardless of where he was placed, Daniels worked constantly, never satisfied until the job was done. The chief saw this in him, along with his ability to solve problems and cases, so Daniels was transferred to detectives after only three years on the force.

Just as his wife treated him like gold, Daniels kept an eye on his family. He drove his old Honda, or a utility truck purchased at a city auction a few years back. He cut costs everywhere, sometimes at the sake of his own pride, to provide the best life possible for his family.

By no means did it make him happy to see his fellow officers driving new sports cars or Harley-Davidson motorcycles while he drove second or third-hand vehicles that frequently needed repair.

He let Cindy have the good car, trying to look at vehicles as little more than transportation. His focus was on the house, which gave him bragging rights over most officers. Just outside of Bloomington, they owned one of the best suburban homes the city had to offer.

Most police officers he knew rented, or bought homes a distance from city limits. Daniels typically thought little of himself when it came to providing a good life for his family.

He provided a good house in an area with safe and respected schools. His appetite for practicality was satisfied with a home so close to work and shopping centers.

"Good morning," Cindy said, walking into the kitchen, planting a kiss on his lips as he read the comics.

"No news is good news," he said, flashing the paper's front page to her.

"Any new leads?"

"Nothing," he said dejectedly. "It has to be someone connected to the hotel, but I don't know who or why."

Cindy went about pouring herself a cup of coffee, prepared for a day of errands with their daughter before she went into work for the phone company. Both were just getting accustomed to full nights of sleep now that their daughter was getting old enough to sleep through the night without crying or needing a change of diapers.

"I got your photos yesterday," she said, handing him a packet from the one-hour photo service at the drug store down the street.

He wondered if the camera he found at the hotel would be his much longer.

Daniels began to open the pack, but a glance at his watch informed him how soon he needed to be at city hall. Standing, he patted himself down, assured everything he needed was on his shoulder holster, or in his pockets.

He opted for a shoulder holster during the winter months when it was necessary to wear a heavier coat. Daniels hated weighting his belt down when he wore heavy clothing. With his strong upper-body, the higher holster often went ignored, whereas a conventional gun belt dug into his side after a long day, and wasn't as easy to conceal.

As he stood, Cindy adjusted his tie for him, using the opportunity to sneak in another kiss, knowing she would not see him until the next morning. He smiled, knowing how little time they had together.

"Want to do something this weekend?" he asked, picking up his winter jacket.

"That would be nice," she said as he put it on, stuffing the photo packet into one of the pockets.

"Give it some thought," he said, opening the door. "When you decide, call a sitter."

***

Daniels walked into the investigative offices to find his partner ready for a morning drive to West Baden. He objected to Kendle's blood-sniffing, since they lacked concrete proof either way.

During the drive south, he said little, simply admiring the countryside view. Several ideas came to mind regarding where he might take his wife for the weekend, but none seemed good enough for her after everything she had done for him.

"I'm going to nail your boy," Kendle said as they pulled into the hotel drive. "Then we'll see how smart you are."

"Whatever," Daniels replied passively as he stepped from the unmarked car, realizing the rift between he and his partner was completely due to a generation gap, intensified by friction in the workplace.

He felt Kendle acted unprofessionally simply to get at him. Around other people, the senior detective kept his professionalism intact, but when it came to Clouse or his only potential protector, the man lost his cool much more easily.

While Kendle spoke to Rusty Cranor, Daniels walked inside, finding several state police officers photographing the stains, and taking samples from the various blood pools. He stepped over the primary puddle at the entrance, noticing someone had not, from the footprint left at one edge.

"Has anything but the blood been found?" he asked one of the troopers.

"We've had the county boys looking inside and upstairs, but nothing yet," one answered.

Daniels stepped outside a moment, looking over several county and state police cars from the veranda. He saw several construction workers approaching with perplexed looks across their faces. The detective couldn't say he blamed them.

He fished a cigarette from his shirt pocket, lighting it as someone approached him from the side. Daniels turned to see Clouse with an unsettling look on his face.

"Why does it seem you're everywhere there's trouble?"

"Just lucky I guess," Clouse replied sarcastically.

"That man wants your ass on his living room mantle," the detective noted, nodding down toward Kendle, who continued speaking with Rusty.

"He might not get the chance. The reconstruction is being closed down until further notice."

"On whose orders?" Daniels asked with a quizzical look.

"Dr. Smith informed both Rusty and I last night that no further construction would take place until the killing ceased, or he could find a buyer for the hotel."

Daniels paced the balcony a moment, pensively thinking about what Clouse had just said.

"Who would be in line to buy such a place?"

"Someone with more money than you and I will ever see," the fireman stated. "You're talking about millions to reconstruct this place."

Daniels pointed his forefinger upward as a revelation raced through his mind, then crossed his face, showing sudden awareness.

"Yes, but what would the *selling* price be?"

Stumped, Clouse drew the same expression the detective had a moment before.

"You know, I'm not sure," Clouse finally answered. "Dr. Smith would probably be more concerned about what the person did with the property than he would about the money."

Without another word, Daniels took a final drag on his cigarette and flicked it over the balcony railing. He stepped inside the hotel, over the initial pool of blood again. Clouse followed, extremely careful to avoid it.

"You know who stepped in that?" Daniels asked.

"I think so," Clouse said in a voice that gave the detective his answer, especially since the print in the puddle looked very much like a cowboy boot. "It was too dark to see."

"Uh-huh."

Walking to Landamere's office, the detective flipped the light switch, illuminating the room. He walked in, surveying the room and the desk flipped over on its side. All of the drawers were removed, while papers strewn across the floor almost served as a carpeting for nearly half the office.

"What would anyone want from in here?" Daniels inquired.

"Hard telling. Dave kept most of his paperwork from the project in this office, but it wasn't anything useful to the layman."

"You have a key to the room, correct?"

"I do, and so does Rusty."

"So neither of you would need to be kicking in doors to look through his belongings," Daniels surmised.

Daniels knelt beside the desk, looking at and around the papers, finding something unusual among the scattered documents.

"Hey, troopers!" he called. "I need some latex in here!"

One of the state troopers brought Daniels a disposable latex glove, allowing the detective to finger through the papers, finally reaching the object that had caught his attention.

Snapping the glove tightly over his right hand, Daniels picked up a ring, smeared partially with blood. One of the troopers held out a plastic bag, allowing him to place it safely within its protective confines.

Taking hold of the bag, he examined the ring, finding a small red stone within a tiny white band that appeared diamond in nature, all encased within a gold frame. He assessed it a rare-looking ring if nothing else.

"Recognize it?" he asked Clouse.

Readily nodding, Clouse felt unhappy and uneasy about the find.

"It belongs to Dave Landamere," he answered. "Dave always wore it opposite his wedding band."

Daniels wondered if the ring had been there an extended period of time, or if Dave Landamere had come back to visit the night before. It looked quite authentic, which meant it was probably valued in the thousands. The ring was not something Dave Landamere would easily forget or drop.

"What do you think?" Clouse inquired, uneasy about the skeptical look on Daniels' face.

"I think I'm going to pay Mrs. Landamere a visit."

A few minutes later the detective and Clouse walked outside, seeing more construction workers gather around the front entrance, unsure of what to do until either Clouse or Rusty told them.

Clouse walked down the steps, giving them a quick briefing on what was found before giving them instructions to pack everything away in protected areas until the construction could commence again. Before dismissing them, he insisted they stay with another worker at all times for safety.

He took two men aside, instructing them to clean up the pools of blood as soon as the police were done, in order to preserve the tile if that was still possible.

"I checked on your grounds keeper," Daniels said once they were somewhat isolated from everyone again.

"And?" Clouse asked curiously.

"His full name is Vernon Black. It seems he's a throwback to the hotel's university days. He's a drunk who's been jailed a few times for disorderly conduct and public intoxication, but nothing remotely close to homicide. I doubt he's our killer."

"It was worth a look," Clouse replied, the hope of clearing his name fading just a bit more.

Clouse looked over to Zach, who was awed by the equipment in a police car.

Luckily, one of the county officers had time to monitor the boy while Clouse spoke with Daniels. Like most boys his age, Zach found police equipment fascinating despite the fact that his father used similar devices on the fire department. There was an intimidating power police officers possessed that kids loved.

"What's going on?" Jane Brooks asked Clouse, brushing past a few construction workers once the meeting was over.

"What are you doing here?" he replied in surprise.

"It's my tour day. What happened?"

"We're not sure. I found pools of blood inside, but the police didn't find much else."

"My God," Jane gasped. "You don't suppose-"

"I hope not," Clouse cut her off. "Let's hope it's just some sort of prank."

He looked over to Brinkman's patrol car, finding little optimism in the situation. The circumstances were unusual, and state troopers didn't just disappear for no reason.

Rusty approached the two with the same worried look he had met Clouse with earlier.

"Sorry to break this up," he said, "but can you take over, Paul? I'd like to see if Missy ever got home, or at least to school."

"Sure, Rusty. Let me know what you find out."

Both watched as the foreman left, shaking his head. For parents, it was easy to understand the concern he felt.

"No matter how old they get, you never stop worrying," Clouse commented.

"I know," Jane replied. "Care for some company until my tour starts?"

Clouse somehow doubted there would be a tour, but he wasn't going to scare off his best company of the morning.

"Sure," he replied. "Can you tell me any good news?"

"I'll try."

"Let me introduce you to my son," Clouse said, walking over to the county officer's car.

Glancing away from the two patrolmen he was speaking to, Larry Kendle took notice of Clouse thanking the county officer standing beside his son, and a lady he did not recognize, who seemed quite concerned about Clouse's well-being.

From his own experience, he knew wives were troublesome when their husbands found someone new, and he wondered how far Paul Clouse might have gone to keep his wife from getting everything, had they divorced.

Kendle suspected Clouse had murdered for money, and perhaps the detective had just stumbled upon an additional motive. He wondered about this woman's identity, and if she was more than just a concerned friend of the prime suspect.

He intended to find out.

***

Susan Portman had second thoughts about working at the hotel when she arrived late in the morning to find patrol cars around the building.

Recently hired to transform the hotel's gift shop, little more than two crates containing post cards and a few small historical books, into an emporium, she had a daunting task ahead of her. Creating merchant accounts and doing enough paperwork to kill several small trees kept her busy enough, but the mental anguish from the strange events surrounding the hotel was almost enough to make her quit before she even started.

Near the second main entrance, what was to become her shop looked like a makeshift warehouse with boxes appearing randomly scattered throughout the room.

She pulled an invoice from one box, studied it, and found herself distracted by voices outside her window. Police were still buzzing over the reported spilled blood. Rumors were already circulating about the missing state trooper. A few of the workers stuck around to put their tools away, but few stayed very long.

Susan heard another rumor that Paul Clouse was the first person to discover the pool of blood. She wasn't sure whether to feel sorry for the man, or suspect him of cold-blooded murder. He seemed to be in the wrong place too many times to be coincidence, but no one had placed him directly at a murder site either.

Like most people involved with the hotel, Susan knew who he was, because she conducted occasional tours. Still, he was a relative newcomer to the restoration project, so she never made presumptions about his character.

Being around such an environment made her nervous, but she had confidence in the security staff, and knew the building like her own house.

An Orange County native, she remembered the various phases the hotel went through, including the time it was abandoned for more than a decade. Overgrown with weeds, the building had faded, lost shingles on its roof, literally fallen down along one exterior wall, and suffered extensive damage to its glass fixtures.

Many statues were missing or broken at that time, and the floor looked deplorable. Tiles were dislodged, stained, and completely gone in chunks, as though someone had removed them with heavy machinery.

She remembered being inside the atrium when it rained through the dome where the glass panels had fallen in from deterioration and vandalism. For a time, the hotel was surrounded by gates containing warnings of dangerous conditions for those who trespassed. Like hundreds of other people, Susan ignored the signs, wanting a look at the hotel for herself.

That was years ago.

Now, she felt lucky to have been a retail store's assistant manager, which helped land her the job as the emporium manager at the hotel. Her position allowed her, and her husband, to remain close to family, while giving her a sense of doing something worthwhile.

Proceeds from the new gift shop benefited the hotel, because funds from the shop and tours kept the electricity paid, with a little extra money for the upkeep of the building and grounds. The store was tied in directly with the National Preservation Society for just such a purpose.

Returning her mind to the task at hand, she picked up another invoice, checked inside the box, then checked off the items as she found them. Many of the current items were related to the hotel's era, while custom books, models, and clothing were being manufactured locally that symbolized the building itself.

Ignoring the chatter outside, she went about her business, glad a dozen or so people lingered behind. The room she stood within was going to be an office one day, where she might keep her paperwork, phone clients and vendors, and make her life easier through the internet.

Using a sharp disposable knife, she slit the tape along the top of another box as a tapping noise, like a dropped pen, came from the hallway.

Her doors were open, so the slightest noise from the atrium or hallway echoed through the first floor, and into her gift shop, as though occurring right beside her.

Hearing no other noise, like footsteps, or chatter, she chose to investigate. Walking to the closest door apprehensively, she figured the noise came from across the atrium, some hundred yards or more away from her.

"Hello?" she called softly. "Anyone there?"

Reaching the door, she realized all five of the doors that would eventually make up the emporium were open to let fresh air inside. New carpeting laid the week before gave off a foul odor due to the adhesive used to bond it with the concrete floor.

The old windows were hard to open, and they were securely fastened with screws through wooden one-inch cubes atop each frame. Martin Smith wanted to make certain no one snuck into the hotel from the outside, so every door and window was secured in one fashion or another.

With stacks of boxes everywhere around her, Susan felt a bit uneasy about someone sneaking into the emporium while she distracted herself with invoices.

Peering into the hallway, Susan found no one in either direction. Writing off the noise as falling particles, she turned to find someone standing beside one stack of boxes, startling her as she let a brief shriek escape her throat before placing her hand over her mouth.

"Brent, you scared me," she quickly apologized to the retired state trooper who sometimes worked morning shift security.

"Sorry," Brent Guthrie said, chuckling. "I just wanted a peek at some of your goods before you put them out."

Susan paused a moment, letting her wits return.

"Have they found anything out about Jason?" she asked of the missing trooper.

"Not yet," Guthrie said solemnly. "I worked with the boy. He's not going to disappear, and he sure as hell isn't going to ignore his duties."

He looked through a box, but Susan read his emotions. Guthrie was passing time, simply keeping himself occupied, and his mind away from the grave matters at hand.

"It just seems things have been bad around here lately," he muttered. "If I was those Bloomington detectives, I'd be taking a hard look at that Paul Clouse."

"I would think they already are," Susan noted.

"One of them seemed awful chummy with him earlier."

Returning to her work, Susan opened another box.

"I'm just glad you're here," she told the retired trooper. "I take it you arrived to find the big mess outside?"

Guthrie shook his head negatively.

"I got here at seven, like usual, and there was already a slew of cops out there. Things aren't looking good for Jason, and I heard Cranor say his daughter never came home last night."

"That's terrible," Susan said, genuinely concerned for the likeable foreman.

She stared into the dimly lit hallway, wondering if things were going to improve around the hotel anytime soon.

If they didn't, all of her hard work to land her new position was destined to be a complete waste of time. Hoping not, she turned her attention to another box needing her attention.

Susan decided to work as long as people were at the hotel. If they all left, she planned to quickly follow their lead.

Chapter 17

It took Daniels nearly three hours to break himself away from Kendle, who was dying to find out the identity of the woman Paul Clouse was with at the hotel.

Though he found it strange, the prime suspect would be seen with *any* woman so soon, Daniels focused on Landamere's disappearance, still convinced Clouse did not swing the scythe, and hopefully had nothing to do with the murders.

When the detective arrived at the Landamere estate between Bedford and Bloomington, near the area his work was based, Daniels could not help but stare at the beautiful landscape as he pulled into the driveway. He felt it was nearly as astounding as the hotel he had just come from as he stepped from his unmarked car.

He began a stroll around the house, taking in details of the yard's beauty, earned from hours of labor and careful planning.

Sparkling with intricate design, the grounds displayed the remains of rich summer flowers, now wilted to tangled vines or pedals. More impressive were the statues, artistic flowerbeds, and benches placed symmetrically across the expansive backyard where Daniels could picture a happy couple strolling leisurely, wasting part of a day in their own backyard.

But the Landameres were not that kind of couple from what he had heard.

Staring at the grounds, he failed to hear anyone walk up behind him in the grass devoid of leaves. Not until Joan Landamere was within a few feet did he actually hear her coming.

"Do you like it?" she asked.

"It's beautiful," Daniels replied, quickly looking her over.

For a lady her age, Joan Landamere looked quite young and firm, even wearing a jumper, which indicated she kept herself that way by design. He could see no lines along her face, and her gray hair, cut stylishly short seemed en vogue if Daniels recalled some of his wife's recent beauty magazine covers correctly.

Though old enough to be his mother, Daniels could not help but find her attractive. He wondered how Landamere could be unhappy with such a woman. From the youthful sparkle in her eyes, which seemed to display her pride, and the way she conducted herself, he had already gauged her to be an intelligent woman.

"I spend my summers working in the garden, finding something new every season to add to its beauty."

Daniels nodded easily, but said nothing.

"I'm here to ask you about your husband," he revealed, returning to his businesslike nature.

He quickly introduced himself, producing credentials.

"I figured," she said, obviously disappointed about having to talk about her husband.

"Can I take it you and your husband don't get along?" he asked, realizing his breath was visible in the cold air.

"You've probably heard we have a marriage of convenience, detective, and I'll save you the trouble of researching. It's true."

Daniels could hardly fathom being in such a situation himself. Perhaps money allowed people luxuries he would never understand as both a police officer and a family man. He considered himself a Christian as well, which usually kept him on the straight and narrow path.

"But you have no idea where he might be?"

"He does this, Detective Daniels. He'll just disappear for a week at a time. It's even in his contract with Kieffer Construction that he can take unannounced personal days for creative integrity."

She said the last words with a lofty wave of her hands, as though her husband received snobby superstar treatment in his contracts.

"So you're not concerned?"

"Are you?" she answered with a question.

Daniels grinned. He had hoped for more of a straightforward interview.

"Let's get in where it's warm, detective," she said, leading him around the front.

"I have some genuine concerns about your husband's safety," Daniels confessed as they stepped inside the lavish three-story house.

It was far more than two people would ever need, and he could picture the couple throwing meaningless grand parties on the weekends, cooking on the industrial grill in the backyard, and swimming in the in-ground pool. By his own definition, it was a mansion.

Daniels couldn't help but look around the house, and he was certain Joan viewed him as a kid in a candy shop. Everywhere he looked sat oriental rugs, hardwood floors, imported art, and more furniture in any given room than he figured his entire house contained. He wondered just how much Dave Landamere earned as a project manager.

"How did you come to get your house if you don't mind me asking?"

"David built it," she said as though it was a simple weekend project. "It took him well over a year with help from a few of his workers."

She noticed him looking up the stairs, then into the doorways of several rooms on the first floor.

"If it puts your mind at ease, you can look through his office," Joan offered, appearing to enjoy the notion of someone rummaging through her husband's things, as though it would agitate him.

"I'll take you up on that. Thanks."

A moment later Daniels walked into the office, finding it much more elegant than the offices at the hotel. Full bookshelves were mounted to the wall, reaching the ceiling in the octagonal room. A lamp sat atop a small stand near one window while the large wooden desk stood beside the other, its top glowing from the light that streamed through the open blinds.

Daniels looked over the books, finding most of them pleasure reading or construction-related. He set into the desk, opening the drawers one by one, seeing little except business letters, personal belongings, and several awards Landamere had won, either for his designs, or his humanitarianism, in efforts to save historic buildings. Apparently, the hotel was not his first preserved landmark.

He glanced over the letters, finding nothing to indicate either danger, or a reason why he would disappear. Still, Daniels felt a nagging sensation he was missing something of interest. He closed the desk drawers, thinking of what he might do if he was fooling around behind Cindy's back.

While he would never do such a thing, Daniels had to think as though he was, and it seemed he would need a place to hide letters or knickknacks if he was concealing a relationship, if indeed that was what Landamere had done.

Daniels opened each of the desk's side drawers, feeling beneath each of them sequentially. On the bottom right drawer, his hand rubbed a piece of tape, then a cold piece of metal.

He peeled the tape back, carefully pulling a gold-colored key from the drawer. Daniels inspected the key momentarily, contemplating how much it would be missed since it was obviously a secret.

He placed it in his pocket and stood to leave.

His day was far from over.

***

Clouse wasted some time playing on the internet, registered as a guest on Angie's computer. He was waiting for Tony Dierker to break the main code, but his fellow firefighter needed to take his wife home from work before coming over.

In the meantime, Clouse ran a search of the worldwide web, trying to locate information about several of the hotel's potential buyers Dr. Smith spoke about.

He had managed to weasel a verbal list of prospects from one of Smith's board members. He used the excuse of possibly meeting several company presidents, wanting to do some research on them ahead of time so he didn't look foolish when they toured the grounds.

Unwittingly, the board member gave Clouse more than he expected, even phone numbers and website addresses in most cases. The companies without much information were the ones he worried about and targeted first in his online search.

Most were nonprofit organizations, set up to restore old buildings, or preserve them. Some specialized in creating museums out of famous houses, or returning buildings to their original state, sometimes making a working exhibit that held true to the time period. Clouse cringed at the thought of someone decimating his hotel.

"Tincher Incorporated," he read a name aloud from his list, unfamiliar with the name or reputation of the company. Ironically, the listing provided a website, but no phone number or address.

Clouse typed in the address, quickly bringing up several impressive before and after photos of restored buildings. There were links to more photos of their interiors, but he passed up the interesting stuff for an information search.

He found an Illinois address, a voicemail phone message number, and an e-mail link for the company, putting several of his fears to rest. Clouse tagged the site for future reference, typing in his e-mail address and personal information under the company's mailing list as he had the rest of the sites, in the hopes of receiving more information through the mail or internet.

In all, Clouse had looked at more than twenty sites that morning, hoping his contracting credentials would get him a response from each company. Every shred of information he obtained about each company would help him determine which, if any, was involved in foul play. He finished looking over his list as a knock came to his front door.

He leapt to answer it, knowing Zach was napping upstairs.

"Tony," he said with a smile after opening the kitchen door.

"Hi, Paul. Finally made it over."

Clouse briefly explained the situation to his fellow fireman, letting Dierker seat himself at the terminal. Clouse grabbed a seat nearby.

Though his colleagues considered him a bit strange, they respected Dierker for his intellect and ability to think through most any situation. In a way, they thought of him as a nerd with his wild, curly red hair, lack of practical common sense, and an ability to focus on a computer screen regardless of what occurred around him.

Clouse figured Dierker could be in the middle of an inferno with his laptop and not flinch. When it came to dragging hose lines into a blazing building, Dierker kept the same intensity as he did with a computer, which earned him respect among other firefighters, even if they did find him a bit standoffish at times.

"This shouldn't be hard," Dierker said, pulling a diskette from his shirt pocket. He popped it into the disk drive, concerning Clouse slightly.

"You're not going to blow it up or anything, are you?"

Dierker chuckled.

"Not unless it's wired to blow if given a wrong password. And even then it would only kill me."

Clouse smiled, finding Dierker's humor entertaining for a change.

"My program will run a series of words, pretty much like a dictionary, then names, then random sequences of letters and numbers until it gets the right one."

"How long will that take?"

"It generates about a million codes per minute, so unless she had a fairly complex sequence of letters and numbers, which is recommended mind you, we should be in within the next ten minutes."

Half an hour later the program continued to run as the two men exchanged stories about fire scenes and some of the people they worked with. Clouse seldom spoke with the computer expert since they worked different shifts and stations.

"I guess Angie had a decent code," Clouse surmised, looking at the tally of codes tried across the screen.

It was over the twenty-million mark.

"You would have been an eternity trying this yourself, Paul," Dierker revealed. "But the good news is the program will tell us the code before entering it so you'll know, and you'll be able to change it if you want."

A few minutes later the computer beeped and a line of code flashed on the screen. It was the password.

"Zach82Mac," Dierker read aloud. "Mean anything?"

"My son's name and the name of his favorite teddy bear, but the number doesn't mean anything. It probably didn't to Angie either. I'd have never gotten that."

Clouse wrote it down for reference while Dierker excused himself, his job being done.

"Thanks a million," Clouse said, tossing the diskette to him.

"Don't mention it. You can build me a house to repay me sometime," Dierker kidded as he left.

For the next half hour, Clouse browsed through Angie's mail messages, her online address book, and messages sent. Everything seemed ordinary except for one message sent, and another received.

Clouse confirmed that he was correct about Michael Hathaway keeping the purchase of the hotel a secret until it was actually done. He told Angie not to say a word to Clouse until the final paperwork was signed, leaving the firefighter to think it was only a possibility of the hotel being bought.

He also realized something that meant the world to him. In a reply message, Angie told Hathaway about their marital trouble, and that she planned to reconcile with Clouse when the time was right. He was overjoyed about the idea of Angie still caring for him, and upset that Kelli mislead him about the facts.

Clouse noticed the late afternoon time on the clock and decided to wake Zach up from his nap. He ran upstairs, nudged his son awake, and walked to the upstairs bathroom, letting the door close partway behind him.

Cupping water in his hands, Clouse splashed his face, feeling a soothing cool as he rubbed his hands and the liquid into his skin. Dripping from the face, Clouse glanced in the mirror, catching a good look of someone standing behind him.

It was Angie in spectral form, dressed in a summer dress, like those she wore when they were first married. Her face held a placid look, taking Clouse back to the times they were happy for the split second before he blinked, losing the image. He looked behind him, seeing nothing; sure he was going mad.

Taking a towel from beside him, Clouse wiped his face, then looked in the mirror again, horrified by what he saw this time. Now his wife stood there, hands by her sides in a position of pleading, wearing a white dress completely stained with blood, accompanied by gashes and cuts across her body.

Her face and hair were sticky with dried blood and pieces of flesh and chunks of internal organs glued by the blood. The dress was torn in numerous areas, and she looked to be anything but peaceful as she mouthed the words "Help me."

Clouse turned away from the mirror, afraid to actually glance behind him. The horror was bad enough in the mirror, but when he looked again the image was gone, replaced by his son. He turned to Zach, who appeared only partly awake, and dropped to hug him. He felt certain he was going mad, and wondered what was wrong with his mind.

"You okay, Daddy?" Zach asked innocently, unsure of why he was the recipient of so many hugs lately.

"I don't know, Zach. I just don't know."

Chapter 18

Early the next morning Clouse fed the animals after his parents left with Zach. He scooped grain into several troughs, contemplating how soon he wanted to put his house up for sale. The images of Angie disturbed him, leaving him to wonder if the house was now haunted, or if he might be losing his mind.

He was dressed in sweat pants, an old T-shirt, and tennis shoes without socks. The combination made for a cool trip outside, but inspired him to hurry with the chores. His hair crossed several directions, feeling oily because he had not yet showered. At least the cold weather now helped him sleep a little better at night.

Taking a look into the field which surrounded his house in nearly every direction, he spied most of the animals in the field, enjoying what little time they had left to walk in the open pastures. Hearing the phone ring inside the house, Clouse tossed the feeding scoop inside the barn and jogged inside, answering it on the third ring.

"Paul," a distraught voice said. "I received a disturbing letter today."

"Dr. Smith, what's wrong?" Clouse asked, recognizing the voice.

"Someone left me a letter ordering me to reopen the hotel or the killing would never cease."

"It's a trick," Clouse stated. "Don't reopen it. Call the police."

"I did," Smith said. "Now they want me to reopen it so they can stake it out and catch him."

Clouse shook his head, unable to believe the killer would make demands the hotel remain open. He was skeptical of police involvement because they would only monitor him all the more, letting the real killer run free.

"I may just take the best bidder I can find and sell the thing," Smith said with obvious tension. "I don't like all of this around me."

Clouse knew the pressure was getting to the doctor. Smith never intended anything but good for the property, but his dreams were being crushed by the insane crusade of one person.

"Do what you have to, doc, but you should give it time. They'll catch whoever's doing this."

"I'll call you when I know something more, Paul. But it looks like we'll be going back to work with a police guard."

Great, Clouse thought sarcastically. He expected at least one officer to monitor his whereabouts at all times.

"This is your dream, doc," Clouse almost pleaded. "Don't let it go that easy."

"I'm trying, Paul. I'm really trying. Goodbye."

"It's my dream too," Clouse commented as the click reached his ear.

He turned the phone off, tossing it to the couch. He hated days that started this badly.

"Goddamn it," he said, heading toward the bathroom for a shower.

As he dried himself several minutes later, he heard a phone ring from the living room, but it was not his cordless phone.

"Cell phone," he said, scurrying from the bathroom without benefit of towel cover. "Hello," he said, clutching it from its charger, still dripping from his shower.

"Hello, Paul," an unfamiliar, but clear voice said from the other end. It could have easily been the voice of a disk jockey, but it seemed too crisp, too unrealistic to be anyone he knew. Clouse wondered if it was a voice-altering device doing the talking.

"Who's this?"

"That's not as important as *where* I am," the male voice replied. "Seems you have some people missing from your hotel. Guests check in, but they don't check out, is that it, Paul?"

"Who the hell is this?" Clouse demanded, sick of phone games. "I'm in no mood for this shit."

"Neither was your wife."

Stunned silence for a few seconds.

"You sick fuck! Why don't you—"

"Seems there's a lot of death around you lately, Paul. Everyone you know is dying, and you're always there. Too bad you weren't quick enough to save Beaman."

"Asshole!" Clouse stammered. "What the hell do you want?"

"I want you to rot in prison, then in hell for the crimes I commit. You've got it coming."

"Listen—"

"No, you listen!" the voice said, breaking its cool, calm demeanor for the first time. "You've got an hour and fifteen minutes to reach your precious hotel or a certain tour guide we both know gets a plot beside Father Ernest on the hill."

Clouse heard the click and froze, unable to move for a few seconds afterward while he pondered the authenticity of the call. Deciding it was real, he dashed to his bedroom to grab some clothes before he raced to West Baden in an unreasonable amount of allotted time.

***

While the bustle of morning work surrounded Mark Daniels, the young detective looked through the file of evidence surrounding the West Baden murders and that of Angie Clouse. His desk, basically a cubicle surrounded by a sea of cubicles, looked rather impersonal because he kept his family photos inside the desk drawers. Often required to interview suspects and prisoners, Daniels didn't want images of his family atop his desk, serving as potential targets for the sick individuals who sometimes invaded his space.

Unfortunately, the morning seemed to be the only time of day the detectives wandered the investigations office like bees, drinking coffee or catching up on the rumor mill. Later, the detectives split up, took long lunches, or conducted work in the field. To Daniels, the office could actually be highly distracting in the morning.

He found little evidence of use inside the file. It seemed the killer was hiding his tracks well, but at the same time manipulated evidence and circumstances. If Daniels' hunch was correct, and Paul Clouse was not committing the murders, someone had gone through great lengths to incriminate him, yet left a lack of physical evidence to link him to the crimes definitively.

Daniels knew how easily someone could have left traces of Father Ernest's corpse in the back of Clouse's truck, or picked a better time to frame him for Angie's murder. At the fire station, he had a fairly potent alibi. There had to be times when Clouse was alone with no witnesses. Perhaps the killer was simply being ambiguous with the fireman's potential guilt.

"Time," Daniels thought aloud, focusing on one of his thoughts.

Suddenly timing seemed the one thing he hadn't given much thought to.

Halloween?

No, nothing else tied into that.

West Baden Springs nearing completion?

Perhaps, but that seemed irrelevant.

Clouse's marital problems?

It seemed a good trigger to start the series of murders with, but held little consequence in the scheme of things.

A potential purchase of the property?

Daniels knew there were interested parties, but how serious they were, and who they might threaten, eluded him. He sat back, pondering where his search would lead him next.

Kendle was busy checking out what Clouse stood to inherit from his wife's death while trying to link physical evidence from the corpses to Clouse. The coroner would be able to determine, more or less, what height the killer was from the depths of the impacts, and whether he was left or right-handed by the angle of the cuts.

Daniels let his hands fall to his sides, slapping against his coat on the chair's backside. He felt a solid lump on the coat's right side, which puzzled him momentarily.

"Oh, the photos," he said to himself, finally remembering them.

Subconsciously he was afraid to look because the photos would probably show several people huddled in a pose, revealing who the owner might be, or perhaps some baby photos from a grandmother who had toured the grounds, accidentally dropping the camera on the way out. Daniels would never keep the photos or the camera if he had the slightest idea how to find its owner.

Reluctantly, he opened the packet.

"Want to go for coffee, Mark?" one of Daniels' old patrol partners asked, passing by his desk. He had just gotten off the midnight shift.

"Sure, Marty," the detective replied, stuffing the packet back into his jacket.

Its contents could wait a little longer.

***

Clouse swerved around several cars on a single-lane road as his unexpected trip to West Baden neared its end. Several cars honked as his truck awkwardly passed at a high rate of speed, but its driver did not care. He could not believe the audacity of the killer, actually phoning him and threatening Jane.

According to the clock on his dashboard, Clouse neared the killer's deadline, leaving him little option but to phone Ken Kaiser, who would hopefully be patrolling the county. He speed-dialed the number, hearing two rings before his friend picked up.

"Hello?"

"Ken, it's Paul. Where are you right now?"

"Working security at the hotel. Why?"

"I need you to find any tours going on, round them up, and get them to a safe place."

"Paul, what's this about?"

Clouse could feel sweat forming between his palm and the cellular phone. He realized how unusually nervous he felt, and must have sounded, to his friend.

"Just do it, Ken. I'll be there in about five minutes to explain."

"What do I tell them?"

"Whatever it takes. Just keep them together, and safe."

When the truck pulled into the hotel's lot, tires squealing from such a sharp turn, Clouse drove immediately to the front door, seeing no one outside. It seemed empty without the workers busily reassembling areas of the building.

Clouse dashed up the stairs, threw open the double doors, and entered, seeing a group huddled inside the atrium with Kaiser standing nearby. The deputy's face showed his displeasure, but a quick glance at him, then the group, failed to reveal Jane. Panic set into Clouse, then he saw the tour guide badge on an older man among the group members.

"Is Jane working today?" he asked the man.

"No, she toured yesterday," he replied.

Kaiser intervened, taking Clouse aside from the group, which probably figured he was the potential danger, and the reason they were corralled by the deputy.

"What's going on?" Kaiser demanded.

"I got a call from the killer, Ken. He said he was going to kill Jane unless I got here in less than an hour and fifteen minutes."

"Why didn't you call sooner?"

"I got spooked," Clouse said. "If the killer saw a cop looking for him, he would surely kill her that much quicker."

Kaiser motioned to the tour guide to let the group continue on their way, afraid they might overhear the conversation. There was enough local media blitz already.

"Did he call you at home?"

"On my cell phone. My God, how could he have known the number, or that I'd be home?"

"Your number is posted in your office, Paul. Someone broke into your room a couple nights ago, remember?"

"Yeah, you're right," Clouse stammered slowly.

Clouse wondered why someone would lead him to West Baden for nothing. He could think of no motive, unless the killer wanted to monitor him, or to keep him out of Bloomington.

"Home," Clouse said aloud, knowing how easily someone could lead him out of Bloomington, only to plant evidence on his property or break into his house. He turned, heading hurriedly toward the entrance.

"Where are you going, Paul?" Kaiser demanded, growing more irritated with Clouse's strange behavior.

"I've got to get home quick, Ken."

"Don't be rushing off, Paul! You just broke every speed limit there was getting here. Stay a minute and cool off."

"I can't, Ken," Clouse said from an atrium doorway. "Can you find out who called my number almost two hours ago?"

"No. I'm not authorized to just check that stuff for fun."

Clouse wondered if his friendship with Kaiser was growing more strained, or maybe his request was simply unrealistic. Perhaps the tension made him overreact, but he darted out to the truck without another word, desperate to outwit whoever made his life a game to be played at will.

***

In a corner booth at a local café, Daniels took a sip of his coffee, and then a drag from his cigarette, realizing how many bad substances went into his body every day. He figured it made little difference anyhow because almost every food he ate held potential hazards.

"Ever notice how everything we eat is bad for us?" he asked Marty Hazen, sitting with his back to a window.

"It's always been bad for us," the officer commented. "When we were kids no one cared. Now they research everything people ever thought about eating or drinking."

"We live and we die," Daniels put it simply. "Guess in the end we choose our poison."

"You going to eat that donut hole?"

"No," Daniels said, taking a look at the local section in the paper.

A small column under current events commented how there was no progress in the investigation of Angela Clouse's murder, and the situation at the West Baden Springs Hotel. He felt lucky the press didn't dog him for comments.

"So, how is the investigation going?" Hazen asked of Daniels, noticing the same article.

"Peachy," the investigator said with disdain. "I've got an obsessive partner, an accused murderer who can't give me a solid alibi, and a slew of murders and disappearances without a single witness."

"Got any vacation time coming?"

Daniels laughed.

"Kendle's already ripping me a new asshole. I'd be giving him ammunition if I took off."

Hazen munched on some bacon, then forked some scrambled eggs into his mouth.

"You sure you don't want patrol again?" he asked between several chews.

Daniels shot him a strange look for talking while eating before he answered.

"I've waited my entire career and most of my life for this. I don't care what the brass think, and I don't care what the good ol' boys in that division think. I'll be damned if I'm going to give up this opportunity and go back to seeing every drunk, drug addict, and wife-beater there is in this town. Not that detectives is an easy division, but it gets me out, and might make a name for me."

"The chief seems pretty high on you," Hazen commented. "A lot of the guys call you his boy."

"Bullshit. He needs more of us young guys in there."

"It is kind of a stale division," Hazen agreed. "The old guys are probably starting rumors so you'll quit."

Daniels wiped his mouth with a napkin after taking a sip of coffee.

"They'll have to do better than that."

"Damn," Hazen said, looking at his watch. "I'd better get home before the wife does, or she'll throw a fit. Let me use the john and I'll walk out with you, Mark."

While his old partner walked away, Daniels pulled out the pictures for a quick look at what he had put off for too long.

Opening the pack, he saw various shots of the hotel and the grounds, quickly assuming they were simply tourist shots of the hotel. If that was the case, he might not be able to identify who owned the camera.

Flipping through the shots, he stopped when he came to an almost pure blue photo, which he realized would be the sky with just a few trees acting as border for the picture.

"Who would take an awful shot like that?" he wondered aloud, flipping to the next one.

His eyes widened as he took in the view of a cloaked figure looming above the camera at a side view, holding what appeared to be a staff, or perhaps a scythe. There was no visible face, and the photo was slightly blurred, but Daniels scanned it for every minute detail. He wondered if there was a possibility the figure in the photo was the killer.

A dark cloak, a potential murder weapon, the hotel as a setting. It all seemed to fit.

There was no visible blade as the staff ran off the visible realm of the picture, but the pose of the figure seemed threatening and calculating. Daniels could hear his breath, unable to look away from the photo for what seemed an eternity. Finally, satisfied there was nothing more to see, he slowly flipped to the next photo.

"Dear God," Daniels said as a horrible spectacle filled his eyes.

A slightly different angle, this time with a scythe in view and a hand clutching it from the victim's perspective filled the color photo. The hand loosely wrapped around the weapon, and it was apparent the camera was falling at this point, catching the last shot or two possible before it hit the ground.

Daniels could see blood on the hand, though most of the photo looked fuzzy. He guessed from the orange hue in the sky's horizon it was late afternoon, probably near sunset, when this occurred. The killer's profile was vague again, giving no real clue to his identity.

Only parts of him were visible in this photo. His arm and part of the torso were the only pieces captured behind the startling image of the weapon and the dying hand taking hold of it.

"Who the hell is taking that picture?" the detective wondered aloud.

Bracing himself, Daniels flipped to the last photo, unsure of what to expect. The result shocked him, and at the same time, sent a chill through his body, knowing there was finally some possible evidence in his case.

"Vacation shots?" Hazen asked, returning from the restroom.

"No," Daniels answered almost blankly. "I've gotta run, Marty," he said, bolting from the table, stuffing a ten-dollar bill into his old partner's hand, implying he didn't have time to pay for the tab.

"Something come up, Mark?"

"You could say that," Daniels said, rushing toward the door. "Something real big."

***

Dust flew as Clouse pulled into the gravel-covered driveway, slamming on the brakes when he reached the end. He nearly crushed his chest on the steering wheel, but didn't care, bolting from the truck once it stopped completely.

Throwing the door shut behind him with one hand, he stormed toward the house, catching a cold crosswind that stopped him for a second as he looked to the barn. Cautiously looking around, he saw no foreign vehicles, nothing disturbed, and no reason to panic.

Yet, he felt highly apprehensive.

Walking to the barn, he rolled the main door aside, letting natural light flood the boat storage area and the stalls in the back as he stepped inside. Unarmed, Clouse felt certain he had no business walking around so boldly, even if he was on his own property. He cautiously looked around every corner, and down every dark, musty hallway ahead of him. A few minutes later he emerged, finding nothing unusual inside. Still, an uneasy feeling controlled him. Someone was toying with him, and his usually cool demeanor was nowhere to be found.

A moment later Clouse stepped inside his house, stopping in the kitchen, listening for any noises before closing the door. His eyes wandered to the ceiling because he knew the history of the second level, so Clouse decided he needed to make a full inspection of the house before he could be satisfied.

Taking his jacket off, Clouse tossed it over a chair before making his way into the downstairs bedroom, then the living room.

Finding nothing out of place in either area, he ventured into the family room, finding several boxes he had sifted through a few nights prior disturbed, their contents strewn across the floor. He started toward the mess, but caught a glimpse of a light to his right, coming from Angie's old office. Clouse turned, finding one of his largest potential leads lying in a heap on the floor beside the desk.

"Her computer," he said aloud, assessing the damage.

From the family room, he could see the computer was a complete loss. Its sides were battered and the monitor appeared smashed beyond recognition. Papers and folders were strewn across the desk and floor, much like the items from the boxes. Clouse was about to inspect the damage when a noise from upstairs distracted him.

Jerking his head toward the noise, he stood a moment, breathing nervously. Deciding the police would probably arrive too late, or screw up his chances of catching the intruder, Clouse scurried to the kitchen, taking a hammer from a utility drawer.

Quickly, but quietly, he took to the stairs, heading up to see who or what was invading his house and destroying everything left in his life. The carpet virtually deadened the usual noise of his boots, allowing him to ascend quietly enough to surprise any unsuspecting intruder upstairs.

Reaching the top, he looked down the hall, seeing nothing. He opened Zach's room, seeing no one inside. A quick inspection revealed nothing in either the closet or under the bed. He left the room, shutting the door behind him.

Next was the guest bedroom.

It too held nothing in plain sight, or in the other areas. Above this room loomed the attic. Clouse listened for a minute but no sound came, assuring him no one would be in this room or above it. He carefully shut the door behind him, walking to the bathroom.

Flipping on the light, Clouse looked to his right where a brown shower curtain obscured the entire tub, showing nothing behind it. He drew in a breath, slowly reached for the curtain, and threw it aside, seeing nothing but typical sundries along the tub's side. He breathed a sigh of relief, turning to run the water in the sink.

Perhaps his paranoia was getting the better of him.

As he bent over, throwing cold water against his face, the noise of the faucet drowned out the squeaking door behind him as the bathroom's only entrance closed. He rubbed his face thoroughly, feeling a sense of relief, thinking he was alone in the house before he had mistakenly called authorities.

Clouse looked up to catch a glimpse of the killer and Zach's baseball bat just before it struck his skull, rendering him unconscious at the killer's mercy.

Chapter 19

Clouse slowly awoke to the sounds of breaking glass and shuffling papers near his living room.

He moaned from the knot growing on his head, though he could not touch it because his hands and feet were tied together behind his back. Being hogtied was about the only way to ensure he would not interfere while the killer finished his business.

Within his scope of vision, everything looked hazy, like a dream in a television soap opera.

He could see none of the activity because the noise came from the kitchen. And he never saw who the killer was because the person was masked when Clouse spied him. Somehow, it didn't surprise the fireman he was in another compromising position, or that he had the misfortune of figuring out the killer's game only to get beaten at it anyhow.

He was unlucky lately.

Adding insult to injury, the attacker stayed even longer to complete whatever objective he had set out to accomplish. Clouse had no idea whether the killer was looking for something to take, or there to destroy evidence the homeowner might have already discovered. If evidence was in his possession, Clouse had no idea what it might be.

In essence, the killer took no chance.

Detective Kendle would simply believe it was an elaborate hoax set up by Clouse to remove blame from himself, and there was no evidence to support any notion otherwise. The killer knew how to avoid detection, and never left physical or trace evidence unless by design.

Clouse barely had time to think about a way out of the ropes, or what he might do if he accomplished such an impossible feat, before a car pulled into the driveway, startling both he and the killer. While he desperately hoped no one he knew would step into jeopardy, the killer bolted for the back entrance, toward the open fields for safety.

Nearly half a minute later, a knock came to the front door. Clouse glanced to the open backdoor before answering, wondering if the killer dared lie in wait for whoever was visiting.

Whatever he was looking for had to be important for him to risk an entanglement with Clouse, but the captive decided not to leave whoever was standing at his door in the same predicament he had put himself in.

"Come in!" Clouse shouted, hoping the front door was open, trying to squirm in that direction.

It opened, and someone stood in his kitchen, obviously waiting for the host to walk into the room.

"In here!" Clouse shouted. "Help!"

He was surprised and relieved when Mark Daniels rushed into the room, though the look on the detective's face displayed total shock.

"Kendle's going to have a bitch of a time pinning this on you," he commented as he began undoing the ropes.

"The killer just bolted out the back door," Clouse announced quickly. "If you'd quit jabbering, you might be able to catch him."

"I know who it is," Daniels said, looking to the door, then heading for it. "He's not getting away again."

"Hey!" Clouse shouted, finding the ropes weren't completely undone. He fought against the straps to free himself, wanting to know everything Daniels knew.

While Clouse tried to free himself, Daniels darted down the shortest field on the property with the killer still in his view. The detective leapt a short wire fence in his initial pursuit, while the darkly clad intruder darted into a short bed of trees, crossing into a neighboring farm.

Daniels found the chase easier since the field consisted of short, dead hay that occasionally stabbed his ankles through his thin dress socks. He sprinted the best he could despite a mild lack of stamina. He hadn't chased any suspects since his days in the uniform division, and it was never after someone of such an athletic nature.

Still, Daniels dodged small trees and hurdled thick brush after the mysterious man with equivalent ease.

He reached a thicket of trees, cautiously slowing down. He could see a white farmhouse and decaying barn ahead, with several small fields to either side, but no sign of the man he pursued. Tree branches whipped him as he pressed past them, noisily crunching the blanket of dry leaves on the ground as he stepped through the small grove.

Looking to the ground, Daniels realized the leafy piles were not thick enough to conceal a person, so he looked at the trees surrounding him, noticing how dark the area appeared compared to the sunlit farm ahead. He passed each looming tree and its thick trunk, which could allow anyone to hide with ease. Because the light breeze and his own feet created noise, Daniels worried about a potential sneak attack from a stalker who didn't have to put forth much effort in hiding.

Reaching into his coat, Daniels unlatched the holster, letting his nine-millimeter slide into the palm of his hand. At the end of the trees the detective looked across the entire farm, seeing no sign of his target.

A truck parked near the house implied people might be home, so his attention fell to the barn where the killer would likely hide, since no one was visible in the fields. Had the killer continued toward the fields, Daniels would have spotted him. It seemed doubtful the killer would have hidden among the trees and doubled back to Clouse's residence.

Daniels reached the barn, finding its main doorway completely open from morning chores. He sucked in a breath, held it, and stepped inside, carefully surveying the troughs on the ground and hayloft above him for any sign of the killer.

Most of the barn was clear of hay bales and tools, so the search was quick and easy as the detective walked from one end of the barn to the other.

At the end, he found an open door leading to a small field that was partially obscured by trees. In the center of the field, he could see a man-made wall of rocks, probably used to divide property, or keep a herd from straying. Daniels started walking toward the rocks, unsure of where the killer might have gone at this point.

Avoiding fresh manure piles, the detective spied the remains of a summer garden beside the rocky wall once he drew closer, his firearm held cautiously to one side, clasped with both hands. The garden was partly obscured by the wall, with a scarecrow centered along the rocky mass to keep the birds from preying on summer vegetables.

Daniels kept a firm grip on his gun as he neared the wall, climbing it when he finally reached it for a better view. He found it was more than a fence-high wall when he scaled it. The foundation also created a small walkway, or area to sit and rest, when the farmer's help grew tired of stacking hay bales in the summer.

As he reached the top, a voice called from behind him, distracting him from the garden, the view, and the scarecrow.

"What are you doing out there?" demanded an older man, most likely the property's owner.

Daniels turned, stuffing his pistol into his pants, ready to display his police shield when the scarecrow came to life, taking up a scythe found in the barn before ambling toward the distracted detective.

Frantically pointing behind Daniels, the farmer realized his real scarecrow was nowhere to be seen, and whoever crept behind the detective meant bodily harm.

"Look out!" the farmer cried too late.

Daniels whirled around in time to grasp the scythe's handle enough to prevent the blade from cutting through him, but it still reached his innards. The detective's pistol popped loose, landing amongst the leafy blanket atop the rock wall.

Though not life-threatening, the injury was serious. Daniels slowly backed away, clutching his wound as he hunched over, trying to contain the bleeding.

He saw what looked like a small chunk of pinkish cotton candy bulging from his side, stained with blood, knowing it was part of a vital organ he would not attempt to put back. Instinct told him to keep pressure on it, preventing it from rolling out further.

Without his gun, Daniels seemed to pose no threat to the killer, who slowly stalked him, noticing the farmer had darted into his house to call for help.

Daniels fell to one knee, luring the killer close enough to strike him in the groin. The blow was potent, but Daniels felt the wound tear further, making his breathing more labored as blood trickled through the gash.

While the killer doubled over, the detective clutched the mask, ripping it from the killer's face. It was just as he had suspected, but it was also too late.

He felt blood reach his mouth from within, and a sudden cold chill shot through his body. Without help, he could not last much longer, and any more attempts to slow the killer would drain his body of what life it still had.

Daniels backed away on one knee as the killer stood, picking up the scythe from the leaf pile. He hoisted the weapon high above his head, ready to swing it like an axe when another disturbance came from near the barn.

"Don't!" Clouse's voice echoed from the old building.

Not looking in that direction for fear he would be identified by the fireman, the killer finished the job, swinging the scythe with enough force to decapitate the detective and destroy Clouse's only hope to end his ordeal.

"No!" Clouse screamed, holding the word out several seconds before charging the rock mound as the killer darted off the other end, running to freedom.

Before Clouse could reach the rock mound, the entire scene faded to white and the world around him began spinning. A pain to the back of his head overtook him as he felt his consciousness wane, or perhaps return.

Chapter 20

Larry Kendle flipped through several files at his desk concerning the recent string of murders at the hotel.

He began to understand his partner's theory about how Clouse would have trouble committing all the murders, but still could not fully buy into it. He suspected Paul Clouse was guilty as sin because he was the only one who stood to gain anything of value.

It also seemed odd the man would be associating with a hotel tour guide, whom he easily could have known for some time before murdering his wife. It appeared quite plausible the man could murder Angela Clouse, inherit all that they shared, and start a new life with someone whose company he preferred.

Though he gave Daniels a hard time, Kendle respected the younger detective's intuition and knack for overlooking the obvious to dig deeper into a case.

Kendle once had the ambition and tenacity to search harder, but after so many cases ending with the obvious suspect in guilt, and the jury going against Kendle's better judgment in those that didn't, the detective simply gave up and went with the flow, letting justice take care of itself.

Kendle spent most of his time gathering what evidence he could against Clouse while Daniels, in his opinion, wasted energy trying to clear the man. Unfortunately for the detective, he found little except circumstantial evidence to go on. He could never place Clouse directly at any scene, and there were no witnesses who could truly prove or disprove his presence.

Kendle did not consider Rusty Cranor credible because he could easily be covering for Clouse in the murder of Scott Beaman.

He wondered why Clouse would involve himself in more murders than Angela's, except to throw authorities off track. He stood to gain nothing in regards to the hotel by killing off construction workers unless he sought to redirect suspicions elsewhere.

The detective had managed to obtain DNA samples for David Landamere through the hospital, and took both the samples, and the bloodstained swab, to a friend at Indiana University for comparison. Earlier that morning his friend had called back with the results.

He and his students had made a positive comparison from the two samples, verifying it was indeed David Landamere's blood found within his own car. Everything seemed to point toward foul play against Landamere, but Kendle wondered if he could possibly be helping or covering up for Clouse.

His loyalty to Clouse remained in question, and needed to be investigated further.

Kendle laid the files down as his phone rang.

"Kendle," he answered.

"Hello, detective," the voice said. "This is Andy Lewis with the coroner's office."

"Oh, hello," Kendle replied, recognizing the name, knowing the man as a forensic pathologist. "Have you got something for me?"

"I was combing the belongings of your latest victim in the West Baden case and found some interesting fibers in the clothing, as well as the body cavity. We've already bagged and tagged everything, but Gary said I should call you first so you could take a look before we ship everything off to the lab, in case you wanted comparisons done."

Gary Singleton, the coroner of seven years in Monroe County, cooperated fully with all police agencies during investigations. Kendle regarded him highly compared to other men who held the position previously because he went out of his way to assist the detective.

"Great," Kendle said, happy the coroner would keep him in mind on such an important case. "I'll be down in a little bit."

***

Half an hour later, the detective descended the stairs to the basement of Bloomington Hospital where the morgue was tucked safely away in a corner.

Nodding to a passing orderly, Kendle took a familiar corner where he found partial darkness in the hallway ahead as the fluorescent light above flickered, nearing its end. The detective knew its ballast was bad because janitors constantly replaced them in the detective division office.

A vibration stopped Kendle in his tracks as his pager buzzed at his side. He plucked it from its case, noting the number from his own office. It was probably Daniels wanting to swap information on their case, but there was no distress code after the entered phone number, so Kendle decided it could wait.

He looked ahead, noticing how dark the corner where the autopsy room's entrance appeared. Usually it was dim, but this was to the point that he could barely find his way to the door. He found it, however, and its numerous hazardous warning signs in bold red print atop a white background, proclaiming the room was indeed for autopsies and unauthorized people were not allowed.

Knowing he was authorized, Kendle gave two quick knocks to the door, then opened it slowly, finding the lights inside were also off. The scene felt wrong because the door was never unlocked without someone there. Yet, it was, and no one seemed to be around.

"What the hell?" he couldn't help but ask aloud as he stepped inside the room, finding an orange glow from inside the main autopsy room further ahead.

Leaving the lights alone for the moment, Kendle slowly stepped ahead, wondering what in the world was going on. He heard the door shut behind him as he walked toward the next room, hearing only his footsteps in the darkness.

He suddenly felt vulnerable standing in the center of a darkened morgue.

Reaching the next room, Kendle's eyes widened as he took in the view of a plastic skeleton, its head covered by a lit jack-o-lantern. Instantly he placed the scenario closely with what he and Daniels envisioned Angela Clouse's murder scene looked like. His body stiffened as a chill of realization ran through him.

He flipped on the lights for a better look at the room as a cold piece of steel slid between his legs without touching the seams of his pants.

As the lights flickered to life, the steel blade of the scythe launched into Kendle's crotch before the detective even knew anyone was behind him. In one swift motion, the killer used both hands to hoist the weapon upward, then ripped it back, letting its sharpened blade act like a sword on its unwitting victim.

Kendle did not know the extent of his injuries as he grabbed what little remained of his groin area. After an initial cry of pain, he groaned intensely, hunching over before dropping to his knees. He fell to the ground in a fetal position, continually groaning from the pain, lying beside a concoction of his own urine and blood, created by his wounds.

He could not have known that his penis was severed beyond repair, or that the remains of his manhood lay beside him in a puddle of organic juice and layers of soft muscle tissue with two lumps of internal flesh that defined, in part, who he was.

Kendle only knew pain, and lots of it.

Groaning intensely, Kendle attempted to reach the gun at his side without looking up to his adversary, who was measuring him with calculating eyes through a dark mask.

Dressed in his black garb, the killer allowed the detective to reach the gun, already knowing what move each of them would make next. As Kendle pulled the gun slowly from its holster, still moaning, the killer waited until it was partly raised before letting the scythe fly again.

It had to look deliberate, the killer thought. It had to look intense and hateful, as though an emotionally invoked crime. There were no rules in crimes of passion.

Only bloodshed, and no conscious means to the act.

This time the weapon lodged itself partway in Kendle's hand, severing every vein in its path, causing a yelp from the detective, followed by an agonized scream as the killer pried the weapon loose. Kendle could not decide whether to clutch his useless hand or his groin, but either way he was at the killer's mercy.

Kendle rolled to his knees in an attempt to stand, and face his adversary if nothing else. Supporting himself with one hand, the detective drew himself to a crawling position, using his good hand to support himself.

Tired of waiting, and afraid someone might have heard Kendle's outbursts, the killer eyed his victim, drew the weapon back in a wood-chopping position, and let the bladed end launch forward.

It made a swoosh sound before piercing the back of its victim, splicing his heart, and landing on the floor beneath him, cracking the linoleum tile below. Blood dripped like a leaky faucet to fill in the crevices.

Acting as the fourth appendage of support, the scythe kept Kendle's body in its knelt position while the killer searched for appropriate means of disposal, opening various cabinets throughout both rooms.

After looking at jar after jar of organs and samples, cutting tools, and paperwork, the killer found exactly what he needed, swiping it from a top shelf.

Walking over to the body, the killer tilted his head for a better examination of his work, stared a few seconds, then blew out the jack-o-lantern's candle, prepared to clean up his mess.

Chapter 21

A brisk wind slapped Clouse in the face as he awoke among overgrown grass, feeling no pain from the brushy straw rubbing against him, because the rest of his body felt like a ball two off-road trucks had used in a game of soccer.

His ribs and face in particular had bruises and swelling. His kidneys felt inflamed as though someone had used them to practice kneading dough. He fought an incredible urge to wet his pants, and barely had the willpower or the physical ability to prevent carrying out such an act.

Clouse knew he had been in and out of consciousness several times, but could not remember details. What exactly was real or conjured up by his mind during his unconscious spells eluded him. Struggling to look around him, he rolled to his stomach, forcing his aching neck to stretch upward, seeing familiar grounds around him.

He was nearly to the top of one of the hills on his own property, and seemed to recall crawling and dragging his way up it during one of his numerous conscious spells. He looked around, taking note of the late afternoon sun, realizing how much of the day had passed.

To his left he saw an open field where several cows grazed, his house was to his right, and in the center stood the barn. In front of the barn, he saw something strung from a rope, swinging slightly in the breeze.

It reminded him of his childhood days, seeing butchered cows hanging from a hoisted hook in front of the open barn doors with nothing but an empty, reddish inside and the open rib cage serving as an entrance point to the hollowed guts.

But this was no cow.

"Benny?"

Dangling in the wind like a porch chime, his favorite dog, a three-year-old Doberman, was gutted just like the cows Clouse remembered as a child, only with his intestines hanging like a knotted rope to the ground. Anger coursed through his body as he reached a hand upward, clawing the cold earth to pull himself to level ground.

Just as he rolled himself onto his yard, still wracked with pain, Clouse heard a car pull up his gravel driveway. At first, he wondered if the killer had returned to finish the job, or if he was supposed to already be dead. Panic froze him as his eyes scanned the driveway to find a county police car drawing to a stop.

Clouse wondered whether Kaiser was friend or foe once he realized who was driving the car. Propped on one elbow, Clouse maintained his position, cautiously watching the deputy's movements as he stepped from the car.

With nothing except a T-shirt and jeans on, Clouse's body was frozen. The socks on his feet were not enough to keep them warm, but he didn't have time to wonder where his boots were. Like a partly domesticated animal he remained perfectly still, observing what one of his best friends did, once outside the car.

Kaiser had parked near the barn, and appeared to instantly notice the gutted dog hanging at the front door. The officer, still in uniform, made a strange face at the sight, as though wondering what sort of strange thoughts might be going through Clouse's mind.

Clouse wondered if it could be an act, if Kaiser was the one who had attacked him and returned to finish the job under the guise of concern. It would be an easy excuse to use after the strange actions numerous people had witnessed Clouse carrying out around the hotel recently.

Hearing the smack of metal against an obstruction, Clouse and Kaiser respectively turned to look toward the house's front door. The storm door was swinging in the breeze, and Clouse had to wonder if the front door might be open, or worse, the killer might still be inside.

"Ken!" Clouse called too weakly for his friend to hear him.

His body was half-frozen from hours in the elements without proper clothing, and his voice was hoarse from being outside so long.

Shivering, Clouse pulled himself further across the yard toward the house and Kaiser, who was crossing the yard to reach the front door. Kaiser reached for his service weapon, obviously alarmed by the open front door.

"Ken!" Clouse shouted again as the front door closed behind the deputy, forbidding the words to enter behind him.

Forcing his aching body to stand, Clouse lumbered toward the house, fighting the pain of his kidneys and stomach. He looked toward the barn, certain he saw something behind his mutilated dog. Clouse had caught only a glimpse of the object, but it looked tall and pure black in color. He wondered if his fear was provoking his imagination, because the object did not appear in his second glance when Clouse reached the front door.

Taking no chances, Clouse pounded on his own front door, turning the knob with little result from his stiff hand. His fingers lacked flexibility enough to perform such a simple task as grasping a knob, but they could still help him make enough noise to bring Kaiser to him.

Clouse's full weight pressed against the door when it opened, sending him barreling into his friend, knocking them both to the ground.

"Goddamn it, Paul!" Kaiser shouted more from surprise than anger.

He immediately noticed the lack of movement from the firefighter and touched Clouse's cold skin, apparently building a mental image of what had transpired. Forced to dial 911 because his dispatch center in Orange County used a different frequency than the one used in Monroe County, Kaiser identified himself and requested police and paramedics. He quickly returned his attention to Clouse, openly concerned about his childhood friend.

"Hang in there, Paul. Help is on the way."

"Thanks, Ken," Clouse muttered.

"Did he do this to you? Was it the killer?"

Clouse simply nodded the affirmative.

"Damn," Kaiser said before dashing to the living room for a blanket, noticing the mess throughout the house. He quickly collected his thoughts and returned to throw the blanket around his shivering friend.

Pulling a business card from his wallet, Kaiser used his friend's cordless phone to call Larry Kendle's number in the investigations division, discovering both Kendle and Daniels were unavailable. He spoke to a Detective Peterson, their supervisor, and requested one of them, if possible, be sent to Clouse's address immediately to investigate an assault and burglary.

"Hang in there, Paul," he told Clouse after hanging up. "We'll find out who did this to you."

***

When Clouse next awoke, he was surrounded by several familiar people as he lay in a soft hospital bed. The blinds were drawn, but Clouse could tell it was probably late evening. His body still felt horrible, but at least it was warm.

He could feel all of his fingers and toes again, but it would be some time before his body recovered from whatever physical abuse it had sustained.

"You're lucky to still have all your body parts," a doctor said, standing closest to him.

Clouse's parents and Zach stood at the foot of the bed while Ken Kaiser stood behind them, still in uniform, holding his hat. Everyone wore an expression of concern, yet they seemed relieved to see him awake.

"We managed to warm your body slowly enough that we saved all of your limbs," the doctor explained. "Too much longer in that weather and we would have been lucky to save you at all."

"Thanks," Clouse said.

"Would you like some time to rest?" the doctor asked.

"Kelli and Roger are waiting outside," his mother jutted in before he could reply.

Clouse drew a smile, though it pained him.

"I'd like to talk to Ken a minute if I could, Mom," he replied. "Then I want to see everyone."

Ushering everyone else out the door before him, the doctor left Kaiser alone with Clouse, as his patient wished. Clouse barely mustered enough energy to speak, but he needed to know something before he could rest easily again.

"Did you see who it was?" Kaiser asked.

"No. He got me from behind."

"I called for Bloomington PD to comb your house for evidence, but they aren't sure what to look for until they speak with you. I told them it could wait until morning."

Clouse coughed involuntarily a moment.

"Ken, I was in and out of consciousness several times this afternoon and I'm not exactly sure what was real, and what might have been a dream."

"That's okay, Paul. What are you getting at?"

"I saw Mark Daniels get beheaded by the killer at my neighbor's farm."

Kaiser chuckled a second.

"Well, lucky for you he was the one who showed up at your house to seal it off until tomorrow."

Clouse rolled his eyes back in relief.

"So you saw him? He's definitely alive?"

"Yes and yes, but we can't seem to find his partner. Daniels said Kendle is probably pissed off, thinking you came up with another way to clear your name, so he won't return pages or anything."

"The consummate professional," Clouse said with a weak chuckle.

"I'll go ahead and get your folks," Kaiser said, probably ready to get home to his own family. "You're lucky I got worried about you after this morning. At least you haven't lost it like I thought you might have."

Clouse grinned.

"You been wearing that uniform all day, Ken?"

"Yeah," the county officer said, pulling lightly on the brown uniform blouse as he looked down at it.

"Smells like it."

Kaiser smirked, giving Clouse the middle finger before turning to the door.

"Ken?" Clouse called before the officer could leave.

"Yeah?"

"Thanks."

"Anytime, pal," Kaiser said before heading into the hallway.

Chapter 22

"You must be fatter than you look," Clouse commented from the passenger seat of Roger Summers' pickup truck as his brother-in-law drove him home the next morning.

He tugged at the sweatshirt Summers had let him borrow until he could get into his own house.

"I buy the shit large in case it shrinks, brother."

"Uh-huh," Clouse said, unconvinced.

Summers was not permitted past the police guard at Clouse's residence until Mark Daniels had a forensic team comb the grounds with Clouse's help, so he had let Clouse borrow some of his own clothing for the ride home from the hospital.

"You sure you're up to this?" Summers asked, turning onto the road that led directly to Clouse's house.

"I want it over with, Rodge," Clouse said, taking short breaths. His rib cage hurt whenever he took a deep breath, but luckily, no bones were broken.

"You don't know where all those injuries came from?"

"I have a good idea," Clouse answered. "I just wasn't awake to see it coming."

Summers grunted skeptically to himself, carefully watching for oncoming traffic around a bend in the deteriorating county road.

"Looks like I go back to work next week," he said.

"Chief call you?" Clouse asked.

"I went in yesterday to talk to him."

"Funny I haven't been invited back yet," Clouse commented, unable to hide the bitter bite of his words.

"Well, the chief thinks-"

"I know what he thinks, Rodge, and he doesn't want to touch me with a ten-foot pole until this whole thing gets cleared up."

"You've got to admit this is some weird-ass stuff happening to you, brother. Time off ain't gonna hurt you," Summers suggested as he pulled into the drive, straight from the road.

"I just want a normal life again. God, what I wouldn't do to set things right."

Several unmarked cars sat beside the driveway as the truck pulled in. Clouse recognized one of the vehicles as the one Daniels drove. He felt a rush of relief when he spied the detective near the barn, but a sense of dread as the dangling body of his favorite dog retained its place, hooked through the jaw, and probably stiff as a steak pulled from the freezer.

As much as he loved the land, Clouse fully realized he needed to sell the house, because everything reminded him of death. There was nowhere left to go where he couldn't think about Angie, his dog, or the bizarre dreams and visions he'd been having around the farm. It was all one big nightmare now.

To make matters worse, his other dog, Spot, had yet to appear on the property, leading Clouse to believe something unspeakable happened to the Dalmatian.

"You okay from here?" Summers asked, stopping near the police cars.

"I'm fine, Rodge. I'll call if I need anything."

Summers nodded as Clouse stepped from the truck. Daniels noticed the fireman's arrival and briskly walked to greet him.

"Heard you had a time of it yesterday," he commented.

"Well, I thought you were dead, so I guess we're both pretty fortunate."

Daniels gave him a puzzled look so Clouse explained the disturbing dream in detail.

"I don't suppose you really know who the killer is?" Clouse asked once he finished.

"No, but I have made some progress. I've got something to show you in a little bit, but first, let's get started on your place and figure out what the killer might have been searching for."

Clouse needed to see the inside of the house again, because he could not recall any memories after his initial blow to the head.

"How do I know this isn't all a dream?" Clouse pondered aloud.

Assured no one was looking, Daniels rapped the fireman on the bicep with the back of his hand.

"Ouch!" Clouse said, not expecting the detective to stray from his usual straight-laced behavior.

"Convinced?" Daniels asked, not breaking stride as they reached the front door. The detective opened it, motioning to Clouse to go first.

"I guess the banged up ribs and kidneys should have been convincing enough," Clouse commented as he reached the inside ruins of his house.

It looked much as he had expected with drawers overturned, papers scattered everywhere, and a tone of thoroughness that fit the theme of hatred the killer seemed to hold for Clouse.

"Where's your partner?" Clouse asked, beginning to look around the disarray.

"I'm kind of worried," Daniels admitted. "No one's seen him since yesterday, and he left no word about where he was going."

"Oh?"

"Left around lunch time and never came back. It's not like him."

Clouse pictured both as by-the-book investigators, and Kendle seemed even more regimented than his partner, so it was strange that he simply dropped from sight. Then again, Dave Landamere pulled it off, he thought.

"Were you doing anything out of the ordinary the last few days that might have worried the killer?" Daniels asked, kneeling to shuffle through some loose papers on the floor.

"Not that I recall," Clouse said, though thinking about his internet search and all the websites where he left information.

Perhaps he was closer than he thought, but telling Daniels meant giving away information he was not supposed to have in the first place. They would question where he found companies querying the hotel's sale and how he gained access to his wife's account.

"You sure?" Daniels asked, still shuffling through papers and scattered items on the floor.

Clouse only stared at him without realizing it.

"What?" the detective inquired, taking notice.

"I was so sure you were dead," Clouse said slowly, only half of his mind located where he stood. "I saw it so clearly."

Daniels stood, slightly agitated and uneasy about Clouse mentioning his death.

"Look, whatever you saw didn't happen," Daniels said sternly. "I'm still here. I don't know what that bastard did to you, but I need your head clear if you're going to help me catch him. I can't go slapping you into reality every time you have these weird lapses."

"Understood," Clouse said, drawing a grin until the pain of his ribs returned.

"He fucked you up, didn't he?" Daniels asked, leading the way into the family room.

"Yeah," Clouse agreed, following. "So what were you going to show me?"

"I've got some new photos you should look at. They're at the office, but they might shed some light on who our killer is if the right person sees them."

"And I'm that person?"

Daniels shrugged. "I'm not sure. Guess it depends on if you know the killer or not."

Both looked around the room a moment, seeing nothing but the mess left by the killer. Through a window, Clouse could see the police crews outside, looking for evidence on the cold, hardened ground. He appreciated Daniels putting so much effort forth in collecting evidence, but doubt clouded his mind about ever finding the killer.

"Do you remember anything?" Daniels asked. "Something I should have the boys check for in here?"

Now that his dream was proven false, Clouse actually could not remember a thing after being knocked unconscious. If he did remember something, he couldn't trust its validity until he checked.

"I can't remember anything concrete," Clouse said. "The guy was wearing a black cloak, like I saw at the hotel. There wasn't a face or anything."

"Nothing after he struck you?"

"No," Clouse answered, closing his eyes, trying to focus on the event. "I know I was in and out of consciousness a few times, but nothing stuck with me."

"What was the point of entry?"

Clouse gave a confused look.

"You know, where he came in?"

"I know," Clouse replied, somewhat insulted. "I'm just not sure he broke in is all."

"Why is that?"

Clouse walked to the back door, turning the knob.

It opened.

"That's why. And I don't remember if I locked it or not."

"And if you didn't, who has keys?"

"Pretty much anyone in my family, and in Angie's for that matter. A lot of them came over to visit, babysit Zach, or keep an eye on the house when we were on vacation."

"So everyone's a suspect."

"You don't really think-"

"Don't close your mind to it, Mr. Clouse," Daniels said evenly. "I think it's someone pretty close to you."

"Then maybe I don't want to know," the firefighter answered. "But who around me would have any interest in the hotel?"

***

Hours later the police finished with his house, so Clouse took time to travel across town to a stretch of road he was familiar with, but not accustomed to visiting. Now he would be a regular until the pain inside his heart and mind went away.

He pulled up to a large archway beside a small church, looking across the rows of granite and concrete with reverence, only now understanding how important the upkeep of cemeteries was to the living. They always seemed so vacant and lonely, and dozens of questions about death and the afterlife always flooded his mind when he visited them.

His truck pulled beside a familiar sports car and he saw Kelli placing flowers on her sister's grave, oblivious to the fact he was there. A fleeting thought told Clouse to leave before she saw him, but he stayed. It would be a wasted trip if he turned back, and Kelli would be crushed if she saw him leave without speaking to her, but he was quite uncomfortable around her at the moment.

"Oh, you scared me!" Kelli stammered when she turned to see Clouse after hearing his approach.

"Sorry," he said, placing a freshly bought set of roses beside Angie's tombstone.

"Are you feeling better?" Kelli asked as she stood.

"A little," he said. "I feel weak and cold, but I'm going to settle in by a big fire tonight."

"Need any company?"

"No, but thanks. I'll probably start cleaning up the house tomorrow."

Kelli looked down at the gravesite and the recently placed sod.

"If you need anything, just call."

"I will."

Hesitating momentarily, Kelli gave him a strange, almost accusatory stare.

"Rumor is you have a new love interest, Paul," she said, catching him entirely by surprise.

"Whoa," he said immediately. "Jane is not a love interest. We've only talked a few times at the hotel. Where the hell did this come from?"

"Around," Kelli answered aloofly.

Clouse was growing frustrated with Kelli and her great interest in his life lately.

"So what exactly is your stand with me lately?"

"What do you mean?" she asked defensively.

"All of this attention since Angie's death. You spend the night, and you keep finding excuses to come over. What gives?"

Kelli's expression changed to one of grave concern, as though Clouse misread her intentions completely.

"I've been taking care of you like a brother, Paul," she answered. "As for spending the night and allegedly getting close to you, I'm going to have to let you in on something."

Clouse stared, waiting for the answer.

"I don't bat that way, Paul."

His look grew slightly confused, matching his thoughts.

"Ever wonder why I didn't marry, Paul?" she said, raising her voice intensely. "I'm gay. And I'm not after your body and your life like you think, and I'm not trying to replace my sister. My interest in you is strictly family concern, and as of right now, I don't have much interest in you at all," she said before storming toward her car, squealing the tires as she left.

"Ah, shit," Clouse said before looking to the grave, then to Kelli's car in the distance. Dust flew behind it as the setting sun in the distance nearly blinded him.

Another long night awaited him.

Chapter 23

Everyone wondered about Larry Kendle's whereabouts, his partner included. Daniels flipped through the set of pictures, now smudged with his fingerprints, looking for any further clues he might have overlooked.

He wished his partner would show up to compare clues with him, but Kendle was missing from work a second consecutive morning. Nothing of consequence had turned up at Paul Clouse's residence the day before, and Daniels would forever wonder if his partner's presence and expertise might have made a difference.

Dressed in one of his many white shirts with blue pinstripes, the detective tossed the photos atop his desk, opting for the file he put together concerning every murder since Angela Clouse's that seemed tied to her husband.

Cindy often teased that he was obsessive compulsive about shirts with blue. If he wasn't wearing a blue dress shirt, it had blue trim. It seemed to go with everything, and being the practical person he was, Daniels liked simplicity.

And he liked blue.

Kendle's wife had phoned him several times already, and it wasn't even lunchtime.

Daniels spoke to her half a dozen times, then had other detectives take messages, none of which he planned to return. It was difficult enough to plan his next move without distractions. He felt certain his partner was fine, probably intently investigating some part of Paul Clouse's deep, dark past. Daniels shook his head at the notions his partner came up with concerning Clouse.

"Kendle's wife called again," another detective said in passing.

"Tell her I was dead?" Daniels asked sarcastically, sick of being considered Kendle's keeper all the sudden.

"No, but it can be arranged," the detective answered with a slight roll of the eyes, indicating he was sick of playing secretary.

Daniels felt no desire to be mean, but he was at work. Being the consummate professional, he wanted to focus on what he was paid to do, and that meant investigating several murders when he wasn't busy preparing for court, or dealing with dozens of lesser crimes. On the rare occasions he found some spare time, Daniels cracked open a cold case file.

He wanted to begin more intense interviews with Clouse's immediate family, especially those on Angela's side. More than ever, he believed Clouse was innocent, but could not piece together a connection between the hotel murders and that of Angie Clouse. He could see that someone was probably framing Clouse, but to what extent, and what purpose?

Daniels picked up the last photo of the bunch, staring at what details he could make out from the blur. Already he had reprinted it, and sent a copy, and the negative, to the state police lab in Indianapolis hoping they could reduce the blurriness or sharpen the image with their computers.

Feeling Clouse was hiding something from him, Daniels did not share the photo with the firefighter. He wanted to see what the lab could pull from the image anyhow, before sharing it with anyone.

He knew the fireman was intelligent, and probably carrying out his own investigation with knowledge beyond what Daniels could legally obtain, so he understood why Clouse would not divulge his sources, but it aggravated him that they could be closer to solving the murder if they didn't keep secrets.

He and Kendle already *had* that working relationship.

Holding the picture firmly, Daniels examined the contents again.

Most of the picture's upper half was a black blur, which Daniels knew was the cloak worn by the killer. From what he made out, after studying the picture for hours since first seeing it at the diner, he could tell the victim's leg had kicked up part of the cloak, revealing the killer's leg from the lower calve muscle up to the knee.

Though Daniels could not see the ankle or foot to determine what footwear the killer wore, he knew it could not be a cowboy boot, which Clouse nearly always wore to the hotel. This furthered his evidence Clouse could not be the killer, assuming the photo was authentic and not a hoax, or a distraction created by the killer himself.

Daniels did not believe it fit into either of those categories.

From what little he saw of the victim's body, he guessed it was Robert Bennett. A few calls confirmed the man was an amateur photographer and indeed owned a decent camera, though no one could inform the detective of its make or model. Bennett and his van hadn't been seen or heard from in a week, so there was no true way to verify the rumors.

What really set the photo apart from the others for Daniels, however, was a visible mark on the killer's right leg. The picture appeared too blurry for him to determine whether it was a bloody spot, a scar, or possibly part of a tattoo. He hoped the lab could clarify the image, making it easier to determine exactly what color and shape the smudge was.

Any identifying mark would put him that much closer to finding the killer.

It would be several days before the lab technicians had anything concrete, since they were backed up with evidence from several other rape and homicide cases. Several recent departures had left the state police lab with a shortage of technicians, increasing the turnaround time on evidence analysis.

In the meantime, Daniels wanted to begin interviewing people around the hotel, now that construction was reopening. Orange County sat two counties away from his jurisdiction, but Daniels had the okay from his supervisors to conduct interviews and probe for evidence down there in the Angie Clouse murder case. He felt the more time he spent at the hotel the less bad things were apt to happen. He knew Smith had little choice in the matter, and he knew county and state police would be keeping a close watch on the place, but he felt a personal touch would also help.

And without Kendle to override his decisions, Daniels could do most anything he wanted, as long as the chief and his sergeant saw results on a regular basis.

***

Clouse had most of his house back to normal by noon. His body ached too much to sleep in, but felt even worse when he moved. He tolerated the pain, ignoring it as best he could after taking a few pain pills.

He had already phoned the fire chief, asking to return to work the next day his shift worked. The chief agreed, but only if he took an assignment with Summers at the same station. Clouse assumed this was at his brother-in-law's request, but the chief would not say.

Now he had two days to clean his house, make arrangements for Zach's babysitting, get a tentative schedule for the hotel, and mentally prepare for everyone to treat him like an outcast at work, despite several people now proclaiming his innocence.

Maybe working with his brother-in-law would be a bonus after all.

After digging through pictures and paperwork, Clouse found several items missing, which he assumed were taken, or destroyed, by the intruder. Most importantly, one page from his list of potential hotel buyers was missing. He was unsure if it was buried beneath some other piles, or stolen, but he assumed the latter.

Now Clouse had to question what the page's contents were. Without the computer he might never find out.

He picked up the remains of the computer from the floor, clearing off the desk with one swipe of his arm before placing it there. Taking a screwdriver from the kitchen, Clouse set to work, undoing the battered shell of the computer, using tin snips where the metal was too badly damaged and dented.

From the looks of the dents, and what Daniels guessed, they were made by a baseball bat or some other blunt object.

Whoever had broken into his house did not want the computer recovered.

Clouse worked up a sweat prying apart the metallic walls of the computer, hoping they did their job enough to protect the hard drive and processor components inside. He knew they were the heart of the unit, and could easily be placed in another body and reused. He wanted to phone Tony Dierker, but feared telling anyone about whatever moves he made in solving Angie's murder.

He trusted no one at this point.

Once the cover was off, now completely beyond repair, Clouse found most of the circuit boards intact. One was broken completely in half, but the rest appeared fine, though that was only from an exterior view. Clouse knew the fragile pieces could be severed or ruptured, rendering them useless. The only thing that ultimately mattered was the hard drive, and it appeared intact, at least from the outside.

When he went into town later, he planned to take them to a computer store for some advice, but wished he could confide in Daniels, having them sent to a secure lab for analysis without fear of the killer stalking him, or trying to destroy what evidence he had gathered.

Clouse left the computer casing on the desk to answer his cordless phone in the other room.

"Hello?" he answered.

"Paul, it's Rusty," the foreman said from the other end.

"How is everything?"

"Terrible," Rusty answered with a sigh.

It sounded as though something was bothering him.

"Any word from Missy yet?"

"No. That's what has me worried."

"Sorry to hear that."

Clouse decided not to probe any deeper, though he felt absolutely terrible for Rusty and helpless to assist in any searches because of his own issues. He knew if Zach ever went missing, he would be beside himself with worry. Rusty was probably sensitive about everyone asking him questions every few minutes.

"You at the hotel?"

"Yeah. I was wondering if you were working this week."

"I'm probably going back to work at the fire department," Clouse replied. "I'll let you know my schedule once it's settled. Everything the same there?"

"I suppose. The workers are scared to death, my daughter and Landamere are still missing, and Dr. Smith has been here all day warning us to stay in groups and leave no one alone, even for a second."

"He's spooked," Clouse said, knowing the feeling all too well.

"He's not the only one, you know. This whole thing is making everyone's lives miserable. I can't take much more of this."

"Hang in there, old man. I'll let you know when I get my schedule."

"Take care," Rusty said, hanging up the phone from Landamere's office, which he now used as his own.

Rusty looked outside the window at several construction workers who were surveying the hotel grounds. He knew they would do almost anything to avoid entering the building if they could help it. They were scared, but they were also protected by police that strategically surrounded the grounds. From several key areas, the county and state police performed surveillance details, but Rusty and his workers felt none the safer.

Taking up his hard hat and clipboard, the foreman left the office, shutting the newly replaced door behind him. It was time to get back to work and appease his police watchdogs.

As he confirmed the lock was set, he heard a noise down the hall, like a stone ricocheting off the trim. No one else should have been inside the hotel at that moment, since it was a day to ready the grounds for winter.

"Hello?" he called down the hall. "Anyone there?"

No answer.

Licking his lips nervously as he thought about investigating, the foreman decided better of it, choosing to join his workers outside instead.

Again, the noise came from down the hall, getting Rusty's attention. He involuntarily stepped toward the echoing noise before his senses caught up with his reflexes. Still, it was too late because the foreman had rounded the first bend.

Rusty wanted to think there was a chance his daughter was playing a prank on him. She sometimes liked to trick him during her younger days, playing hide-and-seek, or just plain hiding. It wasn't like her to run away from home, much less abandon her parents, but her boyfriend had changed her way of thinking. Missy's car never turned up, and neither Missy nor the boyfriend Rusty disliked had left any clues about their intentions. The simple childhood days were long gone between Rusty and his daughter, but he clung to the belief that she loved him enough to trust him with anything.

After taking a few steps down the hall, he knelt beside two pebbles, only inches apart, picking them up as he looked down the hall. Seeing nothing, he wondered if they might have fallen from part of the wall, or been the closest physical evidence to a figment of his imagination.

Either way, Rusty had no intention of staying to figure it out.

A moment later, he stepped out the front entrance, surprised it was such a sunny day in November, yet it was. Strangely, no warmth seemed to strike him as he zipped up his thick work jacket, looking across the landscape as he did, his nerves still tingling from the noises inside.

Rusty panned from one side to another, seeing nothing except usual activity. He saw none of the police officers, implying they were doing their job correctly, and better yet, he saw no sign of danger. He also saw nothing of Vern, the old grounds keeper. The man had been missing for several days, but that in itself was not unusual.

Drawing a deep breath, the foreman thought perhaps things would look up, and the day would pass without incident. Perhaps the police might call to tell him they had found Melissa safe and unharmed.

He could always hope.

***

Feeling somewhat dejected, Clouse continued to clean the rest of his house into the afternoon. With only papers and small debris left to pick up from the floor, he felt a sense of relief that he was nearly done.

Zach was with his parents, which left guilt weighing on his mind. As though it wasn't bad enough he was being accused of murder, Clouse worried about being a negligent father. Truth be told, he simply wanted to keep his son away from any danger.

Looking around to his doors and windows, he still felt unsafe, as though someone might barge into his house any second. Worse yet, he felt virtually defenseless in his battered state.

He wanted to rest and recuperate, but didn't feel tired enough to try sleeping. Seldom did he nap at the fire station, and if he did, it was typically when he felt sick or extremely worn out from a lack of sleep.

As he picked up the last of the computer pieces, he heard a thunderous roar in the distance. Considering his driveway spanned at least the length of a football field, he wondered what caused the noise at the foot of his property.

Drawing close to his kitchen window, Clouse looked outside, spying a motorcycle cautiously navigating his driveway. He knew instantly who the rider was, but wondered why Tim Niemeyer was paying him a visit.

Though they were very close buddies in high school, the two were lucky to see one another twice a year at best.

Ordinarily, Clouse might think his friend was paying him a visit to check on him, but he had good reason to be suspicious of everyone around him at the moment.

Stepping onto his porch, Clouse watched Niemeyer put the cycle's kickstand down before dismounting. Wearing a bandana, half-gloves, and a black leather jacket, Niemeyer looked the part of a renegade biker. He had begun growing a goatee to accompany his mustache since Clouse last saw him at Angie's calling hours.

"Hi, Tim," Clouse said neutrally, offering his hand.

Niemeyer shook it, but only to pull his friend into a long hug.

A big teddy bear. Gentle, caring, and blatantly honest was how Clouse always described Niemeyer to others. Even in high school, he was a stocky individual, but he carried his weight, a solid mix of muscle and girth, very well.

"I was worried about you," the construction owner said, his Southern drawl coming through.

Part of his upbringing meant staying with his grandfather from Tennessee. Since middle school, Niemeyer always spoke with a trace of a drawl.

"Ken told me about what happened," Niemeyer revealed. "I thought you might like to see a friendly face."

Clouse stood awkwardly a moment, contemplating what he truly wanted at the moment. Niemeyer shifted his stance uneasily, licking his bottom lip in obvious anticipation of a reply.

Realizing he looked like a terrible host, Clouse finally decided some company might take his mind off his problems awhile.

"I'm sorry, Tim," he finally apologized. "Come on in."

Leading the way, Clouse closed the door behind them. He walked to the refrigerator, taking out a beer for each of them, opening his own before downing half the can with one upward tip.

"You sure you're okay?" Niemeyer questioned aloud.

"I've been better. I'm just not sure who I can trust these days."

Niemeyer opened his beer, taking a sip before setting it beside him.

"I hate drinking before I ride the bike," he admitted.

"Sorry. It's just instinctive to have a beer around you and Kenny."

Niemeyer smirked.

"I can remember some times when you two were pretty tanked."

"I don't remember all of them," Clouse noted, forcing a grin.

He looked out the window at the new Harley-Davidson sitting in his driveway.

"I take it the construction business is paying pretty well?"

"I do okay," Niemeyer said with an indifferent shrug. "I think I've got Kenny wanting a bike now."

Clouse shook his head slowly. He never had any desire to own a motorcycle. His boat provided adventure enough for him.

"He's always had a stiff one for motorcycles. It's just a matter of time before the wife lets him buy one."

Looking to the beer can beside him, then to Clouse, Niemeyer had a perplexed look.

"Where's your boy?"

"With my folks," Clouse answered. "He's a lot better off with them for the night."

He paused a moment, realizing once again it was strange for his friend to visit him at home.

"Tim, what really brings you out here?" he asked.

"Well, I'm worried about you and Ken."

"Ken?" Clouse asked, leaning against his kitchen counter, folding his arms. "I didn't realize my recent turmoil was causing him grief."

Niemeyer shrugged.

"He's afraid he might lose his second job, and he's more afraid you might be, well, you know."

"Guilty?" Clouse questioned, raising an eyebrow.

"It just looks bad for you," Niemeyer admitted. "I know you'd never do anything crazy. And again, I'm sorry for your loss."

Clouse decided to lighten up toward Niemeyer.

"I appreciate it, Tim. As much as I hate to see the hotel close its doors, it might be safer for Ken, and everyone there, if it did."

"Any ideas who's causing all the trouble?"

"If I was a betting man, I'd say it's the same person who killed Angie. I can't trust anyone around me anymore, Tim. Whoever it is knows my habits and where I'm going to be. It has to be someone who knows me well, like a family member, or a good friend."

Niemeyer swallowed hard, getting the point. He picked up the beer, taking a long drink, before setting it on the counter.

"What's the matter?" Clouse asked, taking notice of his friend's sudden change of heart toward drinking.

"Nothing," Niemeyer said too quickly for his friend's taste.

"It's about Ken, isn't it?"

Stalling for time, Niemeyer took another drink from the beer can.

"He says he's doing it to protect you. To make sure nothing else bad happens there."

"What are you talking about?" Clouse asked sternly.

Looking almost helpless, Niemeyer's face had an expression of grief, as though he was about to open the gates of hell to shove Kaiser through them.

"He's been working a lot of overtime at the hotel."

"Ken works there regularly," Clouse noted aloud. "What's the big deal?"

"I'm not talking about his regular shifts. He's been picking up extra shifts, sometimes working two a day when he's off-duty from the county."

Clouse was puzzled. He felt certain he would know if his best friend was working so many shifts.

"A lot of the shifts are in the overnight hours," Niemeyer stated. "He thinks that's when people are sneaking around the grounds, disrupting things."

"Like graves," Clouse muttered quietly.

"Ken's just not been himself lately. Maybe you can talk to him."

"Yeah," Clouse said almost absently. "Sure."

Based on recent observations, Clouse wondered if Kaiser was hell bent on finding the truth to prove his innocence or send him to prison.

Niemeyer seemed to look uncomfortable, almost as though his sole purpose for visiting was to bear bad news.

"I didn't mean to come out here and dump all this on you," he admitted. "God knows you have enough on your mind without me bugging you."

"It's okay," Clouse assured him. "I didn't mean to be harsh, earlier. Like I said, I'm just wary of everyone right now, but now isn't the time I need to be pushing my friends away. You guys have helped me through a lot of tough times."

Niemeyer nodded in understanding, probably realizing the times Clouse and Kaiser helped him through some ordeals.

"I was worried about you staying alone," Niemeyer confessed. "In this house."

Niemeyer looked to the floor, as though expecting to see bloodstains where Angie was brutally murdered and hacked to pieces. His blue eyes quickly returned to Clouse.

"I'm here for Zach's sake," Clouse said, deciding to address his friend's concern. "He needs something stable in his life until I can put this place on the market."

"Yeah, but he was here that night, wasn't he?" Niemeyer asked hesitantly.

Clouse nodded.

"It's not easy for me either, Tim."

"I know, Paul," Niemeyer said with a regretful expression. "Sorry I brought it up."

Deciding that company wasn't such a bad thing, Clouse wanted to make his friend feel a bit more welcome. Alienating Niemeyer wasn't something he planned on doing, but he was apparently doing just that.

"Let's go have a look at that bike," he said, putting an arm on the burly man's left shoulder as they walked toward the door.

Chapter 24

Ian Briscoe hated calls in the middle of the night.

When he took a deputy coroner position, he knew murders were more common during night hours, but how so many bodies came to be found in the early morning hours baffled him.

Lately, things were slow within Monroe County, but the Angela Clouse murder was still fresh on a number of minds.

Briscoe was now on a call for a rape and murder retrieved in the south end of the city. He had already examined the scene, finding little useful information in the open at the scene. Now he walked with the paramedics who were wheeling the body into the morgue where a thorough examination and autopsy were soon to follow.

He already knew she was killed by a bladed object, but he needed to determine what drugs, if any, were in her system. For that, blood needed to be drawn by the pathologists and sent to the state lab. The victim was a known prostitute who occasionally used drugs, and homicide detectives would throw a fit if the coroner's office failed to dig up any details.

Though dead tired, Briscoe didn't mind doing his job. He was thorough, and enjoyed helping the police however he could. It beat his usual nine to five job at the hospital in the surgical ward where he often specialized in boredom during his internship. He hated having no hands-on experience, but worked diligently at learning everything possible about the medical profession. His diligence was why the coroner picked him as an assistant soon after they shared lunch with a common friend one day.

Barry Andrews, one of the hospital's resident doctors, who also ran his own clinic, took a liking to Briscoe's work ethic, promising the young intern a spot under his wing, and his practice once he was ready. He felt it would be great experience, and a test of sorts, to place him in the morgue examining corpses, while learning about human anatomy up close. The lunch went well and the rest was history.

"Just pop the bag up on the table," he told the paramedics once he had unlocked the morgue.

If he needed it moved to the freezer in the near future, Briscoe planned to recruit the assistance of a security guard, or a male nurse.

Dressed in a wrinkled pair of slacks with a polo shirt, Briscoe intended to be seen at this time of morning only by people in the same condition as him. His long hair was uncombed, looking like a perm gone wrong. It felt disheveled and oily because he had found no time to shower, and probably wouldn't before going to work.

The combination of his hair and the old pair of glasses he found to put on at such an early hour created the look of a terrorist from any number of early Eighties flicks.

Briscoe didn't care, as long as he found ten minutes to sharpen up his look and put his contact lenses in, before his shift began.

He watched as the paramedics placed the black body bag on the exam table, leaving it zipped to ensure no contents spilled out. As they left, Briscoe scanned the room, finding a new odor to his dislike. He saw the room on a weekly basis, but it seemed to change a bit every time he walked in.

Briscoe took notice of the skeleton sitting in the corner atop a stool, apparently set there around Halloween by one of his colleagues. He also saw the remains of a jack-o-lantern in the trash, which explained the smell. Traces of the pumpkin's innards remained atop the skeleton's head, causing him to wonder exactly what went on around the past holiday, since he was out of town.

Other than the smell and the disarray of the plastic skeleton, Briscoe saw no difference in the two rooms forming the morgue. He looked to the two examination tables, side by side, and wondered where to begin. By now, he had observed dozens of autopsies, often conducting the initial bodily examination by himself. The exam required him to examine the clothing and body surface, recording everything he found. With that complete, he bagged and labeled all of the clothing and swabbed any fluids or small objects found atop the victim's skin.

After conducting his examination, Briscoe needed to store the body in one of the coolers if the pathologists hadn't reported to the morgue by then. Briscoe wasn't certified to conduct an autopsy, though he learned quite a bit about anatomy from observation.

Starting with the body bag, Briscoe unzipped it, carefully sliding the body, half at a time, to the adjacent clean table. Assured everything was out of the bag, he took it to the industrial-grade sink where he thoroughly washed it. When he gave items back to police or EMS he preferred they be perfectly clean, so his rapport with their organizations remained equally so.

Once it was clean, he turned it upside down, shook it out, and began looking for a place to store it once it dried.

He looked through several cabinets before recalling where the coroner usually stored objects needing to be returned. There was often a small collection when the coroner waited for the organizations to retrieve their equipment. His relationship with them was not as strong as Briscoe's.

Opening the cabinet, he noticed a space in the right-hand corner. It took a moment before he remembered what was usually there, and ironically, it was the permanent body bag the coroner's office owned.

"Where in the hell is it?" Briscoe wondered aloud, beginning to search drawers, knowing he would be blamed if it came up missing.

Frantically, he searched drawer after drawer, finding nothing except chemicals, preserved body parts, household cleaners, and other things he didn't care to see. His search, however, allowed him to find more evidence of horseplay inside the lab.

He found candle wax atop the steel counter and strange smudges along the floor as though whoever last used the lab did not properly clean it. He knew the lab came clean easily enough, with just a few minutes of work and the correct cleaners.

"Damn it, guys," Briscoe berated his absent colleagues, certain they knew better.

He figured the bag was around somewhere, or someone had broken the golden rule about removing equipment from the lab when it wasn't needed. He checked the paperwork, discovering no one had signed for it.

No one dared break the rules, or the coroner would be on them like flies on shit.

To Briscoe's knowledge, there were no bodies currently in the freezer, but he decided to check all eight doors anyhow.

Inside, each compartment held a sliding steel tray, though none were actually divided by any sort of wall. Briscoe opened the first compartment, peering inside, but only seeing to part of the third compartment due to lack of light. He moved down, opening the last top and bottom doors, finding his body bag inside, apparently filled with something.

"Oh, you guys," he said with a shake of his head, figuring someone had thrown a secret Halloween party in the lab he'd missed, then hidden their mess to delay cleanup for a few days.

Tugging the black bag from the bottom compartment, Briscoe found it heavy until it landed on the floor with a thud.

"Heavy," Briscoe muttered, taking hold of the zipper, prepared to find blackmail material to use against his colleagues for a later date.

He unzipped the bag fully with one swipe, caught the familiar whiff of death, and gasped audibly.

"Holy shit," he said, stumbling back until he hit the exam table, falling to a seated position on the floor, stunned from what he had viewed. It would take several minutes to recover before he could phone for investigators.

At least there was no need to call the coroner's office.

***

No one inside the room could truly keep their cool when the bag was fully unzipped and the body of Larry Kendle was curled up inside, assuming a fetal position. Kendle's suit was wrinkled and soiled with various internal liquids.

Inside one sport coat pocket, and sealed in a plastic bag with an unmarked label were the remains of his testicles, their surrounding tissue, and part of his penis picked up from the floor. They appeared to be marinating in a mix of juices, also cleaned from the tile surface. Every police officer in the room cringed with discomfort when the evidence was viewed.

On more than one level.

"I can't believe this," Mark Daniels said, slumped in a corner stool, staring at the group around his partner. It was all he could do to sit up as nervous shivers ran through his body.

He never envisioned this happening to his partner, or even himself, but now his mortality was laid out before him in a black bag. One simple look at his dead partner broke down Daniels' usually calm, cool demeanor in front of several people he worked closely with on a regular basis.

A blank stare crossed his face, showing the stages of shock, and an inability to cope, that came with someone close to him dying. He didn't care how he appeared, and neither did anyone else in the room, considering they were experiencing the same feeling.

Dressed only in blue jeans, an Indiana University sweatshirt, and tennis shoes, Daniels almost didn't get past the police guard because a new officer failed to recognize the detective. His hair looked somewhat like a bird's nest with strands sticking up in little patches as he sat, hands nervously in his lap, watching as other investigators performed his usual job, examining his partner with the scrutinizing detail he often used at murder scenes.

"You don't have to be here, Mark," one of the other detectives said. "We've got it under control."

Seeing that Daniels would not budge from the corner, his eyes simply staring intently at the body bag, the detective walked away. Daniels folded his arms, not moving his eyes from Larry Kendle's corpse or the helplessness it seemed to exhibit.

He desperately wanted to step outside for a smoke, but he knew once he left the room they would not let him return, and he was determined not to leave his partner, even in death.

Even if they weren't as close as partners should be.

Maybe it's my fault, Daniels caught himself thinking. If we hadn't been so determined to work on this separately, I would have been there for him. But then the killer would have no reason to target him, he deduced. An array of thoughts and emotions ran through his head, but nothing seemed worth dwelling on at the moment.

Within the examination room, Daniels recognized the coroner, two detectives from his division, a forensic photographer, one investigator from the state police, and Ian Briscoe. He could tell that Briscoe desperately wanted out of the room, but the state police investigator was asking him a slew of questions.

Daniels expected some to be asked of him later.

Without him realizing it, his right hand assumed several positions every minute. It would scratch his chin, rub his cheek, set in his lap, and take any number of other positions without him realizing how much nervous fidgeting it did.

Much of the examination and questioning around him was carried out with relative silence. There weren't threats of getting the bastard who did this crime, or other wasteful comments. For the most part everyone went about conducting their jobs professionally, collecting evidence and asking the questions of everyone who might be of help.

Daniels was not thinking like a police officer at the moment. For now, he could only be a supportive partner in the most final sense. His thoughts wandered to investigation tactics occasionally, but they quickly bounced back to Kendle's wife and three children, and how his murder might have been prevented.

For him, the most unfortunate thing was the lack of clues left at this crime scene, and how much that would prolong him in finding the killer when the time came. The one thing Daniels did realize was the nature of the crime and how hateful it appeared.

Insulting Kendle's character by placing the body, and its loose organs the way he had, the killer had set out to write the detective's demise with as much of a humiliating conclusion as possible. Such an end was meant to anger the police, particularly the man's partner.

And it did.

After another fifteen minutes the state police investigator approached Daniels, who was simply waiting for an excuse to leave by then. He was too proud to just walk out on his own accord, subconsciously fearing others would say he left his partner when he didn't have to. Daniels had to see it through with Kendle until they laid him to rest.

"Can you go to the post and answer a few questions?" the state investigator asked Daniels with sensitivity, crouching to look him in the eye.

"Sure."

✳✳✳

After more than an hour of explaining the case to the investigator, Daniels finished, lighting a cigarette as the two walked outside the state police barracks. It was time to talk more informally.

"Could this Clouse have killed your partner?" Investigator Ben Edwards asked of his fellow police officer.

"Highly unlikely," Daniels said before taking a drag. "If he is involved, he's not the one swinging that scythe."

Edwards had grown less formal during the course of their talk. He treated Daniels well, not like a suspect or a lesser investigator. Some troopers considered their organization to be superior, despite the fact that the same academy trained every police officer in Indiana. Many of those troopers with a haughty attitude found themselves working alone, without many friends, because most of the troopers liked interacting with other cops.

Over the past hour, Edwards had loosened his tie and undone the first button of his dress shirt. He now carried his sport coat outside with him, looking more like someone leaving a bar at closing time than a man with arrest powers throughout the state. His thick, black hair remained intact, loosely combed to one side, but his face indicated he might go for a drink before breakfast if his schedule hadn't just been completely filled for the coming day.

"Any chance Clouse might be behind it?" Edwards questioned.

"The more I'm around him, the less likely it seems," Daniels explained. "It would be real hard for anyone to take a beating like he did yesterday, even if he was trying to cover up, and the way his dog was gutted and left hanging, I don't know," the detective said, shaking his head to free his mind from the gory image it harbored.

"He wouldn't really have any motive in the hotel killings, then, other than trying to remove the suspicion of murdering his wife away from himself."

"Even at that, it would be awful risky to orchestrate so many murders," Daniels explained. "And I doubt anyone would do so many hits for what little he could pay them."

"Are we talking two separate sets of murders then?"

"I don't think so," Daniels noted. "Everything we've gotten back from the lab indicates the same person swung that scythe in every murder, that it's a right-handed male around six feet in height, and that he has at least a fairly strong build. That describes Clouse, but at least a tenth of the population fits that profile."

"Our office will likely take this investigation over," Edwards noted cordially. "Or we might work out a joint effort with your chief."

"I know. I've got a few things coming back from the lab I want to look at, then you guys can have everything. I'll help you however I can."

"Thanks."

Edwards never expected the detective to relinquish control of the investigation so easily, but they both knew Daniels would keep searching for the killer on his own. He felt a sense of responsibility to Kendle, as though he had missed something in the case that might have saved his partner's life.

Daniels said a goodbye to Edwards as he walked toward his car, thinking about where to start. He knew the department brass would want him to take time off, which would leave him free enough to investigate the case as he saw fit, with the ability to check on the lab's progress through their photo analysis, and any other evidence in their possession. They would not know he was on leave, and Daniels saw no need to tell them otherwise.

Tomorrow he would begin investigating his way.

Chapter 25

Clouse reached the edge of town in his pickup, anxious to see if any of the computer's components could be salvaged. The morning paper informed him of Kendle's murder, which failed to impact him deeply, but concerned him for several reasons.

Somehow, Clouse knew the killer wanted to implicate him in the murder, because Kendle certainly did not endanger the killer's spree by exclusively investigating the firefighter. Though he did not know the details, Clouse suspected the murder was gruesome and meant to look vengeful, as though he performed it.

Also, it potentially turned Daniels, his only ally of significance, against him, or at least away from finding the truth. This was a last-ditch effort by the killer to keep the public believing Clouse was guilty of murder.

"Where are we going, Daddy?" Zach asked from the passenger seat.

"To see if our computer is fixed," Clouse answered.

After reading the bad news that morning, Clouse took the remains of the computer to a local dealer, then retrieved Zach up from his parents. He had taken time to clean the house and properly bury his dog, though it disturbed him to see Benny treated like a deer cleaned in hunting season.

That was his most loyal dog.

"How did it get broken?"

"It fell on the floor, Zach."

"Grandma said someone bad hurt you. Why would they do that?"

Clouse had to think on a four-year-old level for a moment. There were some things his son simply could not be told yet.

"Some people have something wrong with them, Zach," he explained. "They don't like anyone, and they don't know anything but how to hit people and hurt them. I think I made one of those people mad, and he decided to hurt me."

Zach sat for a moment, accepting what he understood of his father's explanation as gospel before asking another question.

"What does gildy mean?"

"Guilty?"

"Yeah."

"It means someone did something wrong, Zach."

Silence.

"Why?" Clouse asked his son.

"Grandma and Grandpa took me out to eat and someone with a newspaper said you were gildy. Did you do something wrong?"

Shit, Clouse thought. It was times like this he missed having Zach in preschool. When he returned to work for the city in a few days, Zach would return to his school, mostly for his own good. Consistent, familiar surroundings would do the boy good, he thought.

"I haven't done anything wrong, Zach, but some people think I'm the one who made Mommy go away. See, the newspaper doesn't always print what's right."

"So, they're wrong then?"

"They are," Clouse confirmed, pulling into the parking lot of the computer store.

A moment later, he and his son walked into a maze of computer tables and glass cases. Toward the back, the owner saw the cause of his most troublesome repair job in recent memory return, and waved Clouse to the back repair area.

"Welcome back," the man said with a smile that indicated he'd managed to do something right for the firefighter.

Clouse saw a complete computer setup along a long table with printer, scanner, monitor, and several other pieces of hardware he was unable to identify. On the screen were several programs and files Clouse recognized from Angie's computer. Perhaps his luck was getting better.

"Good news and bad news," the owner stated. Clouse still didn't know his name. "Most of your processor parts were damaged, so the computer is a complete loss. The hard drive was pretty dinged up, so I retrieved what information I could from the old one. I managed to salvage about half of the information and got everything downloaded into my system here."

"Do I need to buy your system?" Clouse joked.

"Not quite," the man replied with an understanding smile. "Using an external drive, I downloaded everything inside my computer onto this disk," the man said, handing Clouse a rather large and sturdy diskette. "Is there any place you can use that?"

"I know someone with one of these drives," Clouse replied, thinking of Landamere's computer at the hotel. No one else would be using it.

Clouse walked with the computer expert to the counter and paid him.

"Let me know if you need any more help with that," the man said as Clouse led Zach toward the door.

"Will do," Clouse said with a nod, happy he could set to work on finding his attacker.

***

On the other end of town, Mark Daniels stood across the counter from an old friend in the locksmith business. If anyone knew where the key he took from Dave Landamere's house came from, it would be Lee Colton.

With a stack of locksmith magazines and technical manuals on the shelves behind him, Colton examined the key with a keen eye. Daniels could tell he found it vaguely familiar, but seemed unable to place its origin.

"Safeblock," the locksmith read the name on the key aloud.

As expected, Daniels was called in by the police chief and given a week off from work with pay. Departments bent over backwards to give employees time off with pay because they knew placing stressed employees into work after a traumatic situation sometimes led to potential problems. Sometimes those problems led to lawsuits much greater than one week's pay for any given employee.

Daniels figured he had time to investigate several things on his own that he otherwise might not have, which led him to an old friend.

Colton was one of the few people the detective had known since high school who actually knew what he wanted for a career, stuck with it, and made a good living. With four kids, he apparently had sufficient free time and financial means to support them.

Daniels had never met anyone with such a calm demeanor. The man seldom displayed emotion, and did everything with a deliberate, cautious manner.

His patience was incredible, and in his line of work, it needed to be. He never hurried a project. By the same token, he never seemed to make errors. His product knowledge of locks and keys was the best Daniels had ever seen, even topping forensics experts he'd worked with from much larger departments than his own. The detective had faith his friend would provide an answer much quicker than the heavily burdened state labs.

"What do you think?" he asked Colton, who continued to scrutinize the key.

"Goddamn, it's familiar," the locksmith noted aloud. "Don't know that I've ever seen one of these in person, but it caught my eye in a catalog once," he continued, putting the key down to search for a particular booklet.

Built like a grizzly bear, Colton often intimidated people when he came to fix their lock problems, but Daniels knew the man was far more docile than he appeared.

He could even recall a time when several friends of theirs in high school found fun in taunting a hapless snapping turtle. Despite urging from his friends, Colton would have no part in toying with nature, or a creature that stood no chance against a swarm of teens. He simply objected by standing back and crossing his arms. Eventually the others followed his lead, rather than causing the animal any permanent damage.

Daniels knew Colton as a silent leader. Strong, intelligent, and occasionally witty, the quiet locksmith impressed the detective more as the years passed.

"I don't suppose you ever lose books or files, being the organized police type?" Colton asked, feverishly digging through his magazines for the correct issue.

"No, never," Daniels replied with a sarcastic tone.

At work, everything went through the commanding officer in his division, so organization was easy. At home with a child, however, proved a different story altogether.

"Aha!" the locksmith said after a few minutes, yanking an issue from the bulk stack.

"What have you got?" Daniels asked as his friend flipped through the pages.

"This," Colton said as he folded the magazine over, fronting an advertisement that stumped the detective for a moment. "There's an article about this thing in another magazine, but it'll take me a while to find it."

"Not necessary," Daniels said, staring intently at a large, metal lockbox in the ad.

Shaped much like a footlocker, the box contained several drawers and looked immensely heavy. The box seemed the height of a nightstand, but held three drawers controlled by one lock above a bottom drawer, apparently with its own lock.

The detective read the features listed on the side, and it seemed to be an impressive invention. Made of a lightweight version of the metal used in safes, the box was dent resistant and portable, if used in conjunction with a special wheeled cart.

Daniels looked at the cover of the magazine, finding it dated two years prior. He was lucky Colton knew how to keep relevant information handy.

"Did it help?" the locksmith asked.

"I think it did," Daniels replied, certain he saw no such box at Landamere's residence when he visited.

He thought about it, realizing the box was too industrial to be used in the home. It seemed more appropriate in a garage, or perhaps a hotel renovation.

***

Clouse pulled into the hotel, unsure of what to expect any longer.

He recalled when the job was fun, when he could expect to see Dave Landamere's face within the first few minutes of his arrival, put in several hours of work, and return home to his loving family.

Now he might discover pools of blood, rotted corpses, or his office door kicked in. He no longer enjoyed driving to West Baden. Still, he was drawn to it after spending so many hours laboring there.

Today he needed to be there.

"I thought you weren't coming in," Rusty said as Clouse stepped from his truck, greeted by several unfriendly stares from the construction workers.

Though Rusty now swore his innocence, the workers either refused to buy into it, or just considered Clouse the source of their troubles.

Zach walked around the side of the truck, taking his father's hand.

"I've got to use Dave's computer to read this disk," Clouse replied, holding the diskette firmly. "Any news on Missy yet?"

"Nothing," Rusty said dejectedly. "It's like they both just disappeared. No one's seen her car either."

"I'm sorry to hear that," Clouse said, thinking perhaps no news was good news with two teenagers in love. He wondered if they might have simply run off to escape persecution from their parents.

"I've got to check on some of the workers," Rusty noted. "I'll see you inside in a bit."

Clouse nodded, taking Zach toward the hotel entrance. He had little time to waste, considering the impending events building around him. The next evening was the reading of Angie's will, which would bring no surprises to him, considering they had written it out together less than a year before.

State police wanted an interview with him about Larry Kendle's murder. He hoped to be exhumed from guilt, since the murder apparently took place while he was laid up in the hospital. Still, he was the one Kendle had investigated closely for the better part of two weeks, so Clouse again found himself a prime suspect.

Unlocking the new door to Dave Landamere's office, Clouse let himself and Zach inside, closing the door behind them.

With a clean, new look, the office appeared better than before with the exception of Landamere's papers and books stacked randomly in a corner beside the bookshelf. Toward the back of the office stood an antique hutch as high as the ceiling. To the best of his knowledge, the hutch, and the computer hidden inside it, were never touched or damaged during the break-in, or any other time.

While Zach occupied himself with the globe on Landamere's bookshelf, Clouse walked to the hutch, finding it locked.

"Damn," he said under his breath, knowing it was never actually locked before.

He could hear the computer running inside, which was unusual, since it seldom remained powered up when not in use. Clouse recalled it being off the last time he left the room and actually checked, which was after Landamere disappeared.

Unfortunately, Clouse did not own a key, which explained his unhappiness with the situation, but more importantly, someone did have a key who should not have, or Landamere had come to check on his computer.

Either way, Clouse needed at the computer.

Luckily the hutch had no back to it, and after a few minutes of mustering all of his strength to move it, Clouse had it far enough out that he could reach inside with a small screwdriver and remove the clip from the lock, letting it fall freely out the front.

Assured nothing was permanently damaged, Clouse opened up the front of the hutch, pulling a chair up to the computer as he turned on the monitor. He could hear the hard drive running heavily. Once the monitor's screen warmed up, Clouse saw the computer downloading information from the internet, but a gray message box blocked his view of whatever crucial information might help him identify who had been using the computer.

Clouse knew Landamere could easily be avoiding people, perhaps vacationing or spending some time at a resort. Maybe he was just checking on the hotel from time to time, assuring himself things were running smoothly.

Just maybe, but that did not sound like the Dave Landamere Clouse knew.

If the project manager were abducted, his captor would have access to his keys and everything Landamere knew. With everything he'd seen so far, Clouse felt obligated to fear the worst because he trusted Landamere too much to expect anything less than the man's best effort on the hotel.

To Clouse, the hotel was probably the greatest feat in his life. He understood Landamere had done all sorts of restoration projects, and even a few major saves like the West Baden Springs Hotel, but he could not picture the man as the type to suffer burnout just as a project neared its end, regardless of what the man's wife, or Rusty, thought.

Carefully working around the message box, Clouse looked for indications of what the computer was being used for. He copied down the information from the website address box and whatever other tidbits he could find in various internet boxes that might prove useful.

He debated momentarily whether or not to break the link to the download, and ultimately decided to, knowing he could print the information from his disk and investigate any downloaded information in the appropriate download file.

"Daddy, this is neat," Zach commented.

He had been talking to himself the entire time, but not directly to his father.

"What have you got, kid?" Clouse asked without removing his eyes from the screen.

Momentarily, Zach presented him with a framed certificate made of shiny silver paper, containing black type across it. It was presented to Landamere almost a decade prior in Chicago for his contributions on the restoration of an old school, which became a senior citizen activity building.

Did Dave live in Chicago? Clouse wondered. He recalled Landamere mentioning several areas in which he lived prior to Southern Indiana, including one project overseas that lasted almost a year. In such a profession, one could not expect to remain local, due to funding drawbacks and an eventual lack of work.

Landamere was a journeyman manager by design, so it ultimately made sense he had spent time one state over.

"It's cool," Zach said, staring at the shiny paper, probably wanting to color on it.

"Yeah, it is," Clouse replied, holding a different opinion as to why.

He had always assumed Landamere grew up locally, and figured he always returned home when his projects were done. As he thought about it, there seemed little Clouse truly knew about his boss's past. He knew about Landamere's training and his work, but little about his personal life or work history.

Within a few minutes, Clouse printed the useful information from his disk and began searching the computer hard drive for anything downloaded, but little was legible. He began looking under recently visited websites when the room's door opened.

"Jane," he said as both he and Zach were startled by her presence.

"I was just getting ready to leave for the day when I saw your truck outside," she said. "I hope I'm not interrupting you."

"Just about done," Clouse said, turning to write down the last few sites on the screen.

"Are you getting any closer to the truth?"

"Slowly," he said, taking up the remainder of the papers he would have to sort through later. It would take some time to compare what he had to the new information.

They talked a few minutes about the impending reading of the will, the hotel's progress, and what might happen if Smith decided to sell. Both knew the results would not be good. Smith would be hasty to sell, and probably to the wrong party.

"My brother is an excellent attorney if you need one," Jane suggested.

"I'll keep him in mind," Clouse replied, "but I should be okay."

"Let me know when you're up for breakfast sometime, okay?" Jane said as she headed for the door, knowing he wanted to finish with the computer.

"I will," he said with a sincere grin. "I go back to the fire station in a few days. It's not far from your clinic, you know."

"Good," she said. "Maybe we'll get a chance to talk."

As she left, Clouse turned to click into several more windows, searching for more crucial information about whatever was being downloaded. If Landamere wasn't accessing his computer, someone else was. Clouse realized he was ruining the chance to catch whoever it was. He also knew the police would never monitor the room upon his request, and talking to Daniels was too risky considering the information he had already kept from the detective.

Clouse's options were limited.

If the police perimeter was as tight as they claimed, and someone gained access to the computer, it meant they were someone who actually belonged at the hotel, or had knowledge of how to evade surveillance. Of course, that person would have to know there was a police presence in the first place, and no one outside of the work force was supposed to know about that.

Clouse finished writing down every shred of information he felt might possibly help him discover the user of the computer, and filed the paper in a manila folder. Pocketing the external disk, he grabbed his jacket from the chair and stood, turning around too quickly to avoid bumping chests with Ken Kaiser.

"Hey, Paul," the county officer said. "Doing some computing?"

"Mine's broken," Clouse explained, noticing Zach had been too preoccupied with a jigsaw puzzle on Landamere's shelves to see the door open.

"Did it crash?"

"You could say that," the firefighter said, uneasy with the fact Kaiser stood so close to him, using an almost accusatory tone of voice.

Kaiser finally backed up a few steps, allowing Clouse to gather his things and call over to Zach that it was time to go.

"Feeling any better?" Kaiser asked, following him to the door.

"Somewhat. I've been too busy trying to find the killer to rest much."

"Getting anywhere?" the county officer asked as both stood at the doorway.

"I guess I'm realizing you can't trust anyone."

"No, you really can't," Kaiser said as though it was a golden rule he abided by.

"This job, this hotel was everything I ever dreamed of working on, but now it's just a place where, I don't know, it's-"

"A place where people check in, but they don't check out," Kaiser said in a tone that seemed half joking. "Kind of like that Eagles song, eh?"

Feeling a chill run through his spine, Clouse realized it was past time to leave.

"I've gotta go, Ken," he said to his friend, who suddenly seemed more ominous after uttering the words Clouse had heard over the phone just days prior.

"Take care of yourself, Paul," Kaiser called as Clouse led Zach toward the closest exit. He simply gave a quick glance back.

He only wanted to get home where it was safe to peruse the new information. He was too close to simply give up.

Chapter 26

Settled beside a warm fire, Clouse reviewed the files lying beside him meticulously for any details that might disclose who was using the computer in Landamere's office.

He planned to visit a local copy shop in the morning that rented out computers by the hour for printing or online access. Several key sites continued to plague him as he read through the dozens of laser printouts.

Zach was tucked in for the evening, leaving Clouse feeling less guilty after finally spending a day with his son. He felt safer keeping Zach close to him, especially now that the killer had made the ordeal personal by attacking him. Kids made easy targets for people with hostile intent, and Clouse had no idea how far the game might escalate. At the same time, he felt terrible for denying his son of childhood pleasures and not being an especially personable dad lately.

Most of the information would have to be accessed through the internet when Clouse found a computer to use the next day. Once he plugged in some of the websites, he figured everything would be revealed to him, and he would be that much closer to knowing who was using Landamere's computer.

Hearing a knock at the door, Clouse shoved the papers into a folder, setting them beneath his couch cushion.

"Rodge," he said, finding his brother-in-law on the other side of the door.

"Hey, Paul. Is this a good time to talk?"

"Sure. Come on in."

After the two sat in the family room, Summers talked a few minutes about how he looked forward to working with Clouse again. It was less than two days away, but Clouse didn't feel as optimistic about working around his brother-in-law.

"I came to make sure you were ready to get back to work," Summers confessed from the recliner he chose to sit in. "I didn't want them rushing you back or anything."

"I'll be fine, but I'm not so sure it's a great idea to stick us together, Rodge."

"Sure it is. We haven't been stationed together in almost two years."

"It's not that. It'll just look strange is all."

"Come on, brother. I'm not going to let anyone say one bad word about you. Anyone gets out of line, I'll take care of 'em."

Clouse groaned to himself. He wanted to return to work on his own terms, not saddled with an overly protective brother-in-law who would lay his fellow firemen out if they spoke out against either one of them.

"It seems you managed to piss Kelli off," Summers said almost offhandedly.

"That I did."

"You didn't know?"

Clouse's face flushed red.

"No one ever told me. She's been acting kind of strange lately so I confronted her about it."

"She'll be okay. She just couldn't believe you thought that of her."

"Oops," Clouse said apologetically.

"It's okay. When I got out of the service and started looking for a job, I noticed Kelli didn't act the same as she had when we were kids. It took her almost another five years to fess up to me."

Clouse stood to throw another log on the fire.

"Is Kelli going to forgive me?" he asked, returning to his seat.

"Oh, she'll be fine. I think she was just a little shocked at what you thought." Summers shrugged. "We're all pretty tough in our family. I met people in the service who weren't as tough as that girl."

"What branch were you in again?" Clouse inquired, barely recalling it ever mentioned.

"Navy. I was an engineer. I was lucky enough to stay close to home. They always had some projects going in the Midwest."

"You never got shipped overseas?" Clouse asked.

"A couple of times, but never for more than a few months. I had it pretty easy working for the government."

"But you came back home."

"I had some pretty good offers," Summers admitted. "But I'd already tested for the fire department during my leave time, and decided to wait it out until my name reached the top of the list."

For the next few minutes the two talked about how good it would be to get back to work and move on from Angie's death.

"I'd better get home," Summers said, standing up.

"I'll see you at work in a few days, if not tomorrow," Clouse said, walking him to the door.

"Don't sweat it, brother," Summers said reassuringly. "You'll be fine."

I hope, Clouse thought as he watched his brother-in-law climb into his truck to depart.

After closing out the chilly weather, Clouse locked the door and returned to the paperwork at the couch. With a hi-lighter he went through, marking repeated e-mail addresses and websites. Several addresses continued to appear as places where e-mail was forwarded.

"Orangeco," he read one of the e-mail addresses aloud. From the looks of it, the address belonged to someone who worked in Orange County where Kaiser patrolled.

Of course, Orange County was also where the hotel stood.

He planned on checking the e-mails for a user profile or origin in the morning. Though well before midnight, Clouse decided to turn in early for an early start to the next day.

Chapter 27

Before heading to the copy store the next morning, Clouse decided to take Zach to Deacon Park, at an old church outside of town.

To entice enrollment in their church, the Church of Christ built an extensive playground and daycare facility to draw families to their location. If nothing else, it seemed to provide more funding for the congregation. Others, like Clouse, simply took advantage of the open playground without joining the church.

Recently remodeled, the church was growing. Clouse remembered Angie wanting to join because it was relatively close, without the hassle and detachment of a city church. Clouse never took action on the situation, preferring to keep his Sunday mornings to himself around the house with his family.

As Clouse and his son walked to the park from his truck, he spied someone familiar with a swinging girl behind her.

"Jane?" he asked, drawing closer.

"Paul. What brings you here?"

"I've got Zach all day, so I thought we'd hit the park before I do my busywork."

"Katie and I had the same idea," Jane said, looking to her daughter, happily swinging behind her.

While the children began playing together, Jane walked with Clouse over to a nearby picnic table where parents often monitored their children. They took a seat at the table, each waiting for the other to begin a conversation.

Clouse zipped his jacket halfway, stuffing his hands into its pockets as a gusty wind passed through the park. Leaves shook in the trees as their fallen counterparts danced across the barren, hard ground.

"Are you any closer to what you need?" Jane asked.

"Getting there. Sorry if I seemed distracted yesterday."

Jane looked over to the children, who seemed to be enjoying the merry-go-round as they pushed it to a high rate of speed and jumped on, pretending to cling for dear life. Smiling and laughing, they didn't have a care in the world, unlike their parents.

"They're a handful, aren't they?" Clouse wondered aloud.

"Katie certainly is. She's always wanting to do something, or be somewhere."

"Do you have custody?" Clouse asked, breathing on his hands for warmth.

Jane gave a look of disdain in no particular direction as she thought out her answer.

"Her father sees her once every three or four weeks, and that's *his* choice."

"I see."

"It doesn't help that she asks about Daddy all the time and wonders why he isn't there for her soccer games and karate lessons," Jane said with a disgusted tone. "He's too busy with his projects in other states."

Clouse began to ask what her ex-husband did for a living, but thought better of it. He felt his face begin to flush from the cold wind's assault, and decided to limit how long Zach stayed outside.

"This weather is horrible," he commented.

"It's supposed to be a rough winter. I'll bet that makes for some long days at the fire station."

"It can," Clouse replied. "It's bad enough to begin with, then the water and cold mix for some dangerous conditions. It doesn't take long for the cold to eat through our gear when it gets wet."

Both sat silently a moment, watching the children play on the slides, then the swings.

"Is that detective getting any closer to finding out who killed your wife?" Jane finally asked.

"Haven't really spoken to him lately. Unless he finds forensic evidence, he won't have any more than I do."

"Maybe something will turn up," Jane said, bobbing her hands atop her lap optimistically.

"Maybe," Clouse said doubtfully. "So, it looks like you won't be doing any tours for a while."

"I heard they're shutting the renovation down again so that foreman can search for his daughter. I got the call last night."

"And with me returning to the fire department, they really don't have anyone to manage the construction until Dave Landamere comes back."

Jane gave a quizzical stare.

"Don't you mean *if* he comes back?"

"I think he will," Clouse said. "He's done this sort of thing before."

"But never at such a bad time, has he?"

Clouse shrugged. "I suppose we'll find out soon enough where he's been."

He felt terrible leaving the construction by the wayside, but he had a career to return to, and the hotel was not a safe place for anyone to be, even the police who performed the surveillance. Now, to his understanding, there would be no one working security at the hotel, leaving it entirely unprotected.

Though Clouse hated the idea of an abandoned hotel, he considered human life more important than steel beams and concrete.

After the kids had played a little longer, Clouse decided to begin his errands. He called to Zach, said a goodbye to Jane, and headed for his truck. A full day of activities awaited him.

***

Despite his week of leave from the police department, Daniels felt obligated to check for mail and messages in his office.

Wearing everyday attire, he walked into the investigations office, seeing a few of his colleagues sitting at their desks. The few who weren't at lunch shifted their eyes in other directions when they saw the young detective walk into the office.

Daniels felt uncertain of exactly what they were thinking. Blame could be placed on him for not being closer to Kendle, or they might have simply felt bad because it could just as easily have been their partner killed on an assignment gone wrong.

Ignoring the cold shoulders, Daniels walked to his desk, which appeared just as orderly as he had left it, except for several sheets of paper and a large envelope in the center. The first two messages were inconsequential, but the third, from Dave Landamere's wife, appeared more important. He read, then reread it, thinking he was mistaken.

"David called and spoke to me briefly yesterday," he read it aloud. "Thought you would like to know."

Surrounded by quotation marks, the officer had obviously taken the message verbatim over the phone. Daniels decided to speak with Joan Landamere immediately, but not over the phone. He wanted another opportunity to scope out the grounds and house as much as possible.

As he walked out of the office, Daniels again tried making eye contact with the other detectives, but there was none returned. He slipped his index finger beneath the envelope's flap, prying it open as he reached the stairwell leading down.

He sauntered down the stairs amongst dim lighting, pulling an enlarged and computer-enhanced photo from the envelope, which had arrived from the state police lab that morning.

"That was fast," he commented to himself, pushing the door open to the main floor. Once in better light, he observed the photograph better.

He was amazed how well the lab technicians had removed the blurriness and regained clarity, simply by using a computer. He knew the state bought programs that were ahead of the common market, and Daniels felt this software was one of their better purchases.

Standing beneath a recessed light, the detective peered at the area in question on the killer's calve muscle. Though still rather dark in color, Daniels made it out to be a tattoo of some sort. Much of it seemed to be cut off, but the visible edge appeared to be part of a shamrock, or perhaps the edge of a cross. The photo did little for him except verify that it was a tattoo, which enabled him to eliminate suspects rather easily if he could verify they had no artwork on the bottom of their right leg.

Feeling a bit more confident with new evidence, Daniels walked outside, strolling across the street to his Honda. Opening the door, he felt a strong wind hit him in passing, as though to indicate winter was drawing near. He slid into the driver's seat, starting the car, fully unaware someone in a parked car across the street monitored his every move.

***

Clouse considered himself the most unlucky person on the planet. As he stared into a nearly blank screen, he felt completely dejected.

Neither e-mail address turned up a profile or any sort of true origin. The first three common websites Clouse had found seemed to lead to nothing, because they were mere subdirectories for a larger site. His search ended there in all three instances.

While Zach contented himself with building blocks in a children's area outside the computer bay, Clouse cursed himself for not being able to find anything concrete with so much information already provided. Worse yet, he may have blown the only chance he had to discover who was using Landamere's computer, especially now that the hotel was closed off to everyone.

He searched through the printouts again looking for any key words he might have missed the night before. Knowing how tired he'd felt it might have been easy to overlook something as simple as one key word or an address.

"Tincher Incorporated," he said, finding it five sheets later amongst a pile of paragraphs and gibberish. It would have been easy to ignore the night before in a state of fatigue.

Clouse quickly typed in the website, finding the same images and text as before with an Illinois base-of-operations. He jotted down every shred of information the site provided him, opening every possible window, noting every project the company had claimed to work on, and the organizations it claimed to have worked beside.

The more he wrote, the more Clouse convinced himself the company was a sham, explaining why he had never heard of it before one week ago.

He recalled giving his information to the company the day before he was severely beaten, and his house ransacked. Clouse touched his ribs for proof of the pummeling he had taken. They were nowhere near fully healed, but he could breathe normally again. He knew exactly who to call, and where to check on the legitimacy of Tincher Incorporated. It would take just a few phone calls to some people who owed him some favors.

Armed with a new source of information, Clouse closed down the computer, took up his folder of papers, and walked to the front counter to pay for his computer time. As he called Zach over from the play area, his cellular phone rang.

"Hello," he answered.

"Paul, it's Mark Daniels."

"Hi, detective. I wasn't expecting to hear from you this soon."

"Just have a question for you."

"Shoot," Clouse said, handing his credit card to the unhappily employed teenager on the other side of the counter.

"What kind of tattoos do you have?" Daniels asked pointedly, leaving the question open-ended on purpose.

"I don't have any," Clouse answered quickly enough to assure the detective he wasn't lying. "Any reason?"

Daniels hesitated knowing what he was about to do went against his training and standard police policy. Then again, Clouse was probably the most useful source of information he had, since he could reasonably be eliminated as a suspect.

"If I send you a copy of a photo I received back from the lab today, do you think you might be able to identify some body art for me?"

"I can try. You think I'm into some weird stuff. Don't you?"

"No, it's not that," Daniels explained. "I have a feeling you may know the person responsible for the murders and just don't realize it. There's what I believe to be a tattoo in this photo. Where can I send it?"

Clouse took his credit card back from the counter person and signed the receipt, taking Zach's hand as he left the copy center.

"Well, my computer's broken," he said, exiting through the sliding glass doors. "You could fax it to the fire department and I could pick it up later."

Daniels considered that a bit too public, but no one would probably understand what significance a photo of a leg meant anyhow, especially if he didn't accompany it with any vital information.

"Okay," Daniels agreed. "Give me the number."

Clouse stopped to pull his fire department work calendar from his wallet, then gave the detective the fax number.

"I'll take a look and see if it's familiar," Clouse said. "You think the killer's in this photo?"

"Almost certain, so get back to me if you know something. I don't want you holding out on me," Daniels warned, airing his suspicions.

"I won't," Clouse promised.

Daniels clicked on his phone's talk button and looked to the Landamere house before stepping out of his car. He surveyed the grounds his entire walk up the driveway, seeing little that might lead him to the whereabouts of the lockbox he sought. He could see no storage shed, and their garage was used to house their vehicles, not as a workshop.

Before he even reached the front door, it opened, revealing Joan Landamere.

"Hello, detective. I didn't expect such personal attention."

"I wanted to see you in person because I have a few questions for you," Daniels replied, following her inside.

She led him to the living room where they both took a seat on opposite sofas.

"I suppose you want to know what David said when he called?"

"That would be a good start."

"He said very little really, except that he was out of town and expected to be back within the week. He said there was a project he'd worked on previously that needed some attending to."

"I find it difficult to believe it was too inconvenient for him to let any of his staff know about this," Daniels said somewhat scornfully. "Did he act artificial perhaps, as though someone was forcing him to say those things to you?"

"Not particularly, but David is a rather dry speaker to begin with. If you're implying that someone would abduct him, I seriously doubt it. There's no sensible reason to hold him hostage."

"Not to you and I perhaps, Mrs. Landamere, but one never knows these days."

Walking to the kitchen, Joan pulled a kettle from the stove, pouring a cup of coffee for herself, and another for her guest, almost as though she had expected him. Daniels thought back to several mystery movies he'd watched where guests were poisoned by their hosts, often through coffee or tea. He quickly shook off the notion.

"Did you have another question for me?" she asked, handing him a cup of coffee. "Sugar or cream?" she questioned before he could reply.

"Cream," he answered. "Does your husband have a storage box around here with a bottom drawer that locks separately? It would be a fairly large unit."

"Is it metallic, with about five drawers total?"

"It is."

"He keeps it at the hotel, full of things he doesn't want me to see, I suspect," she replied as though it might contain dirty magazines or things husbands knew their wives hated them having. Daniels could relate from his own marital experience.

Hesitantly, the detective took a mild sip of the coffee before setting it on the coffee table in front of him. He berated himself for being so suspicious, deciding it was time to go.

"I hate to rush off, but I've got a lot of ground to cover, Mrs. Landamere."

"You do what you have to," she said, much like he remembered his grandmother doing. Daniels remembered hating it when she put guilt trips on him as a teenager, as though he was always abandoning her. "You're welcome to drop by anytime."

"There's nothing else you can think of?" he asked as they strolled toward the front door.

"No. Nothing stands out."

"If you think of anything, even if it seems insignificant, please call me."

"I certainly will," she replied, opening the door for him.

"Thanks for your time, Ma'am."

Daniels felt compelled to check on the box at the hotel, despite the nagging feeling he was walking into a dangerous situation. Like Clouse, he felt there was no one left to trust. There were still too many suspects and not enough clues for him to narrow it down.

He hoped to reach the hotel before dark and discover some new evidence in the box, assuming he could find it.

Chapter 28

Daniels was surprised to see the mammoth arched gate of the West Baden Springs Hotel lit by a great number of bulbs when he pulled up to the front entrance. He expected everything about the hotel to be shut down and dead in appearance.

Including the lights.

From the road, he spied no one along the grounds. Several Victorian lamp posts along the brick path leading to the hotel were lit, and the arch entrance held no physical impeding gate, so he would have easy access walking to the hotel. If what he heard was accurate, there would be no security posted anywhere at the hotel, but the doors would be locked.

After befriending locksmith Lee Colton for so long, Daniels knew several tricks about entering buildings without detection, and leaving no signs he was there. Colton let him borrow several lock picks for just such an occasion with the knowledge of how to use them efficiently.

Daniels felt terrible about breaking and entering, but he had no intent to steal anything. He simply wanted to observe, and search for the final pieces of the most difficult puzzle he'd ever been asked to solve. Without department backing, he was desperate to find his partner's killer and put an end to the senseless slaughter before more people wound up dead or missing.

No matter the cost.

At the end of the brick walkway, Daniels stared up at the looming building. Two of the four giant towers appeared to stare back. Behind them, the dome glistened with its curved glass fixtures and new red roof tiles.

An eerie orange glow emitted from the horizon, indicating within minutes it would be fully dark outside. Daniels wanted access to the hotel before nightfall so he could find the lights inside and make his way around the hotel with ease. He already knew how to reach the basement and storage areas, but turning on sources of light would prove more difficult if he could not see.

Daniels reached the first set of steps leading to the main entrance, catching a whiff of some foul odor in the wind. The smell, to him, was that of death. He had worked enough homicides, and grown up around enough hunters, to know what a dead carcass smelled like, human or otherwise. He turned to look at the cemetery in the direction the smell emanated from, saw nothing out of the ordinary, and turned to the double glass entrance doors atop the steps.

A form of deadbolt lock blocked his way to the inside but he was prepared with some helpful advice from Colton.

Within two minutes, he had successfully used lock picks to steadily get inside the lock and move the metal bar toward him, unlocking the door. He replaced the picks to their case, then stuffed them in his jacket pocket before letting himself inside.

"God only knows how I'll lock that up," he muttered to himself.

Stepping inside the main lobby, Daniels looked up to the balcony, then past an arch, into the atrium where half the rooms overlooked the floor where so many social gatherings had occurred over the years. He was amazed at how many of the lights were turned on, able to lead him down any path he chose.

He chose to visit the basement and look for Landamere's chest.

Daniels began to understand why the construction workers referred to the basement as the dungeon. Beneath the hotel, it was much colder, and damp, suited only for the tools they stored there.

He made his way along the dusty concrete floor, looking cautiously around him, seeing nowhere a person might leap out and ambush him. Daniels felt very uneasy entering the hotel, and especially this target area alone, under such conditions.

Various cabinets and doors stood along the walls of the basement, making Daniels' search even more complicated. He suspected the trunk would be found by itself, not surrounded by power tools or building materials. He looked along the floor for the most traveled paths, noticing one particular door had little or no foot traffic leading to it, while the others appeared significantly used.

Daniels prepared to take the pick set from his jacket, but found the door unlocked. He opened it, patting along the wall for a light switch. He found it a few seconds later, illuminating a nearly empty storage room. The only object inside the room was a large metallic storage box, exactly like the one he was searching for.

"Too damn easy," he muttered to himself, his suspicions of foul play reaching a new height.

Digging for the key in his pants pocket, the detective walked toward the box, looking around the room to assure he was alone. Wasting no time, Daniels knelt down at the foot of the box, becoming oblivious to everything around him except the lock, and the key he was about to place inside it.

Before he truly conceived turning the key, the drawer popped open and Daniels realized his mind was not where it should be. He was so consumed with solving the case, his actions superceded his thought process.

Pulling the drawer open, Daniels let the faint light of the room reveal a blanket covering several unidentified objects. Slowly, he pulled the blanket toward him, revealing a soft pad taking up most of the bottom drawer's space with an indentation across it.

An indentation shaped much like that of a scythe blade.

"Shit," Daniels thought aloud. "If it's not here, where is it?"

For a moment, he remained knelt beside the box, looking to the door, listening intently. Nothing broke the silence, so he started toward the door to leave the room, almost convinced Dave Landamere was behind the killings to obtain the hotel for himself.

It made perfect sense for him to draw Clouse into his confidence, learn everything about the man, and use him as a pawn in a scheme to obtain the property potentially worth a small fortune.

Now he had some circumstantial evidence to back his theory.

Daniels carefully headed toward the door, anxious to exit the hotel grounds and return in the morning for some further explanation. He wanted to contact the state police, who were now handling the investigation, to inform them of a tip he had just received about a certain box in the basement of the hotel.

Leaving obscure clues with the new investigative team was about the only power he had left.

Locking the hotel doors and returning the box's key to Landamere's study were issues he could deal with easily enough. Creating the perfect story, complete with evidence to hand the state police investigators would prove more difficult.

Daniels had obtained some of his evidence illegally in the eyes of the court, which would let the killers escape courtroom justice if the case came to that.

As he ascended the stairway toward the main floor, the detective heard several shrill screams and a plea for mercy from a distance. It was a woman's voice, and he thought it sounded much like Joan Landamere, after just visiting with her.

Hurried, but cautious, Daniels reached the top of the staircase, stopping to listen for more screams.

They came once again to his right.

He reached behind him, pulling his duty weapon from the back of his pants where it was tucked. Keeping close to the inside wall of the circular hallway, Daniels continued to listen for any noises, occasionally hearing a few to pull him forward. It seemed as though he was heading toward one of the small corridors leading into the main atrium.

He rounded another bend, finding the corridor, then spotting Joan Landamere lying at the threshold of the atrium entrance. Running to her, he felt for a pulse, discovering she was only unconscious, a few drops of blood under her nose.

Glancing to his right, he found a green staircase leading up to the second floor, and an elevator adjacent to it.

A ring from the elevator sent Daniels dashing to its side, waiting for the door to open. His back almost pressed against the staircase, the detective pointed the firearm at the elevator door, waiting for it to open. He hoped it would reveal the perpetrator of every crime he had dealt with the past two weeks, and the entire ordeal could end.

It didn't.

Just as the doors opened, Daniel raised his weapon, unable to see someone descend the stairs behind him, just far enough to have a solid swing at him with a wooden-handled weapon. Too focused on the contents of the elevator, Daniels would have needed to look completely behind him to see the figure standing there, ready to swing down at him.

"Damn it," the detective uttered before the short-handled garden shovel connected with the back of his head, creating a loud clank before he fell face down on the floor.

Chapter 29

Clouse considered his first morning back to work fairly mundane, much as he expected.

After the usual inspection and cleaning of his assigned truck, he was free to do as he pleased. It was an administrative holiday, so there would be no training, and most of the firefighters were sitting around, watching television upstairs in the living quarters, or working out downstairs, but Clouse found solitude in the game room beside the pool table with his list of things to check, and his cellular phone.

What he was discovering through several phone calls was that Tincher Incorporated had existed less than a year under that name.

It seemed the construction company was indeed real, but there were no known current projects, and none of the listed contact people could be located. Clouse wondered how the company expected to prove legitimacy to buy the hotel if no one could be contacted.

He smelled trouble.

Clouse had asked one of his contacts to cross-reference the jobs Tincher claimed to have done, to jobs done by other companies and individuals. The results would be one solid way of proving legitimacy, or the fraudulent nature of the company.

Due to the Chicago connection, and Landamere's previous experience, Clouse expected to find jobs done by Landamere under an old company name. He was beginning to piece together the likely scenario for the hotel's takeover.

Apparently, Landamere wasn't happy with just managing the construction job. He wanted the property for himself, and intended to bring it down to his price range.

No one else made sense as the killer, at this point.

Clouse wondered why Landamere would want the property. Millions of dollars in renovation remained, and the upkeep alone would be more than the project manager could afford on his salary. There had to be something more to the plan that Clouse had yet to find.

Long ago, the hotel had harbored antiques and art worth a fair amount, but even selling those would never equate the funds necessary to fund a working hotel.

Royalty had visited the grounds at one time, and legends of the jewels and gems they left as gifts passed down through several generations, but the notion they could still be somewhere on the grounds seemed unfathomable to the firefighter.

"What are you working on?" Summers asked, walking into the game room.

"Checking on some construction companies," Clouse replied a half-truth.

"Looking for a new job?" Summers inquired, plucking the pool table's balls from the corner pockets.

He gathered them on one side of the table before racking them, much to Clouse's dismay.

All morning long, Summers had kept his brother-in-law within eyeshot. Clouse didn't need protection from his fellow firefighters, nor did he feel alienated. He kept to himself for a specific reason, and as long as his associates made the necessary phone calls, it would pay off. Clouse trusted no one, because people tended to talk and he knew what could happen when people talked.

While Summers practiced his pool shots, Clouse buried his nose in the papers, searching for overlooked evidence. He was waiting for several important phone calls, with little else to do but bide his time. He thought of something he needed to do, stood, and stuffed the folded papers into his back pocket.

"Where are you going?" Summers asked almost defensively as Clouse walked out of the room.

"I'll be right back, Rodge."

A moment later he returned with shoe polish and an old T-shirt he used as a rag to shine his station shoes. Clouse preferred shiny shoes like military personnel wore, so they were easy to clean. Seldom was polish necessary but he occasionally took the time to spiff them up.

He took his shoes off, opened the cap of black shoe polish and scooped the rag into the polish when the dispatch tones went off.

Without a word, he and Summers looked at one another and started toward the door. Clouse quickly stuffed his papers under a chair cushion before rushing toward the pole where he followed Summers to the truck room below, feeling the brass pole between his arms and legs for the first time in several months. All the other stations Clouse had worked at recently were single story.

Clouse reached the ground wondering how he would react in a fire scene again, or if this was an actual fire. According to the dispatcher, it was a reported working fire, but so many times the trucks were called back to the station after just a few minutes because of false alarms. As he stepped into his protective boots and took hold of his bunker coat, Clouse sensed this wasn't one of those cases.

He was right.

Five minutes later, he found himself standing in the middle of a burning feed store on the south end of town. He, Summers, and two other firefighters stood in the middle of the room armed with an attack hose line and two pike poles. Clad in full gear and breathing apparatus, they were ready to face the challenge before them.

Clouse and Terry Jarvis, the other firefighter riding the pumper truck with him that day, used the charged hose line to smother the growing flames before they consumed the entire store. Summers and his partner, Gary Pierce, were riding the ladder truck, which meant they were extra manpower in this instance.

Using the pike poles, they tore down accessible areas of the wall and ceiling, allowing the water to penetrate and kill off any smoldering areas. The fire itself seemed to provide little threat to the property because most of it was contained within a minute. Parts of it had climbed into the ceiling, making their job a bit tougher.

Made entirely of wood, the feed store carried bags of grain, pellet feed, and lots of hay. Not quite half had been ablaze, making it possible to save the store if the firefighters contained the rogue flames. Summers worked diligently, breaking apart the thin wooden boards along the walls. As Clouse manned the hose with Jarvis supporting the charged line, he heard an officer shouting orders behind them, before heading outside to check the progress of the other crew.

Clouse watched as several flames danced atop the baled hay in front of him, sneaking in from behind the bales where water had not reached. Water streamed in from a hose line above, cascading from the roof to help extinguish the various sets of fires below. Clouse turned the hose several times against different flames inside the building that seemed to cling to life. He knew fire would continue to survive, unless thoroughly soaked, or robbed of oxygen.

There were already too many cracks and crevices in the structure to deplete its oxygen supply.

After making a round with the hose, Clouse and Jarvis paused a moment to remove their facemasks. Now that visibility was much better and the smoke had thinned out with help from the ejector fans, they didn't need them. They traded places so Clouse had to take a break from the nozzle, which got somewhat heavy pumping hundreds of gallons per minute. Supporting the hose for the front man wasn't much easier, but he knew his forearms would feel better in the morning if he wasn't wrestling the nozzle the entire time.

Hearing no activity to his left, Clouse looked over, seeing his brother-in-law standing there, holding the pike pole at his side, simply staring at him. He waited a few seconds, wondering if Summers might be waiting for a cue from him to come help, but it never came.

Summers had stood there too long to be taking a break, and no one had come to relieve his crew yet, so he was technically abandoning his duty.

Clouse quickly analyzed the stare. Summers was burning a hole right through him with the look, as though Clouse had somehow severely wronged him. Clouse sensed his brother-in-law was pondering whether or not to do something. He wondered if he was the object in question, or if Summers simply happened to be eyeing his direction.

"What's the matter, Rodge?" another firefighter finally asked, catching Summers' attention.

As though shaking off a trance, Summers immediately set to work helping his fellow firefighters destroy the blaze with a second attack line that had been dragged inside, sending water streams everywhere they were needed. Few could man a hose as well as Summers. He had both good size and natural instincts when it came to putting out fires.

Clouse set to work again, keeping Summers in the back of his mind. Perhaps his self-doubts were misguided, and Summers was the one who needed more time off. And perhaps putting them together wasn't such a good idea. Clouse knew his job required continuous focus and attentiveness to one's surroundings. Summers knew it too, yet something else was enough to distract him from a fire, a potential life-threatening situation.

Clouse wondered what it was.

***

An hour later, the firefighters settled back into the station. Clouse's truck arrived after his brother-in-law's because their truck provided the necessary tools and water at the scene. Clouse spent half an hour cleaning the insulation and muck from his air pack and mask once he rinsed his gear with a garden hose. It took more time to clean up at the scene and the station than it did to actually put the fire out.

Clouse recognized the unique odor fire scenes left in his bunker gear, but he actually felt happy to have it back. He took off his gear, setting it beside the truck, which dripped water from several areas. The trucks usually left puddles beneath them from the overfill in their water tanks.

Down to his station gear, minus shoes, Clouse started toward the door leading up to the living quarters when Jerry Guinn, the deputy chief, stopped him for a moment, handing him two sheets of paper. He was dressed in gear suitable for fishing, particularly on an administrative holiday.

"These came for you yesterday," he informed Clouse.

"By the time I got here yesterday the office was closed," the firefighter replied. "Thanks, Chief," he added. Guinn simply gave a playful salute and headed out the backdoor, apparently finished with whatever business had brought him into the administrative office for the day.

He was one of the few officers who knew how to have fun, Clouse thought. He had missed the deputy chief the day before because the office closed early for a presentation on the Indiana University campus. It had already been closed when Daniels faxed over the sheets.

As he climbed the stairs Clouse looked at the cover sheet, which said little more than nothing, then to the darkened black and white copy of the original photograph Daniels had sent. Clouse studied it a moment, trying to make out what the photograph was supposed to be before figuring out what Daniels was talking about.

"Damn," Clouse said, realizing what the photo was when he saw the handle of the scythe and the mostly-cloaked leg of the figure.

Like Daniels, he suspected this was Bennett's death.

Clouse reached the top step, almost hit by the door leading to the living quarters as one of the firefighters swung it open to head down.

"Sorry," the man said after Clouse barely caught the door in time to save his face from being rammed.

As he walked through the quarters toward the locker room, Clouse found better light by which to study the copy. He began to make out part of the tattoo, but it was difficult to confirm due to the darkness of the paper.

Clouse walked into the locker room, subconsciously wanting a shower, but still too intent on the photograph to undress. After a few minutes, the edge of the body art began to take shape for him and he realized there were edges, and they appeared to be rounded, but Clouse felt almost certain it was a flaw in the original photo because he knew tattoos could look distorted from a side view with bodily curvatures.

"Could be a cloverleaf," he said doubtfully under his breath, stepping toward the bathroom, realizing there was only one person he knew with a tattoo on the backside of his leg.

"Or a Maltese cross," he thought aloud, looking at the one tattooed on the right leg of his brother-in-law, who was standing in front of a sink, covered only by a towel as he combed his hair now that his shower was over.

For a moment Clouse simply stared, much like Summers had toward him at the fire scene. He asked himself what seemed like a thousand times why his brother-in-law would commit such heinous acts.

There were no ready answers, and Clouse felt compelled to ask Daniels for more proof before he questioned Summers. Somehow, it all seemed to fit, yet Clouse couldn't bring himself to believe the man who was like a big brother to him would kill so many people he worked with and cared about.

He looked to the red and gold Maltese cross permanently etched on Summers' right calve muscle. It seemed ironic someone who wore a symbol depicting protection, worn as a badge of honor, was capable of cold-blooded murder.

"Need something, Paul?" Summers asked, apparently over whatever had bothered him at the fire scene.

"Just seeing if a shower was free," Clouse replied. He stuffed the fax in his back pocket, unbuttoning his shirt. "What kind of engineering did you do in the Navy, Rodge?"

"Structural, brother," Summers replied, turning from the mirror. "We built stuff."

"Oh," Clouse said, satisfied with the answer.

"You sure you're okay?" Summers asked, apparently taking notice of how apathetic Clouse appeared, because mild shock still overwhelmed him.

"I'm fine," Clouse said, undoing the last button on his shirt. "I think I'm going to do a workout before I shower though."

Summers nodded before heading into the locker room to put on his station attire.

A few minutes later Clouse stood downstairs, locked in a restroom with his cell phone, desperately wanting to talk to Daniels.

"What do you mean he didn't come to work this morning?" Clouse asked the detective who answered the phone at the police station. "Did he call in?"

"No, I don't believe he did," the detective said, sounding more than a bit concerned. "He just never showed up."

"And you didn't bother calling him at home?" Clouse asked, somewhat irritated at the lack of forthcoming information.

"I'm sure they tried."

"His number's not listed. Any chance I could get it to give him a ring?"

"Sorry," the detective said. "We can't give out that kind of information, but I'll give him a call, and leave him a message if you want."

"Okay, thanks," the fireman said, hanging up before he said something he might regret to the detective.

Quickly realizing his fellow firefighters were just as protective about personal information, Clouse regained his wits. He didn't blame the man for not believing him, or giving out Daniels' information, but Clouse felt like one of the few people genuinely concerned about the detective. It was already apparent something bad might have happened to his only true protector.

Clouse knew Daniels well enough to believe the man would never skip work without calling in first. He knew of only one place the detective might have gone that would have placed him in danger.

And Clouse had no way of getting there until morning.

He stepped out from the bathroom, literally running into his station's captain.

"Sorry, Captain," Clouse quickly apologized.

"Paul, are you sure you didn't come back too soon?" the older man asked, genuinely concerned. "Rodge says you acted kind of strangely at the feed store fire."

Clouse found it odd his brother-in-law would say such a thing when it was Summers acting out of character.

"Maybe I am still a bit distracted," Clouse told a half-truth, hoping the captain would take the bait.

"I don't need you endangering yourself or the others if you're not mentally ready to do this job. I'm going to call someone in and give you the rest of the day off."

Clouse was overjoyed inside, but couldn't let it show.

"You sure, sir?"

"Yeah. Get your gear and I'll see you in two days."

Clouse nodded.

As the captain left, he took the fax from his back pocket, crumpled it up, and walked outside to the dumpster behind the station, tossing it in. As he returned inside, Clouse looked up to the second story and saw his brother-in-law looking down upon him. Summers had seen him toss the sheet of paper, but probably had no idea what it was.

Anxious to leave the station, Clouse did not bother to retrieve the fax. He simply wanted to locate Daniels and get some concrete answers.

Without saying a word to the others, he gathered up his belongings upstairs and headed away from the station feeling empty inside. The world around him felt like it was caving in, and his guts hurt from anxiety. He hated not knowing the answers, feeling as though Daniels had left him hanging. Clouse had a fleeting thought the detective could simply be toying with him, hoping Clouse would reveal some break in the case to make it easy.

He now trusted Daniels, and knew better deep down.

As Clouse pulled into his driveway, the sun began to set, leaving a strange glow across the fields surrounding his house. After a change of clothes, he would head to the hotel, and hopefully find some answers.

Chapter 30

Dressed in more familiar attire, Clouse drove his truck up the hotel drive, seeing a county police car parked near the hotel's main entrance when his truck's headlights panned that way.

He still felt wary about who to trust and how accurate Daniels' information was. He remembered Kaiser echoing the very same words the killer used the day his house was ransacked and he was beaten half to death.

He had also spied Daniels' car parked at the front gate, glad his hunch was correct, but worried for the detective's safety. There were still a number of possibilities running through Clouse's mind as to who the killer might be. Daniels was the one person he trusted by default. The detective could not have been present during all of the murders due to his job.

As his boots hit the ground Clouse closed his truck door, zipped up his jacket and recognized a smell crossing the sunken garden with the breeze. Perhaps he now knew the smell of death too well, but the fireman felt sure it could be no other odor. Though he barely saw it through the few overhead lights on the grounds, the cemetery sat across the garden.

Climbing the stairs to the main entrance doors, Clouse noticed the wind pick up as though the sky might let loose with precipitation. It seemed deathly cold for rain, and too gusty for snow, but hail or sleet might be possible, he thought.

It also seemed fitting.

Clouse tugged lightly on the entrance doors when he reached the hotel's balcony, expecting them to be locked. He wasn't really surprised when they opened, leaving him extremely leery of what to expect inside.

He walked inside slowly, noticing the lights seemed to be turned on selectively. He could see his way to the atrium, but barely. It was like being in a haunted house, only without any sense of fun. Clouse walked carefully, unsure of what to expect or who he might find, dead or alive. He fought back an urge to turn and run only because he wanted assurance Daniels was alive.

Zach was safe at preschool, Jane was at work, and no one else Clouse knew would be in danger except the detective. Ordinarily Clouse would not be so concerned, but Daniels was the one person who believed in his innocence when no one else did. He felt obligated to return the favor, putting his neck on the line the way the detective had for him.

As Clouse stepped further into the lobby he spied a glimmer from the floor, created by a single row of bulbs along the second floor balcony, selectively turned on above him. After standing frozen a moment Clouse shivered in realization, moving closer to the pool of blood in front of him.

Drawing nearer, the firefighter realized it was more than just blood as a body came into view. He could make out a torso, legs, and shined shoes at the very end.

But there was no head.

Gasping, Clouse took a step back with a deep breath to regain his composure, praying it wasn't his high school friend. Even rescue runs on the fire department never prepared him for something as horrific as finding a dead friend. Seeing a corpse usually did little to faze him because people in his line of work grew hardened to death in time as a psychologically protective measure.

Still, knowing such an act on any human being was intentional chilled him to the bone.

"Damn," Clouse said, reluctantly kneeling near the body for a closer look, careful to avoid the pool of blood where the head had been.

He felt the brown vinyl jacket, looked at the uniform pants, and knew it was a county officer. Lying backside up, the body yielded no clues of who it might be. Warmth emitted from the torso, implying the death was quite recent. The pool of blood came mostly from the neck, but there was a large tear in the jacket with blood bubbling upward.

Clouse figured the officer never saw the blade coming. He also suspected the beheading was done posthumously to intimidate Clouse further upon his arrival.

It worked.

He wanted to know whether it was his friend or not, but figured knowing might scare him out of the hotel completely. Clouse refused to turn the body over to look at the nameplate.

Stepping over the headless corpse, he found the service weapon missing from its holster.

"So much for sense of security," he thought aloud, hoping to have found some form of protection from the fallen officer.

Clouse continued down the hallway, unable to see much except dim light bulbs ahead. He heard the footsteps from his boots echo down the hallway, wondering who else heard them. As he passed an open door, something brushed against him.

Whirling to see what it was, Clouse gasped again as the stiff body of Robert Bennett hung from two ceiling hooks in front of the door. Clouse looked at the blood-covered body, stumbling backwards as he did so.

Two sharp hooks pierced the shoulders of Bennett, giving him the appearance of a beef slab hung for storage. Bennett was fully clothed, but somewhat dirty, as though stored in a basement, or maybe a pile of dirt. The skin appeared ghostly pale, even in low light, and a creaking sound emitted from the hooks where they screwed into the ceiling.

He had only met the electrician once, but remembered Bennett, who spent more than an hour touring the entire facility with Landamere and himself. Soon after that, Bennett had started his work, then disappeared.

Clouse stared, continuing to back up until he felt another bump from behind.

"Shit!" he exclaimed, turning to see Vern, the grounds keeper, hung by the neck from the ceiling, a small gardening shovel still stuck in his abdomen with dried, crusted blood along its edges and his clothing.

His eyes were still open as though asking why he deserved to die, while a dried trickle of blood streamed from his mouth. He appeared as discontent in death as he had life. Clouse never liked the man, but knew he deserved better than the death he received.

Wanting to avoid any more bodies, Clouse hurried his walk down the hall toward the beam of light crossing the hallway from the atrium entrance. At least in the center of the atrium he would be able to see in every direction with ample light, and guard himself from all sides. The area was too big for anyone to surprise him.

He approached the light carefully, looked around the corner, and saw a grand spectacle awaiting him from a distance.

"Dear God," Clouse muttered, horrified, yet obligated to walk inside for a closer look.

Along two portable support posts, Dave and Joan Landamere were tied and gagged, looking to the floor until they heard Clouse's footsteps. They both turned to see him, and gave muffled cries through their gags as he approached. Apparently realizing they might endanger Clouse too, both quickly silenced themselves, certain they had his attention.

Nearby, Clouse saw Daniels lying belly down, hands rope-tied behind his back with a gag as well. He appeared unconscious from what Clouse could tell, but he would not draw any closer until the rest of the horrifying scene in the large atrium was revealed, serving as a grand stage for the killer's sick, playful imagination.

Against one of the marble statues, Melissa Cranor's headless body leaned forward, arms stretched upward as though reaching to the heavens for help. Her boyfriend's body was stuffed inside a giant vase, only his shoulders and head visible above the rim. The body was a bluish hue with the one remaining eye partly open as the head lie slumped against the side of the oversized decorative object like some demented Halloween prop. It was almost like visiting a wax museum, but realistic beyond Clouse's wildest dreams. He never expected to walk into anything as gruesome as the scene before him.

Beside the vase was a jack-o-lantern seated on the floor, flickering from the inside as a candle burned. It was becoming symbolic for death, starting on the creepiest holiday of the year. Clouse realized just how much trouble one person had gone through to set the stage for this final act. One way or another he would find out the answers to every question he had posed the past few weeks.

As he approached Daniels' unconscious form, Clouse spied a state trooper's uniform, previously hidden behind Joan Landamere. Haplessly laid to rest on his front side, arms sprawled out on the floor, Jason Brinkman's corpse appeared stiff, and somewhat dirty, much like Bennett's had been. The eyes were closed, and of the bodies, his appeared the most at peace if there was any such thing for the victims.

Avoiding the Landameres for the time being, Clouse knelt beside Daniels, finding a pulse along the detective's neck as he placed a small blade in Daniels' partly opened hands in case anything happened to Clouse and the detective awoke. At least one of them would hopefully make it out alive. Clouse knew the end was quickly drawing near in one form or another.

"I see you've made it to my little gathering," a voice called from some distance behind Clouse, echoing through the mammoth atrium.

Bolting to his feet, Clouse whirled to see Roger Summers carrying a head in one hand as he crossed the atrium floor toward his brother-in-law.

"Heads up," he said, tossing Melissa Cranor's head to Clouse, who refused to catch it, letting it thump against the floor beside him, leaving bloody patches as it bounced off the ceramic tile.

"You're no fun anymore, Paul," Summers said, acting much more at ease than he had that morning.

Almost fully relaxed in fact.

As though this was all rehearsed.

"You managed to get here quickly," Clouse noted, refusing to let Summers near him.

Summers circled around him, stopping as he drew near Daniels. Clouse also stopped in front of the helpless Landameres, keeping a watchful eye on Summers in case he tried to harm the detective.

"I have some good connections," Summers said. "After all, I'm not the one accused of murdering Angie by everyone in Bloomington, am I?"

"You're smooth all right," Clouse commented bitterly, realizing all of his fears were completely true.

"Somehow you don't seem totally shocked, Paul," Summers commented. "Seems your buddy over here is smarter than you are," he added, walking over to lightly kick Daniels' motionless form. "You should watch what you throw away at the station."

Clouse refused to take his eyes off Summers, not noticing that directly behind him, Landamere was loosening his bonds.

"I'll keep that in mind, brother," Clouse said with a sour tone, mocking how Summers always referred to him.

Dressed in a black cloak, but without the benefit of hood or mask, Summers still appeared creepy in the costume. He was an imposing form, and it was no wonder victims fell so easily at his hand.

"We've got a lot to talk about, Paul," Summers noted. "But it will have to wait."

Before Clouse could ask why it would have to wait, Dave Landamere dropped the ropes from their loose position around his hands, to the floor, taking up a small garden shovel from between his legs. With one swift motion he clocked Clouse in the back of the skull, sending him unconscious to the floor with a thud.

Chapter 31

"I didn't want Roger to have all the fun," Landamere said as Clouse regained consciousness, rubbing his head as he sat on the tiled floor.

Though he was not bound like Joan Landamere and Daniels, the gun in his brother-in-law's hand was enough to keep him motionless.

"Dave, I can understand your stand in this," Clouse said, still feeling his head, "but Roger, I don't get your angle. Why, Roger?"

"Why, Roger, why?" Summers mocked him, waving the gun airily. "Paul, that's the dumbest question you could possibly ask."

Summers paced the floor a moment, thinking about where he wished to begin his tale. He looked to Landamere, smiled, and knelt fairly close to Clouse, the gun dangling in one hand across his knee. He seemed to be having fun with this at Clouse's expense.

"Let's start from the beginning," Summers said. "You already know Dave worked in the Chicago area but what you didn't know was that we met on a common project while I was in the Navy, stationed there. To make a long story short, I moved back, Dave moved back, and we decided to collaborate on a different sort of project. See, we knew if we scared the shit out of the people around this hotel we could drop the price and eventually buy it for pennies on the dollar."

Landamere stepped forward to speak.

"But we knew Smith would never sell to just anyone, so we created Tincher, a company that cared about its work, and the investments it purchased and ran. You probably didn't have much time to research too deeply into that. Did you, Paul? See, the guest book was kind of our tracking system for snoops who might look at Tincher for the wrong reasons."

"The original idea was just to scare the people through the Father Ernest legend and some ghostly sightings," Summers added. "We thought about it though, and decided it would take a little more than just that to scare Dr. Smith and the workers away."

"So you went and hacked people up?" Clouse asked, shocked at the notion of murdering for financial gain.

"Well, Roger did most of it," Landamere said, giving credit. "But I got a little dirty with those two unruly teenagers and that trooper."

"You did pretty well," Summers said with a complementary nod. "I have to admit it was a hell of a lot of fun roughing you up, Paul, and destroying that computer before you could research us anymore. Now, cleaning up after the old detective's body parts proved rather gory, but I managed to itemize everything for the police."

Clouse shook his head in disappointment, amazed the one person he knew and trusted for so long committed such acts. A person completely instrumental in making his life as he knew it go from a dream to a reality.

"And as for the rest of the money to finish up and run this place for an unholy profit, we simply need to have you finish up your rampage of murder right here and now, Paul," Landamere noted. "You see, after you walk in here, dig up all these bodies, and kill both my wife and your detective friend using his own weapon, you'll take your own life because you'll finally realize you've destroyed everyone you love, and life is no longer worth living," he summed up the end of the plan.

Clouse couldn't fathom people truly falling for such bullshit, but the evidence indeed pointed to him.

"You still don't have a concrete alibi for any of the murders, and after you blow away Detective Daniels, there won't be anyone left to dispute your guilt. And no one will even care, Paul," Landamere added with a maniacal grin. "It'll all be swept neatly under a carpet, and no one will care that you, a psychotic, delusional murderer, took his own life."

"Oh," Summers butted in. "We invited your county police friend but he was unable to make it."

"So hospitable of you," Clouse said bitterly, finally realizing where the master plan was heading.

"From the insurance on Mrs. Landamere we should make enough to finish the hotel at cost, or at least enough to take out a large insurance policy," Summers noted. "We play it by ear, see if there's interest in the property, and if the money isn't there, the hotel has an unfortunate accident and we collect the insurance. Both Dave and I know how to work the system, Paul. We would have brought you into this, but you've always been too straight-laced."

"I still want to know exactly what turned you into a scythe-wielding maniac," Clouse insisted.

"Now that's the one part you *should* know," Summers said with a laugh. "You murdered my sister after everything I've done for the both of you, just so you could collect the insurance and have everything to yourself, so I decided to do the same exact thing and take everything from you."

Clouse's shocked look caught Summers off-guard.

"I had nothing to do with Angie's murder, Rodge," Clouse said steadily, looking Summers straight in the eye. "How the *hell* could you ever believe I did?"

"Finish this," Landamere whispered hurriedly to Summers as his fellow conspirator shot him a quizzical stare.

"No," Summers replied. "This needs a proper ending. There's a lot to be said for how things end."

Clouse looked over to Daniels for a moment while the two debated exactly what to do with him. Without looking up, the detective took the small blade Clouse had placed in his hands, and began to work at the rope binding his hands.

"Do you really think I could have gone home and killed Angie when I was working that night, Rodge?" Clouse insisted, purposely barging in on their conversation.

"You could have," Summers said, outwardly growing less certain by the second.

He seemed to still genuinely believe Clouse was to blame for all of his family's problems after Angie's death.

"Angie and I weren't on the outs as someone led you to believe," Clouse noted, shooting a glance toward Landamere. "Who pushed the idea of murdering the workers here, Rodge?" he asked insistently. "Who had the most to gain from this whole thing?"

Slowly, Summers looked to Landamere, who looked from his bound and gagged wife back to his fellow conspirator.

"Finish him, Roger," Landamere insisted with a hiss. "Don't let him lie to you like that."

Summers looked at his hands, and the gun clutched in one, possibly realizing Clouse was correct, or deciding who to aim at before pulling the trigger.

"You've known me ten years, Roger," Landamere stated. "You don't know him that way," he added, pointing to Clouse as though he were a complete stranger to both of them. "Day after day he kept coming to work, telling me his marriage was failing and he didn't know how he would ever pay the bills. I warned you months ahead of time what Paul was capable of, then it happened. He took that insurance policy out on your sister, then killed her for profit."

"Bullshit!" Clouse yelled at Landamere. "You're a piece of work, Dave. You've had this master plan worked out all along," he said, slowly standing up, keeping them both from looking to Daniels, who had cut most of the ropes. "The thing I want to know is when your conscience abandoned you, because it was obviously long before you met me."

"You can't trust him, Roger," Landamere almost pleaded. "Blow him away and let's get on with making millions."

Shaking his head, Summers turned away from them, holding his hands up in frustration. He shook the gun enough to make both Clouse and Landamere nervous. For the first time, he realized he had murdered on the premise of mere words from a man he deeply trusted in the name of revenge and financial gain.

A man he trusted too much, perhaps.

Joan Landamere shrilled from within her gag, uncertain of what to expect as well.

Taking advantage of Summers' distraction, Landamere decided to protect his own interests, pulling the fallen county officer's gun from within his jacket, ready to fire at Summers if necessary.

Clouse shot a quick glance to Daniels, who looked up for the first time, barely lifting his hands behind him to indicate he was free. He returned his attention to Landamere, just as the project manager drew a gun from his jacket. Clouse rushed toward him, knocking it free, back toward the detective.

Turning around to a complete scene of confusion, Summers looked past Clouse, who hit Landamere with a hard right hand, toward Daniels. The detective stood, scrambling for the gun, which provided the only threat to Landamere and Summers pulling off their scheme if they could still coexist.

Taking quick aim, Summers fired the service pistol, missing completely on the first shot, but firing a second directly into Daniels' backside, flooring the detective. As Landamere fell to the floor from a second punch, Clouse looked to Daniels, who lay motionless halfway across the atrium. A blood pool formed atop his back, through his jacket.

"Damn it, Roger," Clouse said quietly, giving a mixed look of shock and disapproval to his brother-in-law. "This has to end."

Clouse didn't care anymore. He would say whatever he chose and face the consequences. Almost everything he knew and cared about had been destroyed during the past two weeks by the man he looked up to and respected like a big brother. Only now did Summers realize the extent of his mistake and his misplaced trust in Landamere.

Now that it was too late.

Frustrated that his emotions were toyed with by Landamere, and that his once good nature was tarnished with utter evil, Summers felt his eyes water, knowing he could not return to a normal life, nor could he finish this lie, this evil ploy with Landamere, knowing it was based completely on greed and deception.

He pointed the gun at Landamere, who held up a foreboding hand with wide eyes, silently begging for mercy.

"You killed my sister," Summers finally spoke what he had come to realize. "All for this," he added, looking up to the glass dome, loosely holding the firearm. A serious look etched itself across his face as he regained his composure.

For what seemed several minutes, the betrayed firefighter took careful aim at Landamere, then turned toward one of the atrium entrances, tossing the gun like a frisbee. It hit the wall, echoing as its metal frame collided with solid concrete.

"I'm sorry," Summers said to Clouse, stumbling away with the realization his life as he knew it was over.

He headed toward one of the atrium exits, possibly wanting it completely over as he stripped away the black cloak from his body, tossing it aside.

Clouse also saw him undo the bulletproof vest beneath it, then toss it against a wall before he exited the atrium. Several stopped slugs were visible from where Timmons, the missing teenager, had shot the reaper several times before his untimely death.

Clouse turned his attention to Landamere for a moment, full of rage he would not be able to contain were he not preoccupied with Summers' new revelation.

"You son-of-a-bitch," Clouse scorned the project manager. "You had this set up from day one," he said, realizing just how long they had worked together. "You bided your time, waiting for the right opportunity. When Angie and I separated, you found out from Roger and put your scheme into action."

"Just admit it, Paul. It was brilliant, was it not?" Landamere said, cracking a slight smile, not bothering to rise from the floor.

Clouse soured even more.

"But now it's over. I'll see this hotel imploded before you ever own it," he said, looking to Daniels, who still lay motionless across the atrium. "You asshole."

Quickly darting over to the detective, Clouse saw the pool of blood emanating from the center of his back, near the spine. Summers was a better shot than Clouse ever imagined. Putting that fact out of his mind, he knelt beside Daniels.

"Talk to me, Mark," Clouse said, avoiding the usual formality in names.

"Can't feel my legs," the detective answered quietly so Landamere would not hear. He was still belly-down on the ground, and stuck that way because Clouse would not risk moving him. Snatching Landamere's gun from its nearby spot on the ground, Clouse placed it in the detective's left hand, assured the man could still grip a weapon.

"I'll be right back, Mark. I'm calling the police and getting Roger before he does something else stupid."

"I'm not going anywhere," the detective answered quietly again, knowing he could do little to protect himself once Clouse left the room. He pulled the gun closer, tucking it beneath his jacket, hoping to avoid using it.

Clouse wanted to stay with the detective, but felt a deeper urgency to save Summers from his own destruction, despite everything his brother-in-law had wrongfully done.

He walked out of the atrium to find Summers under Landamere's watchful eye. The project manager knew he could not confront Clouse without a weapon, and the only useful gun he knew of lay across the atrium against a wall.

Besides, he knew Clouse would be back once he and Summers were finished. He hoped they might kill one another and give him an easy conclusion to an otherwise complex situation.

Chapter 32

Clouse entered the circular hallway, listening for his brother-in-law's footsteps, hoping they weren't in the direction of the dead bodies. He no longer felt any sense of danger confronting Summers, and sensed what frame of mind the man harbored.

Unfortunately, he probably knew the hotel's layout just as well as Clouse.

Down the hall, he heard the elevator door close. Taking off his jacket, Clouse tossed it behind him before running down the hall to discover he was too late for the elevator, which was heading to the top floor.

"Shit," Clouse muttered, knowing two exit points led to the roof above.

This elevator was one.

Another was a long flight of stairs leading to a door on the roof. Clouse had no time to climb six stories before the elevator delivered Summers to his destination. The second elevator, across the atrium, only went to the sixth floor, and not the roof, so Clouse still had a run ahead of him if he tried to use it.

No, he decided. He was waiting for this car to return.

He pushed the up button several times, anxious to discover exactly what Summers was up to.

Down the hall in the atrium, Landamere looked up to his wife from a sitting position where he recovered from Clouse's attack, smiled sadistically as she stared down at him wide-eyed, and stood, slowly crossing the atrium to retrieve the gun Summers had tossed away, assuming Clouse had taken the other weapon with him.

As he picked up the weapon, the project manager strolled toward Daniels first, seeing no movement from the detective. He stopped short of the motionless man, viewing the bodies and the bizarre horror around him. Smells of death and dirt intertwined for an unusually foul odor inside the freshly cleaned atrium.

"Too bad you figured it out too late, detective," Landamere said, kicking Daniels over to his backside, surprised to see him still alive.

"You're still finished," Daniels said between labored breaths, the bullet in his backside plaguing him several different ways.

Being overturned put his back in agony.

"You won't be able to wrap everything up neatly before Clouse calls the police."

"You'd be amazed what I can do," Landamere said confidently. "I have several contributors to this project who will do anything to see it succeed. People you and your pathetic department would have no chance of discovering."

Landamere checked the gun over, released the safety, and pointed at the detective's waist, slowing tracing his torso up to his head.

"Don't worry," he said. "I'll put you out of your misery, just like the wounded animal you are, detective."

Daniels' hand had slowly crept toward his jacket during the course of the conversation, but he would never draw before Landamere put a hole in his head. Still, he had to try. He only needed the murderer to shift his attention for a second.

"Freeze!" he heard from across the atrium, barely able to see the county officer drawing a bead on Landamere with his service pistol.

From what he could see in such a prone, limited position, Daniels thought it was Kaiser, though they had only met once. From the way Summers had spoken, he figured the deputy was dead. Then again, they had been so determined to make Clouse as miserable as possible before they killed him that they probably twisted the truth.

Daniels knew there was no way Landamere would surrender to the county officer, but he felt compelled to keep quiet since a nine-millimeter duty weapon was still pointed directly at his head. For a moment, the three men exchanged glances, almost like the multiple person showdowns in old westerns.

"Drop your weapon, Ken, or the detective gets a lobotomy the hard way," Landamere instructed the familiar officer.

After a few seconds of thought, Kaiser set his weapon to the ground, rising to a standing position, unaware of what Landamere had in mind.

Kaiser failed to react to Landamere's surprise turn of the gun on him. One shot fired from the weapon tore through the officer's chest, flooring him with a thud, as the impact took his feet out from under him. Left groaning in pain, the officer rolled to one side, blood oozing from his chest and shoulder area.

Landamere smiled with the utmost confidence, unaware that shooting Kaiser had left an opening for Daniels to draw the concealed gun from his jacket and aim it upward at him, with as steady an aim as the detective could muster.

Once he saw the pistol pointed at his forehead, Landamere's smile quickly faded at the same moment Daniels pulled the trigger, jerking the project manager's head back as a red spot appeared instantaneously in the center of his forehead.

A shocked look crossed the man's face the second before he died, his fading eyes looking into those of the detective. Landamere was genuinely surprised anything spoiled his plan after so much effort to keep it all together.

His body quivered a second or two before collapsing to the floor in a heap.

Daniels breathed a sigh of relief while Joan Landamere sighed through her gag, looking off in a different direction; apparently glad her ordeal was over.

Strangely, no one in the room was in a position to get help because Kaiser's radio was in his patrol car, since he was officially off-duty for the day. For the first time Daniels noticed Kaiser was dressed in street clothes. Taking a deep breath to calm his mind, Daniels simply remained still, getting some satisfaction knowing justice was served, even if he might never walk again.

He hoped for Clouse to return soon, because no one else was going anywhere.

***

When the elevator finally reached the roof access, Clouse stepped from the car, into a small room containing a door that opened to the roof.

He stepped into the brisk air, finding the black, rubbery surface wet in several spots from the recent rain showers. Treaded mats created a safe walkway along the roof during all seasons, centered along the regular surface. All of the walking areas were black while the dome's roof was finished in red roofing tiles.

A few small buildings atop the black roof contained heating and cooling units, while a few small shacks held ducts for the units. Standing beside the dome, Clouse noticed the windows allowing a peek into the atrium from high above, but ignored them.

A rusty ladder that looked somewhat like a staircase along its bottom portion, led to the top of the dome. A rounded room referred to as the crow's nest provided an access point where lights were changed above the chandelier. Paintings far older than Clouse lined the smooth walls of the old room, and graffiti marred their beauty, identifying people from the hotel's various eras bold enough to sign their names.

Clouse figured Summers had no intention of getting inside the rounded room to dive into the atrium. It was a tricky climb, and getting through the small hatch along the floor of the tiny room was no easy feat.

Instead, Clouse rounded the first bend along the roof, finding a shell of the man he once trusted and loved beside one of the four towers. Summers kept his back to his brother-in-law, probably not hearing anyone approach because the weather and the black walkway deadened nearly every sound.

"Talk to me, Rodge," Clouse said, not getting a response from his somberly pensive brother-in-law.

Summers stared over the edge to the brick walkway below, and several trees that looked to obstruct any jump from such a height.

As the two stood a safe distance from one another, the sky let loose with sleet and rain to accompany the heavy winds sweeping through the hotel grounds. Ordinarily, Clouse liked being on the roof, seeing everything for miles around.

All of the hotel's other buildings, including the spring buildings and the old pavilion, seemed so small below.

For Clouse, nothing compared to the bird's eye view through the glass dome of the atrium, seeing the giant steel rails below, holding up literally tons of glass. It gave him an entirely different perspective of the hotel and what craftsmanship went into building it so many decades earlier. He also marveled at old fire stations the same way.

The same way he once admired his brother-in-law.

"I was so self-involved," Summers said after a minute of silence. "Dave lied to me for so long in setting this up that his word became gospel," he added, a tear coming to his eye, realizing everything he had thrown away.

"He screwed us all, Rodge," Clouse said, desperately thinking of a way to dissuade his brother-in-law from thinking of suicide. "You've got a wife and kids. Let's get out of here and go see them."

"No. They're better off with me dead," Summers said, looking back to the edge from the black roof surface at his feet. "I never realized everything I might throw away. I was so damn bent on revenge and making things right that it never occurred to me it might all be one big lie."

"I'm not letting you do this, Rodge," Clouse said with the greatest voice of confidence he could muster.

"Why? So, you can enjoy watching me rot in prison? Or die in the gas chamber?" Summers asked angrily, finally looking toward Clouse. "I'll be a disgrace to everyone on our department, and my family will know I was partly the cause of Angie's death. I can't live with that, Paul. Let me do this," he said, nodding toward the unforgiving concrete below.

"No," Clouse answered with a foreboding tone, shaking his head in sadness.

At that moment, Summers realized he had lost his big brother role and Clouse was now the responsible one. The one in control. He smiled awkwardly, determined to end his own life rather than face the ones he loved in shame.

There was no explaining what he had done, and there was no going back. He realized what he had to do, and climbed the short wall of the roof to jump.

"No!" Clouse yelled, grabbing his brother-in-law by the seat of the pants to pull him back.

Summers turned suddenly, hitting Clouse with a strong right hook. The younger fireman staggered, trying to shake off the punch.

"Don't make me do this," Summers insisted. "I've already hurt everyone too much. Just let me go."

Without a word, Clouse charged forward, taking Summers down with a football tackle before crossing left and right fists across his face. Though nearly equal in size and strength, Clouse always had more of a tendency to excel when under pressure, frightened, or both. Summers wanted no part of him like this.

Clasping the younger man by the shirt, Summers tossed him away, now ready to fight if necessary. He wiped the blood from his lips as the rain soaked him. The combination of rain and sleet made the surface of the hotel roof slick. He consciously kept track of his footing as the two contemplated their next moves.

Moving toward one another, the two locked stares, each determined to foil the other's intentions. Summers threw a jab first, hitting Clouse in the jaw. The roof surface tripped the younger man, landing him on his posterior as Summers staggered toward the edge of the roof once again.

"Damn it!" Clouse said to himself, regaining his footing enough to run and baseball slide against the wall, catching Summers by the foot before he could lift it over the wall.

"Give it up, Paul. I'm going," Summers stated.

Doing as he said, Summers broke his foot free from Clouse's grasp, pulling himself up to the wall. Once again, Clouse tugged him back, throwing a right hook that landed squarely against Summers' jaw, teetering him back several steps.

Before Clouse could follow up the punch Summers bolted toward one of the four towers alongside the hotel. The slick surface slowed him down enough that Clouse could follow closely, but both lost their footing several times in the trek toward the huge tower as the roof grew icy.

Reaching the tower first, Summers let himself in, slamming the door against Clouse's head. Falling back several steps as he held a hand to his head, Clouse wondered if it was worth such pain to save a man who wished to die.

Nonetheless, he pushed on, bursting through the door in time to see his brother-in-law climbing a ladder to the higher portion of the tower where it would be a cinch to jump without intrusion or interruption. Clouse quickly followed, trying to avoid snagging his cowboy boots against the ladder rungs.

He reached the top level just as Summers leapt over the railing, but managed to dive forward enough to catch one of the man's hands. It was a situation he had experienced only twice as a firefighter where someone's wellbeing hung literally in his hands. This was the first time he recalled the situation definitely being life-threatening.

Bracing his body against the tower railing, Clouse grabbed for Summers' other hand as they both stared down, finding the ground even further than before. Still, Summers showed no fear of dying. Clouse realized it was all but over, refusing to let go of his tight grip.

Catching a foot alongside the tower wall, Summers braced himself, beginning to climb back toward the tower railing as though he had changed his mind. He took a few steps upward while Clouse assisted him, pulling with every bit of strength he had.

Suddenly, Summers paused.

"Let me go, Paul," he insisted, looking up to his brother-in-law, not the ground below.

"You know I can't, Rodge."

Summers closed his eyes a few seconds and nodded in understanding. He would do the same thing if their roles were reversed.

But they weren't.

Placing his feet against the wall, Summers pulled himself up a few more steps and looked at Clouse with a strange grin. Taking hold of Clouse's hands, he crossed them over, making his brother-in-law's grip more difficult.

Summers then let his weight fall entirely downward, smashing Clouse's forearms against the railing. Wracked with pain, immediately thinking a bone in his forearm might be broken, Clouse felt his grip break loose. This sent Summers into a downward spiral, tumbling against the building several times before the deadly impact with the ground arrived.

Clouse slumped against the tower wall, ignoring the pain in his forearm as the emotional pain intensified. Perhaps selfish motivation, remembering the good times gone by, made him want to save Roger Summers, but he felt doubly hurt by the man now.

Summers had always been a man of strong convictions in life, and perhaps those rules he lived by made choosing death easy for a man with so much pride.

Only now did Clouse realize how easily manipulated even the best of men could be. He always planned to teach his own son the value of true friendship and family. In the end, little else mattered.

He stared down at Summers' distorted body, wondering what else was left.

Was it finally over?

Subconsciously he straddled part of the railing, looking down at the spot Summers had hung from, wondering if he could have done anything more to save the man.

"Don't do anything stupid," a voice said from behind him as someone clasped his arm, tugging him back softly.

"I'm not," Clouse answered, turning to see Kaiser standing behind him, using his left arm and a thick towel to put pressure on the wound to his right shoulder. "What happened to you?"

"Got shot by your buddy Landamere."

"And you climbed up here like that just to check on me? I'm flattered," Clouse replied, stepping back into the tower, ready to follow Kaiser down the ladder.

Kaiser gingerly stepped into the hatch first, descending the ladder. Clouse followed, careful to give his friend an ample lead.

"And he's not my buddy anymore," Clouse added as he stepped down, glad the ordeal finally had closure.

Chapter 33

Less than a week later Daniels was able to have visitors other than his family. Though still unable to walk, the prognosis was good. The swelling in his spine had recessed enough that doctors could evaluate him.

Just a few days prior, Daniels had given his statement to state police, corroborating what both Clouse and Joan Landamere attested to. According to Joan, her husband had abducted her after Daniels visited the house, and made haste to the hotel, luring the detective into the end of his plan's very detailed ending.

It appeared Landamere had everything planned far in advance, but didn't want to carry out the ending any sooner than he had to.

"They say I should be up and walking within a few months," Daniels told Clouse from his hospital bed where he sat propped on a few pillows, with a tray of less than desirable food in front of him. "I should regain feeling in my legs within a couple weeks."

Clouse lifted the cast on his forearm, displaying his own battle wound. It was evaluated as a complete fracture of the ulna bone in the center.

"Looks like an excuse to get off work," the detective scoffed.

"God knows I haven't had enough of that," Clouse joked. "I'm just glad to have something I can call a life again."

Both looked past the pleated curtains to the outside, at the season's first real snowfall. The holidays were quickly approaching, and neither planned on having their best time ever among family. Things would never quite be the same for either man.

Without carpet, the hospital room felt chilly. It was another sign that winter had officially arrived. Zach was asking his father to go find a Christmas tree, perhaps in a subtle attempt to put the past further behind them.

"What's this I hear about you being nominated for Police Officer of the Year?" Clouse asked, suddenly recalling an article from the morning paper.

Daniels chuckled.

"My chief jumped right on that one," he said. "It'll be awful hard to sum up my nomination in just one paragraph after all this."

"You'll get it," Clouse said confidently. "After all you've been through, there's no one more deserving."

"Thanks."

"It's me who should be thanking you," the firefighter said. "You were the only one who gave me a chance through this whole thing, and you almost got killed trying to prove my innocence. I can't repay that."

"Then don't try," Daniels said. "But *do* fill me in on some of the details I haven't heard about yet."

"Like what?" Clouse asked with a quizzical look.

"Like where all those bodies were stored, and why the state police never found them."

"Easy enough. Landamere used Father Ernest's gravesite to store them since it was freshly dug, and police usually refrain from disturbing graves. He just piled them inside and discarded the extra dirt in the woods."

Daniels knew the police probably couldn't disturb the gravesite, even if they had suspected it, because a warrant would have been necessary on private property and they were still technically looking for missing people at the time.

"And the vehicles?"

"Landamere had a storage facility in town where utility vehicles were stored for Kieffer Construction. Thing is, they were all summer work vehicles so no one had any reason to visit the building. Both Melissa Cranor's car and Bennett's work van were found there the next day."

"So Landamere knew Roger for a decade and once they found one another in Indiana they devised this plan to scare people off from the hotel?"

"True," Clouse answered, still amazed he never knew a thing about their relationship beforehand. "But things changed when I came to work for Dave. He saw the opportunity to push the scare even further, and used Roger. From almost the time I started the West Baden project, Dave was feeding Roger lies about me and my marriage, establishing a revenge motive early on. When Angie and I split up, he used that fully to his advantage and made me sound desperate for money and a way out of my marriage. Neither was true of course."

Daniels nodded.

"So what's going to happen to the hotel?"

"Dr. Smith is pleased things are back to normal," Clouse answered. "Kieffer Construction is interviewing for a new project manager. If he's up to it, I suspect Rusty will be the man for the job."

"That's horrible what they did to his daughter."

"It's been horrible for all of us," Clouse added. "I wish I could say things will return to normal, but there *isn't* a normal anymore. Roger's family and our department agreed to bury him without ceremony just to keep things quiet. I doubt I'll be on speaking terms with any of his family again."

For a moment, both of them sat silently, each wondering different things.

Daniels seriously questioned the extent of his stay at the hospital, while Clouse thought about the future, and whether or not Angie would want him to move on. He was in no hurry to rebuild his life, but the horrific visions of his wife haunted him. Clouse never wanted to remember her as a bloody mess the way Dave Landamere had left her.

"How did Landamere get into your house that night to murder Angie?" Daniels questioned, as though reading Clouse's mind. "I mean, she did lock the doors, didn't she?"

"He probably lifted Roger's key to my house then returned it, or just copied it. Once you got to know Rodge, he got too trustworthy, even with his possessions."

"Sounds like he had Roger under his thumb."

"A little too much," Clouse admitted. "You were right when you said it was someone close to me."

"But I didn't expect a pair," Daniels noted.

"Me neither. Care if I use the commode before I take off?" Clouse asked, thumbing toward the tiny bathroom.

"Go ahead."

Clouse closed the door behind him, did his business, then washed his face in the sink. When he looked up, a ghostly figure stood behind him dressed in the purest white dress, with the most peaceful smile Clouse had ever seen on her face.

"Ang?" he asked aloud, wondering why on earth his wife's spirit chose a hospital restroom to visit him again.

Perhaps timing was her motive.

Without a sound, the specter looked at him in the mirror's view, blew him a kiss, then disappeared.

There had been no blood, no discontent.

Perhaps Angie was now at peace. Clouse sensed he could move on with his life, even with the possibility his imagination was playing tricks on him.

"Everything okay?" Daniels asked when he emerged from the tiny room staring at his hands.

"Everything's just fine," Clouse replied, a grin crossing his face. "Take care of yourself, detective," he said as he opened the door to leave.

"You too," Daniels said with a voice that echoed the uneasy feeling in his own heart. He watched as Clouse left, wishing he could have emerged from the incident so unscathed.

His destiny would be determined by willpower and months of rehabilitation, but he intended to live a normal life once more.

Epilogue

By August of the following year, things had changed for the better.

The hotel was almost fully renovated, rooms and everything. Clouse was content with both of his jobs, since Rusty had eventually taken the project manager position with Kieffer Construction, and his relationship with Jane was blossoming quite nicely.

In fact, he had set his mind on proposing before the holiday season came. Things could not get much better for the couple and the two children. Clouse had eventually sold his house and moved in with Jane. She lived in town, but the two actively searched for a country home more suited to the lifestyle they preferred.

"I can't believe Dr. Smith actually gave you a personal suite here," Jane commented, seated on a blanket inside the atrium.

Clouse had brought a picnic basket and white wine for a picnic in front of the hotel's grand fireplace, seated on one side of the atrium. It was large enough for several people to stand inside, fully upright.

He had obtained permission from Smith to light a fire for such a special occasion. He was more proud than ever of his achievement at the hotel, now that it neared an end, and wanted this to be the setting where he asked Jane the most important question he could ever ask.

"It's only two small rooms," Clouse said, carefully opening the wine bottle before filling the two wine glasses. "Still, it was a nice gesture."

"I can't believe we have a day without the kids," she commented, looking up at the clear blue sky through the atrium's glass dome, six levels above the blanket they sat upon.

"God, I feel like I own the place," Clouse said, thrilled that Smith had been so generous toward him.

Not only had Smith decided to maintain ownership of the hotel, he had ordered it finished by Kieffer Construction, to be dedicated in late October, and opened soon thereafter.

"You've got the keys," Jane said. "That's the next best thing."

Clouse smiled. He did that quite a bit more lately.

He looked up through the dome for a moment, lost in the sky as Jane had been a moment earlier.

"What are you thinking about?" she questioned.

"How everything seems so right," he said pensively, still looking up.

"You seem so much happier than when I met you," she said, caressing his face with her soft hand, drawing a long kiss from him.

He finally felt comfortable being intimate again, which was part of the reason he could ask Jane the question that had plagued his mind the past few weeks.

Clouse looked at the fire brewing in front of him, wondering why Jane hadn't questioned his lighting a fire in the middle of summer. The recent cold front was temporary, and by no means chilly. It was nothing more than a few days in which people would avoid their swimming pools and eat inside.

"Did you want a sandwich?" Jane asked, searching through the basket.

Now was the moment to ask.

"Jane," he said seriously, gaining her attention. "I want you to stand over here with me."

Clouse led her to the edge of the fireplace, looking into her eyes as the fire reflected within them. Reaching into his jeans pocket, he pulled out a small box before dropping to one knee. He watched the curious nature of her eyes turn to delight as he opened the box to reveal a sparkling diamond ring, enhanced by the glowing orange light from the fireplace.

"Will you take my hand in marriage?" he asked, not so much as blinking when he did so.

He wanted to remember every split second of this occasion.

Her hands cupped her face as she smiled, while tears of joy filled her eyes. She was genuinely speechless, and to his amazement, she seemed surprised.

"Yes," she said after a moment of recovery. "Yes, I will."

Several tears trickled down her face momentarily as she tried to collect herself. For months, she had wondered if the day was coming and it finally had. She never pushed, knowing how tormented Clouse was after his first wife died.

She had wondered if he would ever recover enough to spend his life with another partner. Now Jane was assured Clouse had been thinking about the same topics recently, and finally proved himself able to commit.

She led him back to the blanket with something besides food on her mind. For almost a year since Angie died, Clouse had felt shell shocked about developing a relationship and sharing his life, and his bed, with someone else. Part of it was ensuring Zach's recovery, and how others might look at him.

Once Zach seemed content with the idea of having a stepsister and a new maternal figure in his life, Clouse decided to live for himself and ignore what others thought or said. It was none of their concern.

"Are you okay with this?" she asked, tugging his polo shirt lightly.

"I'm fine," he said, kissing her again.

Simultaneously, the two knelt on the blanket, undressing one another as their breathing came heavier. Clouse felt an urge to look around in case someone might have made their way into the hotel for a free peep show, but his attention was entirely on Jane, and paranoia had left his mind over time.

He gently laid Jane on the blanket, kissing her deeply while he kicked off his boots. At this moment in their lives, nothing could be more perfect, and perhaps it never would be again.

As the couple made love in the grand atrium their passionate moans echoing throughout the hotel, a light along the sixth floor switched on as a shadow crossed the room, finally coming to a stop behind the room's drawn curtains.

Everything around the newly engaged couple seemed much more at ease lately. They could enjoy the children, their own company, and now the idea of a life together. With Clouse's tragic events almost a year behind him, it was time to move on and start over.

Time for a new life.

Life without haunting memories of tragic death.

Memories that might finally stay buried.

And perhaps, some that would not.

RETRIBUTION

Book Two of the West Baden Murders Series

This manuscript is dedicated to Scott Thomas Davis,
a brother firefighter who was taken from us far too soon.

Acknowledgements

I owe many thanks to my usual crew for helping out, and especially to Troy Lobosky and John Leach for their insight.

I also owe thanks to Brad Wiemer, Kelly Reed, Tim Lee, Rick Shellabarger, Korby Sommers, David Dotson, and Stephanie Barber for their assistance.

Cover design by Kendrick L. Shadoan from KLS Digital.

Visit www.klsdigital.com for more information.

Chapter 1

Standing in the living room of his new country home, Paul Clouse took in the view of stacked boxes, clean carpet, and a fresh start to his life. Miles outside of town, he could begin anew, with the house serving as a template for his life.

In August he had proposed to Jane Brooks, and she accepted. The house was their first step in solidifying the idea of being married, particularly since Clouse's first wife had been murdered almost one year prior in his former residence.

After surveying the packaged organization in the form of two-dozen cardboard boxes, Clouse stepped from the living room into the kitchen, hearing the sound of his brown cowboy boots clop against the linoleum floor. He stared at the large room, looking forward to cooking breakfast for the family when he was off weekends.

He crossed the room to walk through the open front door to the large porch, which wrapped partway around the two-story home.

"Not bad," he said of the mid-October weather.

Living almost two miles from Bloomington, Indiana, where he and Jane both worked, Clouse enjoyed having no visible neighbors, and room for his animals to run. She ran a medical clinic, while he worked for the city as a firefighter once every three days.

He loved his schedule, and worked a second job as a design consultant for Kieffer Construction, a company in nearby Bedford that always seemed to have new work for him. He could pick his own hours, sometimes completing designs at the fire station, and he felt as though his college degree wouldn't go to waste.

Wearing jeans and a flannel shirt to accompany his boots, Clouse looked more like a lumberjack than anything else with his brown hair loosely parted, and a thick mustache he planned to trim later in the day before he attended an inaugural dinner that evening.

His blue eyes scanned the empty, tanned fields surrounding his property, and the nearby old barn that housed his boat, his horse, and occasionally, a vehicle. It reminded him of the barn on his old property, except he no longer had space enough to keep his father's seasonal farming machines for winter storage.

Clouse broke away from the scenery just long enough to pour himself a cup of coffee inside.

When he returned to the porch, he took in the new, bare wood. He had yet to pick a color to stain his porch, so he decided to leave it until spring. A few old rocking chairs and some flowerpots were all that adorned the outdoor retreat.

A small tan car pulled up the long drive to the house, and Clouse smiled as he saw Jane return with his son, Zach, and her daughter from a previous marriage, Katie. Part of what made their relationship seem perfect was how the kids, both five years of age, seemed to get along so well. They had both longed for a sibling to identify with, and finally found one.

"Hello," he said, planting a kiss on Jane's lips as she stepped from the car.

She looked as beautiful as ever, taking a bag from inside the car as the kids rushed inside the house to play with whatever toys she had bought them. To him, Jane never looked bad, even on her worst mornings when she dreaded going into public because she felt flawed.

Her medium brown hair flowed in the wind as though she was a supermodel at the edge of the sea, and her slender form might have landed her some parts on television if she lived out west. Clouse suspected Jane was perfectly content being a mother and a doctor. Dressed in blue jeans and a blouse of country beige, she looked the part of a natural country girl today.

If there were an imperfection in her personality, or beauty, he would have to find it later, because he had spent the past year mesmerized by everything about her. She felt the same about him, but Clouse never took to the compliments about his looks.

"You're not going to the dinner like that, are you?" she teased as they walked toward the house.

"I was going to wear a baseball cap too," he kidded before a sip of coffee. "Believe it or not, I do have my tux hanging upstairs, and I'll even take a shower before I get dressed."

"I'm impressed," she said with an easy smile. "So I'm taking the kids over to my parents' house to change before meeting you at the hotel?"

"Yup. I dropped their clothes off there this morning to make it easy on you."

"What are you doing this afternoon?" she asked, apparently forgetting what he had stated the night before.

"I've got to see Mark, then I'm taking the boat out one last time before we put it up for the winter."

"Don't be late," she warned. "You've been waiting almost three years for this night."

"I wouldn't miss it for the world," he said sincerely with a crooked smirk. "I'll take my stuff with me and get ready at Ken's house once I'm finished with the boat."

Ken Kaiser was Clouse's high school pal who worked for the county police in the area of the hotel, and lived fairly close to West Baden. Clouse was no stranger to Kaiser, or the man's family, because he often dropped by when working in the area.

Kieffer Construction had begun work on the West Baden Springs Hotel several years prior, when the National Preservation Society stepped in to save Indiana's first self-supported dome structure, built just after the turn of the 20th century. Bought by Dr. Martin Smith, the hotel was funded for renovation, and eventually redone completely, from the grounds to each individual room.

Clouse took great personal interest in the project, particularly since he had drawn a set of blueprints from scratch for his graduate work at Indiana University. His prints proved quite useful to the company during the reconstruction. The first project manager and now his replacement heeded his advise.

Tonight, a dinner marked the completion of the hotel and the impending grand reopening of the building after decades of use for purposes other than its primary function.

"I'll finish with the boat, change, and meet you at the dinner around seven," Clouse said as the couple walked inside. "They won't start serving and announcing the guests of honor until about seven-thirty."

Clouse pulled Jane in for a kiss, wrapping both arms around her slender form. They locked lips several seconds until the children ran into the kitchen, anxious to be seen and heard.

"Where are you going, Dad?" Zach asked.

Many relatives felt Zach was a spitting image of his father. Others could see Angie's traits from beyond the grave, thinking much of her resided within her son.

"I've got to take the boat for a spin while it's nice out, son."

"Can I go?"

"Nope. You've got to stay with Jane until the party tonight." He knelt beside his son. "Give Dad a kiss?" he asked, despite Zach reaching an age where such an act was no longer kosher.

Zach shook his head, indicating a refusal.

"Oh, come on," Clouse chided him. "Your friends aren't here."

His son finally gave him a hug and a kiss so he could be left alone to play again.

"I'll see you at the dinner, okay?"

Zach nodded an affirmative. In Clouse's opinion, he took to his father's new love interest quite well. In many ways, Jane was like Angie had been. She was beautiful, led a professional life, and acted cordially toward everyone she knew.

Clouse quickly replaced his boots with tennis shoes for the boat outing, and left in his Chevy four-wheel-drive truck, which he considered a must when living outside of town. Since his parents lived on a farm, and his new property was of similar nature, keeping the big truck seemed practical, despite its appetite for fuel.

He pulled out of the driveway, leaving a slight trail of dust behind.

Chapter 2

Clouse stopped at a red light several blocks before Bloomington Hospital, seeing its familiar form illuminated by the afternoon sun. He hated visiting his friend every week at the hospital, but only because it conjured up bad memories from the depths of his mind.

When Clouse's first wife had been murdered the previous year, Detective Mark Daniels was the only one who gave Clouse the benefit of the doubt in his plea of innocence. When it turned out his former employer, the first project manager for Kieffer Construction, was primarily responsible for Angie's death and half a dozen others, Clouse and Daniels were already trapped by Dave Landamere's evil scheme.

Though Clouse escaped the incident without serious injury, Daniels wasn't so lucky. He was shot in the spine while scrambling to retrieve a loose weapon. The injury left him paralyzed from the waist down, and a year later, he continued to battle in rehabilitation for full use of his legs.

Once a week Clouse made the trip to the hospital, feeling obligated to visit the hapless police officer in his personal fight. Ironically, Clouse had never met the man before he was accused of murdering Angie. Now they were on a first name basis and knew each other quite well.

Clouse figured guilt kept him visiting Daniels every week because the man had shown undying devotion to find the truth when no one else made much of an effort. Until the detective walked, Clouse would never truly put his mind to rest. It made him feel horrible that his life had taken such an upswing while Daniels' had basically fallen apart, and Daniels never spoke a negative word about how he had obtained his condition toward Clouse.

He was just that sort of person.

Confined to a wheelchair, the detective was now relegated to dispatch duty. Clouse imagined it ate him up inside, but Daniels never lashed out at him. Somehow, the police department worked it out with the dispatch center to use Daniels as a liaison or trainer for police dispatchers so he didn't get pensioned out on disability. The possibility still lingered, and if Daniels went much longer without improvement, he was likely going to find himself out of police work.

Daniels did not seem to enjoy the firefighter watching him fail week after week in his attempts to walk, but he seemed glad someone aside from his wife cared enough to help him through his burden.

Within a few minutes, Clouse parked his truck and found himself on the fourth floor of the hospital, heading toward one of the therapy rooms where Daniels made his attempt in vain, once a week, to walk again.

As he approached the room, he saw Susan Jameson, the officer's doctor, walking out.

"How is he, doc?"

"His state of mind just isn't positive, Paul," she answered. "He's getting more and more pessimistic about his chances of ever walking again."

"Do you still think his problems stem from his head?" Clouse asked.

She hesitated, glancing into the room as though Daniels might see them speaking.

"Let's sit a moment," the doctor said, leading him to a set of chairs across the hall. "His wife has been working with him daily, conditioning his legs. He should have enough strength to take a few steps, and he's even told me he has most, or all, of the feeling back in them."

"But he can't or won't walk," Clouse summed up the situation.

"I've seen this before," the doctor commented. "Sometimes there's a mental block preventing the patient from fully recovering. Whether it be a deep residing fear of returning to active duty, or some trauma left from the shooting incident, I don't know," she said with an air of frustration. "Most mental blocks don't last this long, but most are usually taken care of through psychotherapy, early in rehab."

"And he won't go, will he?"

Susan shook her head.

"No, he won't. He knows there's nothing physically wrong with him, so he thinks he can do it on his own."

"Can I talk to him?"

"Sure," she said. "He's about to attempt a walk with the support railings."

Clouse and the doctor walked into the therapy room as Daniels supported himself with two parallel braces nearly six feet in length. Susan kept the door from slamming shut for the sake of her patient's concentration as the two watched from behind. Daniels slowly dragged one leg forward, showing slight use. Concentrating fully, he wobbled a bit, jerking his right shoulder forward before dragging the left leg up to him.

"That's good," the female therapist by his side commented. "Are you ready to try full weight on it?" she encouraged, despite the fact he could barely steady his feet beneath him.

Daniels did not answer, but simply steadied himself on the braces, bringing both feet to a standing position as his upper body trembled from supporting all of his weight. He slowly let go of the braces appearing surprised he could stand at all without them. Subconsciously licking his lips in anticipation, the officer lifted one foot to take a step as the therapist moved to the inside of the bars for a better spotting position.

With his left foot off the ground, Daniels attempted to move it forward for his first step, but fell forward instead, his fall broken by the therapist. Luckily, she was accustomed to catching everyone from elderly ladies to burly construction workers, so any bumps and bruises she received from the officer's fall were expected.

"Damn it," Daniels said to himself as she helped him back to his wheelchair.

He shook his head in disgust.

"You're doing better," Clouse commented, walking into the officer's view.

"I just can't get it," Daniels said with a discouraged tone, his eyes showing the hurt he felt inside.

"Let's get out of here a minute," his friend suggested, leading the way to the door before opening it for Daniels.

Both left the room silently, opting for the sunlit hallway outside, with unusual warmth about it.

"Dr. Jameson still thinks your problem lies up here," Clouse said, pointing to the side of his own head for reference.

"She's right," Daniels admitted. "I want to do it, I've been physically able for eleven months, but I just can't get it done."

Clouse took a seat at the edge of the hallway, across from the disgruntled police officer. For a moment he looked Daniels over, noticing a few things different about the man he'd met the year before.

For his rehabilitation, Daniels had quit smoking, which Clouse considered a step in the right direction.

That, coupled with confinement to a chair, led him to put on some additional weight and become a bit more crotchety. He had also grown a full beard thicker than his head of dirty-blond hair.

Other than occasional minor lapses of depression, Daniels still seemed the determined, genuine person Clouse recalled meeting under unimaginable conditions.

"You know, you don't have to come watch me fuck this up every week," Daniels said as he sometimes did.

"I owe you my life," Clouse said. "The very least I can do is support you through this, so quit trying to get rid of me."

Daniels grinned.

"I really do appreciate it, but you've got a life to live. Don't put it on hold for me."

"It's no trouble, Mark. So, tell me what's troubling you this week. Why do you think you're not making progress?"

Daniels shrugged from his wheelchair.

"Dr. Jameson keeps trying new drugs on me every other week. One of them is for my mind. One's to help my muscles and another's to relax me. All I know is my hair is falling out in clumps, and I go through these mood swings worse than I've ever had before."

Daniels had lost some hair over the past year, but Clouse attributed it to male pattern baldness. He never suspected the drugs might be responsible.

"She's switched prescriptions three times, and every new one seems worse," Daniels revealed.

Clouse simply shook his head, suspecting the medical staff knew what was best, and Daniels was just grumpy because of the side effects.

"Overall, are you holding up okay?" Clouse decided to ask.

"Yeah, I suppose. It sucks going to work and being a dispatcher when I used to bust the bad guys. No one talks to me because they feel sorry for me."

Clouse nodded in understanding, and hesitated a moment before asking a favor of his ailing friend.

"I want you to come to that dinner tonight," Clouse told the officer, speaking of the hotel's grand reopening gala.

Daniels sneered at the idea, looking to the wall.

"You *know* I don't want to go near the damned place after what happened."

"I know, but it might do you good to see the source of your problem," Clouse said, knocking on the wheelchair. "You're too damn stubborn to see a shrink, and whatever's plaguing your mind isn't just going to work itself out."

"Why can't I just go down there with you sometime?"

"Because you and Cindy need a night out, and we're both too busy to set a common time. Come on, Mark. You're already invited. You can just sit with me and Jane."

"I don't know," Daniels hesitated.

"It can't hurt, you know. I doubt anyone down there will know you, and if they do, they'll want your autograph."

"Why's that?" Daniels asked, finally drawing a smile.

"Ah, come on, Mark. You won National Police Officer of the Year," Clouse said, playfully punching Daniels' left arm, still solid despite the lack of mobility. "There are thousands of cops in this country and you won."

Daniels rolled his eyes. He had remained extremely modest throughout the entire process, though Cindy once informed Clouse of how proud he acted about the award, away from other people.

"I still think you were instrumental in that."

"A letter here, a letter there," Clouse said with a disarming wave of his hand. "The only thing I did was tell every committee that would listen about the guy who saved my ass, and probably several other lives."

Daniels seemed relaxed enough to debate with Clouse about the evening's plans.

"Is this a formal thing?" he asked.

"Tuxedo, buddy," Clouse said.

"I don't have one of those handy," Daniels countered.

"Yes you do," Clouse informed him, standing from the seat. "I asked Cindy to go pick one up for you."

Daniels lunged at him with a half-hearted punch from the chair, missing as Clouse dodged.

"I am going to kill you for this," he said, followed by a sigh.

"Fine, but you'll have to show up to do it," Clouse said, pointing both index fingers at the officer, stepping backwards toward the elevators. "See you tonight, Mark. I've got to go play on my boat."

"Sure," Daniels said, realizing he was outvoted by his wife and a good friend.

Like it or not, he would have to visit the place that cost him the most important position he had ever held, and a year of his life he could never take back.

Chapter 3

Across Lake Monroe, tiny ripples glided atop the water as a gentle wind passed through the reservoir. Clouse's boat easily navigated the lake, leaving a foamy white trail behind the outboard motor as he captained the craft.

A large boat, it was designed for overnight stays on the lake rather than fishing. Beneath the deck, a comfortable living area provided room enough to sleep, cook, or relax when the boat was idling or stopped. A collapsible canopy could be rolled over the helm to protect the captain and his controls.

No one else dared challenge the wind and quickly cooling water on the lake. Clouse merely wanted to give the boat one last run before winter weather hit the area. He usually ran it almost completely out of gas before toting it home for storage. During the season, the boat remained docked at a marina until he felt the urge to take it out.

Jane was not as enthusiastic about boating as Clouse's first love had been. It used to be a tradition for them to take Zach out overnight, or sometimes leave him with relatives if they wanted time alone on the lake.

He planned on taking the boat home after his next workday at the fire station. His work at the hotel was functionally complete, and he had no major projects pending with Kieffer Construction.

In the back of his mind, he hoped Dr. Smith might give him a chance to run the day-to-day operations of the hotel, but suspected the doctor probably wanted the opportunity to do that personally, at first. There were many people to meet, and so many compliments to receive about the hotel's striking appearance.

Clouse would not pass up the opportunity either.

Noticing the gas meter drew close to empty, Clouse decided to return to the marina. He wanted just enough gas left to load the boat onto his trailer in a few days.

For a few minutes, the craft skimmed across the center of the lake with the greatest of ease, then it hit something that stopped the motor. The outboard sputtered a moment before dying as the boat gracefully coasted along the water, slowly drawing to a complete stop.

"Shit!" he exclaimed, steadying himself once the boat rested, floating in the middle of the lake completely alone.

Even the nearest shore was too far for Clouse to contemplate swimming without a risk of hypothermia setting in. He looked in every direction, seeing no one around, and no way to signal for help.

If the engine failed to restart, he would be alone for some time.

Looking over the back of the boat, Clouse saw a bit of lake vegetation trickling from the back of the outboard motor. This surprised him only because the water's surface was completely clear of debris, the ripples carrying most of the plant life to shore, and the motor's blade reached nowhere near the bottom of the lake.

"What in the hell?" he asked himself, studying the plant life attached to his motor, wondering if it had actually stopped his boat.

Walking to the helm, Clouse turned the key in an attempt to start the vessel. It tried to start, but fell short of actually turning over.

"Damn," he muttered, knowing there was no additional aid because his cellular phone was in the truck, and the boat coasted far too slowly to return him to shore by the dinner's start.

Also, not a soul could be found on the lake.

Returning to the rear of the vessel, he looked over the side, questioning how long he could stay in the water to fix the motor before his body began to freeze. At best, the water temperature stood between forty and fifty degrees. Without adequate covering, he would feel the effects of the cold within minutes. A severe cold would be the lowest form of punishment he might receive for such a foolhardy action.

Unwilling to take a chance in the water just yet, Clouse took up an emergency oar from one side of the vessel. He returned to the rear of the boat, using the oar to prod at the underside of the motor, slowly removing debris from its blades.

While he worked, the craft's captain felt the boat shift slightly to one side, but attributed the motion to the ripples striking one side. He devoted more time to battling the motor housing, barely noticing the rocking motion stop suddenly.

Knowing the ripples in the lake would not simply cease without a good reason, Clouse tensed, suspecting he might not be alone. It seemed far too coincidental the boat got tangled in debris during a season where the plants and brush were mostly gone, or submerged far beneath the surface.

His boat had *never* struck anything in all the years he had taken it on the lake.

Without turning around, Clouse took a few steps back, casually reaching for the second oar as he knelt down, fearing he might need it for additional self-defense. His hand fumbled momentarily for the wooden tool, finding nothing in its usual housing.

Suspecting he was in deep trouble, now hearing the distinct dripping of water along the boat deck behind him, Clouse bolted upward, pivoting away from the potential attacker at the same time.

His action failed to deter his attacker, however, because someone wearing a black wetsuit waited until Clouse was done parrying before swinging the second oar like a baseball bat toward his skull.

Too slow to react, Clouse felt the oar impact the side of his head, which whirled him around into a defenseless position, allowing his assailant to land a second blow against the side of his head, right beside the temple.

Never able to see his attacker's face, Clouse was knocked into the water, where he struck the surface limply. His body turned as it bobbed, his clothes quickly filling with water.

Every bit of consciousness he had left went to hold his breath while viewing the dark form looming over the side of his boat from beneath the water's surface. Ripples and air bubbles along the surface obscured his view of his assailant, who looked mysterious and black in the wetsuit, with no visible face.

Everything grew dark as Clouse slipped further beneath the surface, feeling his consciousness waver as he entered a liquefied oblivion. The only sound entering his ears was that of moving water before he blacked out, unable to keep the aquatic environment from entering his lungs.

Chapter 4

"Goddamn it!" Daniels exclaimed as his wheelchair hit one of the chairs around the kitchen table.

Usually mild-mannered, Daniels found himself a bit more emotionally turbulent with each failure in his rehabilitation.

"What is it, Mark?" his wife, Cindy, asked as she ran into the kitchen from the living room.

"Nothing," he replied with a sour expression, forcefully shoving the chair out of the way.

His entire morning was mired in frustration, especially since he was practically being forced to attend the formal dinner.

As much as he tried, Daniels could not always avoid hurting the most important woman in his life.

He had spent his entire police career sheltering her from the occasional horrors he witnessed, and the everyday aggravations his job brought to him. Now he forced her to deal with a husband who seemed to take out his frustrations on no one except her.

Daniels went to work at the dispatch center, came home, and avoided public contact as much as possible. Even most of his old friends were shut out of his life. She often told him she was tired of him feeling sorry for himself and giving up on so much of his life.

Rearranged to accommodate Daniels' condition, the house looked a bit different, especially after several friends from the police department volunteered to build an entirely new front walkway, complete with a ramp, for his wheelchair. He slept and lived downstairs, by himself most of the time, while Cindy was at work or in bed.

He found strength in the family pictures hung along the living room walls, and lining the shelves closer to him on the ground. Though tidy because he couldn't afford any wheelchair accidents, the house seemed a bit disheveled because of the modifications made specifically for him.

Though Daniels was completely functional, he chose a lonely direction, afraid his performances in bed would not satisfy his wife, though she had urged him to try several times since the shooting.

His fears went far beyond paralysis.

"Why did you volunteer me for this dinner?" he asked Cindy, complacent to wheel the chair beside the table and stare at her.

"You need to get out of the house, Mark. You're so close to walking again, and you need to keep your mind occupied. It's not like you to brood so much."

"Brood?" he questioned, raising an eyebrow. "I get shot in the back, receive a great prognosis that I'm supposed to walk within a few months, and I can't live up to my end of the bargain. How should I feel?"

"There you go again," she said, raising her voice to match his. "Something's keeping you from walking, Mark, and it isn't your legs," Cindy added, showing her frustration. "I spend over a dozen hours every week conditioning your legs and feet, keeping them strong enough so you can walk when the time is right, and something keeps holding you back. It's time you faced your fears and moved on."

"I haven't been back there in a year," he said in a solemn tone, settling down. "Every night I see that damned hotel in my dreams."

Some nights, Daniels dreamed he walked along his street, joined his daughter on the playground, or patrolled a beat at work again.

Simple things like dancing with Cindy or in-and-out use of the bathroom still eluded him in daily life.

Usually he awoke, instinctively trying to swing his legs out of bed, but it never worked. They teased him with occasional twitches, and sometimes he actually swung them out of bed halfway before realizing it. Daniels never brought himself to stand on his own when his legs swung out, and if he tried, fearing his legs would simply buckle from beneath him. It tortured his mind, knowing everything was ready except his mind.

He never told his wife about those failures.

Cindy knelt beside him, taking his hand.

"All the more reason to face this and put it behind you," she encouraged, speaking of the dinner. "Paul moved on with his life. He's getting married again and leaving the past behind him. We've got a baby boy who needs his daddy."

Daniels knew he hadn't been a model father lately. His girl, Renee, was almost three, and his son, Curtis, was only four-months-old. Doctors and friends all told him to concentrate on himself and getting well, but perhaps he had taken it a step too far and left too many friends behind, and more importantly, his family.

Before, his family meant the world to him. He remembered how many sacrifices he made to provide for Cindy and the kids, and to save for his children's eventual college. He realized his self-involvement tore apart his relationship with Cindy and distanced him from the children who needed more than just a mother. He was too good on the inside to realize otherwise.

"Alright, I'll go," he said, knowing he was doing the right thing to be with Cindy in public if nothing else.

Perhaps his fears had gotten the best of him for too long. He would do anything to walk in front of the people who cared for him once again.

And get back to his real job.

***

As Jane Brooks ascended the main stairs of the West Baden Springs Hotel toward the double glass door entrance, she took in the view of the six stories above her, and the mammoth dome topping off the old building. It still amazed her how the hotel remained so sturdy after years of decay and the eventual rebirth of the grounds.

She knew the grounds well after being a volunteer tour guide for nearly two years. Her mother lived in Southern Indiana, so Jane decided to play into her mother's interest. Giving tours was also where she had met Clouse while he helped design the building, appearing on the grounds several times a week, catching her eye.

Several selected rooms had lights on, giving the hotel the appearance of actual use for the evening's visitors. It was the first time everything was complete and actually suitable for us. It was Dr. Smith's way of letting everyone know the hotel was functional and ready for everyday use so they could spread the word to their thrifty friends.

"Where's Paul?" a voice asked Jane, catching her attention as the kids stopped on the steps beside her.

"Hi, Ken," she said to Clouse's friend Ken Kaiser, a local county police officer who happened to be working a security detail for the evening, dressed in a tuxedo of his own. "I didn't see your car anywhere."

"Got a different ride tonight," he said, nodding toward an older, maintained Harley-Davidson just off to the side of the steps below.

Kaiser had recently purchased it from a fellow officer.

"I see," she said.

Clouse had mentioned his friend's recent motorcycle fetish, but wrote it off as an early mid-life crisis phase. Looking the part of a biker, Kaiser had grown in a full beard since the last time Jane recalled seeing him. A training mishap kept him off work for a few weeks, and now his vacation time had kicked in, allowing him to keep the facial hair a bit longer. Clouse told her about heckling his friend for looking like a soap opera villain, but Jane didn't agree with the assessment.

Kaiser typically kept his hair buzzed short, but he had grown it out to accompany the beard of dark brown, almost black color. Clouse once revealed his high school buddy had curly hair, and absolutely hated it, so he buzzed it short whenever it started growing in. Strangely, the man's hair didn't even appear wavy, but Jane knew some people went through physical changes as they grew older.

"Paul should be here by now," she said after a few seconds. "He said he was going to shower and change at your house."

"Never saw him," Kaiser said. "And I've been here about half an hour now."

Jane's perplexed look showed, because nothing would keep her fiancé from attending the dedication of the project he had worked almost three years on, not to mention the hours spent blueprinting before that for his college courses.

"You know Paul," Kaiser said without any outward concern. "He's probably just running behind. The guy has the worst luck of anyone I know."

"But he usually calls, Ken," she stated.

Kaiser shrugged, unsure of where his friend might be.

"I'd better get the kids inside," Jane said, shaking off the notion anything bad kept her future husband.

"Don't worry. I'll let you know if I see the big lug."

Jane gave an appreciative nod.

Two doormen pulled the beautiful double glass doors open for the partial family, then the next set of doors leading to the lobby. Inside the lobby, the children were awe-struck by the array of bulb lights across the overhead balcony and the stained glass windows lining the walls of the lobby. The room was designed to impact guests by giving them a taste of what sort of hotel they were entering.

It worked, time after time.

A circular hallway surrounded a central atrium where all of the inside rooms owned a view downward, into the social center, while the outside rooms overlooked the gardens and red brick walkways outside.

Jane paused a moment, seeing Smith with a few of his guests. They seemed to be speaking to him about the marvelous job he had done with the hotel, but as always, he was modest, giving credit to his designers and the construction workers.

"Hello, dear," he said upon seeing Jane. "So good of you to attend."

"A pleasure," Jane said, putting forth the best smile she could, considering Clouse was running fashionably late.

"Where is your future husband?" Smith inquired.

"Running late, I suppose. I know he wouldn't miss this for the world."

Smith cracked a smile, though his age showed through the lines in his face and the pale nature of his skin. He seemed as happy as a deteriorating man could be. Jane suspected his health had gone downhill after the death of his wife, and if there was more to it, Smith wasn't telling.

He seemed weak, almost frail, compared to the man she met several years earlier, when she first started doing tours at the hotel. Still, she took his hand and gave a reassuring smile, hoping her fiancé would arrive soon.

"You've outdone yourself as always, Dr. Smith," she noted, peeking into the atrium, which looked gorgeous, despite the low lighting.

"It would never be possible without the help of people like Paul and Rusty Cranor," Smith said. "Paul was quite a find when he showed up with his blueprints all those years ago. It's a shame he had to endure so many hardships last year."

Smith's concern showed.

"I can't imagine how he ever got through it," Smith added, "but I'm sure you were about the best therapy he could have ever received."

"Thank you."

To this point, the children had remained patient, but they were beginning to get antsy with the party calling to them from within.

"I guess we'd better get inside so you can tend to your guests," Jane said quickly.

"Thank you," Smith said, giving a reassuring grin. "I'm sure Paul will love what we have planned after this inauguration."

Jane nodded, making her way inside the atrium through a large arch.

As always, Jane was impressed with the hotel's splendor. Especially so when they were led into the atrium where a sea of round tables provided much of the room's lighting from the candle centerpieces on their white tablecloths. An array of saucers and silverware adorned the tables with various colors.

Nearly as long as a football field in any direction straight across, the round atrium held beautiful colors of gold, green, and red trim that the candlelight failed to reveal. With so many tables present, the caterers would be hopping all night long.

She was amazed at the turnout, and how formal the event appeared, with tuxes and gowns everywhere. Her profession made certain she attended numerous galas, but Jane recalled few so grand as this. The atrium looked like something out of a movie, or perhaps an extravagant dinner only seen in Washington and political circles. A collective murmur crossed the large room as people made conversation about the hotel and their contributions.

Apparently, Smith had spared no expense.

Above, a select number of the rooms were lit, teasing with pieces of their beauty inside now that they were finished. Jane heard people speculating about what the rooms contained. Would the massage parlors return, or the saunas? Would the suites contain luxuries in the form of hot tubs, or would they be traditionally maintained?

Even Clouse refused to tell.

A new designer carpet replaced the pattern Jane saw on her last tour. She knew Dr. Smith detested the look of the old carpeting and ordered a new pattern to replace it. To her, this design of vines and various colored roses seemed no more appealing, but the primary colors of gold and forest green matched the colors of the atrium's wall and trim work.

Far above the crowd, a chandelier spread some light from its nest in the center of the glass dome. Supported by a dozen pairs of thick, steel ribs, the mammoth dome remained safe from weather and the elements. During daylight hours light streamed into the atrium, illuminating various artwork and statues at different intervals. At night, the low light hid most of the supporting structure, leaving only a clear view of the stars above through the large glass panels.

Jane, like Clouse, grew to love it more every time she visited.

"Hello, Mark," she said once Daniels and his wife drew her attention with a discreet wave. "I see Paul didn't sneak in."

"He's not with you?" Daniels asked.

"No, and I'm worried. He took the boat out on the lake and I haven't heard anything from him in a few hours."

"Paul won't miss this," Daniels said. "He knows better than to drag me here and not show."

As most of the chairs filled, waiters and waitresses dressed nearly as nicely as the guests rolled trays filled with covered dishes into the atrium. She looked to the itinerary, noticing the guests of honor would soon be introduced with a brief ceremony and announcement before dinner.

Jane looked to the entrance, wondering where her fiancé might be. She pulled out her cellular phone before the meals made their way around, trying Clouse's number, and getting no response.

"Where's Dad?" Zach asked, seated beside her.

"He'll be here, Zach," she answered, not wanting to worry him.

She refused to outwardly show her concern because of the children.

Jane considered walking outside to ask Kaiser for his home phone number, or to call his wife and see if Clouse ever stopped by, but she spied him walking inside with a uniformed officer.

Daniels seemed to recognize the uniform of dark green adorned with tan patches because he raised a skeptical eyebrow.

"Who is that?" Jane inquired.

"He's a conservation officer," Daniels replied. "They patrol the roads sometimes, but their primary responsibility is the state parks and lakes."

The last part about the lakes caused Jane to stiffen slightly since Clouse had taken the boat out on Lake Monroe. She figured there had to be a reasonable explanation why a conservation officer showed up unannounced to the dinner.

"Do you know him?" she asked Daniels.

"Nope."

Both continued to stare at the duo beside the door until Kaiser pointed toward their table and Jane in particular.

"Oh, no," Jane said as the two motioned to her to join them outside the atrium in the hallway.

"Go ahead," Cindy told her. "I'll watch the kids a minute."

Collecting herself and her purse, she stood, walking as discreetly as possible toward the exit. As Jane drew closer, she saw Kaiser look away toward the floor beside him as the conservation officer took a deep breath with a grim look in his eyes. He appeared a veteran of his department, and most conservation officers with seniority transferred to the southern part of the state because it was an ideal retirement area. Regardless of his experience, the officer seemed unable to contain the unhappy emotion painted across his face.

"What is it?" Jane asked, looking back and forth between the two.

"Ma'am, I'm afraid I have some bad news for you," the officer said.

Chapter 5

Above the crowd of people in the atrium, Lucas Rexford made use of the mirror inside Room 404. As a descendant of Charles Rexford, one half of the hotel's husband and wife management team after the turn of the 20th century, he was invited by Dr. Smith to attend the hotel's ceremonial dinner and reopening as a guest of honor.

Though he held no direct ties with the hotel or grounds, his name was important to anyone who knew its history. Smith wanted the ceremony to be much more than just a focus on the new hotel. He wanted historical value added, and with that in mind, he invited numerous descendants of various figureheads from the hotel's past. Smith paid their travel and hotel fare just to bring them to Southern Indiana for his gala.

A dentist in Chicago, Rexford found it easy to make time for the dinner. He knew about the hotel and his link to it from childhood, when his mother told him stories. Though not a direct descendent of Charles Rexford, like a grandson, the dentist was the best Smith could come up with for a relation. It gave him an excuse to take a week off work to travel to the hotel he heard so much about growing up.

Most of the rooms were completely bare of furniture, though sinks, tubs, and mirrors were installed, waiting for the larger pieces to come. Rexford marveled at the detail given to each room's trim work. From below, the people never saw the completed product they were missing. That was part of Smith's plan to sell them on spending a night to see for themselves. The grand reopening would not take place for another few weeks, and by then, everything would be in place.

Outside the room was a mounted balcony painted dark green to match the wall trim. Select rooms had balconies, once used for guests to appear and wave, or simply look down upon the atrium's nightly events. In its day, the hotel drew events every evening. Circuses, seminars, large group meetings, concerts, and many other spectacles convened within its walls.

Rexford peered into the mirror, adjusting the black bow tie to his tuxedo. He could have used the downstairs bathroom, but Smith had a plan for each special guest to appear on a third floor balcony for all to see before dinner. He had a few minutes before the doctor took the microphone, giving his guests their cues.

Being in a large, empty room felt creepy, especially with no furniture, and an echo from every little noise he made. He looked around, seeing nothing but the closet door opened just a crack next to the curtains. The curtains, currently wide-open, could be drawn to cover the glass window and the door to the room's balcony.

As Rexford returned his attention to his tie, they did exactly that.

***

"Please tell me what is going on," Jane demanded, more than asked, of either officer standing at the threshold of the atrium.

"This is Bill Schrader," Kaiser informed her, trying to stall for time.

Jane gave a perplexed sigh.

"Was your husband boating at Lake Monroe this afternoon?" the conservation officer asked.

"Yes."

Jane decided not to mention she wasn't married, because that would only take up more time.

"We had a lakeside resident report the sinking of a boat late this afternoon," the officer informed her. "By the time we arrived the boat was nearly completely beneath the surface but we were able to identify it before it sank." He paused a moment, letting Jane absorb the notion of what she knew was coming. "There was apparently foul play because the boat had several holes punched in the bottom."

"Paul's boat?" she asked nervously, not sure what to expect.

Schrader nodded.

"Where is he?" she asked.

"He's missing," Kaiser said, trying to soften the words, his expression showing he felt Schrader had acted too insensitively.

"We believe someone may have sunk the boat to cover up-"

"No," Jane stopped Schrader short. "If there's no body, you can't believe that," she said frantically, beginning to break down.

As their conversation drew the attention of more than a few guests, Kaiser led Jane further down the hallway, followed by the conservation officer.

"They're looking for him, Jane," Kaiser stated. "But it doesn't look good. Paul's truck was still parked at the dock with his cell phone and briefcase still inside."

"I won't believe it," she replied, ignoring most every spoken word now. "I can't believe it."

"I'm not giving up either," the county officer said. "Paul's tough. He's been through a lot before. They'll find him."

At the bottom of the lake, Schrader seemed to think based on the strange expression crossing his face.

"What can you tell me?" Jane demanded of the officer.

"I was patrolling the lake when I received a call about a sinking boat," Schrader began. "I was able to don my scuba gear and examine the boat before it fell beneath the surface."

He seemed to hesitate.

"And?" Jane insisted.

"There were punctures on the boat's underside. They looked intentional."

Jane sighed nervously, trying to steady her jittery hands by cupping her mouth. Her body felt flush and numb at the same time. Kaiser tried leading her to a nearby chair but she wanted none of it, gently tugging her elbow from his hand.

She simply wanted answers.

"Was there any trace of Paul? Any at all?"

"No," Schrader said slowly. "But we consider that a good thing. Several divers relieved me so I could come out here, and so far as I know, they've found nothing."

Everyone stood awkwardly a moment, apparently unsure of what to say next.

"What's going on?" Daniels asked, finally wheeling himself out of the atrium, apparently to see where Jane had disappeared to.

He likely suspected a conservation officer was out of place at the dinner and wanted to know exactly what they were talking about.

"Hey, Mark," Kaiser said quickly, since the two had met through Clouse. "Paul's boat sunk in Lake Monroe and he hasn't been seen since he left home."

"Oh, no," Daniels gasped. "What do we have to go on?"

Before Kaiser could answer, Schrader shot him a questioning stare.

"It's okay," Kaiser told the conservation officer. "He's Bloomington Police."

"Oh."

"Both the county police and state organizations have divers combing the lake in search of clues to the boat sinking or, God forbid, a body. All of Paul's belongings are still in his truck, and it was found near the marina."

Daniels drew a deep breath.

"Not good," he said before looking to Jane beside him, his wincing face making it obvious he regretted the statement immediately.

Jane, however, felt shock settling into her body, knowing Clouse might very well be settled at the bottom of the lake near his boat. She could not think of any reason why he would not contact her unless he felt her life, or perhaps his own, was still in danger. No one came to mind who would want to sink the boat or bring harm to Clouse.

She felt completely helpless as she walked away from the group to think a moment.

***

Rexford stopped fidgeting with his tie, turning around to find the curtains almost completely drawn. With his cue coming in less than a minute, that would not do. He needed an open path to the framed glass door to step onto the balcony. He also wished to remain obscured from view below until his cue came, per Smith's instructions, so he dared not center himself while drawing them open.

Wondering why the curtains seemed to change positions, or if he was just imagining it, Rexford walked along the back wall toward the drawstring, located near the closet door. As he approached the string, hidden far enough behind the curtain that no one inside the atrium could see him, Rexford heard the first guest of honor's name called.

"Damn," he thought aloud, trying to hurry his pace.

As he reached for the string, the closet door sprung open, revealing a spray nozzle shoved only inches from his face before a stream of gasoline squirted forward, squarely embedding itself in his eyes and face, burning as it blinded him. Rexford screamed aloud when the gasoline struck, his cries muffled by the applause and laughter of the people in the atrium. One of his fellow guests of honor took a bow, amusing the crowd, across the atrium at a different balcony.

He stumbled back to the center of the room unaware of how many times his attacker went about spraying him as his body became drenched in the chemical liquid. Rexford moaned and whimpered, giving the occasional verbal obscenity during the process. The stinging in his eyes was unbearable, and there was little hope of finding his way to the bathroom to wash the chemical from them, even if he felt safe enough to do so.

What seemed like an eternity of blindness played out in less than a minute as Smith kept the guests distracted outside, calling various names as the guests of honor each took a turn from their balcony, waving and smiling for the dinner guests below. As the floor and Rexford reeked of gasoline, the attacker struck a match, setting the hapless guest ablaze, giving him a swift kick toward the glass door leading out to the balcony, ironically as Smith called Rexford's name.

***

An agonizing scream pierced the soft music in the background and any noise the guests made as they whispered at their tables. Everyone swiftly looked around the atrium, then up, in an effort to discover the disruption's origin.

To the surprise of the crowd below, Rexford smashed through the glass door as all eyes turned his way. Everyone gasped as a living ball of fire burst through the glass, onto the balcony. Instantly, horror fixated itself in the guests as they realized the inferno would not stop there. Rexford stumbled toward the edge of the balcony, toppling over the railing.

He fell a short distance through a table where he continued to incinerate. The sizzle of his body reminded many of a campfire, but the odor of burning flesh nauseated everyone nearby until one guest regained composure enough to grab a fire extinguisher and put him out.

"Oh, God," Kaiser said, rushing into the atrium too late, looking up to Room 404 and the broken glass, before charging into the hallway.

He assessed the situation quicker than anyone else deciding what happened to Rexford was no accident. He also knew whoever caused the damage might still be on the fourth floor, or trying to escape. The county officer took the closest flight of stairs, rushing upstairs to search for the perpetrator, or a witness.

Reaching the fourth floor about thirty seconds later, he found nothing to his left or right down the rounded hallway.

"Shit," he muttered, knowing how easily someone might have used one of several other stairwells to head downstairs, easily fitting into the crowd.

In the chaos below, everyone was standing and surrounding the body. Drawing his duty weapon, he began a necessary, but futile search for the assailant, heading directly for the room where the murder originated. He possessed a master key to each room, but he doubted the killer had the same means. Escaping the hotel wasn't going to be a difficult feat, even with heightened security, so the deputy figured he needed to find the killer quickly or lose him in the confusion.

Kaiser didn't see any rooms with an open door on his way to the room where Rexford had been biding his time. Taking a quick peek inside, Kaiser was greeted by a strong, horrid odor crossing his nose. He retreated to the hallway, realizing the killer had not remained inside. Odors of gasoline and burnt flesh followed him like a stalker, but he soon left them behind. Hoping he guessed the direction correctly, because the circular hallway led directly to other means of egress, Kaiser picked up his pace.

He checked each door as he walked, making certain it was locked, his firearm readily clutched in his right hand. After the events of the previous October, Kaiser refused to take any chances. He nearly died once defending his friend, and the thought of someone ruining the West Baden Springs Hotel's reputation once more crossed his mind.

Detecting a noise down the hall a few seconds later, he ran down to check it, and found the conservation officer reaching the top of the nearest flight of stairs. Obviously thinking along the same lines as Kaiser, the officer had chosen a different set of stairs to check. Both realized their search was futile, and over, because the killer had already slipped into the crowd of hundreds below.

Chapter 6

Daniels felt groggy the next morning at work. He continually yawned from the lack of rest two hours of sleep had provided. After Lucas Rexford was pronounced dead at the hotel, guests were stuck there until local and state investigators questioned everyone. In the meantime, Jane Brooks grew more discontent dealing with her fiancé's disappearance. She wanted to head to the lake in case any new developments were discovered.

Fortunately, nothing more of Clouse was found, leaving the dim hope he might still be alive. Last, he knew, Jane planned to take the day off from work and remain at the lake in the hope of an answer, good or bad. She made arrangements during the long wait for the kids to stay with her mother. Daniels thought she performed magnificently with them, not letting on for a moment that anything might be wrong. She left several times, however, to be alone and out of their view. He recalled seeing her on the phone in tears several times, doing her best to remain strong by keeping her emotions away from others.

So far as Daniels knew, the investigation into Rexford's death led nowhere. The murderer might easily have been an uninvited guest who attended in the correct attire, killed the man, and slipped into the crowd, escaping later without notice. Daniels knew of no one missing from the party, although several people failed to show for the dinner. The police would check them for alibis later.

Luckily, the morning proved more mundane than usual. Daniels occasionally fielded a call, then found time to daydream about returning to work on the streets. Already, he felt forgotten by his old mates. Seldom did they stop in to joke with him like they used to, his name was never mentioned in the circles it once was, and the chief was already talking to his assistants about filling Daniels' position on the force if he didn't show improvement soon. All that after the chief nominated his detective for officer of the year and grabbed all the kudos when Daniels won.

"I'll be back," Daniels said to one of the other dispatchers before wheeling himself toward the public restroom of the courthouse, which required a detour outside because the dispatch center was isolated in a basement.

Overall, things looked bad for Daniels.

Taking the trip to the hotel didn't seem to help in the least. While he was there, Daniels fell asleep during the early morning hours, waking an hour later to the recurring dream of being shot in the back. Nothing troubled him more than waking in a cold sweat with heavy, uncontrolled breathing, and the knowledge that he was still disabled.

Clouse, the only person who had stuck with him through his ordeal, was nowhere to be found. Daniels refused to envision him turning up dead, but at the same time, there seemed little alternative, given the circumstances. It plagued him to think Rexford's death and the fireman's disappearance might be connected, but after what he'd experienced the year prior, nothing was impossible.

His thoughts wandered to Clouse, and where the man might be. Throughout the night he watched Kaiser and Jane fret about where he might have gone, while overhearing others speculate how Clouse might have somehow been involved with Rexford's murder. Daniels knew better, but remained quiet, numbed at the thought another murder spree might be in its early stages.

Daniels struggled to pull the bathroom door open and wheel himself inside. He still faced the battle of lifting himself from the chair to the toilet, pulling down his pants without complete use of his legs, then reversing the process before returning to work.

Somehow, he managed to complete the task within a reasonable amount of time, hearing someone else step into the bathroom in the meantime.

Whoever took up the stall beside him sneezed uncontrollably several times, sniffling deeply, intermittently. Daniels listened a bit more intently than usual, hearing no unzipping of pants or drawing of toilet paper to blow a nose. He felt his chest tighten from apprehension as his heartbeat escalated, pounding hard enough that he felt its thumps. Being confined to a wheelchair made him much more aware of his surroundings. He often found it injurious if he wasn't.

And it appeared someone was waiting for him.

Unsure of exactly what to do, Daniels hesitated a moment before opening the stall door, deciding no one else was going to come into the usually frequented restroom. Whoever waited in the neighboring stall probably noticed his indecision, but the officer planned to wheel clear of the person and avoid contact if possible.

He failed.

Before Daniels could even clear his own stall, a solid hand cupped his mouth as someone yanked his chair back far enough to tip it back, landing him on his back, though his assailant cushioned the fall with his other hand.

"You know, the last twenty-four hours I've had nothing to do but think," Paul Clouse said, looming directly over the officer, before releasing a sneeze to his side, keeping one hand over Daniels' mouth a moment more. A hint of temporary insanity seemed to gleam from one of his blue eyes, which were bloodshot from a lack of sleep. "Gives a guy a lot of time to think about who he really trusts and who might want him dead. And I don't know who I can trust now," he said, slowly releasing his hand.

"What the hell happened to you, Paul? Everyone thinks you're at the bottom of the lake."

"I was," the fireman admitted. "I got whacked twice upside my head, fell in, and woke up later, around dark, on the shore beside the lake," he relayed the story in as monotone a voice as Daniels could ever recall, as though the events still crucified the corners of his mind.

"Why did you wait so long to let someone know?" Daniels asked with his usual tone of interrogation.

Clouse gave Daniels a look of distrust.

"Mark, you were one of two people I told about the boat yesterday. I doubt Jane told anyone I was out there, and I hope to God you didn't."

Daniels propped himself to his elbows, knowing Clouse wasn't about to let him up by the way he loomed directly over the officer. He was happy his friend was alive, but not about the man's doubt in him.

"I may have mentioned it to Cindy," Daniels admitted. "I'm not even sure I did that."

"You sure?"

Daniels nodded.

"I'm positive. Now let me the fuck up," he added with a light push to his friend's chest.

Clouse sneezed again to the side, showing the effects of the lake on him. Daniels noticed how ragged he looked, though fully dry. His hair appeared far more disheveled than usual with a dried blood spot on one side matting some of it. A foul smell accompanied Clouse with his return to civilization that only the murky lake might have provided.

"So where have you been?" Daniels asked as his friend finally helped him into his chair, standing it upright.

"Well, my keys are fifty feet underwater so I had no truck," Clouse replied. "I also had no cell phone, or change for a payphone. I wanted to question both you and Jane before I let anyone else know I was alive because obviously I'm not supposed to be."

"How did you wind up on shore? Lake Monroe doesn't exactly have tides and beaches."

"Someone had to have pulled me out," Clouse said. "I don't know who or why, but someone got me out of there. And I'm sorry I haven't been very trusting, but someone did almost kill me."

"I understand."

Daniels felt one of his legs twitch involuntarily. He wondered if the fall had prompted it to accidentally kick. It sometimes happened to him when he was lying in bed.

"So how do you know your boat sank?" he asked, wheeling toward the door.

"The fact that it was gone when I woke up, and this morning's paper," Clouse replied, wheeling his friend toward the door. "I found a lot of time to read this morning, and to think. I understand I missed quite a dinner last night."

"Well, the main course wasn't quite what we expected," Daniels replied as Clouse held the door open for him.

"Do you think it's happening again?" Clouse asked the inevitable question.

Daniels said nothing, just shaking his head.

"I'm going to find out who's investigating the case and see if I can get some answers. Maybe they'll let me help as a consultant because of last year."

Clouse shrugged.

"Can't hurt to try. We need to know what's going on because it's no coincidence I get whacked in the head and that guy winds up dead at a hotel function."

"I'll take the rest of the day off and see what I can dig up," the officer said. "You better fetch Jane from lakeside and let everyone know you're still among us."

Clouse rubbed the side of his head, sneezed, and quickly recovered.

"Yeah. Then I'll sleep for a couple days."

Chapter 7

After talking to a friend of a friend, Daniels discovered a state police detective by the name of McCabe was assigned the case of finding Rexford's murderer. He was from the Bloomington district, so it was easy for Daniels to arrange a meeting with him by that evening. He learned the detective had a favorite haunt after work every night in a predominantly Irish bar called Kelley's, where the nationality was also the theme.

Daniels wheeled inside the door, finding the pub filled with lively music and chatter. He counted more men with red hair than he'd ever seen in one building. Many owned the shining eyes the officer had read about in fable, but he figured most of those were from too many import ales. He knew Kansas City and Chicago had bars dedicated to nationalities, but he never dreamed of it in Bloomington.

For some reason, it worked.

Constructed of old wood, the tavern looked somewhat like a hunting lodge with a mounted deer head along one wall, and torches set about shoulder level along the sides. They were lit by bulbs that looked like flames to avoid any fire hazards, but the fireplace and candles on each table were certainly real.

Daniels' eyes panned the pub for a man who fit the profile of a police detective. Daniels knew too well how to play the part after his stint in Bloomington's investigative division.

Before the shooting.

He felt his right leg twitch again as he searched and quickly held it down forcibly with both hands. The involuntary movements showed his legs were ready to move again, but he wanted to look completely in control when he met McCabe.

Just as he spied a man drinking alone at a table set near a window, the man looked up from his green bottle, smiled, and waved Daniels over.

As he wheeled up, Daniels quickly assessed the detective.

With full head of rustic-brown hair and brown eyes of a creamed coffee tint, the detective remained in dress pants with a plain white dress shirt and loosened tie. His shoulder holster cupped his armpits, looking rather tight against the wrinkly dress shirt. Barely average in height, the man looked stocky, almost like an immovable tank. What little beer belly he owned remained tucked beneath the shirt. McCabe did not appear grossly muscular, but his natural size was enough to keep even remotely intelligent pests away.

"Turlough Casey McCabe," he said, standing to introduce himself boisterously. Daniels assumed everyone in the bar already knew him by his outgoing nature as the two quickly shook hands. "Friends call me Terry or Tug."

"Mark Daniels," the chaired officer countered, unsure of which to call the man.

By the look in the detective's eyes, Daniels assessed he was past his first beer. There was also a slight stagger in the way he stood, but McCabe held liquor remarkably well from what friends told Daniels that morning.

"So I understand you might be able to help me on this new case I've got," McCabe said in a more reserved manner once he sat down. Daniels wasn't positive, but he thought he perceived a hint of Irish tongue in the way the man spoke.

"Before I get to that, why are you investigating the case instead of the detective in Jasper?" Daniels inquired, referring to the state police post closer to Orange County.

"Their investigator is off for heart surgery, so it fell to me."

Daniels nodded in understanding.

"Have you read the reports about the incident last year?" he asked.

"I have. Most interesting it was," the detective said before finishing off the mug. He motioned to a server for another. "Make it two," he said when she arrived, nodding toward Daniels. "Keep the change," he said, tucking a ten-dollar bill into her change pouch.

"What sort of name is Turlough?" Daniels felt compelled to ask.

McCabe flashed a toothy smile.

"If you haven't guessed, I'm big into my heritage," he said. "Turlough is a Celtic name meaning 'broad-shouldered.' In English, it's translated Terence."

"And it reads Turlough on your birth certificate?"

"Yes, sir," McCabe answered. "My mother says she nearly beat my father to death for it, but he wanted his son to have an authentic Irish name on that piece of paper. Even my middle name, Casey, has a meaning of watchful or vigilant. That came from my uncle. I guess Dad knew how to pick fitting names, even at the risk of his own life."

Daniels grinned. He immediately took to McCabe's outgoing personality, though he personally remained reserved around other people. He also realized the man possessed brains enough to sell anyone on what he believed.

"How far up does the family tree go in America?" he asked, now curious about the man's heritage, since he was, in essence, surrounded by it.

"Been here five generations. Great-great-grandfather was a cop in New York City in the early 1900's. Now a couple thousand miles away and a century later I'm doing the same thing. You could say it runs in the family."

"That's neat," Daniels said with a genuine nod.

He sat back in his chair, taking in the sounds of violin, accordion, and drumbeats that combined for a unique Celtic melody. He understood why people wanted to visit this bar once they discovered it. The atmosphere was authentic and unblemished. There was no distracting television, no blaring jukebox, and no parlor games in the background.

Only food, conversation, and fine spirits created the atmosphere, and everyone he saw truly seemed content being there.

"You know, you seem familiar," McCabe noted. "Without the beard you look like the guy I saw in a publication last month."

"Officer of the Year?" Daniels asked, like it was no big deal.

"Yeah," the detective said, a smile of realization crossing his face. "Goddamn, I never put it together. You're the one who investigated that ordeal last year and got shot. The reports don't mention very much of that. They focus more on some guy they were investigating the whole time who got cleared." McCabe stopped a moment to take it all in. "Wow."

"That's what I thought, too."

"I heard you lost your partner," the alcohol prompted the detective to say. His expression showed he regretted the statement before the words finished spilling out. "I didn't mean to, uh..."

"It's okay," Daniels said. "Let's just say last year will never make my top ten."

"Let's get down to business before I say something else stupid," McCabe suggested. "So exactly how do you want to help me on this thing?"

"If what happened to that man last night has any relation to what occurred last year, it needs to be stopped now before more people get slaughtered."

McCabe sipped his beer, his expression showing he wasn't convinced by the statement.

"That seems like a bold statement based on one single murder that wasn't done in the style of those perpetrated last year."

"I'm just saying *if* it has any ramifications from last year. I was in your shoes at the time, and it's not something I care to go through again."

"What do you suggest?"

"Right now I'm stuck dispatching until I finish rehabilitation on my legs. I want out of there in the worst way, and I can be a fantastic information source for you."

McCabe thought a moment, tapping his beer bottle with two fingers.

"I want your help unofficially if nothing else," he finally said. "I'll talk to my supervisor and see what we can do. From the sounds of it, your department won't have trouble loaning you out."

"Is it possible to see the room where it happened?"

"Sure," McCabe shrugged. "There's really nothing to see though. We know he was doused with gasoline by someone, set afire, and shoved off the balcony. Not much to it."

"Any ideas why it was him in particular?"

"We're checking into it. Seems someone went through his hotel room and his belongings. The only thing odd was a small jewelry case with nothing inside. We sent it to the lab for analysis but there was nothing in the room or on Rexford that might have been inside that box. He wasn't wearing anything but a watch and there were no loose articles in the hotel room."

Daniels thought a moment, taking a drink of the unusually strong brew. His eyes widened as his throat tingled. Since starting his rehabilitation, he hadn't touched a drop of alcohol, so his body was a bit unprepared for McCabe's choice in drink.

"Could it have been something other than jewelry?"

"Sure, but we won't know what until we get lab results or his family tells us something. We couldn't reach his wife from the office today. We think she's out of town too."

Daniels finished off his beer rather quickly, deciding it best to get home. He needed rest from the night before, and driving with his condition was no easy task.

Using hand-controlled metal bars was far worse than any driving simulation game he'd ever played. Though his feet were mobile, Daniels could not count on his legs to respond in time for emergency braking, or even to keep consistent speed with the gas pedal.

Professional installation of such bars in his car kept Cindy free to be with the kids, rather than taking Daniels everywhere he needed to be. He drove to work, the hospital, or any fast food drive-thru alone. They were also removable if she needed use of his vehicle.

"Give me a holler tomorrow," he told McCabe, handing him a business card.

"Will do. Either way, you'll hear from me."

Daniels headed for the door, taking in the sounds of musical melodies he would only hear at such a tavern. He rather enjoyed the change of pace there, understanding why McCabe relished his heritage.

Chapter 8

While Clouse lay in bed, his fiancée tended to his wounds, particularly the gash on the side of his head where blood matted his hair after drying into a clump. The warmth of the sheets and two blankets that covered him felt good, but his body shivered, sometimes going numb from so much time spent in the water and cold air.

After speaking with investigators at the Monroe County Sheriff's Depart-ment, he called her cellular phone and told her just the basic facts before she picked him up. She was relieved, of course, but also a bit perturbed he hadn't made contact sooner. For that matter the sheriff's office wasn't thrilled either, after having divers from numerous departments searching the lake for his remains.

Jane gave him what limited outward affection she could without hurting him when they reunited, temporarily forgetting about being upset with him. She drove him home, silent most of the way, which he hoped was her trying to let him rest rather than giving him the cold shoulder. For the last several hours, Clouse had slept as best he could under Jane's orders.

"You should have called me sooner," Jane scolded him, sitting on the side of the bed. "I prayed and prayed you weren't at the bottom of that lake."

"I had to protect you," he said. "Whoever wanted me dead might come after me here if he thought I was still alive."

Luckily, Jane had put off some supplemental interviews from the police until the morning, also taking care of other matters. Clouse was excused from work until he felt able to return. His disappearance was everywhere in the news, drawing speculation from everyone who knew about the past year's events about what might happen. Everyone assumed he was dead, and Clouse might have thought the same if not for some anonymous help.

"I can't believe someone wanted to kill you," Jane said, carefully washing the matted spot in his hair, treating the dried sore with peroxide on a cotton ball.

"Ouch, doc," he told her, feeling the sting of the medicine. "It's kind of cool not having to leave the house for a doctor's excuse," Clouse added, chuckling a bit until it literally hurt.

"Take it easy," she told him. "You're going to need lots of rest to fight off the effects of the lake. Don't even think about leaving this bed until I say you can."

"Yes, ma'am," he replied with a weak smile, growing more tired every second. Jane left the room a moment, probably to fetch something for him.

Sleep had almost overtaken him when Zach tiptoed into the room, as though doing so behind Jane's back. It was the first time he had truly seen his son since returning home, and he felt somewhat uncomfortable letting Zach see him bedridden.

"Jane says you're sick," his son informed him.

"I am," Clouse said with an uncontrolled yawn. "I went for a swim and I shouldn't have."

"It's kinda cold, Dad."

"Yeah, I know." Clouse rubbed a hand through Zach's hair. His son quickly replaced it with a swipe of his own hand. "Were you worried about me?"

"I knew you'd be okay. Something cool happened at the dinner last night."

"I heard. Better not let Jane hear you talk about that."

"About what?" his fiancée asked, returning to the room, carrying a bowl of soup.

"Nothing," both replied simultaneously.

"Good night, Dad," Zach said, scurrying out of the room before he was told to.

"Night, Zach," Clouse called back.

Jane sat on the edge of the bed again pushing Clouse's head back lightly. He recognized the smell of homemade chicken broth, then saw actual chunks of breast meat.

"My mother made this and brought it over while you were sleeping," Jane informed him. "She says to get well soon."

"This will help," he noted. "Please thank her for me."

He shivered as the broth warmed his insides, making him feel even colder externally. His body ached for rest and warmth. Clouse hoped to feel better in the morning, but the chances of that were slim.

He would wait and see.

***

After managing his way inside, Daniels wheeled quietly through the kitchen, trying to remain quiet. He suspected Cindy and the kids were all asleep, though the baby occasionally kept them up at night.

Daniels despised his modified driving, but it beat keeping Cindy from being his personal servant. Neither of them wanted that, and the injured officer made the best of his situation. He never wanted to fully adapt to being in a chair for fear that adaption meant complacency. Daniels fought feeling comfortable in the chair, knowing he was physically capable of walking.

As he entered the living room, one of the chair's wheels hit a doll left beside the doorway, which acted like a doorstop, hurling Daniels forward, out of the chair.

"Damn," he cursed under his breath after an initial cry of pain.

Positioned on his arms and knees, the officer remained perfectly still a moment, assessing something new to him.

He looked down at his knees behind him, realizing the few times he'd fallen out of the chair he landed sprawled out. As though unsure of what to do, Daniels stared at his knees a moment, wondering if he dared chance standing the rest of the way.

Without taking his eyes off it, he drew his right knee toward his torso slowly, as much as it would freely move. It took several minutes, but he drew it close enough that he finally placed the foot flat on the ground, in a position prepared for standing.

Daniels felt his right leg going numb from being bent for so long, so he decided to hurry the process along, taking in a few deep breaths before attempting to move his left leg for a wider base, before he tried standing.

He gained the wide base, felt his muscles tense for the first time in months, and pushed upward with what little muscle strength his right leg could muster. He grunted and groaned from pain as the underused leg attempted to straighten, but he only gained a few more vertical inches before the leg gave out and he collapsed to a sprawled position on the floor, just as he was accustomed to.

Though he tried to contain himself, Daniel let out several curse words under his breath. He was beyond sick and tired of failing at when he tried to walk. Nearly ready to sell his soul to walk again and return his life to normal, the former detective balled one hand into a fist, then thought better of beating down his floor.

Almost in tears from sheer frustration, Daniels dragged the chair over to him, pounding his fist squarely in the seat before deciding just to crawl to bed. He could brush his teeth and take care of other hygiene essentials in the morning. For now, he just wanted to sleep and dream about walking again.

After lying in bed several minutes, Daniels quit berating himself, realizing what a significant leap he'd found toward his recovery. Though still angry with himself, he felt for the first time in a long time walking might prove possible.

He fell asleep with a sense of hope lingering over him.

Chapter 9

Daniels found himself in the break room pouring himself a cup of coffee on his first break. A specially ordered desk held all of the snacks and condiments, assembled at just the correct height for employees confined to wheelchairs. The soda and snack machines offered nothing Daniels cared for, and the odor of a burnt coffee pot from earlier in the morning lingered in the air, almost nauseating him.

The former detective had noticed several new modifications made in city hall and the dispatch center since his return to work. He vowed to never complain about special disability privileges again.

"So you met Tug," Deputy Chief Randy Collins said, walking into the room.

"That I did," Daniels answered with some indifference.

A moment passed while the deputy chief poured himself a cup of coffee, adding sugar and cream before drinking some.

"I worked with him several years ago on a homicide," Collins noted. "We had a murdered girl found in a swamp."

The deputy chief paused a moment, looking outside the window at the parking lot below. Daniels figured the man was thinking back to the days when he wasn't confined to a windowless office, dealing with criminals rather than internal problems.

"She was a mess, covered with algae and fly shit, but we identified her based on missing persons reports. It took us a month or two, but we tracked down her scumbag ex-boyfriend and arrested him."

"What was his story?" Daniels inquired.

"A lover's quarrel I guess," Collins said with a shrug. "She didn't have any money or insurance, so it had to be a spur of the moment thing."

Daniels sat quietly a moment, wondering where this was leading.

"Quite a flighty guy," Collins commented.

"How do you mean?" Daniels inquired, uncertain of whether the man meant McCabe or the arrested murderer.

"You talked to him, didn't you?"

"Sure."

"Tug has a tendency to change a subject faster than you can blink."

Daniels gave a perplexed stare that told he knew nothing of what Collins spoke.

"Oh, he must have been drinking," the chief corrected himself. "If Tug drinks, and he does often, you'll see a cool, collected side of him."

"Sounds like you know him well," Daniels said, understanding the situation now.

"Six months we worked on that case. You get to know people pretty well that way."

Collins paused.

"Been married three times, Tug has."

"He's my age," Daniels commented, a bit surprised.

"He's just carefree about life in general except his job. His work is most of his life, and it consumes him. I don't think he's meant to settle into anything."

Daniels wondered exactly what Collins meant, but ignored the remark, figuring he would find out for himself in due time. He picked a donut from a box, toying with it a moment before speaking.

"Anything else you want to tell me about him?"

"Terrible sense of direction," the deputy chief said with a squeamish look. "Once he's been somewhere, it's etched in his mind, but the first time getting there is rough."

"Interesting," Daniels commented, "but I take it you're not here to talk about old times."

"No," Collins said. "Tug called the chief today asking to borrow you for his latest assignment."

"And?" Daniels inquired with an unblinking stare.

"And, based on your experience with the West Baden Springs Hotel last year and a push from myself to get you doing some real police work again for your own betterment, he reluctantly agreed. You're free to work with him as soon as he's ready for you, but only as a consultant, so don't be carrying a firearm or wearing your badge."

Daniels nodded, cautious not to outwardly show his happiness.

"You're on the bubble, Mark," Collins warned, unable to look the former detective in the eye, stirring his coffee instead. "The chief isn't happy that your condition hasn't improved, and he's talking about adding a man from the new recruit list."

"Mandatory retirement in the form of permanent disability?" Daniels asked with a raised eyebrow, suspecting what the deputy chief had in mind.

"That wouldn't necessarily be the case," Collins said, waving off the notion. "But we've been down a man nearly a year now. If you don't get any closer to walking, you may be finding a more accommodating career."

He walked to the door, stopping just long enough to turn with a few parting words.

"I bought you some time, Mark, and the chief has nothing against you, but even the Board of Public Safety has limits to how long they'll allow the city to pay for a police officer who can't carry out his duties."

"I understand," Daniels answered, though openly displeased.

Giving a dismissing wave, the deputy chief departed, leaving the echo of his footsteps down the empty hallway as he went.

"Damn," Daniels said, sighing heavily, looking to the ceiling above before resting his head atop his open hand. "Damn, damn, damn!"

***

Within two hours, McCabe had called Daniels, picked him up, and taken him down to the hotel. Daniels found what the deputy chief warned him about completely true as he fought to stay awake, guiding McCabe to West Baden, then the hotel.

McCabe had no sense of direction.

"You're a trooper?" Daniels commented halfway through the trip.

"Nobody's perfect," McCabe retorted. "I've never patrolled this area before."

Upon their arrival, Rusty Cranor, the project manager, unlocked the hotel's main entrance and led them to the room where the homicide occurred.

"I should probably just give you a key," Cranor commented to Daniels, remembering him as the detective who investigated several murders at the hotel the previous year.

"I certainly know my way around," Daniels replied.

Daniels followed the detective inside as McCabe held the door open for him. He recalled a bit of information Clouse had shared with him about the project manager.

Cranor was near retirement age, but an offer to manage projects for Kieffer Construction, the same company Clouse worked for part-time kept him working at the job he loved. Helping to rebuild the hotel was his career highlight.

His full head of hair was red, peppered with gray hairs, cut shorter than the last time Daniels saw him. Cranor had also trimmed his beard of the same coloration down to a full goatee. He wore blue jeans, steel-toed boots, and a thick, gray sweater like sailors wore to keep the wind from chilling them. It turned out to be a perfect day for such attire.

Though not a scholar, Cranor's intellect in his field gained him the respect of everyone around him. He talked little about history or world events, and seldom much about anything relating to his hometown. But when it came to his business, no one possessed the vocabulary he did. The men working under him learned quickly or found themselves looking for work elsewhere.

"I'll be downstairs putting some stuff away if you need anything," the older man informed them before leaving the room.

Remaining at the doorway, Daniels looked over the room. He could see several charred spots where carpeting and curtains caught fire from the spray of gasoline. The smell of burned flesh lingered in the room despite efforts by the hotel's remodeling crew to air it out.

"We recovered the gasoline spray can and sent it to forensics," McCabe noted aloud. "Doubt anything will come of it because it was burned pretty badly."

He stared at what little overall damage the room had suffered, but Daniels eyed it both warily and curiously.

"There's really nothing to see in here."

"I didn't expect there to be," Daniels said.

"Authorities in Rexford's hometown spoke with his wife and asked her about what might have been in that case. She wasn't sure, but said she'd look into it."

"I'd imagine she's pretty upset," Daniels commented, looking around the room. "I wonder what he possessed that someone might want."

McCabe looked toward him with a perplexed look.

"Almost as though someone knew he was bringing whatever it was from home."

Daniels agreed, but remained quiet a moment.

"So you've been married three times?" he asked as they concluded their inspection of the room.

"Yeah. Guess I'm not one who likes stability."

Daniels grunted to himself, wheeling into the hallway toward the elevator.

"So how about those Pacers?" McCabe asked, changing the subject, living up to his notorious nature.

"There may be another angle to this case," Daniels suggested as McCabe pushed the down button.

"What's that?"

"There's a myth about this hotel and a Jesuit priest named Father Ernest."

"I've heard of it," McCabe said with a nod. "The papers reprinted the shit out of it last year."

"What if burning Rexford was somehow tied into that?"

As the elevator dinged, indicating the car was heading their way the detective rubbed his chin in thought.

"Could be sending a message," McCabe deduced. "If they simply wanted to steal something from him, they could have broken into his hotel room. As a matter of fact, they did."

Both entered the elevator doors as they opened with another ding.

"That's bad news," Daniels said with a blank stare toward the closing doors, his memory filled with horrifying images of the past year.

"How so?" McCabe asked as they were greeted by a first floor view a moment later.

Daniels refused to answer immediately. He recalled the year before when nearly a dozen people paid the ultimate price in the name of sending a message. He hoped no one would ever carry out that agenda again.

"The guy who let us in here," Daniels said before hesitating. "His daughter."

"Oh," McCabe said, letting the tragic end go unstated.

As the two officers passed the office where Cranor filled out paperwork, he gave a wave, which they both returned.

"Thanks," Daniels called. "We'll let ourselves out."

Cranor nodded before returning to the paperwork at his desk.

***

While the detectives exited the hotel, Cranor found himself too engrossed in his work to really care. Sitting at his desk, he had removed his sweater in lieu of warming temperatures, draping it over the back of his chair. His light-colored plaid work shirt provided just enough warmth inside the hotel.

His office, filled with shelving, contained a great deal of the hotel memorabilia from past and present. Several old serving dishes from a century prior lined his shelves, along with blueprints and some family photographs, several of which contained his deceased daughter. Family problems after her death led to Cranor's wife moving out, leaving him an empty house to return to every night. He offered to move out instead, but she refused. She said she didn't want a divorce, at least not yet, but needed some space.

Staring at his wedding band momentarily, he realized a divorce wasn't what he wanted, but life changed after his only child died. Some parents grew closer when their offspring passed away, but Cranor found the opposite happened for him. He simply threw himself into his work at the hotel while his wife kept busy working for a law firm. Neither blamed the other for their sorrow or their lack of effort in their marriage. Both of them simply refused to live a lie, which Cranor found useful as a coping mechanism.

Just when he thought it was impossible, life threw him another curveball. The Indiana Department of Environmental Management had fined his employers nearly one hundred thousand dollars for illegal dumping of paint chips along several rural roads outside of West Baden. The chips, from old paint that contained high levels of lead, were also transported without a legal permit, adding to Cranor's woes. Two of his trusted employees were responsible for the act, though without his permission. Still, he answered for the actions of his subordinates.

Rubbing his head, Cranor worked on a report to his supervisors. Though troublesome for someone who considered himself limited in the English language, the report was better punishment than filling out a resignation.

For two decades, he had worked with Kieffer Construction under three generations of ownership. He worked his way up from laborer to foreman, then to project manager within the past year. Apparently, the company held as much loyalty toward him as he provided them, since he still had a job.

As he fought for the correct wording in a sentence, Cranor heard the door to the adjacent room slam shut. This startled him, considering he was supposed to be the only person left inside the hotel and all of the doors were *already* supposed to be shut.

Bolting from his seat, he scurried to the door, looking both ways for someone down the rounded hallway. Seeing no one, he walked to the office beside his, opening the door.

"Paul?" he called aloud, seeing the lights turned on as he peeked inside. Clouse occasionally came in to update his blueprints, but he always greeted the project manager first.

He now knew Clouse had survived a strange incident at Lake Monroe, which explained his absence from the tragic festivities a few nights prior.

Police suspected his daughter was murdered in this particular office, so when Cranor became project manager he moved to a different space. The thought of stepping into the room where Melissa breathed her last always plagued him, but police could only *speculate* where she was indeed killed the previous year.

As Cranor stepped fully inside, a knotted rope fell over his neck, beginning to tighten almost immediately. He intercepted the rope with his right hand, quickly ducking out of the hangman's noose, thinking it might be a prank by one of his workers.

He was dead wrong.

Whirling to see who was behind the door operating the noose, Cranor barely caught a glimpse of black before a solid fist struck his jaw. He fell to the floor as his attacker jumped down from a chair, immediately laying into his ribs with a swift kick. Feeling the wind knocked from his lungs, Cranor tried to roll out of the way but his attacker was unrelenting, letting the project manager know this was no Halloween seasonal hoax. Grasped by the collar, Cranor felt his body being dragged toward the door, meaning this person meant to hang him.

Cranor instinctively fought back, pulling against the grip as he tried to free his collar from the dark figure's grasp. When that failed, he struck at the gloved hands, drawing the figure close enough to return the favor and strike him along the side of the face. Grunting, the would-be killer released his grip as Cranor fell to the concrete floor on his rump. For the first time he viewed his attacker from top to bottom, seeing the person dressed in some sort of black robe with a hood that covered most of his face. What wasn't covered by the hood still appeared black because some sort of mask covered the assistant's face to the point that Cranor couldn't even guess the person's ethnicity.

Based on eyewitness accounts and stories in the newspapers, he knew this was the same costume worn by the people who caused problems the last year. Cranor also knew he was in mortal danger if he didn't escape or call for help.

When he tried to stand, the assistant kicked him squarely in the side of the head, stunning him enough that he found himself dragged halfway to the noose before he thought clearly enough to resist again. As though anticipating such a move, the darkly clad attacker kicked him in the ribs again without releasing his collar. With nothing around him to reach for that might fend off the grim reaper, Cranor simply reached out with both hands toward the black boots, upending his assailant with a loud thud when the perpetrator joined him on the floor.

From the sound of the grunt accompanying the thud, Cranor confirmed his attacker was male, which he certainly suspected all along. Both men struggled to clear the cobwebs from their minds as Cranor found both his skull and his ribs aching from the physical attacks. He tried to stand, but the robed man returned the favor by sweeping his legs out from under him, sending Cranor crashing to the unforgiving floor. He tried to soften the landing, which resulted in his head meeting the concrete, rendering him semi-conscious.

This time, Cranor could feel his body being dragged but lacked the ability to fight back right away. Only when he felt the hangman's noose slide over his head did he begin to squirm and put up a fight. He was about to try removing it from his neck when the killer yanked on the rope hard from where it was looped over an air duct near the ceiling level. The rope found little resistance from the paint or the edges of the duct, allowing the man in black to yank the project manager completely off the ground before he could fight back.

While his hands instinctively clutched the rope, already embedding itself into the soft flesh of his neck, the unidentified man tugged harder as the rope shifted over the duct. Cranor kicked for dear life, gasping heavily for breath as the noose tightened and the additional pull of the rope nearly crushed his windpipe.

Now croaking desperately for breath, Cranor aimed a few kicks toward the killer, missing badly both times, and expired several seconds later as the last bit of oxygen inside his lungs was forced out. His body fell limp as his struggle for death ended tragically, the killer coldly looking over his prize as it swung from the rope.

Chapter 10

After ordering Clouse to remain in bed for the duration of the day, Jane proceeded to pick Zach up from school, arriving earlier than Clouse usually did.

She checked with the main office, discovering that Zach had a gifted class on the second floor scheduled to finish in a few minutes. Unsure of whether Zach would be looking for her or not, she decided to venture into the classroom and tour the school in the process, since her daughter would start there the following year. Though Katie was considered the same age as Zach, she barely missed the cutoff birth date for kindergarten.

Considering how much Clouse worked with his son at home, and how much his mother had taught him before her death, Jane was not surprised to discover Zach was in gifted classes so soon. Reaching the room number given by the office, Jane knocked, finding a smiling teacher on the other side of the door.

"Hello," Jane said. "I'm here to pick up Zach."

"We haven't met," the woman said. "You must be his mother."

Jane simply smiled, taking a step inside.

"He's just finishing up in there with one of our teaching aides," the teacher said, pointing to a room with a closed door. "I'm Judy Parker," the teacher said, introducing herself.

Jane shook hands, revealing herself as Zach's expected stepmother. While Judy worked with several students, Jane took time to look around.

Several other children were at a table, working on group projects, which appeared fairly complex. She wondered what sort of task Zach was given.

When the door finally opened, she noticed the room behind the emerging Zach encumbered in darkness. Only the outlines of a desk, computer, and someone cleaning up after the activity were visible. Zach smiled when he saw Jane, because his father seldom came upstairs to pick him up, fearing he disrupted the class by showing up unannounced.

"Dad still sick?" he asked her immediately.

"Yes, and I told him to stay in bed."

"Come and look, Jane," he said, taking her hand, pulling her into the main part of the classroom.

He immediately began showing her some of the completed activities on display, the toys, and several of his friends.

Jane was overwhelmed by the amount of student-created projects hanging on the wall, and covering the tables. It seemed unfair that gifted children had all the fun projects to work on.

Between all of this, Jane snuck a peek behind her, seeing a woman leave the darkened room where Zach had been, cutting out the main door. Without so much as a look back or a goodbye to the other teachers, the woman left, as though trying to leave the premises before the flow of students streamed into the hallway.

Perhaps her womanly intuition got the best of her, but Jane suspected the woman was more than running late. Most teachers and aides openly greeted parents while this one seemed to avoid contact with her altogether. Perhaps it was simply a bad day, or maybe the woman just wanted to get home.

"Look at the fishes," Zach said, regaining her attention, leading her to the room's aquarium.

"They're beautiful," she commented, not taking time to correct him on his plural word usage.

She was too curious about exactly what Zach was working on separately from the other children and the identity of his hurried instructor.

***

Following Jane's orders, Clouse remained in bed all morning and afternoon, despite feeling much better. Occasionally cold chills ran through his body, along with a light feeling in his head that came with viruses. He suffered from either a bad cold or flu, or perhaps a touch of pneumonia as Jane figured, but he hated being so inactive. With two jobs that kept him occupied regularly, his current situation felt too mundane to tolerate.

He spent much of the day on the phone, fielding calls from concerned friends and family, along with several from the press seeking interviews about his experience, undoubtedly so they could exaggerate the final product. He declined until he was well enough to see them in person.

Dr. Smith called him, wanting to know how his favorite designer was coming along. Smith, growing more idle with every year that passed, still took the time and effort to contact his employees and check on their well-being. It impressed Clouse that a man rumored to be worth several billion dollars took it upon himself to save a historical landmark in the West Baden Springs Hotel, and keep tabs on the employees there, in a good way.

Smith seemed to understand just how much Clouse had suffered the year before because the experience was partly shared by both men. He said he wanted Clouse healthy to witness and share in the grand reopening of the building. None of the employees ever dreamed it was possible to see such a day, but Smith continued to surprise them all, spending millions of his own dollars to assist the National Preservation Society in rebuilding the only hotel of its kind.

Half an hour passed while Clouse glanced through a public safety catalog, finding a few items he considered ordering, partly to pass the time. He knew eight hundred numbers meant long waits. He sneezed three consecutive times to the side of the bed, causing a headache while adding to the dizzy feeling already swirling inside his head.

Clouse felt rather scruffy, like a bum, because he hadn't shaven since the incident. He missed doing the little things in everyday life, including readying himself for work and playing with Zach outside. If not for Jane's medical background, he might have decided to stay in the hospital. She recommended doing so, but he refused, trusting her completely. Not since childhood had Clouse felt so helpless and ill.

"Damn," he commented to himself, placing a bookmark in the magazine as the phone rang again. "Hello," he answered with a stuffed nose.

"You sound good," his buddy Ken Kaiser said sarcastically from the other end.

"Thanks. Are you calling to let me know you recovered my boat from the bottom of the lake?"

Kaiser chuckled aloud.

"You can dive for the rust deposits in a couple years, pal," the county officer said. He turned serious for a moment. "The divers did find something weird, though, Paul."

"What's that?"

"The boat's ignition key was still in place. Did you say your other keys were on a ring with it?"

"Yeah, Ken. It was a pretty solid ring. They should have all been together," Clouse replied, hoping to get his other keys back.

"They were gone."

Silence filled both ends of the line for several seconds.

"They could have broke off on impact," the officer suggested.

"No, Ken. They were on there pretty snug."

Both knew what the implications were if the keys were missing.

"So someone could have my keys," Clouse said it aloud, knowing that 'someone' would probably be his attempted murderer.

"Might want to change your locks," Kaiser suggested.

"Thanks," Clouse said with a sharp tongue, already knowing it was a must. Despite his position, Kaiser was little help to him.

"One other thing," the officer noted. "We found evidence in the propeller that your boat didn't get tangled up. Someone basically made certain it ran into a cluster of thick plants, as though a whole patch of that shit was deliberately set there."

"How so?"

"The divers found traces of what was either tape or some sort of strap used to keep the plants together until they housed themselves into your motor."

"No wonder it stopped so quick."

"Hate to cut you off, buddy, but I've got to get to work," Kaiser said. "I'll call you later."

"Okay. Thanks, Ken," Clouse said slowly, realizing how badly someone wanted him stranded in the middle of the lake.

He hung up the phone, picked up his catalog, and read only a few minutes more before the phone rang again.

"Now what?" Clouse wondered aloud before answering. "Hello?"

He instantly recognized the sound of traffic in the background.

Pay phone.

"Paul Clouse?"

"Speaking," he answered, figuring another reporter wanted a scoop, though the man on the other end sounded nervous.

"I have to speak with you," the man said in a matter-of-fact tone, sounding like that of a young man.

"About what?"

"I have information about who tried to kill you."

Clouse's attention belonged to the caller as his body tensed.

"What sort of information?"

"Who wants you dead and why? I know who laid an oar upside your head."

For a moment, Clouse thought it might be a joke until the caller mentioned the specific nature of how he was knocked overboard.

"When can we meet?" he asked.

"Soon," the man answered nervously. "I'll find you when the time is right."

"How do I know you're not putting me on?" Clouse questioned.

"I'm the one who pulled you from the lake," the answer came, followed by a click.

Clouse held the phone, staring at it. Even after the buzzing sound and dial tone followed, he stared at it, stunned by what he had just learned. Several things flooded his mind to ponder, but it felt like too much. His headache worsened, and Clouse decided to lie back, letting the world around him pass by until Jane returned.

***

As the late afternoon sun blazed a trail for his Chevy pickup to follow, Tim Niemeyer stayed along the dirt trail leading to the property he alone took responsibility for maintaining. Though few of the landmarks remained, Beverly Hilton paid him a token wage to check on the property when he saw fit, and to keep trespassers away.

Money was not the issue, nor was a deep loyalty to the widowed woman who asked such a favor of him.

For years, Niemeyer had wanted to buy the land, or at least part of it, from her. She refused to sell, partly he believed, because he continued to mind it for her. Sometimes he felt like the only person who cared at all for the property, mostly from a sense of ownership. He was confident it would someday be his own one way or another.

Owning a small construction business between Bloomington and Bedford gave him the option of calling the shots and making his own hours. In the past three years, several key bids doubled his business, forcing him to hire more employees and put in more hours. He knew missing some of the little things with his family would pay off when he eventually took an early retirement, or let his kids take over when they were old enough.

Niemeyer felt thrilled to be close to his friends and family after watching so many of his high school buddies leave for college, or relocate for better jobs, and never return. He enjoyed the neighborly things, like plowing driveways in the winter, or helping kids by occasionally speaking at a church school class.

Just off Highway 37, north of the turn to West Baden and French Lick, the grounds he sought were overgrown and mired with decrepit buildings. They were a ghostly testament to what once drew visitors to the property.

A red brick drive, now overgrown with weeds, gave way to a parallel muddy path just several feet away, created by off-road truck tires. Several guest cottages barely stood, their splintered wood barely clinging to their frames by rusty nails. One of the roofs revealed several holes from rocks thrown by unwanted trespassers.

Just the types Niemeyer sought out.

With his favorite shotgun nestled in the extended cab behind him, he looked straight ahead, spying a foreign truck parked just past the guest cottages as the old retreat came into view. He stopped short of the old driveway, pulling out his cellular phone. He hoped Ken Kaiser was working the afternoon shift.

"Orange County Police," a female voice answered on the other end.

"This is Tim Niemeyer," he told the woman. "I'm at the old Hilton property and there are some trespassers here."

"Have you seen them?"

Normally Niemeyer spoke softly with just a hint of Southern drawl that stemmed from years on the farm around his grandfather, who came from Tennessee to live with his parents during his youth. He could turn it on and off at will, except when he got angry.

"No, but ah'm about to go and look."

"Stay put, sir. We'll send a unit out."

"Okay," Niemeyer answered with no intent of obeying the order as he clicked the phone off, placing it back in its charger.

Stepping from the truck, Niemeyer pulled the shotgun out, wanting to make a point if he found someone. A burly man, he took jokes easily about his beer belly, and even the ones about protein drinks and steroids causing his brown hair's recession to the point of just a fringe, though he never actually took steroids.

Average in height, he had a barrel chest matched by his stomach, because he liked to eat heartily after working out.

After befriending several police officers, he often worked out with them and took it quite seriously after seeing significant improvement in the size of his upper body. He learned to take their teasing in good nature, and returned fire when chances arose.

Niemeyer was sick and tired of telling teenage punks to stay away from the property. Occasionally, curious adults came to see what had become of the old retreat, once home to so many rich and famous residents of Southern Indiana, but usually trespassers were the bad kind.

Kids shot at the buildings, left trash, got high, drank, and rode motorcycles around the property without regard to its heritage or the fact that someone still owned it. He hated it when they made excuses for being there, despite all the signs warning against trespassing, or the fence they so recklessly threw aside every time they entered.

He hated liars.

With his steel-toed boots already covered in mud, Niemeyer trudged forward, feeling warm in his thick brown leather jacket as sweat dripped down his forehead. Usually a fairly reserved person, he attended church and feared God just as much as the next man, but something about others violating his property, or that of others, lit a fire beneath him. Perhaps being a victim of theft in the past, or a heightened sense of security that came with being a family man, hardened him, but there was no changing his nature.

Seeing no one around, he snuck a look at the old truck parked near the old resort. A temporary license plate stuck inside the back window revealed as little as the cab of the truck did. His sharp blue eyes scanned the area like an eagle, seeing no movement. No strange noises sounded around him either.

It was his nature to remain more calm, collected, and cerebral than even his closest friends realized. He thought of all sorts of topics they had no idea he was versed in.

Right now, he focused on only one of those topics.

"Your truck's about ta get towed!" he yelled a warning, losing his accent through the top of his lungs.

His friends also knew of his temper, how difficult it was to get him mad, and to stay clear when he reached that point.

Steaming, Niemeyer examined the near skeletal frame of the resort, scarred badly by fire several years prior. By all rights it should have been torn to the ground, he thought, but Ms. Hilton wanted it in place to reclaim some of her memories, despite the danger of a lawsuit from anyone hurt inside.

Even if they were technically trespassing.

Beverly Hilton no longer moved around like she had in her younger days. In fact, she barely left her house these days, and when she did, it was for everyday things like groceries or card games with her few remaining friends. Though independent enough to live on her own, the days of her walking the treacherous grounds of the estate were probably long gone. Niemeyer could have built a new hotel on the grounds and she might never have known the better.

Parts of the wooden walls clung to the frame of the long, two-story house. Most of the remaining wood retained its charred appearance, though the smell of fire had long since blown away with the winds that howled through the vacant wreck of a building.

The mix of gray and black wood occasionally gave way along several walls to the view of the dead, overgrown grass behind the building. Seeing streams of daylight through the building still gave Niemeyer chills, just as it had in his younger days.

Knowing his gun was loaded, the independent contractor stepped forward, finding two young men completely dressed in black emerge from the building, not spying him until he was unavoidable. Standing beside their vehicle, Niemeyer simply held the shotgun in one hand, burning holes through them with his stare until they were within several feet.

Neither looked the druggie part he expected, but one had a snake tattoo wrapped around his neck. Niemeyer referred to that as 'trouble.' Dressed in black pants, black turtleneck shirts, and dark military-type boots, the two looked like members of some cult, probably practicing their religion in a secluded area.

Taking a quick glance, Niemeyer looked for any signs of what they might have been doing on the property, or evidence of weapons or drugs.

He could see no trace of any foul play.

"Problem?" the taller of the two asked.

"You're trespassin'," Niemeyer informed them hostilely.

"We had no idea," the other said, doing his best to appear genuine.

"No idea?" Niemeyer retorted, pointing his gun toward one of few remaining signs not victimized by gunfire or run over by four-wheelers. "You two know you're not s'posed to be back here."

"We're sorry," the taller one said without sincerity in his voice. "We'll leave."

"And don't be comin' back," the property manager said before they could turn to go.

Though Niemeyer failed to hear it coming, the two younger men spied a county police car at the edge of the drive. Looking both confused and irritated at the sight of police, they instinctively turned on Niemeyer.

"What's this?" the taller one asked, pointing in the direction of the drive.

"Protection," Niemeyer answered without looking, suspecting Kaiser, or another officer, was on the way.

Timing it perfectly, the same man shoved Niemeyer as he turned to see the progress of the police car down the drive. Caught off-guard and unbalanced, Niemeyer reacted in the manner most natural for him in such a position. Perhaps it was how he saw his grandfather settle farm scuffles as a kid, or the insurance of having a number of local police friends to back him, but Niemeyer stepped out of character.

He struck the taller man with the butt of his shotgun just as Kaiser's patrol car reached the open area of the property, giving him full view of his high school chum's perpetration.

"Get back, Tim!" Kaiser called as he stepped out of the patrol car in the standard brown uniform shirt and earthy light brown duty pants.

Niemeyer slowly obeyed, putting down the shotgun. He felt stunned concerning his actions, like everything was part of a bad dream.

"He went ballistic!" the struck man shouted immediately. "He smashed my jaw!" he added, pointing to the blood oozing from his mouth, though the county officer appeared skeptical of the injury's severity.

"What happened?" Kaiser asked, stepping beside his friend.

"I told them ta leave, they saw you comin', and the one shoved me," Niemeyer explained. "I just went off and hit 'im with the gun."

"Are you two wanting to press charges?" Kaiser asked with a tone implying it would not be in their best interest.

Niemeyer started to speak but the county officer silenced him, holding up a foreboding hand. "I don't have a choice, Tim," he said aside to his friend. "I saw what happened and you never know these days when someone's hiding in the bushes with a video camera. I can't risk my job like that."

"He shoved me," Niemeyer complained just above a whisper.

"I didn't see it," Kaiser insisted.

Niemeyer reluctantly nodded in understanding. Kaiser obviously had too many years on the force to risk his career. He would likely figure out some way to get his friend off the hook later.

"Damn straight we do," the taller one finally answered, much to the amazement of his friend. "Can we do this at the station so I can get this looked at?"

Kaiser hesitated a moment, looking from the two young men to Niemeyer.

"Sorry, Tim. I've got to put you in cuffs."

Niemeyer bobbed his head slowly, understanding, but hoping there was a way to avoid being formally arrested. He knew he had overreacted, but this was going a bit far considering he was in the right.

"Frisk him," the taller one insisted. "I don't want him pulling anything else out on us."

Numbed by the fact his best friend had to arrest him, Niemeyer sighed as Kaiser led him toward the patrol car, instructing him to place his hands on the hood and spread his legs. Niemeyer felt terrible putting his friend in this position, since he had initially called it in. Now he was helpless to do anything but accept whatever hand fate dealt him.

"Ah'm sorry, Ken," he said between the two of them as Kaiser's hand ran up and down each leg, then through his jacket and flannel shirt. "Ah'm so sorry. He shoved me and…"

"You can't go whacking people with shotguns," Kaiser said, equally hushed, cutting off Niemeyer's last statement. "I don't know how I'm going to get you out of this, Tim."

Partly from the embarrassment of the situation and putting his friend in such a predicament, emotion overwhelmed Niemeyer as mist filled his eyes. He refused to show any emotion in front of the lying punks, so he let Kaiser hurry in cuffing him. He wondered how he would tell his wife and kids, and how would they take the news. In the past, his friends were there to stop him when anger took over, but this time Niemeyer realized it was different.

His frustration turned to fear when he saw the young men from the corner of his eye reaching for the discarded shotgun. As the last cuff wrapped around his wrist, Niemeyer began to warn his friend too late as the taller of the two darted toward him, knocking him upside the temple with his own gun while the other apparently went for Kaiser.

Blue sky whirled around the contractor a moment before everything went completely black. His fear of being arrested became the least of his worries in one bleak moment.

Chapter 11

Clouse awoke to find the confining room around him closing in. Between the floral wallpaper, the vase with the plastic red rose, and the facial tissue holder that displayed its stitched design of a kitten playing with a red ball, Clouse felt like he was in a maternity ward.

He looked outside at the Indian summer day, thinking how nice it would be to play with the kids in the afternoon sun. Any number of things sounded better than being stuck in bed, sick as he had ever felt, wishing to get better.

Still staring out the windows, he saw Jane pull into the driveway.

As his son joined Katie outside to play a few minutes later, his fiancée sat on the edge of his bed with a concerned look. Sleepy-eyed, Clouse took hold of her hand as he looked her in the eyes.

"What's the matter?"

"Do you know what kind of project Zach is working on in his gifted class?"

"Not at the moment. He usually doesn't talk about it."

Jane put her free hand up to her chin, tapping it a few times.

"I asked him and he wouldn't give me a good answer," she told Clouse. "I don't know if he can't or won't tell, but they've got him in this dark room by himself with just a computer while the other children work on group projects, Paul."

"That's strange," Clouse agreed. "I'll ask him later."

"So, are you feeling better?" she asked, appearing glad he agreed with her about Zach's school situation.

"Somewhat," he answered, not about to reveal the conversation of his last phone call to her. "I'm still getting cold chills, with just a bit of a headache."

Jane quickly stood.

"I'll get some Tylenol," she said before leaving the room.

Before Clouse could tell her to avoid the drowsy type, the phone rang from beside him. Hesitantly staring at it the first two rings, Clouse decided to answer before someone else in the house did.

"Hello?"

"Paul?" a familiar, mild Southern drawl asked.

"Tim? I haven't heard from you in forever."

"Sorry about that. Listen, I need your help on something," Niemeyer said with the sounds of iron bars clanking behind him.

"Tim, where are you?" Clouse asked curiously.

***

Almost an hour later, completely against Jane's advice, Clouse arrived at the Orange County Jail in Paoli. Though he felt and looked horrible, Clouse refused to let his friend sit in jail for reasons neither of them truly knew. Niemeyer sounded scared, and even confused, because the police were questioning him heavily about Kaiser's whereabouts. The last thing he remembered was being knocked unconscious, then waking up in the jail.

Through a screen separating them in the visitation area, Niemeyer relayed the story to his other high school buddy. The three of them were country boys in their younger days, and a bit of that remained in each of them, though in different ways. They were all raised on farms, forming a pact as early as grade school that they would never part ways. In some ways, they had, but all three resided in the area and loosely kept in touch. There was nothing they wouldn't do for one another.

Nothing.

"These two men," Clouse said after his friend's narrative. "Have you seen them before?"

"Can't say I have," Niemeyer replied. "God, Paul. What could they have done with Ken? They had me dead to rights for arrest. Why would they do that?"

"I don't know, Tim. One of the officers told me his patrol car was still there, you were lying unconscious in handcuffs, and there was no sign of any truck. The last report they had from Ken was when he reached the property. They sent backup when he didn't respond to radio calls and found you there."

"But I didn't do anything," his friend pleaded. "They're just holding me because they don't know what I did. And they won't believe a word I say 'bout those two guys in black."

Clouse felt drained and sicker than ever with the world around him occasionally spinning from an uncontrollable dizziness. He needed rest, not more worries.

"I'll talk to the shift commander and see if I can get you released until something comes up. Either way, I'm going to look for Ken."

"Where could he be?"

"I don't know. You've given me a description of the truck and the two men who took him. I have some ideas."

Clouse was about to stand when his cellular phone rang from inside his jacket pocket. The guards knew him well enough that they let him walk in with it. He was close enough to an external wall for it to work, so he quickly pulled it out, pressing the talk button before answering.

"Clouse."

"Hotel," a voice said before hanging up.

Stunned a moment, Clouse realized it was the same voice who called him earlier stating he knew who had attempted to take his life two days earlier. The warning was too strong to ignore, and the only lead he now had.

"Shit," Clouse said to himself. "I've got to go. I'll be back for you later."

"But, Paul," Niemeyer almost begged, not understanding the situation, unable to finish before Clouse exited the visitation area.

Clouse stopped outside the visitation area to take a final glance at his friend, who simply slumped back in his chair, waiting for the guards to return him to his cell. Though he felt guilty for leaving Niemeyer, Clouse harbored grave concerns about Kaiser's situation.

***

Few lights illuminated the inside of the West Baden Springs Hotel when Clouse unlocked the front door, taking a step inside. He had already alerted the county police and EMS to head toward the building, but he waited until he was almost there before doing so. He simply told the dispatcher there was a threat of life on the property where he worked part-time. Clouse wanted to be the first to see what the caller meant before anyone else arrived.

When he rounded the first corner, Clouse saw a dim light from inside the atrium brighter than he or Rusty Cranor left it when they closed the building. He also heard a dripping sound, like a bathtub faucet slowly releasing droplets into an already filled basin.

Nothing in the atrium contained running water, or even the capacity to hold fluid.

Clouse slowly approached the closest entrance to the grand center, apprehensive about what might be inside. He stood on the opposite side of the doorway, not looking in, just listening to the drips as long as he could bear it. Finally, Clouse stepped through the doorway, finding what appeared to be a work of art set up just for him.

A message.

"God, no," he muttered, taking in a view of the cleared atrium, a pool of blood surrounding one of the statues on the other end.

Drawn to the horrid spectacle, Clouse recognized the pale form of his high school friend laid across the statue, still in his police uniform.

Clouse swore immediately his friend was dead, his form tied by several crude ropes into a lying position across the statue where his left arm, left free to dangle, fed blood through an intravenous tube. Laid across the outstretched arms of the statue, the scene looked almost natural, as though the statue was holding a fallen child in its arms.

Unfortunately, the child happened to be tied helplessly in place with a heavy abundance of straps. The only way Clouse thought his friend might have escaped from the bonds would have been to physically break the statue's arms by thrashing himself around, if that was even possible.

Apparently, that never happened.

He stared at the reddish puddle thinking back to his first responder runs on the fire department, positive his friend had lost too much blood to have survived. His heart sank at the thought of losing a childhood friend so soon.

As he reached the edge of the bloody pool, Clouse saw the needle stuck inside the pale wrist of his friend, feeding blood through the tube, which leaked the fluid into a massive puddle on the floor. A tight cloth strap assured the needle remained in place, even if Kaiser had shifted positions. A clothespin slowed the progress of the blood assuredly to prolong the suffering Kaiser went through before dying.

Immune to the sounds of the EMS personnel and police officers entering the atrium behind him, Clouse stared at the form of his friend closely. Kaiser's eyes were closed, his uniform torn and ragged as though a struggle ensued before he was drained of his lifeblood. Visible cuts and bruises showed along his face and arms, probably from various weapon strikes to subdue him.

Missing were Kaiser's gun and belt. From the looks of the marks, they might have been used against him. Though damaged, every other part of the man's uniform appeared to be on him.

Clouse knew how tough Kaiser was, after watching him in action several times. He now understood what Niemeyer and the deputy experienced was much more than a simple trespassing, but he wondered why.

"Why?" he asked aloud, looking at his friend's pale form, as though Kaiser had already undergone embalming. He couldn't help but wonder if Kaiser had been conscious for any of it. The thought of being slowly bled to death mortified Clouse.

If the medics or police officers asked him any questions, Clouse failed to hear them. Without realizing it, Clouse stepped back from the scene, letting the medics do their job. They carefully pulled the needle from his arm, checking his vitals as they did so. Avoiding the puddle of blood around the statue, they laid Kaiser down in a clean part of the carpeted floor, quickly checking for pulse and blood pressure as Clouse turned away, feeling tears well in his eyes.

Two deputies and a state trooper accompanied the medics into the building, now dividing their attention between the victim and Clouse with questioning eyes. Clouse understood their concern for Kaiser, but none of them cared for the man more than his oldest friend. They could take their suspicious stares and stick them up their asses for all he cared. Tired of being a suspect and a victim, Clouse wanted to find whoever did this and put a bullet through their heart.

"We've got a pulse," one of the medics announced, surprising everyone around him.

Clouse whirled around, equally stunned.

"We've got to move him now!" the senior medic ordered, apparently astounded by the discovery as well.

As the group placed Kaiser on a stretcher, continuing to assess him, they prepared a saline solution to help replenish his lost bodily fluids until a transfusion could be arranged at the hospital. A moment later the medics wheeled the mobile cot past Clouse as he looked to the sky, thankful for such a miracle, though he knew the ordeal was far from over.

"Thank you, Lord," he said uncharacteristically before rushing toward the atrium exit, taking one last look back at the gargantuan puddle of blood before heading out.

Chapter 12

McCabe milled through the photos on his desk, wondering exactly what to make of the Rexford murder. He spent the night at home alone, except for the companionship of a beer, which displayed signs to those who knew him that an important case had come his way.

He told his mother he would call her back later.

He hadn't.

He promised a buddy at work he would attend his daughter's baptism.

One less person witnessed a Catholic tradition.

His friends at the bar expected him as usual once his shift was over.

They might worry a while before drinking enough to forget what they fussed over.

Entering what he called the zone, McCabe put pressure on himself to develop a lead, despite the lack of necessary components.

Witnesses: None that helped.

Motive: None apparent.

Promising leads: A big fat zero.

Usually McCabe entered the zone when he merely lacked a clue, or perhaps a shred of evidence that slammed the door shut on the case. Now he did it from sheer desperation, realizing how quickly murder cases grew cold without solid leads to begin pecking away at.

Daniels gave him a few ideas to work with, but nothing that put him any closer to solving the case. McCabe felt somewhat like a stranger to the case because he knew nothing about the hotel's history or what happened to Daniels and Clouse the previous year.

He wondered if anyone truly knew aside from the few survivors.

As unusual as it was for the detective to avoid socialization, it was equally unusual for him to begin a case with so little information. Everything about it felt strange. McCabe thought it eccentric to murder someone by lighting him on fire. He believed the victim was shoved onto the balcony, thus calling attention to the crime.

Also unusual.

Crosschecking the other names of those on the balconies helped very little. Most were descendant relatives of important hotel figures from years past, making them no more or less likely to be murdered than Rexford. He hoped the stolen property might shed some light on the case if its exact nature was discovered.

"McCabe," the detective said, scooping his phone up after one ring.

"Tug, it's Denny. We've had another situation at the West Baden Springs Hotel."

"Not another murder," he stated more than asked, hoping his reply was true.

Denny Mason, a fellow trooper, had a history of delivering bad news to McCabe from his past marital problems to the cases that gave him fits in his sleep.

"Not yet. County cop ended up in the hospital, drained of most of his blood."

McCabe sat silently a few seconds, wondering what on earth kind of curse plagued that hotel. He would question Daniels more about it later, no matter how much the man felt personally beleaguered by it.

"Did they take him to Bedford?"

"There was no time," Mason replied. "Clinic in Paoli. Need directions?"

"No," McCabe said promptly, not yet ready to swallow his pride. "I'll find it."

After all, Paoli wasn't that big a town.

"There's something else."

"Oh?"

"The Illinois boys called back with some info on your case. The wife remembered him packing a piece of the hotel's old tile floor. She said they asked all the guests to bring something relating to the hotel with them for the dinner if possible."

"What the hell?" McCabe wondered aloud.

"Was there a tile piece in his belongings?" Mason couldn't seem to help asking.

"No, but why would anyone want that?"

His friend chuckled.

"That's why you're the detective, not me."

"Thanks, Denny. See you tomorrow."

"Anytime, buddy."

As he hung up, McCabe wondered where the clinic was in Paoli. He figured he could reach the town in less than an hour with lights and siren, and radio dispatch for specific directions while en route. There was no shame in asking the whereabouts of buildings over the radio, even if people with scanners might hear the request.

It seemed the missing piece of his puzzle was a piece of tile floor. He would spend the next hour questioning how a piece of tile might be at all important to someone, and if it was the reason Rexford had to die. Though it seemed unreasonable, McCabe's experience told him sometimes things just lacked rhyme or reason.

***

When the detective arrived, a man fitting Clouse's description spied him while rolling his sleeve up with a discontent look on his face. Apparently recognizing the detective's mandatory shirt and tie immediately, the man shot him an unfriendly gaze, silently stating that any questions would have to wait.

"You Clouse?" McCabe asked anyway.

"You O-negative?" was the reply.

"Yeah," the detective replied, seeing where the conversation was going.

"Donate a pint and I'll answer any questions you want."

McCabe inquired about the officer's condition, quickly learning that Kaiser's situation looked grim, his only hope being a massive transfusion, which the clinic was not equipped to handle. He was the type of person who would volunteer regardless of the circumstances.

Paramedics from Bloomington were on the scene, ready to transport once the transfusion finished and Kaiser was deemed stable. Several local volunteers rushed to the clinic to donate once they heard. To ensure Kaiser received no foreign particles or unknown diseases the volunteers needed to meet certain criteria.

Despite his illness, Clouse donated a pint, looking paler than some corpses the detective had viewed over his career. McCabe saw him call someone after his donation, apparently arguing about leaving the house in his condition, and why he needed to do so. McCabe understood how women could be, despite not having a steady relationship in over a year.

While McCabe remained on the table, he saw Clouse take two county officers aside, asking them to question Niemeyer officially and release him, since he obviously had nothing to do with the incident. After radioing their commanding officer, they received permission to take Niemeyer's statement and inform him of what happened to Kaiser only after they finished.

Once McCabe finished donating, the clinic staff appeared confident Kaiser could safely be transported to Bloomington, receiving medical attention along the way from a Paoli doctor who volunteered to ride along. Clouse watched helplessly as the procession slowly followed his injured friend into the ambulance.

"Care for a ride to the hospital?" McCabe asked Clouse, rolling his sleeve down with gauze and a synthetic covering over the needle mark.

"Sure."

Five minutes later, both were settled in the unmarked police car and on their way to Bloomington. Clouse thought about nothing except his friend until McCabe broke the silence.

"So what happened?"

"I was talking to my buddy Tim in jail when I got a weird call."

Clouse spent about five minutes explaining the entire situation to the state trooper, shivering most of the time, sneezing between sentences. McCabe had spoken with Daniels about Clouse's attempted murder, so the trooper understood what the man was probably going through.

"You should be in bed," McCabe said after a few minutes of silence.

"I can't sleep with everything going on," Clouse said with a forced laugh.

"Sounds like I want to talk with your buddy, too," the trooper added.

With no reply the trooper looked over to find Clouse dozed off, his body too exhausted to remain awake, despite the dire events surrounding him.

"I don't blame you, man."

Chapter 13

Clouse awoke in a hospital bed the next morning when light peeked through the window blinds, hitting him squarely in the face. Feeling better, he threw the sheets aside, finding himself fully dressed.

"What happened?" he asked Jane after darting into the hallway and finding her seated nearby.

He remembered little from the night before because he and Jane had stood nearby, monitoring Kaiser as closely as the hospital staff would allow. Clouse had fallen in and out of sleep in the uncomfortable waiting room chairs.

"He's stable," Jane answered, seeming to know exactly what his thoughts were. "And the staff was kind enough to provide a room for you, so you wouldn't catch cold."

Jane used her connections, in other words.

"But Ken's okay?"

"He's stable, Paul. It'll be touch and go the next few days."

"Has he woken up?"

"No. His body is extremely weak right now. Even his family isn't allowed to see him."

Clouse paced a moment, still feeling a bit light-headed. Even with nearly a dozen hours of sleep, his initial feeling of better health quickly evaporated.

"Your friend Tim came by after I got you the room. He wanted to thank you."

"I'm glad he's free."

"Why have I never met him?"

Clouse gave a funny smirk.

"Tim and I just run into one another often enough that we don't usually call one another. We were both always tighter with Ken than we were each other. Besides, he lives south of Bedford."

"So does Ken," Jane informed him.

Clouse shrugged for lack of a comeback.

"Mark's upstairs if you want to see him."

"What's he doing here?" Clouse questioned quickly, afraid his friends were all being brutalized.

"He has an appointment with the physical therapist."

Clouse thought a moment. Kaiser's condition was not subject to change in the near future, and there was a possibility he might help Daniels if he went upstairs.

"I'll come get you if anything changes," Jane assured him.

"Okay," he said, giving her a long kiss. "You know I love you."

"I know. Now go get Mark on his feet."

Clouse smiled hesitantly before heading for the elevator.

When he reached the appropriate hallway, he spied Dr. Susan Jameson walking from the rehabilitation room, shaking her head as she clutched her clipboard.

"What's the matter, doc?" Clouse asked when she saw him coming.

"Your friend seems to be getting worse. He wasn't cooperative toward our techniques today," she said, cupping her hand over her chin. "Has he been doing anything on his own?"

"I'm not sure," Clouse answered, shaking his head. "I'll talk to him," he added, seeing the therapist leave the room.

Clouse stepped inside to find Daniels staring at the floor, as though he thought about trying something on his own. The officer shot a strange look his way once he spotted him.

"I hear you're being unruly."

Daniels ignored the remark, looking past Clouse toward the door.

"Paul, I want you to get behind this chair and dump me on the floor."

Now Clouse gave the odd look.

"I suppose you want me to kick you once you're down too?"

"Seriously," Daniels said, growing agitated. "I may be onto something."

Reluctantly Clouse walked behind the chair, grabbing the chair's push bars. He looked around to make certain no one was looking through any of the windows surrounding the room. The last thing he needed was accusations of bullying the handicapped.

"Do it," Daniels ordered, noting the hesitation.

Clouse looked toward the door reluctantly before pulling up on the bars, lurching forward to spill his friend on the floor.

Landing hard, Daniels wasted no time in pushing himself up with his arms before slowly picking up his right leg, trying to position it for standing. Clouse watched in amazement as his friend showed limited use of the appendage for the first time in his presence.

"I've been able to do this before," Daniels spoke in labored breaths.

"That's cheating."

"So sue me," the officer said, reaching for one of the support rails to help support himself. Clouse started toward him. "No. I'll do this myself."

Clasping the rail, Daniels managed to pull himself to one knee, straining to reach a standing position.

"It's in your mind, Mark," Clouse coached. "Put it all behind you and stand up. Get your job back. Your life."

Daniels placed his other foot to a ready position.

"Stand up, Mark. Stand up, damn it."

With several strained, painful sounds, Daniels made his tensed muscles fight for enough energy to stand him up. Giving it one final push Daniels fought to bring the back leg forward.

"Come on, Mark," Clouse encouraged. "While you've still got the energy."

Daniels pushed his body to its physical limits to stand, pulling the rail as he did so. Within a moment, and without realizing Clouse took up his side, Daniels managed to stand enough to lean against the railing. He was not walking, nor was he fully under his own power, but he was using both legs.

Both men watched as Susan walked in, gasping with shock as she witnessed the spectacle. What she had fought with Daniels for months to accomplish, he managed to pull off without professional assistance.

Leaning back against the railing, Daniels casually folded his arms, smiling from ear to ear. It was the first time the injured police officer had genuinely shown a positive attitude in months.

"I'm impressed, Officer Daniels," she said. "I won't ask how you did it, but I'm very impressed."

A few minutes later, Clouse walked from the therapy room nearly as happy as his friend. Walking down the hall, he smiled, giving one look back to the room before a hand cupped him around the mouth, pulling him down a side hallway.

Spinning around defensively, Clouse saw who he thought was his attacker back away, motioning for him to settle down and keep quiet. The man, dressed in black, was several inches shorter and carried nowhere near the muscle to harm the rugged firefighter.

He appeared typical in nature. Free of tattoos or piercings, he could be any young man just out of college. The black attire fit the description of what Niemeyer spoke of the night before. This youngster appeared too harmless to be involved in anything as vile as what happened to Kaiser at the hotel.

Clouse knew too well how appearances were sometimes deceptive.

"Who are you?" he asked, complying with the man's wish for quiet conversation.

"I'm the only one who might be able to save you and everyone around you," the man said nervously, peeking around Clouse's shoulders.

"I suppose I owe you thanks for pulling me from the lake."

"We don't have time for that," the man said. His dark hair appeared wavy throughout, as though not properly combed. Clouse wondered if it might be a current style. "You're still in considerable danger."

"From who?"

A negative shake of the head was the answer.

"I'm part of a group instructed to carry out a list of objectives," the man confessed. "Our leader goes by the name Jacob."

Clouse flailed his hands in frustration, disturbing the dust float through the rays of sunshine streaming in through a nearby window.

"Jacob what? You aren't giving me much here."

"I can't tell you what I don't know," the man said. "I got into this group for the wrong reasons, Mr. Clouse. I no longer believe what they're doing is right. We are called the Coven, our leader's name is simply Jacob, and what you must know and understand is that a list exists which contains your name and the names of others I believe are involved with the hotel. Everyone on this list is to die, and your name was the first."

"Can you tell me who else is on it?"

"No. I only find out as they're scheduled for execution. I managed to save you and your friend Kaiser."

Clouse was taken aback. Systematic execution and a specific list. It sounded like a conspiracy plot from a movie, but he was living it.

"You call that saving him?" Clouse complained.

"Who do you think put the clothespin on that tube to keep him from bleeding to death? I managed to prolong the process long enough for you to get there, didn't I?"

"Alright," Clouse admitted, realizing the true purpose of the clothespin. "You did. But what's the point of this list? The agenda?"

"I'm not privy to that information either. I know your friend Cranor was killed because they wanted something from him."

Clouse took a moment to let the words register.

"Rusty? Dead?"

He started to turn around but the man tugged his arm, getting him to stay.

"I can't believe it."

"I'm sorry," the young man said with a sincere expression. "There was nothing I could do for him. They'll know I came to you," he added, rubbing frustration from his head. "Jacob will have me killed when he discovers we talked."

Clouse sighed aloud, trying to make sense of it all. One moment ago he was thrilled his high school friend was alive and a newer friend could walk again. Now his joy was crushed by the news his colleague was murdered, and he still had no idea why. He found it incredibly strange no one had reported Rusty's demise if the man was indeed dead.

"We cannot meet again. I have to leave," the man said suddenly, pushing past Clouse who clasped his arm with a solid grip.

"What do I call you?"

"Call me Stephen," the man replied.

"And how can I get a copy of this list?"

"I'll get you one. Somehow I'll find it and get you the names."

Clouse let go. As the man scurried away, he wondered what to do next. If what his informant said was true, it seemed prudent to inform the police. Clouse had no one to trust or contact that might begin to understand. Daniels was still in no shape to go chasing down leads with him.

"McCabe," Clouse decided aloud, walking down the hallway.

A strange feeling he was being watched by another party entered his mind, but he put the sensation aside, deciding that dwelling on his paranoia only served to slow him down.

Chapter 14

After a search of the hotel resulted in nothing, Clouse traveled with McCabe to Cranor's house outside the city limits of Bloomington. Under the detective's blanket of request, Clouse had searched the man's office for anything that might be missing.

He found nothing out of the usual.

Because it seemed rather odd to him, and he felt clueless about its significance, McCabe questioned Clouse about the tile floor piece on the way to Cranor's house. He openly revealed a suspicion it might somehow be related.

"I'm not sure what he was doing with it, but when the company started reconstruction they auctioned off the pieces for money to aid in the rebuilding," Clouse answered as he rode in the passenger's seat toward Cranor's house.

For the first time he noticed the odor of a car freshener in the unmarked car, wondering why officers with take-home cars always bought them.

"How would Rexford, a dentist from Chicago, obtain one of those pieces?" McCabe asked, keeping his eyes on the road.

"Mailing list, probably. The hotel has a number of volunteers who keep track of all sorts of things. One list is dedicated to descendants of the hotel's former owners and major contributors."

List, Clouse thought, missing whatever question McCabe asked next. His thoughts about those around him being systematically executed haunted him. He prayed it was all one big lie, or a misunderstanding on his mysterious ally's part. Though there was no answer when he had called, Clouse hoped they might find Cranor at home, alive.

If that was the case, he could theoretically dismiss the boat incident as a trapped thief fighting his way out, and the Rexford murder as some sort of revenge killing.

If only it would prove so simple.

"You okay?" McCabe asked, raising his voice.

"Sorry. I'm just preoccupied with my earlier encounter."

"You didn't say much about that, aside from what he told you about Cranor being dead. Did he give any names, or anything else that might be useful?"

"Not really," Clouse answered quickly.

He felt no urgency to tell McCabe details of the meeting. State police proved of little use to him the year before when he was accused of killing his wife. Clouse also wanted to keep his friends and family from panicking, because he knew the police were sometimes excessively protective. He also wanted to avoid a local media circus.

Clouse would handle it his own way.

He planned to confide in Daniels, because the two shared a bond in such circumstances. Whether his friend shared information with McCabe or not would be up to him. Clouse simply refused to fully trust anyone he didn't know.

Anyone.

"Can you find out who those tiles were sold to?" the detective asked.

"I'll see. Finding who has the record will probably take a while. Getting a copy will be another task altogether."

"I'll give you whatever assistance you need," McCabe encouraged. "Did Cranor have any of those tiles?"

Clouse covered his mouth, exhaling through his nose as he thought.

"Pretty much anyone who worked on the hotel that long ago has at least one. But I still can't imagine what value they are to anyone. You really think that's motive enough to kill someone?"

McCabe shrugged.

"I don't know. It's my job to ask seemingly inane questions."

He paused a moment as Clouse indicated a direction to turn.

"You have any of those tiles?"

"One," the firefighter answered. "Stays inside a curio cabinet at our house."

"Must be quite the display piece," McCabe said. "Rexford kept his inside a jewelry box."

Clouse folded his arms.

"The tiles were imported, but they're pretty much worthless in such small pieces. They hold more sentimental value than anything."

Unlike McCabe, Clouse did not feel like talking. He realized the detective was probably hardened enough that he didn't mind eating or talking through any situation, but the thought of seeing a friend dead disturbed Clouse.

"Why were the tiles brought up?" McCabe asked as they neared Cranor's residence.

"The floor was displaced by water mixing with some of the original materials used to quickly harden the atrium floor. It cracked and buckled in several places, disrupting the tiles. Some of the pieces were stolen or damaged over the years. Enough that piecing together replacements became either too costly, or just impossible artistically," Clouse forced a quick answer. "I'm not sure which."

Once the lone country house with no neighbors for a mile in any direction came into view Clouse tensed. As they came upon the driveway, chills shot up the fireman's spine. He felt no urge to step inside the house, or investigate the property, knowing he might see another person he cared for in a state of death.

Over the past year, Clouse had mentally recovered from the torment laid upon him by David Landamere. Seeing Kaiser so close to death flooded his mind with memories he wanted only to forget. Finding another friend in such condition would only add to the heavy burden weighing on his mind.

"You staying here?" McCabe asked, once parked in the driveway.

Clouse nodded an affirmative.

"I'm going to knock," the detective informed him. "If I don't get an answer, I'll look around and probably go inside."

Clouse watched the next several minutes after no answer came to the front door, and the detective looked around the property, including the backyard and all of the windows.

When he returned, McCabe walked to Clouse's side of the car, forcing himself to contain his initial excitement in his discovery.

"The backdoor is unlocked," McCabe told Clouse before starting around the house for the second time.

"Damn," Clouse said, tired of the detective's tinkering.

He knew McCabe wanted him to look for those damned puzzle pieces, and Clouse wanted the experience over. Opening the car door, he looked to the detective, who seemed to be smiling inwardly like a big kid.

He had gotten his way.

"I knew you couldn't resist," McCabe said, opening the backdoor.

"Like I had much choice."

Much to his surprise, Clouse saw the house exactly as he remembered it. Since Cranor never stayed home, the house usually appeared tidy, with all sorts of remembrances of years past.

In the living room, several photos of the man's deceased daughter lined a shelf. Photos of the hotel, and other major projects Cranor worked on, were displayed in a staircase manner, hanging along one wall.

Knowing what McCabe wanted him to look for, Clouse set about the rest of the living room, searching for several tile pieces he knew his friend usually kept on display. Several shelves and glass display cabinets lined the living room, so Clouse carefully examined each one as McCabe explored the rest of the house.

***

After clearing the downstairs areas, the detective tried the second floor, opening each bedroom and closet door with caution, his service weapon already drawn. Finding nothing in either bedroom, McCabe tried the bathroom, thinking Clouse's source of information was a big hoax. Like the fireman, he hoped it was.

McCabe peeked around the bathroom door, finding nothing disturbed. From what little light followed him inside, he noticed the shower curtain drawn shut. Shielding himself behind the door, the detective flipped a switch, bringing the fluorescent light flickering to life as he took hold of the curtain, yanking it to one side.

Nothing.

McCabe turned around, squarely hitting someone who had come up behind him.

"Shit!" the detective exclaimed, relieved it was Clouse.

"I thought you might like to know I couldn't find those tile pieces Rusty had," he reported. "There's a bare spot in one of the glass cases, and dust surrounding it, implying something was there until very recently."

"You're doing my job," McCabe said almost defensively. "I've looked everywhere and I can't find anything."

He looked up to the ceiling, beyond Clouse.

"Except there."

Down the hallway, a drawstring served to bring down a collapsible ladder leading to the attic. It was the only thing left untouched in the entire house, since there was no full basement. Clouse dreaded the thought of looking up there, preferring to keep hold what little hope remained for Cranor's safe return.

"Stand back," McCabe ordered, placing a hand behind him, keeping Clouse far enough away that he would be at a safe distance if something fell from the attic.

Clutching the string, McCabe gave it a tug.

The ladder tumbled downward, and with it, the stiff carcass of Rusty Cranor. As though placed intentionally to do so, the body slid down the ladder like processed meat, bumping every rung as it went, hitting the floor with a thud, like a sack of groceries, when it landed backside down.

"Aw, shit," Clouse said, turning away from the sight.

He wasted mere seconds before bolting downstairs to collect himself as McCabe examined the bluish form of the dead project manager. McCabe hadn't expected a man so accustomed to death to flee from the sight.

Medically trained firefighters see death almost as regularly as police officers, and McCabe sensed Clouse would be hardened after so many traffic wrecks and bodies seen on first responder calls. That, coupled with the vicious murders around him the year before should have prepared him, but then the detective also understood these were his friends dying around him.

Cranor's lifeless face had a somber expression, his eyes wide open, mouth partly ajar, as though he might have been ambushed, or given up on life to see his daughter.

Rope burns around the neck were outwardly apparent. Without touching the body, McCabe did a visual examination, finding nothing aside from the rope burns that might give any clues. Because the body was dressed in long sleeve clothing, only skin from the face and hands was truly visible. McCabe spotted what he thought was bruising on the face and the right hand, but he wasn't a forensics expert. It was time to call the coroner's office and begin the second phase of his investigation.

Based on the condition of the body, McCabe figured the time of death to be within twenty-four hours, probably soon after he and Daniels had left the hotel the day before.

Perhaps *immediately* after they left.

"Damn," he cursed under his breath, looking down the stairs at Clouse, who sat on a bench, his head buried in his hands.

McCabe wondered what motivated the killings, and how much good Clouse was to him after suffering another loss.

Time would tell, but time was something McCabe found sparse.

Chapter 15

Clouse arrived home hours later to find Jane cleaning upstairs with no kids to be heard or found. Disheartened and still unhealthy, he felt discouraged about life in general. He was powerless to stop the mysterious list from being carried out, and his friends were dying around him, much like they had the previous year.

Running was no option. He might save himself, but it did nothing to help those around him. Since he had no idea who Jacob might be or who he might target next, Clouse decided to speak with Daniels in the morning. He hated the idea of ruining the happiness his friend had just found, but chances were strong his friend's name was on that list.

"What's the matter?" Jane asked, turning from making Zach's bed as her fiancé entered the room.

"Rusty's dead," Clouse simply said, slumping on the bed.

"My God," Jane gasped. "What happened?"

Clouse held up his right hand, throwing a dismissing wave indicating he wasn't ready to speak about it.

"Everything is so wrong," he said, grasping the back of his head with both hands in frustration. "It's just so wrong," he continued, sniffling.

He never let Jane see him this emotional. Usually Clouse acted calm, cool, and rational. She never witnessed a temper, and he was perfect around the kids, even when he felt bad, or had a rough time at work.

She had to know the traumatic things he sometimes saw as a firefighter, like dead children or the misery families suffered that tormented him. As a doctor, she likely witnessed similar scenarios on a regular basis. Never had Clouse let his fiancée see him lose control. On one hand she would probably feel relieved, seeing a new, vulnerable side to the man who tried too hard to be perfect to everyone around him, but at the same time she would likely wonder what demons were running through his mind.

Clouse vowed never to tell her because no one else needed to endure the pain he went through.

"The kids are with my parents for the night," Jane said, sitting beside him. "It's okay. You don't have to be tough for me."

"It's just not fair," Clouse said, between heaved breaths from emotion.

"I'm sorry, Paul," she said, carefully wrapping her arms around him, pulling him close to her warmth.

Feeling too much like a consoled child, Clouse collected himself, looking down at the floor, beyond the carpeting. His thoughts stretched to the hotel and Cranor's house, seeing only horror in each. He wondered why he didn't just quit work on the hotel after the past year. His life might have returned to normal and he might have enjoyed every moment alone with Jane.

"Sometimes I just want to leave," he told her. "I can't believe I ever went back to work there."

"How could you have known?" she asked a question with no answer. "You can't blame yourself for what's happening."

"But somehow I'm the center of it again," Clouse said, frustrated. "Last year I was the suspect. Now everyone close to me is dying."

"Do you want to leave?"

"No. That's not an option. Too many people are stuck here with no way of knowing who's behind it."

"And you think you can find out?" Jane asked skeptically. "You're not a detective, Paul."

"But who knows more about the hotel than me? Or you for that matter. We have to be strong, Jane, and hope to God we catch whoever's doing this before he strikes again."

She seemed to take comfort in his strength with her unblinking eyes and forced grin. If there was one complaint Jane sometimes had about Clouse's personality, it was that he refused to show her every dimension of himself. She had just witnessed his weaker side, and now his ability to pull himself together.

"We'll get through it," she said, pulling him close. "I don't know what I'd do if I ever lost you. Just be careful."

"I've got too much to lose if I'm not," he said before giving her a kiss on the cheek. "There are a lot of possibilities, but Mark and I will figure it out somehow."

Somehow, he mentally assured himself.

***

Without the benefit of full lighting, Stephen left the West Baden Springs Hotel's atrium carefully, so as not to disturb the off-duty state trooper providing security. Though the combing of evidence for Kaiser's attempted murderers was done, the yellow tape remained, sectioning off part of the atrium where blood stained the intricately detailed carpeting and tile floor.

After ensuring Clouse had a realistic chance of finding the list he took so much risk in stealing, Stephen felt better. He knew his position within the Coven was now endangered, even to the point that Jacob might order him dead.

Luckily, Stephen kept one step ahead of the group and its leader.

If not for his foresight in taking Clouse's keys from the boat before it completely sank, Stephen never would have gained access to the hotel. It was one place Jacob could not follow because of security and no means of entry. Stephen entered and immediately locked the doors behind him.

Stephen participated in the attempted murder of Kaiser, though he foiled it in the end. Up to that point, he felt his trust in the group was solidified because he was the shorter of the two men Niemeyer encountered, and ultimately the one who knocked the deputy cold. This allowed them to transport him to the vacant hotel where he spied Jacob coldly toting Cranor's body out of the building.

He felt positive someone ratted on him for lingering behind, which would probably lead Jacob to ultimately discover a traitor in his camp. It showed in his unfeeling eyes.

Unsure of where the guard wandered off to, Stephen left the atrium as quietly as possible, glad the carpeting covered much of the old tile floor. Footsteps, like any sound made in the open area, echoed throughout the six-story dome and alert anyone present. At least his footsteps would go unheard.

Soon after joining the Coven, Stephen realized what a terrible error he'd made in deciphering their motives. What he thought was a relatively dark religious sect turned out to be a group with a much deeper, darker purpose than he ever imagined. Rebelling against the common practices of society was one thing, but murdering a slew of people in the remembrance of one slain long ago was quite another.

Cautiously looking for the guard as he exited the atrium, Stephen made his way down the hallway toward the exits, looking to see if the man might be positioned in the lobby window where he could view most of the grounds. Occasionally the guards did rounds, which this one seemed to be, based on his absence.

Stephen breathed a sigh of relief, seeing a clear path out. He walked past several doors along the way. One of the last was Paul Clouse's office, where Cranor was killed. It was the one murder he was unable to prevent. It was planned in such a way that Stephen had no knowledge beforehand. Jacob claimed to have entered the hotel while the doors were unlocked and everyone was distracted during the daytime. He carried out the murder himself, taking the body directly to Cranor's residence where he claimed he would search for something "necessary to the cause."

A flicker of light from beneath the office door caught Stephen's attention. Like a moth, he was drawn to the odd, orange flicker. Clouse's keys included a master key, which opened any door in the hotel, but the door was already unlocked when Stephen tried it.

When the door swung in with a creaking sound, Stephen was shocked by an eerie jack-o-lantern set atop Cranor's desk, not because it was out of season, but because it meant death for anyone who saw it.

He knew the Coven's calling card all too well.

Beside the jack-o-lantern came flickering shadows along the walls, looking like black specters prepared to grab Stephen at any moment.

"So nice of you to join me," Jacob's voice whispered as he clasped Stephen's mouth, holding him completely still by threat of breaking his neck from behind, following a brief struggle. "I have quite a little surprise in store for you."

Stephen objected through muffled cries.

"Believe me, Stephen, your treachery hasn't gone unnoticed. You aren't the only one who acquired keys to this place."

Held helplessly still by Jacob, Stephen could barely resist as his taller, stronger captor pried his mouth open, using a dropper to place several drops of clear liquid on Stephen's tongue. Held a moment longer until the drug's effects began to kick in, Stephen quit resisting, feeling quite a bit more relaxed. Jacob let him go, where he soon fell to the floor, seating himself against the wall in an almost fetal position.

Stephen knew the calm before the storm had set in. Soon his mental journey would take a winding road, because he knew what was happening to him through

Jacob's previous threats. The potent brew of modified LSD was already sending Stephen down a road of madness, allowing Jacob to be the driver.

As Stephen began to shake and shiver, his twitches indicated he would soon be seeing things no one else could. His eyes began to take in everything around him, factual or not. The real world called it a bad trip, and it set in rather quickly.

"What's the matter, Stephen?" Jacob asked, kneeling down beside him.

Even in such close proximity, Jacob's form was obscured by shadows. Stephen always wondered exactly who he was. Where did he fit into normal society, and as whom?

"I see bugs everywhere," the apprentice answered nervously, seeing them everywhere above him — on the ceiling, on the walls, around the jack-o-lantern on the desk.

"There's one," Jacob said, pointing to Stephen's arm.

"Ah! Get it off me!" Stephen cried.

"One just crawled inside your neck," Jacob said with remarkable calm, pointing toward Stephen's face.

"No!" Stephen defied, clawing at his cheeks and neck intensely, drawing blood immediately.

"You'll never get them that way," Jacob informed him. "Dig harder. Deeper."

Stephen did so, madly drawing more blood, feeling nothing as he tore strips of skin and blood from his face. Beneath his fingernails, the tissue balled up, making them useless as scraping or digging tools. His progress slowed when he saw bugs crawl up his arms, into his open wounds, stopping to feed in swarms at the blood from the gashes. He heard incessant bug chatter as they gnawed his flesh away within his mind.

"No," he moaned, rather than fight his imaginary enemy.

Fantasy and reality meshed into one horrifying setting for Stephen. Spying open cuts on his arms, Stephen saw puss ooze from air pockets. Like boiling spaghetti sauce atop a stove, they rose, then burst, spilling a mix of soupy red and yellow. After each rupture, Stephen saw the tip of a fly larva surface for air, then disappear beneath his skin again.

"Maggot," Stephen whispered to himself, wide-eyed, positive he felt the wiggles under his flesh. Disgusted and frightened, the thought of such creatures festering within his body overwhelmed him. Like a child, he moaned and sobbed, rocking back and forth. Now he was afraid to touch or reach for anything.

"What's the matter, Stephen?" Jacob asked, feigning sympathy. "You're not digging deep enough to stop them, are you?"

After opening a thick blanket beside Stephen, Jacob placed latex gloves over his hands, snapping them into place. He turned to pull a hammer with a jagged ripping claw out from behind him.

"Let's dig together, shall we?"

Chapter 16

Returning to the hotel was not how Clouse planned to begin his day, but a call from Dr. Smith and his new quest of finding whoever purchased or took pieces of the atrium's old tile floor forced the issue.

Using his spare key to the hotel's main entrance, Clouse let himself in. Considering the hotel was like his second house it seemed fitting that he kept a spare.

While waiting for Smith to arrive, Clouse opened Cranor's office, finding everything in order. He then walked into his own office, not wanting to touch anything, pending McCabe's search for evidence, though seeking any advance notice of foul play. The detective would want to check both rooms thoroughly, so Clouse touched nothing in either.

A distinct smell of candle wax entered his nostrils when he stepped inside. Clouse took a moment to sniff the air, certain of the odor. He wandered into the room, seeing no sign of candle activity or anything out of place.

Remembering what McCabe told him of the visit to the hotel, and knowing how Cranor died, Clouse panned the ceiling for something solid enough to support a man's weight while he dangled, struggling for life. The visual picture of his friend dying perturbed him, but he contained his emotion, even after seeing the solid gas line above and several areas of chafed paint where friction burns had occurred.

"Knew it," he said to himself, climbing atop a chair for a better look. He planned to report his find to Daniels or McCabe.

Climbing down from the chair, he heard his boot clop against the floor, then nearly trip him up as its smooth leather sole slid a bit from something on the floor.

Usually ice or any liquid similar to water gave his boots poor traction. It just so happened blood did the same thing.

"What?" he asked himself, kneeling down to scoop a few droplets of blood onto his forefingers, examining the substance close up.

Only several spots remained along the floor, seemingly fresh. Such small drops certainly should have dried, had they been Cranor's. Clouse could only wonder what events had transpired at the hotel during his absence, because nothing else in the room provided any clues.

Deciding to leave the room alone, he stood and walked out the door, bumping into someone as he closed it.

"Dr. Smith," he said, regaining his composure after the initial scare and spinning to confront the person.

"Paul. Nice to see you're in good health," the man his grandfather's age replied.

Smith made his fortune early, amassing his net worth in the billions according to many locals, supported by several magazines focused on the nation's wealthiest people. To Clouse he seemed common enough, like any other local business owner the fireman knew. He put so much finance and effort into the hotel's reconstruction that it couldn't help but succeed.

Success came at a price, however, as the efforts and events from the past year, surrounding the first batch of murders took a toll on the doctor's health. Once as healthy as men Clouse's age, the doctor now looked much older, even decrepit to some. His walk seemed more hunched, and he brought a staff with him to aid him when his back failed.

"I'm doing fine," Clouse replied to the comment about his health. "Yourself?"

Smith simply nodded an affirmative, his dark gray hair set upon a face drawn inward from worsened health. He appeared in good spirits, but physically the doctor seemed on a downward spiral compared to the man Clouse had met a few years prior.

Clouse knew another major episode at the man's favorite landmark would probably do irreparable damage. Smith had considered selling the property during the tumultuous period the year before.

"Is it happening again?" he asked Clouse.

"It may be, but this time I've got some clues and I need your help, doc."

"How can I help?" the doctor asked, walking toward the atrium where sounds of work emanated. They walked to the door then stopped, watching several workers remove the carpet from the floor and thoroughly clean the statue where Kaiser had been placed. "How is your friend?"

"He still hasn't regained consciousness," Clouse answered. "The doctors fear the worst."

He hesitated a moment, seeing Daniels make it through the front door with heavy use of crutches. Clouse was amazed his friend left his chair behind at all, so soon after regaining use of his legs.

"You were saying?" Smith asked.

"I need to know who acquired the old tiles from the atrium floor," Clouse answered as Daniels slowly made his way up, depending heavily on his right leg over the left. "Is there any record of who purchased the tiles?"

"Somewhat," Smith answered. "We had a ceremony several years back where many of the tiles were sold. Most everyone who attended put their name on a list, whether they purchased or not. Many put addresses and phone numbers down for contact purposes."

"Who has that list?"

Smith's eyes rolled as he tried to recall.

"You might check with Joan Landamere," the doctor answered. "I think she was in charge of most of the hotel's fund-raising back then."

Clouse felt a chill run through him, hearing that name, and Daniels' face appeared to lose color as he drew an apprehensive expression. Though she was as much a victim as they were the year before, the duo dreaded the idea of having to speak with her again. Daniels knew her more personally after interviewing her several times during the course of his investigation the year before.

"That's all you," Clouse said, passing the buck.

"Thanks," Daniels said with no sincerity. "Impressed?" he asked, looking down at his crutches.

"Walking involves both feet, Mark. You might try using the left one too."

"I'm working on it, hard-ass. Dr. Jameson said I was lucky to even think about using these so soon, but Cindy's kept my legs in great shape."

"Have you felt any cramps yet?" Smith asked, apparently familiar with how difficult walking after a layoff was from his experience in the medical field.

"Oh, yes," Daniels said emphatically. "I still use the chair around the house."

He looked up to the second floor momentarily, as though reflecting on the tragic events from the year prior.

"If you'll excuse me, I've got something upstairs to look at."

"Careful, gimpy," Clouse playfully warned, catching a disapproving shake of the head in return. "He's loosened up around me," Clouse informed Smith quietly, "but the guy's too serious all the time. It's not healthy."

Smith grinned.

"I know a certain firefighter under my employment who once acted much the same."

Clouse smirked, shaking his head. He did not feel he had ever acted quite so seriously on a regular basis.

"Another one of those reporters called me this week wanting exclusive rights to an official account of the events from last year," the doctor said. "I told him where to stick his exclusive."

"I know. They call me almost every week, too. It'll get worse once they find out what's going on now."

Everywhere, unofficial books lined the shelves, attempting to tell the story of the West Baden murders the year before. Most times events were completely wrong or characters were misrepresented. One account made Clouse's character sound like the fugitive from the television series, running to prove his innocence. Another placed Daniels as a determined Hispanic detective, fighting to gain the respect of his white counterparts while solving a case with their jealous eyes watching.

Neither account had any merit.

Names were always changed, and the facts completely misleading, but the newspapers provided so much public information that the books were usually correct in part, with some creative writing used to spice up the characters and details.

Only a few people knew the entire truth, and they weren't talking.

"So how are you holding up these days, doc?" Clouse asked as they walked away from the atrium entrance.

"I'm doing fine," Smith answered. "Rusty's death leaves me at a complete loss. It just seems everyone I've cared about since this project started has either betrayed me or died in the process."

"I know the feeling," Clouse said solemnly. "I promise you I will find out who's behind this before anyone else gets hurt or the hotel's reputation gets tarnished."

"You may be too late for that. You and I are all that's left of the people who care about this place that deeply."

Clouse shook his head.

"There are others. You'd be amazed at the community spirit toward this building."

"But they didn't put it back together," Smith noted. "You and I did. Rusty and David did too, but they're gone." He lost himself in thought a moment. "But if finding who bought those tile pieces can help you, talk to Joan Landamere about some of those fund-raising events and she will probably have some sort of list for you."

List.

Again, the word haunted Clouse. Such a simple word, used by so many people in so many ways. Quickly the word became synonymous with death.

"I'll have Mark check into it," Clouse said. "Somehow we'll figure out who's behind this."

***

Daniels felt compelled to check the Rexford murder room once more. It amazed him how close the hotel came to opening again, only to have more trouble rear its ugly head. Being inside the building conjured bad memories for him, but he was on his feet again, and able to get around.

Sort of.

Riding the elevator to the second floor, Daniels heard a ding as the doors opened, letting him crutch his way out. For a moment, he simply stared down the hallway, which was lit with lights mounted along the walls. Unlike ordinary hotels, the West Baden Springs Hotel was circular in design, so he could only see so far until the hallway curved in either direction.

Decorative carpet lined the floors, matching the gold and forest green decor throughout the atrium. Mostly consisting of leaves and plant life, the designs on the carpet were enchanting, keeping a person's eyes on them instead of the freshly painted walls or decorative doorways.

As he ambled toward the room with the click of crutches under his arms, Daniels rounded a hallway, seeing a glimpse of a dark flash ahead of him, like someone streaking across the hall.

Saying nothing, the officer ignored the room for the time being, staying close to the wall as he struggled toward the area where the person appeared. A perplexed look came across his face when he rounded the next bend, finding nothing. Hearing something behind him from one of the rooms he'd already passed,

Daniels whirled around, nearly losing his balance as his crutches fumbled to gain traction on the carpeting.

Someone streaked down the hall the other way.

"Paul?" Daniels called. "You know better than to fuck with me."

Clouse did know better, leading Daniels to think he was alone on the second floor with someone far less friendly.

Even so, the former detective was between two elevators, neither much closer than the other. Despite an eerie feeling someone was on the second floor with him, he decided to check the murder room anyway, because he was in no condition for a quick escape.

Daniels started back toward the murder room, feeling his muscles tense, and his breathing become heavier. He was almost a dozen rooms away from the closest elevator, and the stairs simply were not an option. The stairs were the only open area where sound might travel to the first floor. Even so, the hotel's vast interior would probably serve to prevent anyone from hearing the officer if he tried calling for help.

Reaching the open door of the Rexford murder room, Daniels slowly peeked inside, wondering where the streak had ended up. Leaning against the doorway, Daniels carefully peered inside the room, hearing another door fling open.

Across the hall.

Barely ducking a scythe planted in the wall where his head had been, with the sound of an ax splitting wood, Daniels fell to the floor. He lost one crutch, clinging to the other for dear life. He looked up, wide-eyed, at his attacker. Dressed in a robe befitting the grim reaper, no face was visible, nor any features to provide any clues. It was the same disguise used the year prior in the West Baden murders.

Without ample means to defend himself, Daniels desperately crawled toward the elevator, boot camp style. He gained several feet, crawling without use of his legs, before the killer pried the weapon from the wall, giving chase.

Hearing footsteps behind him, Daniels instinctively rolled to one side. The scythe sliced through the new carpet like a knife through butter, sticking once again. Rolling to one side, Daniels swung the crutch with what force he could muster, striking the person's knee. As the killer clasped his injured knee, collapsing to the floor, Daniels started toward the elevator once more.

Without his footing, the officer crawled at what felt like a snail's pace toward the elevator, which seemed to grow no closer. Adrenaline kept him from feeling the skin rubbed nearly raw on his elbows as they swung forward, one after another, moving him along. He failed to hear the killer resume the chase until he neared his escape route.

Knowing he would not make it, Daniels used the crutch to punch at the down button on the elevator, but missed. He quickly glanced, seeing the killer slowly rise from the floor, still clasping his knee, but having the presence of mind to retrieve the scythe, yanking it from the floor.

"Shit," Daniels muttered to himself, using the crutch to punch at the down button again.

Once more, it missed.

Now the killer was shaking his knee, trying to lessen the pain. He obviously felt confident Daniels was not going to escape, or perhaps he was playing a game of cat and mouse.

Nervous, but steady enough to try once again, Daniels wriggled himself a bit closer to the elevator and held the crutch firm, finally punching the down button. He then crawled into a small waiting area, just to the right of the elevator doors. He hoped it might offer shelter or offer something useful for self-defense.

Wrong on both counts.

"Damn," Daniels said, realizing the killer was directly behind him as he reached a three-foot jut in the hall where a large glass window provided a view of the atrium for guests while they waited for the elevator to arrive.

It served as a tiny lobby area of sorts, because there was extra room available when former rooms were converted into the elevator shaft on each floor.

Crawling as far in as he could, Daniels flipped over to his backside just as the killer reached the end of the hallway, holding the scythe. With nowhere to run or hide, Daniels used his hands to crab-walk back to the glass, leaving his crutch out of range. There was simply nothing to do except watch as the killer raised the weapon over his head, delaying a few seconds before letting it fly.

Chapter 17

Daniels cringed as the weapon made its way downward. Using both hands, he pulled his head forward of the blade's intended target area. He was shocked to hear a crunching sound, thankful the blade embedded itself in something other than his cranium. He prayed the commotion caught the attention of Clouse, below in the atrium.

The glass cobwebbed where the scythe landed in its center, just above his friend's head. Beyond the obscured surface, he spied the reaper imposter looming above Daniels.

"No!" Daniels heard Clouse exclaim from below, virtually assuring him help was on the way.

Shocked he was still alive Daniels lunged forward for his crutch, thankful the killer failed to hit another mark. As he snagged the crutch, the elevator dinged, indicating it was ready for him. While the killer tried freeing the weapon from the glass, Daniels used the crutch's wide end as a battering ram, striking his attacker squarely in the testicles. While the disguised man hunched over and fell back, Daniels seized the opportunity, crawling toward the elevator.

He quickly found himself inside its serene confines as the doors began to shut. A hand jutted through, preventing their closure as the killer pried them open, now wielding a double-edged knife in his other hand, ready to end the officer's life one way or another.

Daniels forced himself back, quickly raising the crutch, striking the killer's jaw as he did so, clearing the elevator. When the doors closed, Daniels breathed a sigh of relief, unable to imagine who wanted him dead, or why. One thing appeared certain.

Last year was repeating itself.

When the elevator reached the first floor, the door opened, revealing someone racing down the stairs nearby. Tensing in fear, Daniels drew the crutch close, unsure of how many more attacks he could weather.

"Mark," Clouse said, revealing himself from behind the stairwell. "What the hell happened?"

"He came after me," Daniels said between labored breaths, trembling as his friend helped him to his feet. "I think that was our killer."

"Let me get your crutch," Clouse said, starting for the stairs.

"Don't," Daniels said quickly. "Don't go alone."

Clouse hesitated momentarily, with apprehension written in his face before he decided to take the elevator with Daniels.

"I didn't see anyone up there," Clouse said on the way up. "Where was he when you last saw him?"

"I don't know. I hit him, then he fell back. I don't know where he went."

Clouse looked discouraged, being so close to nabbing the killer, and angered that the person dared assault Daniels just a day after the man regained use of his legs.

"How are the legs?" he asked, his hands clenched in fists from his obvious fury.

"Fine," Daniels said, using Clouse almost entirely for support. "They can't hold me up yet."

"I know it might be against protocol, but you might want to keep your piece with you," Clouse warned as the doors opened.

"I plan to," Daniels replied. "Believe me."

***

"What do we have?" McCabe asked a local officer as he sidestepped down the hill toward the cordoned crime scene.

He had already completed an inspection and analysis of the roadside area.

Every track and footprint was now collectively placed in police evidence through photography and other means of preservation.

All morning clouds had hovered overhead, threatening precipitation, adding to the gloomy feeling inside the state trooper's gut when he received the call.

McCabe originally planned to spend his morning investigating Cranor's death, combing through the man's office at the hotel. Things grew more eerie when a call came over his radio pertaining to a body found outside the Paoli town limits, a mere fifteen minutes from the hotel by car.

"Hard to tell what happened," the officer said, staring down at a lump rolled inside a dark blanket. "Found this guy inside the blanket. Coroner's office already pronounced him. Ugly marks all over his arms, and there's basically no face left."

"Any ID?"

"Nothing whatsoever. A number of teeth are knocked out too."

"A bitch to identify him," McCabe commented, pulling latex gloves over each of his hands. "Anything else?" the detective asked, taking the final few steps toward the body, ready to examine it personally.

"A strip of his skin was removed from one arm."

McCabe lifted the blanket, partially saturated with blood, to reveal a skull containing a misty red core in most areas, tatters of skin and fleshy tissue in others. Everything appeared moist, telling him the murder was recent. Parts of the organic material looked like meat chunks from the deli, ready to be plucked off and bagged.

One eye remained, loosely embedded in a chunk of tissue, looking blankly forward at the detective, sending an uneasy feeling through him. The other hung halfway down the cheek, attached only by a few veins protruding from the eye socket. He noticed something was used to pry the man's face to the bone in some areas. The facial area looked a bit like one of the muscle and skeletal illustrations used in science books and classrooms, only with random damage spread throughout. Despite the lack of damage symmetry, McCabe assumed the blows were delivered very purposefully.

Both eyes seemed placed, almost staged deliberately for effect. The face was apparently carved to give the most disturbing appearance possible. It felt like a piece of artwork, perhaps even a grave message meant for McCabe to pass along to Daniels and Clouse. Mafia families were known for sending such abstract and gruesome warnings, but he quickly dismissed that hunch.

"I'd say more than a strip was removed," he added, looking at the claw marks, apparently from fingernails, along each arm.

Based on the mounds of skin beneath the victim's fingernails, McCabe wondered if the wounds were self-inflicted.

"Flip it over," the officer said, speaking of the left arm.

McCabe did so, finding a perfectly rectangular bloody patch along the arm where the skin had been surgically removed, probably to conceal some tattoo or distinguishing mark from authorities. Aside from the cranium, neck area, and the arms, the body appeared practically untouched. Blood saturated the clothing, which appeared intact, though disheveled because the killer needed access to the appendages.

The detective decided to fetch his photography equipment and a radio to summon some forensics experts, suspecting more than a random homicide or robbery cover-up was afoot. With so little to go on, he could ill afford to miss any shred of evidence.

"Who found the body?" he asked the officer.

"Farmer came down here to repair his fence and found this instead."

"He still here?"

"No, but we interviewed him and took his information. Said he'd be home all day. The guys are checking with the neighbors now."

"Good," McCabe said before turning to the body with a thoughtful gaze.

"What's wrong?"

"Nothing," the detective replied, thinking it too coincidental that a person turned up dead with so many identifying marks ripped away. In the wake of the other murders, it didn't seem to fit, but each death scene contained entirely separate clues to begin with. "I need the area sealed off from the road to the body and twenty feet every direction around it," he instructed the officer, since no official crime scene information was apparent.

"Okay, detective," the officer said, ready to rally several of his buddies to assist him.

Accustomed to taking charge, McCabe rather enjoyed being the only state police detective in the area. It kept him busy, but also gave him a sense of purpose and phenomenal opportunity to grow in his profession.

It also frustrated him knowing how the system worked. As fast and accurately as he was able to perform his job, forensics and the brass above him often slowed the process. It often took months, if not a full year, for lab results to make their way back to him. Sure, there were alternatives like the university's labs, or friends in the right places who might occasionally move things along, but McCabe's uses for them came few and far between. He tended to save his favors until no other alternatives remained.

He looked around the body, thumbing through the blanket for anything that stood out. McCabe found nothing in the blanket except dust and several hairs forensic scientists would collect and put in storage until he found them a suspect for comparison.

"Shit," he muttered, checking the victim's genital area for any signs of sexual activity including semen or marks, carefully shielding the body's area from the horde of reporters above, in case they lacked a sense of decency.

Finding nothing, McCabe discovered the murder had something in common with the others after all.

It appeared unsolvable.

***

Seated at a local café, two men desperately tried to piece together the numerous leads that might inevitably help them save several lives, including their own.

"Are you sure you want to do this?" Clouse asked Daniels, concerned for his friend so soon after a near-death experience.

"Positive," the answer came immediately. "I want to find out who that was and chase *him* around with a weapon," Daniels added with a quiver in his voice that came from a controlled anger. "So who are our suspects and their motives?" he asked while Clouse tapped a pencil against the pad of paper he brought from his truck.

"There's always revenge," Clouse said. "They've gone after me, Ken, Rusty, and now you. It's like unfinished business from last year."

"Motive, but who falls in that list of suspects?"

"Any of Angie's family," Clouse said, speaking of his first wife. "I haven't really spoken with any of them since her death and they never seemed to believe in my innocence last year."

"Who else?" Daniels pushed.

"I don't know."

"Who else is around you?"

"Jane, you, Ken, Dr. Smith, people from work sometimes. I don't think anyone around me would do this."

Daniels grimaced.

"That's what you thought last year. What about your pal Tim?"

"Tim? He'd never do something like that. We grew up together. He goes to church picnics, takes his family to Disneyland, and keeps his work close to home."

"He was carrying a shotgun."

"Yeah, but-"

"And doesn't he work construction?"

"Damn it, Mark. He doesn't have it in him. I'm sure you're going to think it was all just a bit too coincidental that he was with Ken when he got abducted by those freaks, and all he got was a bump upside the head, but he's no killer. Speaking of which, you're not paying much attention to the possible occult aspect. What about the guy who approached me with information?"

Daniels showed his indifference about the subject by looking away momentarily.

"It may be bullshit, Paul. A Coven? Stephen? Jacob? You're throwing these names at me because they're what he said. There's no proof of occult involvement in this."

"And there's none to the contrary."

Clouse put his hands up defensively, showing his palms.

"Alright, back to your revenge theory. What if it's someone seeking retribution for a slain relative last year?"

"Rusty Cranor's daughter was murdered," Daniels thought aloud. "So was her boyfriend. The list just goes on. You've got a point, but that's a lot of people to check out."

"I know," Clouse said. "I also want to know how these tile floor pieces tie into everything. There has to be a reason they're so important. You know what Dr. Smith said about that."

"Yeah," the officer said reluctantly. "It means I get to talk to Mrs. Landamere."

"The sooner the better," Clouse added, jotting down several more ideas for leads on the notepad. "We're running out of time."

"What do you mean?" Daniels asked after a sip of coffee.

"Have you thought about what holiday we're coming up to?"

Daniels drifted off in thought a moment of the things brought by the fall season, taking a quick look outside. Fallen leaves, bare lawns, chilly breezes, and cloudy skies. They culminated for the perfect witching season.

"Halloween," he answered, realizing how significant it was the year before.

If the possibility of occult participation proved true, it became all the more important to stop the killer from striking again, especially with such a critical date impending.

"Let's go talk to Mrs. Landamere," Daniels said, reaching for his crutches.

Chapter 18

Clouse phoned Jane to have her pick Zach up from school again, knowing he would not be home until after dark. He wished things could be normal again as a view of colorful leaves blurred past the driver's side window, their beauty virtually unnoticed by Clouse in his distracted state. Picking his son up from school ordinarily seemed mundane, but now it felt rather dear to him as friends and colleagues died around him or remained steadily unconscious in hospital beds.

Daniels seemed disappointed not to hear from McCabe all day, but both he and Clouse had come to realize it was up to them, and them alone, to find the killer's identity before they joined the list of casualties.

"How do you do it?" Daniels asked from the passenger seat as they neared Joan Landamere's house, which sat in the midst of abundant nature.

"Do what?"

"Go on with everyday life knowing someone is out there wanting you or everyone around you dead?"

"You're sounding abstract. You know? It's not like your situation is any different."

Daniels gave no reply, so Clouse spoke first.

"Truthfully, I worry more about those around me than I do myself. People can't go on living any sense of normal life thinking every corner might reveal a serial killer. I'm a big boy, Mark. I take care of myself and worry more about others."

Silence for a moment.

"Did you cry when Angie died last year?"

Clouse exhaled a sigh, letting the disturbing nature of the question show. It was out of character for Daniels to inquire about Clouse's personal life, even as good of friends as they had become. Perhaps the idea of their own mortality weighed heavily on each of them.

"Why are you asking that?"

"It's just that everyone had you made out to be some greedy son-of-a-bitch out to kill his own wife for the benefit of a life insurance policy. When my partner and I questioned you, you really kept it together and acted stoic. I want to know how the real Paul Clouse reacted behind closed doors."

Clouse nodded. Daniels' forward nature surprised him, but he felt comfortable enough to give an answer because a year later he knew the man as a friend instead of a cop.

"Alright. I cried myself to sleep that night, Mark. After you and your partner hounded me for answers that I couldn't give, I put my boy to bed and I cried my ass off. Are you happy?"

Daniels glanced over for just a second before returning his eyes to the road.

"While we're clearing the air, I'm going to ask you something, buddy," Clouse said.

"Fire away."

"You spent a year in that wheelchair. Unable to walk, couldn't go out with the wife and kids, couldn't recover your life the way I did. All this because you were the only one with guts enough to believe me and search for the truth. Do you blame me for what happened?"

Daniels thought a moment. The question apparently hit equally as hard as any inquisition he threw at Clouse.

"No, I don't blame you," Daniels answered slowly, as though not entirely sure he believed his own words. "I don't regret sticking up for you, taking a bullet in the back, or missing a year's worth of work, or even putting a bullet in Dave Landamere's head. The only thing I regret is putting myself in such a lonely spot for so long."

"What do you mean?"

"I fell into a trap of self-pity and shut out everything important to me."

Both reflected on the answers a moment.

"Feel better?" Clouse asked, pulling into the appropriate driveway.

"Not really."

"Me neither."

Both remained silent as the house came into view beyond a large iron gate.

"You know, I stopped taking my medication," Daniels revealed, as though Clouse was the only person he might confide in.

"Why?"

"I feel better without it. Don't tell Cindy or she'll flip out, but I don't feel as tired and groggy now that I'm off it."

"Then don't take it," Clouse agreed.

As dusk approached the gorgeous property, encumbered by unique shrubs and highly detailed stone figurines, mainly in the picket fenced rear, the two men approached the front door. Daniels hesitated before knocking, but gave three quick raps. Both knew they were being viewed through the peep hole in the door momentarily, then several deadbolts unlocked and the electronic beeps of a security system being deactivated were audible from their position.

"Mrs. Landamere," Daniels said, viewing the older woman from head to toe as Clouse did the same.

Conservative, short gray hair took nothing away from an unusually youthful figure. Dressed in a light blouse with dark slacks and off-white tennis shoes that worked perfectly for casual dress, a flood of yellow light emitted by the numerous ornate lamps almost silhouetted her in the doorway. In her right hand, she cupped a short glass filled with what appeared to be a strong alcoholic beverage.

"Detective," she said, recognizing Daniels instantly, despite the crutches supporting him. "Do come in."

Daniels seemed a bit uncomfortable as he followed Clouse inside.

Clouse recalled Daniels telling him stories about how Joan flirted with him briefly the previous fall, despite being his mother's age. The former detective apparently hoped to avoid such conversation again, trying to keep his eyes strictly to himself.

"Have a seat," she said, inviting them into the spacious living room, waving them toward any number of couches or love seats. "How may I help you two?"

"It's started again, Mrs. Landamere," Daniels said after settling into a couch, placing the crutches beside him.

"I heard," she said, slumping herself into a chair across from both of them, taking a long, stiff drink from the glass. "I prayed it wasn't true. I hoped and prayed."

"Mrs. Landamere," Daniels said. "I know this may be difficult, but we need to ask about a list that might help us stop the killer before he strikes again."

"Before you ask me to help you on this, detective, I want to explain to you exactly what the last year of my life has been like," she said matter-of-factly, much like Bette Davis might have in any number of her movies. "You both think you know what David put me through, but I've never told anyone, including the press, including the police, exactly what happened to me that day."

Daniels nodded as he sat back, trying to find a comfortable position before hearing the tale both men genuinely wanted to hear.

"The day everything happened, David already had Detective Daniels safely tucked in the hotel," she began, looking to Clouse. "David comes home acting as cheerful as he can be, considering he missed two weeks of work, giving me only a phone call between visits."

She shifted uneasily in her seat before continuing.

"Well, I think little of it until he says he wants to check on the hotel's condition in his absence. He wants me to go with him," Joan said, the glass in her hand trembling slightly. The words came uneasily and she paused before restarting her story.

"Naturally I'm a bit reluctant because he never asks me to go with him on business, and everyone there knew we were a marriage of convenience. It was no secret, and I was wondering exactly what he was up to."

She took another drink from the glass, taking time to refill it at the nearby bar.

"Care for any?" she asked her guests, both refusing with open palms.

After settling back into her chair, she prepared to continue.

"This is my strength now," she said of the drink in her hand. "Every day I live with a security system on, every night with the front gates locked. I knew it wouldn't stop with David's death."

"Why did you go with him?" Daniels asked, prompting her to return to the narrative.

"I was concerned for my safety if I didn't," she said. "After all, he made the money and left me to the life I always wanted, surrounded by the garden and tranquility I loved. Though he never said it, the ability was his to remove it all in a heartbeat. Something about his eyes let me know there would be consequences if I did not go. Or he would force me to go anyway."

"Was Roger there?" Clouse asked of Landamere's accomplice.

Roger Summers was Clouse's brother-in-law, and a fellow firefighter, who attempted to frame him for the murders.

"He didn't show up until later," Joan answered. "It was when we reached the hotel and everyone was gone that he set up the final scenario. He dragged Detective Daniels out from the back," she noted, causing Daniels to uncomfortably look anywhere except toward the two other people in the room, remembering how helpless he was for two days at the hands of Landamere, bound and gagged in a secluded room.

"The two took great pleasure in tying me up to the post before they gagged me," Joan continued. "David then told me everything he planned to do, including how he planned to kill me and pin everything on you, Mr. Clouse. Until you arrived, I was the subject of taunts and revelations even the devil might cower at," she noted, closing her eyes to block the emotion.

"At that point I realized they were both insane, and almost nothing would stop their plan. They had it worked out in such detail, that I questioned how anyone would ever believe otherwise once all three of us were dead." She quietly trembled for a moment. "I truly believed none of us were going to make it out of there alive."

"Inadvertently we all contributed to their scheme," Clouse said. "We all survived a horrible ordeal."

"What I'm about to say is the part I've never told anyone else," Joan said, putting the glass down on a small table beside her.

Both Clouse and Daniels leaned forward in anticipation.

"When David spoke of contributors to his potential purchase of the hotel, I think he spoke of some very powerful businessmen."

"I thought he was talking about investors or stock holders," Clouse said.

"No," Joan said. "A different sort of power."

"Are you speaking of mafia involvement?" Daniels questioned.

"Perhaps. He told me they were people who could get things done. That's what he said."

Daniels and Clouse locked eyes for a moment, knowing what sorts of things were getting done by the mysterious presence.

All three sat silently a moment longer.

"We came to see if you might have a list," Clouse said. "A list of people who might have purchased pieces of the old tile floor, or even names and addresses of hotel visitors. People who toured and bought at the souvenir shop. Anything."

Joan held up a finger, stood, and walked into the parlor. Clouse and Daniels exchanged looks again as she shuffled through a desk drawer.

"This should help," she said, returning with a worn notebook, several of its pages clinging to life inside the wire binding.

"What is it?" Clouse inquired.

"Several years ago we sold the pieces during an auction at a hotel gathering. It was before you started work with Kieffer Construction, Mr. Clouse. I hope it helps with whatever you're looking for," she said with a look of empathy, and a certain emptiness in her eyes they both related to.

"It will," Clouse said. "Could anyone else have seen this list?"

"David would have had access to it," she said, all three outwardly realizing the dire consequences of Landamere's access. "The previous secretary had that notebook, but of course she passed away. Poor thing was eighty-five."

"You've been a great help," Daniels said, balancing himself to his feet with the crutches. "Be careful, Mrs. Landamere," he added, giving her one of his old cards. "If you need anything, just call me."

"I will, detective. And I'll be sure to watch the news. With any luck at all, I'll see you apprehending the killer instead of more senseless killings. Why that one this morning was the worst yet."

"What?" Clouse asked, looking from her to Daniels, who seemed equally clueless about the homicide.

"The young man they found outside of Paoli. The news man said his face and arms were nearly torn off."

Clouse and Daniels quickly said departing words, ready to contact McCabe and discover just what they had missed.

***

While waiting for Clouse's return, Jane sat down with a magazine after unpacking more of their belongings. After a day at the clinic, and organizing the house, she felt drained. She worried about her fiancé and everything happening around him. They met soon after his wife had died the past year, and though they did not court for some time after that, she felt close to him during the ordeal the first time through.

She heard sounds of laughter behind her from the backyard as the kids played during the last few minutes of sunlight. Soon she would put them to bed with the hope that Clouse might be home in time to read them a bedtime story. Beside her, a fire roared in the fireplace, countering the cold drafts their large house allowed to roam throughout its two stories.

Feeling a slight chill run through her, Jane found herself in the mood for some hot chicken soup. She walked to the kitchen, taking a few minutes to open the can and heat it on the stovetop. Placing the burner on a simmering temperature, she decided to call the kids inside.

Before she reached the front door, a disturbance came from the back bedroom in the form of the stereo she had unpacked and set up just a few hours prior. Sounding like one of the hard rock songs Clouse often listened to, Jane found it difficult to tell whether it was a CD or the radio kicking on because the stereo system's volume was so high.

She did not recall placing any compact discs in the stereo or turning it on. Whether or not she even plugged the device in was in question. Still, she made her way back to the room, wincing from the deafening tones as she turned the volume control down, then turned the stereo off completely, looking around for what might have brought it to life.

From the back bedroom, one hallway led back to the kitchen while the adjacent hallway led to a bathroom, then the family room. She decided not to search that hallway.

A bit nervous, she turned all the lights on as she walked toward the kitchen. A door creaked open, causing her to rush her pace.

"Paul?" she called, reaching the kitchen, realizing the front door was closed. "Damn," she said, turning off the stove as the soup bubbled.

Turning her attention to the family room, Jane knew the creaking door had to be the house's side exit. Slowly, she stepped toward the doorway to the family room where the fire could not curtail the draft pushing through to the kitchen. Her fear was realized when she saw the door swung open from the edge of the room, feeling almost positive someone else was in the house.

Or at least had been.

Without turning her attention from the family room, she stepped back. Her destination, the front door, seemed several nervous breaths away as she frantically looked around her, feeding into the paranoia Clouse was all too familiar with. Never again would Jane doubt anything he said about creepy experiences.

Kids, she suddenly thought, oblivious the past few minutes to any sounds around her, except those of creaking doors. Her eyes focused on the family room and the open door, swinging lightly with the breeze from outside, thumping against the wall.

Reaching behind her for the doorknob, Jane refused to wait any longer. She turned to open it as a hand clasped her own.

She shrieked until realizing her potential attacker was her future stepson. Jane cupped her mouth to both apologize and muffle her fear as she collected herself.

"Zach, where is Katie?" she asked, still trembling.

"She's outside. We saw the side door open."

"Katie!" she called, defensively taking Zach by the hand. "Come here, sweetie!"

Little Katie came running through the same side door Zach had, taking the long way around the winding hallway where the back bedroom was located. If someone had turned on the stereo in the bedroom, he could have easily slipped around the back hallway and exited through the side door before Jane realized it. The blaring music distracted her long enough to keep her from finding the person, and scared her enough to keep the kids close.

She intended to keep Clouse much closer too. Someone violated her life and her house, and Jane would be damned if she let it happen again.

Taking up a knife from the nearest kitchen drawer, Jane walked into the family room, closing the door when she reached it. She looked around the room, then to the bedrooms and upstairs. The kids followed her every step, wondering what the commotion was about, and why she clutched the knife when she reached the base of the darkened stairwell.

"Stay right here," Jane instructed the children.

The light atop the staircase was burned out from her numerous trips up and down that day while cleaning house and she had no intentions of searching a darkened hallway without protection. She slowly ascended the stairs, looking down periodically to ensure the children remained still, and safe, while she listened for any noises out of place above her. Several thoughts of how someone murdered Clouse's first wife almost a year to the date roamed unchecked through her mind, especially with the strange goings-on around the couple lately. Someone lured her to the top of the stairs, and Jane seemed to recall something about a light bulb not working.

Clasping a flashlight along the wall when she reached the top of the stairs, Jane quickly checked Zach's room and breathed a sigh of relief after finding nothing disturbed. Of course her future stepson's usual mess was present because his father refused to enforce rules too strictly. She tried to tell Clouse that Zach needed structure, but her fiancé seemed to think his son was like an egg, easily cracked so soon after his mother's death if pushed too hard.

Looking down the stairs, she made certain both children were in the same spot before moving to the next room. The door opened with a creaking sound, allowing her to peer inside with the flashlight's guidance. This being Katie's room, peach-colored translucent curtains wafted from the gentle breeze barging into the house. Jane recalled opening the windows because the afternoon sun left the house a bit warm while she cleaned.

Deciding to check the room a bit more thoroughly, Jane shut the window before kneeling down to look under the bed. Perhaps past viewing of too many horror movies set the image of someone stabbing at her eyes from beneath the bed, so she cautious kept her distance while shining the light from headboard to footboard. Seeing nothing except a few thin books and a doll, Jane exhaled as she stood. She next slid the folding closet doors open, seeing only hung clothes and some organizational dividers along the floor. Content that her daughter's room was safe, Jane quickly inspected the shared bathroom and the guest room to find nothing out of the ordinary.

Satisfied the house was clear of any intruders, Jane quickly returned downstairs with thoughts that maybe she was paranoid and nothing strange really happened. But the more she thought about it the most certain she felt that the stereo was unplugged that afternoon. Taking no chances, she made certain each door was locked, turning each one's deadbolt to assure heightened security until Clouse returned.

Starting the next day, she planned to make some lifestyle changes for the better.

Chapter 19

Clouse spent the next morning on the computer, searching for any ties to the Coven or his secret helper. When he and Daniels parted ways they photocopied the notebook so each possessed a copy. Daniels vowed to meet with McCabe and discover more about the murder they heard about through Joan Landamere.

He had returned home to find Jane awake by the fireplace, too upset to sleep. They talked about how she thought someone might have been inside the house, despite Clouse thinking it was the kids all along. He refused to doubt her entirely, because experience had taught him better. Raising the security around his family seemed the logical solution, and Jane said she wanted him around the house more, instead of seeking out the killer.

A feeling of responsibility toward potential victims, including his own family, pushed him forward in the investigation. He knew hesitation usually resulted in countless deaths and put himself and those around him at risk. Jane needed to understand why he and Daniels sought out the killer.

They had lived through it once before.

Clouse had already taken several steps in securing his family, including a call to a local electronic security firm. He planned to purchase a handgun and permit in town later that day. Indiana law would probably force him to wait a week before taking the gun home, but he would feel more secure.

Letting his dogs stay in the house provided another layer of protection. If he made Jane feel secure again, she might open up to the idea of him pursuing the killer.

He still doubted that was *ever* going to happen.

As he sat before the computer monitor, the phone rang.

"Hello?"

"Paul, it's Mark."

"What's new?"

"McCabe told me the body was unidentified and they don't have a clue who it might be. Too many teeth and distinguishing marks are missing."

"Makes it tough, doesn't it?"

"Somewhat. You have time to do some legwork on this list of ours today?"

"It seems I've been grounded."

"How's that?"

Clouse quickly explained Jane's story from the night before.

"She wants me here all the time."

"Maybe I can talk to her for you."

"Not a good idea, Mark. I'm trying to heighten her sense of security so I can get out of here. We both know sitting around won't help a bit."

"You're right about that. I'm trying to cross-reference some of the names on this list with any crimes. If these people bought pieces of that tile floor, they may have been burglarized in the past couple years, or someone might have contacted them asking to purchase the pieces."

"Or they might have met with foul play," Clouse suggested.

"I'll find out soon enough. So, what have you been working on?"

"Playing on the internet to see if I can track this Coven or anything about it down. I go back to work tomorrow, so I'll see Tony Dierker. He's a computer whiz who can probably track down stuff I can't."

"He can't do any worse than we are."

"Let me know if you come up with anything on that list, Mark."

"I will. Tug might want you to look at that body later. He thinks it might be someone you know if it's related to the hotel."

"So you two are on first name basis, huh?"

"Jealous?"

"I'll get over it," Clouse replied dryly. "Call me if you find anything."

"Will do," Daniels said before hanging up.

Clouse spent a few more minutes searching through related websites, relying on keywords to guide him. With the computer calling up any listing of "coven" or any references to the occult, the firefighter looked at a potential of spending days tracking down any realistic lead.

"You've got mail," the computer voice of his server said.

"Thanks," Clouse said more to himself than the voice, clicking out of another fruitless website to view his mail.

He saw the message from StephenCov was sent as a delayed message, received only at the current time specified. The message box read: "Valuable information."

Slightly apprehensive, Clouse clicked on the message.

> Paul,
>
> After our meeting the other day, I realized Jacob had me figured out. I couldn't risk sending you something in the mail for fear he would intercept it. Even this could be intercepted, so I delayed it. Unfortunately, the message I leave you is somewhat encrypted because I know you will figure it out before anyone else.
>
> At this point I am probably dead, but I won't give you any hints about myself, the Coven, or their objectives because my family would be both horrified and ashamed at what I've done and affiliated myself with.
>
> In closing, I give you the location of your list, though you will need to think a bit before understanding it.
>
> Look in the place where the puzzle pieces most.
>
> Best of luck,
> Stephen

"What the hell?" Clouse asked after closing the message, certain to save it for the next day in case Dierker could help him track it down.

Granted, Stephen would not make it easy for authorities to track him, but Clouse wanted to know who the man was, where he came from, and everything he could about the Coven. McCabe and Daniels could doubt Stephen's words all they wanted, but Clouse was a believer.

"Where the puzzle pieces most," Clouse repeated the riddle to himself.

What puzzle?

What pieces?

Clouse harbored urges to knock Stephen silly if he found the man again, if he wasn't already among the recently deceased. Somehow he suspected the body McCabe busily investigated was probably that of Stephen, but it sounded like they might never know.

If what Stephen wrote was true, his family knew nothing about his affiliation with the alleged group, so perhaps his family considered him missing. If so, investigators were probably already looking for him, perhaps under a different identity, but a match would identify him and lead Clouse closer to the truth.

He decided to call Daniels with his discovery later that afternoon, but he wanted to do some more searching on the internet for the Coven or any missing persons between the ages of eighteen and twenty-five before he did so.

A yawn forced his mouth open, hinting that his day might be longer than he suspected.

***

"No, Mr. Barnett, you cannot see the patient unless you are with the family," the nurse scolded the unwanted guest.

"I have a story to do and I need to talk with *someone*," the local black newspaper reporter retorted. "It's eight o'clock and my deadline is almost here."

"No one but family is allowed to see Officer Kaiser," the nurse replied.

"Is any of the family here? I'll settle for anyone at this point."

"No. They've all left for the night," the thick-bodied veteran nurse said. "And I'm going to have to ask you to do the same."

Everyone in Bloomington knew Jerome Barnett from the *Bloomington Post* as a household name after his coverage of the West Baden slayings the year before. Unlike several other reporters, he failed to capitalize on the events by publishing a book, but it wasn't for lack of effort.

After failing to secure interviews with Clouse, Daniels, Smith, or any of the other key witnesses to the finale of the murders, he aggressively sought current related events, especially when the murders began again. His articles, accompanied by his photo, and his beaming, almost insincere smile, were an everyday occurrence in the *Post*.

It was as though he knew whatever words rested beside his photograph and byline were going to be exaggerations used to sell newspapers.

"Visiting hours are over," the nurse said sternly. "As you can see, no one else is here," she said, waving a hand toward the vacant hallway on either side of them. Only she and one other nurse remained on the floor for the remainder of their shift.

"But I-"

"*Over*," she repeated sternly as someone stepped from Kaiser's room, instantly catching the reporter's attention.

"He's not family," Barnett said, pointing to Tim Niemeyer, who slowly ambled toward them, ready to leave after a long day of visiting his comatose friend. His eyes seemed to follow the dark lines of the floor as he walked toward the elevator.

"He has family permission to be here," the nurse said.

She looked to the other nurse, a younger redhead, who had just returned from rounds.

"Lisa, would you please see that Mr. Barnett leaves the floor before I have to call security?"

Niemeyer, hearing the escalating volume of the conversation, looked up. He recognized the reporter, cursed under his breath, and turned around, heading for a flight of stairs as an alternate means of egress.

"Mr. Niemeyer," Barnett said, giving chase. "How do you feel about police speculation that you might be the new West Baden killer?" he asked a piercing, though unfounded question to gain the attention of the stocky construction boss.

It worked.

Niemeyer turned around, readying his right hand into a fist, but stood perfectly still, knowing better than to punch Barnett or give in to the man's preposterous claims. As the nurse blocked the reporter's path, Niemeyer simply turned around, heading for the staircase.

In doing so, he passed Kaiser's room again, tuning out the taunts Barnett threw at him from afar.

Niemeyer apparently had other things to worry about, but the reporter had planted a seed that would likely help him later.

***

Inside the room, Kaiser groaned and mumbled in his sleep, showing the first signs of life in several days. Constant visits kept his mind working, even if his body refused to cooperate. Now, after hearing Niemeyer's voice so close for hours, and a disturbance in the hall, Kaiser's body decided to return to the real world.

His brown eyes fluttered momentarily, adjusting to the dark room, which seemed intently bright after days of unconsciousness. He could see everything around him clearly, feeling the tubes inside his nose. For a moment he simply breathed, lived, and took in the room around him, remembering the horror of being beaten and laid upon the statue, barely conscious from the intense pain.

He remembered the needle being plunged into his arm and looking down at the faces of the three people attempting to kill him, almost positive he recognized one of them through the blinding pain. As the man who referred to himself as Jacob commanded the other two, Kaiser stole a glance at the list, seeing which name fell after his own.

Feeling parched in the throat, Kaiser reached for the phone, unsure of whether or not he was capable of speech. Swallowing to regain some moisture in his vocal chords, Kaiser slowly dialed the number to Clouse's cellular phone. It rang three times before his friend picked up.

"Hello?"

Kaiser tried to speak, but only muffled, coarse groans emitted from his throat.

"Hello?" Clouse asked again, a bit more emphatic this time.

Kaiser attempted to speak again, but it took several seconds before he was able to utter a word.

"Paul," he said as a click reached his ear.

Already exhausted, Kaiser let the phone fall to the floor from his limp hand. He looked around him, trying to find the pager to summon a nurse. He patted down the side of the bed with his hand until he found the device, pushing on it. Soon he would be free of the hospital bed, and perhaps able to help Clouse find the real killer before the person struck again.

Though it took several minutes, someone walked through the door, with several items in hand. Kaiser looked through dizzied eyes as a womanly figure walked toward him, and he saw a gleam of metal as she raised something from beside her waist.

Something that might be sharp.

"No!" Kaiser yelled, squirming away from the nurse who tried to place the stethoscope near his heart.

"Settle down, sir," the redheaded nurse said calmly. "You've been through a traumatic experience. I'm here to help."

"I need to talk to Paul Clouse," Kaiser stammered.

"There will be time for that later," the nurse assured him. "I'm going to fetch a doctor to have a look at you."

Before Kaiser could utter any defiance, a streak of darkness entered the room, clasping the nurse's mouth. To the officer's horror, the killer raised a dual-edged knife, its blade gleaming from what little light entered the room from the hallway. Despite the nurse's muffled cries, she was at the mercy of the shadowy figure.

Wasting little time, he rammed the knife through the woman's backside. Its blade pierced her chest at the sternum, the tip covered in shiny blood, which trickled down her uniform blouse before her lifeless form was dropped to the floor with a thud.

Horrified, Kaiser shrank back toward the edge of the bed, watching as the killer wiped the knife on his own dark costume. The officer recognized the grim reaper costume from past experience, but until the killer placed a knife within a sheath at his side and drew out a small, modified scythe, Kaiser did not feel sheer terror about his own mortality.

"Shit," he said, falling back from the bed, pulling the entanglement of tubes from his nose by force.

He landed awkwardly on the floor, quickly regaining his footing, despite a weak, dizzy feeling throughout his body.

Staying in a crouched position, Kaiser quickly surveyed the room, seeing the killer nowhere in sight. Weaponless, and in no condition to do battle, the officer spied a vase beside him on a table. Seeing few other alternatives, he snatched it, slowly walking around the hospital bed toward the door, cautiously looking around him as he stayed low to the ground.

Wearing nothing more than a hospital gown, Kaiser felt even more disadvantaged. Bare feet and scanty clothing would not get him far. On sheer adrenaline he walked around the edge of the bed, carefully stepping over the nurse's body, hearing a creak from somewhere in the room.

His own nervous breathing drowned out most every other noise in the room, but he stopped momentarily, holding his breath, to listen intently.

Less than a second passed before the entire bed came springing upright from the floor toward him, pinning him against the wall. The vase fell to the floor, shattering into what seemed a million pieces. Kaiser felt the air depart his lungs as the killer's seemingly faceless form rose from behind the bed, drawing the knife from its sheath once again, drawing back to stab at the officer's throat.

Using what little energy he possessed, and one free hand, Kaiser punched the killer through the faceless hood, connecting with what he thought was a real nose. With no force behind it, the bed fell to the floor as the killer stumbled back.

Kaiser started toward the door, feeling the equivalent pain of a thousand pins and needles batter his feet. The vase's shards of glass pierced the tender skin, making it almost impossible to walk. He gave in, falling to the floor in a quick attempt to crawl into the hallway and pick the glass splinters from his feet in the process.

He managed to open the door and reach the hallway, attempting to crawl away as his attacker neared him, scythe in hand. Kaiser evaded one swing of the weapon, rolling himself against a wall. Using one of the shards pried from his feet he cut the killer along the ankle, trying for the Achilles heel. The costumed reaper reacted, clasping the ankle, but soon picked up the pace, taking the scythe and marching toward Kaiser once more.

Feeling a kick to his ribs that probably cracked one or more, Kaiser rolled against the wall, taking another kick from some form of hard footwear. It felt military-grade, much like the police issue boots he usually wore on patrol. He groaned, feeling another swift kick to his kidney, rolling to his back, facing the killer who loomed directly above him.

Looking down the hallway, Kaiser spied an empty nurses' station. Knowing the nurse who attempted to assist him couldn't be the only one on the floor, he tried to let out a cry for help as the killer yanked his feet, dragging him into the room. Kaiser managed a single bellow for assistance that went unheard as the door slammed shut and the glass shards pierced his back, turning his "Help!" into more of a pitiful loud groan.

Bleeding from his feet and back, and losing what little strength he originally possessed, Kaiser took one last good kick at his assailant, striking the person's leg beneath the knee. The move bought him a few seconds as the cloaked attacker went down to one knee, and Kaiser tried to roll himself over to crawl for the door once again.

Kaiser only managed a foot or two at best before the killer caught up, rolling him to his back before raking him over the broken glass again. Moaning in agony from the dozens of miniature knives stabbing him, Kaiser slowly looked upward, devoid of any strength necessary to fight back.

He saw the killer already holding the scythe behind his head, ready to swing it down upon him.

"Fuck you," Kaiser muttered, suspecting who his killer was before the blade hurled toward his chest.

Chapter 20

McCabe arrived shortly after ten o'clock at the hospital. He was nearly finished at his favorite bar when the vibration from his pager took him from a card game. Since he was winning, it seemed fishy to the other players his job suddenly summoned him.

"When Lisa didn't come back after half an hour I started searching the rooms," he overheard a black nurse tell one of the Bloomington detectives in a broken voice as he passed the nurses' station.

A camera bag at his side, he focused exclusively on Daniels and the open door ahead. McCabe knew which room it was after several personal visits to Kaiser, but he was given no details about what to expect. Because he was already investigating several other related murders, including the first attempt on Kaiser, Bloomington officers immediately requested him.

Outside the room, a slight bloody streak became visible along the edge of the wall, only if a person studied the floor carefully. Where the trail appeared to have started before a brief cleansing, a large chunk of the floor tile appeared forcibly dislodged. McCabe knew which clues to search for, even when alcohol did some of his thinking for him.

"It's not pretty," Daniels commented as they stood at the door's threshold.

"Anyone been inside?"

"Only the nurse who found the bodies."

"Bodies?"

Daniels nodded solemnly.

"Our killer took out Kaiser and a nurse."

McCabe let out a belch, controlled by the closed fist applied to his mouth.

"You been out?" Daniels asked him, aside from the other cops.

"Yes," the detective answered the silent accusation. "Don't worry. I'm fine."

Daniels probably wasn't concerned how well the man held his alcohol, but rather how efficient he would be at performing job tasks. Any speck of evidence overlooked would never be recovered. Daniels appeared rather uncomfortable being around the Bloomington detectives he once worked with on a daily basis. He failed to fit in, wearing jeans and a hooded sweatshirt, a bulge seated beneath his right shoulder.

"You packing?" McCabe asked, noticing the protrusion.

"After what happened yesterday, I won't leave my house unarmed," Daniels replied. "I've got a family to worry about."

"Your buddies won't say anything?" McCabe inquired, knowing one of the stipulations of Daniels working with him was that he remain unarmed and carry no identification affiliating him with the Bloomington Police Department until his rehabilitation was complete.

In other words, he was to act merely as a source of information.

"They won't care," Daniels said. "I worked with all of them before my accident last year."

McCabe let out another quiet belch, looking around this time for anyone who might have heard. Most of the officers were mingling in small groups, or questioning hospital staff. Only a few people were even visible on the floor, although a deputy coroner was one of them.

Assured everyone was too occupied to have noticed the sound, McCabe looked inside the room.

"Any witnesses?" he asked Daniels.

"None."

"What about security cameras?"

"They tape a sequential pattern from floor to floor. We've got officers reviewing the tape, but it seems unlikely they caught the right moment."

McCabe thought a moment about his bad luck, finally deciding to make the best of what he had.

"Let's do this," he said, leading the way inside where he stopped just past the door, able to survey the carnage.

Daniels appeared unmoved by the scene, but McCabe took in the chaotic mess for the first time, carefully panning the room. The overturned bed, the pools of blood, the white-heeled shoes of the nurse, still attached to unmoving, smooth legs. All at once, the view flooded his mind, leaving him with any number of ideas about where to begin his search for clues.

"Did you know Kaiser?" McCabe asked, looking over to the overturned body of the county officer, face-down on the tile floor, one hand placed upon the heating unit as though reaching for something to save him.

The detective knew Kaiser's body was positioned after death from the blood he spied in the hallway. A path of blood led across the fallen bed mattress from the direction of the hallway, leading him to believe the killer again sent a message, leaving the county officer in such a prone position.

"Knew him a little through Paul."

"He was a good guy from what I understand," McCabe replied. "Never had a chance to work with him, but a lot of the guys said he was an outstanding officer."

"That I can vouch for," Daniels said, remembering the year before when Kaiser saved him from a bullet in the head at the hands of David Landamere.

McCabe further examined the room without benefit of moving. He pulled his camera from the bag, attached the flash, and began scrutinizing through the lens with each push of the button.

First shot.

Ignoring the untouched wall to the left of the door, the shot included part of the overturned, bloodstained mattress, and the lower half of Kaiser's body.

His bare feet protruded from the hospital gown. Spatters of blood speckled the gown, mostly from a weapon's impact, but some from moving the body. The tubes formerly providing Kaiser sustenance and oxygen lay to the left of his body, hastily discarded in McCabe's opinion.

He began to assess exactly what happened.

Second shot.

Finishing the view of the overturned mattress, the shot included Kaiser's torso. His left hand was placed atop the heating unit as the rest of him lay flat on the floor, face down. A cavernous, bloody pool stained the clothing. Through the blood and shredded area of cloth, McCabe saw some flesh color, including strips of skin dangling from the open wound. The weapon exited through the officer's back, thus chipping the floor as McCabe noticed in the hallway.

"Whoever did this cleaned it awfully quick," McCabe noted aloud.

"I smelled a cleaning agent of some sort," Daniels said. "I asked one of the detectives to check their closest janitorial closet, but he hasn't come back yet."

"Good thinking," McCabe noted, realizing he missed the smell, or it had diminished too much by the time he arrived.

Third shot.

Moving the camera to a completely different area of the room, directly to his right, McCabe photographed the dead nurse, hands lying open on either side of her body, as though placed in a holy position. Her head looked awkwardly angled to one side.

She was dead before she even hit the floor. From the blood stains in her white uniform McCabe deduced what happened, but the mess seemed extremely conservative compared to Kaiser's wounds.

He recalled Daniels' story of the killer pulling a knife on him in the hotel elevator. Compared to last year, the killings seemed far less predictable. Various weapons and no clear motive left McCabe wondering where to begin, even after half a dozen murders.

"I'll be right back," Daniels said as McCabe focused exclusively on the room.

"Okay."

***

Growing tired of McCabe's silent, mental calculations of the scene, Daniels stepped into the hall, finding a distraught, well-dressed man approaching the edge of the police line where several uniformed officers and detectives halted his approach, although the hospital security officer seemed to know him.

"I'm Barry Andrews," the man said as Daniels quickly looked him over, wondering why a doctor would be so despondent.

He had noticed the man's hospital identification badge pinned to his knitted gray sweater.

With brown hair, laced with streaks of gray, and a smooth face accented by greenish hazel eyes, he looked like the type of person cast for a Lifetime Channel original movie as a caring husband and father. His fluent, deep voice would nearly guarantee him a role.

"I was downstairs," he began to explain. "I heard someone was murdered and my girlfriend works up here."

Daniels moved forward with the assistance of his crutches.

"Can I talk to him?" he asked the lead detective.

An affirmative nod allowed Daniels to proceed. Too busy with the case at hand, and not wanting to be bothered with an irrelevant interview, the detectives were happy to let Daniels take the man aside.

"Follow me, sir," he instructed the doctor as he looked for a place for them to talk.

A moment later, he found several nearby chairs in a waiting area. Realizing he looked out of place, especially with crutches, Daniels decided to begin the conversation appropriately, with a slight lie.

"I'm Detective Mark Daniels," he said, despite his inactive role. He took out a notepad, flipping it open. "And you are?"

"Barry Andrews. I work in the surgical ward."

"Who is your girlfriend, Dr. Andrews?"

"Lisa Terrell. She was working the floor and I heard someone was killed up here and there were police everywhere. Have you seen her?"

Daniels finished writing several notes.

"I'm afraid I have bad news for you," he said, struggling to look directly at the doctor.

"Oh, God. Is it true?" Andrews questioned, his eyes wide with anticipation and fear.

"Yes. She and a patient were murdered within the last two hours," Daniels decided to reveal.

"No," the doctor muttered, shaking his head. "I just saw her before her shift started."

"I have some questions I'd like to ask you, sir."

Andrews shook his head violently.

"Can it wait until tomorrow, detective?" Andrews pleaded, bolting from the chair, running his hands through his hair in an obvious frenzied state. "I really can't even think right now."

"Sure," Daniels replied, knowing none of his questions were directly related to the murder.

He suspected Lisa Terrell was by no means the actual target of the killer.

"Doc, do not tell anyone about the information I've shared with you here," he warned, knowing he should not have leaked a few of the details. "The coroner's office will have to notify the next of kin before we can release her name to the public."

Andrews nodded in understanding.

"Where can I reach you tomorrow afternoon?" Daniels asked, regaining his footing with the use of the crutches.

"At my clinic, or at home," the doctor answered as Daniels began to hobble toward the crowd.

Before the officer could ask him where the clinic was, Andrews underwent what appeared to be a nervous breakdown. Daniels decided to simply call the hospital in the morning for information.

Daniels hobbled down the hall, stopping to speak with the officer he'd asked to check the janitorial closet before returning to the bloodied room. He received an answer before continuing onward to check on McCabe's progress.

"Find anything?" McCabe asked when Daniels returned.

"Found the boyfriend of our dead nurse. A surgical doctor here. He won't be much help tonight, so I'll interview him tomorrow."

"I doubt he can give us anything important if his alibi checks out," McCabe deduced. "She was probably just collateral damage in the killer's way. I'm done with the photos, so I'm going to get some forensics people in here with the fading hope they might find something useful."

"Whoever we're dealing with knows how to cover things up. Speaking of which, my buddies found the janitorial closet and it looks like some form of bleach was used to clean up the mess."

"So we've got a killer who knows how to avoid leaving any trace of evidence, and knows the quickest way to the cleaning supplies," McCabe decided.

"It probably doesn't take a genius to find where the stuff is kept."

"Still, we're talking about someone who had at least some familiarity with this hospital and where things were located."

"Kaiser was here a few days. Maybe our killer took his time and staked out the floor."

"And knew exactly where Kaiser was?"

"Follow one of his family or friends up here and it's easy. We can interview them to see if anyone strange was around, or followed them up here."

"They'll be shook up for a while," McCabe said. "I'll get a list of who has been here to visit, and start interviews first thing tomorrow. You can speak with that doctor. See if he's noticed anything strange up here since he probably visited his girlfriend a lot."

"I'm going to give Paul a call. I don't want him finding out about this from someone else first."

"How close were they?" McCabe questioned.

"Paul and Kaiser? They went to high school together. They were pretty much best friends."

"Send him my condolences," the detective said with a look of genuine sincerity. "And tell him somehow we'll find the bastard behind this."

***

An hour later Clouse sat at the kitchen table alone, thumbing through his high school senior yearbook. Daniels had phoned from the hospital to inform him of Kaiser's death before the press received any information.

Clouse looked at the photos of himself, Niemeyer, and Kaiser. It was a time when Niemeyer still had hair, and shortly after the time Kaiser kept his continually buzzed. Clouse chuckled, thinking how his friend hated having wavy hair so he constantly trimmed it, often nearly to the scalp, just to keep people from remembering what it looked like.

One photo depicted all three beside Niemeyer's pickup truck. Since all three were country boys, each owned a truck almost from the time they could drive. None of them had a problem wearing cowboy boots to school because no one dared tease them about it.

Clouse played basketball, Kaiser was destined to be a cop from a young age, showing it throughout high school, and Niemeyer had a quick temper. Being the largest of the three, he played football, often spending his off-season working on the farm or chasing girls.

Soon after Daniels called with the tragic news Clouse decided to use a sick day and miss work the next morning. He figured either the chief or another of the fire department brass would call and tell him to return to work when he decided to. The year before they worked around him, partly because he was accused of murdering his wife and they wanted to keep their hands clean in case he was guilty. At the same time, they were supportive by giving him time to work things out.

He hoped for the same now.

"How are you?" Jane asked, joining him at the kitchen table after making certain the kids were asleep.

"I'm okay," he lied. "I just have this overwhelming urge to find whoever's doing this and squeeze the life from them with my bare hands."

Jane took hold of his thick forearm.

"I won't pretend to understand what you're going through, but if you need anything at all, just let me know."

Clouse felt a tear slip past his right eye, dripping down his cheek. His emotions were getting the better of him.

"I'm going to need freedom, Jane. I need time to work with Mark and find whoever's behind this."

Jane appeared to feel more secure after they installed an alarm system on the house and Clouse took several other steps in raising the security of their house, including a change of the door locks and letting the dogs run free outside, or in the house. Luckily, no neighbors were within a half mile of their property, so the dogs would know their boundaries and avoid straying too far.

"You do what you have to," Jane insisted. "When you're stuck here, you're restless and unsure of what to do with yourself. I can't expect us to live normal lives until this is all over."

He gave her a quick kiss on the cheek.

"You know I love you."

"I know," she replied. "A week ago we were planning the final details of our wedding, and now we're living in fear for our lives."

"Don't worry about me," Clouse assured her.

"I can't help it. Every minute you're away from here I worry someone might try and kill you again."

"I know, but Mark and I know what to expect. We keep an eye on one another."

A knock at the door interrupted the conversation, leaving both to wonder who might visit their property at such an hour.

"Tim?" Clouse asked, opening the door to find his friend on the other side.

One look at his buddy told him Niemeyer already knew about Kaiser. In his left hand, he clasped a high school yearbook, apparently thinking like Clouse. His eyes appeared red, puffy, and moist. Clouse was unsure whether mourning or alcohol could be held accountable for the state of his high school pal.

"Feel like getting drunk?" Niemeyer asked, giving a partial answer.

Clouse looked to Jane, then back to his friend, knowing it was time to exercise some of his newfound freedom.

"Actually, I do."

***

Half an hour later the two sat at a table, away from the bar and the televisions that caused most of the commotion inside a local bar and grill. Clouse stared at the onion rings placed before him momentarily, not particularly hungry, but needing something to absorb the alcohol in his stomach. Like every other table, theirs held a centerpiece oil lamp that seemed to provide most of the light around them.

For a weeknight, the pub bustled with activity. Country music blared from surrounding speakers while occupants of several tables cheered, or yelled at the basketball game's results on the big screen television. Others played electronic trivia, and some simply sat off to the side, away from the noise to hold quieter conversations.

"A friend of mine working security at the hospital told me," Niemeyer stated. "I couldn't believe it. I just visited Ken tonight."

"Was he awake at all?"

"No. I hope for his sake he never woke up."

Niemeyer chugged down the last of his fourth beer. His speech was noticeably slurred, and his eyes a bit more red than before. Though he was big enough to hold alcohol in bulk, even Niemeyer had a limit.

"You remember the time we all brought a pig to school for homecoming?" Clouse asked, sipping his second beer. He tried to contain himself to be a designated driver for Niemeyer.

"I thought Mr. Evans was going to shit himself," Niemeyer said with a bit of his drawl coming through, cussing uncharacteristically with a crooked grin.

When provoked or drunk he tended to swear more, and treat some ordinary events as threats.

Clouse picked an onion ring from the basket, biting off an edge as he thought about how the three of them were never as close after high school.

"Why didn't you and I talk more after we graduated?" he simply asked.

"We did," Niemeyer objected, looking at his empty bottle. "I guess things just get in the way sometimes."

"I guess."

Both men seemed to stay closer to Kaiser than one another, though they never became strangers.

"What can I do to help you find whoever's behind this, Paul?"

"I don't want you to do anything, Tim. I've already lost enough friends to this maniac."

Niemeyer massaged the bald area of his head while he groaned.

"What's wrong?" Clouse inquired.

"This loud music is givin' me a headache."

Clouse sighed to himself, trying to remember what he was about to say before his friend developed a headache.

"I just want you to be careful and keep an eye on your family," he finally said. "Are you still working in Bedford?"

"We're buildin' a new shoppin' complex at the edge of town."

"Good. Stay away from West Baden and Bloomington, Tim. I don't want anything happening to you."

After calling for another beer, Niemeyer took out a cigar, puffing it to life as he lit it with a match. When the beer arrived, he tipped the waitress, exhaling directly above him. He returned a glassy-eyed stare in Clouse's direction.

"Since when did you start that habit?" Clouse asked.

"Ah, a couple of my weightliftin' buddies smoke stogies when we play cards or go out."

"You're giving in to peer pressure at our age?"

"I ain't givin' in," Niemeyer said defensively. "No one forces anything on me, and there ain't nothin' wrong with enjoying a good cigar once in a while," he added, letting his grammar and his drawl slip a bit further.

Clouse shrugged indifferently. He didn't want the conversation taking any more of a negative run than it already had.

"What can you tell me about the two men who attacked you and Ken?"

Niemeyer spent a few minutes relating the story to his friend, giving details about the two men, including the serpent tattoo on the taller one. Clouse felt certain the other was his secret helper, Stephen, whom he feared was murdered. He felt positive a snake tattoo would stand out in public, or its owner needed to constantly wear concealing clothing.

"Who do you think is behind it, Paul?"

"I don't know," Clouse answered, shaking his head slowly. "Last time it was someone closer to me than I thought, but this time I just don't know, Tim. I just hope I figure it out before more people get hurt."

"Me too."

Clouse took a sip from his beer bottle, wondering if some of the answers he needed weren't already around him. Somehow, he would get the time off work and begin his own search.

Chapter 21

Despite the agony of leg cramps, Daniels refused to use the wheelchair the next morning when he found Barry Andrews' clinic in Paoli. Strangely, it was the same clinic that treated Kaiser after he was discovered inside the hotel. One phone call to the hospital gave him the location of the clinic, sending a strange chill through him.

It felt a little too close to home.

When he walked inside the small clinic he saw several employees walking around, tidying up the place, but no Andrews.

"How can I help you?" a young lady asked, looking up from some papers on her desk from behind a glass shield.

Daniels felt certain she thought he was a patient, despite him donning a suit to look more the part of a police detective. His firearm remained holstered beneath his left shoulder, in the event that danger crossed his path again.

"Is Dr. Andrews in?" he asked.

"He's not available at the moment," she replied, glancing behind her.

"It's police business," he said, displaying his credentials.

"Oh," she said, pointing toward a door. Daniels made his way over with the crutches, entering the back of the clinic. "I'll get him for you," she said, leaving him centered in a sea of examination tables and chairs, all empty at the moment.

Though small, the clinic obviously served a purpose, and seemed fully functional, as though an extension of the local hospital. It probably gave local residents a sense of having a family doctor around in a small town.

Everything appeared new and clean, and mostly light in color. Though he had grown to detest hospitals, Daniels felt more at home inside the clinic than in his own rehabilitation room in Bloomington.

"How long have you known Dr. Andrews?" he asked a young man who cleaned one of the nearby tables.

"Almost 21 years," the tall, stout employee answered. "He's my father."

"Are you studying medicine too?"

With a chuckle, the young man ceased his mopping to shake Daniels' hand. He looked very little like his father with light, stringy hair that reached his shoulders. Not the type of kid one expected to work in a medical clinic.

"No, that is *not* my field of study. I just work here for extra spending money, and to help my father out. He's taking Lisa's death pretty badly if that's what you're here about."

"Yeah, it is."

Daniels let the younger Andrews return to his work as the father emerged from the back office.

"I know this is difficult, but we have to talk," Daniels told him.

"Of course," Andrews said, motioning to Daniels to follow him back to his office.

"It's nice that your clinic is a family affair."

"Have a seat, detective," Andrews said when they entered the office, giving the impression he was uninterested in small talk.

He closed the door behind him.

"My daughter, Kenya, is about to enter the nursing program after her freshman year at college, while my son, Ryan, has decided to pursue acting in his college studies."

"Is he any good?"

"Oh, he's very good, but he works here out of financial necessity while my daughter considers it a paid internship of sorts."

"I see," Daniels said, taking out a notebook and pen, trying to force a grin.

Taking a seat behind his desk, Andrews waved toward a seat, which the detective gladly took to be off his feet a moment. Daniels waited until the doctor made eye contact again before asking his first question.

"Can you tell me where you were last night around eight o'clock?"

Andrews told the detective he was in his office working on some overdue reports. He went on to state that he and Lisa Terrell had been dating almost two years. Andrews was divorced, though he assured Daniels the relationship with the nurse followed the proceedings. Daniels believed Andrews was truthful, and sincerely grieving, but the coincidence of the clinic, the hospital, and the murder of the nurse, along with Kaiser's death all being intertwined, plagued him.

"How familiar are you with the West Baden Springs Hotel?" Daniels asked, blazing a new path of questioning.

"Somewhat. Lisa and I used to take tours there sometimes."

"Did you ever purchase any pieces of the tile floor when it was broken up and sold as souvenirs several years ago?"

"As a matter of fact we bought one, but it came up missing sometime last year."

"Can you give me an approximate month or time?"

"Around the holidays. I know it was after that murder spree down there, because I went to look for it and it was gone. Strangest thing, too. We kept it in one of our kitchen windows with some jars and it just disappeared."

"Disappeared?"

"Well, I leave the window open sometimes when I cook. I'm not a very good cook, so I take precautions. One day I just noticed it was missing."

Daniels went on to inquire about any possible enemies Lisa might have had, finding no leads there. He tried to ask if she had any connection to Kaiser outside of the hospital, discovering she did not to the doctor's knowledge. Andrews claimed he hadn't seen anyone strange on her floor, saying he visited it only a few times a week to keep workplace gossip to a minimum since they didn't work in the same ward. It began to appear that Kaiser was indeed the intended target and Lisa Terrell was a victim of circumstance.

Bad circumstance.

Daniels flipped his notebook closed.

"I guess that about covers it," he said, reaching for his crutches.

"May I ask what happened to your legs?"

"I was shot in the line of duty. I'm on a rehab assignment, assisting the state police with their investigation."

"I didn't think beards were allowed in police departments," Andrews noted, as though testing Daniels' legitimacy.

"They aren't," Daniels said, forcing a grin. "Again, I'm just assisting. I'm not on active duty yet. But we need as many legs as we can afford to get this solved, even if they aren't one hundred percent good. You could say I have an insider's perspective on this latest string of murders."

"I see," Andrews said with a tone of acceptance. "I want you to find who killed Lisa, detective. If I can help in any other way, please don't hesitate to call me."

Daniels nodded, pulling himself to a standing position.

"I'll show myself out, Dr. Andrews."

***

Daniels struggled through the front door of his house later that afternoon to find his wife holding their son in her arms.

"What's going on?" he asked, knowing she had planned to leave the kids with her mother so they could have a night together.

"He's running a fever," she replied, looking up.

"Oh," Daniels replied, looking for the cordless phone.

"It's over there," Cindy said with a tone admonishing him for paying little attention to their son's sickness.

He knew she felt he was growing obsessive about the new set of murders.

It was the same as last year, only far more dangerous. A year ago, she was outwardly proud of him for working toward solving the crime. Now he was a potential victim, not fully healthy, and in danger of losing the strong support, she provided over the past year.

Forever.

She had made statements recently about her frustration, helping a man who refused to help himself. Occasionally she dropped questions and comments that implied she thought Daniels might be happier alone, but he always indicated he would not be.

Cindy paid him little attention as he spoke with McCabe, discovering the detective had no luck with the hospital's cameras, or with security officers on the double homicide. Daniels hung up the phone, unhappy with the lack of leads.

"How's my boy?" he finally asked, sitting beside his wife, feeling Curtis' forehead. "Wow, he *is* warm."

As Daniels settled into the couch, she handed the moaning boy over to him, heading for the kitchen. From her rigid walk, he began to realize she was displeased. He heard several pots and pans clanging from around the corner, providing further evidence of her unhappiness. Apparently knowing he could not readily get up to confront her, she waited several minutes before returning to the living room.

"I thought we were going out tonight," he said.

"We were until Curt ran a fever this morning."

"Did you take him to the doctor's office?"

"I called. They gave me a prescription."

Daniels held his son close a moment, simply touching Curt's tiny fingers and watching how his baby fussed and moaned, refusing to cry. He inherited the strong will of his parents, refusing to let life's obstacles keep him down.

"Are we going to make a night of it?" he asked as she placed Curtis in the crib on the other side of the room.

"Do you actually plan to stay here tonight?"

"What's that supposed to mean? I planned to go out tonight, with you."

"I don't know, Mark," she said, exasperated. "It's almost like you use this whole murder spree to avoid me. There is absolutely no sense in you chasing down a killer when you can't even walk yet."

Daniels sighed.

"I'm in no danger-"

"No danger? You nearly got killed at the hotel a few days ago and you're in no danger?"

"Paul was there. It wasn't that bad."

"Yes, it *was*," Cindy said, sitting beside him, taking hold of his hand while hers nervously shivered. "If you won't do it for me, do it for the two children who want to grow up knowing their daddy."

"Do what?"

"Give up this chase of yours. You aren't a detective anymore."

Daniels simply sat stunned as the words pierced his heart and soul. He couldn't believe his wife ever thought of him as anything less than the job title that consumed him. At the same time, he realized perhaps too much of his life intertwined with his career.

"I cannot give this up while Paul is still in danger. Until I find this supposed list, I don't know who's in danger, and there won't be any telling who the killer might be. Cindy, this is no different than last year."

"Yes, it is. Last year you were on the outside looking in. Now someone wants you and Paul out of the way for stopping Dave Landamere. I don't want to see you hurt again."

She cupped his bearded cheek in her hand as their eyes locked. He felt disheartened and vulnerable, but knew his assistance to McCabe could not stop until the case was solved. He wanted so much to promise Cindy everything would be fine, but he knew better. The memories of a bullet ripping into his backside haunted him, though he never actually saw it coming.

"I can't promise-"

She shushed him, placing her hand over his mouth, replacing it with a deep kiss. Romance had disappeared from their lives over the past year, and Cindy realized her last hope was to win him back, and keep him home.

"Can you make it upstairs?" she asked, planting another kiss on him, arousing him now that the shock had passed.

A smile crossed his face.

"Oh, I think I can." He looked to the crib. "What about Curt?"

"He'll be okay for ten minutes."

"After a year that's all I get?" Daniels asked, reaching for a single crutch, knowing the baby monitor worked perfectly from hearing their son's cries most every night. He planned on making his return trip to the upstairs worthwhile.

"We'll see," she answered. "You'll have to earn it."

Daniels uncharacteristically let out a tiger-like growl as he hobbled up the stairs behind his wife.

***

Clouse walked up the stairs to his son's final class at the elementary school, feeling somewhat better after a talk with the fire chief about him taking a few weeks off until things settled down. The following day, Kaiser's calling hours and funeral would keep him busy. It seems his family had already planned some of the arrangements in case he never awoke from his coma. After the funeral, Clouse could stay home with his family and leave the investigation to the police.

He hoped.

A feeling of helplessness overwhelmed him. Clouse tended to believe if he could confront the killer, he could overtake him. Like before, the killer was always one step ahead of him, taunting him. He picked on those around the firefighter, adding to his guilty conscience by making them suffer. Clouse's entire life felt violated because someone wanted at him and everyone around him.

"If only I could find that list," he muttered to himself, reaching the classroom door.

He knocked, finding Zach's gifted and talented teacher, Judy Parker, waiting on the other side. She smiled, knowing she hadn't seen Clouse in some time, or often enough. She probably wondered how involved Zach's father was in his life, not realizing the strange schedule of Clouse's jobs, or that his son meant everything to him.

"Here to pick up Zach?" she asked, leading him into the classroom where several restless children were anxious for school to let out.

"Yes," Clouse answered, looking around. "Where is he?"

"He's working with Mrs. Teague on the computer," Judy said, looking toward a closed door.

Clouse recalled Jane's statement about Zach working behind closed doors, away from the other students.

"Who is Mrs. Teague?" he questioned, recalling Jane's mention of a teacher scurrying off the other day. Clouse felt obligated to be suspicious of everyone and everything.

"One of our teaching aides. She's here three days a week."

As the bell rang and the kids dashed for the door, only to be halted by another teaching aide who insisted they walk rationally, Clouse took off his brown leather jacket. He laid it across one arm as he inspected the classroom.

"Why is Zach being kept separate from the other students?" he asked Judy without looking away from the fish tank.

"Apparently this time of year is rather difficult for your son, Mr. Clouse. The other kids have sensed it, and give Zach a hard time about certain things."

"Angie," Clouse said his deceased wife's name under his breath.

He couldn't believe other kids were so mean-spirited at such a young age, but he knew children sometimes acted before taking a person's feelings into account.

"We decided to keep Zach on some special projects until the season blew over," Judy informed him. "Perhaps if you spent more time with him-"

"I *do* spend time with him," Clouse insisted, taking a defensive tone. "This isn't exactly a great time of year for me either, but you don't see me shelled up at home. If Zach is alienated from every kid in school, every year like this, he'll never grow up normal. I don't want him thinking he needs to spend the month of October holed up like some hermit."

"I didn't mean to imply that you didn't spend time with him, Mr. Clouse. He just needs as much support as he can get right now."

"And he'll have it," Clouse assured the teacher.

"He's been doing well with the computer education so we stuck with it."

"Fine, but please get him out of there once in a while, Mrs. Parker. I don't want to tell you how to do your job, but he needs normal experiences."

Any further conversation ceased as the door opened and Zach walked out, followed by Mrs. Teague, an older lady Clouse took as a retired teacher or bored grandmother. She was little more than a silhouette, barely illuminated by a desk lamp on the computer table as the overhead light remained off. Zach immediately ran over to his father's embrace, apparently happy to see someone who understood the demons caged within him.

"How are you, sport?"

"Fine, Dad. Can we stop at the store on the way home?" Zach asked, referring to the only worthwhile drugstore on their way out to the country.

"Sure, kid. Get your coat and backpack."

Clouse stood, looking to Judy while Zach crossed the room.

"I didn't mean to get out of line, but Zach is about all I have left. I'd never let anything happen to him, or neglect him."

Judy let a smile creep across her face.

"I know. I'm sorry, too. I would just like to see you here more often so we could talk about problems when they arise."

Clouse nodded as Zach returned to his side.

"I will. Take care."

They walked together outside the room, and Clouse tried to sneak a peek inside the computer room, but the door was only open a crack, and he decided not to appear nosy. He simply walked outside the school with his son, greeted by a cool autumn day and falling leaves from nearby trees.

Neighboring houses had pumpkins lining their porches, along with bales of straw, and corn stalks tied to pillars. Artificial cobwebs hung from tree to tree, and some families had gotten creative enough to place miniature cemeteries in their yards.

Clouse looked at the scenes, but Halloween would never be a chipper holiday for him again. Candy and pranks took a backseat to the haunting images burned within his mind.

He helped Zach into his truck and turned away from the yards, knowing his family life would never be as normal as the picture perfect families living near the school.

***

Almost a mile from the road they lived on, Clouse's truck pulled into the KTS Drugstore upon Zach's request.

"Why are we stopping here, Zach?" the fireman asked his son, genuinely uncertain, but more than willing to accommodate the boy's wishes.

"I want to look at costumes."

Clouse pulled into the store's small parking lot, stepping out as his son dashed inside. He tried calling to Zach, but it was too late. The boy had slipped past the electronic door.

"Why the change of heart on Halloween, kid?" Clouse asked, once he found his son sorting through the costume rack, framing his words so he didn't squash Zach's enthusiasm.

"All the other kids are going out on Halloween. They all think I'm weird," Zach replied, a pouting look across his face.

Clouse knelt down, looking into his boy's blue eyes.

"You're not weird. I think you're a pretty cool kid."

"That's not what they think."

Clouse smirked, forcing a grin from his son.

"I know this past year has been rough on you, but I want you to know I love you, and I'm never going to leave you. You're the most important thing in my life right now."

"Even more important than Jane and Katie?"

Clouse hesitated a second, deciding to answer honestly.

"Yes, you are. And I miss your mom just as much as you do, Zach."

"Is she really in a better place?"

"It's called heaven, son. She's with God, and someday I'll tell you all about it."

"Promise?"

"I promise. And if you want to go out on Halloween, we'll go out."

Zach nodded, his childhood innocence showing through his grin. He grew up too fast for Clouse to keep pace. It seemed just a year ago, he could barely speak an entire sentence, and now they could carry on brief conversations.

"Pick out whichever one you want, kid. I'm going to grab a few groceries."

Since the entire drug store was in view from any vantage point, Clouse felt secure leaving his son alone momentarily, especially since no one else was visible except the store's owner and a pharmacist.

As Clouse sauntered down the aisle, he thought about what a horrible time of year it truly was for the both of them. When his wife was murdered, Clouse had been at work while Zach was inside the house when his mother's blood spilled. Clouse was immediately accused of the murder and interrogated by two detectives, one of whom was now a good friend.

Between the investigation, the press, and the fact that he could never properly mourn Angie while being a single father, he harbored a bad taste about the season in general. His faith in those around him crumpled as the murder of his wife, and every other killing around the hotel, could be traced to greed.

He sensed the same cycle recurring, but this time a hint of revenge seemed obvious, since he was apparently the first choice to die. Unfortunately, Clouse felt certain the man who saved his life had suffered the fate meant for those on the alleged list.

Looking over the various potato chips for the brands the kids preferred, he considered the possibilities of those around him being the killer and how several had survived apparent close encounters with the killer, coming away with far better health than Clouse after his unintentional swim in the lake.

Niemeyer escaped with a severe headache from a rifle butt after seeing the person who was, quite possibly, the killer. He was also the last person to see Ken Kaiser alive. Clouse felt his friend had no motivation to kill anyone, shaking off the notion that an old high school chum could commit such an act.

Daniels avoided what should have been an obvious death in Clouse's view. Perhaps the killer was inexperienced with a scythe, or perhaps Daniels escaped unharmed for a different reason. Clouse knew the best alibi for not being the killer would be a third party viewing that person next to the killer. He focused on the chips again, trying not to think of the coincidences thrown his way the past several days.

Even Jane had told him several odd stories, making him leery of even the woman he planned to marry. Zach's solo education was satisfactorily explained in his view, and the stereo incident in the house was probably just the kids accidentally turning it on and refusing to take any blame for their misuse of appliances. Clouse wondered about everything and everyone around him, almost constantly.

Perhaps, in part, the killer was getting what he wanted.

At one point, Clouse mistrusted Kaiser, and perhaps vice versa, when Angie was murdered, but their skepticism was later put to rest. Still, it was someone close to him committing murder the first time, and he felt obligated to be wary of everyone again.

Clouse picked up some popcorn and soda for the kids before Zach ran up to him, carrying a costume with a familiar appearance.

"Can I be a fireman for Halloween, Dad?"

"It's awfully dangerous work, Zach," Clouse said, kneeling down beside his son. "Sure you can handle it?"

"Yeah. I need a hose too."

"That can be arranged," Clouse said with a chuckle, knowing there were some old leftover garden hoses in the barn.

Clouse playfully messed up his son's hair, taking a look at the costume. He found it odd how all firefighter costumes looked more like unfashionable raincoats of bright red and yellow than the real thing. They always came with a tacky plastic helmet shaped somewhat correctly to give the costume a minor look of authenticity.

He looked at the elevated drug store price on the costume.

"I'll need a second mortgage to pay for this," he muttered to himself as they proceeded toward the checkout counter.

Chapter 22

A feeling of despondence overcame Clouse as he tugged his tie into place the next morning. His best friend would be laid to rest in a few hours while he felt certain something more could have been done to prevent Kaiser's death.

A guard at the door.

More investigators assigned to the case.

Quicker follow-up on leads.

Faster forensics.

He realized none of this was easily feasible, and that police were doing the best job possible given the circumstances. Clouse wondered what more he could do.

With the funeral drawing closer, the consequences of his best friend's death truly hit him. He would have to face the man's family and know that somehow, no matter how inadvertently, he was part of the problem.

"Almost ready, Paul?" Jane asked as she walked past the dresser where he stood, straight into the bathroom.

"Just about," he replied, dabbing the mist from his eyes, realizing all the times he and Kaiser shared remained in memory and photos alone. Two children would grow up without a father because Clouse wasn't there to protect his friend.

"What's the matter?" she asked, returning from the bathroom, finding him sitting on the edge of the bed, his hands limp atop his lap.

"I feel like it's my fault."

She sat beside him caressing his shoulder. He wasn't looking for sympathy or support per se, but he wasn't sure how much more loss he could bear. Clouse's stomach hurt from not eating and from his body convulsing when he sobbed away from Jane and the kids. His mind refused to stray from Kaiser, or his death, for more than a minute or two, regardless of what else transpired around him.

"There is nothing you could have done for him. Whoever did this knew exactly what they were doing, and exactly when to do it. You know Tim had to leave when visitation was up, and he couldn't have done anything either."

"But at least Tim was there."

"And he feels the same way you do. Both of you need to realize someone with no conscience, no heart, is doing this to us. Start worrying about your family and the friends you have left."

Clouse knew why she made such a good doctor. Her spirit and general outlook on life made her one of the strongest women he had ever met. He admired her ability to shrug off the bad and continue with life.

"Do you know Barry Andrews?" he asked, wanting to quickly change the subject.

"Of course. His clinic is a lot like mine."

"The murdered nurse was his girlfriend."

"I know. They were the talk of the hospital."

"How so?" Clouse asked, standing to find a tie clip.

"They were off and on for the longest time."

"Off and on how?" he asked, clipping the tie before searching for his sport coat.

"Every so often they broke up and he found a new girl for a few weeks. It was mostly to make Lisa jealous I think."

Clouse grunted quietly, scoffing the idea of such a relationship.

"Don't worry," she said, wrapping her arms around him as he looked in the dresser's mirror at his tie. "I would never treat you that way."

"I think we've gone a little too far to play around now."

She kissed his neck, apparently sensing the rigid, tense nature of his entire body. Jane had experienced him accused of murder, and now losing friend after friend. Understanding exactly how he felt was virtually impossible, so she supported him the best she could.

"I've got another question for you," Clouse said, satisfied with his attire. He sat on the bed again, putting his shined black shoes on. "Those tiles they removed from the hotel floor and auctioned off. Do you know anything about those things that I might not?"

Jane had volunteered as a tour guide at the West Baden Springs Hotel for two seasons, learning much about its rich history. She shared her knowledge on tours, but she kept lots of little shreds of information in her mind. Often the tours were pressed for time, which meant much of her knowledge was never shared.

Her volunteer work had enabled her to meet Clouse the year before while he worked on the hotel's interior, soon after his wife was murdered. His knowledge was vast, considering he was a buff of the landmark, but Jane had access to a completely different array of people.

"Lillian and Charles Rexford took over the hotel in 1916 and had the tile put down."

Rexford. The name caught Clouse's attention once again and he cursed his distracted mind for not following up on its importance earlier.

"Anything special about the tile?"

"It was imported, put in by the Cassini Mosaic Tile Company. They were Italian craftsmen out of Cincinnati."

"Probably the best available. Anything else special about the floor?"

"Not that I know of, but if you want to hear from someone who actually watched it put down, old Charlie Winters can tell you firsthand how the process went."

"Who's he?"

"He was a local teenager who did grounds work for the hotel when it came under new ownership. He's seen about everything new there since it was rebuilt. He even gave tours before the hotel was declared a landmark."

"I might want a chat with him this week."

Jane glanced at the clock on the wall. Her sister had already stopped by to babysit the kids, so things were in order.

"We'd better get going," she told her fiancé. "It won't look good if we're late."

Clouse looked himself over in the mirror one last time before following Jane out of the bedroom. A tear dripped from his eye as the realization that his best friend, soon to be his best man, would never be around him again. He felt selfish, knowing how many other friends and relatives Kaiser left behind, but the deputy was the closest friend he could possibly lose.

He sniffled, collected himself, and followed Jane.

***

At the mortuary, Clouse found himself numbly shaking hands with old friends and people he had never met. As a pallbearer, he was stuck in the spotlight, not far from Kaiser's wife and two children much of the time. He stole glances at Sandra and the kids, thinking how similar his friend's situation was to his own. His own death would have left Jane with Zach and Katie, all by herself.

Throughout the course of the calling hours, Clouse spied Daniels and McCabe at separate intervals. When each went by, he asked them to stay through the funeral so they could talk afterward. Daniels would be able to give him a ride home, since they both lived in the Bloomington area. Clouse felt the three, collectively sharing information, might speed up the process of discovering who was behind the murders.

Since Tim Niemeyer was another pallbearer, the two spent most of their time exchanging glances until the guests began to thin out, preparing to head for the cemetery. Niemeyer gave him curious glances when he spoke to each of the officers at some length. His friend soon crossed the aisle, taking Clouse aside.

"I hate this," Niemeyer confessed. "We're not supposed to do this now. Good God, we're supposed to be grandparents before we start burying one another."

"Not fair, is it?" Clouse asked, slumping into a chair, since most of the visitors were already outside.

"I feel so responsible. Like I could have done something different."

"Yeah, I know how that goes, Tim."

"I guess you would after losing so many friends," Niemeyer said, immediately realizing how terrible his words sounded by the look on his face. Clouse gave a questioning glare. "Sorry, I didn't mean it like that."

Clouse's expression lightened as he stood and slapped his friend on the back.

"You never were much for words, Timmy. If I die before you, let someone else do my eulogy, okay?"

"No problem. I hate public speaking."

Both walked toward the casket, peering in to see their friend, a bit paler than he was in life, at eternal rest. Wearing a suit never quite matched Kaiser's personality. Even when he worked detective details he wore a polo shirt and slacks instead of a tie. An avid outdoorsman, he appeared happiest on a motorcycle, or camping for a weekend. Clouse couldn't have asked for a more devoted friend, and Kaiser risked his own life, quite literally, to keep Clouse safe the previous year.

So many memories flooded the heads of both men that his visitors, even his closest relatives, would never share. Most never truly knew Ken Kaiser and what he stood for.

They were oblivious to his undying devotion to his family and to just causes. Kaiser always fought the good fight, and Clouse felt a tear run down his cheek as he prayed his friend might see them from above, knowing they cared, loving him like a brother.

"God, I remember the day he got married," Niemeyer stated, sniffling a bit. "Kenny got so drunk he could barely stand, and we had to cover up for him so his police buddies wouldn't badger him later."

"When it came down to it, we were always the guys there for him. Like the time he got stranded in Indianapolis. Who did he call?"

Niemeyer chuckled.

"He called you because my wife thought it was a prank and hung up on him."

"Poor Ken," Clouse said with a grin. "There'll never be another."

Realizing it was truly goodbye, Clouse looked at the body of his best friend one last time, trying to contain himself. Kaiser had so much to live for, and so many people who cared about him. Unfair, Clouse thought of his death. He was young, in his prime, and died simply for doing what was right. He played by the rules.

Those rules have to change, Clouse thought angrily. He began to understand part of where the killings came from, but discovering who was actually swinging the scythe proved more difficult. No matter what it took, or how many laws required bending, Clouse vowed to find the killer before other innocent victims, himself included, were laid in coffins.

"Are you two ready?" the mortician asked, bringing the other pallbearers into the room, ready to transport the coffin.

"Yeah," Clouse answered, able to stop a flood of emotion before it began.

***

During the trip to the cemetery, Clouse felt mentally numb as lights blurred past him on the overcast day. Neither he, nor Jane, spoke during the brief trip. He replayed all of the good and bad memories with Kaiser inside his mind, ready to lay his friend to rest before setting out to find the killer.

A bit of misty rain further dampened the spirits of those surrounding the burial site as the coffin lay atop the lowering device and a fairly large gathering listened to the pastor give some final words. Clouse heard and felt little through the proceedings until Kaiser's department members, along with a slew of various officers, gave their final respectful salutes to their fallen comrade. Each gave a salute while the flag from the coffin was handed over to Kaiser's wife as his two children sat idly by, unsure of why their father was not coming home.

Clouse lost all sense of whom or what surrounded him, mourning his friend quietly, tearfully, as he dragged himself away from the group no sooner than the mortuary people began mechanically lowering the casket into the ground. Thankful Zach was not part of the funeral, or witness to the lack of his father's usual strong composure, Clouse stumbled through the rainy mist toward a boulder seated at the edge of the graveyard.

By himself, he took a seat, buried his head inside his hands and cried the next several minutes, hoping everyone else was too busy to notice. Occasional glances showed he wasn't the only person openly mourning as Kaiser's fellow officers and lots of friends and family wept, walking toward their vehicles.

Jane walked among them, viewing her future husband from a distance. To her, he probably looked like a person lost to the world, obviously hurt over the loss of such a close friend. It was another part of his vulnerable side she would see for the first time. She veered from the group, taking a walk toward him.

"Maybe I'm just a selfish bastard," Clouse said, sniffling and wiping his eyes dry as Jane approached him. "God, I miss him."

"You're just doing what comes natural. You're human."

"I guess so. I just can't believe he's gone."

Jane sighed to herself, at an apparent loss for words.

"Mark said he could take you home," she said, kneeling beside him, placing her hand on his knee. "Are you sure you'll be okay?"

Clouse nodded, still too choked up to speak at length.

Quickly giving him a gentle kiss on the forehead, Jane turned to leave. She would have plenty of projects to keep herself busy the rest of the day.

A moment passed before Daniels and McCabe headed toward him. McCabe let Daniels amble ahead of him to speak with Clouse first. Clouse pulled out a pair of sunglasses, putting them on to mask his grief despite the gloomy weather.

"You sure you still want to talk?" Daniels asked, approaching apprehensively.

"I'm fine," the firefighter answered, wiping away the remaining moisture from under the shades.

"This can wait, you know."

"No," Clouse said defiantly. "It can't."

McCabe stepped forward.

"Where are we going then?"

Both men shrugged.

"I know a place."

"No bars," Clouse and Daniels said simultaneously, looking squarely at him.

"I promise, no bars," the state trooper replied defensively, raising his hands. "I do occasionally frequent other establishments."

Clouse's attention turned from the two officers.

"What the hell is he doing here?" Clouse asked under his breath, seeing Jerome Barnett some distance away, overlooking the remains of the proceedings from beneath a shady tree.

Before he contemplated an answer, Clouse glanced further to his left as he removed his sunglasses, adding to his distress.

"Oh, shit," he said, rising from the boulder.

He saw Niemeyer marching in the direction of the mettlesome reporter, unsure of whether Barnett saw him, or what the burly contractor might do when he reached him.

Before the two officers understood the problem, Clouse darted in the direction of his friend, hoping to cut him off at the pass.

He made it just in time, as Niemeyer began screaming several choice words at the reporter, even before he drew close enough to slug the man.

"You have no right to be here!" he yelled as Clouse physically restrained him from stepping any closer, fearing Niemeyer's temper might lead to a discharged fist. It took every bit of strength the firefighter could muster to keep his larger friend away from Barnett.

"I'm not here for any trouble," the reporter said defensively. "I just came to pay my respects."

"And see what scoop you could get," Niemeyer fired back. "You son-of-a-bitch! You've done nothin' but capitalize on all of us this en'tar time and you expect me to believe that?"

"I'm sorry. I'll leave," Barnett said, turning to go.

Niemeyer struggled to get at the man, virtually ignoring Clouse's physical restraint.

"This isn't the time, Tim," Clouse said sternly. "Leave it alone."

"He's nothin' but a piece of shit, Paul," Niemeyer said, letting his drawl slip into his speech through the pent up anger.

Barnett turned just long enough to get in some parting words.

"Yes, Mr. Clouse. You probably should keep an eye on him and that *killer* instinct of his," he said, inferring once again that Niemeyer was perfectly capable of murder.

Infuriated, Niemeyer lunged forward again, prompting McCabe to assist in keeping him at bay, particularly since several stragglers from the funeral watched from a distance.

"Easy, big guy," the state trooper said, grasping one of the contractor's arms until Niemeyer finally settled down, Barnett too far from his reach.

"Damn, Paul, I'm sorry," Niemeyer apologized. "It just pisses me off every t'ahm I see him after what he put you and everyone else through last year."

"He doesn't need to be pointing fingers," McCabe noted. "It's not the press's job to wildly throw out names of suspects."

Niemeyer gave a strange look to McCabe, as though asking if he was truly a suspect, or if it was a slip on the trooper's part. McCabe turned away with Daniels while Clouse took his friend aside momentarily.

"You okay now, Tim?"

"Yeah. Ah'm fine."

"Good. I feel like I'm playing big brother to you lately. Start worrying about yourself and your family, and leave everything else to the police, okay?"

"Alright. I'll let it go," Niemeyer reluctantly agreed.

"Thanks. Now I've got to have a chat with Mark and his buddy to see what we can find out about Ken's killer. Just go home and relax a little while," Clouse said with a hearty slap to his friend's back.

Niemeyer nodded.

"And one other thing, Tim."

"Yeah?"

"You aren't that bad at public speaking."

A short-lived grin slipped across the contractor's face as he turned to leave. Like Clouse, he probably felt a void in his life without his high school buddy. He was obviously infuriated about being publically accused of murder, twice at that.

Chapter 23

While McCabe insisted on changing in the restroom of the café the three men stopped at, Clouse ordered coffee, catching glimpses of a peculiar grin forming on his friend's mouth every minute or so.

"What's got you so giddy?" he finally asked Daniels.

"Nothing."

"Don't give me that. You've been acting weird all day." He paused to sip from his coffee mug. "Mark, you're the most grim, serious person I know. Today it's like you're a kid getting a trip to the candy store."

"Thanks for the kind words."

Clouse gave a sarcastic complimentary nod.

"Despite my hollow and boring life, I got home last night and made my way upstairs for the first time in a year."

Clouse gave a puzzled look.

"You know," Daniels said in a lower voice. "Upstairs. Where my bed is."

"I still don't see where you're going with this."

"Because I haven't been able to walk for a year, I've been sleeping downstairs alone, where wheelchair access is easier. Cindy took me upstairs last night."

Clouse thought a moment before what his friend stated finally materialized in his mind.

"Oh," he said with a momentary hesitation. "You mean you've gone a whole year without it?"

Daniels nodded, the relief showing in his face.

"Guess I'd be pretty chipper too."

McCabe emerged from the restroom carrying his covered suit, wearing jeans and a T-shirt depicting the statement: *You can always tell an Irishman when you see him, but you can't tell him much.* He settled into the booth beside Daniels, draping his suit over the seat.

"Welcome back, Turlough," Daniels said, teasing the detective about his heritage, and his personal obsession with it.

"At least my last name doesn't have a hundred listings in the phone book," McCabe retorted. "There's nothing wrong with a man's roots."

"And there's nothing wrong with us getting this over with," Clouse stated. "We've got a lot to cover."

Both officers looked at one another guiltily, forgetting momentarily whose funeral they had just come from.

"Okay," McCabe began. "I'm having no luck whatsoever on this *Coven* your informant told you about," he said to Clouse. "Either the group doesn't exist, or they're so underground that no police organization has ever heard of them. And that is highly unlikely."

"It sounded regional," Clouse recalled aloud. "Local, perhaps."

"I'll keep checking, but it doesn't look promising."

"What about suspects?" Daniels inquired.

"I've eliminated all of the Summers family," McCabe said, referring to relatives of Clouse's deceased wife. "Our revenge theory is probably out the window."

"Unless of course it's revenge for someone other than Roger Summers," Daniels noted.

"Are you speaking of David Landamere?" McCabe inquired.

"Not necessarily. Maybe someone's loved one got axed last year and they hold Paul and me responsible, so they're taking out everyone else involved, saving us for last."

"So knocking me unconscious off my boat was just a strong foreshadowing?" Clouse asked his friend with skepticism and a raised eyebrow.

"Who knows? Maybe they intended to pull you out so you would think you're very lucky. Maybe this whole informant thing you've got is one big lie."

Clouse shook his head.

"I don't think so." He looked to McCabe. "I think my informant is that mutilated body you found roadside a few days ago."

As their waitress returned, each quickly placed a light order, quickly returning to the business at hand.

"Seems we're a bit shorthanded on suspects," the state detective told Clouse. "Your buddy Tim and that reporter guy were both placed at the hospital just minutes before the murder occurred. Granted, the cameras didn't catch anyone else snooping around that floor, but it would be awfully tough to completely avoid detection while wandering hospital floors."

Daniels sipped some orange juice before speaking.

"Not that tough. After visiting hours the place is like a ghost town on some floors."

"And if it isn't Tim or Barnett, then it's probably someone who has familiarity with the hospital," Clouse said. "Maybe he works there, or had time to study it. You might ask their staff if anyone unusual has been snooping around."

"Already have," McCabe replied. "They said no one stuck out."

Daniels sipped his juice, probably thinking of what clues they already possessed, and how to further check them before speaking again.

"Assuming Paul's buddy is truthful about those two teenagers wearing black, it might be worth checking out some of the local tattoo parlors. A snake tattoo with someone's neck as a template shouldn't be too hard to trace."

McCabe nodded in agreement.

"Are you pretty certain the person who attacked you on your boat wore diving equipment, Mr. Clouse?"

"What little I saw was black and rubbery," Clouse recalled. "And it was a little chilly to be wearing swim trunks."

"Okay. I'll check the local outposts and see about purchases made in the last year. Maybe I'll get lucky and snag a recent purchase that seems fishy."

"Don't hold your breath," Daniels commented with a strange smirk, knowing how scarce lucky breaks were the previous year.

"Ah, a pun," McCabe said. "I like that."

Clouse found it amusing that Daniels could only be funny completely on accident. Even before the shooting, his friend was quiet, and often emotionally detached from everything around him. He often wondered what caused the former detective to find so little in life entertaining.

"So tell me what you're both thinking," the state trooper requested.

"I think this Coven doesn't exist and Paul's informant led him down the wrong track to begin with," Daniels began. "Our killer probably has a deep-seated interest in the hotel, much like Landamere and Summers did last year."

McCabe nodded, looking to Clouse.

"I think the murders are very personal," Clouse began. "The Coven could be bogus, but I think these tile floor pieces are extremely important to the killer. If we are dealing with an underground faction, it could be difficult, but I don't think any leader is going to trust multiple people with carrying out several murders. We're probably dealing with one to three people, tops. I think the killer waited until this season, picked out the important survivors from last year, and set to it."

"And you're a fireman?" McCabe asked, eyebrow raised. "We may have to recruit you."

"Sorry. I'm perfectly content where I work."

Daniels paused until the waitress placed their food on the table before speaking.

"You might also check out campus apartments that have been vacated, or missing roommates in case my informant was a college kid," Clouse told McCabe.

"I can try," the detective noted doubtfully, "but your informant could have been from any number of towns around here. I'll glance through the missing persons reports."

"While you check out your leads, I want to go with Paul to speak with the people who bought those pieces several years ago, so we can check them out. Since Paul's an acting manager for the hotel, it'll be perfectly legit."

McCabe thought a moment.

"Good idea. Make sure you photograph each piece, front and back, so we can see if there's anything about them worth killing for."

"We can start tomorrow," Clouse said. "Mark and I need to spend a day with our families to appease the womenfolk."

"Good," Daniels said, obviously feeling better, knowing his friend took some scolding at home, much like he did.

"That's fine," McCabe said. "I'm going to do some interviews and find a good bar where I can organize my findings."

He gave Clouse and Daniels a slightly devious grin before digging into his breakfast platter.

Chapter 24

Most of the next morning seemed spent in vain for Daniels and Clouse as they followed a route of their own planning, trying to reach as many tile buyers as possible before dusk. By late afternoon, they were on the tenth name.

Four had moved, one turned out to be a false name and address altogether, and the other four owned only singular pieces of the tile. For the most part, they were happy to see Clouse, hear about the hotel, and allow their pieces to be photographed for what Clouse called "preservation purposes."

To both men, none of the pieces held any significance whatsoever. Clouse noticed the pieces were like new on their shiny side, where either forest green or white were predominantly the colors. The backs showed nothing but dull gray, and occasionally specks of the adhesive used to put it down almost a century before.

As he navigated a typical county road outside of Paoli, Clouse spied everything possible to remind him of the season at one time or another.

"I hate this time of year," he muttered.

"It's not my favorite either," Daniels replied.

"Are we getting close?"

"About another half mile or so," Daniels replied, reading house numbers under his breath as they went.

Clouse spied a lit jack-o-lantern on someone's front steps, reminding him of how his first wife died, and the entire setup of the first batch of murders.

"Does this whole thing ever make you wonder about how you might die?" he asked Daniels as they drew closer to the house.

"I know none of the people who were murdered ever expected it. You and I know better, and that's why we're hunting instead of being the hunted."

"I can't believe the killer came after you when you couldn't even walk."

"That's the whole idea," Daniels explained. "Catch people when they're off-guard, or at their weakest. If we sit around our homes thinking we're safe, we'll be as vulnerable as everyone else, if not more so."

From a distance, the two men spied an isolated farmhouse with a rickety unpainted barn in the backyard, looking close to a central collapse. Clothesline was strung across the back of the house to the barn, and several large toys, such as toddler peddling tricycles were strewn across the yard.

Clouse pulled into the drive, spying several pumpkins set along the porch. A scarecrow, stuffed awkwardly, sat in a chair with a large, rusted scythe resting atop his lap. A shrieking ghost, like the one he and his first wife had, swung from atop the porch, giving signs that children probably lived in this household, unaware of the suffering the Halloween season brought to some people.

Though dressed in slacks and a tie, Daniels did not bring along his firearm. He simply played along with his friend's charade, revealing nothing about his police background unless absolutely necessary to obtain information. To this point, it mattered little what he did, because they were no further than they had been that morning.

"Take a look," Clouse said, pointing out a sign that displayed the house was guarded by a security agency, making it difficult for any potential thieves to steal the pieces, assuming the family and the pieces resided here.

"Maybe we'll get lucky," Daniels noted.

Before knocking, Clouse took the list out from his pocket to assure himself the address and name were both correct. He found Gerald Thompson had purchased four pieces during the sale of the tile fragments.

He knocked.

"Hello?" a man slightly older than the two visitors asked when he answered the door, figuring he was being harassed by peddlers.

A sour look of dismay crossed his face as he prepared to ask them to leave.

"Mr. Thompson?" Clouse asked.

"Yes."

"I have somewhat of a strange request for you, if we could have a moment of your time," Clouse asked of the man.

Several minutes later, they found themselves seated in the living room as Clouse explained a partly fictitious account of why they were visiting.

Considering the yard looked to be in shambles, the house's interior was quite the opposite.

A redone Victorian house, the place possessed a spotless interior with vast shelves and curio cabinets filled with antiques and collectable plates. Most of the house lacked carpet in order to display the original wood flooring. Even family photographs were framed in antique wood, continuing the look of the house's restoration.

"So, you think there's something on the back of these pieces that was overlooked before they were sold?" Thompson asked when Clouse finished his explanation of why they were visiting.

"Yes, possibly the designer's name, or exactly where they were imported from."

"I have to admit I've never really examined the back of the things. Kim, can you get those out of the cabinet?" he asked his wife.

She left the room to fetch the tiles.

"Can I get you two anything to drink?"

"No thanks," Clouse answered for both.

"So you're really one of the top dogs in the reconstruction?" Thompson asked Clouse, interested in the hotel's condition, like many local residents familiar with the structure.

"I am, when I'm not putting out fires in Bloomington," Clouse explained. "I work for the city, and tend to the hotel on my days off."

Thompson nodded.

"I sell agricultural machinery to farmers," he explained. "I was a volunteer firefighter when I lived closer to city limits. Addictive, isn't it?"

Clouse agreed with a friendly smirk. He noticed Daniels perk up when Kim Thompson returned with four tile pieces in hand.

"Here you are," she said, carefully handing them to him.

Clouse examined them momentarily, finding something unique on the flipside of two fragments. Daniels took up the camera, snapping shots of each side as Clouse held them in position. The former detective also seemed to notice the peculiar markings.

Marks in the form of several lines seemed to cover part of the two pieces, one of them containing part of what looked to be an "X" near one edge. Clouse set the fragments on the nearby coffee table, seeing if they formed any sort of pattern.

"How did these come?" he asked Thompson, unsure since he started the hotel project years later.

"They were in a box," the salesman recalled. "I just remember picking out four on top, trying to get the largest chunks I could. We got extras in case the kids ever got interested in the place."

Clouse noticed the two pieces containing markings fit together at one corner, but like a jigsaw, several other pieces were necessary to complete whatever map or design was to be studied. Even as he noticed a snug fit along a one-inch surface where the lines connected perfectly, he wondered if it was truly possible that the pieces belonged together, from a batch of potentially hundreds of fragments.

"Photograph that," he told Daniels, who was already poised.

"What do you make of it?" Thompson asked, assuming Clouse had some sort of expert opinion far beyond his own.

"I'm not sure. It's a lot more than I expected to find." He stood, ready to continue his quest with newfound initiative. "I appreciate you taking the time to help us."

"It's been enlightening," Thompson said with a sincere smile. "Let me know if there's anything else we can do for you."

"Thanks," Clouse said, shaking the man's hand. "I just might do that."

A few minutes later the two friends headed down the road, feeling a sense of accomplishment because their search finally paid dividends.

"What do you really think?" Daniels inquired, apparently under the impression his friend held out on the Thompson family.

"I really don't know. But at least I feel like there's some information on the tiles. Why it's worth killing for is beyond me, but it must be important."

Daniels rewound the film in his camera.

"So what now?"

"We'll drop that off at a one-hour lab and I'll get you home."

"And you?"

"There are a couple other things I want to take care of before I call it a night."

***

Most of his little cottage appeared dark as Charlie Winters read in his favorite plush chair, using only the light from a nearby lamp to skim the words of *The Scarlet Letter*.

He often read classic novels, thinking every modern book was nothing more than a mutation of previous works. Only the names and slight plot details ever seemed to change when he read such drivel. To him, nothing was more frightening than the details and realism of classic horror and drama, written long before even he was brought into the world.

Over the years Winters found respect for antiques and the way the world once was. He remembered two World Wars, the Great Depression, and the Reagan years. To him, nothing remained fonder in his memory than his youth, and how good it felt to be reckless, without a care in the world.

By today's standards, he thought, his notion of recklessness was quite tame. Vandalism, murder, and taking guns to school just didn't happen in his day. Teenagers stayed to themselves, or in small packs, never aiming to bother or harm anyone. Things had changed, he pondered as a knock came to his front door.

"Who on earth could that be?" he asked aloud, setting his book down to see who his unexpected visitor might be.

"Hello," a young man answered from the other side, holding a notebook and pen. "My name is Paul Clouse. I'm working on the restoration of the West Baden Springs Hotel. My fiancée said you might have some information to help me in a particular search I'm conducting."

"What kind of search?" Winters asked curiously as he waved the younger man inside.

For a man of his advanced age, Winters' voice and even his posture remained remarkably intact.

"I'm looking for pieces to the atrium's tile floor that were sold off years ago. I think they might have a message, or something the restoration crew overlooked before selling them. I understand you worked at the hotel when the Rexfords took over?"

"I did," Winters replied. "Have a seat, Mr. Clouse," he added, taking refuge in his favorite chair again. "Would you like to take your coat off?"

"No thanks. I won't take up too much of your time."

"So, you work at the hotel, eh?"

"I've been there several years," the visitor replied. "We finished the place up this year, and were prepared to have a grand opening when a tragic accident happened last week."

"Yes, I heard," Winters replied. "So what exactly do you do there?"

"I'm a design consultant. I created blueprints of the hotel, then got hired to help research and restore the hotel to its original appearance."

"I see. I'm glad you take such interest in that beautiful building."

"That I do."

A moment passed while Winters watched his visitor open the notebook and ready the pen.

"So, what can you tell me?" he asked at last.

"Many years ago, when I was younger than yourself, I watched them put that floor down."

"So you weren't actually part of the crew?"

"No. I was just there to do odd jobs. My job there was basically political, since my mother knew the Rexfords and wanted to keep me busy during the summer."

"What can you tell me about that floor?"

"Very little, other than the fact that it was stunning. They put it in, piece by piece," the old man recalled, running a thoughtful hand through his uncombed thicket of gray hair.

His beard looked to be about a week old, as though it slipped his mind to shave within that time.

"So you're saying each little one inch piece was placed by itself?"

"Well, most all of them."

"What?" Winters' guest asked inquisitively, setting the pen down. "Was there an exception?"

Winters groaned a moment, unwilling to automatically tell his guest the secret he kept locked inside his mind for so many decades.

"If I tell you something, will you take it to your grave as I've sworn to?" the old man asked, as though relieving himself of a deep, dark secret on his deathbed.

"If it helps me in my search, I'll make certain it never leaves this room."

Winters pondered a moment, knowing what a can of worms letting his secret out might create. For years, the hotel lay in decay, with declining public interest, and even less help in its struggle to retain any of the beauty remaining from its glory days. Now, with things looking better, and near the anniversary of the murder spree, he wondered if the man before him could truly be trusted. He also realized this might be the last person he could reveal his secret to, who might have the slightest comprehension of his tale. After all, every year he continued to live and read his books proved a blessing at this point in his life.

"Very well," Winters said, clasping his hands in his lap, deciding he had nothing to lose by telling the story to someone connected to the hotel. "Toward the end of the floor's completion, a bare spot about three feet around stood with no covering for several days. One morning, as I was making my way around several rooms upstairs, I heard a conversation from the atrium between Mr. Rexford and several workers. I peeked from a balcony room to see the four men below, two of them carrying the last tiles for the floor, only this time they were in one solid piece, cut perfectly to fill the empty space."

Winters paused, taking a sip of water from a nearby cup.

"On the other side of the tiling appeared a detailed sketch, which I took to be some sort of map. Several lines led to a few distinct marks, almost like a pirate treasure map. It drew my attention, enough to make me follow Mr. Rexford after the conversation ended, and the floor was being finished."

Winters looked to his hands, then to his visitor.

"He returned to his room, taking a small chest out from a closet. After opening it, he removed a canvas bag, which appeared somewhat weighted. He made some comment about keeping it safe, and set about replacing it into the box, which he locked."

After writing several notes, the visitor closed his notebook, giving Winters a curious glance.

"Did you ever see the bag again? Or its contents?"

"Never on either count. But I'm sure they hid it wherever that map led to."

"If they hid the contents, why would they leave a map to its whereabouts?"

Winters shrugged.

"I suppose so that a later generation might find it. Perhaps it was their personal memoirs they wanted saved for later, or valuables they felt would fall into the wrong hands at the time. They were a different sort, the Rexfords. Of course their marriage didn't end well, but I'm sure you know about that."

The last statement went virtually ignored as his guest focused on only the flooring.

"But you feel certain the map led to whatever Mr. Rexford possessed that day?"

"Of that I have no doubt. He gave an impassioned soliloquy about keeping its contents safe from harm and his wife's family."

"I appreciate you confiding in me, Mr. Winters. That certainly does help my cause."

"Is there anything else I can do for you?" Winters asked as his guest stood to leave.

"You've been quite a help already. Thanks for your time."

As his guest turned toward the door, Winters noticed an unusual marking atop the skin along the collar of the man's jacket. He drew closer, seeing it partially covered by the jacket, and by a black turtleneck sweater.

"Oh, there is one other thing," his guest said, turning around as Winters made out the serpentine tattoo along his neck.

Before he contemplated a reaction the knife blade rammed beneath his sternum with the force and speed of a charging bull. He groaned and lurched forward while blood spewed from his open mouth. His murderer heartlessly tossed him to the floor, the blood emptying from Winters' abdomen as he slowly bled out, convulsing almost immediately from blood loss and shock.

He listened as the door opened and the man known to others as Jacob left the residence. In all his years, he never expected such an end, and Winters supposed the element of surprise was all part of life.

One thing remained certain.

His secret would never leave the room.

Chapter 25

McCabe finished his second beer at Kelley's pub as he glanced over the paperwork from that morning. He had checked tattoo parlors with little success.

Most of the serpent design customers were bikers passing through town, or college kids. Both were nearly impossible to trace because the parlors kept no detailed records of their customers.

He called most of the major apartment rental companies in Bloomington and the surrounding area, gathering a short list of male renters who had recently disappeared, either because they found new apartments, moved home, couldn't pay their rent, or simply disappeared for no reason.

He planned on visiting the former roommates, and family members, starting the next morning, to discover the whereabouts of the missing renters.

For the moment, he occupied himself by reviewing a list of people who had purchased scuba equipment the past five years, and the information they left behind. He could only search for promising names and locations initially, and if that resulted in nothing, McCabe would probe deeper, interviewing suspects in the order of apparent relevance.

Ordinarily he never brought work to the pub, but he felt more relaxed, seated at his own table with Celtic music in the background. Some regulars thought he was some sort of accountant, or in business for himself. He seldom wore his gun or badge inside, and never told people his profession unless they asked. McCabe simply wanted to fit in the best he could, and when others knew he was an officer of the law, they tended to be less accepting, and less comfortable.

Raising his hand, he motioned to one of the waitresses for another beer, tipping her when it reached his table. He took a sip, looking at the thicket of papers in front of him. Sorting through them required hours of concentration. He sighed aloud, deciding to visit the restroom before getting started.

Shuffling his papers into one neat pile he stood, draping his sport coat over the chair to ensure everyone knew he would return momentarily. He sauntered into the tiny, one-stall men's room, hearing a noise from outside the window.

After zipping his pants, McCabe walked to the window, opening it further than the inch it was already cracked, looking out to the back of the pub where several cars sat in the darkness. Cold air hit his face, reminding him of why it was better indoors.

He grunted to himself before returning to the music and festivity of the tavern.

McCabe seated himself, sipping from the beer bottle before sifting through the papers, making certain everything was there. He began to look over the first inventory sheet when the pub's door opened, revealing a man dressed almost entirely in black, stepping inside. He looked around momentarily, as though looking for something.

Or someone.

To the detective, he appeared completely out of place. He was too young, and he didn't look the least bit Irish. His hair was black, perhaps dyed, judging by the strange gleam it seemed to produce.

His clothes, except for the turtleneck, appeared out of place. He wore heavy black boots, almost of a military issue, that were hip in some dance clubs. The young man could easily have been a model in any teen magazine with his slender build and smooth face. McCabe was about to start reviewing his paperwork when their eyes locked and the young man acted as though he'd found what he came for.

"Are you Detective McCabe?" the young man asked as he approached.

"I am."

Looking nervously around, the young man pulled out a chair beside the detective.

"May I?" he asked.

McCabe waved him into the seat.

"My name is Stephen," the young man revealed. "I've spoken several times with Paul Clouse about my involvement with a certain, um, faction. He told me where to find you."

"What brings you to me?" the detective asked with a hint of suspicion.

"It's getting too dangerous for me to keep sneaking out on the group. I'll tell you everything you need to know about these people if you'll protect me. Put me in witness relocation, give me a new identity, something."

McCabe sighed aloud, taking another sip of his beer before shifting the papers into one stack, using a paperclip to bind them.

"What can you tell me?" he asked, sitting back.

"Oh, no," the young man said, looking around. "We can't talk here."

"What did you have in mind?"

"There's something at the hotel you really need to see. Something I couldn't tell Clouse. I can't tell you everyone who's involved, but I can tell you what they're after. And I can show you exactly where it is."

McCabe pondered the situation a moment, knowing how safe a public place was compared to the outside. His gun rested in the trunk of his patrol car, allowing quick access if necessary. His tendency to trust the young man wavered against the knowledge that Clouse's informant may very well have been the mutilated body discovered outside Paoli.

"Okay," McCabe said after a moment. "I'll be right back," he said, taking his beer up to the bar with him, gulping it on the way.

Setting the half-empty bottle on the bar, McCabe tapped the bartender on the shoulder. Shawn Kelley had known the trooper several years, especially since McCabe had helped him keep the bar safe from trouble over the years.

Some locals weren't entirely willing to accept a theme pub after it opened, but McCabe ensured Kelley's maintained peace anytime he was there. The trooper also received free drinks on occasion, practically guaranteeing his continued patronage.

"What is it, Tug?" the owner asked, an authentic accent acquired from his father, coming through.

"Shawn, can you call my local post and have them send a unit over here once I'm outside? My radio's out in the car and I don't want to make a scene," he said, shifting his eyes behind him without moving his head.

"Problem?" Kelley asked.

"Not at all," McCabe answered, using a slight accent of his own.

"That kid came in for a moment while you were in the restroom, acting like he was looking for something."

"That a fact?"

"Yeah. Walked over to your table like he was supposed to meet you or something. Got a confused look on his face and walked back out. Be careful, Tug."

"Always am," the trooper replied, stepping away from the bar, his feet feeling a bit rubbery beneath him.

Two beers never even fazed the trooper.

Never.

Perhaps it was unsteady nerves, but McCabe's walk was not as hearty as usual when he returned to the table.

"Had to tell my friend I was leaving," McCabe lied to the young man when he reached the table, taking up the collection of papers from the scuba gear dealerships.

He snatched his sport coat from the chair, putting it on for protection from the brisk weather.

Giving a nervous nod, the young man followed McCabe's lead out the door. A wall of cold air hit them both instantly, leaving McCabe fighting for his senses. He reached for his keys, intending to retrieve his gun from the trunk, but dropped them on the ground as his fingers began to shiver.

"Feeling a bit disoriented?" the young man asked, his voice sounding much more certain than before.

The shift of control still eluded McCabe as he reached for the keys, stumbling a bit as he did so.

"Allow me," the young man said, snatching them from the ground, quickly finding the key to the trunk.

McCabe shot him a confused stare, knowing somehow he was drugged or poisoned, but uncertain of how. Kelley's words echoed through his head, speaking of when the man walked into the pub, searching for something. McCabe had left his beer on the table when he used the restroom, leaving ample opportunity to slip something into it.

Suddenly the noise out back made sense.

"I know what you're thinking," the young man said, opening the trunk with ease, keeping his focus on McCabe, rather than what the trunk held. McCabe spied his service weapon, holstered beneath his briefcase.

"You want to know who I am and exactly what I put in your beer that's giving you a drunken feeling you probably haven't experienced since college. We'll have time for that a little bit later. First, I have to show you that 'important something' at the hotel."

McCabe stumbled over toward the young man, his mind as groggy as his body. The younger man pulled the turtleneck down, revealing a marking McCabe had only been familiar with through description until now. Without much thought or provocation, he swung at the man he knew to be the mysterious Jacob, and missed. Giving a slight laugh of amusement, Jacob shoved the detective into the trunk, ready to close the lid when McCabe lunged with another fist, receiving the trunk against the top of his head as a reward for his effort, knocking him cold.

***

Russell Hinds walked the grounds of the West Baden Springs Hotel for only his third night.

One of four private security guards hired by Dr. Martin Smith, he had the graveyard shift. After the incidents the previous year, combined with Ken Kaiser's bizarre death, Smith decided to hire private guards, having them sign waivers, rather than risk contracting state or local police.

He wanted to ensure his guards were full-time, knowing the grounds and the hotel they patrolled like their own backyards. It took some of the liability away when they signed contracts assuring they, or their family, could not sue for loss of life, or injury, because they knew beforehand, the hotel was a dangerous assignment.

Strangely enough, Hinds was a local reserve officer from the neighboring town of Orleans, who worked mornings at a factory job. Tall, dark-haired, and strong, he looked the part of a cop with his mustache and slight gut, which coffee and donuts occasionally contributed to.

The plain blue uniform did little to inspire Hinds, and he refused to wear the cap Smith provided with its generic silver emblem. A horrid yellow stripe down either pant leg would have made the uniform completely intolerable for the guard, but he was simply in it for extra money, figuring no one would ever see him at such late hours.

He might have done regular police work if the factory didn't pay so well. Money never seemed abundant enough though.

Following two divorces, the security guard had two children and little free time on his hands. Child support kept him working two jobs, though his oldest was nearly out of high school, giving him a reprieve to look forward to the next year.

As he walked the grounds, customary of the first hour every night he worked, his steely blue eyes peered through the thin frames of his glasses, over the sunken garden as his old leather holster creaked at his side. Both the holster, and the .357

Magnum it held, were gifts from his grandfather soon after his first marriage. Upon signing with Smith to guard the hotel, he was instructed never to fire the weapon unless his life appeared immediately threatened.

After signing the insult of a waiver, Hinds decided he would fire the weapon whenever his police training dictated it was appropriate. By no means was he putting himself in the path of a flying scythe.

Passing the cemetery, Hinds looked up to the bland stone markers, knowing one of them contained the legendary Father Ernest, who had been dug up for a few days the year before, during the murder spree. A grave set apart from the others, it seemed undisturbed to this point, despite the witching holiday drawing near.

Across the sunken garden, near the hotel's main entrance, Hinds spied a car pulling up the long driveway, after somehow bypassing the chain at the front gate.

"Ah, damn," he cursed, beginning the long walk back toward the hotel, ready to bark at whomever had enough indecency to barge through an obvious gate and make their way onto private property at such a late hour.

When Hinds reached the concrete steps leading up to the hotel lobby from the brick driveway, he found the car parked at the base of the stairs. Its rear end faced him, and as he drew closer, keys shimmered from beneath the trunk. Several of the old, antique lampposts loomed overhead, giving him a good perspective of the car and the entire driveway.

"Strange," he muttered to himself, picking them up, noticing the car's red and blue lights mounted inside the car's windows.

A look at the plate confirmed it was an unmarked state police car, but where was the owner?

Using his flashlight, Hinds peered inside the vehicle, finding nothing. He shined the light around the area, seeing nothing more than trees, shrubs, lamps, and the mammoth hotel behind him. He unzipped his nylon jacket, reaching for the portable radio he'd forgotten to bring in his hurry to work.

"Shit," he said, finding nothing to grasp inside the jacket.

There was no base, or another officer for him to contact anyhow. His only use for the radio was for emergency calls to local police departments, and he could do that from any phone.

"Fuck," he muttered, breathing a bit more nervously now. "Anyone out there?" he called in a controlled tone, certain he heard a slight echo from the grove of trees seated behind the hotel.

With no response, he decided to open the trunk, fearing something odd was afoot. Either way it was his watch, and he needed to discover why a state police car was parked in the lot. To this point, he felt no immediate danger to his life, though the tranquility surrounding him made him feel his well-being was subject to change.

As he placed the key in the trunk, a noise reached his eardrum. Unable to decide whether it was below or behind him, Hinds placed his right hand on his sidearm, ready to draw if necessary. With his free hand, he turned the key slowly, letting the trunk pop open as he stepped back.

***

From inside the trunk McCabe barely saw through the drug's effects to spy Jacob running up on the unsuspecting security guard, knife in hand. The wide eyes of both officers locked for an instant, shocked to see one another. His gun already drawn, the trooper fired two shots through double vision, both nailing Hinds in the right side of the chest, just missing the intended target behind him.

"Oh, shit!" McCabe cursed to himself aloud for screwing up his one opportunity for an easy escape, and hitting a fellow officer.

Hinds whirled around in pain, and in an instant, Jacob lunged forward, swung his right arm, and knocked the gun from McCabe's impaired fingers.

Certain the trooper was no longer a threat to him, Jacob ran to Hinds, jabbing him in the side with the knife, forcing a painful groan from the guard, before using both hands to clasp the guard's jacket and drag him up the stairs to the first landing. Keeping hold of the jacket the entire time, the masked assailant launched Hinds off the concrete walkway, down the cold steps where he heard several of the guard's bones break on the way.

During the first few tumbles, Hinds grumbled and yelped in pain, but nearly halfway down, he made no sound, even as his body tumbled end over end onto the brick driveway.

Jacob watched the guard land awkwardly at the bottom of the steps, feeling certain the man was dead. Even if he wasn't, he would be before daybreak. The cold weather would do little to sooth his open wounds as his warm blood slowly leaked onto the already red bricks.

"See?" the young man asked, returning to McCabe. "That wasn't so bad, was it?"

"Fuck you," the detective replied as he was hoisted from the trunk with some degree of difficulty. "What did you do to me?"

"Oh, it's all about you, isn't it? You just shot and killed a fellow police officer, and you're thinking about yourself?"

"You bastard. That's not true," McCabe replied with a drunken sort of slur.

"Ah, I see your condition is worsening. I'd better get on with explaining my master plan before you completely pass out, hadn't I?"

Only a spiteful mutter came from McCabe.

"You see," Jacob said, practically dragging the detective toward the hotel entrance, "I slipped you a drug known as GHB, or gamma-hydroxybutyrate, while you visited the restroom. I'm sure you know it as a date rape drug, but believe me, I have no intention of carrying out such acts on you."

"That's a relief," McCabe mumbled, unable to bear his own weight any longer, much less put up a fight.

He knew GHB acted very much like alcohol, only much more intense, even in small doses. There was no telling how much his body took in, even though he never finished the beer. Symptoms included dizziness, difficulty focusing the eyes, slurring of speech, grogginess, and positive mood swings.

Except for a good mood, he had experienced them all.

"They say large doses can kill a person, and I did give you a rather frightful amount, but it seems you'll live, at least for the time being. Even if you had died, it would have served my purpose. We can't have you tracking me through all the local merchants, now can we?"

McCabe felt himself being dragged up a flight of stairs, probably toward the hotel's main entrance. He wondered exactly what Jacob had in store for him, or if he would remain conscious to experience it.

"And, as for that body you found, that was my former protégé, Stephen. It seems he didn't like playing by my rules. It's so hard to find team players these days," he continued, opening the glass front doors, leading the way into the hotel.

A moment later, McCabe realized he was being dragged into the basement. Despite a size and power advantage over his captor, the drug made him powerless to retaliate. Every ounce of energy he possessed went to keeping himself conscious long enough to figure out a measure of escape. His survival depended on observation, now that his best chance of killing Jacob was foiled.

"Don't worry, detective. I have far worse fates in store for your newfound friends," Jacob continued as he pulled McCabe into a small corridor, separate from the supplies stored in the basement.

A stack of bricks and mortar mix were waiting nearby, and McCabe sensed his ultimate fate.

Even as shackles cupped his wrists, attached to the thick concrete walls of the hotel, he could put up no fight. His consciousness faltered over the next few hours while a brick wall grew before him, sealing him in what would become a tomb devoid of sound, and possibly air. A candle placed on his end of the new wall burned brightly, then dimmed over the course of time as the wall went up.

McCabe regretted never getting to the radio in his front seat, and accidentally shooting Hinds, but his few measures of escape seemed far out of reach as the final bricks went up, leaving the candle to die slowly as it melted away. McCabe had no way to touch the wall, call for help, or hope to escape such a predicament.

Even as the effects of the drug wore off, and he realized how dire the situation was, he could only rattle the chains, bolted tightly to the wall, and think how similar this was to a story he'd read while in high school. He never much cared for Poe, or the man's eerie horror stories, but now he was living one, realizing the cold, calculating process Jacob must have gone through to pull off such a plan.

Through the wall, he could barely hear Jacob whistling to himself, obviously happy with his plan's evil result as he left the room.

Chapter 26

"You know, we should probably just see about getting a couple suites at this place," Daniels commented as he pulled into the hotel's drive, no longer using any devices to help him drive. "We're certainly down here enough."

Clouse stared ahead at the flood of police cars and ambulances.

"Quit bellyaching. You getting me up at the crack of dawn isn't my idea of fun either."

What Daniels knew to this point was something about a grisly discovery made by the supply manager when he came to find Hinds for access to the hotel. Though few details were released to the former detective, he knew McCabe had somehow been involved, and feared for the trooper's life.

After calling for a state police escort that took him most of the way down to West Baden, Daniels made good time, allowing him to get there before he missed anything important. His limited investigative powers came with his allegiance to McCabe, and if the trooper was missing as they said, or worse, he and Clouse would be powerless to conduct any sort of legitimate investigation. The thought of having no law enforcement power, with a killer after him, worried Daniels greatly.

Both stepped from the car, greeted by a county officer who recognized Clouse. He started to hold up a foreboding hand but Daniels showed him his old badge. Though he still used both crutches, Daniels' mobility increased each day. He passed as a working detective.

"I'm working with Trooper Tug McCabe on the homicides. He's with me," Daniels said of Clouse.

"Okay," the officer said. "We don't have a homicide here, but it's pretty fucked up."

"Who's in charge?"

"Sergeant Williams," the officer said, pointing to another county officer with stripes on the sleeve of his duty jacket.

Daniels led the way, introducing himself, and Clouse, to the sergeant before asking what they were looking at on the base of the stairs, at the foot of the sunken garden.

"Luke Williams," the sergeant said, exchanging handshakes first. "We had a security guard shot and busted up," the officer said. "He's not making much sense. We think he might have some internal bleeding, and possibly a broken spine. That's why they're taking so long moving him."

"Has he said anything?"

"Something about getting shot by a state trooper. We've had men searching the grounds all morning and we haven't seen a damn thing. No bodies, no state vehicle, no nothing."

"How about inside the hotel?" Clouse asked.

"We had some men check in there too, but with six-hundred rooms, or whatever it has, there's no way we're going find anyone who doesn't want to be found."

Clouse thought of how the original hotel supposedly had over seven hundred rooms, but research indicated they were tiny and crowded. The new design called for less than half that number, creating larger rooms worthy of five-star consideration. He took notice of a man off to the side, standing by himself at the base of the building's main entrance.

"Who's that?" Daniels asked.

"Carl Welch, the hotel's shipping and receiving manager. He comes in early two days a week to check inventory and unlock the back gate for the supply drivers."

"He probably found the poor security guard."

Clouse nodded.

"I'll be back, Mark," he said, excusing himself.

***

"Hi, Paul," Welch said, happy to see a familiar face after a barrage of police questioning.

"How are you holding up, Carl?"

"Doing okay, I suppose. It's not every day you come to work and find what you think is a dead body."

Clouse understood, knowing it got less traumatic each time.

"So what happened?"

"I came to work through the front gate and found the chain down. When I got out of my truck to look, I saw it was cut with bolt cutters. Well, I knew something wasn't right, so I hurried up to the main entrance, and that's when I heard a groaning sound from that area near the sunken garden."

He nodded toward the group of people now standing there.

"One of the guards was laying down there on his back and I saw a bone sticking out of his left arm, so I knew it was bad. I just told him to lay still and went to call for help."

"Did you talk to him at all?" Clouse inquired.

"I tried, but he was in a lot of pain. Said something about a state trooper's car up here and being shot by the trooper. He got stabbed and tossed down the landing, but he wasn't sure who did that to him."

Clouse felt completely lost. All attempts to locate McCabe that morning had proved unsuccessful. He failed to respond to telephone calls, pages, or his radio. Clouse worried something might have happened to the trooper, especially if he drew too close to the truth.

Something terrible.

"But there was no sign of any other vehicle, or other people, when you got here?"

"No," Welch answered. "Like I said, the chain was cut, but other than that, everything else seemed in order."

Clouse was about to inquire about the front doors when a noise from behind the two men startled them. A loud diesel engine roared at the back gate as a truck parked at the locked structure, its driver impatiently stepping on the gas while it was in neutral to attract attention.

"Asshole," Welch said of the driver. "Figures he'd show up an hour late and still be as much of a prick as always."

"Who is it?" Clouse asked, unaccustomed to being on hotel grounds so early.

"One of our usual delivery drivers. His name is James, and he's quite a piece of work," Welch answered, leading the way to the locked gate.

"What's his problem?" Clouse asked, following.

"The world, I think. Just watch."

Welch approached the gate as the driver of the truck, donning a stained, tan college baseball cap of some sort, looked down on the two men.

"About time you got over here," he said to Welch.

"It's not my fault you're two hours late," the supply manager replied, unlocking the gate.

Grunting, the driver noticed the commotion inside the hotel grounds.

"What's going on over there?"

"An accident," Welch said.

"Damn, this place is cursed."

Welch stared at the driver a moment, indicating he wanted no further mention of the hotel's checkered past.

Both walked with the truck as the driver backed it to the cafeteria doors, which provided the quickest route to the basement where supplies were delivered and stored.

"No partner today?" Welch questioned when the driver stepped down from the cab.

"Nope. Small shipment."

Clouse decided to test whether or not the driver was as much of a jerk as his colleague described.

"Paul Clouse," he said, extending his hand as the man walked toward him.

"James Hartley," the driver replied, simply walking past, his eyes never wavering from their gaze at the hotel's cafeteria entrance.

Clouse spent a moment observing the man, noticing his navy blue shirt, nylon back support, steel-toed boots, and tattered blue jeans. His brown hair made way for flecks of gray, and his eyes seemed fixed a bit closer together than those of most people Clouse met, but he seemed ordinary enough. There was no wedding band on his left hand, and Clouse had some ideas why, but he wondered what made some people miserable toward everyone they met.

Probably no older than the firefighter, Hartley seemed to walk with an arrogant stride that resembled a hunched gorilla with his protruding belly and thick arms. Clouse observed him for a moment at Welch's side as he shoved a mechanical lift like those used in retail stores, beneath a stack wrapped in heavy plastic. He wasn't about to do any more work than necessary.

"When he does make a joke, it's always bad," Welch noted aloud.

"There's too much stuff here to fit in the storage room," Hartley complained, pulling the cart out from the truck, rolling it down a ramp.

"It'll fit."

"You're wrong. I'll come get you when it doesn't, so you can tell me where you want it."

"Asshole," Welch muttered.

He noticed a strange bundle settled toward the edge of the truck, wrapped in heavy plastic atop a strong skid.

"Did you order bricks?" Welch asked Clouse.

"I've never personally ordered *anything*, Carl. Why?"

"Probably a shipping error. I don't feel like dealing with James again today. Let's see if they've made any progress with the security guard."

Clouse snickered and walked beside his co-worker, then remembered why he was there to begin with as they approached the scene. He noticed the guard now atop the stairs at the sunken garden, strapped into a stretcher. Daniels was speaking with the injured man, despite the anxiety on the faces of the emergency medical technicians.

"Hold on just a second," Daniels said to the paramedic in charge. "What I need to ask him concerns life and death for someone else."

All eyes fell upon Hinds, who appeared fully conscious, despite the brace around his neck.

"Hurry it up," the paramedic replied. "He's got several broken bones, possibly including his pelvis."

The medics had determined his back and neck were probably fine, but the arm and pelvic bones were definitely in bad shape. Despite several things Hinds had forgotten to bring to work, a bulletproof vest was not one of them. His vest stopped both slugs from hitting anything vital, and actually stopped the knife from gaining full access to his ribs.

"What happened, Russ?" Daniels asked, using the man's first name now that he knew it.

"I swear to God there was a state police car parked in front of the hotel," the man said between labored breaths. "The keys were at the base of the car, so I opened the trunk slowly. Before I could draw my revolver he fired two shots, and I spun around."

Hinds drew of few painful breaths before continuing.

"Next thing I know is I'm getting jabbed with a knife and tossed off the front stairs where I lay unconscious most of the night."

Daniels scribbled mental notes as he went, trying to think of vital questions.

"Do you think the man in the trunk was the state trooper?"

"I think so."

"Is he the one who tossed you down the steps?"

"I don't know. It happened so fast that I never saw who it was. Thank God I've got insurance for this."

Before Daniels could invoke any further questioning, the paramedics rolled Hinds off to the ambulance where he would likely be transported to a larger medical facility than the Paoli clinic.

"Damn," Daniels muttered.

"What do you think?" Clouse asked, leaving Welch to join his friend.

"I think either way we look at it Tug is in some major trouble."

"You don't think he-"

"No," Daniels halted the question. "I think Tug was locked in his trunk, fired his weapon, and for some reason, missed the intended target."

Clouse sighed heavily, rubbing his chin.

"Where could he be?"

"I'd like to know that myself," Daniels replied. "He must have been too close to the truth, and someone wanted him silenced, but I have no idea what happened here."

***

Taking the final load into the basement, Hartley placed it outside of the usual storage area before lowering the cart's fork arms, and took one final look around the area, satisfied he was correct.

"Told him it wouldn't all fit in there," he muttered to himself.

A faint jingling sound caught his attention as it had several times earlier during the unloading process. At first Hartley dismissed it as noise from workers upstairs, but he remembered no further work was being done at the hotel until after its official grand opening, whenever that happened. This time the noise seemed closer to him, almost from an adjacent room.

But there were no adjacent rooms.

About to dismiss it and leave the creepy hotel, he heard a jingling noise once more, almost like chains clanging against concrete.

"What the hell?" he asked himself, stepping toward where he believed the noise originated.

Hartley thought the storage area looked somewhat smaller, but failed to notice one particular area freshly adorned in bricks.

Until now.

He approached the wall, examining it from top to bottom as he did so. The type of brick used was smaller than any other concrete blocks used in the hotel's basement, giving the impression they were older or newer. Feeling almost positive it was new, he touched the mortar, discovering it wasn't fully set.

Part of it rubbed off to the touch, showing it had yet to cure. A sudden rattle of chains behind the fixture caused Hartley to jump back, startled at the thought of someone being inside. He immediately wondered if he was the butt of some joke, or the hotel might very well be living up to its reputation.

Using the fingers on his right hand, he gently pushed one brick, watching it give almost a centimeter. He pushed a bit harder, causing the entire brick to fall into the other side of the wall, leaving him to wonder how solid the rest of the wall remained.

"Help me," he heard a voice murmur from inside, as though dehydrated to the point there was barely a voice left.

"Help yourself," Hartley said, ready to bolt from the room and leave the hotel grounds for fear of his life.

Bumping into a solid body halted him as he looked up into a faceless mask, held in place by someone wearing a grim reaper costume. He felt his breathing come in heaves.

Death itself had come for him.

Both hands, covered in the same black nylon as the rest of the costume, wrapped themselves around Hartley's neck, squeezing momentarily before launching him face-first into the stack of bricks he had just delivered, breaking his nose, stunning him, and setting him up for the kill.

Moaning in pain, and too shocked to move, Hartley slumped against the covered bricks until the reaper came forward, grasping him by the back brace, yanking him to his feet. This time the killer hurled him toward a solid wall, letting his face hit first, cracking his jaw. His ankle twisted when he fell to the ground, leaving him no chance of running away.

Hartley nearly lost consciousness, staggering to regain his footing with what little sense the killer hadn't knocked from his head and his one good foot.

Taking a moment to collect himself, the driver looked through mildly blurred vision around the room, seeing no one. Several stacks of bundled goods loomed around him, each potentially hiding someone. He heard his nervous breathing as his eyes darted around the room, looking for any possible hindrance to his escape.

Hartley wanted nothing more than to hop in his truck and get out of the hotel forever, and let the police deal with whatever psychopath lurked in the basement.

Mentally mapping the safest route out of the room, Hartley tested his foot briefly and limped toward the entrance to the storage area, looking around him as he gingerly trotted toward daylight and the cafeteria above.

In his haste he looked behind him for anyone lurking behind the bundles, distracting him momentarily from the entrance where a large, curved blade swung upward, making a swoosh sound as it did so.

No, Hartley thought as he turned around too late, the blade already in motion toward his abdomen. He caught a glimpse of the steel as it pierced his soft muscle tissue and organs, creating a gap too big for even modern medical miracles to heal. To ensure quicker death, the killer tugged the blade to the side, opening the wound further. Blood and intestines leaked from the driver's stomach, unrolling like a small carpet sample.

He looked upward, seeing the empty black of the mask staring back at him, almost certain he saw a smile behind it. Death was not as he expected. It was cold and hallow, and no bright light or family members from the other side were there to greet him. His life ebbed quickly as the pool of blood grew along the concrete floor, and soon his lifeless eyes stared at the wall he had accidentally punctured just moments before.

The very reason he died.

***

"It's about time," Welch said as the delivery truck drove away several minutes later, a dusty trail rising from the barren back lot of the hotel.

Welch and Clouse stood in the sunken garden. Daniels had left to search the grounds for clues while the other two talked momentarily.

"Guess he had enough room," Clouse noted.

"That or he was too big of a prick to tell me," Welch replied. "God, there's times I just wish he would fall off the face of the earth."

Clouse turned his attention to Daniels, who knelt over where the concrete steps met the grassy edge of the garden. He took his friend's side, wondering if Daniels might have found something important.

"Nothing yet," the former detective noted, still examining the ground. "You know, I would have expected to find a spent casing or something."

"When they get those bullets out of the guard, won't you be able to do a comparison?"

"Not without his weapon, unless the state police have a ballistics record for his service weapon already on file."

Without McCabe's car or weapon, and without any trace evidence in the form of blood, bullet casings, or fingerprints, Daniels would have a short trail to follow.

For the sake of covering bases, he had asked one of the local police officers to scrape samples of the blood atop the walkway and the stairs, where Hinds landed, for DNA testing, though he seemed to feel positive it all belonged to the security guard.

"I guess I should lock this place up," Welch said, ready to depart.

"Go on home, Carl. I'll lock up for you."

"You sure?"

"Positive. We'd like to take a look around first, anyway."

A few minutes later, Daniels' crutches clacked behind Clouse while he locked the back gate. He wanted to make certain the doors around the cafeteria and the lobby doors were all secure as well.

"I should probably check downstairs and make sure the delivery guy left us an invoice, and left everything he should have."

"That's not your job, is it?" Daniels inquired.

"No, but someone needs to do it."

Clouse soon made his way down the basement stairs while Daniels waited in the old dining area. Most of the hallway was dark because most of the overhead light bulbs were smashed.

"Ah, shit," Daniels heard his friend say from below in the darkness.

"What?"

"Son-of-a-bitch," Clouse cursed from the entrance of the supply room.

"What?" Daniels insisted more intensely this time with a concerned tone.

"That asshole spilled an entire shipment of bricks all over this room," Clouse yelled down the hall, staring at a pile that scattered across most of the room, nearly half his own height. It would take some time to clean up such a mess. "And he smashed almost every light bulb down here. I almost fell on my face twice."

Clouse cussed under his breath, turning to leave the storage area. The mess could sit another day or two until the company returned with the next shipment.

Infuriated, Clouse had no intention of forcing his own people to clean up the bricks, or replace the bulbs.

"I'm going to give his supervisor such a bad report the guy will have to leave the state to find work," Clouse spouted on his way up the stairs.

Simply shaking his head, Daniels made it clear he had no idea what his friend was talking about.

"You don't need to be worrying about the little things right now," the officer said.

"I know," Clouse replied. "It just seems like whenever it rains, it pours."

Chapter 27

While Clouse went to check on some leads at the hospital, Daniels managed to derive enough courage to step into city hall, and Deputy Chief Randy Collins' office. He barely used his crutches at all when the secretary showed him in.

"Mark, looks like you're doing well," the deputy chief noted upon inspection of the former detective.

"Doing better these days," he replied, taking a seat across from Collins, who stood to pour a cup of coffee.

"How do you take yours, Mark?"

"Cream, please."

Collins set the coffee down for Daniels, noticing the concerned look across the man's face.

This was no social visit.

"Something the matter, Mark?"

Daniels hesitated a moment, unsure of how to place his words, or ask the favor he desperately needed.

"It seems there was an accident last night at the West Baden Springs Hotel," Daniels began. "A guard was shot, and it appears Tug may somehow be involved."

"You mean, in the shooting?" Collins questioned skeptically.

"Well, perhaps, but not intentionally. I think someone set Tug up, and he's nowhere to be found. We've called, paged him, talked to his post, spoken with his commanding officer, and tried his radio. Hell, I even tried his favorite bar. Nothing."

Collins sat a moment, thinking with a poker face. Daniels said nothing, patiently waiting for the deputy chief to speak.

"Any idea why he would have disappeared?" the question finally came.

"I think he was close to discovering who the murderer is. My guess is he's either dead or incapacitated. We were in pretty close contact and he hasn't made any attempt to reach me."

"And I suppose you want my blessing to let you continue the investigation without Tug if necessary?"

Daniels nodded slowly.

"Some form of credentials would be nice," he added.

Bobbing his head in thought, the deputy chief arrived at his only feasible conclusion.

"I can't give you clearance to investigate, much less use departmental equipment of any kind," Collins said.

Daniels began to object, but refrained when a foreboding finger raised before him.

"Furthermore, only a doctor can release you medically to active duty, and it doesn't seem to me that you've been very consistent in your rehabilitation appointments."

"But, sir, I have to-"

"I know what you're up against, Mark, and I know there are some demons in your past holding you back. But it sounds to me like you're looking for a legal way to protect yourself because you're scared for your life. Am I at all correct?"

Daniels swallowed his pride along with a sip of coffee.

"You're partly correct, sir. I've already been attacked once, and barely lived to tell about it."

Collins acknowledged Daniels silently.

"I don't know what else to do, Chief. I won't sit at home and let myself be a target for this asshole. Too many people have already died, and like it or not, I may be one of the few people left who can stop this maniac before any more innocent people get hacked up," Daniels said emphatically, showing a rare sign of both heated emotion and confidence in his abilities.

"Legally, there's nothing we can do, Mark. The chief filled your spot in detectives officially this week with Brent Jones."

Daniels gave a disgusted face.

"Jones is a fuckup, and a lackluster patrolman to begin with. I wouldn't let him investigate missing pets," he said with a frustrated wave of his hand. "He's a lawsuit waiting to happen the way he handles people."

"Apparently the chief saw the same thing in him that he saw in you a couple years ago," Collins retorted.

Grabbing his crutches, Daniels pried himself from the seat. Perhaps the chief was suffering some acute blindness when it came to his personnel.

"Even the chief makes mistakes."

He headed for the door, unhappy with his current situation in every way.

"Mark," Collins called, stopping him at the doorway.

"Sir?"

"Do what you have to, but don't go dragging the department into it, or you won't have a job left to come back to. Understood?"

Daniels nodded.

"Perfectly."

***

Clouse walked up to a particular office in the hospital, finding the door closed. He read the name "Barry Andrews" on the metal nameplate, knowing he was correct. After a few knocks and no answer, he decided to move on.

He wanted to ask Andrews several questions pertaining to the man's care for Kaiser in Paoli, under the guise of a concerned friend. Discovering where the doctor had been the night before would also satisfy Clouse's nagging doubt about the physician's potential involvement in the murders. Andrews' timing and placement felt a bit too coincidental to dismiss.

A walk down the hallway left him at an office he knew even better, and it was his other reason for visiting the hospital that morning.

"Hello," he said, calling to his fiancée from the doorway while she filled out several papers across her desk.

"Paul," Jane answered, her face outwardly showing the joy of seeing her future husband, since their paths had never crossed that morning. "Where have you been?" she asked, rising to hug him.

"It appears my problems with the killer just got worse. We had a security guard attacked at the hotel last night."

Jane's expression changed.

"What happened?" she asked with concern.

"We're not quite sure. Is Barry Andrews here today, by chance?"

"Haven't seen him. Did you try his clinic?"

"Mark and I tried this morning, but he wasn't in. I'm beginning to wonder about him."

"Barry's good," Jane stated. "I don't think he could ever hurt anyone."

Clouse nodded, knowing how people were sometimes deceptive. He considered his brother-in-law a good man the year before.

"Where are the kids?" he asked.

"Your mother picked them up. She said they could stay with them for the night."

"That's fine," he said with an uncontrollable yawn.

"God, you look tired," she said, rubbing his face, staring at the dark patches beneath his eyes. "You need some rest."

"Are those doctor's orders?" he asked, giving her a flirtatious kiss on the cheek.

"Those are," she said, pushing him away gently with a smile while she looked around her. "Not at work, Paul," she scolded him in a hushed voice. "It's hard enough keeping respect around here."

He took hold of her hand.

"You know I love you," he said, like so many times before. "When this is all over, you and I will spend a week together. I don't care where, I don't care how much it costs. You will be treated like a queen when this is over."

Jane laughed, apparently already knowing he would reward her for her patience.

"So, let me get this straight," she said. "I'll have choice of where and how we spend this alleged week?"

"You will."

She flung her head back with a chuckle. Clouse figured she was thinking of the various ways in which she could spend a week with the only man who meant so much to her.

"I think I see dollar signs."

"Oh, no," she replied, fingering his chest, certain no one was looking. "I have some *very* intense ideas for you and I."

"Oh, do you," he stated more than questioned, pulling her close, though the timing was nowhere near right.

Not caring if anyone was looking or not, he gave her a long kiss, knowing it might be some time before they could spend any time alone.

"I've got to go track down Dr. Andrews," he said afterward.

"Are you planning to talk with Charlie Winters anytime soon?" she inquired.

"Maybe tonight. You want to go?"

"Sure," she said, valuing any time she had with him.

He kissed her goodbye before starting down the hallway.

"Good luck," Jane called after him.

"I'll need it," he replied, turning only for a second.

***

"Ouch!" Cindy Daniels heard from the bathroom as she walked upstairs.

"What are you doing, Mark?" she asked, reaching the doorway.

Dressed only in his underwear, Daniels ran a razor along his cheek, finishing off the stubbly remains of his beard, heading toward a completely clean-shaven appearance. Several thin, bloody cuts lined his chin and cheeks, indicating how tender the skin was after months without shaving.

"I decided it's time to shave the rug, now that I'm recovering."

"Does that mean you'll be back on the force soon?"

Daniels hesitated momentarily before answering.

"Not exactly."

"Then what does that mean?"

"It means I need to look that part."

Cindy took a seat on the bed, watching him finish before he put peroxide on his wounds and toweled his face dry. He looked completely different without a layer of hair along his face. She preferred him that way.

"You aren't planning on investigating this under false pretenses, are you?"

"If I have to."

"Mark, you could lose your job altogether," Cindy noted with obvious concern.

He had fought too hard, and too long, to throw away his career.

"It beats losing my life," he said, walking slowly without crutches to the bed, in great discomfort before gently sitting.

He awkwardly placed his right leg to one side, pulling up a pair of dress pants within a few minutes.

"Is Paul putting you up to this?" Cindy asked, afraid her husband had lost his mind, or at least his common sense.

"No," Daniels answered sternly, buttoning his shirt. "This isn't just about me, Cindy. And it isn't about Paul either. It's about me protecting you, protecting

Renee, and protecting Curt. This is just like last year. You know how badly I wanted to stop that madman and keep all those innocent people safe. You know the consequences if I don't do anything."

Cindy scooted over beside him.

"I don't want our children growing up without their dad," she confessed, clasping his arm. "You're finally walking again, Mark. Everything looks so right, yet you're willing to toss it by the wayside and chase this madman by yourself."

Daniels squeezed her hand.

"I'm not by myself," he said in a calmer voice. "Paul isn't going to let anything happen to me, and I'll be damned if I let any homicidal maniac get to him. We're so close to finding the killer, and I can't just stop now."

"But you could. You could let someone else do the searching."

"Yes, I could, but I would be letting Paul down. I'd be letting myself down." He kissed her cheek, caressing it with his hand. "Cindy, I'm too damn close to stop now, and if we put pressure on this bastard he'll make a mistake. Then he'll be mine."

Cindy took a deep breath, sighing aloud. Knowing there was no changing his mind, and unwilling to put undue pressure on him by threatening separation, or something more drastic, she simply gave in.

"Please, just be careful," she pleaded.

"Always," he said, grabbing his crutches from beside the bed. "I'm starting to feel like a new man."

***

Clouse entered an auditorium on the Indiana University campus, finding a rehearsal of *Caesar* already in progress. He watched for a moment as the climactic scene of Caesar's death unfolded. He folded his arms, leaning on a pillar in the floor section as the actor portraying the great leader took several dagger shots from other actors around him, a shocked look crossing his face as his pretense friends and allies murdered him.

Echoes of the actors' voices boomed through the vacant auditorium as the visitor strolled down the row between the seating columns toward the stage.

Everything was dark except the stage itself, and the actors were too busy in their work to notice him at first. Even the director, off to the side, was consumed by the college kids playing out their roles.

Clouse watched Caesar's violent death on stage, eerily familiar with stabbing deaths as goose bumps crawled up his arms. Flashbacks from so many deaths the past year flooded his mind, and he felt his hands tremble subconsciously. As though the director wanted to challenge both the students in their acting and Clouse's tolerance for violence, he ordered the stabbing sequences done another five times, each time barking out orders to individual actors who didn't meet expectations. Clouse's stomach quivered a bit more each time and salivation crept into his mouth, a nervous tick that was sometimes a prelude to vomiting in his case.

Feeling a sudden urge to leave and separate himself from the chilling scene, Clouse turned as the director took notice and called for him.

"Sir, can we help you?"

He turned, deciding to finish what he came for.

"I'm looking for Ryan Andrews," he stated, hoping the trip proved worthwhile.

"Right here," the young man said, dressed in a toga and sandals fashioned in that particular era of Greece.

The director ordered everyone to take a five-minute break since the students were already beginning to disperse.

Ryan placed a dagger down on the wooden floor, alongside a script, before sliding off the stage to Clouse's level. "How can I help you?"

"My name is Paul Clouse. I need to speak with your father as soon as possible. It concerns the murder of his girlfriend," Clouse told a partial fib.

"Have you tried the clinic, or the hospital?" the son asked, apparently assuming Clouse was part of McCabe's investigative crew.

"Both. No sign of him at either."

"If he's not home, there's only one place he might be. We have a cottage down by the lake. Sometimes he'll go there for time alone, or if we have a family outing."

Clouse nodded.

"You make it sound like you don't have too many family events."

"Not much anymore," the younger Andrews answered. "Things have changed since my sister and I left home."

Clouse glanced at the stage where most of the actors were parting for their break, carrying their scripts and props with them.

"Who do you play?"

Andrews looked at his own script, and the dagger sitting upon the stage. He chuckled a moment.

"I play Marcus Brutus, the man who forms a conspiracy and betrays his ruler," he said with a laid back air of knowledge. "He acts with no thought for his own safety, and without hopes of gaining widespread power. He puts men and country before his own well-being."

"Does he die for his treachery?"

"You'll just have to buy a ticket and find out."

Clouse grinned.

"Maybe I will."

He gave a wave, turning to leave.

"Need directions to the cottage?"

"I'll be alright," Clouse said, already prepared to let Daniels search for the doctor.

He had other leads to follow.

***

A few hours later, Clouse picked Jane up from work, prepared to get some answers from Charlie Winters about the tiles and their significance.

"I can't believe I'm actually helping you on this," Jane commented, rather excited about the notion of aiding in something so important. Her everyday life as a doctor grew rather tiresome in its routine, though she truly loved her work because it made a difference for so many families.

"You're only helping because this is a safe trip," Clouse replied, half-kidding. "Most of the time I go somewhere wondering if I'll be jumped from behind, or find a corpse."

"We're almost there," Jane said, changing the subject as they neared the small residence.

As the words came out of Jane's mouth, rain began to pour from above, pounding the windshield of Clouse's pickup truck. He flipped on the wipers, surprised at the sudden nature of the weather.

"I didn't even notice it was that cloudy," he stated, looking skyward. "Did they say rain in the forecast?"

"Unfortunately," Jane replied. "Didn't you notice how windy it was, or the difference in the humidity?"

"I'm not noticing much these days," Clouse said in a somber tone as he pulled into the driveway, following Jane's pointing finger. "Life isn't as much fun when you find all of your friends dying around you."

Despite the pouring rain, both emerged from the truck seconds later, dashing through the merciless onslaught toward the small cabin where a light glowed from inside the residence.

Clouse knocked as Jane took his side, cringing beneath the small eave above them, which provided little protection from the rain. Waiting several seconds with no answer, he knocked again, prompting Jane to lean over toward a window despite getting drenched in the process. It was too late to save her from the involuntary shower.

"No answer," Clouse said as she stared through steamed windows, which made it impossible to see inside.

"His car's in the drive, Paul," she noted. "I can't see inside, but the lights are on."

Without much thought to it, Clouse tried the doorknob, finding it unlocked. He slowly pushed the door in, wondering what to expect once inside.

"This is creepy," Jane said, stepping in first as her husband ushered with his arm.

The lights flickered as lightning flashed outside, startling them both.

"Mr. Winters?" she called with no answer.

Noticing a kerosene lantern on the table, Clouse darted over to it as the lights flickered again, sensing the power might go out any moment. He found a book of matches near it, and brought it to life momentarily.

"This feels weird," Jane said, looking around the abandoned house, which, for all intents and purposes, should have revealed its owner by now. "Oh my God," she said, kneeling down where several drops of blood sat atop the stained wooden floor.

"What?" Clouse asked, coming over.

"This," she said, fingering the blood from the floor, still somewhat moist in the form of large droplets.

"Great, just great," Clouse said sarcastically, looking around the room a bit more frantically, wondering just what to expect.

Before he contemplated his next move, his cellular phone rang from its holder on his belt.

"Hello," he answered quickly as the lights flickered again.

"Paul, it's Tim. You got a minute?"

"That's about all I've got," Clouse said a bit impatiently. "What do you need?"

"I've been thinking about Beverly Hilton's old estate and how I found those two punks screwin' around out there. They might have been lookin' for something, so I wanted to go out and explore the grounds, but since the buildings are so crumbly, and well, you know…Paul, I don't really want to go out there alone."

Any other time, Clouse would have taken time to badger his friend about acting like a frightened schoolgirl, but this was not the time for joking around.

"Alright, Tim. I'll go out there with you, but I've got somewhat of a situation on my hands right now. Can I call you back when this storm is over?"

"Sure, Paul, sure. Talk to ya later."

"Bye," Clouse said, clicking the phone off, looking to Jane, who seemed more interested in moving on than hearing his conversation.

"You want to go outside?" he asked, offering her a way out.

"Not a chance," she replied, looking out at the downpour, knowing all too well what they might find within the small cabin.

"I want to know how in the hell everyone knows my cell phone number, hon," Clouse complained vehemently. "Is it listed in the phone book or something? It's not like I leave it up at either job anymore."

"You didn't give it to Tim?"

"I don't remember giving it to him," Clouse said, starting toward the back of the house. "And everyone from friends and family to psychotic killers get the number to call me. It's a bit strange, don't you think?"

"Maybe Ken had given Tim your number."

"Could be," Clouse said as he opened several closet doors.

He could not see inside as the lights went out for good with a dying hum.

"Ah, shit."

He held the lantern up to the closets, expecting a ghostly white face to meet his from inside, but only clothes and several small trunks lined the interiors.

"Here, hold this," Clouse requested, handing the lantern to Jane while he looked around the kitchen for a flashlight.

While he searched, Jane backed into a wall where objects were stored above in a low-budget storage bin created by the home's owner to house memorabilia he seldom viewed. Spying several small boxes above, she reached for one, as something smacked against her head from the other side.

Clouse saw and felt it, too, turning to observe the action by the dim light of the lantern. Whirling the lantern toward the source of the hit, Jane found an arm dangling from above her, obviously dislodged during her attempt at viewing the box. Jane shrieked, then screamed, experiencing her first corpse outside of the hospital, especially since this one was brutally murdered.

Clouse took hold of the lantern while his fiancée shrunk back, shining the light up into the rafter where Charlie Winters' pale face stared back at him, eyes wide open, completely devoid of life. Though much of the body was obscured by boxes, Clouse noticed that blood stained much of the man's shirt, showing the murder was no different than any other slaying the firefighter recalled from the past year.

"Damn," Clouse said, pulling his cellular phone from its holder once more to phone the police.

***

As thunder rolled outside and lightning occasionally gave his house better lighting, Daniels sat on the couch downstairs, feeding his son, who cradled himself in his father's lap. With power lines down there was no television, and little else to provide entertainment.

Candles burned in the living room, and on the kitchen table, providing just enough light for him to find his way around. Seldom did the power go out during storms in town, but there were times power lines actually snapped, or a tree fell on them, breaking the circuit.

With little else to do, the disabled officer simply replayed the recent events of his case through his mind.

Speaking with Barry Andrews, as Clouse had asked of him, provided little information. Andrews' alibi was suitable, though not perfect. It seemed the man spent much of his time to himself, or at the clinic. His work apparently took a backseat to his mourning.

In reality, the alibi mattered little. After speaking with people at Kelley's, Daniels felt convinced the young man with the snake tattoo was responsible for McCabe's disappearance, and possibly the murders. He might have requested a sketch artist, but placing a sketch on television or the newspapers would automatically tip the man off that Daniels was close. He felt extremely close to discovering who the man was, so Daniels opted to hold off a bit longer.

After speaking with Hinds, Daniels knew the officer's shooting and McCabe were tied in somehow. He pieced together what he felt was a fairly accurate scenario of what had occurred, though uncertain of where McCabe or his unmarked car might be.

In the meantime, he discovered Smith had canceled all security measures at the hotel, opting to lock up every gate and suspend all activity there until further notice. When he last spoke with Clouse, Daniels discovered his friend had a meeting with Smith in the morning to finalize a plan to suspend the hotel's opening indefinitely, if not permanently.

Good, Daniels thought. He would sleep better knowing the cursed grounds were sealed off, unable to invoke more deaths.

As his son finished off the bottle and began moaning, the officer gently placed Curtis over his shoulder, patting his back solidly for a belch. While he waited, a vehicle pulled to the front of his house in the pouring rain, prompting Daniels to stand agonizingly.

"Who the hell could that be?" he wondered aloud.

"Want me to get it?" Cindy called from the kitchen.

Daniels sensed the visitor was probably there for him. He decided he wanted to keep his wife from his affairs, or danger, if that was still possible.

"No, just hold Curt, please."

While she took their son from his arms, Daniels grimaced as he hobbled toward the door. He expected to see someone familiar on the other side, but found a denim-clad, burly man he felt certain was a biker. His reddish beard looked overgrown and unkempt while black square-toed boots kept the rain from soaking his feet. A black Harley-Davidson shirt peeked through his thick, faded denim jacket as the man waited for the officer to say something.

"Can I help you?" Daniels finally asked, figuring the man needed directions.

Noticing Cindy holding the baby, the man appeared a bit shy about speaking his intent. He looked behind him, since the rain had begun to dissipate.

"I need to speak with you about Detective McCabe's disappearance," the man said.

"Oh, okay," Daniels replied, recalling the man from the tavern where he had asked questions that morning.

He had probably raised a few eyebrows when he asked questions of a few patrons outside the pub about a certain snake tattoo.

"Outside," the man insisted, holding the door for Daniels, who motioned to Cindy that everything was fine.

"What can you tell me?" the former detective asked of the man, not asking for a name, because he doubted a truthful reply would be forthcoming.

Daniels stepped down the front steps gingerly, his legs cramping more with every second of use. He felt the dissipating rain peck at his head and shoulders as it refused to completely subside.

A few minutes outside and his clothes would be drenched.

Pacing a moment, the larger man seemed to contemplate what he wanted to say, as though carefully choosing the correct words to use, probably to keep himself out of danger, or trouble with his peers.

"First off, I wasn't at the bar last night when McCabe disappeared. They say that guy with the snake tattoo came in and acted like he was looking for the trooper. They also say he probably slipped something into the man's drink."

"Who is *they*?" Daniels felt compelled to ask.

"Just people at the bar."

"Do *they* all know he's a state police officer?"

"Some do. Most just think he's a business man of some sort."

Daniels knew from talking with the owner the basic story of what occurred the night before. The part about the man slipping something into his drink was new.

"What else do you have?"

"That guy with the snake tattoo might be someone I've met before."

"Where?"

"About six months ago we had a rally up near Indianapolis and this younger guy came into my buddy's tattoo parlor looking at the displays on the walls. Well, he kept looking at the snakes and touching his neck, like he was wondering how one of those might look wrapped around it."

"Did he give any information about himself, or get any work done?"

"He didn't get anything done, but he did say he was passing through, heading south."

To Daniels, that made sense. It also opened up the possibility that the killer was not local, or part of Clouse's alleged Coven for that matter. Things were possibly about to get much more complicated.

"Did you see what he drove, or remember what he wore?"

"I was getting some work done on my posterior," the man confessed with a crooked grin. "So I wasn't in a position to see a whole lot. I don't remember him really looking the part of a biker, though. He wore jeans, an old long-sleeve shirt, and what looked to be hiking boots. Almost like he'd been in the woods doing something."

Burying a body maybe, Daniels thought grimly.

"Please let me know if you think of anything else," Daniels said.

The man nodded, starting to leave when Daniels produced another question.

"Hey, did you know McCabe or something?"

"Not very well. But he's a great guy, and I hope you can find him."

"Me too," Daniels said with a courteous nod, returning to the comfort of his house.

Chapter 28

Several birds too stubborn to head south let Clouse know he was not entirely alone on the hotel grounds as he waited for Smith to show up the next morning. He knew what the meeting concerned, and he felt both depressed and relieved at the same time.

Closing the grounds ensured no more innocent blood was shed, but it would close off a historical chapter of the town for an indefinite amount of time. It was also an important part of the last three years of his life.

Thoughts of the rainy previous night continued to run through his mind. Now a reluctant sun peered around several remaining clouds, illuminating the garden and brick driveway where Clouse stood. He kicked his cowboy boot heels against the brick, hearing a clop that let him know he stood in the real world and not some nightmarish dream that didn't seem to end. Sleep eluded him most of the night because he answered police questions and consoled Jane for much of the overnight. The few hours he tried to sleep were plagued with images of Charlie Winters staring at him through a glazed death trance.

Shaking his head, Clouse tried freeing his mind of the horrific memories.

At the foot of the entrance stairs Clouse waited, looking around him at the beauty of the trees, and the six-story building looming over him in its colorful splendor. He fished his key ring from his pocket, picking out a particular golden key from the set. He wondered if he would have to surrender it to Smith, or if the hotel would still be like his own property.

His thoughts abruptly ended with a chill piercing his unzipped jacket. Just barely sunny, the morning was cool enough to keep him from waiting outside.

He ascended the stairs toward the hotel, thinking of all the good and bad times over the past several years. Several of his closest friends died on the grounds, all as a result of greed and manipulation, though never on their part.

A moment later Clouse walked into his office, looking at the list of phone numbers along the wall, looking for the distribution center where Welch's supplies came from. Finding the number a moment later, he dialed.

"Carson Distribution," the man answered on the other end.

"Hello, can I speak to the distribution manager, please."

"This is Billy Carson. I'm the owner."

Clouse introduced himself and explained the situation as he saw it from the day before. He inquired about the driver's ethics and courtesy.

"Well, Mr. Clouse, James never came back from that run. After calling your hotel and getting no answer there, I alerted authorities because I thought something might have happened to him. They said they'd keep an eye out for his truck, but they've yet to get back with me."

"Do you think he took off?"

"No, no," Carson scoffed over the line. "James is probably the most reliable driver I have, and he's actually a very good guy when you get to know him. I guess he had a rough upbringing. You know, teased a lot by other kids and stuff. So he's a bit crass, and maybe backwards in some ways, but he would never just disappear like that. In fact, he missed his final two runs yesterday."

"So this was the last run he actually made?"

"Yes, sir. And he never checked in afterwards, so this is the first I've heard of him even being there. Like I said, I tried calling, but there was no answer."

Clouse's mind raced, beginning to worry that the driver met with foul play on the hotel grounds. It happened the year before with an unwitting electrician.

"Well, things have been a bit slow here," he explained. "We're dealing with a few internal problems right now. But if I hear anything, I'll let you know."

"I'd appreciate it."

Clouse hung up the phone, wondering about the mess downstairs. He felt negligent not checking the bricks or the storage room more thoroughly. Locking his office as he stepped into the hallway, he decided to look downstairs when a plea for help on one of the floors above caught his attention.

Frozen, he listened a few seconds more, then another cry for help came, this time sounding more familiar to him.

"Dr. Smith?" he questioned aloud, wondering when the doctor had slipped in, and what the problem could possibly be.

Forgetting about the business of the hotel, Clouse sprang toward the nearest stairway, listening for further cries. He started up the stairs, hearing another terrified plea from what sounded like several floors above.

Echoes rang through the vacant hallways, so he could only take an educated guess where the noise originated.

"Doc?" he yelled up the stairs. "Is that you?"

He heard nothing as he ascended the stairs, spiraling his way up. Each floor came and went without utterance, or any sign of life. Clouse finally reached the sixth floor, peering in every direction as he might have in a search and rescue routine. With nothing in sight, he chose the hallway on his right because more openings, including the access to any of the four towers, and two restrooms, would be accessible.

Clouse started down the hallway, unsure of whether he even had the right floor, much less which rooms to begin checking.

"Dr. Smith?" he called down the rounded hallway, continuing his walk.

As though in answer to his query, he heard a door shut further down the hall. Most of the rooms were locked on the higher floors, which left only the restrooms or the towers, where Clouse truly feared visiting after the results of the previous year. It was where he confronted his brother-in-law for the last time.

Four towers stood along two sides of the hotel, each with only one hatch leading up to its top area, which looked much like a gazebo from anywhere but within. Each tower barely held four people, and the drop down to the main roof would hurt to say the least. Clouse knew the towers were a dangerous place to be, particularly on a windy day.

Cautiously opening the doorway into a small room with a metal ladder mounted to the wall, Clouse peeked around, certain no one hid behind the door before proceeding up the ladder, unsure of what sort of trap or predicament he might be rushing into.

With experienced quickness, the firefighter scaled the ladder, finding the hatch above already open. He looked above him, then around the tower once his head pierced the surface, finding a horrifying sight, just beyond his control and reach.

Climbing up the roof ledge, Smith used his last means of distancing himself from the reaper pursuing him with a scythe. Clouse saw a bloody slash along the doctor's side as the elderly man stumbled onto the ledge, possibly unaware that only a foot of ledge stood between him and a six-story drop.

"Doc!" Clouse yelled, catching the attention of both his employer and the faceless killer.

Both looked at him, but as Clouse went to climb the last few steps, his boot slipped, allowing the killer to return his attention to his prey. Clouse stumbled up to the tower's top, and sprawled out along the roof, forced to watch an action that threatened to haunt him the rest of his life.

Taking a final swipe with the scythe, the reaper missed, but Clouse was forced to helplessly watch as his employer lost his footing, realizing too late that nothing except air was behind him. Clouse watched the doctor's horrified face as he began a six-story plummet, hearing the terrified scream for a second or two until the dreadful impact came, silencing the man. Clouse scrambled to his feet, beginning to rush toward the ledge for a look.

His eyes met the blank, drooping mask of the killer, and Clouse quickly changed his mind as the reaper pulled a knife from a sheath along his side, holding it out for Clouse to see while he turned it threateningly.

"Bastard," Clouse muttered, blinded by fury toward someone so cowardly.

He wondered how anyone could attack someone as kind, giving, and defenseless as the doctor.

Wary of the blade, but fearing little for his own safety, Clouse kept both eyes fixated on the murderer. What seemed a minute passed with both men staring one another down before the killer charged him, forcing Clouse to dodge the blade or be stabbed through his innards.

Whirling to face his adversary, Clouse quickly realized the attack was nothing more than a feign to get him out of the way for an easy escape. He watched as the killer slid down the ladder hatch with incredible ease, forced to choose between giving chase and viewing the unsightly body of Smith.

He ran to the edge, seeing the twisted corpse six stories down, a pool of blood draining beside the body. For a moment, his body felt numb. His heart sank, but his mood quickly returned to its previous state. Infuriated, he bolted toward the hatch, streaking down the ladder in pursuit of the killer. Once he hit the floor, Clouse darted out the roof entry into the sixth floor, listening for any sound leading to the killer.

He heard an elevator ding in the distance.

"Shit," he muttered under his breath, taking the closest staircase down.

Clouse flew down the stairs, reaching the ground level as the elevator car arrived, dinging as it arrived, pausing momentarily. Waiting several seconds, Clouse poised himself outside the elevator until the door opened, revealing nothing.

"No," he stammered, realizing he'd been duped and the killer might very well be on a different floor or leaving the hotel altogether.

There were any number of staircases the murderer might have taken, and Clouse was too late to check any of them.

Desperately searching around him, he looked for any sign of the killer, hearing a slight hiss from one of the tension springs on the ornate glass doors on the other side of the atrium. He sprinted to the other side of the hotel, taking in every angle of the hotel grounds once he reached the cold outdoors, finding no trace of the reaper.

"Damn it," he said, emotionally drained as he reached for his cellular phone, his fingers trembling from the thought of losing another person he considered a dear friend.

He would call for police, who would in turn call the coroner out to the grounds.

Again.

***

Daniels ambled into the third floor of the newspaper office on his crutches, finding a beehive of activity as people darted from desk to desk, typed, answered phones, and did a bit of horseplay in between.

He already felt grossly negligent, and somewhat corrupt, using his old badge to gain access to the news room where an impending deadline for the morning paper had reporters, photographers, and editors scrambling in the late afternoon to make all the pieces become one cohesive unit.

Daniels understood pressure, and working under a deadline. He knew how homicides worked, and how putting off any work might result in the killer remaining free. To this point, he had no fantastic leads, no real suspects, and the only person of any official, real help to him had disappeared.

"I'm looking for Jerome Barnett," he told a female reporter, obviously too busy to help him as she shrugged haplessly, talking on the phone and typing as she did so.

Daniels felt a bit rude after interrupting her, but carried on nonetheless, panning the room for the reporter. When he saw Barnett emerge from a conference room, Daniels quickly hobbled over to the man's desk, tossing several papers down as Barnett took a seat.

"Yes?" the reporter asked, viewing the headlines he had manufactured the past year.

"I'd like to have a talk with you about some of your recent headlines," Daniels said, taking a seat across from the confused reporter.

"Are you feeling left out of my stories?" Barnett inquired. "I've been meaning to include some pieces about your investigation into these murders, despite the lack of departmental backing."

"I've had departmental backing," Daniels retorted. "I've been working with state police as a consultant."

"And carrying a gun," Barnett noted.

Daniels gave an irritated sigh.

"Where exactly do you get your facts, Barnett? I'm very curious about the source from which you draw conclusions."

"My sources remain anonymous."

"You know, you would be a lot more help to the public if you'd focus on the real issues at hand, rather than trivial facts that no one gives a rat's ass about."

Barnett held up one of the papers from the previous year announcing Paul Clouse as the main suspect in his wife's murder, despite little more than circumstantial evidence. Daniels fully remembered investigating the case and giving very little to the press.

"It's the little things the public likes to hear about, Mark. May I call you Mark?" Barnett asked without waiting for an answer before setting into his next discourse. "See, it's much like a soap opera. We provide little hints and clues to keep the public interested. In a manner of speaking, you, Paul Clouse, Tim Niemeyer, and Detective McCabe are simply bit players in this story I unfold for public consumption."

"Speaking of which, you seem awful quick to point fingers at Niemeyer for no apparent reason."

Barnett flashed an exaggerated smile, similar to his photo in the newspaper.

"I accuse no one. The facts speak for themselves. Tim Niemeyer was there the night his friend and that nurse were murdered. He also lacks a solid alibi for every other murder to this point."

"*You* were there the night they were murdered too, but I don't see you mentioning that in any of your articles."

"But I can account for my whereabouts during the Rexford murder, Cranor's murder, and even this morning's latest slaying."

Daniels' face registered his ignorance on the latest slaying.

"Oh, you didn't know Dr. Martin Smith was thrown off the West Baden Springs Hotel this morning, detective?"

"I had no idea," Daniels replied slowly, unsure of how to take the news.

"Strangely, your friend was there and witnessed the entire thing. Sounds like déjà vu, does it not?" Barnett added, knowing how the killer teased Clouse the year before, allowing him to view parts of the murders in order to lure him in, trying to frame him for the killings.

"So how can I be sure you weren't at the hotel, pushing the good doctor off to add some much needed drama to your soap opera?"

"Because I was at work, detective," Barnett said with a grin. "Oh, I keep slipping with that title, don't I?" the reporter added, acting sarcastically apologetic. "What is your working title these days? Is disabled police officer politically correct?" he asked, trying to push the right buttons.

"I prefer *recovering* police officer, myself," Daniels said before taking up the newspapers he brought. "You can jack with Niemeyer all you want, but you're not going to get me to play your media games. I've got useful work to do."

That said, Daniels hobbled from the room to carry on his investigation as Barnett shot a strange stare toward the former detective.

***

Clouse sat at his kitchen table with papers strewn everywhere, trying to figure out where to begin with his former employer's funeral plans.

Actually, he had little to plan because once the coroner pronounced Smith dead at the scene he informed the firefighter of the man's friendship with a local funeral director out of the Bedford area. One call later, Clouse discovered Smith had sense enough to pre-plan his funeral since he left no living relatives, a wife, or children. It was up to Clouse to inform everyone important in the doctor's life that a visit to Bloomington was necessary in two days.

He felt bad for Smith after losing his wife several years back, and leaving behind a legacy, along with a fortune, to no one in particular. Toward the end, the doctor led a truly sad and desolate life, living only for those around him with nothing left to spend his fortune on.

He dedicated much of his time and money to the hotel renovation, though his motivation never came to light. Perhaps the doctor had a childhood connection to the land, or he was a closet history buff, or maybe he held a fascination for the hotel itself. Either way, Clouse would never know why Smith chose to devote his finances to the landmark.

Clouse wondered what would become of the hotel. It could become state property, or be fully taken over by the National Preservation Society, or perhaps transformed into a tourist attraction. None of the options sounded optimal, but he saw no other way for the hotel to see completion.

In between phone calls Clouse had touched base with Niemeyer, assuring his friend he had not forgotten to inspect the resort ruins along Highway 37 with him the next afternoon. He also planned on visiting the hotel the next day, once the task of calling everyone in Smith's book was complete. Fearful of what he might find there, Clouse planned to ask Niemeyer to return the favor and tag along with him.

As he skimmed the doctor's old address book for phone numbers and acquaintances he hoped might be able to attend the calling hours, the phone rang.

"Hello?"

"Paul, it's Mark."

"What's up?"

"Nothing here. Is it true about the doctor?"

"Unfortunately."

"I'm sorry, man. Anything I can do?"

"Just attend the calling hours and funeral in a couple days. Maybe we'll get lucky and dig up some clues."

Daniels hesitated before his next question.

"Is it true that you saw it?"

"Yes," came the equally hesitant answer.

"What did the killer look like?" Daniels asked for the sake of comparison.

"Same as last year. Grim reaper outfit. I couldn't see the eyes or face at all."

"Any ideas?"

"Nothing more than before."

"Don't take this the wrong way, but could it be your pal Tim?"

"No, Mark. Tim is neither thin nor nimble enough to chase people around a hotel."

"That disguise hides a lot, you know."

"I'm aware of that, but no. You're starting to sound like that reporter."

No reply.

"You didn't go talk to the man, did you?" Clouse pressed.

"Well, I did it on my own terms."

"And?"

"I'm not convinced he's innocent either."

"How so?"

"I have a feeling every alibi he gives will be work-related. You know reporters are in and out of their offices all the time."

"As are detectives," Clouse noted.

"Yes, but detectives usually lack motive to go on killing sprees. Barnett is thinking newspaper prizes, a book deal, maybe a movie of the week."

"You know what they say. Fact is stranger than fiction. He could write an accurate account a lot easier if he was in on the action."

"You got it. And by the way, detectives don't sit around all day doing nothing like firefighters."

"No, they only have eight hour shifts to sit around their offices and complain about the rest of the world," Clouse said, deciding to give his friend a ribbing. "In between bitching and complaining, they call home to check on the kids. After that, they get to go home and sit around griping about what a rough day they had at work."

"Hey, be nice. We're like you, when we have to work, we really earn our paycheck."

"Okay, I'll give you that much, Mark." Clouse looked down at his booklet of names and numbers. "I hate to cut this short, ol' buddy, but I've got about a hundred phone calls to make tonight for this funeral."

"Alright. I'll call you when I have something new."

"Okay, bye," Clouse said, clicking the end button on his phone, contemplating just what was required to prevent anyone else's death before returning to the contents of the address book.

Chapter 29

Clouse spent much of that night and the next morning calling people listed in Smith's book, surprised by the ratio of success to failure. He contacted nearly everyone, despite the book's age, and most were not surprised Smith had died, but all seemed shocked about how he met his end.

He put off his search with Niemeyer once more, realizing it was too late into the afternoon to make the trip to both the resort ruins and the hotel. He phoned his friend, assuring him they would make the trip the next day after the funeral. Niemeyer seemed unhappy about waiting yet another day, but reassured Clouse he would not make the trip alone after what happened to Kaiser.

After a quiet supper with Jane and the kids, Clouse felt confident he had contacted everyone possible from the book, and from his memory. Every employee at the hotel, including construction crewmembers, had been contacted, and most would attend the calling hours. If anyone had been excluded, he knew he had tried his best to invite everyone in Smith's life.

Once the table was cleared and the kids ran off to play outside, Clouse started the dishes without saying a word. Jane seemed to sense he was somber after Smith's death. As he washed a bowl, she wrapped her arms around him from behind, leaning tightly against his back.

"Want to talk about it?"

"What's to talk about?" he replied. "I can't keep anyone around me alive."

"You're being too hard on yourself. It's not like you're the cause of all this."

"Not directly, but I keep wondering if all this would have happened if I had just died in the lake."

She spun him around to see the look in his eyes. He sounded fairly serious about the notion, which visibly disturbed her.

"Blaming yourself, or wishing you had sacrificed your life to help everyone else is not going to solve your problems. Whoever keeps killing these people has an agenda. And he's going after everyone who survived last year's attacks."

"That's why I'm going to visit Mrs. Landamere tonight, Jane," he said with a tone that indicated he might do a little good. "She's one of the last remaining people who made it through that ordeal last year. After that, it's basically just Mark and myself."

Jane tapped his chest a few times.

"Aren't you forgetting something?"

"What?" he asked, genuinely unsure.

"Zach has parent-teacher conference tonight. You signed up to be there."

He closed his eyes, shaking his head in mild defiance.

"I can't go *now*."

"I'll go for you," his fiancée volunteered. "I want to see the school again, and I can get the scoop on Zach for you."

Clouse forced a grin.

"You sure?"

"Of course I am. Maybe I can get some ideas on what to start teaching Katie for next fall. I don't want her to be behind the other kids."

He planted a kiss on her lips, knowing he could not ask for anything better at home, even if the rest of his life's story read like a Shakespearean tragedy.

"Are you going to take the kids with you?" he asked.

"I can drop them off at my sister's house. I don't think an hour with Cassie will hurt them. In fact, they love her rabbits."

He turned to place the bowl in the drainer.

"Speaking of domestic animals, have you been taking my horse out lately?"

"Bucky? You lied about that horse. I've worked with him the past two weeks and he's as docile a ride as any horse I've ever been on."

"You sure we're talking about the same horse?" Clouse asked skeptically.

"Positive. I just don't think you know how to work with animals," she chided.

"That, coupled with the fact I'm never home long enough to train them."

"Well, you'll just have to try him again sometime."

Clouse chuckled, a first for the day.

Once a weekend cowboy, he had let that part of his life slip away because his first wife enjoyed different kinds of recreation. Bucky became more of a pasture horse than a pleasant country ride on Sunday mornings.

"I'll take him out when I get the chance," Clouse said. "But for right now, I need to get started if I'm going to catch Mrs. Landamere at home," he said, giving her a quick kiss. "Thank you."

"For what?" Jane inquired.

"For being here with me. For putting up with me, even when I act like a complete moron."

"You're welcome. Just be careful out there."

"I will, and you do the same. There's no telling when and where this asshole might strike next. As long as you're around me, you and the kids could be in danger."

Both looked out the window momentarily as the kids pushed one another on the swing set, content to enjoy the fall sunset, unaware of all the grownup dangers around them.

***

Somehow, the school seemed less like an elementary school at night. Encumbered by adults as Jane walked through its quiet hallways, it seemed overly peaceful. Passing several other parents as she made her way upstairs, Jane headed toward the gifted and talented room where Zach finished each day.

She was over the dead body from the cabin, but the encounter forced her to realize the mortal danger Clouse placed himself in every single time he went to the hotel alone.

Putting any negative thoughts behind her, Jane walked down the hall, remembering her own school days with the lockers and bland floor tiles everywhere.

Zach's primary teacher had nothing but praise for the way he carried out activities and finished his work ahead of most students, but pointed out his interaction with other children still seemed shaky. Perhaps, Jane thought, Clouse set an accidental bad example by straying from several of his friends, and seldom having company over to the house. Both seemed most comfortable at home, and who could blame them?

Home typically provided a safe haven for them.

Jane wondered if the gifted program was the best thing for Zach, considering the way he behaved around others. Most gifted classes involved self-awareness and independence, which it seemed Zach needed little of at this point. She suddenly questioned her fiancé's involvement in his son's life and studies for allowing him to enroll in such a class. Perhaps Clouse only saw the positive attributes of the program, and not how they might harm Zach's maturation.

Like most others, the gifted class's door was ajar, welcoming any parents inside. Paintings, drawings, simple writing tasks, and art projects lined the walls, displaying the achievements of every child in the class. As she walked inside, Jane noticed a cluster of parents speaking with the teachers in the opposite corner. Off to her left sat the room where Zach seemed to work by himself, the door closed.

Quickly deciding to investigate the room, Jane tried the door, thinking she would say she was looking for her child if anyone was inside.

No one was.

Certain no one spied her movements, she scurried into the room, shutting the door behind her before turning on the computer without benefit of an overhead light. She hoped leaving the light off served to keep anyone from entering the room, though she knew it would appear terribly suspicious if anyone walked in.

Her finger nervously trembled as she turned the computer on, waiting for what seemed an eternity for it to boot up. As the screen slowly showed signs of life, laughter and brief chatter passed by the door as the parents and teachers walked into the hallway.

As the computer finalized its load sequence, she clicked on the hard drive directory, reading the available files as she went.

"Simulator, Spelling Bee, Fun with Benny the Hamster, Games, Math Master, Spanish Translator, Reading with Lady Bug. Oh, boy," she commented, noticing how many directories were before her.

Deciding to wade through some of the jargon, she clicked over to the recent documents folder, trying to see which programs had been utilized the past few days.

Finding only text and photo files fell into the appropriate category, she decided to do a search through the find command by most recent date, getting several responses for the past week. Most appeared to be games or educational software. Two stuck out in particular because they sounded like they had nothing to do with school.

"Lock," she said, clicking to open the file.

After a few seconds of loading, then reading the file before her, Jane felt horrified, even sickened at what she read. *Behind Locked Doors* was apparently the title for an adult book. From the first chapter she read, Jane deduced it was written by one of the teachers in her spare time. An obviously steamy, and poorly written text, Jane saw little chance of its success, except in a fantasy store alongside sex toys and blowup dolls.

"Maze," she said, trying the other file, simply because it was not attached to a childish title and seemed to be more of an actual program than the other files.

As it loaded, using a larger program to run the file called "Maze" Jane saw a computerized animated cavernous opening come to life. Using the arrow keys on the keyboard, she followed the entrance in, finding several choices in caverns, noticing something strange along one side of the cavern entrance that stuck with her as she progressed through the program.

It was small, perhaps even insignificant, but a small strip of gold and forest green stuck in her mind as she walked through the computerized cavern, unsure of where it was leading, or why there seemed to be no variance in the walls.

"Good Lord this is boring," she said under her breath, deciding the journey led nowhere in particular.

A sudden absence of light from underneath the door and the locking of the main door outside led Jane to believe her time to leave had definitely come.

"Oh, no," she said, rising from the chair after switching off the computer and monitor with the simple push of a button.

She quickly exited the computer room, finding her way out of the main classroom momentarily.

Waiting a moment for all other noises to cease, she quietly stepped into the hallway, looking both ways before darting for the nearest stairwell as the lights shut off around her. Forced to wait a moment for her eyes to adjust to the darker setting, she ventured toward the stairs, finding a railing just as she spied the steps.

Once she reached the bottom, voices were audible at the other end of the building as teachers left for the night, probably anxious to get home after such a long evening. Spying an exit door, Jane pushed on it, only to realize an inner security bar held the doors in place, foiling any attempts to levy the bar down from the outside. Only janitors typically had keys for such devices, and Jane could not budge the system.

"Damn," she cursed uncharacteristically, heading in the opposite direction for another door.

She found herself partly down the school's main hallway when the sound of footsteps echoed behind her, with no voices or any other form of comfort remaining.

Hoping a teacher had simply run late in leaving, Jane spun around, expecting to see a friendly face.

Instead, there was no face almost the distance of two cars away. A shadowy figure stood behind her silently, perfectly still a moment, until a gleam of metal caught her attention.

It shimmered as a single beam of light from down the hallway caught it. To her it looked like nothing except a knife.

Gasping, Jane darted toward the opposite door, fearful for her own life the very first time since Clouse's ordeal had begun.

She rounded a corner, seeing the means of her escape straight ahead as she burst through the double metallic doors, into the waiting arms of a dark figure.

"Whoa there, miss," a local police officer said, holding her at a distance from himself.

He was a brawny black man who wasn't about to let her go. Jane felt nervous being outside the building, but still in potential danger.

"You get lost in there?"

"No," she said quickly. "There was someone behind me."

"Probably my partner Darren," the officer said, looking beyond Jane toward the empty hallway. "Darren, you there?" he called.

For a moment, nothing happened, then a figure emerged from around the corner and Jane saw the gleam of metal one more time. The person hesitated, then stalked forward toward the two. Jane felt her body tense with fear. Oh my God, she thought, unsure of whether this was the partner or someone far more diabolical.

"Lady, you had me scared to death," the second officer said as he came into view.

Jane was relieved her imagination was working so hard, and that she was out of the school.

"Why did you run like that?"

"I had no idea who you were," Jane said. "I got caught up in looking around the school and the next thing I knew the lights were getting shut off," she told a partial fib.

"I'm glad we checked it over," the first officer said. "You could have been stuck there all night if the custodians secured all the exit doors."

"Thank God for small miracles," she said, hoping her fiancé had better luck and fewer scares in his ventures.

***

In the darkness, Joan Landamere's rural paradise looked far less appealing compared to the times Clouse visited during daytime hours. The garden, statues, and beautifully trimmed bushes failed to show their splendor at night, but the landscaped front yard and iron gate before the house were prominent as the off-duty firefighter pulled up to the front gate, seeing that some lights were on.

Surprised that the front gate was open, he drove up the paved driveway, slowly exiting his truck as he looked around the grounds, listening for any strange noises.

He knocked on the door a moment later, greeted by several deadbolts unlocking, then a hesitantly opened door.

"Mr. Clouse," Joan Landamere said, instantly recognizing him through the small opening from behind the door. "What brings you out here?"

"I believe you might be in danger, Mrs. Landamere. Can I talk to you a moment?"

"Certainly," she replied, opening the door. "Come in."

A moment later, she fixed them both coffee and Clouse found himself seated across from her, still amazed by the size of the house. Though a participant in mass murder, David Landamere had taken care of his wife, building a sizable house nearing mansion status before his death. Much of the work reminded Clouse of the man he once respected and worked for, but the manner in which Landamere betrayed him left Clouse skeptical of fully trusting anyone again.

"What makes you think I'm in danger?" Joan asked, stirring some cream into her coffee.

"All of the verified murders seem to be people who survived last year's attacks. I've been attacked, and Mark Daniels nearly got killed. The two of us, and you, are about the only people left who survived."

She shook her head sadly.

"I heard about Dr. Smith."

"It's been rough on everyone, ma'am. Will you be at the funeral tomorrow?"

"Yes. And I'm curious what will become of his estate."

"Did he have any distant relatives who might stand to inherit?"

"I don't believe he did. He never had children, and no one really knows much about him. Still, Dr. Smith must have drawn up some sort of will."

Clouse shrugged.

"I'm sure we'll find out soon enough."

Joan took a sip from her coffee mug.

"I appreciate your concern for my health, but I can't do much else to protect myself. I don't go outside after dark, I leave my security systems on constantly, and I keep my dog out back to prevent anyone from sneaking in."

"Are you sure you're fine out here?" Clouse asked, not wanting to leave until he felt certain she was safe on her own.

"I'm fine. No one can get in here to get me, and I have no plans on leaving the house until this whole mess is resolved. Well, aside from the funeral tomorrow, of course."

Clouse stood, setting his coffee cup on the nearby table.

Guilt plagued him for leaving so soon, but his objective was accomplished, and there were any number of things he needed to prepare for the next morning. The funeral, from the number of people he confirmed were coming by phone, would be a rather large event. Clouse had to stop by the funeral home before heading home to finalize details with the director concerning the casket, flowers, and the arranged final resting place to see if there was anything he needed to do.

His overnight rest would be limited.

"I have to go plan for the funeral," he revealed as he stood. "If you need anything, anything at all, just call me or Mark."

"I will," Joan assured him. "And I appreciate everything you two have done for me."

Clouse nodded before heading awkwardly toward the front door. Joan stood to open it for him, and as he stepped outside, he heard the locking of several deadbolts from within. He hoped her security measures would prove enough to keep her safe until some sort of resolution was reached concerning the murders.

Chapter 30

Similar to most of his nights, Clouse ended up sleeping very little before the calling hours the next morning. When he found a rare opportunity to sleep, he tossed and turned with a fitful mind, and even a usual night of full rest never seemed to restore him to full strength.

"How do you feel?" Jane asked as he finished tugging his tie in the bathroom. Feeling sluggish, he took an unusually long time getting dressed.

"I'm okay," he said, not up to an extended conversation.

If the choice was his, he might have slept into the afternoon and spent the day around the house with his fiancée and the kids.

Clouse snatched his sport coat from atop the bed, ready to start what was certain to be one of the worst days of his life. Strangely, he sensed things were about to look up. No rhyme or reason, just an instinctive feeling nagged him that something good would happen soon. He hoped more than anything the killer's identity might come his way.

Jane had already taken Katie to stay with her parents, and Zach to school, which Clouse constantly thought about. He hated leaving the kids out of his sight one second, especially with Halloween only a day away. Things looked more dangerous for Clouse, Daniels, and their families with each passing day.

"Is Mark going to be there?"

"Yeah," Clouse answered in short.

He made it obvious he felt rather bad in spirit. She drew close to him, placing a hand on his shoulder.

"It's okay. I know you must be dead tired, Paul," Jane noted, wrapping her arms around him momentarily. "Take the day off after the funeral. You don't see

Mark running to Paoli every day checking for clues. Do what he does and stay home with us."

Clouse winced, partly from a building headache, and partly because he was tired of hearing how many things Mark failed to help him with, when he knew full well his friend was covering every angle he wasn't.

"Mark is putting his career on the line by investigating these murders, Jane. If he wasn't checking the leads he had, I couldn't check most of the ones I've got. We feed off one another to get closer to the truth."

"Which is?" she demanded.

"What do you mean?"

"Is it a truth you're actually seeking? A person? A justification for what's going on around you? I'm starting to lose track of exactly what it is you're after. I know you've lost a lot of friends, but instead of protecting them and your family, you track this ghost of a killer. This damn reaper in your mind."

Clouse simply burned a hole through Jane with his stare. Stunned, she finally called him on his obsession with finding the killer.

"That's it, isn't it?" she prodded further. "You're actually caught up in the fact that you're chasing this spectral figure, as though no one else in the world can do it."

"No one else in the world seems to be trying, or they're dead," he said sternly, still in control of his emotions, despite the whirlwind of thoughts dancing through his mind. His head hurt too much for the start of any day, particularly this one. "And I realize I'm making personal sacrifices by leaving all of you here so much, but it's only because of my concern for your safety. Don't think for a second that you and the kids aren't on my mind every single time I step out of this house."

"I don't want to argue about this," Jane said after a moment.

"Then please don't bring it up. This funeral is important to me."

"I'm sorry. I realize Dr. Smith meant a lot to you."

Clouse put his sport coat on, adjusting the fit.

"Yes, he did. And I'm actually hoping to see if the killer shows up. Mark and I are going to watch everyone carefully. Last night the funeral director gave us permission to place a camera inside the funeral home for the calling hours."

Jane started to speak but he put a foreboding finger between them.

"Let's just go."

***

On the way to the funeral home, Jane related the story of the night before at the school to Clouse, letting him know about the strange program she encountered, and how much part of it looked like the architecture at the hotel. He asked if it was the program Zach might be using, but she was uncertain, though the dates indicated it had been used more often, and more recently, than most other programs.

Clouse nodded, thinking it odd that Zach was learning from a program that seemed to give endless tunnels that never changed. If he had time, he would go to the school and question the teacher to find out what type of program it was, and if Zach was actually using it.

At the calling hours, Clouse immediately met up with Daniels, leaving Jane to mingle with Cindy and several other acquaintances. His friend was without crutches, but noticeably suffering the effects of labored walking, and the cramps that accompanied it.

"You okay?" he asked the former detective.

"Sure. It gets a little easier every day."

Clouse panned the room, seeing a flood of people waiting to pay their respects to the late doctor. The room contained lawyers, doctors, construction workers, cops, and people from nearly every walk of life. More importantly to Clouse was something he spied in abundant numbers he did not expect.

"Notice how many women are here?" he asked Daniels.

"Some are particularly young, aren't they?" the officer observed.

"And strangely enough, I don't remember calling too many women on the phone."

"You're about to get married, Paul. That could get you in trouble."

Clouse grinned. After his bout with Jane, he wondered just how blissful their future together was going to be. Still, she was looking out for him, and that seemed healthy enough.

"See anything else unusual?" he asked Daniels.

"Nothing noteworthy, except for this one fella who keeps eyeing you every so often."

Clouse's glance followed his friend's. He spied a man dressed in an expensive suit leaning against a corner post, simply staring his way, distanced from everyone else in the room. He appeared very professional, and probably old enough to be Clouse's father, though he could not recall ever having met the man.

He seemed to have a deeper purpose than paying respects to Smith. He also appeared oblivious to the stream of people walking up to the coffin for a final look or to say a prayer. Clouse was amazed they had pieced enough of the doctor together for an open casket after the fall had reportedly shattered nearly every bone in his body.

"He does seem to be staring our way," Daniels noted. "Maybe he's a secret admirer of yours."

"Doubtful," Clouse replied, noting the man's gaze was not especially friendly.

"Maybe he's interested."

"Hardly," the firefighter said, smacking his friend's arm, not enjoying his unusual display of bad humor. "I think maybe it's time I have a talk with our friend," he said, starting to walk across the room.

"Don't get too chummy. We still have work to do."

Clouse looked above his friend at the hidden camera.

"That's what we have that for."

As Clouse drew closer, the man did not shy away or even look in another direction. He appeared as though his wish had finally come true, grinning slightly as Clouse approached him.

"Harold Simms," he introduced himself, arms folded, still leaning against the corner post. "I already know who you are."

"And how is that?" Clouse asked, occupying the other edge of the post, leaning a shoulder against it, enabling a view of the crowd while he spoke to Simms.

"I'm Martin Smith's lawyer."

Giving a questioning stare, Clouse ignored everything around him, wondering what interest Smith's lawyer might have in him, other than a pending lawsuit for mishandling the funeral arrangements.

"What can I do for you, Mr. Simms?"

"Actually, I was hoping to talk to you after everything was over today, but since you approached me first, I feel obligated to tell you. Can we step outside a moment?"

Clouse looked over to Daniels, giving a wave as he followed Simms toward the door, indicating everything was fine, and his conversation would be brief. A wisp of cold air hit the two men as they reached the outdoor balcony of the funeral home, taking in a view of the city block as they did so.

Clouse would not have held the funeral processions in Bloomington, but he followed the doctor's wishes to the letter, including the burial later that day outside of French Lick.

"So, how do you know who I am?" Clouse asked, breathing the cool morning air, noticing patches of fog stretching to the next block.

An eerie gray sky loomed overhead, setting up the witching holiday perfectly.

"Martin told me lots about you, Mr. Clouse. He was very fond of you, and your work. So much so that he named you in his will."

Clouse's attention was captured.

"He named you *alone* in his will, sir," Simms said, shaping his forefinger and thumb like a gun, aimed at a stunned Clouse, who stood there almost a minute in disbelief, fumbling for the balcony railing to steady himself.

A certain realization hit him with Simms' words.

"You're telling me he had no living relatives anywhere?" he asked, a straight arm clasping the railing to support his buckling knees.

"I'm telling you it doesn't even matter. He named you the executive heir to everything he owned, including a theme park, hundreds of acres of land, a hospital ward, and even the hotel you both worked on together. This is all unofficial to this point, of course."

"Of course," Clouse said numbly, wondering if this might be a dream, or some sort of cruel hoax. "Can you prove any of this to me?" he asked Simms.

"Not right now. Come to my office at your convenience and I'll show you the paperwork," Simms said, flipping out a card which Clouse took and examined. "I know my timing is bad, but it was important to talk to you in person."

Clouse regained his composure.

"That's fine. I'll probably see you in a day or two."

Simms turned to go inside.

"I'll pay my respects and make a brief appearance at the funeral," he informed Clouse. "Stop by my office when you're ready."

As Simms stepped inside, Daniels brushed past him onto the balcony. He noticed his friend appeared a bit befuddled.

"What's up?"

"I'm not quite sure."

"What does that mean?"

"I was just informed that Dr. Smith's estate falls into my hands."

Daniels blinked several times, seemingly unsure of what he heard. He had always trusted Clouse wouldn't lie to him, but he apparently required further clarify about what his friend's words meant.

"You mean you inherited everything the man owns?"

Clouse nodded slowly, leaning uneasily against the balcony rail.

"It appears so. I'll get the proof in a day or two."

"Smith's lawyer?" Daniels asked, thumbing back toward the room where Simms had just returned.

"Yeah."

A smile crossed his friend's face.

"Wow, Paul. So I'm going to know the wealthiest man in the state?"

"We'll see about that," Clouse quickly offset his friend's assertion. "Even if I do stand to inherit Dr. Smith's estate, the taxes will probably eat me alive."

"Still, that's incredible."

Clouse gave a dismissing wave, still not sold on the fact he stood to inherit millions, perhaps billions of dollars from his employer's estate.

"We better get back inside," he told Daniels, ready to proceed with his day as planned, if that was still possible.

Niemeyer still wanted to see the land he oversaw with the security that companionship offered. Not one to break promises, Clouse would go because he felt the lives of his friends were very much his responsibility.

His high school buddy had waited long enough to look at his land, and Clouse felt an urgency to check the hotel, especially now that it might be his property.

***

An hour after the funeral Clouse pulled into Niemeyer's driveway, deciding to let his friend drive, considering he was in a race against any number of pending matters. Niemeyer took a scenic route to the resort ruins, giving the two an opportunity to talk. Both noticed the number of colorful leaves fallen along the untended road, creating a perfect fall day. With little sun and continued brisk temperatures, both men wore sweatshirts beneath their jackets.

Clouse neglected to mention his potential inheritance until he received absolute proof. He dreaded telling people about his good fortune since it could be false information. He sensed the will might be contested in court by some unknown relative coming forward, whether the claim proved true or not.

"Your week been pretty bad?" Niemeyer asked, taking a winding curve.

"Not entirely."

"Mine hasn't been worth mentioning," Niemeyer noted with enough frustration to bring out his drawl.

Clouse couldn't help but chuckle.

"What's so bad about it?"

"We're behind schedule on my new project, and your buddy who did your hotel landscaping couldn't make it, so now the owners are wantin' ta sue me for a breach of contract just because I missed a tentative deadline, even though it wasn't in the contract."

"Sounds like fun," Clouse said sarcastically. "So Brian canceled on you?" he asked, knowing Niemeyer referred to Brian Kern, the landscaper contracted to do the sunken garden and surrounding plant life at the hotel.

Most of the landscaping at the hotel was complete, so Kern had moved on to other projects, recommended heavily to Niemeyer by Clouse.

"At least he's good enough to call," Niemeyer said. "Most of those guys just show up when they feel like it and don't think you'll have the balls to call anyone else in."

"That's what contracts are for, Tim," Clouse said evenly, trying to get a rise from his friend.

"Don't even talk ta me about them damn things. That's gonna be my sore spot for quite a while, Ah'm afraid."

Clouse observed the resort ruins from half a mile away in the form of the burned hull of the main building and the surrounding buildings in their desolate form. It was a reminder of what neglect sometimes did to even the most beautiful of grounds.

"What exactly is this place's history?" Clouse asked as Niemeyer pulled into the makeshift drive, merely a muddy trail where trucks had come and gone beside the overgrown brick drive that once provided elegance leading up to a gorgeous resort.

"Beverly Hilton owned it back in the Fifties," Niemeyer began as they stepped from his truck.

He took the lead toward the hull of the building, its boards creaking with the late morning wind as the remainder of a dewy fog lifted from behind. The scene unnerved both men, though neither would confess it.

"I guess it rivaled some of the great hotels in the area, including yours down in West Baden. Take a look back here," Niemeyer said, leading Clouse around the huge remains to the back where the ruins of the large indoor pool and its surrounding villa stood a short distance behind.

Clouse noticed ornate designs through the charred surface of several stones along a path leading toward the pool. They paralleled those of the hotel he worked on, and now possibly owned. With the fog lifting, Clouse saw the few remaining details of the villa walls surrounding the pool, and the intricate detail put into the wood and glass surviving the fire and later the vandals who plagued the resort. Beyond all of it, he spied a sizable body of water he considered to qualify as a lake, though he had never taken it in from this angle.

"Guests had a pool, game rooms, a cigar room," Niemeyer noted, taking out a cigar of his own and lighting it before continuing the tour. "They even had access to the lake back here by boat, or they could swim along the beach. Hell, a lot of guests even fished I guess."

"So this was a fully functional grand resort, huh?"

"It was. And Beverly expanded it after her husband's death in the Eighties. It burned down just a few years ago during a summer renovation," Niemeyer said, leading Clouse around the front, where several boards swayed and creaked overhead, threatening to break loose and land on their heads as they passed. "Luckily no guests were around."

"So what actually happened?"

"With the fire?" Niemeyer asked before taking a moment to think, thumbing the cigar at his side. "Well, I heard one of the caretakers was doing some work late one night, got a little tipsy, and accidentally burned himself, and the entire resort up with a cigarette dropped on a mattress. They found his remains a couple of days later in the ashes. Happens all too often, doesn't it?"

"Yeah," Clouse honestly replied after seeing several such incidents where discarded cigarettes sent apartments or houses into fully developed blazes. "But you're telling me this entire place caught fire because of that, and no one got here in time to save it?"

"This building is close to a century old, Paul. They didn't have fireproof materials when they built it."

"I thought you said Mrs. Hilton owned it in the Fifties."

"Sure, but she bought it from someone."

While his friend thoughtfully puffed on his cigar a moment, Clouse looked at the rickety boards above them, noticing the frame of the main doorway they stood beside. Like part of the villa near the pool, the wood showed signs of artistic detail. No paint survived the fire, but Clouse recognized the decor of the frame as similar to that of the hotel. He wondered if the same architects were used for both projects, since they would have been erected around the same time.

"Can you check some history on this place, Tim?"

"What do you want to know?"

"Who designed and built it? And the dates of construction if possible."

"That shouldn't be too difficult," Niemeyer said with a shrug. "Let's get inside and get this over with."

Clouse followed his friend through the doorway as the door hung awkwardly to one side on a single hinge, unable to perform its function ever again. Despite the daylight streaming through the broken boards of the resort, the inside remained fairly dark. Clouse noticed the remains of divider walls where rooms once stood, and sensed the size of the lobby, even though it was nothing except gray ashes and a charred block where the reception desk once stood.

Above were boards and support beams clinging to the walls where several floors once occupied guests. The two could see all the way up to the roof, and in the distance, one of the staircases remained just intact enough to decipher what it was. By all rights, and probably in a legal sense, the place should have been torn down immediately after the fire in Clouse's estimation. For Niemeyer's sake, he hoped his friend could talk Mrs. Hilton into demolishing the building, or she potentially faced a lawsuit when someone got killed or injured inside the structure, even if they trespassed first.

"What about the insurance?" Clouse inquired. "Surely she had a sizeable policy on a resort this size."

"She collected, but she put the money to other uses," Niemeyer replied. "I think she was uninspired to rebuild the lodge and run it at her age, so she just left it this way."

He knocked against a support beam with his knuckles.

"It's still solid," the contractor noted, looking around at the walls before drawing on his cigar. "It was a beautiful place, Paul."

"But you're more concerned about the land, aren't you, Tim?"

"Hell, yeah. This resort was a great place, but this is where I wanna come home every night, buddy. When I retire, I'll be sittin' on the porch of my dream house, lookin' out at that lake. You can even fish here if you want."

Clouse didn't plan on boat travel again in the near future. Any fishing would be done from solid ground.

Holes in the roof revealed bird nests in the few remaining rafters. Clouse felt uneasy beneath a flat roof, knowing they usually gave rather quickly once their support beams were burned, but apparently, the boards above were strong enough to keep it intact. The three stories of flooring that had burned and fallen to the ground and were now crisp debris all around him, were what concerned him. If they had disintegrated, the roof probably wouldn't be far behind.

"What are we looking for?" Clouse asked, starting to step forward, the wooden remains nearly up to his knees in some areas. "Glad I wore my old boots," he thought aloud.

"I'm trying to figure out what those two punks were doin' in here," Niemeyer said. "Whatever it was, they came out empty-handed."

Clouse's eyes panned the room.

"And you think *we're* going to find it?"

"Sure," Niemeyer said, unrealistically optimistic in Clouse's opinion.

Clouse doubted that seriously as he began stepping through the debris toward one of the room hulls, seeing nothing except an endless trail of ash and burned wood. Ignoring the wind howling through the holes, and the empty streams of light entering the building's weak points, he quickly changed direction to head for what was the main hallway stemming from the lobby.

"Can't you get some sort of injunction to have this place torn down?" he asked his friend.

"Mrs. Hilton would never speak to me again."

"Do it anonymously," Clouse suggested. "Then her fading memories are history and she'll sell you the land."

"You're devious, Paul," Niemeyer said as they waded through the debris toward the back of the building.

"I just have your best interest in mind, pal. And by the way, where are we heading?"

"Toward the basement."

Clouse stopped, staring at his friend with utter curiosity. His look indicated that he was positive Niemeyer approached utter madness.

"There's a hatch leadin' to the basement, but I doubt those creeps found it," Niemeyer stated, chomping his cigar.

"And I doubt we will either."

Niemeyer chuckled a moment, knowing he was close, but not positive where the basement door might be.

"When the hotel was operating, according to Mrs. Hilton, the hatch was flush with the floor, hidden 'neath a large carpet."

"You can't expect us to find this hatch without shovels, Tim," Clouse said. "There has to be a foot of this shit in here, and we're going to get busted up if we dig by hand."

"Any ideas?"

"Let's go to the hotel. I can get us some tools there, and do my stuff, then we can come back and dig around."

"We will come back, right? I don't want you doin' your thing, then denyin' me the chance to help you find out what the hell is goin' on around here."

Clouse looked at the debris surrounding his feet, and throughout the room. It was a battle the duo would not win under present conditions.

"I promise, Tim. Let's go."

Chapter 31

Clouse unlocked the front door of the hotel, stepping inside with his friend close right behind. As gray clouds loomed outside, the inside of the domed building seemed dark and imposing.

As the friends entered the lobby, they cautiously looked up to the ceiling and one of the balconies above, as though sensing they might not be alone.

Though no evidence showed otherwise, such as a car outside, or strange noises, the two detected a peculiar difference in the building. Even Niemeyer, who had only visited the place a few times, seemed to feel something odd in the air. He stepped in carefully behind Clouse, jumping slightly when the glass door closed behind him.

"Nervous?" Clouse asked.

"A bit."

Lightning flashed outside, providing them with an even worse feeling. It seemed fitting so close to Halloween, but a bright sunny day might have made the trip more tolerable. His boots clopped against the floor, echoing throughout the large hotel, as he crossed the lobby to a light switch, flipping it upward.

Nothing.

"Shit. Power must be out."

"No backup generator?"

"Not yet," Clouse said. "It's on our 'to do' list."

He looked around, then down the winding hallway toward the offices. He started toward his office, Niemeyer quickly following. The contractor seemed to fear remaining in the lobby alone, given the circumstances.

Clouse barely found his way to the office as the hotel grew darker with each step away from the daylight in the lobby. Niemeyer followed unusually close behind, even stepping on Clouse's heel at one point.

"Sorry, Paul."

"Hang on a second, Tim. I'll get in here and get us some flashlights."

Niemeyer waited in the hallway as Clouse fumbled around inside the office, finally reaching the cabinet where several flashlights, and other pieces of equipment, were stored. He emerged a moment later, handing his friend a light while bringing his to life.

"What exactly are we here for again?" Niemeyer questioned.

"Two things. First off, someone gave me a riddle to solve, and I've had time to think about it with a clear head the past couple days."

"A riddle?"

"This supposed list of victims can apparently be found where the puzzle pieces most."

"What in the hell does that mean?" Niemeyer asked skeptically, his accent showing through.

"Now that I know what the pieces are, Tim, I may have an idea where to look."

Niemeyer followed Clouse's lead toward the atrium with a perplexed look on his face. Keeping up with his friend's life had apparently become a major chore.

"What pieces are you talking about?"

"The tile pieces that used to be in the atrium. They got sold when renovation began, and now I'm finding out they have some kind of weird puzzle on the back."

"Puzzle?"

Clouse shook his head, shining his flashlight into the atrium entrance as they reached it. Above them, the dome allowed some gray light to enter, but shadows predominantly covered the atrium's new carpet floor and the statues placed neatly around it.

"I'll explain later."

Clouse looked around him, knowing the pieces of the floor came from the atrium, where they were all originally concentrated. Even so, he was unsure if Stephen had meant the atrium, or wherever the pieces now resided. Considering the pieces resided in several hundred different homes, he hoped he stood close to the answer.

"If you were a list, where would you be?" he asked Niemeyer.

"Probably hidden where two people idiotic enough to come in when there's no power would come lookin' for me."

Clouse ignored his friend's ill humor, looking around the room until he thought he spied the answer in one of the statues. Suddenly everything made sense to him.

"I think I've got it," he stated, envisioning how Stephen might have returned to the room in his efforts to save Kaiser, leaving hastily out another exit.

One of the exits contained a statue beside its arch, twice the size of either man. It had an elongated horn just above Clouse's field of vision. To be precise, it looked like some sort of leprechaun holding a horn while on the lookout with a great purpose. Clouse approached it, sizing it up and staring at the horn, which appeared to be the only area on any statue where the potential for stuffing a piece of paper might exist.

He reached up, finding the horn too deep for him to reach on his own. No chairs, or other lightweight objects adorned the atrium yet, leaving him only one way to extend his reach.

"Give me a boost," he told his friend.

"Ah, damn," Niemeyer protested, clasping his hands together for Clouse to use as a step.

His weightlifting strength was about to be tested.

With considerable ease, he boosted Clouse another couple feet off the ground, enabling the firefighter to feel around inside the horn until his index finger received a paper cut. The joy of finding his objective outweighed any pain he might have felt as he carefully tugged the paper from its cubbyhole.

"Find it?" Niemeyer asked, the strain of hoisting his friend's weight residing in his voice.

"Yeah," Clouse no more than said before he felt his friend let go of the support.

Landing on his feet, Clouse tucked the piece of paper into his jacket pocket, finding a shocked look on Niemeyer's face.

"You ain't even gonna look at it?"

"Not yet. I have to check on something downstairs first."

"You have another revelation or something?" Niemeyer asked, half joking, still unsure of where Clouse suddenly came up with all the answers.

"I've been up some late nights, Tim," Clouse said, starting toward the basement access door. "When you have nothing to do but think, all sorts of possibilities start coming to you."

Momentarily Clouse led the way down the stairs to the basement, following the row of broken bulbs above him, shining his flashlight toward the room at the end where all the bricks lay in a heap. Drawing closer to the room, both men noticed an odor growing more intense. What might have been the smell of a dead animal now seemed much larger in proportion.

"Good Lord," Niemeyer commented as his friend stepped into the room, making his way around several bricks toward the back wall. "What in the hell is that smell?"

"I don't know, but it's a lot stronger in here," Clouse said, stepping on several bricks, hiking toward the top of the hill. "Hey, Tim, do you want to go down the hall and pick out some shovels and equipment for our trip back to your resort?"

"Sure," Niemeyer said, turning to head down the hall. "I'll be right back."

Clouse quickly reassessed the situation.

"Tim, wait," he called while his friend was still within earshot.

A moment passed with no sound or visual contact with his friend. Clouse started down the hill of bricks when his high school pal rounded the corner.

"I saw some red marks along the wall," Niemeyer reported.

"Blood?"

"That's what I thought at first, but they're some sort of rust drips from the I-beams. What's the matter?"

"Nothing. I just changed my mind about having you run off by yourself."

"They're just down the hall," Niemeyer stated, ready to head that way again.

"I know," Clouse said with genuine concern. "I've already lost enough friends and I'm not taking any chances with those I have left."

Niemeyer chuckled at the notion of Clouse's overprotectiveness.

"I can take care of myself, Paul."

"I know, Tim, but Ken was a cop and look what that asshole did to him. When we're alone is when we're the most vulnerable. You can help me by keeping your light aimed up here so I can find my way around."

Niemeyer shrugged, keeping his light beam aimed into the room where his friend walked, trying to guide Clouse along. Occasionally he peeked around the pile, wondering if there was anything important to see. The secondary flashlight beam seemed to follow his friend's eyes, so Clouse relied primarily on his own light.

He chose an edge to start with on the other side, walking down to it, then around the pile until something strange caught his attention. Along with the rustic color of the bricks, two bluish pipes seemed to emerge at one edge, too close to the wall to be in any light but that of Clouse's flashlight. Kneeling down, he shined the beam across the objects, discovering they were human fingertips, protruding from the stack of masonry, discolored from days of decay.

"Got your cell phone?" he asked Niemeyer.

"Yeah, why?" his friend asked, peering around the bricks, unable to see what Clouse had discovered.

"Call the police, and tell them we need the county coroner down here," Clouse said as though it was second nature to him.

He hated thinking another death had come at the hotel he cherished rebuilding.

"Damn it," he said under his breath.

"What do I tell them?" Niemeyer asked as he dialed, obviously clueless about what his friend had found.

"Tell them we have a buried body in the hotel basement, and I think it might be a missing delivery man," Clouse said as he continued to circle the edge of the bricks, hearing a faint noise from one side, though he couldn't tell where. "Hear that?" he asked Niemeyer, who asked his friend to shut up with a hand motion while turning away to hear whatever the 911 operator was saying.

Letting his friend complete the call, Clouse turned completely around, then around again, trying to determine where the noise might have originated.

Again, the noise echoed throughout the room, sounding like shackles, or some sort of chain to the firefighter. Clouse looked up to the solid ceiling above him, made of concrete and steel, knowing no sound ever pierced it. Anything outside the room Niemeyer would have heard before he did. Solid concrete enclosed the room except for one brick side, which appeared much more fresh to the designer, and it struck him that the wall seemed out of place, even if he wasn't in the hotel's basement often enough to be familiar with it.

"Police are on their way," Niemeyer announced, putting his phone away.

He saw Clouse feeling along the wall with his hands, beginning to think his friend had developed psychic powers after making several amazing discoveries, and possibly working on another.

"What on earth are you doing, Paul?"

"I keep hearing this noise. Sounds like shackles or something."

"There's a brick loose on your right," Niemeyer said, pointing to the brick sticking out several inches with his flashlight.

Clouse walked to it, tugging on it until it broke free of the wall, allowing air to rush into the sealed makeshift room. The sound of jingling chains grew louder as he placed his flashlight up to the hole, trying to look inside.

"Oh, God," he said, finding a familiar state trooper close to death. "Tim, call 911 again, and tell them to send EMS. We've got a live one."

Chapter 32

After hours of intense questioning from authorities, as usual, Clouse and Niemeyer drove to the hospital to check on McCabe's condition. Other than severe dehydration and some weight loss, the trooper appeared fine once the local volunteer fire department dug him out of the makeshift wall, careful not to rain bricks down on him. The trooper's ability to talk and think straight came soon after he was hooked to some intravenous fluids.

Strangely enough, he asked if Russell Hinds, the security guard he had accidentally shot, was still in the hospital. When he found out the guard's wounds, primarily the stab wound, had kept him there, McCabe asked to be wheeled to his room.

Clouse and Niemeyer walked with him to Hinds' room, then met up with Daniels, who had been there when the trooper arrived, thanks to a phone call from Clouse. The three stood outside to talk a moment and finally reviewed the list found in the statue. Inside the room, McCabe, weak as he was, smiled when he saw the security guard sitting up in bed, grinning the same way, obviously happy the detective had survived to give him an explanation.

Both men were dressed in hospital gowns, so there was no shame in them being wheeled around, or feeling like invalids.

"I can't tell you how sorry I am for shooting you," McCabe began. "That son-of-a-bitch had me so drugged up I couldn't see straight."

"Your buddy Daniels told me what probably happened," Hinds said. "I didn't figure you were aiming for me."

"How are you coming along?"

"I'm healing pretty well except for the knife wound. They said it came close to some vital organs. Got a broken arm, and a disc in my back got screwed up, but they say I'm healing pretty quick. I was lucky I didn't have a broken pelvis like they first thought."

"Sounds it."

"They still don't know who that guy was that stabbed me."

"No, but we may be getting closer," McCabe said, glancing out to the hallway where three of his acquaintances talked.

"I can't believe you got the list," Daniels said with contained excitement. "So, what's it say?"

"Oh," Clouse said, realizing he had yet to even read its contents. "I haven't even had time to look."

Taking it out from his jacket pocket, Clouse unfolded it, looking at several scribbled names, as though Stephen had jotted them down hurriedly before Jacob caught him. He sensed his informant was always in a hurry to avoid detection, and therefore, always in grave danger.

Both of his friends looked over his shoulder while he read the list under his breath. In order, the names read:

> Paul Clouse
>
> Lucas Rexford
>
> Rusty Cranor
>
> Ken Kaiser
>
> Martin Smith
>
> Brian Kern
>
> Tim Niemeyer
>
> Mark Daniels

"Glad to know I'm not excluded," Daniels commented, seeing his name.

"What the hell am I doing on there?" Niemeyer exclaimed, never thinking his voluntary assistance to Clouse would land him on a list, ignorant of the fact it was created long before his actual involvement.

"I don't know, Tim, but it seems to be in order of who was supposed to die."

"You sure?" Daniels questioned.

"Pretty sure. If you don't count my miraculous survival, that is chronological order."

Daniels studied the list again.

"Then Brian Kern would be next," the former detective noted. "Who is *he*?"

In reply, Clouse gave a worried look, glanced at the detective and security guard inside the room, and plucked his cellular phone from his side.

***

A leafy blanket covered the spacious lawn of the Kern residence. An old white farmhouse with a majestic picket fence enclosed the front yard while a gray barn guarded it from behind, accessed by a winding driveway. A mailbox in the shape of a barn stood at the edge of the driveway for the mailman to place letters into every afternoon before gazing at the beauty of the property the landscape contractor had made the talk of the neighborhood.

Ordinarily the leaves were already raked and mulched, but the owner left them just long enough for the Halloween season this year, with plans to dispose of them the first day of November.

Despite the cooler fall climate, shrubs and flowers bloomed around the house while a front porch encompassed two sides of the two-story house. Several jack-o-lanterns sat along the porch, their carved faces staring into the country road out front.

A large maple tree stood between the house and the road, providing shade in the summer, and a place to hang decorations during the holidays. To the side of the house an old Ford tractor sat with a hay wagon hitched to its back. All the fields had been harvested during the early fall, leaving it little to do except lead occasional tours around the farm.

Beside it, several large fir trees sat at the edge of a wooded area, domesticated by the owner and his family to become a pretense haunted woods during the fall, with signs leading to it from every highway and town within a twenty-mile radius. Every year Brian Kern took time off from his construction work to provide Bedford and several surrounding communities a good time around Halloween.

With only tonight and Halloween left, he worked on repairing several key locations in the haunted woods, which had either failed or broken the prior evening.

The morning thunderstorm came and went rather quickly, Kern thought, but gloomy gray skies remained overhead, threatening to bring more of the same.

His usual work involved planting shrubs, flowers, and trees, but it sometimes meant excavating with a bulldozer, or even laying down entire brick walkways to suitable houses. A tall man with a strong build, Kern could usually be found wearing steel-toed boots, jeans, and one of his blue T-shirts. His summer tan had yet to fade, nearly as golden as the thick wedding band on his left hand.

His brown hair, as well as the blond-colored mustache and eyebrows that accompanied it, had also faded from summer sunlight, but Kern took care of himself by wearing suntan lotion after hearing numerous reports about skin cancer. Most people would think of him as a lumberjack before they considered him a local businessman who might relocate plant life in their yard.

Always wanting to be outside as a kid, Kern built his own tree house at a young age with his father, planted shrubs and plants with his mother, and made certain the area animals had plenty to eat while he was growing up.

He never dealt with computers or business classes until he had decided what his profession would be. Though he might have been perfectly happy working in a park, or as a conservation officer, he never would have been satisfied with the income.

His job allowed him to help people, making them happier with their living conditions, while saving enough money to beautify and expand his own place for his family. He also loved entertaining, which seldom proved frugal once the bills for cooking supplies, snacks, and beer were tallied.

With his kids in school and his wife picking up several vital supplies in town, Kern worked on repairing a hangman's noose where a dummy strategically fell during the haunted woods tour. Depending on the age of the visitors and size of the tour, Kern sometimes let them walk through, or used the tractor to pull a large group with the hay wagon.

Alone, and involved in his work, he had left his cell phone inside the house to avoid being disturbed. While the dummy stared at him blankly from its resting spot on the ground, Kern tightened the noose to his own specifications, ready to test it out.

While he went to work on another nearby display, which triggered the noose, Kern heard several cars pass along the road behind him before hearing one slow down. Through the trees he looked out to his driveway to see if he had company, but no car was visible.

"Huh," he said to himself, returning to the mechanical triggering device.

In the next few minutes, everything around him and the house seemed to grow quieter. No birds or insects made any noise, prompting him to quit tinkering with the mechanical device on the ground momentarily. He checked his watch, knowing his wife would be gone at least half an hour more, and no one had informed him they were dropping by.

He looked out toward the house one more time, seeing no activity whatsoever. What sounded like a tree branch snapped behind him caused him to whirl around, again finding nothing out of place. Kern took up the claw hammer he'd been using on one of the repairs, clasping it in his right hand, still feeling as though he wasn't alone on his property.

"Anyone there?" he asked out loud, giving someone a final chance to show themselves before he searched further.

Few men he knew matched his size and strength, but even Kern was reluctant to go searching his own haunted woods. Still, he stepped forward to investigate.

***

"Getting anywhere?" Daniels asked Niemeyer as he tried the number to Kern's house one last time.

"No. It just keeps ringing and ringing. Brian has an answering machine. It should click over like I told Paul."

Clouse had left for Kern's house after the first failed calling attempt, fearing the worst. Daniels, especially, felt a sense of dread, knowing they were the final two on the list, with only half a day left before Halloween, the anniversary of last year's first brutal slaying. One by one, the survivors had been hacked down, along with a few other people in between, leaving only a handful of suspects, which he wanted to pursue the remainder of the day.

Standing at the edge of the hallway, out of earshot from Hinds and McCabe, the two men spied Jerome Barnett speaking with the doctor who had treated the trooper.

Like a bull, Niemeyer saw red.

"He's *dead*," the contractor declared to the former detective, surging forward.

"No, no," Daniels said, physically restraining Niemeyer. "Let's see what he does."

Niemeyer obeyed, knowing the reporter could not see them because he appeared too involved in conversation with the doctor. He took down several notes, then headed for the room where McCabe and Hinds were still talking. The doctor quickly told him he was not permitted to enter that room and pointed in the other direction. Both watched as Barnett hesitantly obeyed.

"I truly *hate* the man," Niemeyer stated.

"Hate is a strong word, my friend."

"I'm not takin' it back if that's what you want. He's nothin' but a snake in the grass who thinks only about getting paid for a story."

"I agree, but he's doing a job, just like we do."

Daniels eased up a bit after Niemeyer settled down, then both headed back to the room to check on McCabe. Daniels felt more strength in his legs than before, and cramping came a lot less often. Though his steps were slow and gingerly, his improvement was obvious.

"Now that I know he's going to be okay, I'm headed home to be with the wife and kids," Niemeyer said when they reached the room, referring to McCabe. "I wish Paul wouldn't have insisted on goin' out there alone."

"He knows what he's doing," Daniels said. "Paul won't do anything too dangerous."

"He's not afraid to take chances, and that's what worries me the most," Niemeyer said with obvious concern. "Take care," he added with a quick wave before heading for the elevator.

***

On the ground level, Jerome Barnett talked with an interested fan and her son, who had just been released from the hospital for a gash on his arm suffered on the playground at school. Her son remembered Barnett from school where his teacher spoke highly of him, especially during Black History Month.

"So, you don't plan on releasing your own book?" the woman asked. "It seems a man of your talent would almost have to."

"I don't want to publish anything less than the facts, and the witnesses from last year's ordeal have been reluctant to speak about their trauma," Barnett replied.

"Can't blame them," the woman replied.

In his thoughts, the reporter disagreed, but he nodded affirmatively.

"So, you've been reporting on the new set of murders?"

"I have," Barnett said. "It seems quite a bit like last year's, but there might be some random killings they have yet to pin on the killer."

"Oh, really?"

"Yes. Several murders have yet to be tied directly, but I believe the police are holding back information."

Nodding anxiously, the woman seemed delighted about the opportunity to speak with the local reporter.

"It's so nice to know people like you are a fixture in our black communities, doing such a great job for the public. Tyrone just kept talking about what an influence you were on his class when you came and spoke last year."

"I appreciate that," Barnett said, looking from mother to child. Her son simply smiled, affirming what his mother said in the reporter's opinion. "It's good to know I have a few fans."

"Oh, our whole community has always loved your work. You're about the only one who tells it the way it is anymore."

Barnett realized he had several errands to run before his deadline. One included some personal research at his house. He quickly excused himself and headed out the hospital to the parking garage.

Fifteen minutes later he slid through his front door, quickly closing it behind him. Everywhere around him looked the part of an average home in the Bloomington area.

Beautiful leather furniture, antique cabinets and desks, a new computer, and a modern kitchen that would make Martha Stewart green with envy. He made a fair living, and with his wife working as a vice president at a local bank, they more than made ends meet.

With his wife at work and daughter halfway across the state at college, he could do as he pleased with his time.

He chose to play the part of a killer.

Darting into his bedroom, Barnett reached beneath his bed, pulling out a flat trunk containing several black garments and a rather long weapon. Feeling a tingle shoot throughout his body, he slowly pulled the black robe over his head, feeling the hood snugly caress his face while keeping it from the view of anyone who might spy him through his window blinds.

He then donned a pure black mask, just like Roger Summers had worn the year before to keep his face from any possible detection. The mask, made of pure black, had woven, plastic threads sewn over the eye slots allowing limited visibility out, but none inside. He wondered how Summers had managed to stalk and kill so many people when his eyes received less than half the normal amount of light through the mask.

A complete feeling of secrecy and power overcame him as he took the scythe from the box, knowing exactly how a serial killer might feel, chasing around hapless victims, or slicing unsuspecting townsfolk in the abdomen before they were able to react. He could kill at will beneath a cloak of secrecy, no one ever seeing his face, much less guessing his identity.

He wanted to understand the power the killer felt before he began his next piece. Knowing such a mindset would aid Barnett in creating some of his best work yet. Still, one thing was missing in the reporter's perception of the killer that he never quite grasped. The one emotion about to bring about his downfall.

Killer instinct.

Barnett heard a creaking noise from the floor behind him. Yanking off the mask and hood, he whirled around to find the true killer standing there, immediately embedding a sharpened, deadly scythe upside down into his waist, yanking it upward without hesitation. He saw no eyes, and no emotion on the killer's face because the mask concealed his identity perfectly, just as Barnett always suspected. As the killer gave one final jerk of the weapon, rubbing steel against bone, the reporter had few thoughts left.

He felt his organs sever as the blade journeyed to his sternum, allowing the blood to drain from his lower torso like a leaky carton of milk. His final gasps traveled with the blood running up his throat, flowing out of his mouth as his eyes glazed and he realized he would soon be one of the highlights he relished writing about the past year.

***

Clouse pulled into Brian Kern's driveway to find nothing indicative of foul play. He saw the tractor beside the driveway and recognized the man's work truck parked behind the house. Slowly climbing from his own truck, Clouse looked around, hearing only the wind rustling the leaves along the nearby grove. He walked up to the house, ringing the doorbell and knocking several times before trying the knob, finding it locked.

Seeing no indication of anyone staying inside, he went around back and tried the other door, finding it locked as well. Sighing as he stepped from the porch, he noticed the signs pointing toward the haunted forest, wondering if Kern might be working on something inside the natural thicket.

"Brian?" he called. "You around?"

No answer.

Hesitantly, he walked into the entrance of the grove, spying what he figured were spooky decorations for the nighttime run through the haunted woods. Several scarecrows, a reaper, jack-o-lanterns, and what appeared to be a pile of fake intestines beside a witch took up the first main drag of the tour, distracting Clouse until he rounded the corner, tripping a wire.

From above, the sound of heavy rope rounding a pulley drew his attention as something large descended quickly, jerking beside him as it came to an abrupt end of its line. Clouse spied the steel-toed boots beside his head first, slowly looking up to see what dangled from the noose as he stumbled back.

"Oh, shit," he said, thankful the victim was simply a dummy constructed for the haunted woods.

He exhaled a sigh of relief, backing into a solid object.

Whirling around, he found the land's occupant smiling from ear to ear.

"Brian. What the hell?"

"Gotcha good. Didn't I?" the landscape contractor replied. "My favorite part of the whole show, Paul," he added, tugging the dummy's leg to make sure everything remained intact after the plunge. "Happy Halloween."

Upset, not from the scare, but rather his friend's ignorance of the recent danger surrounding them both, Clouse shook his head.

"I've been trying to call you almost an hour now," he said. "No one answered, and the machine didn't pick up."

Kern gave a puzzled look.

"It always picks up after three rings."

"It didn't."

Kern started toward the house, wondering how that could be.

"Did you leave both doors locked?"

"I did," Kern replied.

"Then I think I know what happened," Clouse noted, heading for the house's front, then around to the far side. "Where is your phone line out here?"

"Over there," Kern said, pointing to a line, painted over as though part of the house's original construction.

Before reaching it, Clouse could tell it was cut clean through, probably by a knife or wire cutters. Kern noticed the damage as well, but still seemed unaware of what danger he might be in.

"Shit," Clouse said, happy Kern was alive, but curious why someone made the trip out to the man's house just to cut a line. "When your family gets home, keep them inside, Brian," he warned.

"But I've got the woods running tonight. I can't just hole myself up and skip it."

"I understand. Just be careful, Brian. The same person who cut your line is probably the same one who's been killing people at the hotel these past few weeks."

"Paul, you've got to give me some idea of what's going on here," Kern stated emphatically, openly confused about the scraps of information thrown his way. "You came all the way out here to check on me and you haven't said one word about what you think might happen to me."

Clouse wondered why someone bothered to cut the line unless they suspected he had freed McCabe, or knew he had the list. Either scenario jeopardized the killer's identity and plan to some extent. He thought about who might have seen either situation, then realized more importantly, he was squarely between the hotel and his own residence, unable to reach either before the killer might.

As Clouse thought about his own situation, Kern's expression showed he began to realize what his former colleague was worried about.

"You think this wacky son-of-a-bitch might come out here again?" Kern questioned as Clouse pondered the danger surrounding his own family.

"I don't think so, Brian," he said numbly, knowing what his next move had to be.

"Why not?"

"Because I think he's coming after my friends and family now," Clouse answered, starting toward his truck. "Be careful!" he called back, praying he was wrong in his theory, knowing what a dangerous game he might be playing.

Chapter 33

Standing on the side of a hill, Daniels watched as a crane hoisted the dripping wreckage of McCabe's patrol car from a large pond just outside of Paoli. Ordinarily the discovery of a vehicle beneath water failed to create major local headlines, but when divers discovered it was a police vehicle from the license plate, and it was later verified as McCabe's, the state police wasted little time in getting a local crane operator to the site to extract possible evidence in the attempted murder of one of their own.

Moments later the car was examined, and the trunk opened. Every shred of paper appeared waterlogged, and any equipment left inside was certainly rendered useless. Daniels realized what the state investigators would soon discover. No evidence remained inside the vehicle of value to them, and any documents would now be impossible to read.

Monitoring his scanner was about the only way Daniels knew about such events. He retained several ties at the local and state level who occasionally fed him information, but putting himself too close to the events too often was a good way of asking for trouble.

"What do you make of it?" one of the investigators asked him, apparently considering his opinion of some value.

Daniels knew the man's last name as Hansen, only because they had taken the same class about basic forensic science few years back.

"I doubt you'll find anything of use. Our killer hasn't left anything yet."

"It must be weird having to go through this stuff all the time," the man said, fidgeting with his tie, something Daniels often did while a detective. "Do you ever get used to it?"

"You mean the gruesome killings, losing people I care about, or the fact that the killer never leaves me any clues?" Daniels answered with his own question, sprinkled with sarcasm.

"Well, death is never easy. It just seems like the motives are crazier than ever," the detective commented. "I mean, kids kill because their parents piss them off, or because they saw it in a movie and decided to go experiment. The worst part is, they get away with it. Go to court and blam-o, you're free as a bird when the defense pleads temporary insanity, or blames society for the kid's upbringing. Makes you wonder."

"Yeah, it does," Daniels said, watching as officers searched the trunk, pulling a firearm from the sludge lining the interior, all dripping wet.

"We found McCabe's gun," one of them announced, recognizing the issue as that of state police troopers. The serial number instantly proved true possession of the firearm.

Fazed little by the discovery, Daniels watched a moment longer before heading back to his car, stopping halfway as the officers made another discovery, this one more profound.

"A knife," one of them said aloud as the former detective hobbled down the hill to see them holding up a peculiar weapon by latex glove, which he believed would only be a weapon with the right intent.

"Actually, a scalpel," Hansen said, apparently the detective in charge of the scene.

"Actually, a post-mortem knife," Daniels corrected him.

"What's the difference?"

"Ever been to an autopsy?" Daniels asked.

He had attended over a dozen as a detective before growing tired of seeing bodies treated like meat. Most investigators left the autopsies entirely to the coroners and their technicians. His desire to be the best investigator possible had constantly kept him curious about the workings of the human body.

"Never one in progress," Hansen confessed.

State police often missed out on the fun stuff, Daniels thought. Hansen tossed Daniels a latex glove, noticing the inactive officer wanted a closer look at the blade.

Daniels took hold of the potential weapon, looking it over on both sides. He made mental notes during his examination of the blade, finding some modifications that made an ordinary knife into a deadly weapon.

"Your typical scalpel isn't a very large blade," he finally said, pointing to the length and width of the blade, screwed into a die-cast handle. "During an autopsy you need a larger blade to cut rib meat and small bones. This one has been modified to accommodate two blades, reversed from one another, giving it a double edge. I think the reason our security guard pulled through, aside from luck, is the fact that this knife couldn't enter his side far enough to reach any vital areas. The handle is too thick to allow penetration beyond the blade."

"So did someone from the medical field abduct McCabe?" the detective deduced aloud, trying to save face in front of his peers.

"Possibly. With internet sales and the possibility someone stole the blade, it's hard to tell. It's likely someone modified the blade for another purpose, such as scraping or dissection, then found himself forced to use it. A lab might be able to find traces of something on there."

"How was it modified?" Hansen asked Daniels, getting the weapon back.

"Ordinarily the blades work like those of a utility knife. You can screw one in, and it stays pretty snug. If you look at this closely, you can see the edges where someone grinded down the securing ends, kind of like key makers might do if a key is too thick for a lock."

Nodding in agreement with the assessment, Hansen studied the ends, which were thick enough not to break while providing stability enough to carve, stab, or scrape. Made of heavy-duty carbon steel, the blades were meant to last despite fairly rugged use.

With such a smooth handle, it made for an impractical weapon, backing Daniels' theory that it might never have been intended as a weapon, until necessary. Besides, the killer's main weapon of choice was a scythe, which provided much quicker death than any modified scalpel.

Daniels felt he had seen enough to satisfy him. He turned to walk away when Hansen's voice got his attention.

"You think our killer left this here as a calling card, or by accident?"

To this point, the killer, or Jacob, or whatever people wanted to call him, had left nothing to chance. Daniels knew the person behind the murders, and the assault on McCabe and Hinds, if indeed the same individual, was no fool.

"Calling card," he said before trudging up the hill.

***

Feeling a chill run through the barn at her new property, Jane pulled the saddle down from Bucky, Clouse's horse, straddling it across a nearby partition as she led the animal into his stall. Each time she rode him the horse grew tamer from being around a human being, proving her fiancé wrong about its behavior.

Covered in a colorful wool pullover, Jane felt protected from the wind and cold, though the tingling of her face and runny nose told her otherwise. She wore lace-up boots when she rode because they were easily freed from the saddle in a hurry, and comfortable to walk in if necessary.

She glanced at her watch, noticing she had almost half an hour before Zach finished school. A hot cup of coffee would revive her before making the trip into town to pick up her future stepson while his father searched what seemed like all of Indiana to find the reaper.

Jane had gone all morning without seeing or hearing from Clouse. Under ordinary conditions, he was the best father and future husband she could ask for, but the murders changed him, taking him away from her. She hated being alone so much, especially when the kids kept asking where Clouse had gone, and Jane could not explain the situation to them.

As she scooped some feed from a nearby bag, a creaking noise from the hayloft above her caught her attention. Freezing a moment, Jane heard nothing before finally proceeding to line Bucky's trough with the feed.

Winds picked up outside, causing several doors along the barn to flap in and out, banging against the solid structure. She heard howling as the winds darted through the open cracks of the old barn. Several broken windows let in the cold chill, and sounds seemed to come from everywhere in the old building.

Another strange creak came from above, this time sounding like a heavy footstep along the bare, wooden floor.

Without a word, Jane took a hatchet down from the selection of farm tools along one wall. A rake dropped to the ground, tumbling toward the open entrance door. She climbed a stationary wooden ladder, which she guessed was part of the farm's original construction, because it was solidly mounted to the hatchway above. With no hatch to hinder her progress, Jane reached the top, sticking her head through the square opening, keeping the hatchet ready for self-defense.

After a quick glance around, she found no one in the loft. The only available hiding place was beneath a dozen hay bales. Deciding not to pursue her search any further, Jane climbed down the ladder, prepared to pick up Zach. She took out her cellular phone to call her husband, which someone hiding from her might have interpreted as a call to the police.

As she headed for the door, phone cupped to her ear, a cloaked figure emerged from the shadows, cupping her mouth from behind as the phone dropped to the concrete, breaking on contact. Her attacker's other arm wrapped around her free arm, keeping her close to him, entangled enough for him to pull a knife from a sheath along his waist, much to her dismay as her muffled cries went unheard.

Spying the gleam of the knife above her, fearful of where it might plunge, Jane drew close to a wall, kicking with both feet against the solid surface. Both Jane and her unknown assailant tumbled backwards, the cloaked man taking the fall for both of them as he landed neck and head first against the barn's cold, concrete foundation. Jane regained her footing first, darting for the open door of the barn.

Far ahead of the dark figure, Jane looked back to assure herself she could make it, but tripped over the fallen rake at the foot of the doorway. She landed hard, knocking the wind from her lungs and cracking a bone in one wrist.

Regaining her composure, Jane turned herself over, staring into what looked like an empty hood, dripping black cloth all the way down to her legs. She drew a horrified breath as the stalker held up a long knife, tracing the blade with both his index finger and thumb. Wasting no time, Jane attempted to stand up, but the figure stepped on her ankle, threatening to snap it with his industrial-grade black boot if she made any further moves.

Knowing escape was nearly impossible, Jane stared upward, uncertain of what her fate might be as the assailant stared a moment, then swooped down on her.

***

Clouse reached the top of the stairs at his son's school, unsure of what to believe was happening. His cellular phone rang briefly during the ride there, but when he answered, no one responded. He tried the automatic redial function, which dialed Jane's number, but he got no answer only seconds after the initial call.

Unsure of what move to make next, Clouse had contacted Daniels, telling the detective to check on his own family before meeting him. The two quickly exchanged their findings, deciding their course of action for the remainder of the day would probably determine how many people might be saved from certain death.

Concerned for both Jane and Zach, he stopped by the school first, knowing it was closer. He decided to check on his son's whereabouts first, rather than backtrack, wasting time and miles if he found nothing wrong at the farm.

Finding the school recently abandoned of all activity, most of the doors remained open as teachers gathered their notes and ungraded assignments before heading out for the evening.

Clouse walked in as one of the gifted and talented teachers was about to lock her door and head out. He startled her as she closed the door, prepared to lock it. She appeared young, as though just out of college, with cheeks the color of fall apples.

"Sorry," he apologized quickly for the scare. "I'm Zach's father."

"Oh, I recognize you," she replied. "When neither of you showed to pick Zach up at three, Mrs. Morgan called your house."

Clouse's surprise showed, for good reason.

"Jane didn't show up?"

"No, but she asked Mrs. Morgan to take Zach home."

"Who is Mrs. Morgan?"

"She's one of our teaching aides. A very sweet widow who dedicates herself to our class three times a week, especially with your son."

A chill shot through Clouse.

"Did you talk to Jane on the phone?" Clouse asked, genuinely concerned at this point.

What he was hearing of his fiancée sounded very much unlike Jane's behavior.

"Yes, I verified it. And Mrs. Morgan said it was right on her way home."

I'll bet she did, Clouse thought, beginning to realize what might be happening.

"What's going on?" Daniels asked, walking up on the situation.

He was dressed in slacks and a tie with his shoulder holster, just as Clouse had requested, in case they needed some official police access. Daniels had already made it clear that he would rather lose his job than see anyone lose his or her life.

"Do you have any photos with Mrs. Morgan in them?" Clouse asked the teacher, who seemed perplexed by the entire situation.

He turned to speak aside to his friend.

"Jane never came to pick up Zach."

"Shit," Daniels muttered as the teacher unlocked the door.

Once inside the room, Clouse requested his friend boot up the computer while he and the teacher searched for any photos containing the mysterious teaching aide. Digging through a stack of photos buried in a desk drawer, the teacher seemed to sense Clouse's urgency, though she probably failed to understand it.

"Mrs. Morgan isn't very much for photos," she commented. "She just likes to be in the background helping the kids. Is that man a police officer?" she asked Clouse a virtually rhetorical question.

"Yeah. A friend of mine."

"I don't think you have much to worry about," she commented, continuing to flip through the stack of photos. "Mrs. Morgan is a very sweet lady."

Clouse reserved his judgment.

"Here we are," she said, pulling out a mildly out of focus picture, taken outside the Indianapolis Zoo about a month earlier on a field trip.

Singling out Mrs. Morgan in the photo, Clouse took a hard look, finding his fears confirmed instantly, despite the woman in question turning from the camera, as though trying to avoid being photographed altogether. Clouse would not be fooled, and he began to sense exactly what her scheme might be.

"Mrs. Landamere," he said, drawing a confused look from the teacher.

He stormed off toward the computer room, ready to grab Daniels and head toward his farm. Knowing better than to expect Jane and his son to be safe and sound at home, it was much closer than the West Baden Springs Hotel. By default, he needed to check there first.

"Come on, Mark," he virtually ordered, standing in the doorway of the small room.

"Take a look at this real quick, Paul," Daniels said, intrigued by whatever he had found on the computer.

Clouse swung around the desk, finding the same program Jane had viewed just a few days before. Daniels reset the program, causing the hotel's blueprint designer to take an interest in the virtual reality grate located at the forefront of a tunnel system. It appeared filled with intricate designs Clouse instantly recognized after the painstaking renovation at the hotel.

"That's the hotel's emblem," he said, pointing to one particular pattern as Daniels traced the tunnel to one end.

"I keep taking different routes," Daniels commented. "Every time I can only get so far, regardless of what path I take, then it seems to suddenly end, as though it isn't complete. This one here *seems* complete," he said, reaching the end of the fourth of four paths, finding only an empty space for his trouble. "It's as though the program isn't finished."

"It wouldn't be if you didn't have all the puzzle pieces to finish it," Clouse commented, motioning for the seat. "This program looks awfully familiar."

Daniels complied, letting his friend sort through the program, exiting the simulation until he reached the main program itself. There, he discovered a familiar copyright symbol, along with the name of the designers and title. In the lower right-hand corner, he found exactly what he thought he would. The program, *Trailblazer*, was created at Indiana University in the exact same architecture building he once attended as a student, and later as a graduate student. It looked as though the program hadn't changed since he last used it.

He thought of only one person he knew who might have access and knowledge enough to correctly use the program, though he hoped he was wrong.

Suddenly everything fit.

It would take a phone call or two to verify his theory on who was behind the murders and why, but it could be done. He probably needed to ask the man beside him to stretch his pretentious credentials just a bit further.

Daniels looked at Clouse as though he spied the wheels working inside his friend's head while Clouse stared at the computer monitor.

"What are you thinking, buddy?"

"I'm thinking I know exactly who's behind this and why, Mark. And we need to get going right now."

Chapter 34

Niemeyer burst through his front door, disrupting both his wife and two children, who were watching television. He stepped inside, only socks on his feet, not bothering to unzip his thick leather jacket, despite the heat cranked inside the house. All three realized the look on his face was not that of a happy man.

Not the least bit chipper.

"Where are your boots?" his wife, Vicky, asked as she stood from the couch, referring to the pair of work boots he usually wore on the job.

"Outside," he replied in short. "They're muddy."

He stepped past the kids without a word, entirely uncharacteristic for the family man. Heading straight for his gun cabinet, he unlocked it and took out a riot gun, similar to the shotguns used in police or security work, which one of his police buddies had encouraged him to buy. Throwing it over his shoulder, Niemeyer freed one arm to snatch a box of shells, which he dumped into his jacket pocket, letting a few carelessly fall to the floor.

Picking the loose shells up from the floor, he stuffed them into the other pocket, not looking to Vicky or the kids even a second before crossing the room toward the closet. Vicky stood, obviously concerned about her husband's irrational behavior. Never had he entered the house in such a hurry, or given them the silent treatment when doing so. He never hunted without his brother, so this was not a quickened search for wild game.

"Tim, what on earth are you doing?" she implored as he swung the closet door open, his eyes wildly searching for some new footwear.

"I can't talk about it," he answered abruptly.

Given the choice between hole-ridden tennis shoes or the pair of cowboy boots he sometimes wore to church, he chose the latter. He put the shotgun down just long enough to pull them on, then stood, ready to leave again.

Vicky stood in his way, glancing to the children. Niemeyer looked, seeing the confusion in his son's and his daughter's eyes. Despite his hurry, he decided to take a moment with his family, uncertain of what his future held. For all he knew, he could wind up in jail or worse before the day was through.

"Come here, kids," he said, kneeling to pull them into a hug. They ran over, each grabbing one of his thick arms. "Daddy has something to take care of," he told them, feeling a tear coming to his eye. "Remember, I love you both, and I always will. Now go watch the television and don't worry about me."

Both slowly responded, allowing him to confront his wife at the front door.

"What is going on, Tim?" she demanded quietly enough that the kids would not hear.

"I have to do something," he said, clutching the shotgun. "An old friend and I have some business we need to finish. If anything happens to me, you call Randy," he instructed, speaking of his younger brother.

"That's not going to cut it," Vicky insisted. "You're acting like you're going off to war and we may never see you again."

"It's all I can give you right now. This will all be over with very soon, I promise, and I'll be home for trick-or-treat with the kids tomorrow."

Vicky gave him a skeptical look.

"I love you," he said abruptly before heading out the door toward his pickup truck.

He pulled out of the driveway, knowing he had never let his wife and kids see his aggressive nature at its worst. Niemeyer hoped to see them again after taking care of some business.

***

At dark, Clouse pulled into the hotel's long brick path, leading up to the hotel. He saw no other vehicles outside the building, but the two jack-o-lanterns sitting on the grand staircase left little doubt he had reached his final destination.

"Looks like the party's just starting," Daniels noted from the passenger seat.

"If they hurt Jane or my son, someone is going to die," Clouse said, anxious to get inside the hotel.

"Whoa there, Paul," Daniels said, physically keeping his friend in the truck once it was turned off. "Remember, we can't go running in there with both guns blazing. We've got a plan, remember?" His words made sense, and Clouse settled into his seat for the moment. "You *sure* you don't want to call the police on this?"

"I'm not risking the lives of my future wife and child, Mark. Besides, what if this is another false alarm? What if police sirens tip off the killers and let them escape, or worse yet, they hurt Jane or Zach? I'm not taking any risks. We've got the plan, so let's do it."

Clouse had taken Daniels with him to the house, finding no sign of Jane or Zach, as he suspected. Katie was safe with her grandparents, leaving him one less worry, though a world of burden rested on Clouse's shoulders at the moment. Jane's car remained in the driveway at their house, and everything else seemed in order. Even the mail had been left on the table, and the dogs fed in their pens. It was almost as though his fiancée had left and never returned.

From there, both decided to head to crucial locations they knew about, beginning with the resort Niemeyer looked after. Clouse found similar design patterns in the charred remains of the building, leaving him to think the trap door his friend spoke of might have been the answer, since the hotel's basement had no obvious tunnel system beneath it. Though it seemed plausible the hotel kept a few secrets from him, Clouse could not think of anywhere the tunnel entrance might be hidden. Even so, someone had managed to put a brick wall up without him immediately realizing it.

After traveling to the decimated resort, where Clouse expected to find the center of criminal activity, and finding nothing but a cleared area where the trap door seemed to be, he felt absolutely disappointed and anxious.

Someone had beaten them to it.

When he and Daniels descended a ladder from the trap door into an elaborate tunnel system, remarkably similar to that of the computer system, they quickly found why a child had been selected to learn and carry out the details of the actual mission.

Four distinct directions were evident, but each quickly narrowed, leaving an adult only several feet of walking or crawling space before he or she would be stuck in the shrinking walls. Along the settled dust in the tunnel floors, he saw footprints heading in and returning to where he stood at the narrowing edge.

He felt certain Zach had been there.

The tunnels were made of dirt, but the years, and the destructive fire, had baked them into a hardened clay that would take a man and his tools literally years to dig through.

A child seemed the only possibility of getting to the end of the elaborate ducts. After seeing so many of his friends and colleagues die around him, Clouse knew why his child had been chosen. It was simply the climax to the personal hell the killer chose to put him through.

Clouse called several times for his son with no response, wondering if Zach had been forced inside, never to return. He desperately tested the walls with his fist, drawing blood on several knuckles as he shined a light inside, able to see nothing. It paralleled any number of fire scenes he had worked on, where sight and hearing were sometimes of little use to him. Often instinct got firefighters through dangerous situations, but he sensed this was a waste of time.

After several minutes of calling with no reply, and with urging from Daniels, the two decided to move on to the West Baden Springs Hotel with the hope of finding Zach and Jane unharmed, even if it meant confronting the source of their investigation head on.

"You know how to use this?" Daniels asked, handing him a semi-automatic pistol, similar to his police department issue.

"Yeah, but it's been awhile. My aim is terrible."

"With any luck we won't need them," the officer said, checking his own firearm. "I still can't believe Mrs. Landamere has anything to do with this," he commented, shaking his head. "You sure she wasn't being a protective guardian or something?"

"I'm awfully sure," Clouse replied sternly. "I don't see why else a person would force a kid to learn a maze and abduct him from school unless their motivation was at least a little bit evil."

Daniels nodded.

"Alright, let's do this. You said it yourself there might be two of them, so watch it, Paul. I'll go around back and try getting myself on a higher floor in case anything happens. I'm not going to be too mobile if something goes wrong, so be careful."

"Good luck," Clouse said, climbing from the truck, wasting little time as Daniels looked around cautiously before stepping out. If he were spotted, their splitting up would be pointless. If he made it, he could begin to look for Joan Landamere or the person Clouse suspected of being her partner.

While Daniels made his way around back, as quickly as possible with rehabilitating legs, Clouse climbed the stairway, eyeing the gutted vegetables as he passed them. The candles inside flickered, and he knew what their symbolism entailed. A jack-o-lantern was one of the last objects his wife had seen on Halloween night the year before. Moments later, she was ripped apart with a scythe, left mutilated across his kitchen floor for his son to find the next morning.

He felt no desire in sharing her fate.

Stepping inside the double glass doors a moment later, Clouse felt the firearm tucked into his belt along his back, concealed by his jacket. He wondered if he possessed skill enough to save his own life with it if necessary. The last time he recalled firing any sort of pistol was long before he joined the Bloomington Fire Department.

He entered the lobby, seeing a light down the hall, probably from the atrium where he expected to find the center of the action like he had the year prior when his brother-in-law revealed himself as the murderer, and David Landamere as his partner. Clouse still had nightmares about the ordeal, and how he allowed himself to be tricked by two people he trusted so much.

Not this year.

Careful to step quietly so his boots would not give him away, Clouse found himself at a crossroads in the hallway, unsure of which direction to take. The entire hotel was rounded, so it did not matter in the sense of a destination, because he could reach anyplace in due time by walking around the circular hallway. He wondered where he might gain an advantage over the abductors of his son and fiancée before they could do him harm.

Before he decided, he heard the glass doors close behind him when the compression springs meant to keep the doors from slamming activated.

Taking a deep breath, Clouse turned around, finding a shotgun held by its butt, with the barrel aimed straight at his chest.

"I didn't expect you so soon, Paul," Niemeyer said in a voice somewhat above a whisper to keep from gaining unwanted attention.

Clouse swallowed, unsure of whether his assessment about Joan Landamere's potential partner was entirely accurate, particularly after he had called the contractor to help him.

"I don't like wasting time, Tim," he decided to say. "Let's say we get on with this."

"Okay," his friend said, lowering the riot gun, which he had simply used to point, and assure himself it was Clouse before proceeding.

To this point, Niemeyer knew only as much as Clouse and Daniels, but the firefighter felt a bit more secure knowing his high school buddy had made an effort to arrive so quickly.

"It makes perfect sense why I'm on that list now," Niemeyer commented. "I stood between them and whatever they were looking for on the property."

"I know it isn't safe to do this, but we need to split up, Tim," Clouse deduced in a whisper. "I think there's two of them, and hopefully three of us can somehow overtake them before anyone else gets hurt."

"Only two?"

"I hope," Clouse said with a shrug.

Niemeyer gave a short, parting wave, heading down the hallway on the left, while Clouse opted to head the other way, hoping to sneak a peek inside the atrium.

***

Niemeyer found a set of stairs down his hallway, deciding to get a view from above, much like Daniels had. Quietly as possible, the stocky contractor rounded the stairway until he reached the second floor. Finding it dark, he carefully looked both ways before stepping out to the carpeted floor.

He only heard his nervous breaths as his eyes panned the floor. He tried several of the closest doors, finding every room closed and locked, except one. A few doors down on his right, Niemeyer saw a door open just a crack. He wondered if it might be a setup or his only chance to overlook the atrium from above.

Approaching the door cautiously, Niemeyer held out his shotgun, opening the door the remainder of the way. A dim sliver of light from the hallway's wall-mounted light fixtures grew as he opened the door. He could not risk flipping the light switch because he might compromise his position to anyone down the hall or in the atrium below.

He found it easy to check the room because no furniture had been placed inside yet. Without benefit of the light, Niemeyer checked behind the door, then crept over to the closet, which had a sliding door.

Holding the shotgun with one hand aimed at the closet, he slowly slid it open, breathing nervously with the few breaths he dared draw. Making just a little noise, the door slid open, revealing complete vacancy inside.

Niemeyer silently sighed relief, walking over the curtains, peeking through a small space between the adjoining sets to the atrium below, finding a scene worse than he hoped.

"Oh, no," he whispered, hearing a step behind him, allowed by his momentary lapse of caution.

Niemeyer whirled around, allowing his cloaked adversary to grasp his shotgun, ramming the length of its steel and wood against his forehead. A loud thwack sounded as his head met the stock of the weapon, nearly knocking him unconscious in one swift motion.

Too stunned to retaliate against his much quicker opponent, the contractor was grasped by his jacket collar and rammed head-first into the far wall with a running start, his shotgun falling to the ground too far away to aid him.

Blood trickled from the center of his fringe, but he was too close to unconsciousness to realize it. His footing wobbled momentarily as the shadowy figure regained his grip on the jacket, leading Niemeyer toward the window.

There was no balcony to this room, which left only a two-story drop to the atrium below. The decorative carpet below provided little cushioning as the contractor was hurled through the large window, landing hard on his back, sprawled along the atrium floor. An audible moan stemmed from his mouth as his head fell limp to one side and he remained motionless.

***

From one of the four entrances to the atrium along the ground floor, Clouse observed his friend's ill fate, disturbed because a member of his team had already fallen prey to the evil he meant to stop. He was more upset about his wife and child sitting tied up and gagged in the middle of the atrium while a cloaked figure stalked the other side of the mammoth room, keeping another victim close by, hands tied behind his back.

He could not tell who the person was because he faced the other way. After assessing the situation, Clouse knew entering the room meant putting himself at the mercy of at least one conspirator.

He looked to Jane and Zach, thankful both were alive and unharmed from what he observed. His eyes moved to Niemeyer, who lay motionless across the room, blood oozing from the cuts on his head. It was impossible to tell whether or not he survived the fall.

"Oh, shit," he told himself, momentarily uncertain of what to do.

A completely nervous state overcame his mind and body as he paced the hallway, out of sight and earshot of anyone else. He could not risk putting himself in danger if he was their last chance at survival, and he refused to stand around waiting and hoping for Daniels to come through. Perhaps his friend simply needed a distraction so he could act, leaving Clouse the decision of whether to be the last hope or the sacrificial lamb who drew the attention of the killers.

"Fuck it," he concluded suddenly, marching into the atrium to confront whoever was behind the mask at the other end of the circular chamber.

Either way, this would end very soon.

Chapter 35

The clop of Clouse's boots announced his arrival to the atrium before the dark figure even spotted him. He purposely left his jacket unzipped for easier access to the gun, unsure of where Daniels might have gone. His eyes stared straight ahead as they locked with the mask of one of the conspirators.

As though instinctively, the cloaked person pulled out a knife, taking up the nearby hostage, holding Barry Andrews in front, a knife to his throat. Clouse made some quick, keen observations about the knife's wielder. Andrews was definitely taller, as the killer had to pull him back like a bow to threaten his throat area. Clouse knew who the person was immediately, but waited until he drew closer before engaging in conversation.

"Give it up, Mrs. Landamere," he said without hesitation, drawing as close as possible. "I know it's you, and you're the brains behind this operation. I want some answers before we settle this."

"You're in no position to order me around," Joan Landamere's voice said as she pulled the hood back on her black cloak, removing a solid black mask from underneath.

The mask explained why no one ever saw a face beyond the cloak, making the wearer incredibly mysterious and intimidating, but Clouse knew only ordinary people like himself were behind the killings. No longer would he be intimidated.

"It's over," he said, stepping closer.

"Stay back," she ordered with a vicious sneer he never imagined the widow possessing. "I'll slit the good doctor's throat in a heartbeat," she added, positioning herself to walk back toward Jane and Zach, who were tied helplessly in the center of the atrium.

Clouse started toward her to view her up and down, searching for any signs of vulnerability, or any other weapons. She seemed to take note of his keen observations.

"Are you wondering?" she asked, pausing for an answer.

When none came, she continued.

"Do you wonder if the good doctor might be my partner, just posing as an innocent victim like David did last year?"

Clouse refused to answer, remembering how easily he had been duped by the duo of killers before. It haunted him almost daily.

"Can you take that chance, Paul?" she asked, an evil smile forming along her lips.

Somewhere along the line, Joan had snapped, or she was extremely good at containing her psychotic tendencies the entire time Clouse had known her.

She drew dangerously close to his fiancée and son, making him want to draw the gun and blow her away, but he wasn't convinced of the doctor's position. Andrews appeared to be drugged, or in shock. His eyes looked glazed, and he responded little to the fact his life was in danger.

A trick?

Or worse, the real thing.

Clouse felt he was in a battle he could not win.

"I know who your accomplice is, Mrs. Landamere, and it is not Dr. Andrews," he said without falter, daring to call her bluff as she stopped at the feet of Jane, who was too terrified to do anything but look up from the insane widow to her future husband.

Joan's face showed little emotion as she pondered what he said, thinking of her next move. She wanted to shock Clouse, to show she meant business. At the same time, she did not want to exhaust all of her cards in this human game of chess.

"Then you won't mind this a bit," she said, callously drawing the blade across Andrews' exposed throat, leaving a trail of red in its wake.

Gurgling a moment before he died, Andrews slumped to the floor, convulsing as the life and blood ebbed from his body. Hands bound, and quite possibly doped up by medications, he never stood a chance against the psychotic woman. While Clouse watched in horror as the doctor met a cruel end, blood pooling on the floor from his opened throat, Joan snatched up Zach from the floor, holding him in a similar position before Clouse called her several adjectives her senseless murder brought to mind. She simply grinned, apparently satisfied she had shocked a man accustomed to death and trauma.

He looked from the dead doctor to his fiancée, then to his son, held close to the blade dripping of Andrews' blood. Unlike Andrews, Zach squirmed and moaned, wanting freedom from this insane, hostile environment.

Few choices remained.

"Don't do this," Clouse pleaded. "What is it you want, Mrs. Landamere?"

"I want my husband back, Paul. I can call you Paul, can't I?" she said more than asked with a knife pressed against his son's throat, assuring no objections were uttered. "Let me tell you a little story about exactly what happened last year, and how things should have gone."

Clouse stood a safe distance from her, keeping his eyes focused on Zach, knowing the gun was accessible, but of little use to him if he reached for it under the circumstances. He would never draw and fire quickly enough to keep his son from harm, even if his aim was true.

"It's time for a little story, Paul," she said, continually moving in a pattern that kept Clouse at a safe distance from her and both of her hostages. "I'm going to tell you exactly why I want everyone in your life dead, because you and your fucking detective friend killed my husband last year. Kind of a shame," she said, as though feeling a bit of regret. "That Daniels is rather cute. That's why I wanted to save him for last."

"Your husband wanted to kill you, Joan," Clouse said, trying to reason with her. "Why the hell would you want to avenge his death?"

"Because you don't know the whole story," she said bitterly, as though he should have. "David's cover-up was only part of the plan, my dear," Joan began, waving the knife in front of Zach, terrifying the kindergartner further. "David had told Roger Summers they were partners until the end, splitting the money from my life insurance policy between them. In reality, David and I planned to kill Roger, our simple pawn, blame him for everything, be the sole survivors, and destroy Martin Smith in claims court, taking everything he had, including the hotel. After all, it was his ultimate refusal of closing down the West Baden construction that led to so many murders, and would have nearly cost my husband and I our very lives," she said with a bit of artistic license. "Smith was weak, and he would have settled out of court, giving us everything we wanted."

"So exactly what *are* you after?" Clouse insisted, wanting a concrete motive.

"This time, I'm after revenge. And I also want those jewels buried by Charles Rexford oh so many years ago. I think they would make it worth my trouble."

Clouse wasn't exactly positive what Joan meant about the jewels, but he was intelligent to fill in the gaps. Perhaps Rexford sensed his rocky marriage might leave him short of finances, so he decided to bury some financial insurance.

"You mean you don't have them?"

"No, my partner has the loot. He saw fit to leave me your son before heading off to dispose of any other snoops."

Everyone looked over to Niemeyer, who remained motionless where he originally landed.

"What makes you think he won't run off with the prize and leave you hanging like you did your husband?"

"Fuck you!" she exclaimed, gnashing her teeth. "When your friend shot my husband, my heart nearly stopped, but I knew at that very moment I would carry out our plan. I would own this hotel and Dr. Smith, and I would have complete ownership of the tile pieces. See, David and I did some research when we found a few of those pieces a couple years ago, and we found out what they led to and where they might be."

She smiled, waving the knife in front of Zach again, disturbing his father greatly. Clouse's mind scrambled for ways to continue the conversation and distract Joan.

"So you knew about the tiles that long ago?"

"Oh, yes. We only had a few by this time last year, but with ownership of the hotel we planned to buy the others back at any cost and make our fortune with the lost Rexford jewels. Every account I've ever read says they were imported, and quite valuable. They were merely hidden away because of Rexford's overbearing nature, and his impending divorce. He stood to lose a great deal in the divorce proceedings, including the jewels."

"And you figured out the Rexford family owned a retreat not far down the road, and the jewels might be hidden below?"

"It wasn't easy, but we secretly retrieved enough of the pieces to make a map, no matter the cost," she said with a wry smile. "So you see, between the hotel and the jewels, David and I had it made. We would have become one of the richest couples in the country, retired early, and led happy lives in seclusion after selling our newfound goods at a robust calling price. Everything was perfect until you and your detective friend murdered my David."

"Pardon me for surviving," Clouse said, knowing full well he was forced to participate in the final charade the year before, just as he was now.

At the moment, his chances looked worse, considering the scenario.

Clouse glanced around, seeing no sign of her partner, or his own for that matter. He felt as though he knew, and to an extent, understood Joan's motive, but he wanted to know for certain if he was right about the partner, and if so, what motivated that person.

"Where are you, Mark?" he wondered under his breath, glancing around the atrium and its surrounding facade.

***

From across the atrium Daniels surveyed everything below, including the hostage crisis and Niemeyer's condition, which seemed shaky at best. Unlike the contractor, he had picked the lock of a room, closing the door behind him. Careful to leave the lights off, he spied the scene below, unsure of what his best move might be.

It felt like watching a movie where he was helpless to determine the outcome, but he decided a move closer to the action might change that.

His legs felt rubbery, partly from so much use. Nerves had an impact on how well he functioned as well. He carefully opened the door, looking around outside before stepping, his gun drawn for both threat and protection. He needed to watch every step with caution, but something instinctive alerted him that he was already being watched.

Perhaps even stalked.

To his right, a streak of black seemed to zip by. He turned, but it was already past, perhaps into another corridor, perhaps a figment of his imagination. The last time he experienced such a feeling, his head had nearly lost a permanent fit with his neck. Assuring himself the safety was off, he took careful hold of the gun, looking in every direction before advancing up the hallway.

Again, he thought something moved behind him.

Again he turned.

"Damn it," he muttered, seeing nothing.

He returned his attention to the hallway and the multitude of doors before him. As though he paddled down a winding stream, they were his shore, showing him where to go. He quickened his pace, despite the discomfort in his legs. He would literally have to walk nearly a quarter of a mile to help his friend considering the vast space of the atrium and the hallways necessary to reach it. Getting there presented more of a challenge than just the walk.

Rounding the first set of rooms, Daniels felt halfway home, but a gut feeling told him something dangerous drew near. He stopped his walk, turning around completely to look at the dimmed hallway he had just come from.

Nothing visible.

He had nearly shaken off the notion of anyone pursuing him when a door burst open to his side, revealing a black shape too fast for him to shoot before it rammed him against the wall, knocking the wind from his lungs.

And the gun from his right hand.

Though larger and stronger than his foe, Daniels could not match quickness with the cloaked figure as he grasped the person's throat, only to receive several knees to his groin for the effort. Daniels slumped to the floor, taking several more kicks to his ribs, each hurting more than the one before.

He audibly hurt, seeing his gun only a few feet away through dizzied vision. The thought of reaching it died as the figure pulled him to his feet, pulling a knife in an attempt to finish his work.

Seeing well enough to detect the shine of the blade, Daniels clasped the stalker's hand at the wrist, preventing any action from the weapon. With his other hand, the former detective struck the figure's head, spinning him back.

The cloaked figure immediately retaliated with a charge led by the blade. Daniels dodged, hurling the killer forcefully into the wall as he dove for his gun. His legs failed him as he fell short of grasping the weapon he so desperately needed. He began to crawl toward the firearm, but felt a sharp pain in one leg as the killer plunged the knife into the back of his calve muscle. The weapon immediately pulled free, but Daniels rolled over, grasping his new wound while the killer took up his gun.

Knowing he was unarmed and at a heavy disadvantage, the officer struggled along the floor toward the shadows, hoping to make some sort of defense for himself. He nervously wiped his head once, streaking it with the blood from his wound. Within seconds, the killer loomed over him, fully masked, entirely unknown, and holding the officer's firearm. Daniels drew in a horrified breath, knowing what mortal danger he faced.

He could only watch as a shot fired, aimed at his abdomen. His hands reacted before his thoughts, clutching the area in question, taking up a pool of blood in each palm as he stared at his hands, a combination of a gasp and moan emitting from his open mouth. His eyes panned the cloaked legs up to the faceless mask of the person wanting him dead. In the shadows, neither could really see much expression from the other, but the stalker was apparently in no mood to fool around.

He watched a moment as the detective gasped for breath, which came in heaves due to the fresh abdominal wound. Blood trickled through Daniels' hands, spurting quickly enough from the wound that the killer felt content the man was nearing the end of his life. Kneeling down, the killer quickly searched the former detective for additional items, finding a cell phone, which he pocketed to ensure no assistance was called. Pointing the gun at the wounded officer's head a moment, the killer apparently decided his prey deserved a slow, agonizing death, rather than a quick, painless headshot.

Daniels could only watch the killer exit the hallway from his prone position.

Chapter 36

When Clouse heard a gunshot echo throughout the hotel he wondered if Daniels had evened the playing field, or if another of his friends had fallen to the killing duo.

He helplessly watched as the partner entered the atrium, with no sign of Daniels, or any other form of help left. He carried several objects, including Niemeyer's shotgun and an aged book of some sort, with a reddish ribbon protruding from its middle.

His situation paralleled the year before so closely it felt like a dream, as though entirely inconceivable. Once again, he felt abandoned, left to the wolves. His gun pressed at his backside, as though to remind him of its potential help. Clouse could only monitor everything in the room one frame at a time, like sequential security cameras in a retail store.

Zach held hostage by Joan.

Niemeyer lying perfectly still, blood oozing from his head.

A cloaked figure drawing closer, his footsteps preceding him in the form of echoes.

Jane tied up, seated helplessly on the floor with Clouse as her only salvation.

The hotel's mammoth frame surrounding him, offering no protection, anywhere to hide or even put up a fair fight.

No matter which frame he viewed, no hope peered back.

As the other killer approached, Clouse took a step back, carefully surveying the person beneath the guise of the reaper, trying to assure himself he was correct in the person's identity. He felt certain he was.

"Have you come to terms with death, Paul?" Joan asked, keeping Zach too close for him to think about anything except his son's safety.

"I'm done with you," Clouse replied, choosing to play the remainder of the game his way.

He turned his attention to the other person, now standing before him holding the shotgun in one hand, the book in the other.

"I want to see Jacob now. You owe me a peek after everything you've put me through."

"This isn't a very comfortable getup anyway," the young man said, taking off the mask to reveal a head of black hair and the snake tattoo Clouse had heard so much about. "Very hard to see, too. I almost let your two friends get the best of me," he said, looking with cold eyes at Clouse, whose lips twitched from anxiety and a building fury. He wanted so badly to take a chance on using the pistol, but he had to follow the plan to the end, even if Daniels was removed from the equation.

"Let's get down to who you really are," Clouse said evenly.

"Ah, first let's get down to disarming you. I know your friend would never let you come in here unarmed. Let me see what you have."

Clouse lifted his jacket, revealing no holster to Jacob. The young man simply smirked at his attempt to further conceal the weapon.

"Come on, Paul. I know where you have it. I saw him give it to you."

Giving in, Clouse slowly reached behind him for the weapon, seeing Niemeyer's shotgun aimed at him in Jacob's hands while his son moaned with a knife against his throat.

Realistic chances of escape were running out.

"Careful now," Jacob warned as Clouse pulled the gun from his backside, setting it on the ground softly. "Kick it over here."

Clouse obeyed.

Jacob let it jet past him without an attempt to retrieve it. After all, he was already armed.

"So, you want to know exactly who I am?"

"I already do. What I really want to know is why you're involved with that psycho bitch over there."

"Well," Jacob said, forcefully shoving his finger into his hairline to help remove the realistic black wig. "For me, it was all about family, and getting my little group involved," he said, removing the wig to reveal a natural brown hair color beneath, showing Clouse exactly who he thought he would see. When the serpentine tattoo peeled off with just a hint of effort, he knew who he was dealing with, and how their plan came to fruition.

"Why did you conspire to do this, and let her murder your father, Ryan?" Clouse asked the son of Barry Andrews, who lie dead on the floor just a few feet away from either of them.

Any makeup, special effects, costumes, and even several various roles pulled off by one person could be explained by Ryan Andrews' experience in the theater, but several other things had yet to be revealed.

Knowledge and access to the hospital were explained, the use and access to a coroner's blade were explained, and with Joan as his partner, he could easily have gained access to the hotel and any lists necessary to track down the pieces of tile and their current owners. She had masterminded the entire scheme, and he had carried it out, but why?

"Why did I allow my father to be murdered?" Ryan repeated the question, as though he needed to truly think of the answer. The tone in his voice gave Clouse the hint that the boy, sane as he may have portrayed himself, was in the same state of mind as Joan. "See, Barry here wasn't really my dad. He just adopted me when I was an infant and lied to me for 21 years. He never intended to tell me the truth, but I found some people who would tell the truth, and they hooked me up with Joan."

"A few years ago Ryan was a sweet, innocent kid just looking for an education," Joan explained. "I certainly gave him one when the Coven introduced me to him last year after they discovered what happened to David."

"I don't believe there is any *Coven*," Clouse almost spat the words. "I have yet to see or hear of anyone except for you two, and Stephen, whom you murdered."

Ryan let out a short laugh.

"Oh, they exist. We're sort of a fraternal group that doesn't like public recognition. There are always eight of us, and lately it seems we've had a lot of turnover. Joan wanted in, but we were full at the time, so we settled for a working relationship. The group is talking about expansion, but you know how group voting goes. Anyway, the Coven listened to her plight and I took time out of my busy college schedule to help her."

"He's so much more creative than my husband was," Joan commented so conversationally that Clouse truly believed her to be insane. "I mean, setting people on fire, stabbing them, using the scythe, sealing a person up inside a wall. It takes genius to use so many techniques. Ryan was quite a find for me, and his group."

"You two are both sick," Clouse commented with disgust. "You treat this like some sort of game where you can just knock off anyone you want, just to get your precious gems without any consequences. So, are you the leader of this little clan, Ryan?"

Ryan walked over toward Jane, casually carrying the shotgun at his side. He softly patted her head, apparently to let her know she had not been forgotten, and to keep Clouse in check.

"I'm the interim leader while our great one is away on business. And you may wonder exactly what it is my group stands for or worships. Well, we worship the Lord of the Underworld, Mephistopheles, the Devil, Satan, Lucifer, or whatever other name you may want to call him. We especially pay homage to Father Ernest, who in his own way, left a legacy for us to follow. He alone tried to show those asshole Jesuit priests the path to follow, but they wouldn't listen. And you see how many graves there are on that hill out there," Ryan finished, pointing out toward the cemetery at the edge of the hotel grounds.

"This all sounds farfetched," Clouse said. "Worshiping the devil? To what purpose?"

"You can't possibly understand, Paul," Ryan replied. "You may think we're off our rockers, but there is power you can't possibly conceive within the objects we seek. Objects this hotel has been hiding for almost a century. Objects those men, buried on that hill, fought to keep secret."

He paused a moment deliberately for emphasis.

"But we have a member who figured out what they were hiding, and even their weak religion cannot stop us from fulfilling our destiny as a collective group."

Clouse had often wondered how so many graves appeared during the few decades the Jesuits owned the hotel, but simply figured many were advanced in age, dying of natural causes. He knew some of the men requested burial on the grounds, regardless of where they passed away, but he never suspected foul play.

"Those priests died of natural causes," Clouse said. "I don't know where you get this bullshit from, Ryan, but you're wrong on all counts."

"No, you're wrong! If we had time, I would fill you in on the entire story, but it's probably best kept within the confines of my group anyway." He shook part of the black robe, letting some cool air reach his skin within. "So while we're being so forthcoming, how did you figure it out, Paul?"

"Joan was easy once she kidnapped Zach from the school. A teacher managed to show me a picture with part of her in it, taken at the zoo."

"I always hate photos," Joan said, as though sincere. "They never catch you in the right light."

"No, I don't suppose they would show you as a murderous bitch, would they?" Clouse deduced aloud.

With only a glare in response, he decided to continue his story.

"I figured you out from the computer program you two used to teach my son that tunnel system," he told Ryan. "I remembered using that program too, and I remember how constantly annoyed I was by the theater department being so close to the building I worked in."

He looked to the fresh corpse of Barry Andrews.

"I had eliminated your adopted father as a suspect, so that left only people close to the hospital, or working there. So, I had Mark do some checking on you, Ryan. Turns out you're minoring in architecture. What an interesting combination you've picked if you never wanted to land a job, or you were simply fueling your knowledge for a project of revenge. We also found out your roommate from last year, Rudolph Stephen Tenney, was listed missing a few weeks ago by campus police. Guess with a name like that I would have gone with my middle name too."

Clouse paused, glancing over toward Niemeyer, who still appeared dead or unconscious. He prayed one of his friends was somehow alive to help him momentarily.

"Just too many coincidences with the hospital, the cutting blade, and McCabe's investigation into the diving equipment, which I'd imagine you hadn't purchased that long ago. Turns out your entire family took diving lessons last spring, so you probably had a good enough alibi, but you weren't taking any chances, were you?"

"One can never be too careful," Ryan replied, apparently impressed by Clouse's detective work. "I worked awfully hard to pack that state trooper away only to have you two pricks dig him out."

Clouse shrugged, as though to apologize.

"Your father had an alibi, so we figured someone close to him might be behind the killings, especially with his girlfriend conveniently getting axed."

"Don't call that son-of-a-bitch my father," Ryan ordered. "My real father showed me the truth, showed me what I had to do to claim what was rightfully mine."

Clouse paused a moment, taking a few steps to one side.

"So what is your *real* motivation in this?" he had to ask Ryan.

"My real motivation was to find these jewels for Joan, eventually obtain the deed to this property, and live a happy existence with the occasional ceremony to worship my dark lord and carry out his wishes with my group. You can't begin to understand the power we've already unearthed, and that's just the beginning. We make quite a difference in society, as you can already tell. Everyone in the Coven has a professional job. Lawyers, doctors, teachers — you name it, we've got it. Well, we don't take to firemen and cops too well, as you might guess."

He looked to Joan, who returned a sinister smirk.

"But you gotta admit, this place makes one hell of a church, doesn't it?" he asked, looking up to the grand dome, six stories above them, the stars in the sky visible through its thick glass. "Hell, I could start my own ministry here. This place is already a temple for evil, and there's room for improvement. And I have you to thank for putting it back together, Paul."

Clouse looked to both Joan and Ryan, one final question burning inside his mind.

"So where are these jewels I keep hearing about?"

Ryan looked to the book on the floor, then in the direction of Joan and her hostage.

"Seems your boy isn't very good at following orders," Ryan commented. "He said this book was all he found in the tunnels. Swears it. If you like reading about some bullshit account of Father Ernest, it's a great read, but when you're looking for something, for a quick way to get rich, it's a waste of fucking time."

Clouse began to realize the significance of the Father Ernest theme in more ways than one. Not only did Ryan aspire to dress and possibly act like the priest, but Ernest's actual past may have prevented the finish to his plan. The priests, or someone, may very well have found the jewels decades earlier and finished the job, leaving only a book behind.

"So someone beat you to it?" Clouse asked.

"Or your boy is lying," Ryan countered. "Little kids like to take things for themselves and keep secrets. I know I certainly did," he added, drawing a double-edged knife from beneath the cloak. He set the shotgun down, sliding it over to Joan. "Let's see what truths the boy tells when I cut his daddy up."

Clouse felt tense throughout his body. The time to bring the ordeal to a close had come, and he felt unprepared. He stripped off his jacket, letting it fall to the floor behind him as he defensively circled the Coven's temporary leader, ready to defend himself.

"One wrong move, your boy dies," the younger man warned before thrusting the knife at Clouse.

Dodging, Clouse simply stepped aside, wondering how long he could avoid being cut. Another slash missed him, then Clouse caught the knife, knocking it loose before Ryan used it. Ryan looked at Joan for a moment, as though he might actually tell her to harm the boy, but seemed to realize he might need Zach healthy for other reasons. He refocused his attention on Clouse with a visual warning not to prevent any further injury to himself.

For his trouble, Clouse received a knee to the stomach, then a barrage of fists striking everything from his jaw to his ribs, then his kidneys. He groaned in agony with each unshielded blow, fighting to remain conscious with some form of strength reserve in case he found an opportunity to fight back. For Zach's sake, he did not dare strike Ryan after knocking the knife away, which served as his first and only act of defiance.

He only glanced to his son and future wife once, finding them both utterly horrified and terrified at their predicament. Clouse fought to remain conscious long enough to hope for some form of rescue, suspecting his second chances were gone.

Ryan openly delighted himself in knocking the firefighter around, toying with his prey. Clouse found nothing respectable in how a person beat another senseless in a one-sided battle. He knew this was the same person who had snuck up on others and launched a scythe into their guts before they could possibly defend themselves.

Nothing respectable whatsoever.

Clouse felt blood drip from his nose, and an open cut on his jaw, as his body fell to the floor, staggered by a body blow from Ryan. The younger man picked him up, launching several more fists into his abdomen, nearly causing Clouse to vomit from the hunched position he was held in. After half a dozen fists, he let the firefighter fall to the floor where his body naturally wanted to go. Taking a slow, deliberate walk toward the knife, Ryan turned to see Joan holding Zach hostage before staring at Clouse.

"It's too bad you really can't fight back," he said, bending down to pick up the knife. He was ready for the kill now that Clouse was too battered to retaliate against an easy death. "Once you're gone, and we're done with your boy, who knows what we'll do with him."

"Motherfucker," Clouse addressed him between heaved breaths, lying on his back. "If you hurt him in any way, you will die."

"You're not in much of a position to make threats," Ryan said, standing over him, knife in hand.

Poising himself, Ryan pointed the knife's blade down at a battered Clouse. He prepared to launch the knife downward, into his adversary's chest, relishing the moment.

A gunshot suddenly rang through the atrium, catching everyone by surprise. Like everyone else, Clouse perked up to see where the shot had come from, and where it landed.

To his surprise, Joan let out a strange moan, her knife arm falling away from Zach as her eyes slowly rolled back into her head as her arms, followed by her body, went limp. She slumped to the floor in a heap, nearly taking the boy down with her.

Blood trickled from her back as the knife fell several feet from her body. Zach scurried away from the dead woman, hurriedly rushing back to Jane, knowing his father was too close to the killer to protect him.

All eyes looked behind Joan's position, seeing Daniels standing at the door, a pistol held at his side. He walked in with a limp due to the stabbing of his calve muscle, slowly drawing close enough to protect Clouse if necessary, and to assess the situation for himself.

"You died," Ryan said, positive his eyes were not failing him.

"You're not the only one who can act, asshole," Daniels replied, holding up his wrists to reveal two slit plastic packs along the inside of each wrist. Both were lined with red where fake blood had spewed upon contact with small blades pressed against their sides. "Kind of an old professional wrestling trick," the officer said with a grin. "That gun you and I were fighting so viciously over was filled with blanks, son. Some good timing and a little fake blood, and you weren't too hard to fool."

He held his firearm up for the murderous young man to see.

"This one doesn't have blanks."

Clouse struggled to his feet, backing away from Ryan toward his friend.

"Might want to drop that knife," he told the young man.

Ryan obeyed, a smile crossing his face.

"So what are you going to do now? Kill me?"

"Actually," Daniels said, looking to Clouse who was recovering from his beating, "I think it's your turn, buddy," he said, implying that his friend should give some of what he had received.

"Suits me fine," Clouse said, launching a fist into the younger man's stomach, then another across his jaw.

He picked Ryan up, launching several more fists into his abdomen with vengeance on his mind. Not for himself, but for everyone he could never speak to again.

"This is for Kenny, and Rusty, and Dr. Smith," he said with a name for each thrust to the gut.

Ramming a knee into the younger man's sternum, he heard a painfully forced exhale from the killer. Clouse finally threw Ryan several feet further into the atrium, ready to tend to other priorities.

"Keep an eye on him," Clouse told Daniels as he walked over to Niemeyer.

His friend had not made a sound during the entire ordeal, lying motionless on his back. Clouse approached cautiously, checking his friend like he had so many patients on first responder runs. Though a certified EMT through his department, Clouse had reservations about handling his own friends, afraid his nerves might keep him from giving them adequate care.

"Come on, Tim," he said, kneeling beside his friend. "You're too dumb to die on me," he said, about to feel for a pulse.

"I heard that," Niemeyer said through the intense pain that came with regaining consciousness. "I'm only dumb because I followed you into this."

"Where does it hurt?" Clouse asked after a brief chuckle, beginning to examine his high school pal.

"Everywhere, but I don't think anything is broken."

"You're lucky you have so much padding, Tim," Clouse added with a bit of humor since his friend could do little about it.

"Just wait until I get my shotgun back, Paul. Then we'll see who's funny."

Clouse slowly felt around his friend's head, trying to discover if Niemeyer had any spinal or head injuries beyond a mild concussion. A large bump protruded from the construction worker's head along the back, but he doubted Niemeyer had suffered any life-threatening injuries.

"Lie still," Clouse ordered, taking precautions. "You might have a spinal injury, and I'm not taking any chances until we get some paramedics here."

"I'm fine," Niemeyer insisted, trying to rise from the ground.

"Down," Clouse said, pushing lightly on his friend's chest to keep Niemeyer on the ground. "This is no time to be macho."

"Okay, okay," Niemeyer reluctantly agreed.

Clouse turned momentarily to see if the area remained secure.

Daniels kept an eye on Ryan while he untied Jane and Zach, letting them ease away from the killer, who kept amazingly still. He seemed to expect Ryan to make a final attempt at fleeing, or possibly charge him. Neither he nor Clouse envisioned bringing a murderer of such proportion into custody without further struggle.

"So where is your little faction when you need them?" he asked the young man.

"If you heard me talk about that, then you heard me say this was my project," Ryan answered. "Don't worry, regardless of what happens to me, you'll be hearing from them."

"I'm sure," Daniels said, turning his back momentarily to see Niemeyer's condition.

In the brief second or two the officer turned, Ryan charged him from behind, knowing the exits were all too far away for a clean escape. Confrontation was the only way he might still obtain victory, no matter the cost.

To Daniels, the sound of footsteps, Jane's shriek, and the sight of Clouse desperately pointing, flooded his mind simultaneously, alerting him to Ryan's movement. Instinct and previous experience told him the young man would attempt to flee, so Daniels turned deliberately, ready to fire across the atrium if necessary. He seemed to have no idea Ryan was already on his feet when he turned.

Ryan had already launched himself at the detective as everyone, including Clouse, watched helplessly.

Clouse saw the gun leave the officer's grip as the young man knocked it free. Daniels' legs would not allow much close quarters action and Ryan sensed it. He knocked the recovering officer down by punching at one knee. As Daniels fell to his back, the wind knocked from him, he felt a fist bury itself in his jaw, followed by two hands clamping around his neck like vises, throwing his head repeatedly back against the carpet, and concrete floor beneath it. His consciousness quickly faltered, but he felt the weight atop his body leave, along with the hands across his windpipe.

"You've done enough damage," he heard Clouse say as Ryan stood to confront him.

He backed the young man across the atrium a bit, but read the insanity in the younger man's eyes, positive Ryan would charge him, or dash toward the nearby exit Clouse had backed him toward.

Glancing behind him, Ryan seemed to defy running, wanting another chance to finish the job and kill Clouse. His body rocked back and forth, as though he was prepared to attempt a tackle of his larger adversary, despite the firearm aimed at his chest.

"I'm not leaving here without claiming a life," Ryan muttered, prepared to charge Clouse for his final stand, apparently confident his father would carry out the remainder of the plan.

He began reaching toward his backside, perhaps for a weapon, causing Clouse's hand to quiver as it held the gun, forcing him to make a decision he had never made before.

To murder, or not?

"Maybe it's time *you* die," Clouse finally said, firing a shot into the younger man's abdomen, sending him stumbling back until he hit the floor, lying motionless.

"Not bad," Daniels said as Clouse walked back to check on him.

"A little low," Clouse confessed, looking over the bruises on his friend's face. "You're not very good at this conflict resolution stuff, are you?"

"Hey, I'm getting a little better. I'll take a stab wound and a good beating to paralysis any day."

"Damn," Clouse said under his breath, looking up from his friend a moment.

Daniels seemed to already know what had happened.

From the spot where he fell, Ryan had disappeared altogether, most likely scrambling out the nearest atrium entrance. This time, however, a broken trail of blood left something to follow, and Clouse knew he had clipped the killer sufficiently.

"I'll be right back," Clouse said before storming out the exit door in pursuit.

"No!" Jane called, worried for his safety with good reason.

"I'll be fine," Clouse insisted, not wavering from his pursuit one second, and not turning to see any of his friends or family, fearing he might change his mind.

He followed the blood trail to the front of the hotel where it led outside. Thunder echoed in the distance as lightning illuminated the sky outside. Without fear of either, Clouse stepped outside, into the storm, looking around for any sign of Ryan. The wind howled around him, and rain smacked his face and neck mercilessly as the cold droplets found their way inside his shirt, pressing into his chest like the cold, stiff fingers of death itself.

A small trail of blood seemed to lead outside, then dissipate with the puddles and crashing rain drops. Any drips of blood were quickly washing away, leaving him nothing to follow. The weather showered him with rain and cold, reminding him of why intelligent people remained indoors. He took one last look around, certain Ryan had run off to die somewhere, rather than face the humiliation of being arrested. He probably felt defensive about his group, not wanting the police to divulge any information from him.

Insanity caused people to do strange things, Clouse decided.

"Anything?" Daniels asked when Clouse returned to the atrium.

"No. I don't think he'll make it far, though."

Niemeyer sat up at this point, indicating he would be fine after some pain relievers, and everyone else seemed all right in Clouse's eyes, other than being universally shaken. He walked over to his fiancée and son, taking them both into a much needed hug.

"You okay?" he asked Jane. Her reply came in the form of a weak nod. "I'm so sorry you had to go through this."

He looked around the room, keeping his arms wrapped around Jane. All the death, the remaining nightmares to relive night after night, and the wounds they had all suffered, left him wondering. Somehow the answers Joan gave him seemed to make sense, but there was something about Ryan Andrews that remained a mystery. He wondered exactly what had prompted the young man to commit serial murder. He also questioned where the Rexford jewels had gone, and why a diary was left in their place. Clouse planned to read the diary soon, and learn what he could about the hotel's past.

"Want me to call the police?" Daniels asked, walking over to Clouse and his family rather gingerly because of his wounded leg.

"Whenever," the reply came.

Clouse felt no interest in talking to the police again. Nor did he want to leave such a moment of serenity, now that a resolution had finally come.

He hoped tranquility might finally enter his life on a regular basis, but so many questions burned at his mind, and Clouse wondered what price he needed to pay for peace of mind. He may have inherited Smith's fortune, but even that money would not buy him happiness and a normal life if any issues with the Coven weren't fully resolved.

"Is it over, Daddy?" Zach asked, drawing close to his father.

"Yes, Zach, it's over," Clouse replied with absolution in his voice and a gnawing at his soul.

Chapter 37

A week later, Clouse finally left his house to meet Daniels and McCabe at the state trooper's favorite pub for a drink one evening. Things looked up as more answers came to light, but several unanswered questions plagued the three men.

"There's been no sign of Ryan Andrews," McCabe said, now in his third day of regular duty after being incarcerated inside the hotel basement.

Apparently he and Russell Hinds had formed somewhat of a guarded friendship, even after the irregular way in which they met. McCabe promised the security guard a night filled with booze and women whenever he felt up to it. Being divorced, with the typical frame of mind that accompanied men in law enforcement, Hinds accepted.

"I don't think he could have survived that bullet wound if he didn't check into a hospital," Clouse noted, speaking of Ryan Andrews. "Without surgery, there's no way he could have gotten that bullet out of there."

"I agree," Daniels said. "But that boy certainly is crafty. There's no telling what tricks he might have had up his sleeve. If he wasn't lying, there might have been a doctor in that group of his who did a private surgery."

"We did find Mrs. Landamere's stash of tile pieces," McCabe boasted, taking a gulp from his beer mug. "Man, they must have had about two-hundred of those things in their basement, and most of them were useless."

"Actually, they were all useless," Clouse said. "It turned out one of the priests moved the jewels in an attempt to keep them out of the wrong hands. That diary they found was a pretty interesting read."

"What else did it say?" Daniels asked.

Clouse sipped from his second beer bottle, thinking a moment.

"It was kind of odd for a journal, because the entire time I felt like the writer was still keeping secrets. And to be honest, I never did figure out exactly who the writer was. It briefly mentioned some odd troubles with Father Ernest, and how the priests came to regret buying the hotel after some time. Strangely, the journal ends, talking about how the jewels must be hidden, and leaves off, like there's another edition to follow."

"Is there?" McCabe inquired.

"Well, this one was listed number three, so there are obviously others, but I don't know where. Did anything like that show up in your search of the Landamere property?"

"No, but we were just searching for the tile pieces and some notebooks with relevant facts. They probably overlooked everything else."

Daniels had managed to convince authorities he had not used his police credentials in any way during the past week, to keep his job secure. Clouse knew he had also visited Susan Jameson, and discovered his prognosis looked good. He planned to finish rehabilitation and rejoin the force, hopefully taking little time to earn his spot in the investigative division back. With his life back to normal, he had taken the week off to enjoy his son a bit more, knowing he would be able to help Curtis with his own first steps.

"So what are you going to do?" the officer asked McCabe.

"I'm transferring to the north end of the state, and getting back on the road," the trooper said, as though he felt disdain for his current assignment. "Up there you just deal with speeders and the occasional horse and buggy, not serial killers. About the most excitement I'll get from now on will be searching cars for drugs near Gary."

"You'll miss your bars," Daniels said.

"I'll be near Chicago, Mark," McCabe replied with a chuckle.

He turned his attention to Clouse.

"And what are you going to do with your newfound fortune?" the trooper asked the career firefighter, already knowing what Daniels had planned in his near future, since the man had informed them both early on.

Clouse sighed. Indeed, what Harold Simms told him at the funeral was true, and Clouse stood to inherit a net worth of a couple billion dollars.

Perhaps.

"Probably nothing for quite some time. It seems I'm going to be held up in court over some new injunctions, and it may be a while before they figure out exactly what Dr. Smith owed the government. In the meantime, I'll go back to my job after I spend a little more time with my family."

"Did you ever figure out anything about Ryan Andrews' background?" Daniels asked McCabe.

"No. It seems he was left at the hospital's emergency room entrance as an infant and Dr. Andrews was the one who found him. No one had any clue who his original parents might have been. To be honest, I can't understand how that boy could be so indifferent about Joan slitting his father's throat after he disowned the man completely. Something really wrong must have happened there."

"And there's been no trace of the group he was talking about," Daniels stated. "If he wasn't lying, it sure is a secretive bunch."

Clouse took another sip of beer, noticing the bottle felt warmer. The conversation was keeping them from drinking.

"I asked Zach if he checked every tunnel of the hallowed resort when he was down there, and he seems certain he did. If that journal is accurate, someone beat them to the jewels, and they murdered a lot of innocent people for absolutely no good reason."

"There's no *good* reason," Daniels commented. "And I don't see why they couldn't have accomplished their objective without killing anyone?"

"Because there's no revenge in that," Clouse noted. "Joan had it in for you, Mark. When you shot her husband between the eyes she just snapped."

Daniels closed his eyes a few seconds, most likely reliving the experience from the year before by the pained look on his face.

Back then, the answers came clearer in the end. This year, something seemed to be missing from the whole puzzle. Granted, the investigation was not fully shut, but it was winding down. Clouse knew Daniels planned to work with McCabe in finding what few answers remained to be discovered, and hoped they succeeded in finding them.

At least until the trooper moved away.

"Guys, I need to get out of here and see the soon-to-be wife and kids," Clouse said, standing from the table.

Both nodded a farewell as he left a few dollar bills on the table and headed for the door.

Outside, the weather threatened snow with a formidable cold wind that forced Clouse to immediately zip his jacket. He looked around at the leaves swirling in the air, and saw a bleak night sky around him, like so many others he had just experienced.

Strangely, his dilemma felt unresolved, but the only thing to do was wait. Stay home, protect his family, and wait for answers. He headed across the parking lot, feeling determined to put his life back together and take the positive things he had left and make them work. He would play the waiting game, be patient, and take what life offered him, not worrying about the future, or who might come after him. Each day the demons fell a bit further behind him.

And that's where they belonged.

SINS OF THE FATHER

Book Three of the West Baden Murders Series

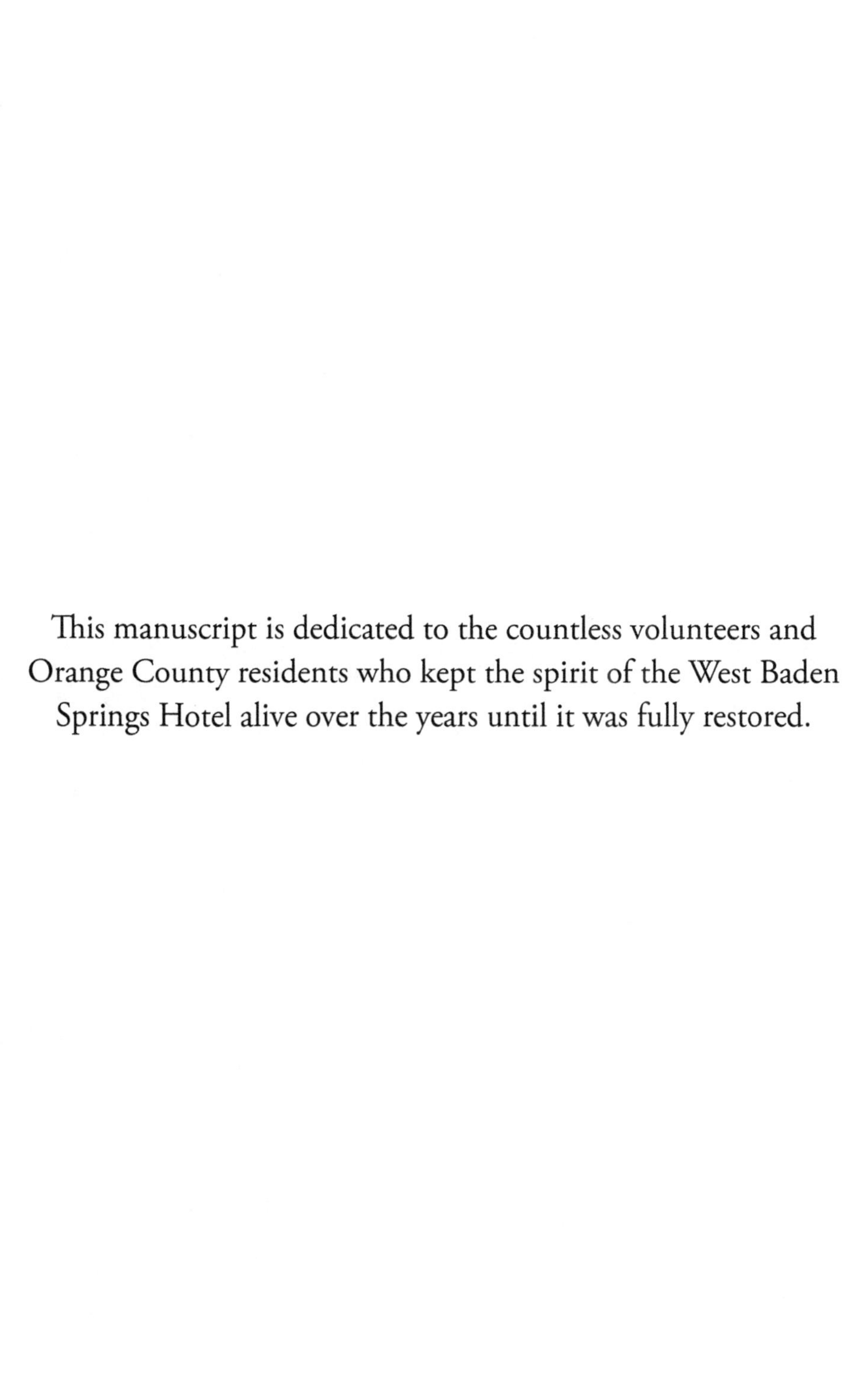

This manuscript is dedicated to the countless volunteers and Orange County residents who kept the spirit of the West Baden Springs Hotel alive over the years until it was fully restored.

Acknowledgements

I owe thanks to Bob Chambers, Donald Williamson, Erica Cosgrove, Shawn Cosgrove, and Jimmy Gibson for their assistance.

Thanks to Troy Lobosky and John Leach for their insight from the very beginning of this lengthy project.

Special thanks as always to Nannette Bell and Carol Pyle for keeping me from being knee-deep in typos and helping me make sense of my own work. Also thanks to Brad Wiemer and Korby Sommers.

As always, thank you Kendrick at KLS Digital for creating a cover to showcase all of my hard work. Visit KLS Digital at www.klsdigital.com.

Chapter 1

aturday night.

In the middle of town, kids scurried in costume from door to door with chaperones keeping vigil. A brisk, breezy night, trees rustled in the wind, though not under the threat of rain despite the bleak weather.

Unofficially Halloween, it seemed more practical in the city of Bloomington, Indiana to have trick-or-treat on a weekend evening, rather than Sunday. Both safety and educational concerns told city officials to hold it the day prior to the actual holiday.

Amongst the flowing traffic of elementary school kids, disguised in various wares, Jamie Vosburgh took time to make certain the two children under her care were warm enough, and that their costumes were fully intact.

"This is great!" Zach Clouse told his babysitter as she examined his costume. "I haven't been out on Halloween in forever."

Actually, Jamie had become much more than a sitter for Zach and his stepsister Katie. When their parents were married around the holidays the year before, the new couple needed someone to take care of the children while they went on their honeymoon, and on the occasional weekend when they went out.

Jamie, a senior in high school, and the daughter of their neighbors down the road, seemed the type of reliable, sweet girl they were looking for to take care of their children. She never let them out of her sight, she put them to bed when they needed to be, and if anything seemed out of the ordinary, she never hesitated to call or page Paul or Jane Clouse.

"Are you two ready to get some more candy?" she asked, receiving anxious nods from both Zach and Katie.

She watched a moment as they ran up the stairs to the next house, spouting "trick-or-treat" with rehearsed ease before receiving a handful of candy in their plastic sacks. A grin crossed her face as she saw the smiles on theirs, returning to her from the house. Their faces seemed to glow with anticipation for what the rest of the evening held.

Everywhere people had decorated their yards with cobwebs, skeletons, jack-o-lanterns, and coffins. For several years, it seemed people had strayed from actively celebrating Halloween, but the spirit appeared to be back in her fair city.

As they approached the next yard, she noticed a pair of tennis shoes dangling in front of her as she turned, startling her a bit. Looking up, she noticed they belonged to a dummy stuffed with old rags, swaying in the breeze, his button eyes staring blankly down at her.

Wearing her high school letter jacket, she walked behind the kids, keeping close watch. An honor student at Bloomington North High School, she participated in several sports, keeping active, and enjoying her last year in school to the fullest. She had finished her cross-country season above expectations, now preparing herself for gymnastics.

Tonight she took the children out while their parents spent the night at a high school basketball game. Jane Clouse wanted her husband to attend the game with her because her nephew was playing. The timing seemed odd, but the couple, as well as the kids, felt perfectly comfortable letting Jamie take them out for the evening. Zach especially dreaded the Halloween season after his mother's untimely death two years prior, but with help from Jamie and unwavering support from his new family, the boy was adjusting well.

The curls in her lengthy red hair bounced as she strolled with the kids to the next house. Her smile came easily, especially when she spent time with them, and she never grew tired or irritated when they were around. She was more of a nanny than a babysitter sometimes, taking time from her busy schedule to be around the kids. Of course, the money was good too, because Paul Clouse had come across some good fortune the previous year when he received an unexpected inheritance.

He tended to treat Jamie like a niece.

"Are you guys having fun?" she asked between houses.

"Awesome," Katie said, having picked up on the word from television lately.

"Good. We've got about another half hour before we have to head home," she said as though she lived with them. Sometimes it felt as though she did. With a key to the Clouse household, the code to their home security system, and unlimited use of the facilities, including the pool and spa, she was like an extended part of the family.

Jamie heard stories about Paul and Jane Clouse, and what they had experienced the past few years. She paid little attention to the rumors, figuring no one could *really* go through what people said they had. They were fantastic people in her view, and she required some concrete proof to sway that opinion.

Her evening plans included earning their trust by getting the kids home early, watching a scary movie, and calling her boyfriend once they were in bed. She expected to enjoy a relatively uneventful Halloween Eve.

***

While most people celebrated the unofficial holiday, Tim Niemeyer drove his four-wheel-drive Chevy work truck down a quiet street in Bedford, a town just south of Bloomington. He spied costumes, light sticks, and jack-o-lanterns at nearly every house. Kids, just like his son and daughter, skipped up and down the street in anticipation of sweet snacks.

His wife agreed to take their children out since this was probably the last year both kids would seek candy. They were rising through the grade school ranks, growing too fast for his taste. Soon they would enter junior high, leaving childhood completely behind.

Niemeyer and his younger brother, Randy, worked at restoring their church inside the city limits every Saturday night. Typically the only night the brothers saw one another, they spent Saturdays working on the church with several other parishioners, often grabbing dinner at one of their favorite restaurants afterwards.

Most times, Niemeyer picked his brother up before or after the church work since Randy lived in town, and he did not. Either way, he had to drive, so he saved his little brother any additional burden.

In business for himself, Niemeyer owned a growing construction company that specialized in building for businesses. His friends and associates all agreed that he knew what he wanted from life, and where he was heading, more than anyone else they knew.

Despite his business savvy and prosperous nature, Niemeyer toted his redneck background with him. A Tennessee accent picked up from his grandfather as a child remained, especially when he was drinking, or angry. He often carried a loaded shotgun in the cab of his truck, much to his wife's dismay. Equipped with a quick temper and little tolerance for alternative lifestyles, Niemeyer took most people some time to get used to.

A burly man with just enough hair left to make a fringe with strands in between, he worked out with several police buddies. He often found himself teased about losing his hair to steroids. They knew Niemeyer was an all-natural weight lifter, but they had fun with him at his expense. For those who knew him, getting a rise out of Niemeyer was one of the funniest things about him.

By conventional means, Niemeyer was immovable. Furnished with forearms as thick and solid as small trees, and broad shoulders, most people considered him a threat to their well-being just in passing. In reality, he attended church, loved his family, and took care to involve everyone he knew in the good aspects of his life. By no means would Niemeyer hurt anyone unless they threatened him or those he loved.

No time was available to change between work at the church and supper with his brother. Niemeyer wore steel-toe boots, as he typically did in his construction business, and a red flannel shirt beneath a black nylon jacket depicting his construction business logo. Business was good enough that he never minded advertising for himself.

Pulling into his brother's driveway, he noticed the fallen leaves of various colors on every lawn up the street. Some families had decorative bags in their yards storing the abundant piles, and most houses were decorated for the season. His brother's house showed no sign of decoration, and very little light from within.

While observing the neighborhood, Niemeyer spied several trick-or-treaters walking behind his truck, as though they considered throwing eggs or some other substance on it. They probably figured him to be the owner of the house who refused to give out candy or welcome them to the door with festive decorations. He growled to himself, not enjoying the idea of his truck getting messy, but the kids moved on without incident. Distracted by their sauntering down the street, Niemeyer was caught off-guard when the passenger side door of his truck flew open.

"Damn it, Randy," he said upon seeing his younger brother, his drawl coming out more than usual. "You scared the shit out of me."

"Sorry," his brother replied.

Strangely, the two were three years apart in age, but looked remarkably similar in the face and their stocky builds. Still, there were differences.

Like his older brother, Randy had two kids, but he was recently divorced, leaving his children in the hands of his ex-wife for the night. He avoided anything to do with Halloween if possible, including handing out candy after a night of working on the church.

"I noticed you had your lights out," Tim noted.

"You know I hate Halloween, Tim. And if any kids came up, I don't know what I'd give them. About the only food I have in the house is frozen dinners."

His brother grunted a laugh.

"That would go over well."

Randy worked two jobs while attending Indiana University a few nights a week in his pursuit of a criminal justice degree. He planned to enter the private security field or go further into a law degree, possibly even police work, depending on which field he eventually decided was more worth his time. Using his divorce as a source of newfound freedom and inspiration, he followed the path of his dreams rather than detouring toward practicality.

Randy sometimes carried a semiautomatic pistol tucked into his belt, which some people attributed to his country upbringing, just like his brother. Tonight he had left it home, since they were just eating and visiting the church.

"How hungry are you?" Tim asked as he reversed the truck from the driveway.

"Very. I missed lunch because I spent all day at the library doing research before we met at the church."

"Good. My treat tonight."

"Special occasion?"

"No, I just figure if the only thing you have to eat is frozen dinners, your wallet must be shrinking."

Randy laughed.

"It will be as long as I'm taking classes."

"I'll take care of you, little brother."

Tim pulled into the parking lot of his own bank, as he always did on Saturday night before they ate. The bank sat in the rear of the parking lot beside a vacant store. Lighting was poor, provided only by a nearby streetlight. In the distance behind them, several fast food restaurants were flooded with hungry patrons. A few cars appeared abandoned just behind his truck as he pulled up to the ATM, ready to finance an evening out with his kin.

"You really hate carrying cash, don't you?" Randy asked his older brother.

"The way things are today, you bet."

"To everyone their own."

Tim grinned, opening his truck door.

He whistled to himself as he stepped up to the cash machine, encumbered by darkness aside from the tiny light mounted atop the ATM. As the breeze picked up, brushing past him, he felt a sudden chill. The feeling wasn't so much related to the weather as it was the impending holiday. While Tim didn't much mind the fall, he disliked Halloween and the local stigma attached to him and his good friend Paul Clouse from the previous year. The high school friends lost someone very near and dear to them in a brutal homicide.

Nearby bushes rustled in the breeze as shadows seemed to pass the construction owner who was in the middle of his cash transaction. Sensing something different around him, Niemeyer looked up to see someone emerge from around the bush. He quickly turned his head, trying to avoid being rude by staring, to finish the transaction and move along.

To the other side of him he spied another shadow interrupting the dim lighting. He felt his face flush from nervousness as he swallowed hard.

"What the hell is going on?" he asked himself under his breath.

***

After a full night of receiving candy and more than a few pranks, Jamie and the kids ended up back in the Clouse household. While the kids were upstairs getting ready for bed, she took a moment to call her boyfriend on the phone.

She had dressed down after the festivities, wearing tight jeans that accented her posterior region, despite a school policy in their handbook stating no pants should be worn that revealed the movement or outline of the buttocks. She felt compelled to rebel in small ways, and her athletic form was one of the main attractions to the boys she dated.

Despite rumors spoken of her around school, Jamie liked dating boys of the opposite race. Her best friend was African-American, and she enjoyed how black men treated her, showing her more respect than anyone else in her school. Her one fling with an older white man, just a few years removed from graduation, ended bitterly for her. He constantly thought she looked at other men while she thought he was overbearing, wanting too much out of their relationship.

The past two months she had dated Trent, a high school jock, recruited by several colleges for basketball, and a few more for track and field. Like Jamie, he was studious, and worked a job to pay for his car and save for college. More so than most black teenagers she dated, Trent was a complete package, and ready for the real world. Her previous boyfriends simply fantasized about taking hold of her posterior for the evening until they accomplished their goal.

Her past relationships had been shallow. Boys seemed to want her for her car, for sex, or for cheap advancement in school studies. Trent seemed different, but she would never put herself in a position to be vulnerable, or hurt, if the relationship ended.

For the first time in her life, despite some open criticism from friends and family, Jamie felt truly happy. As she listened to the cordless phone's receiver after dialing her boyfriend's number, Jamie walked onto the porch. Cold wood touched her feet, reminding her of how cold the fall evenings grew after dark.

The porch wrapped around the front and one side of the house, but before she strolled too far Jamie took notice of the jack-o-lantern at her feet, a candle flickering within its toothy frame. She pulled the top off, now scorched from the flame, and blew out the candle, letting the wax drip down its side as it cooled. While she knelt, a shadow blocked the light coming from the open door for a second, but when she looked, she saw nothing. Jamie figured the kids were downstairs to beg for a snack.

"Hello?" a voice finally answered as she stepped inside, closing the door and locking it.

"Hey, baby," she replied, turning to make some popcorn. She planned on watching a few horror movies before the Clouse family came home.

"What are you doing?"

"I'm getting ready to put the kids to bed."

"Can you put me to bed later?"

Jamie's devotion to keeping her virginity bothered most of her boyfriends, but Trent seemed a bit more understanding.

And patient.

He still kidded her sometimes, but never put pressure on her when it came to sex.

She considered herself worth waiting for, and no one could tell her otherwise. Though it seemed to be the cause of most of her relationship breakdowns, Jamie kept waiting, knowing the right man would someday walk into her life.

"I think you've had enough fun for the night. How was Renita's Halloween party?" Jamie asked, pulling the sleeves of her sweater up now that she was adapted to the warmth of the house.

"Terrible. It was the largest collection of pointless party games I've ever seen."

"Well, we got candy, and some rotten eggs thrown at us. I can't believe people our age have no consideration for little kids."

Trent laughed.

"I bet you weren't so defensive before you became that family's nanny."

"I'm just a babysitter. I do *not* clean house or do windows."

"Sure, Jamie. Whatever you say."

Jamie listened to his tale about the party while she put some popcorn in the microwave. After that, she walked over to the movie selection atop the television, choosing between them.

"I know you love scary movies," Trent said, as though reading her mind. "What are you watching tonight?"

"I've got *Halloween*, or some B-movie I picked out."

"Man, you know, black people always die in those movies."

"Is it a Hollywood tradition or a stereotype no writer wants to break?"

"It could be a subtle form of racism. You ever notice the brothers always get the worst treatment in those films? White people get to run around and check out strange noises while black people are getting hacked up behind their houses. You'd *never* see a black man follow bloody footprints back into the house."

Jamie giggled, taking the unknown movie from its case. She popped it in the player, noticing the security light outside activate. Extremely sensitive, the light could be triggered by one of the dogs getting loose, or a branch blown by the wind. She walked over to the front door unlocking it as she heard the kids come downstairs.

"Jamie, can we watch a movie with you?" she heard Katie ask from the bottom step, Zach beside her.

"No," she called back, cupping the phone. "Go upstairs, guys. I'll be there in a minute."

"Everything okay?" Trent asked across the line.

"I think so," she replied, stepping onto the porch, looking around the yard. Nothing seemed out of place.

Occasionally after the kids were in bed she would allow whomever she dated at the time to come over for a minute. It mildly violated her employer's trust, but she never let anything immoral happen. She just hated being alone for too long.

A flickering light at her feet caught her attention. Jamie knelt beside the jack-o-lantern, noticing the candle inside had been lit a second time. Positive the candle was incapable of reigniting itself, she nervously looked around the yard, seeing no one. All the dogs seemed to be chained up in the backyard, most of them lying beside their protective houses.

"What's up, baby?" Trent asked.

"I think someone's trying to-"

Jamie never finished her sentence before the line went dead.

"Hello? Hello?" she asked frantically, trying to get the phone to show signs of life. "Oh, God," she said, blowing out the candle again, running inside the house for cover.

Someone had cut the phone line and toyed with the jack-o-lantern. Perhaps this was a huge joke, but in the middle of nowhere, and with two kids to think of, Jamie took no chances as she locked the door, setting the alarm system immediately after. She threw the phone to the empty couch, ready to check on the kids when the video playing in the machine caught her attention.

Instead of some straight-to-video release like she expected, the television showed scenes of her own life, particularly a distanced view of her and the kids out trick-or-treating earlier that night. Horrified, she knew of only one way the tapes might have been switched.

Someone was already inside the house.

Suddenly the rumors she remembered hearing about the Clouse family's torment, Zach's mother murdered inside her own house, and the stalker who dressed like the grim reaper in honor of a priest who allegedly burned himself alive all came to her. It wasn't until a dark figure emerged from the dimmed light of the kitchen, however, that she felt certain her life was in mortal danger.

Letting a shriek emerge from the depths of her throat, Jamie looked for something to protect herself with, or an object to hide behind as the dark figure stepped forward, revealing no face. Instead, a black robe concealed his identity, and a drooping mask covered any facial features.

Indeed, he was the grim reaper, and he held a small, modified version of a scythe across the front of his body.

"Oh, God," Jamie gasped, seeing nothing of use to her in the living room. Every piece of furniture hugged a wall, no knives or weapons were around, and the kids were at the bottom of the stairs, blocking her only good escape route. "Run!" she screamed at them, not wanting to follow them for fear she might put them in danger.

Scared for their lives after seeing the dark figure, they quickly obeyed, dashing up the stairs like squirrels up a tree.

In the meantime, Jamie waited for the stalker to draw closer before dodging her way around him, running for the kitchen. There, she flipped on the light, grabbing a frying pan from the stove, whacking her pursuer upside the head as he entered the room, sending him into a heap atop the floor. Jamie pulled a knife from a nearby drawer, shrinking away from the motionless body atop the linoleum tile.

Breathing heavily, and sobbing to herself, she observed the figure and his black military style boots. Whoever he was, this was no joke, and she had no idea what to do next.

Without warning, the attacker sprang up, ready to chase her around the cooking island centered in the kitchen. She faked one direction, quickly choosing the other, thinking she could make a clean getaway. He dove at her, clasping her ankle in one hand as both fell to the floor.

Tripped up, Jamie quickly swung the knife in his direction, forcing the release of her leg before the knife met her attacker's flesh. She stood, but accidentally dropped the knife, which he picked up in his pursuit. Seeing the side door through the living room as her only means of escape, Jamie crossed the living room with her athletic speed. Still, the killer caught her as she pulled the door open a crack, ramming the knife through her backside, cutting one lung and tearing through her chest.

She gasped several breaths, looking down at her chest, spying the edge of the blade, stained with dripping crimson from her insides.

Her body landed in a heap along the plush carpet, but he wasn't done yet. Taking her by the sweater, he picked her body upright, surprised when she turned on him, using her last bit of life to kick him in the groin in an attempt to throw him away from her.

He evaded her attack easily, despite the feeling a sledgehammer had connected below his waist, punching her across the face before hurling her through the side window of the house. Shards of glass entered her soft insides, coming out the backside covered with blood, allowing streaks of the red substance to flow down the eggshell walls. After admiring his work a moment, the killer took up the scythe, heading in the direction of the stairs when the home security alarm began blaring, catching his attention. He stared at the box, unable to recall the code she typed in, leaving him precious few minutes to escape.

Jamie's dying act of opening the door broke one of the magnetic seals that set off the alarm within thirty seconds if the code was not entered. The killer failed to hear the beeps indicating the alarm was armed, and now had to choose between pursuing the children or escaping before the police arrived.

Looking at the door, then to the stairs, he made his choice. Scythe in tow, he darted upstairs in hopes of more fun.

Chapter 2

Tim Niemeyer stood at the ATM, waiting patiently for his money to emerge. As usual, the machine ran slow because of the online connection to the bank's main branch. While he waited, Tim spied a dark figure approaching a few feet behind him. With little light from the machine or the building, he could not make out any features on the person.

"I'll be just a second," he informed the stranger.

While the machine spit out his money, then took its time processing the receipt, another figure emerged to his left, opposite the other. Niemeyer quickly peeked at the other stranger, wondering why the ATM suddenly seemed so popular.

Even the headlights from his truck did not help distinguish who the people were because they stood off to the side, covered in shadows. He grunted to himself, hoping the machine would hurry and let him be on his way.

"Takes forever," he commented to no one in particular, glancing to see another figure, then another come up from behind him, away from the light. A breeze blew some leaves past his feet, as it penetrated his jacket between the buttons.

Significantly more nervous, Tim snatched his money from the machine, suspecting he was about to play victim to a mugging, or perhaps some Halloween joke. A gleam of light from his truck headlights illuminated one side, allowing him a decent look at one of the figures.

Dressed completely in black, and with his head partly concealed by a hood left down around the neck area, the man wore some sort of strange cross around his neck, as though part of some bizarre religious cult. A robe draped around his feet, which barely protruded, but appeared to be covered by plain sandals.

Still, he saw the man's face. If Tim's hunch played true, the only reason a person might let himself be revealed is, if he didn't care who saw him, or he planned to kill the observer to destroy any chance of him being revealed. No security camera was visible at the ATM, but that didn't mean there wasn't one. Regardless, identifying the man positively wouldn't help him at that moment. Besides, who would possibly be monitoring, or ever see, a camera at an isolated machine, he pondered. The tape probably rolled over anyhow, never used or recovered unless a crime was reported.

His nervousness intensified as all of the possibilities ran through his head.

When a sixth figure appeared behind him, the group moved forward, much to the shock of Randy, who had watched this odd encounter take place from inside the truck, as though it was a drive-in movie. The momentary thought of his brother playing a Halloween trick on him crossed his mind, but Tim wasn't much of a prankster and enlisting the assistance of six people seemed farfetched. Randy reached behind the seat for Tim's shotgun, too late to prevent what his older brother was about to endure.

As Tim took his card and statement from the machine, he felt a sharp pain in his kidney area where a dagger pierced his jacket.

Time seemed to freeze as he realized he was surrounded by six creepy, dark figures. All were standing around him with blades in their hands, too far away for him to take a swing at any of them. Spying blood on the dagger of his attacker, he threw a punch anyway, missing wildly.

He cried in pain as another dagger entered his side, then more blades pierced what little protection his jacket offered. He whirled in agony, feeling blood ooze from each wound as more were inflicted. Whenever he tried to fight off an attacker, he found himself jabbed from a different direction.

All six took turns stabbing him repeatedly.

A jab to the kidneys.

A stab to his side.

A blade rammed into his stomach.

Blood smeared the outside lining of his jacket, refusing to soak in. His skin ripped apart with each blade's entrance, leaving less and less hope of his survival. His body jolted painfully with each wound as though a surge of electricity shot through it.

While Randy's fingers found the metal of the shotgun in the extended cab, he saw Tim's face as his brother slumped against the front of his own truck, staring at Randy without a distinctive emotion, blood smeared everywhere across his face and clothes. Tim's shocked expression did not emanate from being ambushed, or even that he was stabbed repeatedly after a miraculous survival from a horrific incident the year before.

It came from the knowledge that he was about to die.

"Jesus!" Randy gasped as he saw his brother's right hand extended as though trying to escape or claw for help.

Tim spit up some blood on the hood of his truck as his face froze into a perplexed stare, his blue eyes dulling to a cloudy gray that Randy recognized as a death trance. Leaving a bloody trail in its wake, Tim's body slid toward the ground, disappearing beyond the hood with a thump.

All six pairs of eyes turned on Randy as he grasped the shotgun. Their hostile intent now peered in his direction like hawks eyeing their prey, and he prayed his brother's shotgun was loaded as usual. He pulled it up to him, taking aim at one of the conspirators.

***

An uproar emitted from the basketball home crowd surrounding Paul and Jane Clouse as they sat in the middle section of bleachers. They watched her nephew on the Bloomington North High School squad assist his team in their lead of a rival Martinsville team.

As the third quarter played out, and the home team retained a significant lead, Clouse looked around, trying to see if anyone he knew might be in the crowd. A packed gymnasium left him surrounded by a sea of faces, unable to distinguish one from another beyond a certain distance.

Not much for the holiday, or even the season, he preferred to accompany his new wife to her nephew's first exhibition home game, rather than be out among the festivities. After all, his first wife, and several of his friends had been murdered the last two Halloween seasons, leaving him wary of the holiday, if not extremely concerned.

"Getting bored?" Jane asked him, noticing his distant looks. To him, she was the perfect wife. Pretty, attentive, and as intelligent as they came.

As a medical doctor she needed the intelligence, while some of her other qualities sometimes acted as hindrances in her field.

"Just seeing if anyone I know might be here," he replied, rubbing the new gold band on his left hand. "We don't get out much anymore."

After receiving a significant inheritance of undisclosed millions, some of which was still tied up in court, Clouse's life changed. Assured he had enough money to last the rest of his life, he quit his job at the Bloomington Fire Department and devoted himself full-time to his family and his few remaining friends.

Working for the city provided benefits and insurance, but he now had enough money to pay for any operation or medication he or his family ever needed. He had tried to work for the fire department a few months after the inheritance was settled in court, but when the tones sounded, it became more of a burden than a calling. When that happened, he knew it was time to quit. Clouse always figured when he lost the desire to do the job he loved, it would be time to get out.

"Want to get some popcorn or a hotdog?" Jane asked.

"I might in a minute."

"Jeremy is doing great tonight," she said of her nephew, who already had several of the team's points and a few rebounds.

"He is," Clouse said, somewhat mentally distanced from the game. "You suppose the kids are okay?" he asked out of nowhere.

Jane put her arm around her husband, pulling him close. She whispered in his ear.

"Quit worrying. Jamie is going to take great care of the kids tonight."

"I can't help it," he replied. "I can't help thinking Ryan Andrews is somewhere out there, waiting for us to let our guard down."

Before replying, Jane made certain to keep her words between just them.

"His picture has been plastered on every major television station there is, Paul. We've gone a year without anyone seeing or hearing from him. No one can lay low for an entire year. He has to be dead. Very few people survive bullet wounds to the abdomen from such close range without medical assistance."

Clouse relied on his wife's expertise often, but he tended to remain cautious when it came to the maniac who nearly killed him the previous year.

"Then where's the body?" Clouse asked under his breath.

His mind flashed to the horrific images of Andrews' partner, Joan Landamere, holding his son hostage the year before, on Halloween to be exact, threatening to slit Zach's throat if the father attempted to save him.

She died, the memory didn't.

Typical of his attire, Clouse wore brown cowboy boots, jeans, and a new chocolate brown leather jacket over one of his old fire department sweatshirts. He left the department on good terms, kept friendships, and used some of his newfound wealth to help his old comrades by getting them safer equipment and additional supplies above and beyond what the city provided.

Most people never recognized Clouse in public because he kept his good fortune and his name out of public view. He still wore his brown hair in a disheveled part, maintained a thick mustache of the same color, and worked around his farm enough that he kept in excellent physical shape. Nothing about his appearance had changed, but enough tragedy in his life kept him living in farm country, away from the city, away from people, and hopefully, away from more deaths. People would never see his blue eyes, or any of his other features, in the local paper.

"Should I call the house?" he asked, looking down to his cellular phone.

"No," Jane said vehemently. "The kids are fine. Just enjoy the game, Paul."

Clouse watched the game momentarily before his eyes wandered again. By chance, he spied his friend, Mark Daniels, a city police officer, walking along the opposite gym wall. Dressed in Bloomington's light blue work blouse and dark blue pants, he stood out as he approached another officer, shaking hands briefly before the other officer walked out where Daniels had come in.

Feeling certain he would have noticed his friend earlier, Clouse wondered where Daniels had been standing the entire game. It had been almost a month since the two talked, so he decided it might be time to get the snacks his wife referred to.

"Want anything from the concession stand?" he asked.

"Sure. Some popcorn please," Jane replied, barely taking her eyes off the game.

While the two friends were both fairly tall, with equally strong builds, their similarities ended there. Clouse had always been geared toward leadership and success, not afraid to talk his way in or out of situations. As a firefighter, he had always been aggressive, ready to finish the job quickly and properly, no matter what task lie ahead.

Daniels had to be the most laid back man Clouse had ever met, especially in his line of work. Usually quiet and mild-mannered, he seemed to mentally size up everything before speaking. He had the unfortunate distinction of being the only person to survive both of the last two years of horror with Clouse. Bad luck seemed to be one of the officer's closest companions at times.

Carefully skirting along the hallway behind the bleachers, trying not to bump other paying customers, Clouse edged his way toward the section of the gym where his friend had taken a post. From the door leading to the narrow side of the gym, where the home team's backboard currently resided, he could see Daniels, back against the wall, hands cupped behind him. The officer viewed everything from the game to the spectators, though he seemed assured nothing bad would happen during an exhibition game, even if the teams were rivals.

Clouse observed the nine-millimeter pistol holstered at his friend's side as he approached. It seemed odd to see him in uniform since Daniels had been a detective when they first met, and most of the time since. Daniels possessed less hair than himself, partly from recession, aided by a bald spot growing in diameter a little more each year. A dirty-blond color, it rested in a careful part atop his head. Daniels was clean-shaven, with a look of serious nature that was his trademark scrawled across his face.

"What's new?" Clouse asked, appearing to catch his friend by surprise.

"Hey, Paul," was the reply with a quick smile and an extended hand. "God, I haven't seen you much since the wedding. You still living in seclusion?"

"Pretty much. Jane wanted to see her nephew play tonight in the home opener so we let the babysitter have the kids."

Daniels gave an uncertain look.

"Is that wise, considering what tonight is?"

"You're here," Clouse pointed out, realizing neither of them was home to guard their children from a scythe-wielding nutcase.

"Yeah, but I'm confident Ryan Andrews is dead and gone."

"I suppose I am too," Clouse said, staring blankly toward the game momentarily.

"The way you shot him in the gut and he took off, no one could have survived unless they got to a hospital."

"You sound like Jane."

And Andrews was never reported from any hospitals or clinics after a police bulletin was issued. In fact, he was never reported anywhere, at any given time. It seemed as though the earth had swallowed him whole during his escape.

"So what are you up to these days?" Clouse inquired.

"I'm back in the detective division," Daniels said with an air of unusually profound happiness. "The guy they replaced me with got suspended without pay after he mishandled a case file. He'll probably be fired at the next Public Safety Committee meeting."

"What are you doing here tonight?"

"Easy overtime, my friend. I'm off every Saturday and Sunday now, so I can pick up extra hours."

Both watched the game a moment, seeing little of consequence unfold. The third quarter drew to a close, assuring Daniels a mob of people would head for the restrooms and concession stands. He wanted to beat the crowd out of the gym.

"Let's go outside for a few," he told Clouse.

Once they exited a side door, Daniels fished a cigarette out of his breast pocket, lighting it within a few seconds.

"I thought you quit."

"Hanging around you drove me back to it. I get jittery dealing with all your problems."

"Don't hang your excuses on me," Clouse replied with half a grin. "I think you just lack willpower."

"That, and my rehab's over."

Daniels spoke of rehabilitation to walk again after being shot in the back two years earlier. During his stint in a wheelchair, he fought any number of demons.

Daniels had been a groomsman in Clouse's recent wedding in Tennessee, soon after he started back with the Bloomington Police Department. Though typically quiet and introverted, Daniels would open up and talk around Clouse. The two had a friendship, even a strange bond, that linked them after nearly being killed simultaneously twice. At one time they had joked about who had the easier city job. Now, like Clouse, the detective had taken more time than ever to spend with his family and assure them he would always be there for them.

"What do you and Jane have planned?"

"Nothing concrete. I'm still getting used to this money thing."

"Did they finally settle?"

Clouse sighed.

"I got about half the money and all of the property. There's a lot to deal with owning a theme park, a hotel, and some other notables."

Daniels took a drag off the cigarette, looking skyward as he exhaled toward the stars. Though clear, the night brought a crisp air and stark breeze with it.

"I heard you bought the Landamere estate at auction. You don't seriously plan on living there, do you?"

"Not at all. I plan on searching everything they owned for any clues about last year. I want to know everything I can, Mark, so we don't have to live through that shit again."

"You're beating a dead horse, Paul. You've got to let go."

Clouse shook his head defiantly.

"No, not if I can keep our families safe. I realize the only thing you want to do is put it all behind us and pretend it's over, and hope Ryan Andrews is lying in a ditch dead somewhere, but the truth is, we don't know, Mark. That kinda scares me. Almost every night I wake up in a cold sweat after a nightmare about my brother-in-law or the Landameres trying to kill me."

"I do want it behind me," Daniels said, finishing his smoke, flicking the butt toward the side of the building. "You can't live the rest of your life in fear or you won't have a life at all. Hell, I guess you could move about anywhere you wanted to, Paul."

"I could, but my family is here, and everything I care about is here. And if someone wants to get to me, they'll find me no matter where I go."

Daniels led the way back to the high school's side entrance; glad to see the chunk of wood he left to keep the door slightly ajar remained in place.

"If I can get through tomorrow night without any problems I'll feel a lot better," Clouse confessed. "Maybe then I'll be able to put some of it behind me."

"You can't protect everyone in your life, Paul. There is a limit to how much you can extend yourself. And if someone wants to come after us, you're right, all those millions you just inherited won't help us," Daniels said as he opened the door for his friend, letting the sounds of the cheering fans escape the building.

Clouse swallowed hard, knowing his friend was correct. He kept telling himself making it through the official Halloween would make everything a bit easier.

If only he could be so lucky.

Chapter 3

Half an hour later Clouse pulled into his driveway, seeing the house in a completely different light than when he had left it.

A lake of red and blue lights swirled in his yard beside the house as police officers came and went from the front door. He recognized the tan and brown cars as those from the Monroe County Sheriff's Department since he escaped city jurisdiction by over a mile.

Clouse parked the truck a distance away from the house, finding himself greeted by a county deputy immediately upon stepping from his pickup. A shorter, stocky man, the long-sleeve shirt recently donned by the deputies seemed to cover most of the abundant hair on his arms. His face appeared serious and gruff, and his attitude read pretty much the same almost immediately.

"You the owner?" he asked Clouse.

"Yeah. What's going on?" he asked, trying to push past the deputy, concerned about the welfare of the kids.

"Hold on, sir," the deputy said, putting a thick, foreboding arm between Clouse and his home as Jane took his side.

"Are the kids okay?" she asked.

"We think so."

"*Think* so?" Clouse demanded, trying to push forward again.

Again, he was held back.

He could see an officer dressed in plain clothes emerge from the house. He recognized Troy Tackett, his neighbor who owned horses, broke in young steeds, and occasionally visited on horseback. Usually Tackett would come over to say hello or ask if any of their family wanted to go horseback riding on the seemingly endless acreage around their properties.

Often his boots were covered in a layer of dirt or manure. Around his farm, Tackett's blue jeans were always worn and faded, and his black cowboy hat was often speckled with dust. His chest and arms were solid from so much work around his farm, and he was as nice a person as Clouse had ever met, despite the grim nature of his profession.

But Clouse was uncertain of his neighbor's capacity tonight. A detective with Monroe County, Tackett had earned his position prior to joining the county force as an officer in another town. Clouse stared a moment as Tackett spoke with a uniformed officer, then stepped down from the porch.

Tonight Tackett wore black cowboy boots with a glossy shine, dress pants and shirt, and a suitable tie. He bore the look of a detective, including a shoulder holster nestled beneath his armpits, which offered protection from the criminal who might have still been on the premises. Clouse might ordinarily have thought it odd that the detective could get himself dressed so quickly, but his mind was on only one thing.

"Hello, Paul," Tackett said, offering his hand as the patrolman moved aside.

"What's going on, Troy?" Clouse asked, shaking it absently. Jane remained beside him, listening intently.

"We found a teenage girl inside, stabbed to death."

"Jamie?"

"Is she a relative?"

"No, our babysitter," Clouse replied, thinking how bad the situation might be. "The Vosburghs live just down the road."

Tackett's face registered the name, but he wasn't entirely familiar with most of his other neighbors.

"So the kids were home?" he asked, sticking to the business at hand.

Clouse nodded slowly.

A bit shorter than Clouse, Tackett appeared more like the typical shop teacher who coached football, except for the thick handlebar mustache reaching beneath his lips in traditional fashion of the cowboy. His dark hair usually remained buzzed longer than military standard and he wore his emotions on his sleeve, never hiding how he felt. Tackett enjoyed being a detective because it allowed him to be himself and steer away from dress code a bit.

"There was no sign of the kids?" Clouse inquired.

"Follow me," the investigator instructed Clouse after a puzzled look. "Tom, can you speak to Mrs. Clouse for me?" he asked the patrolman, who nodded in response. Despite Jane's initial objection, she remained behind.

Tackett plowed the way through a sea of officers and EMS personnel into the house, which appeared undisturbed through the doorway, up to the living room area.

"Oh my God," Clouse said, seeing the lifeless body of Jamie Vosburgh draped over his broken window. Blood streaked down the wall, pooling along the floor where a technician examined it, taking swabs and placing them into carefully marked bags.

He felt completely numb.

A patrolman took photos of the body, flooding the corpse with an intense splash of white light from the flash every few seconds. It stunned Clouse to think the girl he entrusted to watch his children, the *only* person he entrusted, was so brutally murdered. His fears of the Halloween holiday were realized, and he wondered what other damage he might discover.

"Come on," Tackett said, leading Clouse up his own stairwell.

"Are the kids okay?" he asked, hesitant to follow if they weren't.

"We can't tell," Tackett replied. "We got a 911 call out here after your security provider couldn't reach anyone. An officer found the body from the outside, got the code, and shut off your alarm system. We haven't actually seen the kids because we think they barricaded themselves in your attic," the detective added, stopping atop the stairs to peer toward a door riddled with holes.

"Shit," Clouse muttered.

A barrage of vertical cuts littered the surface of the white door, leading to his walk-in closet. They did not appear like any bullet holes Clouse recalled ever seeing, but rather jagged, splintered holes created by stabs with a sharp object, probably terrifying any unfortunate children trapped inside.

He pushed the door, but it was somehow barricaded from within.

"We didn't have any luck with it either," Tackett said.

Clouse nodded.

"Zach?" he asked with a slow, uncertain voice.

Several seconds passed with no sound before he heard a thump from within, as though someone bumped one of the stored boxes, or tripped over something.

"Katie?" he called, louder this time. "If you're there kids, open the door. It's safe, I promise."

Half a minute passed before he heard anything more than hushed whispers. Finally something behind the door slid noisily along the floor, and the knob on the door pulled inward, revealing the dark, windowless room behind the attic's two occupants.

Simultaneously the heads of both his son and stepdaughter appeared at the door. Both he and Tackett breathed a sigh of relief, seeing the children were unharmed, despite the obvious attempts by the murderer to get to them. They ran into Clouse's arms for an embrace as he shot Tackett a somewhat despondent look.

***

Among the beehive at the crime scene with officers and several men in plain clothes scurrying around, a distraught man sat on a curb alone, taking in the view of two blankets, each stained with blood, not far from him. A thick hand draped against the ground from beneath one covering, the wedding band around one finger reminding Randy Niemeyer of how many people his brother touched in life.

Tim Niemeyer had been proclaimed dead immediately by the Lawrence County coroner, and Randy could rest assured at least one of the killers lay dead close by. Strangely, several officers seemed to recognize the killer Randy had shot with his brother's weapon, but no one had taken time to interview him yet, or reveal the dead man's identity.

Immediately after Randy shot the man, the other conspirators scattered, running in every direction once Randy stepped from the truck. He remembered kicking the shot murderer to see if he was indeed dead. Verifying he was, Randy checked on his brother's condition, disappointed and heartbroken, but not shocked by what he found.

Lying face-up, eyes wide open, Tim had died when he slumped against the truck. Randy noticed a small pool of blood spreading beneath his brother. At that point Randy looked for the closest payphone, seeing a phone booth near the store, half a block down. He dialed 911 a moment later.

Randy had related his story to the first Bedford police officer on the scene, and now spied the man talking to a detective, who walked toward him after the conversation ended.

Both turned to look at the young man who aspired to be like them in some sense when he finished his education. Unlike his older brother, the younger Niemeyer looked like a police officer, or military man, especially since he spent several weekends a year in the National Guard. Very rigid in his walk and mannerism, he had lost more hair than his brother, keeping his fringe shaved nearly to the scalp at all times. He enjoyed challenges, even in trying to beat nature to taking his hair.

A reddish-brown goatee, trimmed just a bit longer than his other hair, and of the same shade, encircled his lips. Unlike the concerned, soft eyes of his brother, a devoted family man, Niemeyer did not smile easily, nor did the steely glint of his blue eyes often leave. He sometimes stared holes through some of the toughest people in his weekend regiment, but he could also lighten his expression at the drop of a hat when his children came for visits.

"You the younger brother?" the detective asked upon reaching Niemeyer. He looked like someone who had already experienced a full evening.

"Yeah."

"Detective Harold Unger, Bedford Police," the man introduced himself, his clothes looking as though he had run in them all evening. "You say six people came up behind your brother and every one of them helped in stabbing him?"

Niemeyer nodded.

"What happened then?" Unger asked, sitting on the curb beside him, pulling a notebook and pen from his shirt pocket. The lack of a sport coat showed off the wrinkles of his shirt enough that people might mistake him for a vagrant if not for the badge clipped to his belt.

"I reached for Tim's shotgun behind my seat, stepped from the truck, and fired at one of the motherfuckers."

"Are you aware of who you shot?"

"No," Niemeyer answered with a puzzled look. "Should I be?"

"The man you shot is none other than Ted Lovett, the owner of Lovett Realty."

"The real estate guy?"

Unger nodded an affirmative.

Lovett's for sale signs were in front of nearly every local house on the market. He and his wife constantly appeared in home-finder magazines, and the man must have amassed a small fortune from all of his business. Niemeyer wondered how or why the man would possibly be involved with his brother's death. The desire to contemplate any truth was drowned by his desire to leave the scene and be with his family after witnessing such a tragedy.

"Can you think of any reason anyone would want your brother dead?" the detective chimed in, breaking his thoughts like a raindrop dispersing a puddle's surface.

"No. Tim didn't have any enemies, unless you count last year."

"Last year?" the detective asked, genuinely stunned.

"He was involved with that whole mess at West Baden Springs when Ryan Andrews nearly killed him and a few other people."

Unger nodded. He probably recalled reading about it in every local paper he picked up the past year.

"Andrews was never found," Niemeyer added, mirroring the detective's thoughts.

"So you think he could have been involved with this?"

"Hard telling," Niemeyer replied, tired of questions. He tried to rub the ache from his head. "You should probably ask Paul Clouse or his wife about that. They were there too."

Unger jotted down the names. He would pursue every avenue possible, and possibly team with Bloomington police who were involved the year before. From his shirt pocket, he fished out a photograph safely sealed within a plastic bag. He handed it to Niemeyer.

"We found this tucked inside your brother's jacket. We think it was placed there by the killers, because there were no holes in it and no blood stains. Any idea when it was taken?"

Niemeyer examined the photo a moment, seeing it was of his older brother dressed in a full suit, walking amongst other people dressed in similar fashion. It would not be church because they never dressed that formally, except for holidays, and Tim had never been one to wear a suit for anything except funerals and weddings.

"I think it might be Ken Kaiser's funeral," he finally answered after some thought.

"How can you tell?"

"This photo is recent, after Tim starting hitting the weights and putting on a few pounds," Niemeyer explained. "And last year Tim had a mustache," he said, pointing the fact out in the photo. "He shaved it off earlier this year."

"Was Ken Kaiser the county officer killed last year?"

"Yeah. He and Tim went to high school together."

Unger had another new avenue to check.

"Have you ever seen anything like it?" Randy asked almost blankly, hoping deep down for some kind of reassurance this detective was worth his pay.

"Never in twelve years," Unger confessed. "I've seen animal mutilations and murdered kids, but I've never seen six people team up to kill another human being before. I'm very sorry for your loss if I didn't already say it. I know it's not going to be easy, but I need you to stick with me on this."

"Okay," Randy promised.

Unger looked to the pad he held in his right hand, then back to his interviewee with concerned eyes.

"Was it habit for you and your brother to go out on Saturday nights?" he asked, beginning to conjure up every important question he could think to ask.

"Yeah, pretty much."

"Where did you usually eat?"

"We ate at a lot of different places. Every week one of us would pick something new."

"And was it your brother's habit to stop here at the ATM?"

Niemeyer thought a moment.

"Yes. Tim had something against carrying a lot of cash, yet he liked to pay cash when we ate out."

Unger was about to fire another question when a uniformed officer approached him, hunched over, and whispered something in his ear.

"Excuse me a moment," Unger said, standing to follow the officer a few feet away.

Niemeyer overheard the detective say something to the officer about it being impossible, but could not determine what. When Unger pointed, Niemeyer followed the direction of the detective's finger to a camera, barely visible unless searched for.

"How could the fucking tape be missing?" he understood the man say through both lip reading and broken bits of sound.

"Oh, shit," Niemeyer said to himself, knowing without any witnesses, or any tape to back up his story, his account of what happened sounded farfetched. A feeling of dread loomed over him like a cloud as he dropped his head, staring at the cracked pavement beside his feet.

***

Clouse watched as Tackett finished interviewing the children from across the room. He knew from seeing the detective with his own daughter that he would treat them well. Occasionally he drew a smile from one or both kids, and he managed to calm their fears while eliciting useful answers from them. His holster and badge sat hidden behind him, to further ease the children into believing he was there for their safety.

Never had Clouse seen an interview so tactfully done as this one. He had friends in police work, but usually they charged into things with a brazen, even careless nature at times. He never recalled seeing Tackett visibly upset, on or off the job. The man kept his emotions in check, carried himself professionally, and never took sides, even in debates between his friends. Some people wrote him off as a glorified hick doing police work, but Tackett's devotion to his job and every person he knew carried him far beyond that stereotype.

Whether he talked to children or adults, the detective always seemed to speak in a controlled, steady voice. He sounded like grandparents do when they give their grandchildren the "Now you know what you did was wrong" speech. Tackett sounded nothing like he looked. There was no southern accent or drawl, and he spoke proper English better than any of his colleagues on the county police force.

A few details had emerged in the past hour since Clouse arrived home. He knew about the tape in the machine, watching it over the shoulder of an unknowing officer before it was ejected and placed in an evidence bag.

He had witnessed Jamie's body being placed inside a body bag and carted out through his living room after all forensic analysis was complete. He felt terrible for Jamie, and her parents, as though he had somehow betrayed them, or at the very least misled them by not disclosing the full details of his past.

How could Clouse have known the murders would continue?

Was he wrong for trying to start anew a second time?

Carefully impaled on a shard of glass beside Jamie's body was a picture of her and the children at the state fair a few months prior. Clouse had already identified it for police after some deliberation about exactly where and when it was taken. Both he and Jane were questioned separately while the children were left to Tackett, their testimony the most delicate, and important.

"Were they any help?" Clouse asked the detective a few minutes later as Tackett returned to him, replacing his badge and holster.

"They were," he acknowledged. "And it seems from the description that you may have a return from last year's killer. They said the man was dressed in black from head to toe, and there was no visible face."

Clouse closed his eyes sadly and sighed, feeling his nightmare would never end.

"Not to fear," Tackett added. "I've got some good leads to start with. The killer left that picture of her, and more importantly, that videotape. I want you and your wife to sit down with me and identify some of the people handing out candy on there. Maybe, just maybe, they saw something strange, or might have seen who was holding the video camera."

"If we could be so lucky," Clouse said with a hint of pessimism.

"Where are you staying tonight?" the detective asked with concern.

"Probably a hotel, Troy," Clouse said, making sure no one was around when he used the man's first name. He felt comfortable with his own neighbor investigating the case, but wanted to make certain Tackett's fellow officers didn't notice.

Historically, officers investigating anything to do with West Baden or Paul Clouse had a tendency to wind up dead or severely injured. Clouse would do everything possible to make certain Tackett avoided such a fate.

"You're more than welcome to spend the night at my ranch," Tackett said. "I've got all sorts of spare bedrooms."

"I appreciate it, but I don't want to put you out."

"It's no trouble," Tackett insisted.

"I don't want to get you in any trouble," Clouse said, trying to put it another way.

Tackett chuckled mischievously.

"I'm the only investigator my department has. They're not going to replace me."

"I know, but getting involved with this makes you a target, Troy. The last thing I want to see is for you to get hurt."

Shrugging, the detective gave up.

"That's fine, but I want to talk with you about this hotel of yours, and what happened there last year. Tomorrow."

"Okay," Clouse agreed, weary of such interviews over the past few Halloween seasons.

Tackett handed him a card with the county police address and phone number on it. He took it back a moment to write his home phone number and pager number on the back in case Clouse had misplaced either.

"I'll be at home most of tomorrow," Tackett said. "I'm wanting to come back here and mop up any details when there's better light. Call me and we'll do lunch."

"You better plan on going buffet with everything I could tell you," Clouse said, hating the idea of recalling every miserable detail of the past two years.

Tackett took somewhat of a defensive stance.

"You know, we've been neighbors now for almost a year and you haven't mentioned one word about any of this to me. It always helps to tell somebody."

Clouse grinned, sensing distrust from his neighbor.

"It's not easy to talk about," he admitted. "I trust you enough to tell you everything, but you're getting yourself into one hell of a roller coaster ride, Troy, and this will be your last chance to get off."

"I'll take my chances."

A disturbance from outside cut their conversation short as Jane shuttled the kids into the living room near her husband and Tackett. Clouse followed the detective to the front door where the Vosburghs were visibly upset after seeing the ambulance leave with a body bag. Their concern about so many police cars in the neighboring yard became heightened when they discovered through some leak that their daughter was lying inside the concealing black bag.

"There's the reason our daughter is dead!" Tina Vosburgh shouted, pointing at Clouse as he stood in the doorway, almost defensively behind Tackett. "We should have listened to the rumors about that bastard and never let our daughter near him!"

Clouse shrunk back into the house, listening to the fading voices outside trying to calm the family down. He slumped into a kitchen chair, wishing it all could be over, or that he had moved far enough away to avoid being stalked by the killer ghosts of his past.

Even worse, whoever killed Jamie had planned to for some time. The photograph beside her body was two months old, and someone had probably waited since the past Halloween to enact revenge on this particular night. Clouse prayed it would end before he lost more friends and loved ones to this new homicidal maniac.

Chapter 4

Clouse awoke the next morning, stiff as a board, when his pager beside the bed vibrated enough to fall from the nightstand to his pillow, nearly hitting him in the face. He looked at the number a moment before rolling over to see Jane still asleep in the accommodating motel bed.

He yawned, carefully sitting up.

It was Sunday, officially Halloween, and he had any number of problems to solve, including hiring some cleaners to have the house done by the end of the day. He figured if he flashed enough green paper, he might have new living room carpet and a new window installed by nightfall.

Clouse wanted the memories of his dead neighbor out of his mind. Knowing that was impossible, he figured the next logical step was to remove any reminders of her gruesome death in his own house. Thoughts of installing a panic room also crossed his mind, but he wasn't sure what his residential plans included long-term.

After he called the number on his pager, he would phone some installers to see what kind of motivation they needed to work on a weekend. No matter what, it would get done.

He rolled out of bed, threw on a pair of jeans and a shirt, then sauntered down the hall with sleepy eyes. It only took one ring for the person on the other end of the phone line to pick up.

"Hello," the voice said at the other end when he called, expecting the call.

"You paged?" Clouse asked, still uncertain of who paged him, though he imagined the person was with a police agency.

Using the motel's courtesy phone at the front counter, he leaned against the marble surface, looking outside to the early morning view.

"Yeah, Paul. It's Troy Tackett."

Clouse rubbed the sleepiness from his eyes.

"I thought I was supposed to call *you* for lunch."

"You were. Look, something happened last night I thought you should know about since no one else knew where to find you. I didn't want you to hear it on the news."

He hesitated. Clouse sensed it.

"What is it?"

"Your friend, Tim Niemeyer."

Tackett let his sentence end there.

Clouse felt a tingle run through his back. Oh, God, he thought, knowing what the end of this conversation would be. Niemeyer was his last remaining high school buddy. To lose him meant Clouse losing a majority of his past and the opportunities to relive it. The previous year his friend Ken Kaiser had been killed with a scythe, along with several other close acquaintances.

Somehow, he sensed what Tackett was getting to, but the uncertainty of details forced him to ask.

"What happened, Troy?"

"He, he was stabbed to death in a parking lot last night by six assailants, Paul."

"Six?" Clouse stammered, feeling his body shimmer and his knees buckle at the words stating his friend's official demise. "What the hell happened?"

"We're not sure. His younger brother was with him, claiming six people snuck up from the shadows and knifed him to death. His brother also killed one of the suspects with a shotgun."

"Is Randy okay?"

"He's fine. The Bedford Police are still holding him for questioning because there's a lack of evidence to back up his story."

Clouse felt a hundred emotions and thoughts packed inside his head like sardines, trying to escape all at once. He could not think of what more to ask, where to go, or how to help Niemeyer's younger brother.

"Paul? You okay?" Tackett asked after a moment of silence.

"I'm okay. Is Randy going to need bail or anything?"

"No. I think they're going to let him go in a little bit. There were no witnesses and the videotape that monitors the ATM was missing."

"How could it be missing?"

"I suppose it was an isolated machine with the surveillance equipment locked inside one of those little compartments. Someone probably knew where it was and cut the lock."

"I can't believe it," Clouse said, his voice drifting off, his thoughts returning to his old high school pal.

"I'm sorry," Tackett finally said. "I just thought you should know before you saw it somewhere else. The news is making a big fuss about it."

Clouse looked around the lobby, almost expecting a dozen reporters to flood the area any moment. Everything around the motel seemed quiet as the Asian owner sat behind the desk calculating some totals, and several birds chirped outside, perched upon some wiring.

"Are they digging up last year's events?"

"Oh, yeah. The comparisons have already been drawn."

"Shit," Clouse said, rubbing his head. "Look, let's grab a late breakfast, okay?"

"Sure. How does the Waffle King sound?"

"Fine. Meet me there in an hour."

Clouse hung up the phone, realizing his eating habits had changed little since becoming an instant millionaire. He didn't particularly feel like eating, but buying an hour to contemplate the reality of Tim's death and jot down some questions for Tackett seemed the ideal thing to do. He needed a shower simply to be alone and think if nothing else, wondering why his world fell apart around him every fall.

Just when life returned to normal in nearly every aspect, the past reared its ugly head once again. The circumstances under which he obtained his money would probably be something of speculation for the media in the next few days. He dreaded the thought of putting his family through another tragic ordeal for the third straight year. Even worse, he feared for everyone with any relationship or contact with him because the murders never occurred with straightforward motives. He needed time and assistance to discover why someone wanted his good friend and his babysitter dead.

***

Clouse had already started with some coffee when he saw Tackett walk in, dressed in a Southwestern style shirt with faded jeans. As the detective set his black hat atop the table beside a nearly emptied bottle of soda and drew a seat, Clouse could only conclude that the detective was taking the day off, at least from an official standpoint.

"Any good news?" he asked.

"Not yet," Tackett replied. "We asked the state police lab in Indianapolis to examine the forensic evidence, but that may take some time. I've got to ask for your opinion on Jamie Vosburgh's murder, now that you've had time to think about it."

"Obviously Ryan Andrews is my guess," Clouse said. "I shot him square in the gut last year and he bled like a stuck pig out of that hotel. By all rights he should have died."

"No one has seen or heard from him during the past year. If he *is* dead, who else is there?"

Clouse rubbed his face in his hands, trying to think.

"God, you've got to think of two years' worth of suspects. Anyone could be seeking revenge for the Landameres, or Roger Summers, or even Ryan Andrews. One thing that comes to mind, Troy, is what Ryan said last year when he had us all captive. He said Barry Andrews wasn't his real father."

"That's worth checking into," Tackett noted aloud.

Clouse took a sip of coffee, not really in the mood for conversation, but knowing how important it was to cooperate and help nail the killer, or killers. He had tried to phone Daniels, to no avail, between talks with Tackett.

The notion of six people taking part in murdering his friend plagued him. He truly wondered what on earth was happening in that bizarre circumstance.

"I want to ask you about the picture," Tackett said. "Bedford P.D. said they found a picture of Niemeyer tucked into his jacket. His brother concluded it was probably taken at Ken Kaiser's funeral from last year."

"I don't know," Clouse said. "Jamie's was dated about two months ago. You're talking right around a year ago if Randy was accurate on the photo."

"I'll see if I can get you a copy to look at, since you were there."

Clouse nodded.

"If that's true, then someone has been planning to do this for a long time," he deduced. "I don't remember seeing anyone at the funeral except for reporters in the distance."

"Were they all together? No stragglers?"

Clouse thought a moment.

"They were together in a group. It was drizzling outside, and they were camped out in some sort of lean-to. Mostly television reporters, I think. When I see the photo, maybe I can pinpoint which part of the cemetery it was taken from."

Tackett pulled a small notepad from his breast pocket, jotting several notes as Clouse finished his coffee. The waitress stopped by, listing the small orders each man made for breakfast before scurrying back to the counter. From the corner of his eye Clouse spied her motioning for another waitress, whispering something before pointing quickly in his direction.

"He's the one they thought killed his wife," he could almost hear her say. The other waitress formed a shocked expression before both whispered something else and carried on with their work.

Clouse hated to think everyone knew about his checkered past, but the media made him paranoid by bringing up his name whenever someone died around Halloween.

"So Randy killed one of the six assailants?" he asked Tackett, moving past the dark thoughts.

"Turns out it was a real estate tycoon in Bedford," the detective noted. "That's part of the reason they're grilling him about the details. It's like they don't believe someone like that might be involved in a murder plot."

"Bedford's a conservative place. Any murder around there is big news. You throw in the notion that one of their finest is involved in a cult and they might go nuts."

Tackett looked up from his notepad.

"Cult?"

"Well, you know."

"No, what do you mean?"

"I flipped on the TV before I left," Clouse said. "They implied a cult theory. And come to think of it, Ryan Andrews said something last year about others aiding in his cause."

Tackett looked him in the eye a moment.

"Did he say anything more than that?"

"Not really. He hinted around that they were well-to-do people, but nothing more than that. Dave Landamere said the same thing before he died, but I think he was just talking about his wife."

"Who turned out to be an accomplice in last year's murders," Tackett clarified for his own assurance.

Clouse nodded.

"This is really a rough start," the detective said, giving the waitress a flirtatious grin when she set the food down in front of them. She seemed to respond, giving a wink directly aimed at Tackett. "Not too bad," he commented, his eyes following her firm buttocks as she sauntered back to the counter.

"She probably just wants a good tip."

"I'll give her a tip all right," Tackett said, returning his attention to Clouse, almost immediately chiding himself for losing his professional edge, even though he was not officially on duty.

"How long have you been with the county?" Clouse asked of the detective between bites of his egg and bacon combo.

"Three years."

"And you're already doing investigations?"

"Oh, I have almost ten years of law enforcement experience," he said, as though wanting to cease further talks on the subject.

Clouse gave him a puzzled look, as though trying to remember where he had seen or heard of Tackett before becoming his neighbor.

"I worked for a small police department in Salem," Tackett said, realizing Clouse was about to recall his past police occupation, wanting to set the record straight. "Well, we had a jerk for a mayor back then, and the police chief was his lap dog."

Tackett cleared his throat before continuing.

"Turns out when I tried to pull over an elderly woman for doing almost eighty in a thirty-five zone, she decided to hightail it outside of city limits. Naturally, I gave chase, even though city limits were supposed to be *my* limits. It was early in the morning, and most county and state patrols weren't on the road, or at least anywhere near me, so I decided to pursue her anyway. I finally pulled her over two miles later, arrested her, and had the county boys run her up to the jail."

Tackett grinned, as though implying the best was yet to come.

"Big mistake?" Clouse asked.

Nodding, Tackett continued after a bite from his sausage link.

"Later that morning it seems the mayor and my chief wanted a little talk with me. Turns out the old lady was one of the mayor's high school teachers. They wanted me to dismiss all charges and tear up the tickets I wrote, or I'd face some 'unfortunate' disciplinary measures as they put it."

"Ah, politics," Clouse noted, familiar with a few situations from his firefighting days. He had always maintained a safe distance from the power players in Bloomington.

"Yeah, politics. They immediately took away my sergeant stripes and told me I could choose from a five-day suspension, a hearing before the public board, or I could resign and take the easy way out. Needless to say, my options ranged a bit, but I decided to take the five-day suspension and see what happened."

He paused to take another sausage bite.

"Did they fuck you over?" Clouse asked, knowing how ruthless city officials could be when it came to sending messages. It was almost militaristic how they singled out people as examples to other would be rule breakers simply doing their jobs.

"They certainly did. Because I'd done my job the right way and pulled people over when I should have, I got a reputation for being the bad cop in town. For years, the mayor had wanted to get rid of me anyway, and after the last election, he placed his buddies in the power positions of our department.

"They used their police handbook like a hammer when they nailed me in front of the board. When they got done, you would have thought I murdered the Pope. I put my house up for sale and weighed my options even before the board returned its final verdict. I knew what was coming, and quit before they could officially kick me off the force.

"After it was over, I considered a lot of options. There were other departments, but none were hiring. I thought I could try trucking again, or maybe work with horses full-time. Either way I was leaving town as soon as possible. Hell, they disgraced me, no matter how much the local paper tried to justify my actions."

"It wasn't your fault, Troy."

"Oh, I told myself that a hundred times a day, but it didn't help. God, I considered moving back to Kentucky with my dad, or moving to another state, but I only saw my daughter a few times a month after my divorce as it was. There were a couple of times I even wondered what the world would be like without me."

Clouse gave a questioning stare.

"I'm not kidding," Tackett said evenly. "My life was going nowhere fast, and I couldn't picture myself doing anything but police work, even though I began to despise police officers just as badly as the assholes we put behind bars."

"What do you mean?"

"I hated what everyone around me did. My fellow officers did up my truck and house with shaving cream and certain bodily excrements I won't mention. They also turned on me like rats just to get in with the chief and get their stripes that much quicker. People I thought were my friends, my brothers in blue, back-stabbed me and hung me out to dry."

"And then the county job came along?"

"Just in time," Tackett confessed. "Bobby Pearce had just been elected sheriff and set out to have the department's first unbiased testing process in years. I finished second overall, got appointed right away, and the sheriff took to me. He sent me to almost every training class you could think of and let me slide into the investigator's spot when it came open last year."

"Sounds like things really worked out well."

"Patience is a virtue," Tackett said, reaching to his back pocket for a pouch of chewing tobacco. He took out a wad, shoving it into one cheek before opening the nearly empty bottle of soda to spit in. "Everyone's entitled to one bad habit," he told Clouse with practiced speech around the bulge in his cheek.

Clouse couldn't help but think Tackett was meant to be a small town sheriff somewhere in a southern state. As professional as he was at work, he was a true cowboy on the side. On several occasions, Clouse had seen the man break his own horses, and parts of himself, doing so. Often Tackett suffered pulled muscles, minor fractures, or even concussions after being bucked from his own livestock. He went around the state to small rodeos, trying to break even after paying entry fees, often receiving additional injuries.

Sure, he could make money if he rode well enough, but Clouse sensed his neighbor was more of a daredevil than a man in need of extra cash. Most cops took part-time security jobs at schools, hospitals, or bowling alleys. Tackett chose one that cost him more than he made in travel expenses and hospital bills.

"You don't do that at crime scenes, do you?" he asked Tackett of the chewing tobacco.

"Hell, no. That's what snuff's for."

Tackett was all about image. Losing his old job publically, even if he was in the right, had probably just about done him in. Neatness and pride were another two major contributors to his personality. At least he seemed pleased about the man he became after such an ordeal. To Clouse, Tackett was a person genuinely good in nature who would do anything his friends and neighbors asked of him. In fact, he was good to strangers in need too. Despite his hardships, Tackett was giving of his time, and a self-defined good ol' boy.

"This job definitely suits me better," he confessed. "The sheriff treats me like an officer under his command instead of a part of his political structure. That's rare these days."

"I'll say," Clouse agreed. He pulled out his wallet, throwing significantly more than the total of both of their bills on the table. "Any other questions I can answer for you, Troy?"

"Nothing at the moment. I'm going to interview her parents later to see if the connection could possibly be with Jamie, and not yourself."

"No chance of that," Clouse said assuredly, knowing better. "Jamie was a great girl with a bright future. She didn't deserve to die because someone wants to get back at me."

Tackett stood, reaching for his wallet.

"I've got it," Clouse said, waving off the notion.

"You sure?"

"Yeah. And I'm going to have my house cleaned up by tonight if you're done with it."

"We should be done. The forensics team should have had everything they needed by this morning."

"Good luck," he said, shaking Tackett's hand.

"Thanks. What are you going to be doing today?"

"I've got some things to unpack," Clouse informed the detective. "And they just might be of help in finding our killer."

Tackett raised a questioning eyebrow.

"Don't worry. I'll call if I find anything important."

"Please do."

Chapter 5

As dusk reached the outskirts of Bloomington a group of four people gathered in a leased office building, barely larger than the room they occupied. Only a restroom and small kitchenette filled out the commercial space. A rectangular table, with a dozen chairs surrounding it, centered in the room provided a full view for any lectures or speeches given, allowing any participants to see the lecturer without obstruction.

While three of the people sat at the table with pretense calm, the fourth, a wiry man with glasses and a patch of thinning hair centered atop his scalp, branching desperately out to a fringe, paced near a Plexiglas window. He made the others more agitated from his nervous walk as they began tapping fingers atop the meeting table or shifting uncomfortably in their seats.

"Why did that son-of-a-bitch have to shoot Ted?" he asked the two men, and the lady present, who watched him with chastising eyes. "We had it worked out perfectly, then he had to pull that little stunt. It wasn't like we were going to kill him too."

"Who would have thought there would be a loaded shotgun in the back seat?" a beefy man asked from his seat. Several rings, most including diamonds or gold, encircled his pudgy fingers. They glistened beneath the pool of fluorescent light from above.

"Look," the woman said, looking far less harmless in a pair of light slacks and a New England style sweater than she had in a black hooded robe. "We did our part. We killed Niemeyer and got rid of all the evidence we could. There's no way they're going to link Ted to the rest of us."

"Unless one of us talks," the last man said, seated beside the woman.

"You know the oath," the pacing man said. "If one of us talks, we die. We've all upheld the rules of the Coven so far, and there's no reason to think we won't continue to do so."

For a moment, the group sat silently, waiting for their fifth and sixth remaining members to show. Minutes seemed like hours as they sat. They tried to pass the time by staring at the corpses of flies, trapped in the plastic shields of the lights above, or looking out any of the several large windows to the clear skies above.

"What's taking them so long?" the large man with the rings asked, a briefcase planted beside him atop the table.

Everyone else shrugged, or simply looked out the window for the answer. They had committed to their group almost two years prior, promised wealth, power, and access to places most people had never even dreamed of visiting. Their leader, never wishing his name to be spoken aloud, had always paid them in money orders or other methods difficult to trace back to him. He took every precaution to cover up his identity, and with their help, he had secretly made Paul Clouse's life miserable since the group's inception.

Changing that notion was nowhere in the plans.

Yes, their dreams had all been fulfilled, but that was before the Coven was compromised. Now everything hinged on the meeting they were attending by mandatory decree.

Each had carried out his or her role in the murder perfectly, but rather than flee in separate directions as they planned, they hesitated when Lovett was gunned down by Randy Niemeyer, hoping he might be capable of walking with assistance. Once they were certain he was dead, they scattered in various directions for their own vehicles parked some distance away.

"The plan was so carefully thought out," the nervous standing man said. "We spent months watching Niemeyer's Saturday night plans, only to have this happen. I know the leader won't be happy with us, but it wasn't our fault."

"Quit babbling," the man with the rings bellowed. "We are all professionals here, and we have all benefited from this organization. The leader will understand, and we will pick up the pieces and move on."

An eerie quiet spread through the room as headlights appeared in the distance. The building, set a fair distance from the street, and on the outskirts of town, gave them ample opportunity to survey any people or vehicles approaching.

In such a quiet state, the thin, standing man looked out the window as the car pulled closer to the building. It was not their leader, but rather their fifth member. As he stood still, watching, he heard a strange click behind him. He whirled around, seeing none of the other members had moved an inch, and nothing atop the table, or across the room, could have made such a noise.

A puzzled look crossed his face before he instinctively dropped to his knees, peering beneath the table, then up to its underside. There he spied a strange device he felt certain he had only seen in movies. A small timer and several wires appeared to be connected to a large chunk of clay, or C-4 as he believed it might be referred to in the military or on a construction site.

Regardless, it was deadly, and there was no telling who might have set it. He watched the second hand on the miniature clock near its destination with no time to contemplate who would want the conspirators dead, except for their leader, because they had faltered.

"Oh, shit," he said seconds before the device detonated, obliterating everyone in the room.

The blast sent every shred of glass bursting outward, basically leaving the office building as nothing more than a hollowed, burned out shell for investigators to inspect when they arrived within the hour.

Their meeting had been adjourned before it began.

***

No matter how many times Clouse visited the place, he felt amazed by the beauty of the Landamere estate. Not only had David Landamere, a prosperous contractor, built his own estate, but he let it flourish with a remarkable layout of statues and gardens surrounding his property. Clouse stood in the front yard a moment, feeling more like he was surrounded by a cemetery rather than a residence worthy of a documentary.

With wilting flowers, sagging trees, and an untended yard, it looked more like a cross between a cemetery and a ghostly castle than living quarters. He looked to the wrought iron gates behind him, seeing flakes of rust appear on their neglected poles. He pulled the key from his pocket and walked to the front door, entering the house for the first time since it came into his possession.

Inside the house gave little relief from the chill of the fall weather. Clouse had paid the electricity the past year, knowing he would explore the house, and the urgency of the situation gave him satisfaction he had done so.

He flipped a light switch, illuminating the beautiful den and all of its furniture. He walked along the solid wood floor, his boots echoing throughout the large house with every step. Observing the exquisite detail of the place, he slowly made his way toward the kitchen where a white door stood out from the antiques and assorted dishes hanging from a pot rack centered in the room over a cooking island. He saw dishes, still unwashed, waiting in the sink for an owner that would never use them again.

Out the sliding backdoor, he spied the corpse of a jack-o-lantern left from the previous year, its orange husk reduced to a pile of seeds and black slime. Only the candle standing in the middle of the heap indicated the substance's identity. Clouse looked around the kitchen once more, noticing how layers of dust coated everything as evidence of what happened when houses were left unoccupied.

He turned his attention to the white door, opening it to reveal the cellar below. He found another light switch, but little light came from below when he flipped it. Seeing little more than a hazy outline below, he quickly searched the kitchen for a flashlight or bulbs, finding both in a cabinet. He carefully walked down the stairs, replacing several bulbs as he went, using the light to guide him until he reached the damp cellar, surrounded by boxes of every shape, make, and size.

"Good God," he said, unsure of where to begin.

Unconcerned with replacing the items inside the boxes, he began dumping them on the floor in separate piles, trying to decipher the contents of each box. He found photo albums, awards, certificates, letters, books, and all sorts of clothing.

Some of the documents, he soon found, concerned Tincher Incorporated, Landamere's fake company in his attempt to purchase the hotel from its owner two years earlier. He had gone so far as to mail letters of inquiry about buying the hotel, damaged goods at the time with all the murders occurring, but the owner did little more than contemplate selling the land, prompting Landamere to double his efforts.

If only Clouse had discovered the true source of Tincher Incorporated sooner, he could have stopped Landamere from assisting in the murders of almost a dozen people.

After half an hour of sorting through most of the boxes, he took a seat with a small metal chest atop an unfinished chair. Clouse tried several times to open the box, but a built-in lock kept him out.

Knowing the lock would be too sturdy to pick, he looked for something useful to break or pry the lock instead. He shook the box during his search, attempting to guess what might be inside. He heard a strange, fragile rattle from within, as though glass or fine china might be harbored beneath its thick sides.

He found a small pry bar near the stairs, set the box down, and managed to undo the top with his first attempt, amazed at what he found.

"So there you are," he said with a mild awe, staring at a small pile of ceramic imported tile that had plagued him the year before.

Each contained markings on the back, which, when put together made a puzzle. Joan Landamere had recovered enough of the pieces to create a map after her husband's death, completing the plan they formed together. She abducted Clouse's son, forcing him to crawl beneath the tunnels of an old resort to find what would have been rare jewels, if they had not been switched with a diary written by a Jesuit priest.

Clouse had read the diary, but without the other parts, which he hoped to find here, it made little sense to him. He expected to find various souvenirs from the West Baden Springs Hotel within the Landamere household because David Landamere had been one of the first people to work on the restoration of the building. The man knew a great many secrets before he ever hired Clouse as his design consultant.

With a degree in architecture, Clouse had blueprinted the hotel as a final project for one of his classes. Because the blueprints of the hotel were long since destroyed or lost, Landamere contacted him after discovering he had made his own set, very accurate and to scale, asking him to work on the project.

Clouse could not refuse.

As he sifted through the puzzle pieces, Clouse heard the door atop the stairs creak. It tapped against the wall as though a breeze pushed it. He walked cautiously to the bottom step, looked up, and saw nothing unusual.

He set the metal box aside, determined to search the few remaining cardboard boxes before leaving. He pulled a heavy box from the corner, opening it to reveal a stack of books inside. Along the top, he saw several hardcover novels by noted authors. He pulled them out in bulk, determined to see everything in the box before moving on. Clouse had no intention of returning to the Landamere basement again.

Near the bottom of the stacks Clouse felt himself shiver as he came face to face with a book as red as blood, with gold trim. He felt certain he knew what the book was, but until he picked it up and opened to its center, he had no verification.

"Fantastic," he said under his breath with delight, realizing he had found another one of the diaries, hopefully in sequence with the one he obtained the year before.

He dug further, finding two more at the bottom of the box. He took each out, setting them carefully aside. A quick examination of the final cardboard box ended in him finding assorted plates and dishes.

Clouse was about to take his spoils and leave when he heard a different sort of creak from the door atop the stairs. This time the door hit the wall several times, then bounced itself closed as he reached the stairway, metal box and diaries in hand.

"Ah, shit," he said, making his way up the stairs toward the closed door, wondering how it closed by itself.

His answer came on the other side as he stepped into the kitchen, finding the front door wide open, a steady wind entering the house behind it. Certain he had closed the door after entering he looked around warily, seeing no sign of anyone else in the house. Exercising caution, Clouse walked toward the front door, his loot in hand, and peeked outside, seeing only shrubs and leaves tumbling across the yard before pitch black blocked his view.

Suddenly visiting the house at such a late hour didn't seem like a wise idea.

He stepped out slowly, keeping vigilant watch around him as he closed the door, making certain it was locked. Only his Chevy pickup sat in the driveway, leading him to wonder what caused the door to open. Someone was keeping tabs on all of his friends, and undoubtedly monitoring him. From the pictures found on the corpses, he felt someone had planned revenge, or something much larger, for quite some time.

Just *what* remained the mystery.

Clouse climbed into his truck, set the objects aside to the passenger seat and prepared to head home where his family would anxiously await his return. As much as he hated leaving them for any length of time, he felt obligated to find the killer before more innocent people were slaughtered by the madman.

He started the truck and backed out of the driveway, giving one final look to the neglected grounds, hoping he could find enough information from what he had uncovered to move on and put the estate up for sale. Ridding himself of it would be another tragic portion of his memory he could file away.

Forever.

Chapter 6

Flames quickly died out as the Bloomington Fire Department used a fog stream to douse the remaining flames from the business office wreckage on the outskirts of town. Most of the building lay in collapsed chunks, barely decipherable as parts of the flat roof or interior drywall. Only the kitchen and restroom areas stood in part, their frames still smoldering as the only evidence that a building, in fact, stood at this location.

Almost forming a fence around the scene, police and fire vehicles stood in the way of onlookers and reporters who wanted a closer view. Four ownerless cars remained in the small parking lot beside the building, leading the battalion chief to speculate at least four people met untimely ends within the wreckage, regardless of how it went.

He immediately phoned for the fire investigator on call, along with Bloomington police. Whether there were deaths or not, the possibility of arson seemed extremely high, especially if it was an explosion as he reasoned.

Mark Daniels stepped out of his own vehicle, wearing wrinkled slacks and a shirt and tie he had snatched from a desk chair, thrown down a few days prior. His tie remained loose around his neck from a hurried knot, and the badge clipped to his belt looked as though it might fall off any second from its hastened placement.

He had been paged by headquarters since he was the detective on call for Sunday. He felt somewhat unofficial approaching the scene in black tennis shoes and grease residue covering his hands, but he had spent most of the day assisting his brother-in-law with some engine work.

"Happy Halloween," he grumbled to himself, stepping past a couple uniformed officers. "What do we have?" he asked one, staring intently at the scene.

"Fire department says it was an explosion. They think someone might have been inside."

Daniels nodded his appreciation and moved to the battalion chief who had delegated command to his captain so he could step aside. He wore his white helmet and tan bunker coat, more for recognition than for personal safety.

Holding a radio in one hand, a clipboard in the other, it became apparent this commander had rolled with the changes, becoming more of a general on his battlefield. He gave orders, leaving the field command to his captains as modern times delegated. Battalion chiefs were expected to survey and stand back, able to communicate with everyone under their command.

"You the detective?" he asked Daniels, eyeing the detective from head to toe as though wondering where the police department's dress code had gone.

"I am. What do we have, Chief?"

"Got four vehicles in the parking lot and no owners. I'm fearing the worst here."

Daniels surveyed the area. A building on the outskirts of town with nothing else surrounding it. A small shopping plaza sat within walking distance, but none of the shops were open and it seemed ridiculous to park at the office building and walk so far when each shop had parking spaces right in front.

"Anyone see anything?"

"Not that we know of," the chief replied. "All of these people showed up about the same time we did," he said of the group restrained by the line of emergency vehicles.

"Any idea what was going on here?"

"None. The call came in as a structure fire, possible explosion. We got here and the fire had pretty much put itself out."

Daniels watched the firefighters at work a moment before heading over to the vehicles to see if they revealed any clues about who the owners might be, and if there was any chance they were alive.

Perhaps some people had chosen this parking lot to meet before carpooling to a sporting event or gathering. Maybe they had gone power-walking or jogging together. Or perhaps they were charred corpses inside the blackened remains of the office building to his side.

He looked at each car, noticing none of them were realistically within his price range as a family man. These people apparently had good jobs or rich relatives. Either way, they fared better than a city detective financially.

All of the plates were local, but nothing inside any car revealed anything useful to him. As he jotted down each of the license plate numbers, Daniels envisioned a setup, with an intentionally lethal end. As the firefighters sorted through the wreckage with pike poles, shifting boards and charred plasterboard aside, he expected them to meet with a foul surprise within a few minutes, considering the building's small original size.

He guessed right.

"Uh, Chief," one of the younger firemen said. "We've got, uh, something here," he continued, trying to be discreet.

Waving Daniels over, the battalion chief clambered over the varying debris toward his men, turning his head slightly when the smell of burnt flesh entered his nostrils. Daniels had always questioned whether or not firefighters grew accustomed to the terrible smells they encountered.

Now he knew.

Like the outside of a hotdog grilled too long, only tenfold sickening in smell, human flesh peeled and flaked off just as easily, leaving its mark inside many a mind who viewed it.

Almost as though he was accustomed to it, Daniels knelt beside the body, breathing through his mouth to avoid the smell. Most of the body was covered by debris, but he spied the area where the pike pole had rammed through the charred coating, into the tender tissue beneath. A pool of pink flesh and blood spots was easily discernible from the rest of the corpse.

He looked up to the four firefighters around him.

"Any of you guys got latex gloves?" he asked, knowing they always carried them on their trucks for rescue scenes to avoid contaminants.

One pulled a film container from his coat pocket, handing it to the detective. Daniels opened the container, which made perfect storage for disposable gloves, and pulled a pair out. He snapped them over his wrists, taking hold of one arm on the body, pulling it up to examine the underside.

As he expected, the flesh along the other side was red, even burned in a few areas, but not charred like the rest. In other words, the body had not burned up. Rather, this person had been killed in an intense fireball only lasting a few seconds before the rubble burned itself out, mostly before the fire department arrived.

"Keep digging, guys," the battalion chief ordered, apparently sensing there would be more bodies to find.

"Can you notify the coroner?" Daniels asked, lacking a radio of his own.

"Sure. Anything else?"

"No. I'm going to contact my sergeant and see how he wants me to proceed. He'll want the forensics team out here right away, I'm sure. And I'll want to speak with your investigator as soon as he arrives."

"He's here," the chief said, looking over to a car with red lights pulling up to the scene. The driver stepped out, younger than Daniels expected him to be. Then again, he was younger than most detectives on his department. Turnover was more frequent than the old days. People took second jobs and invested for their future, retiring earlier than ever.

"I'll have the boys take care of crowd control," Daniels said of the patrol officers standing guard beside the emergency vehicles. "Please tell your guys not to move any of the bodies until we examine them."

The chief nodded quickly.

"Any ideas?"

"No. But someone went out of their way to make sure this place went up. And I have a feeling we need to start checking with any and everyone who was related to or close to the victims."

***

After spending the rest of the evening with Jane and the kids, Clouse decided to call it a night and start fresh in the morning. He made speaking with Daniels his number one priority. After that, he planned to find Tackett. Though Daniels would probably show little interest in helping him find the party responsible for Jamie's death, Tackett seemed overly trustworthy and helpful — two traits that made Clouse wary.

Twice he had been fooled by people in his life that drew close to him, only to destroy his friends, and nearly himself. He could not picture Tackett as a man who would be anything than what he showed at face value, but anything was possible.

Clouse was happy to find his house in perfectly restored condition. The high dollar amount spent in the repair meant nothing to a man who now possessed millions, and the safety and happiness of his family took priority.

With a new security code, he had entered the house to find no blood stains on the carpet, and a new window in place, with no traces of the gruesome death from the night before. He felt like a prisoner in his own house, locking the doors behind him and using the security code whether he and Jane were home or away.

Despite renovations giving the house a fresh look, Clouse couldn't sweep away the horrific images of Jamie's death from his mind so easily. With the house's security compromised once, and Jamie's folks living just down the road, he wondered how much longer his family could realistically live there. He didn't want to burden his or Jane's parents by staying with them, or hole up in some apartment or hotel room where security would be sketchy. The kids weren't exactly thrilled about returning to the house after their ordeal, and Clouse understood perfectly, but he felt it was the safest option for them.

He suspected one or both would join them in the master bedroom before dawn from bad dreams or a need for parental protection.

While Jane tucked in the kids, Clouse removed his cowboy boots and jeans, setting them beside the bed. He unbuttoned his shirt, tossing it atop the jeans before curling himself into the king size bed. He turned on the lamp beside the bed, taking up the first of the diaries, determined to see what information they might provide in his search for the hotel's history and what someone might be after.

No matter what, in some way the murders always tied into the hotel, and he felt clueless, and powerless, to do anything about it.

He read several installments before Jane came to bed. In his mind, he could envision the events as they unfolded according to Father Joseph Runnels, the senior pastor at the hotel during the Jesuit era.

***

During the fall of 1934, the Jesuits assumed residence in the hotel, wasting little time altering the interior design to suit their needs. Stained glass replaced the modest windows in the lobby, the original statues were removed and a life-size replica of Christ was centered in the atrium of the six-story domed hotel. Any luxurious drapes, carpeting and furniture were removed to make room for an expanded library. Rooms and the atrium were partitioned for prayer and lecture during classes.

With much of their tax base and job revenue cut, the residents of West Baden were upset with the sale of the hotel to the Jesuit sect. Despite a petition in an attempt to block Ed Ballard's sale of the hotel property for a mere dollar, the sale went through and the priests moved in shortly thereafter.

Father Runnels was concerned about the Jesuit standing in the community, and immediately set to work smoothing things over with people who openly opposed them occupying their local historic landmark.

He set up opportunities for the public to view the hotel and its new look with priests, both instructors and students alike as tour guides. Around the holidays, they threw parties where they served refreshments and performed skits for visitors. Slowly, it seemed, the public took to their Catholic way of life and their residence in the mammoth landmark.

It took a few years for the town's people to accept the priests and the West Baden College, particularly since Southern Indiana was primarily Baptist in religion. For some, the changes made to the hotel were unsettling. To others, it was simply a progression in the history of the hotel. Another chapter as some would put it.

After Ballard's death in 1936, things began to settle at the college, and in the town, after the elaborate funeral. Even the priests could not recall a time when so many people attended calling hours, which were centered in the hotel's atrium, and the funeral at a site several miles outside of town. After everything Ballard had done to guide the hotel, and further its cause by selling it to a religious faction when it might otherwise have fallen to the wayside, it seemed unfair for him to meet such a violent end.

His own business partner shot him in a hotel room in Arkansas. In the end, it seemed neither would benefit from their partnership, nor their holdings in Florida. It did, however, bring the community and the Jesuits one step closer, allowing the college to expand without intervention or ill-intent.

"Father Runnels," a priest in middle-age said as he walked into the director's office one day, extending his hand. As senior priest, Runnels performed any important masses, and dedicated most of his time to overseeing the affairs of the college, though seldom directly involving himself. "I am Father Ernest from Cincinnati."

"Of course," Runnels said, remembering the request he had made for someone to permanently take over the Sunday mass schedule. The Cincinnati office responded to his inquiry by stating Father Ernest, no last name ever given, would transfer immediately to the college. With the campus expanding, the Catholic bishops were happy to accommodate. "Did you just get in?"

"Yes. I would have been here sooner but the train was held up by an extended stop."

"I take it your ride was good?"

"Pleasant. It's a very beautiful area you have down here. In Ohio the leaves are nowhere near as splendorous."

"Would you like me to arrange a tour of the campus, or do you prefer to see your quarters first?"

Ernest looked behind him at the simple suitcase sitting on the floor. Despite a longing to see the grounds he'd heard so much about, he wanted to see what room he could call home.

"I'd like to see my room first, then the grand tour if possible," he requested.

"Of course," Runnels replied. "I'll have Benjamin show you around. He's one of our brothers who knows the layout and the history of the grounds rather well. He also gives many of our tours to the local residents who pass through."

"Residents?"

"Yes. We have the local people come through here on tours as somewhat of a peace offering. They were by no means overjoyed when we moved into their landmark."

"The Eighth Wonder of the World as they call it?" Ernest chimed.

"Yes, indeed. And it is a remarkable building. I think you'll find it quite a match for our plans. We've converted much of what we need into classroom and chapel areas. There is space here for both solitude and gatherings. You could say it's the best of both worlds."

To Runnels, Father Ernest seemed eager enough to begin his tenure on the grounds. A priest younger than himself, Ernest appeared driven by their religion, but distant, even reserved in a way that worried the senior priest. He appeared to always be thinking, right from the first day they met, about things quite possibly beyond their religion.

He watched as young Benjamin showed Ernest around the grounds from a room on the second floor of the hotel on that Indian summer day. The new priest seemed interested in a few odd areas of the grounds. These areas included where the West Baden Springs Hotel church had stood years before, and the old bowling alley, which he believed would make a splendid area of worship, just a short walk from the hotel itself.

Ernest seemed a visionary of sorts, but Runnels questioned just what types of ideas the man brought from Cincinnati.

Runnels was a traditional, old-school Catholic, and it seemed readily apparent that Ernest was not, and never would be.

***

Time would tell if the two could find some common ground, but Clouse learned the first few days, even during a feeling out process, they had varying ideas about how the church, even the college, could be improved in days to come.

Clouse closed the first diary about halfway through. Most of the reading had been about the setting of the area, changing the hotel's layout, and several new staff members, including Ernest, being brought to the grounds. Most of what he read he already knew. He loved learning details of the hotel, which he had helped in restoring during a four-year span.

Now the domed building sat waiting for residents to occupy it once again, as it had for a year. Doctor Martin Smith, the previous owner, contracted his construction company to complete the restoration with the intent of reopening the hotel for business, rather than just tours. On the night of what was to be the grand commencement. terrible things began to happen for the second year in a row.

Clouse never attended because someone made an attempt on his life, and a man was burned alive in the middle of a dinner party along the atrium floor. Later, Smith was chased by the killer to the hotel roof and plummeted to a six-story death. This sequence of events caused Clouse to inherit Smith's entire estate, as his will dictated, though courts tied up the process until the past few months. Only then, did Clouse learn exactly what he owned and exactly how much money he was worth after the government took its share.

Both he and Jane would have done well in life regardless, but Smith had appreciated all of Clouse's work in making the hotel's reopening a reality. They shared a vision of what the landmark needed to look like. David Landamere had shared that vision too, but he saw beyond it, to owning the hotel. His greed cost him his life and a once impeccable reputation. Clouse, however, endured the painful events placed before him and saw the project through.

That, coupled with the fact that Smith had no wife or children to leave his estate to, made Clouse a millionaire overnight.

"Are you going to turn that light out anytime soon?" Jane asked sleepily from her side of the bed, obviously trying in vain to sleep.

"Sorry," Clouse said, realizing he had been sitting up in bed, thinking about the tragedies of his life the last several minutes after laying the book down. "Did you ever think you were marrying a rich guy?"

"No," she replied without turning over. "I thought I was marrying a fireman going through a few hard times."

Clouse chuckled, knowing his hard times were far from over.

"Boy, were you wrong."

"I know, but the adventurous side of you is nice too. Good night, hon."

Clouse slid comfortably under the flannel sheets.

"Good night."

Chapter 7

Clouse barely waited until the investigative division of the Bloomington Police Department was open before he slipped into their office. He noticed a room filled with desks, each equipped with a phone, computer, filing stacker, and cubicle walls on two sides, providing a false sense of isolation for the detectives.

He saw a herd of detectives talking sports or something comical from the night before at one end of the room. Behind them, he spied a young detective with black, prematurely graying hair cropped short atop his head, his eyes panning through a case file. He dressed in perfectly pressed black pants and shined shoes, and appeared former military. His eyes narrowly focused on the file like an eagle searching the ground for movement.

Or food.

Even his jaw appeared unbreakable as it jutted like that of a drill sergeant. Clouse had the impression someone stupid enough to strike the man's face would walk away with a broken hand. His entire face appeared chiseled like stone. He sat three desks away from Clouse's intended target, Mark Daniels.

Daniels reviewed a case file of his own, possibly one in the same, ignoring the world around him. As Clouse moved across the room, and around desks, he could hear the chatter slow, then stop, before awkwardly beginning again. He sensed they were probably now talking about him, but he did not care.

As he approached his friend, he noticed Daniels wearing black slacks and shoes, along with a black shirt and gray tie, almost like a mortician from days gone by. He literally sat across the room from the other detectives, as though excluded from the group like a bookworm on a playground. Too engrossed in his reading, the detective never heard Clouse approach until he spoke.

"You look like you've been to a funeral."

"In a manner of speaking, I have," Daniels replied before looking up from the case file. When he noticed it was Clouse standing before him, Daniels looked around as though his cover had been blown. "Damn it, Paul," he said, standing from his desk. "Let's go outside," he said, ushering Clouse toward the door, away from the other detectives.

A moment later, the two stood outside of city hall. Daniels fished a cigarette from his shirt's breast pocket. He paced a second while lighting it, apparently upset about something.

"I can't believe you came here," he told Clouse.

"What in the hell is wrong with you?"

"Those guys already think I'm some sort of pariah because my partner got killed two years ago. And they know we're friends."

"So?" Clouse demanded.

"So none of them want to work with me. They saddled the rookie in there with me because they all figure I'll do something to get *him* killed. They think I'm on some sort of suicide mission by hanging out with you, and I've been doing my damnedest to fit in ever since I got back," the detective replied, taking a deep drag from his cigarette. "God, you've probably set me back two or three months with them by showing up like this."

Clouse stepped back from his friend, eyeing him with concern. Daniels had never been so unhappy to see him before. Then again, he had never been outcast from his own division either.

"So, when you said things were going well around here you lied?"

"I didn't lie," Daniels retorted. "It's just, well, going slower than I expected. I didn't expect these guys to be afraid of working with me. And now I find out I've got this reputation around the younger guys that I'm almost suicidal with no regard for myself or my partners."

"And you're blaming me for this?"

"If I hadn't helped you a second time and gotten more battle scars, I never would have gotten this label, and gotten stuck with the ex-Marine up there. And you know full well he doesn't want to be saddled with me."

"So you're saying it wasn't worth it to help me out?" Clouse said defensively, wondering if his time was wasted talking to Daniels. He had yet to make it to his point for visiting.

"No, it's just not wise for you to come over here. I'm having enough trouble gaining acceptance from these guys. Now my sergeant gave me that case about the explosion last night. I'm trying to track down who these people were and it's not easy."

Clouse looked at the newspaper machine beside him, seeing the headline of the four deaths from the night before. He had already seen it on the local morning news before leaving the house.

"I tried to call you this weekend," he finally said. "It's starting again."

Daniels took a final drag from his smoke, flicking it into the trashcan ashtray combination beside the door.

"You say that like you know for certain. And I got all of your messages. I was out with Cindy and the kids until I got called back to investigate this mess."

"My babysitter gets stabbed and thrown through my picture window for my kids to see and you act like it's unrelated? Goddamn, Mark, I was a firefighter and I think I've got this one figured out a little quicker than you."

Daniels shivered a second as though he felt a chill run through him with the wind and winter-like fronts moving through. He silently cursed himself for not grabbing a jacket before stepping outside.

"Even if it is happening again, I've got my own case to work on, Paul. I can't go running around with you again trying to figure out who the grim reaper is this time. I've already lost too much of my life the past two years, and I'm not leaving my family's side again."

Clouse understood, but he also feared for Daniels' safety if the detective failed to realize the danger could easily follow him home if he chose not to chase it.

"I'm not going to ask for your help," Clouse said, although that was his sole reason for coming in the first place. "I just want you to be careful out there because someone killed my babysitter and the only high school friend I had left."

"Sorry to hear about that," Daniels said genuinely, looking inside the glass doors of the building as though expecting his fellow detectives to spy on him. "So what are you going to do?"

"Tonight Jane is taking Katie to a dance show while Zach and I spend a guys' evening out. He wants to go to that pizza place with all the games and rides. Poor kid deserves it after what he's been through."

Daniels tapped his foot against the ground, either from nervous jitters or the cold chills shooting through him.

"I heard Troy Tackett is investigating the murder of your babysitter," he said, opening the door for Clouse so they could escape the cold long enough to finish their conversation.

"Yeah. I'm talking with him later."

"He called this morning wanting a chat with me. I guess you told him I might be able to provide some background information."

"And I suppose you told him to fuck off too?"

Daniels grinned.

"No. Out of professional courtesy I'll talk to him once, but after that I don't want to hear about any murders but the ones I'm investigating."

Clouse looked outside, ready to head back to his family before they all awoke. The kids were not going to school for a few days, and Jane took personal time at the medical center. Clouse felt sorely disappointed that his friend refused to openly help, but understood why.

"You know," he said to Daniels before pushing on the exit door. "The one thing that pisses me off most about this whole thing is that the killer doesn't have the balls to face me like a man. What kind of bastard murders a man's friends and family and doesn't have the guts to face the person he really wants?"

Daniels shrugged.

"That's the way it goes. The killer wants you to suffer before he tries to kill you. He wants you to think about how you're going to die, and wonder exactly when."

"I wish the cowardly son-of-a-bitch would just face me and be done with it," Clouse said. "I don't want to go through this again," he said with emphatic emotion, as though approaching an emotional breakdown.

A deep frown crossed his friend's face.

"I know, Paul. Just hang in there and let Troy do his job. He's an excellent investigator."

"Yeah, sure. Take care, Mark," Clouse said, leaving the building, and his friend to do a grisly job with the murder victims.

Daniels searched for optimism, but found as little as Clouse. A few bright spots from the explosion were in the hands of the state police forensics team. In the wreckage, a leather briefcase, a partially destroyed videotape, and some documents had been found, but whether anything from any of those objects could be recovered or not remained in question.

He opened the door, letting himself back into a world of reluctant acceptance.

***

After spending the morning with his family, and attending a rather large funeral service for Tim Niemeyer, Clouse met Tackett at the sheriff's office where the investigator had it much better than Daniels. He had his own enclosed office with a door, blinds, and the option of being as public as he chose.

"Have a seat, Paul," he said, closing the door behind them. "I checked out Ryan Andrews' birth records, or tried to," he said, sitting behind his desk.

"They wouldn't let you examine them?"

"Well, there was nothing to go by," Tackett admitted. "He was left in front of an emergency room as an infant and there's no record of his real father or mother. The Andrews family adopted him soon after that from the adoption agency."

"So we may never know who his real parents were."

"No, but I did get a copy of this," Tackett said, pulling out a duplicate photo of the one found on Tim Niemeyer's body.

Clouse examined it a moment, trying to recall where the photographer would have stood, and if he had seen anything. He knew for certain it was during Ken Kaiser's funeral the year before, but nothing useful came to mind.

"It's definitely the funeral, like Randy said."

"No ideas other than that?"

"No."

Tackett put the photo away obviously wishing he had more to go on. Usually, he would question neighbors of a crime scene, but the Vosburgh family had nothing to add and he was the other neighbor in this case. He had been outside most of the evening tending to his horses. He had followed up on residences familiar in the tape, but none of the people handing out candy in the film had seen anyone or anything unusual. The killer appeared very adept at concealing himself through tree branches and unlit areas around houses.

With so little to go on, the detective felt like he was back to square one.

"Have you come up with any other ideas who might have motivation to get back at you? Think of the past two years, Paul. Let's start with the motives."

"Revenge and hopes of obtaining the West Baden Springs Hotel are the most recent motives."

"Good. Now name me people who survived these ordeals, or might be pissed because their family member was the psycho who got killed."

"Oh, cripes. Mark Daniels and I survived last year. My wife and son were there too. Brian Kern, the landscaper for the hotel, was on the list, but they never messed with him. Tim survived, but you know what happened there. Oh, Russ Hinds, the security guard at the hotel was nearly killed, but he pulled through, and Tug McCabe, the state trooper, he made it."

"Okay," Tackett said, quickly jotting down the names. "What about people interested in the hotel?"

"The only one I can think of is a friend of my first wife and myself, Michael Hathaway. He has millions from his own business, but he was only interested because of me."

"All right. The revenge angle?"

"Any of Roger Summers' family, or anyone who might be associated with the Landameres, or even related to Ryan Andrews, for what little good that will do."

"No other ideas?"

"Not really. I don't think anyone would do this if they thought I'd figure it out this quickly."

Tackett shrugged. He pulled out the photos from both of the crime scenes.

"Someone has planned this for some time," he declared. "He's playing psychological games with you, and anyone who has time to stalk everyone you know has to have a few marbles loose. Who would know everyone in your life, right down to your babysitter?"

"Damn, Troy, I don't know. I would imagine it wasn't someone involved in the funeral, so that would eliminate Daniels, and certainly my wife. And when it comes down to it, Hinds and Kern wouldn't have been involved at all back then."

"So we could be dealing with someone who planned this from the very beginning," Tackett surmised.

Clouse nodded reluctantly in agreement, though imagining such an intricate plan overwhelmed him.

"It doesn't look like the state forensics people are going to turn up anything, at least not right away. All of the fingerprints seem to match people in your family, or the victim. I honestly don't have much to go on, Paul."

"There is one thing, if Mark hasn't thrown it out," Clouse pondered aloud. "Last year during Dr. Smith's funeral we were given permission to videotape the proceedings in secret by the funeral director. Mark may still have that tape."

"And the killer could very well have been someone who attended."

"It's possible."

"You talked about eliminating suspects, yet both sets of previous murders have been done by a pair of killers."

Clouse thought a second about what Tackett was saying.

"True, but one was always predominantly the killer while the other came up with the plan."

"But what I'm saying is we can't rule anyone out yet."

Clouse shrugged helplessly, knowing Daniels and his wife could not be involved. They had suffered just like he and Jane.

"Can you think of *anything* else that might help?" Tackett asked again.

"I'm reading through some old diaries concerning the hotel and the Father Ernest legend these murders have been based on," Clouse revealed. "I don't know if they'll provide any good information or not, but they might help me discover more of a motive about why someone would want the hotel."

"I remember hearing something about precious jewels left from the original owners hidden somewhere," Tackett said.

Not exactly the *original* owners, Clouse thought, though he didn't contradict his neighbor verbally.

"Yeah, but they've never been recovered, if that's even true."

"Alright," the detective finally said. "I'll keep checking around to see what I can find."

"I appreciate it, Troy," Clouse said, standing and shaking Tackett's hand. "I'm going to try and take my family's mind off of this tonight. They could use a break before any other bad news hits us."

Tackett grinned weakly.

"Good luck. I'll let you know if I find anything."

Clouse left the sheriff's department feeling no more reassured than when he entered. He felt certain his neighbor was working diligently at finding the party responsible for Jamie's death, but he knew from experience the killer would be smart, and probably not alone. If someone truly had planned Clouse's torment through the killings and photographs for over a year, he or she would be nearly impossible to find.

A year was a long time to plan the perfect crime, and psychotic or not, no one wanted to be caught. As he walked to his truck, a flood of ideas came and went through his mind, none of them concrete enough to warrant further thought.

His idea of peace and tranquility would have to wait.

Chapter 8

After finishing his pizza supper that evening, Clouse watched as Zach went to play in the maze of attractions, rides, and games available at the Pizza Plaza. Several minutes beforehand, he saw Randy Niemeyer enter the facility with his two children, which bothered him somewhat.

At Tim Niemeyer's calling hours in the afternoon the two had spoken, and Clouse had made mention of he and Zach spending the evening at the theme restaurant. He had sensed Niemeyer had something to talk about, but his duties at the funeral home kept distracting him. A feeling of guilt plagued Clouse, and he did not want to speak to the surviving brother of his high school friend.

Tim had been the best man at his wedding several months prior, and at the time, it seemed everything in Clouse's life was coming together. He had settled most of the inheritance issue, he and Jane were married almost two years after they had met, and his new house was a model of tranquility. He even had good neighbors on either side and seemingly endless acres for the kids to play and grow up on.

Clouse eyed Niemeyer warily as the man set his kids to playing on some of the attractions Zach had already enjoyed. He shifted uneasily when the man came over to sit with him, expecting a possible cussing or further placing of blame.

"Can I sit down?" Niemeyer asked as Clouse looked up to him. He had a rigid, almost frightening way of dealing with people, even when he was being sincere and friendly, hiding his emotions behind a stoic countenance poker players would pay dearly to own.

"Sure," Clouse replied, waving his hand toward an empty seat.

Niemeyer sat, looked to his children playing in the distance, then stared at Clouse a moment, his expression revealing nothing.

"I want to help you find who killed my brother," he said flatly. "I know you aren't going to rest until you find out, and I know what's happened the last two years."

"Then you know what you're asking is extremely dangerous."

"I know, and I don't care."

Clouse shifted in his seat again, looking to a clock. The night was still too young for him to interrupt his son's good time.

"I don't want to see anything happen to you," he said. "It's bad enough I lost my last childhood friend in your brother. Getting you killed certainly won't make me feel any better."

"I have no intention of getting killed," Niemeyer said, his voice rising slightly.

"Neither did Tim or my babysitter." Niemeyer started to speak but Clouse cut him off by holding up an open palm. "Besides, I don't have anything to go on yet. We could be talking about two completely separate instances here since they occurred at the same time."

"But we're not. I read about this Coven in last year's papers, and I know they never found that Ryan Andrews guy. We both know this is all the work of one group."

"I know you're studying to become a cop, but this isn't the way to get experience," Clouse insisted. "If you get involved you become a target, and you've got two kids over there who don't want to lose their daddy."

Niemeyer looked over to his kids, happy as could be in the net of plastic balls, jumping up and down through the pool of multicolored plastic. He had to know the risk involved, but probably felt confident he could not be surprised by any killer.

"You're going to search. What about *your* son?"

"What makes you so sure I'll search? About the only people left to target that I care about would be my family, and I plan on keeping close watch over them."

"So, you don't care who killed Tim?"

"I never said that."

"You implied it," Niemeyer said with the same unmoving expression.

Clouse sighed.

"Fine, Randy. Honestly, I'm going to look for the killer, or killers, but I don't need to put you at risk. I owe it to Tim to keep you out of harm's way."

"I'm not Tim's kid brother anymore, Paul. And I may be about the only person willing to help you search for the truth. And if there's a group of them, I'm willing to dish out vengeance my own way."

Clouse looked over to the kids playing once again. He understood the inherent danger involved with tracking the Coven and Ryan Andrews, if the man was indeed alive. Seeing his father talking with someone he didn't know, Zach made his way back toward the table.

"Hey, kid," Clouse said as his son approached. "You tired out?"

"Not yet."

"You remember my friend Tim, don't you?"

Zach nodded.

"Well, this is his brother, Randy."

Niemeyer forced a smile and a slight wave. Zach still perceived him as a complete stranger, his face not registering any friendliness. He also didn't act shy as he once had toward new people, indicating life's bumps had matured him quickly.

"Go ahead and play some more, if you want," Clouse encouraged his son.

Zach ran off to redo the rides and games once more.

"My phone number is on here," Niemeyer said, sliding Clouse a card. "My cell number too. If you decide you want my help, don't hesitate to call."

Clouse eyed it, placing it in his shirt pocket. He had mixed feelings about Niemeyer's help in any form. Taking responsibility for his friend's brother was more burden than he cared to undertake.

"Okay," he finally said. "If I get anything concrete, I'll give you a call."

"Good, and thanks," the younger man said before walking off to find his own children. Clouse rested his chin on his thumbs in thought, wondering just what he needed to do before more people he cared for died.

***

While his wife made certain the kids were in bed Mark Daniels reviewed several sheets and photos pertaining to the new investigation thrown in his lap. His first major case would have to be a multiple homicide, he thought sarcastically of the department brass.

By no means did he have the experience to carry such an investigation through without some doubts in his own ability. He had several years of police experience, but only one in the investigative division, and that was before his year of inactivity when he was shot. He also thought it strange the brass paired him with a rookie detective, as though setting him up to fail. Naturally, the rest of the division carried out interviews and evidence examination, but his supervisor made Daniels the lead investigator. Such a move would either garner respect for him or make the other investigators despise him all the more.

Daniels knew the explosion was no accident, and he knew how it was devised. Someone with some experience in demolition had probably set the charge after obtaining the C-4 through a construction company, or through military means.

Thanks to the license plate numbers, he knew who the victims probably were, but he would have to wait for lab results to be certain. One of the potential victims was someone he knew rather well, but he could not imagine why she would be a victim of foul play.

For one full year, Dr. Susan Jameson had helped him mentally and physically overcome the challenges of walking again after being shot in the spine. Could she actually be one of the grotesque bodies found twisted and charred by the sudden explosion within the office building? So much of the corpses had been blackened in the front or obliterated that only dental records or DNA could conclusively identify them.

It turned out each of the four people who owned the vehicles were indeed missing, indicating Daniels would have little time to wait for the results he expected.

Each of the four only carried documents pertinent to their work or leisure in their vehicles. He had no idea why a doctor, a coroner, a banker, and an undertaker would be meeting in such an isolated area. Perhaps they were in business together with stocks or trust funds, or perhaps they were part of a social club since all had prestigious careers.

By now, media outlets across the state were having a field day with the Bloomington area. Two murders and an explosion killing four people, all within a two-day span, sent them on a sensationalism tailspin with implications of conspiracy to occult groups living out their Halloween fantasies.

"Are you going to be up awhile?" Cindy, his wife of seven years, asked.

She stood in the living room doorway, dressed only in her nightgown. Her nipples showed through the thin material without the barrier of a bra to confine them. She had let down her cream-colored hair, which drooped against her shoulders. He sensed she wanted to be near him during such a perilous time, but she would have to wait until he was ready for a study break before he ventured up to the bedroom.

"I just need a few more minutes," he said, eyeing her from head to toe. "I'm trying to sort out some details on this new case before I go to work tomorrow."

"I'm glad you refused Paul," she said, sliding into the empty cushion beside him on the couch. He had told her what Clouse relayed to him that morning. "I don't want you doing anything that dangerous again."

With a daughter in school and his son, just over a year old now, Daniels needed to be extra careful to make certain he walked through his front door every night to be a father. He could separate his career from his family life now, whereas in the past he lived with his job or brought it home with him. Only in preeminent cases such as this would he bother to bring materials from work. In this case, he needed every possible lead he could come up with because a lack of motive and suspects plagued him already.

"What if Paul is right?" he questioned his wife. "What if it is happening again?"

"You go to work, you come home. It's as simple as that."

"And pretend as though some mentally disturbed murderer might not come after me? After you? It's not that easy, Cindy. I just know somehow I'm going to get dragged into this."

"It's not your place to investigate this time. You said it yourself, the county police are investigating the death of Paul's babysitter."

Daniels flipped through the case files in front of him, feeling a sense of hopelessness encompass his body. A lack of physical evidence and witnesses would prevent quick closure of the case, but he felt compelled to check out each of the four victims and their possible connection, if any, to one another.

He stood to leave.

"Where are you going?" his wife asked as he grabbed a jacket from the coat rack.

"I've got a few things to check on," he said. "I won't be too long."

Cindy watched with a bit of confusion, and much more concern as her husband left the house. She sensed he would somehow involve himself in Clouse's dangerous situation again, despite what he told her.

When he first took a job with the police, she constantly worried about him, but eventually learned how cautious and instinctive he was as an officer. She never feared for his safety so intensely again, until he took a certain case two years ago concerning a historical hotel and a certain firefighter accused of murdering his own wife.

And she had never stopped worrying since.

***

Clouse pulled into his driveway, finding no sign of his wife's car. Jane and Katie had apparently found something to do after the musical ended. He parked his truck near the house, letting Zach run ahead to the door. Clouse followed, taking time to survey the darkened property from end to end. Even the security light triggered by his son's movement failed to illuminate much around the vast acreage of his estate.

He let Zach run inside first, quickly typing in the numbers for the security code before closing and locking the door with its deadbolt. Zach ran upstairs to his room while Clouse took off his jacket, tossing it to a nearby chair in the living room. He turned on the television with a remote, watching for weather reports and sports updates.

In the meantime, he checked messages on the answering machine, finding nothing except a few insignificant rambles from Jane's family members. He left them for her to find later, opting to pick up around the house when he heard a thump, then a crashing noise from above.

"Zach?" he called, expecting his son to be guilty of something first-graders might do.

No answer.

Clouse called upstairs again, this time reaching the base of the incline, looking up into a dark hallway. He saw a strand of light against one wall from his son's room before the stream disappeared suddenly, reappearing momentarily.

Zach knew better than to try scaring his father. He had lived through most of the same traumatic events, but in many ways, he moved on better than Clouse had. Then again, most of his friends hadn't been slit open with a large blade.

With a great deal of caution and focus, Clouse ascended the stairs, looking for any signs of trouble, afraid to call for Zach again as his heart pounded inside his chest. Ordinarily his parental instinct would tell him to rush up the stairs and see what was the matter, but he knew someone might be out to kill him, and he had no doubt the person could probably get into his house, no matter how secure he felt.

Experience had taught him well.

Clouse wanted to snatch something to defend himself with, but the fireplace accessories were below, and he could think of no useful equipment above him. He crept up the stairs to the top, rounding the corner to find a large silhouette blocking his son's bedroom door, the flickering light of a jack-o-lantern seeping around the dark form he assumed was the killer.

"No," Clouse gasped, seeing the form of his son lying on the floor behind the shape. He could not tell if Zach was alive, or even intact, but his blood boiled at the thought of anyone even touching his boy.

As his eyes quickly adjusted to the dark, he saw the black form for what it was. Again, someone had donned the identity of the grim reaper, hiding his face beneath the cloak, his entire body bathed in black cloth. Held before him was a shortened scythe, good for quick swings at a person's head or chest, inflicting damage quickly and repeatedly.

Enraged, Clouse charged the killer, unconcerned about whether the person held a blade, or even a gun. For his trouble, he received a high knee to the stomach, then another to the sternum, flooring him in a heap.

Clouse groaned, rolling over to his back just in time to avoid the scythe planted in the floor beside his head. As the killer struggled to retrieve the weapon from the floor's grasp, Clouse fired his foot upward, catching the person squarely in the forehead with the toe of his cowboy boot. He saw the scythe drop to the ground beside him.

While the killer stumbled back, Clouse regained his footing, charging him like a football player, planting the killer's back into the doorway behind him. He quickly realized the masked man was his size and strength. A punch thrown into his jaw by the mysterious stranger proved it. Clouse returned the same type of fist, but the mask beneath the hood absorbed part of the blow.

Clouse wrapped his hands around the killer's throat. He started to squeeze when a knee bolted into his stomach, causing him to double over. The killer bent over to reach for the scythe lying beside him, but Clouse took hold of the killer's foot, tripping him up. Clouse started to regain his own footing, finding his adversary ready to strike, despite the fall.

A solid black boot kicked him in the forehead before Clouse stood completely erect, whipping his head back into the wall. The killer quickly rose, grasping him by the back of the head, ramming him into the opposite wall several times, drawing a pained groan the first few times, then no sound. The killer had knocked him unconscious, rendering their battle over. He took hold of the scythe, looked to his motionless adversary, and turned his attention to the boy lying in the next room. Despite the unexpectedly long delay, his objective was complete.

Chapter 9

Clouse awoke to a throbbing head and a silent house, unable to recall exactly what happened for a second or two. He stood, rubbing his aching head as he looked into his son's room. The inside revealed nothing, even after he turned on the light. He knelt along the spot where Zach had been lying when he reached the top of the stairs, seeing no blood, or other evidence his son had been slain.

"Zach?" he called, standing once again.

He marched down the hall at a frenzied pace, trying to find any sign of his child. No answer came back.

"Zach?" he called more desperately this time.

Again, no answer.

He ran downstairs, giving a quick search of the house, feeling a crisp breeze from somewhere nearby. When he reached the kitchen, he discovered the front door wide open, with no alarm system wailing.

The son-of-a-bitch knew my code, Clouse thought as he walked toward the door, realizing his son was probably abducted by the person he had fought with just minutes, or hours ago. Time eluded him during his unconscious state. A quick look to the clock revealed almost half an hour had passed. Too long to hope he might find the culprit responsible.

He stepped out on the porch, frantically looking around his property for answers, but nothing looked different than when he had come home almost an hour before. In the distance he saw Tackett's porch light on, and thought one of the inside lights might be on as well. Perhaps his neighbor had seen something.

Perhaps he had not been home all night.

Desperate, and at his wit's end, he felt a tear draw to his eye. He felt completely at fault for his son's apparent abduction, and now there was nothing he could do. Heavy breaths came and went from his body as anxiety tensed his every muscle. He could not keep up with the numerous thoughts flooding his brain as he looked in every direction.

Clouse turned, nearly running his face into a startling discovery tacked to his door in the form of a theme park pamphlet. He took the glossy paper down from the door, recognizing it as the park he had just inherited, down in the Nashville region of Tennessee.

In a manner of speaking, it was a note, summoning him to just that place if he wanted to see his son again. Clouse closed his eyes, taking in a deep, thoughtful breath. Now the game was in his court, and he was given a false sense of control.

He already knew the rules.

Bring no police.

Come unarmed.

Remember who's truly in control.

You will eventually die.

Clouse took up his jacket, placed the brochure inside a pocket, and reached for the phone. He would call Tackett first, but not to fill out a police report. Time was not a luxury he could afford, and if he reached the park first, he might be able to initiate his own plan. He also wanted Tackett to monitor his house, and to ask him if he had seen anything relevant in the past hour.

Next, he would partially inform Jane of his intent to leave the state, and about what happened to Zach, even though he felt uninformed regarding his son's condition. Still, he needed to tell Jane to change the security code again and remain in the house when she was not at work. She would probably want to personally take Katie to and from school as well, if she dared let the girl return.

Staying in the house no longer seemed safe, but he owned several dogs. It was definitely time to let them free in the house since they loved his children and barked religiously when strangers came around.

Currently they were too far from the house to make a difference, and if they barked, he usually dismissed it as an animal wandering through his fields.

No longer would he ignore them.

Despite his reservations in speaking to Daniels, he trusted the officer enough to inform him about the trip and ask for his advice. He knew his friend would not come along, and that he was devoted to returning his own life to normal, but any help would be useful at this point.

"I don't have time to hang around here," Clouse told himself, tossing his jacket back to the chair long enough to head toward his bedroom to gather up some clothes for the impromptu trip. He filled a duffel bag and picked up the phone one more time to call someone he knew would want to take this trip with him.

***

"I'm only taking you with me if you promise to stay by my side every second," Clouse informed Randy Niemeyer as he drove toward Daniels' house.

"Fine, but I don't understand why you're so concerned about my safety," Niemeyer replied as he pulled a nine-millimeter from a shoulder holster to examine it and the magazine inside its metal body.

"It's bad enough I lost Tim. I'm not going to let him down by losing you too. And where the hell did you get that gun?"

Niemeyer quickly stuffed it back into the holster, clipping it securely shut.

"I was a police reserve."

Niemeyer had let his girlfriend keep his kids while he traveled with Clouse. They had dated for years and planned to be married the following spring. He had no reservations in letting her baby-sit while he was away for a day or two.

"I didn't think you'd call," Niemeyer confessed as they neared the detective's residence.

Clouse looked straight ahead, keeping his eyes on the road.

"No one else will go with me," he confessed. "I didn't have much choice unless I wanted to risk going alone."

"Did you even call the police?"

"Not this time. This is the only way to get Zach back."

"You act like you got a list of instructions or something. Is there something you're keeping from me?"

"No," Clouse said. "Once you've been through this, you know how it goes. There are certain rules you have to follow because the person we're dealing with isn't going to make mistakes. He's been planning this for a very long time."

"God, how did you get so unlucky?" Niemeyer commented, forgetting about his own personal tragedy momentarily.

"It's like they say, shit rolls downhill. You kill the psycho trying to kill you, then someone wants revenge, so you kill them. It just goes on and on."

Clouse finally spied his friend's house. He pulled the truck along the curb since the driveway was easily filled with both of Daniels' vehicles. Seeing the lights on inside the house, he stepped from the truck, quickly finding himself ringing the doorbell.

"Paul," Daniels said when he answered the door, apparently surprised to see his friend. "What's the matter?"

Clouse quickly explained the situation, and what happened, including how he called Jane on her cellular phone to avoid confronting her directly. He knew she would never want him to make the trip, and this way he could inform her and still make the trip since he was already on the road.

"Who's that?" Daniels inquired of Niemeyer.

"Tim's little brother. He wants to come along."

"You told him it was dangerous. Right?"

"A hundred times. He won't take no for an answer."

Daniels stepped outside, shutting the door behind him, despite the chilly weather.

"You know I can't help you on this."

"Yeah, I understand. What I want to know is what I should look for. Do you make anything of these trinkets he keeps leaving me?"

"Not really. It sounds to me like he's jerking your chain."

"But why kidnap Zach? What's the motive there?"

"I don't know. Maybe it's a father connection, like we let someone's son get killed so they're taking it out on you."

Clouse thought a second.

"Ryan Andrews?" he pondered aloud.

"He was someone's son, and he might have died. We know Barry Andrews wasn't his real father."

"True. But we don't know who is, either."

Daniels shrugged helplessly.

"Troy is working on that," Clouse pondered aloud. "And do you have anything new?" he asked, looking behind him anxiously.

He was ready for his trip south.

"Nothing spectacular. I think Dr. Jameson was one of the victims."

"Your doctor?"

"Yeah. Her car was one of those parked outside the building."

"Damn," Clouse said sympathetically. He wondered a moment about possible connections, despite the fact he had known her very little. Somehow, every time a person was killed he could almost bet it was connected to the hotel and his dilemma. Thinking of nothing particular, he turned to see Niemeyer looking a bit impatient in his truck. "Look, I've got to get started. We're due to catch a train in an hour."

"A train? Why not fly?"

"Randy wants to bring his nine-millimeter for protection. I'm not going to disagree with that."

Daniels obviously questioned the decision in one regard or another by the look on his face. He started back into the house.

"I'll be right back," he told Clouse, closing the door behind him.

A moment later, he emerged with a plastic case which he popped open to reveal a .357 Magnum and some spare ammunition.

"Those are hollow point bullets," he informed his friend, pointing to the extra rounds. "I know you don't particularly like firearms, but I want you to take this for your own protection. Those rounds are designed to rip apart any soft tissue they encounter and no psycho killer is going to want those hitting his chest."

"You sure about this?"

Daniels nodded.

"I don't use it. You might as well have something to defend yourself with. I just wish you'd call the police when you get down there."

"No way," Clouse said, shaking his head. "I've got to finish this myself."

"What if it's a trap?"

Clouse shrugged, knowing he had no choice.

"I have to go. Whoever this asshole is, he has Zach. I've got to get my son back no matter what it takes." He looked to the truck, seeing Niemeyer grow even more impatient as he fidgeted with his thumbs. "Look, I gotta go."

The two shook hands.

"Good luck, and give me a call when you find something," Daniels said.

"I will," Clouse said before returning to his truck to begin the journey.

***

An hour later the train departed from the south end of Indianapolis with Clouse and Niemeyer in a coach room, bought from a couple willing to delay their own trip for triple what they had paid for the tickets. Clouse hated the notion of throwing his money around, but he had it, and the life of his son was at stake.

Niemeyer understood what his newfound partner was going through, having two children of his own. Clouse would think of nothing but finding Zach until he did so.

"You think they would hurt your boy?" Niemeyer asked as he placed his suitcase inside a storage closet.

"Not if I comply," Clouse replied, taking out one of the diaries from his own luggage. He planned to study more of the West Baden Springs Hotel's history on the way. At this point, time was one luxury he could not afford, and reading would help preoccupy him.

"Any idea why they would want you to go to this theme park?"

"Other than the fact that I now own it, no."

In a manner of speaking, travel by train would almost be as quick as flying. Without the hassles and delays of the airport, the train could make a direct route to Nashville without needing to stop. There was no risk of traffic jams, and Clouse would not have to worry about receiving a speeding ticket or causing an accident due to his state of mind.

"I don't know what to expect when we get there," he told Niemeyer. "It could be a trap, or he could just continue to jerk me around until he's ready to show himself. We could be getting ourselves into any number of things."

"I don't know about you, but I'm getting myself into a tall bottle of beer from the next car," Niemeyer said, speaking of the bar linked to their car. "You want anything?"

"No thanks," Clouse said, looking at the diary. "Be careful, and look for anyone suspicious over there."

"Will do," the younger man replied with an informal salute.

Clouse watched as his colleague in revenge left the car, then opened the diary to the point where he left off, gaining more understanding of the hotel's past.

***

Shortly after Father Ernest's tenure at the hotel began, the priests adopted a young homeless boy whom they named Henry. The boy spoke not a word to the priests and brothers, but complied with everything they asked of him, and soon he fit into their scheme of things, apparently a young brother in training.

At first, the move appeared temporary as Father Runnels searched the state through adoption agencies, police departments, and newspapers. Nothing turned up, and no one stepped forward to claim the boy. In 1937, adoption was a much easier process, and the boy simply became a ward of the Jesuit state. After spending two months with the Jesuits, social services gave him the option of remaining, or being placed in foster care.

Henry vehemently disagreed through shakes of his head with the notion of being taken away. In his own way, he fit in with the Catholic faction. He seldom spoke a word, and worked with as much vigor as anyone there.

In the meantime, things seemed to go well with Father Ernest as the regular priest for services. He had started several new programs, which everyone seemed to enjoy. Ernest initiated more trust with the local residents by putting on larger holiday programs, or having designated days for the locals to help maintain the garden during the spring and summer, a task too monumental for even several dozen priests and brothers who had other matters requiring their attention.

Henry, it seemed, had taken quite a liking to Ernest. Though he was never seen speaking to Ernest, he followed him like a lost puppy, and the two developed a peculiar set of hand signals between them, like sign language, to help them communicate. Ernest had become highly familiar with the grounds, and showed Henry the hotel's historic areas.

One subject Father Ernest and Father Runnels seemed to disagree upon was the remodeling of the hotel, or "desecration" as Ernest put it. A history buff, Ernest hated seeing the hotel altered so drastically for the needs of their religion when it was such a beautiful work of art. He understood the need to live a simple life, but disliked ripping the heart and soul of the building away, like memories lost to amnesia.

With Ernest's opinion seemed to go Henry's. In fact, Runnels began noticing a change of mood amongst the residents toward himself as they enjoyed more of Ernest's ideas than those of his own. At one point, he considered bringing in another regular mass priest, but Ernest seemed to catch the mistrust from Runnels, showing newfound respect for the senior pastor, although it sometimes lacked genuine feel, or might be laced with an undermining tone.

Though the public never saw the inner workings of religious politics, it prevailed as much in the Catholic religion as any other.

In all, Runnels felt Ernest knew his place and abided by it. Why the priest felt a need to express himself so outwardly was beyond him. He understood Ernest's views, and really could not dispute them.

Over the course of the next year, and into 1938, Ernest and Henry were like father and son. It seemed Ernest had fulfilled an obligation of fatherhood the priesthood had denied him. Henry was never seen speaking to anyone, including Ernest, but the rest of the transformed hotel's residents seemed to pick up on the unique sign language, pleasing the boy when they communicated with him using their hands.

Aside from injury grunts or restless sleep, not a soul ever heard a sound from the boy's mouth. Some speculated he was abandoned, others thought he ran away from an abusive home. Back then, kids disappeared and sometimes parents thought it a good thing. Either way he wasn't talking, and, on the day a local couple brought him to the brothers, he had nothing except the clothes he wore, and they bore no clue to his identity.

During the summer, Ernest and Henry set about digging through some of the hotel's remnants for pieces of historical value. They eventually came upon a crate containing some strange artifacts they believed to have belonged to Ed Ballard, and perhaps the hotel's former owners before him.

Ernest claimed he found a wooden cross that contained several engravings and a strange red cube among the items in the collection. The cube was embedded toward the bottom of the long piece where Christ's feet might be nailed if his likeness was fixed upon the crucifix. A gemstone garnet color radiated throughout its semitransparent likeness as though the cube itself were a precious gem. Ernest carried it with him at all times as his personal cross and a bearer of good fortune.

His good fortune ended the next spring when he became gravely ill. A visit to the hospital revealed his body was teeming with bone cancer. He was diagnosed with less than a year to live.

***

"Damn," Clouse said, closing the second diary almost a third of the way through.

Niemeyer had long since come back and gone to sleep after a few beers. Clouse wanted to rest, but a glance at the clock showed he only had an hour before he reached Nashville.

Arriving would be easy. Getting a rental car and directions to his theme park would be a bit more difficult.

The park, named Escape Island, was new within the last five years, and a place Clouse had considered taking his family before he owned it. Being out of season, he had spoken with the park's manager several times about plans for the spring, including renovation, new rides, and safety mandates, choosing to leave most of the important decisions to management for the time being. He hadn't made any solid plans to meet with the park manager and put his two cents in, though Clouse made a tentative plan to travel there in January.

Now he had little choice.

Reaching it at the stroke of midnight was not what he had in mind, but he felt certain he would find something of use there. If he arrived and the gates were still locked, he would feel certain he had arrived first and outdone the killer, but the chances were slim.

Some careful planning and a lot of luck could bring him a long way, and right now he needed good timing as well.

Chapter 10

Tackett felt his heavy eyelids trying to close, even as he drove his pickup toward the cemetery on the outskirts of Bloomington. When a call failed to rouse him, county dispatch paged him. The incessant buzzing of his pager forced him to wake up from the beginning of a good sleep to call and see what problem required his attention.

As he approached the wrought iron bars surrounding the cemetery, the voice of the dispatcher replayed inside his head. He could hear her state that a county patrol officer found a grave dug up at Hillcrest Cemetery with a tombstone bearing a name that would probably interest Tackett greatly in his investigation.

The only remaining flowers along or inside the area were plastic. Any other flowers had to be fresh, or a wilting form of dead from the first frosts of the fall season. Rows of grave markers led Tackett's eyes to the back of the cemetery, a place sectioned off from the rest of the area reserved for especially important people.

He spied an old rustic truck and a county police car parked outside the area, and an open grave resting at a somewhat tilted position inside its plot. Tackett stepped from his truck, seeing his breath in the cold, midnight air. He barely had time to put on his boots and an old work shirt before leaving the house. Considering the nature of the call, there was no need to get well-dressed.

"What do we have?" he asked Wendell Stephens, the officer who found the grave. Behind him stood a man dressed in overalls, who apparently hadn't bothered to shave, but seemed visibly shaken as his blond hair strayed from beneath a John Deere cap.

"Bill over there found a disturbance about an hour ago when he came out to prepare a grave area for a funeral."

Tackett gave a funny smirk, based on the time of day Bill decided to section off a grave and the fact that no one had noticed anything sooner.

"He says this area of the cemetery is hidden by that row of trees over there. It would be hard to notice, even from the regular area."

"Maybe."

"The reason I called you out here is the name on the grave," Stephens said, walking the detective toward the tombstone.

Tackett walked toward the marker, unable to see anything except its blunt shape until a stream of light from Stephens' flashlight illuminated the stone. The detective studied the marker momentarily until the lighting moved away from the name so he could finally read it without it being whited out. All at once, the breath left his body and the cold air around him seemed to overtake the inside of his body. He exhaled a short burst of breath before he could bring himself to speak.

"Holy shit. Martin Smith?" he asked aloud of the name before him.

"He *is* the one who owned that hotel, isn't he?" Stephens asked.

"Yeah. He died there too."

"Could this have anything to do with your investigation?"

"It very well might," Tackett replied, looking over the empty grave carefully. He stood up suddenly, wanting some equipment from his truck before he could thoroughly inspect the robbed area. "Can you question Bill for me, Wendell?" he asked with a sarcastic tone on the grave keeper's name, implying the man was too ignorant of his surroundings to be much help.

Stephens nodded an affirmative and Tackett walked to his truck, taking out a flashlight and a camera case before heading back to examine the site.

Shining the light over the empty grave and casket, he noticed some of the bedding inside disturbed and the casket laid at a strange angle, as though the grave robber actually pulled one end up to get at the body better. Grunting to himself, he began sifting through the bedding slowly, methodically, to uncover any further clues. Latex gloves would not prove necessary for such an investigation since forensic evidence would never be used in court on a grave robbing case. Only murders and rape cases took such precedence for DNA evidence to be collected and used.

Tackett felt around the pillow area, noticing little in the line of hair or skin fibers. In most cases where bodies were exhumed such fibers would be found, possibly in abundance, in the area where hair decayed and fell from the skull. Of course, most of those bodies were older, so it was difficult for him to tell for certain without a more experienced opinion. He planned to ask the coroner's opinion later.

Around the grave, he spotted regular shovel marks, but no traces of cloth, or even tire treads. Apparently, the robber had chosen to remain parked on the paved drive, leaving no clues for Tackett to trace.

"Damn it," he said to himself, watching Stephens interview the cemetery's keeper.

He wondered why anyone would want to steal the doctor's body, and what good it might do. Somehow it was affixed with everything he was investigating, but exactly how remained a mystery. He stared at the full moon above him, seeing his breath in the air, wondering just what it would take to discover who was behind the murders and who the next victim might be.

***

Just inside the gates of Escape Island, security guard Joe Williamson looked beyond the iron bars to the sea of black pavement, divided by painted white lines, devoid of all vehicles this time of year.

The inside looked no better.

During the park's off-season the only visitors it saw were security guards and the occasional construction person, whether a designer or worker. Usually heavy renovation began in the fall, took a short winter break, and commenced again in February or March. Nothing big was being built for the spring opening, leaving the park more desolate than usual.

The bigwigs in the corporate office only came to the park during weekdays, usually to meet corporate sponsors and take extended lunches. After October the park became a ghost town, so for the time being Williamson had the park to himself. Being alone in so much acreage worried him in two different ways.

One, he was miles from realistic help in an emergency situation.

Two, there was too much area, and too many hiding places, for one security guard to effectively and safely patrol.

Somewhat of a loner, the security guard had never made time for a family. He worked two jobs and provided himself a spacious apartment and four-wheel-drive truck, the essentials in his life. He had also amassed enough firearms to concern any neighbors who saw him move in. Some thought he might be a separationist who dared the government to come get him.

Actually, he was a simple man exercising his Second Amendment rights.

A bit overweight, with a sizeable bald spot, Williamson found his chances of being married by middle age decreasing. He had spent so long enjoying bachelorhood that he forgot to take time for any sort of lasting relationship. His weekends consisted of taverns and local clubs in the Nashville area, but he never learned, or didn't care, that every Saturday and Sunday morning he woke up alone.

During the regular season, Williamson had served as a supervisor for the security force. He often assigned patrol areas, assisted in the hiring process of new employees, and helped develop new ideas for improved security in the park. Unfortunately, during the season none of the guards were allowed to carry fire-arms, much to his disappointment.

Now he carried a nine-millimeter at his side with several extra magazines clinging to his gun belt.

Though the park management took most of his suggestions into consider-ation, they felt some were unnecessary, hence him working alone in the off-season with no additional security.

Walking along one of the wrought iron gates he could see several water rides looming behind wooden fences further down the walkway. One would be torn down in the spring after a mere three years of operation to make room for a newer log ride with greater height, more splashes, and several more twists and turns. It would feature creative scenes of mechanical loggers who would divert the atten-tion of riders long enough to make them forget about the large drop ahead.

He remembered the old ride having several problems, including a few incidents of the logs getting stuck along the peak of the ride, which paralleled the tree line. Some people publicly swore off the ride after that, and the media blew the situation out of proportion. Soon after, the state launched an investigation of the park, including the log ride. It seemed several bolts were missing that tied the plastic tracks together.

Management explained not every single hole needed to be bolted to keep the tracks in line, but the media crucified them again, despite the park passing every safety standard necessary in the state of Tennessee.

As he walked along, Williamson fingered his firearm and steel baton resting at either side of his gun belt. A stiff wind continually darted across the park from the vacant parking lots through the equally empty concrete paths, which would be lined with visitors the following spring.

Several overhead lamps reflected light off the puddles in the path ahead. He wondered if they might freeze over with the wind chill factor. He zipped his nylon jacket almost to the top and adjusted his security baseball cap for a more comfort-able fit. It would be a miserable midnight shift if he stayed outside much longer.

Having access to any of the buildings helped keep him safe from the ele-ments, and running the attractions could be momentarily amusing, but none of the buildings provided much warmth unless he wanted to wait an eternity for the heating units to do their job. Usually it proved easier to head for the security office, but it was across the park, and the numb feeling along his earlobes told him he needed to get inside soon.

Williamson quickly unlocked the door to the nursery where infants played and lost children were brought during the regular season. Pastel colors lined the walls around him while boxes of building blocks and miscellaneous toys were stacked in a corner.

His thoughts turned to the guard shack and the idea of a hot cup of coffee. He reached for the light switch, staring out the window as he did so. Lights glimmered across the puddles of water sitting outside before a dark figure blocked the streams of light momentarily. Williamson's finger froze at the bottom of the light switch as his eyes followed a man dressed in black darting across the walkway.

Unsure of how a person could slip through the fencing that encircled the entire park, the guard decided to play it cool and quietly step outside. He wanted to know why someone would want to sneak into the park, especially in such abominable weather.

Adrenaline flowed through him as he pursued the unwary trespasser along the concrete strip. The person seemed very deliberate in the path he took, and he seemed to know the layout of the park, walking without hesitation in a heated pace, as though on a time limit.

Finally, the man reached the information center, finding the booth in front to his liking. He took out what appeared to be several sheets of paper, perhaps postcards, and tacked them up along the information board outside the booth.

"What in the hell?" Williamson asked himself, amazed this was the objective of the trespasser, who set some sort of garden tool along the booth as he finished his work. The long, wooden handle gave it away.

As far from evil as the person's intent seemed, Williamson felt obligated to stop him and call the police. He unlatched his holster, ready to draw his firearm when the trespasser heard the noise, spun around and saw the unexpected guard standing only the length of a bus from him. His work already finished, he took up the handled tool and darted off behind the information building down another path before Williamson could even think of firing the gun.

He gave chase, running down the path to discover it fingered off into three separate paths with the stranger nowhere in sight.

"He's not that fast," the guard commented to himself, certain the perpetrator had found a nearby building or ride to hide behind. There were several along either path he chose.

Williamson darted to the first building on his left, finding nothing behind it. He quickly scurried to several more, carefully holding his gun at his chest, ready to fire if necessary. He had no idea what else the trespasser might have in mind.

He switched to the next path, looking in every direction as he passed through. Checking building after building with no success, he found himself left with a small restroom area off to one side. He approached with caution, checking the women's stall first, finding nothing except drained, winterized toilets. The men's side provided more of the same.

After stepping outside, the guard grew frustrated, feeling certain the man had gotten away. He stood motionless, listening against the wind howling through the vacant rides and attractions as though it might give him some clues.

He had just about given up hope when he heard a muffled cough from behind the restroom area. Williamson stood still momentarily, finally deciding to go around the opposite way to surprise the trespasser. He quietly set to sneaking around the restroom area, trying desperately to keep his breathing in check because he was winded from so much running.

Stopping for only a second a few yards short of the last corner, Williamson held his firearm close, ready to do whatever might be necessary to keep the trespasser at bay. He sucked in his breath and sprang toward the last corner, hoping to catch his quarry by surprise.

Williamson rounded the corner to find a sharp pain in his abdomen as the combined force of his run, along with the powerful swing of a scythe, combined for a fatal blow. An odd groan, then a gurgle came from deep inside his throat before he felt warm blood trickle out of his mouth from internal bleeding. His gun clacked against the ground, lying as motionless as he soon would.

Wasting little precious time, the killer scooped up the gun, using the scythe to drag the guard along behind him. Blood streaks lined the paths as Williamson was toted along, moaning and slowly dying from blood loss and the gaping wound in his stomach. The wounds were broadened by the dragging, causing him greater agony before he finally expired about halfway through the journey to the killer's destination.

The night's events were just beginning, and the killer had many more places to visit before he was done.

Chapter 11

On the way out of the car rental shop, Clouse used his portable phone to call Jane back at the farm. It rang twice before she answered with a tone of grave concern, as though she hoped he would check in with her.

"Jane, it's me," he said as Niemeyer drove, following the map Clouse had asked the car rental salesman to draw.

"It's about time you called," she scolded him. "I've been worried sick about you."

"I'm sorry. I knew you'd be upset if I told you before I left. There's no other way to do this, Jane."

"Any word on Zach yet?"

"No, but the bastard wouldn't dare kill him. I'm the one he's after, and he's got me playing his little game, just like he wants."

"I just wish you wouldn't have left like that."

"Don't worry about me. I'll be fine."

Jane paced through the living room knowing Katie was sleeping upstairs and the house was secure from any unwanted visitors.

"How can I not worry? You take off in the middle of the afternoon and just leave me a note that your son has been kidnapped. How on earth did he get inside?"

"He knew our code. Did you change it like I asked?" Clouse inquired, speaking about the note he left his wife.

"I got it changed. It's the first code we had out here, only backwards."

"Good. I should be back tomorrow. I'll call if I find anything useful."

"Be careful, Paul. Do you have anyone with you?"

"I've got Randy Niemeyer. Tim's little brother."

Jane stopped her pacing a moment, unsure if she had ever met him.

"Can you trust him?" she questioned in a hushed tone. She knew her husband's trust had been broken twice before by people close to him, nearly to the point of death.

"I think so, considering the circumstances," he replied, referring to his friend's untimely death.

"Okay. Be careful, Paul. It could be a trap."

"I will. Make sure you keep the dogs around you at all times."

"They're in here."

"Good. Love you."

"Love you too."

Clouse hung up the phone and turned his attention to Niemeyer, whose eyes were glued to the road ahead.

"Might want to slow down a bit there, Randy," Clouse said, noticing the speedometer significantly higher than the posted limit. "We don't need to be getting pulled over when we're this close."

"Sorry," Niemeyer replied. "We're just a few minutes away though."

"We'll get there. Two minutes won't matter much. And we might already be too late for whatever that asshole has in mind."

Almost ten minutes later the car pulled into the parking lot of the theme park, its lights glistening against the wrought iron poles, secured by both electronic and padlock devices. Sharp tips atop the iron bars dared trespassers to climb them without being impaled or hurt from the jump to the other side.

"Feeling energetic?" Clouse asked as he stepped from the car.

"Not in the suicidal sense, no."

Both walked up to the fence, tracing its path down the parking lot, seeing if there was an end to the treacherous points. To their left the fence flowed into a grove of trees, turning into a mesh fence with barbwire at the top, as tall as a tractor trailer.

"God, I've inherited a concentration camp," Clouse muttered as he approached the fence. "See if there's anything we can throw over that fence," he told Niemeyer.

"You don't have a set of keys to this place?"

"Unfortunately, no. It's one of those little things my lawyer and I were going to work out later. We're going to have to do some climbing, Randy."

Five minutes and several bumps and bruises later, the two men found themselves inside the main gate of the theme park. Clouse wasted little time in pushing forward toward the main entrance and the attractions inside, waiting to see what was in store for him. As he stepped through the main entrance, he found a boulevard of things to do when the park was open, ranging from theme stores to instant photo booths.

"This could take forever," Niemeyer commented.

"Or maybe we've beaten him here. I don't know how else he would have gotten past the gates."

"This is a big park, Paul. I'm sure if you walk the perimeter you'll find an easier way in."

"True," Clouse said, pushing forward. "But it would take some time doing it."

As hopeful as he might be, Clouse still knew the killer was meticulous and always one step ahead of him. Somehow, he felt, an opportunity would present itself where he could outsmart the killer and find his son.

Much like any theme park, it held several roller coasters, a variety of eating venues, rides for younger children, and all kinds of games meant to rob people of their money by having them throw a ball or ring into a nearly impossible target. Most were closed to virtual shells of their normal appearance, some even boarded up to protect them from the impending winter season.

Clouse noticed a wooden roller coaster looming almost two hundred feet above them in the distance, wondering briefly what the drop was like. He also realized the place was too vast to find one individual easily.

The two men rounded the first corner to find a glossy streak along the path, as though to guide them somewhere. Clouse looked around, noticing the dark streak was only along this path, and somewhat broken several times down the line. He knelt to examine the substance, rubbing his fingertips along it before looking at them.

"Blood," he said with no surprise in his voice. He already felt a certain remorse knowing someone had died, and that he had not beaten the killer at his own game.

"It leads down here," Niemeyer said, walking first toward a cluster of attractions centered by the information booth.

Both slowed their pace when they found Williamson's body slumped against the booth, ending the trail of blood designed to lead them right to the very spot where the killer had left the next clue. While Niemeyer confirmed no life existed in the guard's body, Clouse looked up to the tacked glossy sheets.

He plucked them from their tack, noticing multiple photographs this time. He flipped through the stack, realizing the shots were taken as though from a surveillance position, and they were of his wedding ceremony and honeymoon, all of which had taken place, coincidentally, in Tennessee.

"Holy shit," he said, finding five pictures in total, the last being the most recent.

"What?" Niemeyer asked, bolting to his feet for a look.

"Isn't this your older brother?" Clouse asked, recalling how he had just met Scott Niemeyer at Tim's funeral.

Niemeyer examined it a few seconds. The photo appeared to be taken at the funeral itself, showing Scott walking out from the funeral home surrounded by family, but he was obviously the focal point of the picture.

"It *is* Scott."

Clouse flipped the photos over for any further evidence. On the last photo of his honeymoon experience, he found the words, "Relive your honeymoon." And on the photo of Niemeyer's older brother he saw the words, "or save a life."

"Damn it," Clouse said, realizing the killer knew more about his every move than he could possibly have imagined. "He's trying to split us up."

"I have to check on Scott," Niemeyer said immediately.

"Call him."

"I will. But I'm going to make sure he's safe too," Niemeyer insisted.

"Then our killer has his wish," Clouse said to himself, "because I have to check on the cabins where I had my honeymoon."

Clouse briefly considered taking the guard's keys for an easy exit, but decided he didn't want to touch the body in any way. After all, he was not supposed to be at the park, and he wanted to avoid the police in every possible sense at the moment.

As the two headed toward their entrance point, they discussed what plan of action might suit them best.

"Are you going to call the police?" Niemeyer asked, referring to the corpse at the information center.

"No. It'll slow us down and get us more involved. We don't have time to deal with the police and fill out reports. Someone will report him missing and find the body."

"And how are we going to go separate ways with one car?"

"You can drop me off at the next rental place we find and I'll get another car. I won't be able to talk to anyone at the cabins until morning anyhow. You need to make sure your brother is okay."

Clouse understood the importance of family, and how his son was being used as a pawn to ensure he played the game of life and death one last time. He was losing patience for the conclusion of the game, but left with little choice except to follow the clues.

"Once I'm sure Scott and his family are safe, we'll find out who this son-of-a-bitch is," Niemeyer vowed once they neared the rental car after scaling the fence.

"You do what you have to," Clouse said. "Your family has to come first, and I don't want to put you at risk any more than I have to."

As they left the parking lot, Clouse wondered how much more death would be laid at his feet before the killer was content.

Chapter 12

At the crack of dawn Mike Carter crossed the field of a friend's property to find his tree stand in the distant woods, prepared to conduct some deer hunting. At the outskirts of Bloomington, it was by no means an inconvenience for Carter to drive there.

Perhaps hunting wasn't completely accurate since he just basically sat around waiting for unsuspecting deer to approach so he could ambush them with an arrow through the heart. Either way, he enjoyed the sport testing the limits of his patience and endurance, waiting for the kill.

Most days he was an accountant, and this was his yearly release of energy, a vacation of sorts. He was in the middle of a two-week break from work, and the seasonal growth of his beard had begun.

Dressed in full camouflage, cap and face net included, he trudged through the field to the area he usually enjoyed hunting. A tree stand was available, but often he would pick a spot on the ground against a tree, downwind, to sit and wait. Granted unlimited use of the property, Carter exercised the privilege and made excellent use of the land.

As he reached the end of the field, Carter tested the wind direction and decided where he needed to sit to avoid his scent traveling to any sensitive noses. Though his friend was away, he would be able to use the four-wheeler and car located next to the barn several hundred yards up from the house.

At the edge of the woods sat a blanket of dry leaves in every direction. He carefully stepped into the fray, hoping to avoid making too much noise. Soon enough he found a tree large enough to conceal him, and near an open area where deer might feed and drink since a small stream ran past, all within perfect view.

While he made himself comfortable for a several-hour sit, Carter peered around him, seeing little except naked trees and an overcast sky. Minutes passed as he examined the leaves, a few of which still fell from above. A cracking branch in the distance drew a quick look from the hunter, but he saw nothing except nature.

He didn't particularly like hunting alone when no one was around for miles. An impending danger of being shot by another hunter always loomed, and one never knew about the strange happenings inside wooded areas. Too many times, he had read about people disappearing into the woods, never to return, or shallow graves quickly being dug by child molesters or serial killers.

Carter squinted questionably when something odd caught his attention in the open area, sticking up from a thin layer of leaves. He stared intently, but could not decipher the object entirely, though it's grayish color clashed with the natural colors of the woods. A few minutes passed as his curiosity grew, and finally he decided to risk setting back his deer kill by investigating the object that seemed out of place on his friend's property.

Momentarily, he approached the object, which looked more like a bony arm with fingers reaching toward the sky as he drew closer. When he finally looked down on the entity, he confirmed it was an arm he'd spied from a distance. Only it and a skull, partly mummified, pierced the soil and the leafy blanket atop the ground.

The skull's mouth was open, as though this person had died in agony. Most of the skin was intact, though drawn tightly, like the husk of a grape drying into a raisin. Dark hair tufts were trapped beneath the skull, indicating part of it had been dug up for some time. Claw marks around the body indicated dogs or wildlife had begun to dig the body up from its shallow grave recently, but probably before the fall.

Carter took a deep breath as he stared into the eye sockets, noticing the eyes were intact, but gray in color and sinking back into the skull. He was amazed how preserved the body appeared, but its condition left him questioning exactly how long the victim had been dead, and exactly how the body had made its way to his friend's property.

He carefully stepped backward, keeping his eyes fixed on the body in the hope of remembering its location when he brought the police back. Shock and horror took a few minutes to catch up with his body, but he suddenly felt panicked and numb at the same time, wanting some distance between himself and the unidentified corpse.

"Oh...my God," he murmured as he reached the end of the field, ready to dart for his Bronco parked in the distance. The realization of what he had discovered fully set in when he got away from the secretive woods.

If this person was brutally murdered, who was to say there weren't more bodies? And if multiple bodies littered the woods, what little provocation did a serial killer need to bump off a witness to his makeshift cemetery?

Carter opened the door to his vehicle, reaching for his cellular phone as he looked down the road, seeing the closest house half a mile away on either side. Carter remembered seeing a conservation officer down the road, at a park, ticketing some fishermen, probably due to a lack of license. He put the phone down, deciding to see if the officer might still be in the area.

***

Clouse had camped out most of the morning on the steps of the Heartful Lodge registration area where he knew most of the wedding chapel business was operated. Most of the night into the morning had been spent examining the photos, wondering who took them and retracing every step of his recent marriage and honeymoon.

"Damn it," he said in frustration as he flipped through the set.

Niemeyer had phoned to inform him his brother and family were fine, but he was staying with them until he felt certain they were safe. Clouse understood, especially after the loss of so many friends and family in his own life.

It seemed the killer wanted to make certain Clouse was alone during the remainder of his journey, using Niemeyer's brother as a red herring to separate them.

Clouse recalled that his wedding had been simple and quick. With the recent inheritance, he easily afforded to fly his friends and family down. Looking around, he saw the chapel and its surrounding furnishings still very much the same. The coating of leaves along the ground and the pumpkins seated atop hay bales gave it a different look than the blooming flowers and leafy trees he remembered from the spring, but it was equally beautiful.

He peered at the first photo of his wedding party and guests standing in front of the chapel while he and Jane took the customary carriage ride around the square. It looked as though they were just about to leave, or just returning from the ride, since people surrounded the carriage snapping photos.

Someone had taken one from quite a bit further away, but the details were clear, and the image was close enough to determine someone had used a telephoto lens, but stood close enough to the group to take a quality picture. Clouse tried to recall who might have been standing in the distance, but he was too involved with his own bliss to have looked.

He tried to remember every detail of his wedding, wondering where and when the four photos had been taken.

On the day of the wedding, he and Jane had been scheduled for a four o'clock ceremony.

Each wedding was hurried along to fit within an hour's time. Clouse had paid double for two hours of time so relatives and friends could take all the photos they wanted and spend more time at the chapel itself, rather than rush off to the reception.

Simply put, he wanted to enjoy his day.

For the longest time he and Jane had debated whether to do a western style wedding or traditional. Since both had done the traditional wedding once, and considering the beautiful area in which they would be wed, they ultimately decided to have a casual wedding where guests could wear blue jeans or whatever they desired. Clouse had reached a point in his life where he wanted to do things his own way without constantly having to worry about what other people thought.

When he and Jane first pulled up to the chapel in his truck, he remembered seeing one couple returning from their carriage ride. He observed them from the chapel's exterior balcony while he gathered his essentials for the marriage. As the bride stood on a green mat in front of the river for her family to take photos, he recalled the groom nervously puffing on a cigarette, probably relieved after the longest hour of his life coming to a close.

Minutes later Clouse and his groomsmen, including Tim Niemeyer, were ushered inside while another ceremony finished inside the chapel. In a back room, they were able to change clothes and talk with the minister about what would take place.

A short, hunched man of about seventy years, he spoke with what seemed to be a drunken slur, although there were no indications he was intoxicated. He unveiled the ceremony's events in a comical way, keeping the wedding party on their toes and maintaining their comfort level at the same time, as though he were a fatherly officer about to lead them to battle.

No matter what, they were in it together.

Soon enough the ceremony took place, and Clouse could not recall anyone present he was not introduced to. Everyone in attendance was either a friend or relative to Clouse or his bride. Whoever took the four pictures was not someone he had consciously noticed.

The next photo showed him and Jane outside their reception building in an intimate kiss. This particular shot would have been easy, since it was during a ten-minute break the two took from the festivities inside.

He remembered what a mistake Jane's parents had made, chancing the reception entertainment on a Karaoke disk jockey. The mistake wasn't in the choice of music, but rather the fact that the man himself did all the singing. Almost halfway through the reception most of the guests departed to the bar downstairs to watch a baseball game on television or sing with an actual Karaoke machine where they could request nearly any song they wanted.

Amongst all this, when people were paying more attention to the alcohol or picking out a song to sing, the newlyweds snuck outside for a private moment.

"Is this everything you wanted?" Clouse remembered asking his new wife.

"And then some," she replied, planting a kiss on his lips.

Both looked down to the lake hugging the shore where the reception was held. Several boats sped by the dock down the hill. Sometimes people would rent the building simply for use of the boats docked there. Clouse had enough boating in Bloomington with his own craft, a small yacht he had bought with his newfound fortune to replace the boat buried in silt along Lake Monroe's bottom.

An attempt on his life the year before resulted in the loss of his beloved boat at the end of the boating season.

"Are you glad we did it this way?" Jane asked him as they stared at the ripples in the lake, the music from above filling the air around them.

"Yeah, I'm glad. There's no sense drawing it out and making everyone go through the trouble of a big wedding. It feels good to finally have it out of the way."

The two had already been living together for over a year with both children. Their marriage was simply a legal sanctification of the lives they already led.

"You're forgetting we just made everyone drive all the way to Tennessee for our wedding," Jane pointed out.

"And some flew out here. At least we paid for everything."

"So you're *really* happy?"

"I am," Clouse said, wrapping her in his arms. "It finally feels like my life is complete again."

They kissed a few more times before Tim Niemeyer came out to inform them the song they requested was loaded in the machine. Neither husband nor wife had sung in front of so many people before, and Clouse vowed he would never do so again.

Clouse sighed, recalling nothing of use from the reception. The photo could easily have been taken from a car or somewhere in the woods on the side opposite the lake. Again, the person's intent was obviously not to be seen.

He stared at the next, and most invading of the photos. It depicted him and Jane seated before a large fire at the cabin's fireplace the first night of their honeymoon. He knew it was the first night of the four because that was the only night they actually sat on the floor in front of the fireplace.

What had been a special night, now burned inside his mind and his gut. He recalled preparing the fire, filling the whirlpool hot tub, and having catered food delivered to make their first married night together special.

Starting simply enough, Clouse lit several candles and the fire while Jane changed in one of the bedrooms. The cabin, adorned with birdhouses and works of art lining several permanent shelves built into one wall, felt homey.

Soon enough the two were seated before the fire feeding one another cheese balls and drinking red wine. They kissed while beginning to undress one another. Being a warm night, the windows were all open, though veiled curtains blew aside with the breeze crossing through the cabin. Clouse felt mildly uncomfortable in such an open setting, so he broke away long enough to run hot water into the whirlpool spa.

Since the living area of the cabin was on the second story, and only two stairwells led up to it, Clouse wondered what sort of strange noise he might be hearing from the outside. As he filled the Jacuzzi, another creaking noise pierced the wall from outside, alerting him that something might not be right.

He walked out of the room and toward the door as though he had a normal purpose, to ensure Jane was not falsely alarmed.

"What are you doing?" she asked, obviously perplexed by him stepping out for a moment after their few passionate minutes.

"Getting some firewood," he replied, referring to the stack at the bottom of the outside front stairs.

"We have plenty," Jane retorted with a strange grin.

"Just to make sure," Clouse said with a convincing smile before he stepped outside.

He recalled finding nothing outside, and no traces of any trespassers. His fears subsided, but he felt unnerved most of the evening. Clouse closed the windows when he returned inside, and locked the doors before he and Jane spent the rest of the night together, away from the past and the cares of the world.

Again, nothing of tangible significance came to mind, and the photo of he and Jane at the airport as they prepared to leave Tennessee triggered no recollection either. He began to wonder just who would hate him enough to plan the abduction of his child and the personal hell he was now forced to endure for a year.

His attention returned to the setting around him, and he found some solace when a white SUV pulled into the drive and he saw the owner step out, giving him a curious look.

Perhaps some of his questions would finally be answered.

***

"I can't believe you actually found a body back here," the conservation officer told Carter as they walked from their vehicles toward the area where the body was partially unearthed.

"It's back here. I swear it," Carter said, his camouflage mask removed, and his sweater replaced with a jacket of the same pattern. He left his compound bow and arrows with his vehicle to assure this officer his mindset was not foul play.

The conservation officer's forest green uniform hardly blended in with the tan and orange colors of the fall around him as the two approached the area. He wore a thick vinyl jacket of the same color and a brimmed hat like Smokey the Bear. On his right side, a gun remained holstered beside his handcuffs, and his portable radio rested opposite those items. Like most other men in his profession, he remained slender because so much of his time was spent on foot amongst nature, hardly ever taking lunch breaks at fast food restaurants.

"There," Carter said, seeing the arm sticking up from the ground ahead.

Squinting, the officer saw the partly decomposed remains soon after, a look of both apprehension and intrigue showing in his face. It was, after all, the first time he had been the first officer to view a corpse at a crime scene in over a decade of law enforcement.

Naturally, conservation officers usually dealt with hunters, fishermen, and wild game more than standard police issues. They were trained to be loners with a strong sense of independence and survival instincts that kept them away from mainstream police work and the situations most officers were drawn to.

He referred to himself and other such officers as the cowboys of law enforcement, and rightfully so in most instances.

"I'll be damned," he said, standing beside Carter as they both stared at the tormented body, frozen eternally in a painful struggle with death, which he had already lost. His soul enjoyed no rest as he lay atop hardened soil, unable to enjoy the peaceful slumber that waited beneath.

"Holy Mother of God," the officer said, stepping over to a tree as he reached for his radio. "I've got to call this in and get the coroner out here."

As the officer touched the button to his radio an arrow whistled through the air, pinning his back against the tree after piercing his abdomen through the front. He cried out in pain, though the wound wouldn't place him in mortal danger for some time. In a nearly helpless position, with Carter looking on in terror, the officer reached for his gun, unlatching the holster as another arrow pierced the morning air, missing wildly as the officer saw his attacker in the distance.

After wasting valuable time trying to pry the lodged arrow loose from his abdomen, the officer once again turned to drawing his duty weapon, seeing his attacker draw closer. He began pulling it from the holster when another arrow sailed through the air with incredible speed, finding its mark in the center of his throat.

"Oh, shit!" Carter said, watching the last few seconds of the officer's life end with him gurgling blood in his throat, and choking to death in a futile attempt to breathe.

If not for the mortified feeling overtaking his senses, the hunter might have run a few seconds sooner, but his mind simply couldn't register why anyone would dare attack an officer of the law. Carter now watched as the murderer, dressed in black, but revealed to him plainly, reached for another arrow from the pack beside him.

The hunter's own bow and arrows.

"God, no!" he yelled as he bolted into the woods, trying to escape what seemed an inevitable death.

Taking chase, the killer stalked him through the woods, trying to get a good aim, but unable to lock in through the brush and trees. He quickly discarded the strung weapon and arrows, unsheathing a knife from beside him as he darted into a different thicket than the hunter.

Considering the role reversal Carter experienced, he did not handle it well. A monger for control, he felt helpless running from the killer with no weapon left to defend himself, still assuming an arrow could crack his sternum at any moment.

Looking frantically around, Carter saw nothing except bare trees and mounds of leaves and dirt. He stood still momentarily, afraid to move in any direction. Turning clockwise he peered into the woods, listening for any movement. It seemed a cracking branch or strange wind could be heard everywhere he turned, but he saw no sign of the killer.

"Holy shit," he muttered, unsure of which direction to choose.

He could dart for the edge of the field in the hope of getting to his truck, and possibly get ambushed, or he could run further into the woods and risk losing himself in the plentiful acreage, which also put him in harm's way.

Deciding on a neutral course, Carter bolted along the edge of the field away from his truck for the time being. He was too far back to see the road or any sign of civilization, but he had an idea of just how far he had traveled.

As he ran, Carter tried to look in each direction, particularly behind him. As a thicket of trees drew closer to him, he took one last look behind, seeing nothing, but tripping over a large branch as he did so.

With the wind knocked out of him, the hunter slowly posted his arms, trying to regain his footing when a dark pair of pants loomed at eye level as he knelt. A look further upward revealed the shimmer of a knife before it lodged itself in the back of his torso, on the left side where it would surely render fatal damage.

Carter's eyes filled with the agony his insides felt, then rolled back as he slumped to the ground, unable to move as blood gushed from his wound, pooling on the ground beside him. For a moment, the killer stared at the knife, wondering whether or not to yank it out for one more stab, just to make certain his prey never moved again.

As several weak moans from the dying hunter rose from his horizontal body, along with steam no more abundant than that from a cup of coffee, police sirens echoed in the background. The killer quickly realized his efforts had been for nothing because the conservation officer had keyed his radio.

Even though he never spoke to his dispatcher, simply touching the radio would emit a signal to dispatchers, and they would obviously reply and receive no answers. Based on the officer's last location it would take no time to find his vehicle, and subsequently, his body.

Instead of keeping the identity of the corpse a secret as planned, the killer had just added to the death toll needlessly and endangered his plan in the process. Taking up the knife from Carter's backside, he drew another groan from the hunter before stomping off further into the woods to contemplate the next phase of his devious scheme.

Chapter 13

Clouse approached the vehicle with caution as an older gentleman, easily old enough to be his father, stepped from the white off-road vehicle. He gave a quizzical look to his disheveled visitor, wondering if an expectant groom might be in haste of reserving a cabin for his honeymoon.

"Can I help you?" the man asked, grabbing a briefcase and a separate bundle of papers from inside his vehicle.

"I'm not sure how to ask this," Clouse said as the two walked toward the largest of the log cabins, which acted merely as a main office where paperwork was stored, checks were collected, and appointments fulfilled.

"Ask what?" the man asked as he unlocked the front door.

Clouse looked around him for a moment, seeing a few of the resort cabins in the distance, surrounded by woods as far as he could see. His honeymoon cabin would be further down the road.

"I need to see the cabin where I stayed for my honeymoon," Clouse almost implored immediately as the two stepped inside.

"Lose something?"

"Kind of."

"We have a lost and found, you know? How long ago are we talking?"

"Back in May."

The older man shot him a strange look as he put the papers atop a desk. Already Clouse considered the consequences of disclosing the entire truth, but it seemed too bizarre for even him to accept, much less a complete stranger.

But he would do whatever it took to see that cabin.

"May was a while back. What is it you're looking for?"

A clue, Clouse thought.

"It was cabin fifteen," he said instead. "I'll pay you whatever it takes for a look around."

"It may be occupied," the owner said with a look of genuine concern, as though Clouse's intent might be sinister. He knew men would attempt drastic measures for a drug stash or valuables. In his best interest, he decided to comply as best he could.

Leafing through a file cabinet beside the desk, he pulled the file for cabin fifteen, discovering it was rented for the next two days. He wanted to know the name of his visitor in case a police report was necessary later.

"What did you say the name was?"

"Clouse. It was under Clouse."

A peculiar look crossed the man's face as he skimmed the sheet for the May date, finding it, then finding a listing for the same name again.

"It says you've already reserved it for today," he stammered slowly. "Paid for in cash."

"What?" the distraught father inquired. "Who paid in cash? Who reserved that room? I have to know."

"According to the initials, I took that order," the old man stated. "I take it from the way you're acting, you aren't the one who reserved it?"

"Not at all. Whoever did, sir, is leading me on a wild goose chase, and I want to know who's messing with me. *Can* you help me?" Clouse asked with a serious determination that let the man know he was fully truthful.

"Well, I don't know if–"

"Try to remember who paid cash for that room and when, please."

After thinking for a moment, the owner stared at the paper until something in his eyes showed that he remembered.

"It was a phone call," he said slowly. "The man said he and his wife hadn't gotten enough of the place the first time around and wanted a few more days to rekindle the flame."

"That's how he said it?"

"Yeah, exactly how he said it."

"How did you receive the payment?"

"It was mailed to me a few days after the confirmation of his room."

"That didn't strike you as odd?" Clouse inquired.

"Of course it did. He said something about having a little bit of money to throw around. Acted like the money wasn't really his, and he wasn't entitled to it, but he'd happily spend it."

Another figurative slap in the face. Now the killer apparently felt Clouse in no way deserved the inheritance he received from Dr. Smith the year before. Considering he was not blood relation to the doctor, the notion was partly in the right.

"Can I have the key to the room?"

"Sure," the owner said, taking it from under the front counter. "While you're over there, I'll see if there's anything else I can find about whoever rented the cabin."

"Thanks," Clouse said, heading out to his rental car. He wondered what was in store for him inside the cabin.

***

Troy Tackett had just walked in the door of the sheriff's department when the dispatcher received word about the dead conservation officer at the edge of town. They requested whatever investigative unit was available, meaning Tackett, or someone from the city if necessary. He wasted little time in returning to his warm unmarked car and headed out to the residence where the body was reportedly found.

When he arrived, he found Mark Daniels hunched over the corpse sticking halfway out from the ground, examining how it was positioned.

"What are you doing here?" he asked the city detective.

"Dispatch called me and Lipscomb in, thinking you might be indisposed. We're borderline city limits here."

"Where is your partner?"

"He's back in the woods looking around," Daniels said of the rookie detective.

"And the coroner's office?"

"They've been notified. They said to do our thing since the body was so old, but they'll be here with EMS to transport it when we're done."

Tackett stepped back to the body pinned to the tree by arrows, blood slowly dripping to the ground from the wounds. It had slowed to a trickling drop every few seconds like a faucet with a worn seal.

He had been itching to see the body since his arrival, despite the officer being someone he knew. On several occasions, he had worked with Kendall Jones during instances which required a conservation officer.

Like state police, conservation officers possessed arrest powers throughout the state, and dealt with situations of every kind. Often county officers would call them if state troopers were not available for backup, or for unusual circumstances.

"Knew him?" Daniels asked, walking over.

"I did," Tackett replied, realizing the killer was not only demented, and devoid of any conscience, but he was versatile. "Did you find anything useful?"

Daniels looked and pointed to several areas.

"We've got some footprints, and I ran the plate number on the truck over there. Came back as a Michael Carter, no priors, and there's absolutely no sign of him."

"Check that," Brad Lipscomb said, emerging from the woods. "He's taking a dirt nap in the woods back there, a fresh wound in his back, probably from a knife."

"He's a quick study," Tackett said, aside to Daniels.

"He's probably making guesses based on the training videos," Daniels replied.

"I heard that," Lipscomb said. "You don't get blood flow like that unless there's a fairly large exit wound. Junior high biology teaches *that*."

Tackett shrugged, walking toward the aged corpse.

"All I ever learned about was dissecting worms and frogs. And they didn't have any blood, but I sure left some exit wounds before I was done."

He knelt beside the body, putting on latex gloves before touching the head, particularly around the hairline.

"Have you photographed any of this yet?" he asked Daniels.

"No. I was waiting to see what Brad found."

"I'll get the camera," Lipscomb volunteered.

"Do that," Daniels said with a testy tone, just loud enough that his partner heard it.

Tackett looked down the torso, following it to the legs where he touched the dirt, feeling it crumble in his hands. With the recent frigid weather, most of the dirt, particularly atop the ground, was solid.

This was not.

"I think someone was digging this body up," he surmised.

"Why's that?"

"The soil is loose, and I have a hunch the body wasn't buried with its top half sticking out of the ground."

"You're right," Daniels said, looking behind him as Lipscomb returned with the photography equipment. "Can you find out who owns this property, Brad?"

"Sure. How do you want me to go about it?"

"You might start by looking on the mailbox, or maybe knocking on the front door."

"I was asking if you wanted me to be discreet," the new detective retorted.

"No. Just find out who owns it."

Lipscomb marched off to complete his undesired objective.

"Are you playing alpha male detective for a reason?" Tackett asked.

"What?"

"You're being awful hard on the kid, Mark."

"He doesn't want to be saddled with me, and the feeling is mutual."

Tackett felt along the body, looking for any unusual details.

"Still, he's a fellow officer. You could give him a little respect."

"You don't want to give too much too fast. About three years ago I was saddled with a veteran detective who didn't want my ideas and my optimism. Now I understand why he was hardened the way he was. It's the only way you can cope with the death and the bullshit lies people tell you every day. It gets a little harder every night to go home and keep those problems to myself."

"I know," Tackett said. "I'm divorced."

He tried lifting the right arm, finding it too rigid to move. It seemed literally stuck to the body.

"So are you going to tell me about the crap you and Clouse went through the last couple years or not?"

"Over a cup of coffee. It'll take a while."

Tackett noticed Daniels looking at the body's face, almost as though he knew who it might be, or feared knowing who it was, but he said nothing. He continued prying at the arm until it came free from the body, revealing a strange dark spot in the lower abdomen. Upon Tackett's touch, the spot gave no resistance while his finger slid inside nearly an inch before he yanked it out, looking at his hand, then the hole.

A bullet hole.

"Oh, shit," Daniels said, rising to his feet. He walked away from the body with Tackett hurrying after him.

"What is it you're not telling me, Mark? Whose body is that?" Tackett demanded, seeing how pale his fellow detective's face turned at the revelation of the bullet wound.

"I think that might be Ryan Andrews' body," Daniels said, unable to look back at the stiffened corpse.

"You seem a little more sure than you're letting on, Mark. You kept staring at that face like you recognized him. Is that hole the same one Clouse put in him last year?"

"It's the same area, yeah."

"Then what the hell's he doing buried out here?"

Daniels reached for a cigarette. His nerves were getting the better of him.

"I have no idea. And if he's not committing all those murders you're investigating, that means anyone could be."

Tackett's face showed the same cold, pale realization his fellow officer's had a moment before. He had literally been chasing a ghost, and now he stood figuratively lost in his investigation. With so few leads, and an equally low number of clues, his investigation would soon draw to a standstill.

"I found the owner," Lipscomb announced, returning to the detectives. Both turned to see what the answer might be. "There were a couple pieces of mail in his mailbox."

"So what's the name?" Daniels inquired, notably irritated.

"Russell Hinds."

"Oh, shit," the city detective stammered, wondering if his day could get any worse.

***

Clouse parked in the cabin's short driveway, examining the area around it as he approached. He climbed the stained wooden stairs to the front door, picturing his honeymoon night as he did so. Images of him carrying Jane up the stairs and inside the cabin's gorgeous living quarters flooded his mind, followed by the memory of the whirlpool, then making love on the king-sized bed in the next room.

A shiver of apprehension ran through him as he turned the knob to walk inside.

To his surprise, the cabin looked as normal as he remembered it, except for an envelope atop the coffee table, and a videotape beside it.

Without saying a word, he stepped inside, peering into each room quickly before turning his attention to the items. Assured he was alone, he picked up the packet of photos, then set them down, opting for a look at the video cassette first.

Fortunately, the cabins came standard with televisions and viewing devices. He took the tape from the box, seeing no label on either. It seemed as plain and clueless as everything else he received from the killer, but he felt certain it would be something he cared nothing to see.

As the tape started, he saw pitch black grow into a mildly lit room. Only outlines could be seen because the only light in the room came from beams streaming through drawn curtains. Finally, he spied a small form huddled in one corner of the room. Whimpers and cries came from the corner and he recognized the form as a boy.

Zach.

"Damn it," he muttered as he watched the boy call for his captor and beg him to set him free, but there came no reply, no appearance from the killer.

No clues whatsoever.

Several minutes passed as Clouse intently watched the tape, studying everything about the room, looking for any sort of reflection that might give him a hint about the location, but there were no mirrors, no glass objects. The camera never moved, indicating the killer was likely not present during the taping, and that perhaps the video recorder was hidden from Zach's view.

"Dad, where are you?" Zach cried in the corner, not moving except to wipe the tears from his eyes.

Clouse felt his chest grow heavy, as though a large boulder was placed there to keep him from finding his son. He breathed slow, pained breaths, feeling tears well up in his eyes. Still, he studied the tape further with determination.

Something about the size of the room and its decor sparked a hint of familiarity within the distraught father. He fought his emotions to remain calm and study the video, despite his intense hatred toward whoever had stolen his only child.

At least Zach is safe, he thought as his eyes darted from one corner of the screen toward the next, looking the room over without blinking. He saw the closet door before studying the carpet of a deep green color. The lighting was too shallow to determine the rest of the carpet's makeup, but he could tell other colors streamed in patterns throughout the green.

"What am I missing?" he asked himself, staring at his son, who rolled over just a bit to his right, revealing the wall plate for an electrical plug, but only for a second before the video turned to snow across the screen. "No," he pleaded to unhearing ears, rewinding the tape to look at the wall again.

Using the remote control, he waited until the very second Zach moved to freeze the frame and stare at the wall plate, confirming exactly what he thought he might have seen. The plate was no ordinary electrical covering. He could not see the ornate designs laid atop its beige color, but the unique shape told him exactly what the room was, and in which building it could be found.

He just prayed he wasn't too late.

Chapter 14

"So exactly who the hell is Russell Hinds?" Tackett asked Daniels as crime technicians from the state police combed the area for clues, some of which were accidentally destroyed by the detectives in their quest for answers and survivors.

He had radioed state police when he first arrived on the scene and their people arrived before he could continue his conversation with a certain detective who seemed to be holding out on him better than some drug snitches he had the displeasure of meeting.

"He was the security guard who lived through a stabbing and shooting last year at the hotel," Daniels replied, looking to Lipscomb in the distance as the rookie detective observed the state's fine tooth combing for evidence.

He had a stronger interest in forensics than Daniels, but he hurried through some of the basics during his investigations. Daniels had to correct that problem before his partner jeopardized his new, coveted position.

Advising a partner who seemed intimidated, if not downright hateful, about working with him would be a task in itself. Gaining Lipscomb's trust was his first objective.

"Tough guy if he lived through that," Tackett said. "What would Ryan Andrews' body be doing on his property? Could they have been working together?"

"Highly unlikely," Daniels replied. "Andrews was the one who shot and stabbed him."

"Oh," Tackett said. "Then what's your theory?"

"I don't have one. You might want to talk to Hinds."

As the two sat on the bumper of Tackett's unmarked car, the county detective looked from the scene of three bodies to his city counterpart. His eyebrow raised, as some harrowing thoughts crossed his mind and Daniels saw his expression, but waited until Tackett stood and began to walk away before speaking.

"What are you thinking, Troy?"

Tackett turned toward him.

"I'm thinking you're not telling me everything about this case because you're either scared, or you're somehow part of it."

Daniels' look of shock failed to display the countless number of feelings running through his mind.

"*Me?* Murdering two men in cold blood?"

"It was awful strange how you beat me here," Tackett explained. "Even more odd how you and your partner drove separate cars," he added, looking to both city vehicles.

"We don't exactly get along," Daniels said emphatically, holding his arms in an exasperated fashion by his side. "You honestly think I'm somehow in on this?"

"I don't know, Mark. You're not very forthcoming, and I don't want this investigation compromised by me talking to you if you won't cooperate."

Daniels shook his head in disbelief. He felt the walls closing in on him, unable to believe a fellow police officer would think such things.

"All right, Troy. Let's go have a talk."

"Good," Tackett said, obviously relieved. "First, let's see what the state guys have come up with."

Since the forensics team had little to show for their efforts, and what they did find would have to be bagged and examined, the two detectives rode in Tackett's car down the road to the pond where the conservation officer had been earlier. Several picnic tables offered them a place to sit and talk in the open.

While Daniels fished a cigarette from his pocket, Tackett took the opportunity to pull a wad of chewing tobacco from his back pocket. The two paced a moment before either could find the words to start their conversation.

Daniels fumed over the fact Tackett thought he could be involved while the county detective tried to think of evidence to the contrary. Both felt awkward about their jobs, as though they were doing battle rather than working toward a solution.

"What do you want to know?" Daniels finally asked, seating himself at one of the tables.

"Everything. I want to know how this whole mess got started, who our suspects might be, and what your angle is," Tackett replied, setting a boot-clad foot atop the seat of the picnic table bench so he could lean down on one knee.

"This could take a while."

Daniels began by explaining the murder of Clouse's first wife and how the parties responsible wanted the West Baden Springs Hotel and its property for their own. Subsequently the murders the next year were out of revenge for the slain murderer in the first spree. Ryan Andrews had escaped after his partner was shot, but apparently hadn't survived on his own.

"Still, someone took time to bury him, even if it wasn't a good job," Tackett noted.

"He made mention of carrying out his real father's work," Daniels said. "We know he was adopted, but we never found the birth parents. Turned out he was left in front of an emergency room anonymously."

"So we might be looking for the real dad?"

"Or mother."

Tackett looked out to the pond and its tranquil water a moment. He spat a wad of tobacco juice to the ground before continuing.

"This seems awful personal with the killer leaving photos and kidnapping Paul's kid. Even Paul said some of those photos date back a year or so. That's an awful long time to plot someone's demise."

"You just said it, Troy. How many concrete clues or leads do we have?"

Tackett made a zero indicator with his fingers and thumb. He paced around the table a moment, spitting another glob of brown juice as he did so.

"We're getting an idea of what's happening, but we don't know where to look. Can we check the adoption agency and see if they know anything?"

Daniels shook his head.

"I tried. The lady who was in charge almost the past thirty years retired a couple years back." Tackett started to say something. "Then she died."

"Shit. What about the records? Any indication of visitation? If he knows who his real father is, he must have met him at some point."

"Nothing. He was adopted at a *very* early age."

"Have you talked to his adoptive mother?"

Daniels smirked.

"She won't give us the time of day. After her adopted kid slit her husband's throat can you blame her?"

"But basically what you're saying is everything to this point revolves around the hotel?"

"Pretty much. Mrs. Landamere had planned all along to take it over with her husband, but he was killed two years ago when he tried to off Paul and me."

"How'd that happen?"

"I shot him in the head."

Tackett simply nodded. He was thinking about what steps to take next when his pager went off. He looked down at it, realizing he could not shrug it off for conversation, no matter how important the backstory might prove in his investigation.

"It's our dispatch," he said, realizing his radio was sitting in the backseat of his car. "Let me get them on the radio and see what's up."

He returned in a moment with a look of distress.

"What?" Daniels asked.

"They patched an emergency call through to me from Clouse. He said he got a video and some photos from the killer in Tennessee."

"And?"

"And he feels positive that hotel you were talking about is where they're keeping his son, or at least they were."

"Let's go," Daniels said, bolting from the table.

***

Clouse felt helpless as he boarded the train back to Indianapolis. After receiving the photos and the tape, he decided it best to hurry back. He would quickly get a rental car long enough to retrieve his truck. By then, he hoped to learn what Tackett discovered at the hotel.

Their conversation had been brief, but Clouse made his point clear. Tackett would have to practically go alone to avoid alerting anyone, and he would have to be extremely careful. Clouse took a seat next to the window and thought about what a waste the building was until he found time to reopen or sell it.

Soon after beginning work on his master's degree at Indiana University, Clouse had joined the fire department and begun work with Kieffer Construction in Southern Indiana on the hotel. The blueprints he designed for his final undergraduate project were imperative in the rebuilding of the hotel, or so he was led to believe. At the time he had no idea what torment the project would cause him, or how many friends he would lose because of one simple misunderstanding.

Despite the losses and personal suffering, including the death of his first wife, Clouse pushed forward and eventually saw the end of the construction the year before. It was during the grand reopening ceremony that things began to go astray for the second time, when a special guest was set on fire and pushed off a balcony to the terror of the guests below.

Since that time the hotel had remained completed, but unopened. Somehow, Clouse suspected he might see more problems again this Halloween season, and his prediction came truer than he had possibly imagined. Every room at the hotel stood ready for use with functional bathrooms, heat, lighting, and beds. The atrium blossomed with intricate paint schemes, carpets, and statues, filled with much of the unique flavor that made it one of a kind.

For all it was worth, the hotel might as well have served as a vacated building for local clubs to hold meetings on a rental basis.

Clouse thought about the hotel and its idle nature before he looked at the photos of the old building. One depicted the graveyard on the opposite side of the grounds while another showed the grand atrium inside. Yet, another depicted the basement where several memorable incidents from the past two years had transpired.

He set them aside, taking up the next diary in the set. This was the diary he had already read, but in the sequence of four, it would make more sense. The remainder of the second diary had provided little useful information, so he hoped for better results. He took a deep breath, opened the book and read for the next hour or so, deciphering everything Father Runnels had written with his own hand.

***

As quickly as it seemed Ernest had been diagnosed with less than a year to live, his relationship with the boy became strained. While Henry wanted to support his mentor, Ernest appeared to want more time to himself, usually to contemplate what to do with the remainder of his life.

His sermons grew more intent on living one's life to the fullest and doing as much good as possible. He appeared more emphatic during his speeches, but also tired more quickly as time passed. One day the two priests met in the garden, Ernest cherished working on during his spare time.

"Henry has been spending more and more time by himself these days," Runnels noted as Ernest pulled weeds, his hands covered in black soil.

He noticed the wooden cross tucked neatly at Ernest's side, but said nothing for the time being. The cross never left the sight of the priest, as though it was a winning lottery ticket or a monumental treasure Ernest could not afford to chance leaving elsewhere.

Ernest gave no reply about Henry, but continued his work.

"How are you feeling today?"

"The usual," Ernest replied. "I'll be thoroughly worn out after this bit of gardening. I put my faith in God because modern medicine won't be much use to me."

"Do you plan on spending time with Henry? He seems rather despondent lately."

"He needs room to grow," Ernest said. "The boy must realize I won't be here much longer to take care of him."

Runnels sighed, looking around him as the sun warmed the garden and the surrounding brick walkways. While most of the brothers were stuck inside schooling, he and Ernest had the luxury of basking in the unusually comfortable day.

"If you're so concerned about him, you should spend time with him. He needs to realize how much you care while you're, well, while you're-"

"Still alive, Joseph?"

"Well, yes."

Ernest stopped his digging for a moment, leaving the weeds some peace from his intense annihilation of their existence.

"Very well. I'll take the time to explain to him exactly what is happening to me. The intense pain I feel every miserable day of my life, and how terrified I am of leaving this world behind. Would that satisfy you?"

"It would, Ernest, but why do you fear death when you know there's something better waiting for you on the other side?"

"Do I, Joseph? When one is faced with death, he begins to wonder about a great number of things. I wonder how long my family tree will continue since I never fathered any children, I wonder who will really care when I'm dead, and I find myself wondering if there really *is* someplace better for us to go, and if we're all let into that eternal happiness."

Runnels' surprise was evident in a silent gasp. Perhaps his devotion was stronger than his colleague's, but then again he was not faced with an inevitable, slow death.

"What more does it take to alleviate your fears, Ernest? You know the Bible and the scriptures as well as anyone I've met."

"Yes, I've recited the texts a thousand times over, and even told every soul around me, Joseph, but what have I really seen? What have I really experienced?" He stood to look Runnels in the eye. "God has never spoken to me, I've never seen any revelations, and I'm not so sure these days that words written thousands of years ago, handed down by generations, edited for content by generations, is really what I should believe."

Runnels could not help but show his astonishment now. His jaw dropped open for several seconds before he collected himself. It was apparent he struggled for the right words to say at such a moment. He knew what he was supposed to say, and how he was supposed to comfort Ernest and tell him everything would be fine, but the priest seemed to have thought his ideas through. With so much time to think lately, and little else to do, Ernest had apparently set himself in questioning the word of God and the established Jesuit beliefs.

"Don't act so surprised, Joseph," Ernest said. "If your death isn't sudden, you'll have lots of time to contemplate just what lies ahead, too."

"Yes, but my faith will keep me strong enough to believe in the afterlife and the notion that I've earned my spot in Heaven."

Ernest scooped up his cross from the ground as though he suddenly remembered it and someone might sneak along any second to steal it from him. It seemed the one thing left in his life that mattered.

"I've done nothing to earn this disease I've been cursed with," Ernest said. "I'm too young to be concerning myself with dying. Most of our kind search narrowly for the next week's good word or spend their time idly with the community thinking of the good they must be causing. I'm left with my own thoughts on mortality and nothing else."

Runnels thought of Ernest as somewhat selfish, but understood the meaning of the younger priest's words.

"It doesn't have to be that way, Ernest," he assured him. "Be strong. You're being tested by a greater power. He doesn't show Himself because he wants you to find your own way. You *know* this already."

"If I'm being tested, then I'm certainly going to fail," Ernest said before marching off toward the converted seminary.

Runnels shook his head and collected his thoughts, wondering what he was going to do with his disheartened and disillusioned brother.

Returning to the real world, Clouse felt his eyes grow heavy about halfway through the diary. He marked the page, set it beside him, and dozed off for some much needed sleep while the train's wheels made a comforting rhythmic sound beneath him.

***

As Daniels and Tackett emerged from Tackett's car in front of the hotel, each looked up to the six-story building, painted a bright yellow with white trim and distinctly red roof, much like a Mexican villa with its original bricks barely peeking through the paint. They started up the front staircase leading toward the double glass entrance doors where the true luxurious look of the hotel began.

"It's a good thing you thought to stop at Clouse's house to get a key or we might never have gotten inside," Tackett noted.

"We're lucky his wife had the spare."

Clouse had two copies of a master key, which opened every room of the hotel. Only Clouse, Martin Smith, and two of the hotel's head construction managers had such keys, and the other three men had been killed during the past two years of mayhem.

"You don't like this place, do you?" Tackett asked, seeing how tentative Daniels was about going inside.

Daniels unlocked the door, holding it for his newfound partner.

"No, I don't."

"What's so bad about it?" Tackett asked in a hushed voice once they were inside the prestigious lobby, surrounded by large white bulbs and gold paint atop green trim. A balcony loomed over them where someone could easily listen to their conversation without being seen.

Tackett felt especially awed by the hotel, and though Daniels had been there before, he stared at the building that doubled as a work of art. Tiles less than an inch square combined in the thousands to cover the very floor they stood upon. Individual bulbs seemed to be everywhere around the balcony above, and they all came to life when Daniels flipped the switch.

"What's so bad about it?" Daniels repeated the question as they both stood, staring at the beautiful decor around them. "Other than the fact that over a dozen people have been killed here, most of whom I knew or had met, nothing."

"That would do it," Tackett said to himself. "How should we do this search?"

Daniels knew from experience splitting up could be suicide, but he did not want to look cowardly, and time was of the essence.

"You take the top three floors and I'll get the bottom three. Go room to room since Paul had no idea which room, and meet me back here in fifteen minutes whether you're done or not."

"Okay," Tackett said, turning for the stairway.

"And be *very* careful," Daniels said with a look that showed he meant it.

Within ten minutes, Tackett had searched most of the top two floors with no success. All of the doors were unlocked, granting him easy access. Checking bathrooms and closets took the most time, and every room had them. There were a few specialty rooms to check, including a massage area, whirlpool room, and several suites, but they only took up a little more time.

He kept a close eye on his watch, but felt certain he was wasting his time. No signs of life were evident in or around the hotel. No cars were parked outside, and all of the exterior doors were locked. He wondered if Clouse was accurate in his interpretation of the video, or if his imagination was working overtime. According to Daniels, a slew of negative things had occurred in this building and the distraught father could easily be thinking too much into the situation.

With each door he opened, the detective grew a bit more lax, expecting to find nothing. He walked out of the last room on the fifth floor positive Clouse was wrong. He found the dome-shaped hotel rather odd with its circular floors and rooms on both sides of the winding hallways. While the outer half faced the garden, or the forest behind the hotel, the inner half looked down upon the large atrium below, spanning nearly the length of a football field with a glimmering chandelier above.

As he rounded the corner, taking a precautionary look behind him, Tackett bumped into something that would have put a smaller man on the floor.

"Mark, what the hell are you doing up here?" he asked, realizing his fellow detective had accidentally bumped him on his way into the hallway.

"I got worried," Daniels replied. "The first two floors didn't have anything, and I figured if the killer was still here it's a lot easier to pick us off."

Tackett realized the city detective's logic.

"Okay. Let's do these last two floors together."

Ten minutes later, the two had finished their search of the entire building, except the basement, and another five allowed a thorough search of all its inner workings. Strangely, no signs of trespass or Clouse's son having been there recently presented themselves. Both investigators stood at the front door wondering what to do next, feeling as though they had been distracted from the real mystery in Bloomington.

"What now?" Tackett asked, obviously displeased.

"I want to talk with Russ Hinds," Daniels said. "You want to see if the state boys turned up anything useful?"

"Worth a shot. If Clouse was right, the kidnapper got out of here in a hurry. He said the date on that tape was yesterday."

"But dates and times can be forged," Daniels noted. "There's no telling what time the tape was actually made."

"I believe he felt he was right when he said the hotel. I'm just not sure what his state of mind is right now."

Daniels lit a cigarette. After searching the entire hotel he needed something to calm his nerves. He felt lucky not to have encountered a blade-wielding maniac.

"If our day gets much worse I may put in for vacation," he said, starting toward the car. "Between my rookie partner and getting dragged into this mess, I'm due for one."

Chapter 15

In the absence of her husband, Jane Clouse had nearly gone insane. Based on the vague note he left her, and the phone calls, which provided little more information, she dared not leave the house or have her daughter, Katie, go outside for even a second.

Much of her time was spent cleaning the house, watching television, or waiting by the phone with the hope of her husband calling.

She hated him being so independent, and especially leaving her behind. Jane understood the danger, but wanted to be by his side regardless. She also understood the desire burning inside him to find Zach alive and unharmed. After watching several nightly shows on child abduction and the seldom happy endings, she began to wonder if her stepson might be lost forever.

"Mom, what's for breakfast?" Katie asked as she emerged from her bedroom.

Jane sighed, then smiled, looking to the kitchen with an array of groceries still atop the counter from her shopping spree. She had loaded up on canned goods and other food items that would last awhile after Clouse called with his intent to travel out-of-state.

"How about eggs and bacon, kiddo?" she asked from her seat on the couch.

Several good talk shows were on in the morning, a few with topics about kids hating their parents. She wondered when her own daughter would go through that phase of questioning everything Jane asked of her.

"Okay. Can I have English muffins, too?" Katie asked with an innocent smile and a childhood gleam in her hazel eyes. She had no idea about Zach's abduction, and to this point, had not put up much fuss about staying in the house, probably because she got to miss school.

Jane stood to fix breakfast as the cordless phone rang. She scooped it up on her way to the kitchen, pressing the talk button as she snatched a few eggs from the refrigerator.

"Hello?"

"Jane, it's me," Clouse's voice said from the other end. She could hear the clacking sound of a train in the background.

"I hope you're on your way back."

"I am. The trip was a complete disaster. The killer just left me more clues, including a videotape of Zach locked in a hotel room dated yesterday."

"Oh my God. Was he okay?"

"He looked fine. I think the tape was real, but Troy and Mark went out there and didn't find anything. The son-of-a-bitch stays one step ahead of me every time. I thought for sure I might find something in Tennessee."

Jane stood at the counter a moment, thinking about her husband's predicament, unable to share fully in his pain because he would not let her into his search, and all of his life.

"Are you getting in soon?"

"I'm on my way. I don't have anything left to check on."

"He didn't leave any pictures this time?"

"He did, but they were of the hotel. Troy and Mark checked everywhere I told them to. They didn't see any sign of Zach."

Katie walked into the kitchen so Jane stepped casually into the living room to avoid her daughter overhearing the conversation. Kindergartners tended to ask too many questions about too many things in her opinion. Katie already wondered where Clouse and Zach had been, and Jane had put off the truth as long as possible.

"What now?" Jane asked.

"I don't know. He doesn't want Zach. He wants to torture me. He'll let me know what's next. The ball's in his court."

Jane was about to ask another question when several evenly spaced knocks came at the front door. She froze at the sound, knowing she was surrounded by empty fields with no help for miles.

Who would be at the front door so early in the morning?

"What was that?" Clouse asked over the line.

"Someone's at the front door, Paul."

Katie started toward the door from the kitchen.

"No, sweetie!" Jane called to her in a desperate tone. Katie stopped instantly, unsure of why her mother would not let her answer the door this time.

"Look out the window," Clouse urged over the phone, his tension equaling Jane's.

"I am," she said, scooting up to the window against the wall, unable to see anyone at the front door. Her view was partly obscured by a shrub. "There's no one there. What should I do?"

"Don't answer it."

Again, several knocks came. This time they were in quicker succession.

"I still don't see anyone," she said more nervously, seeing no one at the front door despite the knocks.

"Mommy!" Katie pleaded, wanting to answer the door.

"Go upstairs!" Jane ordered in a manner showing a bit more fear than she wanted. Katie realized this and put up no resistance as she darted off to her room.

Jane moved slowly toward the door, the phone still to her ear, and peered through the peephole, seeing nothing except the garage to the side and empty fields everywhere else. She slowly unlatched the door, taking up a baseball bat she had specially placed there in case of an emergency.

"Be careful," Clouse said.

"I am," Jane retorted sternly, wanting silence as she revealed the knocker.

As she swung the door open, bat raised, she received the biggest surprise she could have ever anticipated on the other side. Looking weary, flush, and perhaps a little roughed up from the elements, stood a child the same age as her daughter. Her expression went from fearful rage to a tender shock as she dropped to one knee and pulled the boy into her arms.

"Zach? I can't believe it's you!" she exclaimed to the amazement of her husband half a state away.

"What?" she heard a surprised Clouse yell over the line.

***

Tackett and Daniels found Russ Hinds at work by early afternoon after the man had finished his lunch at the factory's cafeteria. The two detectives gained clearance from a foreman to speak with Hinds in a break room where the three could have some privacy. Since Hinds would not be charged with anything, and this would simply be a series of questions related to his property, they could hold a brief conversation at work.

If he was guilty in any way, this would put pressure on him when coworkers saw him speak with police, and it could make him do any number of rash things to further incriminate himself.

From what Daniels remembered, Hinds had been a die-cast operator for a certain motor vehicle company who worked part-time for the Orleans Police Department the past year. He secured a position working security at the West Baden Springs Hotel the year before and nearly died as a result of Ryan Andrews' murderous rampage. Soon after, Hinds quit police work altogether and disappeared from the area.

"So why is it you moved up here?" Daniels asked first, once they were all seated at an aged table in the break room. Its top was decorated with any number of scrapes, nicks, and carved remarks.

"From *Orleans?*" Hinds scoffed.

Seeing neither of the detectives crack so much as a grin from his remark, he quickly lost his own smirk. His glasses appeared steamed up, perhaps from nervousness.

"Okay. Once my divorce was final and I decided it was a bit dangerous living down there, I moved up here to be closer to my job."

"How long have you worked here?" Tackett inquired.

"About six years. You guys really haven't told me what this is about."

Each detective looked to the other, deciding it was time for the questions with more impact. They would go slow to see what Hinds might reveal.

"Two men were found dead on your property today, Russ," Daniels said, being a bit more informal since he had met Hinds the past year.

"Shit!" Hinds reacted by leaning back slightly. "What happened?"

"We were hoping you could tell us," Tackett said.

"I came to work at five this morning. The only thing I know is my buddy Mike Carter wanted to go hunting on-"

Hinds stopped short, a realization creeping into his mind.

"Mike didn't, I mean, he wasn't one of the-"

Both detectives nodded slowly, and each grew to believe from the man's sorrowful expression he had nothing to do with Carter's murder. Still, they had to see what Hinds could tell them, and if he knew about the partially decayed body beyond his field.

"Oh God. Mike said he had the day off. He wanted to use my woods for hunting since bow season just started."

"I'll say it did," Tackett said half under his breath.

"What does that mean?" Hinds demanded.

Daniels portrayed his usual calm demeanor, trying to settle Hinds.

"It means a conversation officer was shot with your friend's bow and arrows. Mr. Carter was stabbed to death further back in the woods."

"Who could have done it?" Hinds wondered aloud. His face showed remorse, then realization. "Is it that Ryan Andrews?"

Daniels shook his head. It was time to see what Hinds really knew, if anything.

"We found a body half buried in your woods. Your buddy may have stumbled onto it, which is probably why he was murdered."

"Do you know anything about this body?" Tackett asked.

A blank look crossed the factory worker's face.

"No. I have no idea why any body would be buried on my land."

Tackett turned away, apparently unconvinced by the answer. Daniels sensed he wanted to play good cop, bad cop.

"Are you aware of anything strange about the property since you bought it?" Daniels inquired, ignoring Tackett's ploy. He could see it would lead them nowhere.

"No. And I bought it from an old farmer, so there's nothing weird about the former owner," Hinds added.

Tackett stared at the vending machines and the remaining food products no one seemed to want. He always wondered why the vending people left such food items at the police station, but now he saw that bad taste in snacks knew no bounds.

"Did you ever see anyone trespass on your field?" Daniels asked.

"Nothing stands out," Hinds said. "Pretty much everyone knew I owned guns, so they stayed clear."

"Did you ever see Ryan Andrews after the incident at the hotel?"

"No," Hinds said vehemently. "I would have reported it. That fucker tried to kill me!"

"Any tire tracks or anyone walking out in your field that shouldn't have been?"

"I don't walk out there very much, and I would have remembered if someone was on my property. I'm a little jumpy after what happened last year."

Daniels noted the comments in his pocket notebook, setting both it and the pen on the table.

"We think his body might be the one we found on your property," the detective revealed, surprising both Hinds and Tackett, who opted to take a seat and watch Daniels work the interview his own way.

"Why would he be buried on my property?"

"We'd like to know the same thing. You're not planning on leaving town anytime soon, are you?"

"Am I a suspect?"

"No, but we may have more questions for you."

"I doubt I'll be going home, but I won't be leaving town."

"Our people should be off the property by the time you leave work if you want to get personal effects from your house."

Hinds nodded before a realization showed in his eyes.

"Could I be a target now?"

Tackett let out a disbelieving sigh, as though to imply Hinds was cleverly covering his tracks. Daniels, though, knew the history of the West Baden murders of the past two years. If history repeated itself, Hinds would certainly be a target.

"You may be, if you're telling us the truth about the body."

"Of course I'm telling the truth. What the hell should I do?"

Join the club, Daniels thought. He stood up, looking to Tackett to indicate he was ready.

"If I were you, I'd get as far from the area as you can until this is resolved," Daniels advised. "If you have to stay, make sure you go somewhere no one else knows about."

"Great," Hinds said sarcastically as the two detectives left the room. "Your advice isn't going to help me very much."

Chapter 16

Clouse was thankful for the return of his son, regardless of the circumstances. After a brief dinner by mid-afternoon he sat with Zach atop his lap while they watched a movie on the big screen television that took up nearly half of one family room wall. It had home theater equipment plugged into various ports around it.

Unfortunately, Zach had little to tell about his two-day disappearance. He never saw his abductor's face, never knew exactly where he was, and said he was never hurt in any way. Strangely, the killer who had brutally murdered several people already, including a park security guard, and unbeknownst to Clouse, a conservation officer, showed utter compassion toward Zach.

Considering he had never filed a police report when Zach was kidnapped, Clouse did not bother telling anyone his boy was back. Several attempts to reach Tackett or Daniels had failed, and he would not spend more than a minute away from his son.

A quick slew of questions provided few answers, and Clouse realized the killer had once again covered his tracks very well.

With one arm wrapped around his son, Clouse vowed he would never let anything happen to Zach again. He planned to keep especially careful watch over his son while the killer was loose.

"Dad, you're hugging too tight," Zach said, prying on his father's thick arm.

"Sorry, kid," Clouse said, loosening his grip. "I'm just glad to have you back."

"I wasn't really scared," Zach said, trying to act brave, following the example Clouse set a little too well.

"I know."

Clouse usually tried to select family films for Katie and Zach to watch. His son still awoke in the middle of the night from nightmarish images of his dead mother or the victims of Ryan Andrews he saw the year before. He figured Zach had seen enough real life death, so he avoided it on film and the television whenever possible.

Today Zach had chosen a Disney cartoon to watch while he relaxed with his father. Jane had gone upstairs with Katie to give the two some alone time. Every morning Clouse found another small part of Zach that resembled himself, even though his own parents thought he was imagining most of it.

"Did you look for me, Dad?"

Clouse was taken aback, but understood how kids thought only what they saw in front of them.

"Of course I did."

"You didn't find me."

Clouse grinned, knowing this quirky argument could go on all afternoon.

"Okay, Zach, where were you?"

"I don't know."

"Well, neither did I. That bad man took you and hid you from me."

Zach shifted slightly in his father's lap.

"He wasn't that bad."

"What do you mean?" Clouse asked, an inquisitive look crossing his face.

"He gave me cookies and Pepsi."

Now it seemed the abductor had been almost too hospitable.

"But you never saw him?"

"No."

"Why not?"

"He always wore a hood."

Clouse was left with two clues. The abductor was white and male, because Zach would have noted any differences immediately, as all kids do.

While one of the movie's better parts kept Zach's attention, Clouse reached for the cordless phone, trying to reach Daniels at home.

***

What Clouse would soon learn was his friend took both of his own kids to a nearby park to play on an unseasonably warm evening. His daughter, Renee, had just turned four, and Curtis, his son, was nearing two years.

While his wife went to work for the phone company, Daniels had been left with both children for the evening. After a quick fast food supper, he took them to the park to burn off some of their newfound energy. Renee, especially, could use most of the rides and attractions at the city park, including the monkey bars and slides.

Curt, however, would have to be content sitting atop his father's lap on the swing set for a few minutes. Bundled to the hilt, Curt giggled and swung his open hands wildly in front of him as he felt the adrenaline rush of swaying forward and back.

"You like that?" Daniels asked in his best baby voice. "You like that, Curt?"

He kept an eye on Renee, who tried out every piece of equipment in the park. It was nearing dark, and soon both kids would have to go to bed, but for one night, he wanted them to have their fun.

With so much demand on his work schedule lately, it had been difficult to spend time with them. Daniels sometimes found it difficult to juggle career and family matters, but he knew he only had one chance to raise his children. There would be opportunities for overtime later in life.

Beneath his jacket, Daniels felt his shoulder holster rub against his armpits where the straps wrapped around. He vowed to never leave home without some sort of protection again. Twice he had nearly died helping Clouse find the killer, and the one year spent in a wheelchair was considered the longest waste of time in his life.

The thought of that year caused him to remember the four victims of the explosion. His doctor during that time was one of the four, and he wondered how he had been so easily sidetracked from the investigation. Granted, there were very few leads, but helping Clouse and investigating the two deaths on Hinds' property had detained him long enough.

Daniels stood with Curt in his arms from the swing, looking to Renee, who had just reached the bottom of the slide. He placed Curt in one of the plastic toddler swings, secured it, and gave his son a small push to start the swing. While Curt giggled and waved at the air around him, the detective went to spend a moment with his daughter.

"Having fun?" he asked Renee, placing her atop the merry-go-round.

She nodded an affirmative as he helped her sit down, then gave it a gentle push. Once she was settled, grasping the bars, she seemed unhappy with the speed.

"Faster, Daddy," she demanded.

"Okay," he said with a grin. He pushed a bit faster, remembering how intimidating such rides were until a kid tried them. Then they were never fast enough.

"Faster!" she said again after two more pushes. He reluctantly agreed, giving a strong push this time as the merry-go-round whirled around like a top.

"Getting dizzy?" he asked her once the ride had been going a moment.

"Yeah," she replied, but obviously didn't care if it stopped or not.

Daniels looked behind him, having heard nothing from Curt, and found an empty toddler seat swaying in the breeze with no Curt, and no sign of anyone else around. A parentally based terror shot through the detective as he darted toward the swing set, finding no clues around it. He whirled around, wondering where his son had gone, almost certain no child could have undone the restraints himself.

"Oh, shit," he muttered under his breath.

Daniels scoured the entire playground area, feeling a panic unlike any he had ever experienced. He understood what Clouse had been through, but never figured it could happen to him. Perhaps the killer wanted to include him in his vengeful, devious plot, but Daniels would not endure the games Clouse had. His kids meant everything to him, and he knew he would go insane if anything happened to either of them.

His breathing grew heavy and he felt an intense rage boil through his veins for whoever had taken his son. He looked around, fists clenched, as darkness swept over the playground and the surrounding area, masking whatever malicious activity a merciless killer might undertake.

"Daddy, what's wrong?" he heard Renee ask from behind him.

"Come here, Renee," he said. "Curt's gone. We've got to try and find him."

Daniels started toward the storage shed in the distance, seeing a bundle, light in color, piercing the darkness. Curt had been wearing light clothes, and as Daniels approached, he felt positive those were his son's clothes, and probably his son lying atop a concrete slab beside the shed. Two questions remained.

How had Curt gotten that far away?

Was he still alive and well?

A cry in the dark soon let him know Curt was fine, and he verified it for himself when he scooped his son from the slab, holding him close to his chest, patting him on the back.

As he did so, he heard a crinkling noise between his and Curt's bodies. He pulled his son far enough off his chest to retrieve the piece of paper between them, and read it as Curt clutched at the material on the back of his jacket, happy to be found.

"I own you and your family. Don't forget it," Daniels read the note aloud to himself. It was a combination of magazine and newspaper headline letters, leaving no clue about the killer, including his handwriting. Daniels folded the piece of paper, pocketed it, and prepared to take both children home where it would be safe.

He hoped.

***

Tackett walked through the Monroe County Police Department, hoping to find some useful mail from the state forensics office. Several deputies were milling around, picking up or leaving paperwork. It appeared most of the morning shift had left, including the secretary.

Before checking his mailbox or using his office, Tackett decided to see if the midnight sergeant might be cleaning his car in the garage bay. The two had patrolled the same shift when Tackett joined the county police and quickly became buddies, usually taking their lunch hour together. It was his habit to clean his car inside and out when he was off duty at least once a week.

He opened a door leading from the county building to the adjoining garage bay, finding the mechanic's area empty and dark. A few overhead lights remained on permanently, allowing Tackett a view of an unmarked car glimmering from across the bay. It looked to be in pristine condition like most of their department's vehicles.

Except for a few spots.

"What in the hell?" he asked, flipping on the lights as the door shut behind him.

Several major scuffmarks lined the car's right side, accompanied by dings and dents to either side. What struck Tackett as odd was how the paint along the scuffs was not directly sheared off, but rather seared and partly melted, as though it had come in contact with something hot instead of a collision.

Tackett took his time circling the car for a full inspection. While the other side was completely devoid of marks or dents, he found more strange blemishes in the maroon paint of the car. Several dots appeared black in the center, surrounded by darkened paint, as though something hot had embedded itself into the car, like a cigarette burn mark, only more intense.

"What's up, Troy?" the afternoon sergeant, a broad-shouldered man a few years older than Tackett asked as he walked through the door. He immediately opened the drawer of a toolbox at the front of the garage, looking for something particular.

"Not much, Jerry. Any idea what happened to our unmarked car, here?"

"Not really sure," the sergeant answered. "It just came back a couple days ago like that."

"Who had it signed out?"

The sergeant shrugged, pulling a tape measure from the toolbox.

"Last person who signed it out was Murphy on that surveillance detail a few weeks back. Looks like someone had a joyride and didn't come clean."

Tackett looked the car over as the sergeant returned inside. The only people with access to those keys were the three shift sergeants, the sheriff, the training officer, and himself. He knew *he* hadn't used the car or let anyone gain access to the keys, so that left five people who might have.

When he returned to the offices, he found the sheriff's light on. Ordinarily Bobby Pearce was a sheriff who put in his time and went straight home to the wife and kids. A relatively young sheriff in his mid-forties, Pearce did his job on the straight and narrow, devoid of politics. Of course it was his first term, with reelection coming in a year's time, but Tackett respected the job his sheriff had done so far, and secretly thanked the man for not giving up on him in a time when Tackett had lost any hope of ever doing police work again.

"Bobby?" Tackett asked with a quick knock, then a turn of the knob. He and Pearce were fairly informal considering their positions.

"I'll call you back in a few minutes," Pearce said quickly, waving his detective inside.

Tackett slid into the seat across from the sheriff's desk, realizing they had spoken little since the murders began. In part because of the detective's exhaustive investigation, and partly because Pearce had been doing personal appearances at several functions. Tackett imagined he needed to meet the right people and convince them of the excellent service he provided as sheriff.

"I didn't mean to interrupt," Tackett stated.

"Oh, no," Pearce said, waving off the notion. "That's one of the bankers I'm meeting at tomorrow's social dinner. I've got to start thinking about that election next year. You know? Much as I hate to."

Tackett nodded.

"So, how's the investigation? Haven't seen much of you lately."

"It's not for the lack of hours I'm putting in. It's really an odd situation, Bob. I feel more like I'm intruding than investigating."

"How so?"

"Well, I have no doubt Paul Clouse is the intended victim in all of this, but it's like the killer wants to play this game with him. Clouse and the killer both know how it's supposed to go, but Clouse isn't letting me in on the secret and I've yet to identify the killer."

"Is Clouse being uncooperative?"

"It's not that, Bob. It's like he's keeping me out of it for my own good, or because he doesn't think I can help."

"You *are* his neighbor, aren't you?"

"Yeah. He knows I'm right there, and he's asked me to keep an eye on his family, but he won't let me know everything about his past. And somehow, I feel the past has everything to do with this case."

Pearce grinned.

"It usually does. I know exactly what you're talking about. Have you tried back issues of the newspapers? Those West Baden murders were heavily covered the past two years."

"I haven't had time to get to the library. And the one guy aside from Clouse who could help me isn't very forthcoming, either. And he's a cop for Christ's sake."

"It's never easy," Pearce said, unable to give much more advice on a case he was not knowledgeable about.

Tackett sat a moment, feeling as though he might be keeping Pearce from something important. He was about to excuse himself when a thought entered his mind. The reason for him stopping by, as a matter of fact.

"Do you know about the unmarked car?" he asked Pearce.

The sheriff's face twisted in thought for a moment, as though trying to recall, or perhaps look for the correct answer.

"Well, it came back a few days ago like that, but it appears no one signed it out. I've asked Fred to check it out, but he hasn't come up with anything yet."

Tackett nodded.

"I guess we can take you off the list since you already have a car, and haven't had time for any stakeouts, eh?"

"Yeah, I guess you can," Tackett replied slowly as he stood. "Good luck with your fund-raising, Sheriff."

"Thanks," Pearce said. "I'll need all the help I can get."

On his way out, Tackett found Jerry Alder, the afternoon sergeant, and another county officer at their cars, feet propped on their respective bumpers, smoking while they carried out their conversation. Tackett hardly considered the sight a great boost for departmental public relations while several early evening commuters passed the station.

"Hey, Jerry, has anyone asked you any questions about the unmarked car in there?" he asked Alder.

"No," the sergeant answered. "It doesn't sound like much of anything is getting done about it. *You* sure are taking an interest in it."

"Those are burn marks on that car, Jerry. It's not a hit-and-run accident. Someone drove that thing near something *very* hot. So you're sure Fred hasn't talked to you about it yet?"

"Yeah, I'm sure," Alder said. "In fact, he thought the sheriff would have you check into it, but those murders probably have you pretty tied up. Don't they?"

Tackett nodded with sigh.

"Yeah, maybe too tied up to see what's going on around here," Tackett said, giving a wave before heading toward his own unmarked car, knowing he would be held accountable in the event it was damaged.

"What's that supposed to mean?" the deputy asked Alder.

"Beats me. I'm starting to think Troy's taking a few too many bull hooves upside his noggin."

Chapter 17

Daniels waited until Cindy returned home before leaving for the office just hours after the incident at the park. As he walked into city hall, a number of things crossed his mind. They flew past him like the dimly lit hallways of the building where he worked eight hours a day, solving the problems of everyone else's life and never his own. The selfless act of solving crimes kept him motivated, never stopping to think about his own problems.

Now his problems *were* those crimes he fought so hard to solve.

He knew the killer was either possessive or worried. His attention had been solely directed toward Clouse until this evening. Did the killer want Daniels away from the case, or was this simply the next step in his intricate plan?

If the killer wanted Daniels away from Clouse's troubles, he would get his wish, at least on the surface. The detective planned to skim every detail, take every piece of forensic evidence from the bombing case and the murders, and make them his life, even if they went home with him the next few days.

He would take no chances with his family, calling in sick the next few days until the weekend came. At home, however, he would scrutinize every detail in the possibly related cases for personal reasons equaling those of his professional realm.

The strange connection between Tim Niemeyer's death and the bombing victims puzzled him. Everything about the murder indicated six assailants, five of whom escaped with their lives. In the bombing, there were four victims, just short of five. He found it incredibly difficult to believe the four known professionals might be involved in a stabbing death, but the coincidence felt too strong to ignore.

As he stepped into the office, several afternoon detectives shot strange glares his way. He ignored them, walking straight to his desk and picking up the files before heading toward the copy machine. Taking case files home was against standard operating procedure and many ethical codes of conduct. Daniels, however, would bend the stated rules by taking only copies of certain documents.

Midway through the stack of selected documents one of the detectives came to the door, startling Daniels. He felt certain he was about to be accused of stealing documents, or worse, but the man simply handed him a slip of paper.

"This came in a couple hours ago," the older detective explained. "Guy called about meeting you at his residence to collect his belongings."

Daniels saw the name Russ Hinds scribbled on the piece of paper with a phone number.

"Did he say when he would be there?"

"Don't think he said. Just said he wanted you there when he collected his stuff."

"Thanks," Daniels said before returning to his copies. He worried Hinds would try entering his residence alone. By no means a small man, Hinds was capable of defending himself, but the killer was crafty and versatile enough to kill with any given number of methods.

A few minutes later the copies were finished. He set a file stuffed with the warm papers beside the door, out of sight, before returning the original files to his desk. He was about to smuggle the papers out when one of the detectives called his name.

"What is it?" Daniels asked, turning to see the man holding up a phone receiver.

"For you."

Daniels picked up the nearest phone, pressing the button for the line on hold. "Daniels."

"Detective, this is Russ Hinds. Look, I've been waiting two hours for you to call back and I've got a flight to St. Louis in the morning. I've got to get in there and get my stuff."

"Wait for me, Mr. Hinds. I'm just a few minutes away."

"Fine. I'm outside my house using my cell phone. Damn, I think the battery's going dead."

"Don't move. I'll be right there."

"Okay. I'll wait for-"

The line cut off suddenly.

"Shit," Daniels said. "Hinds? Russ?" he asked with no response.

Daniels hung up the phone, walked to the folder, and swiped it into his arms without notice. He hoped the battery in the former reserve officer's phone had simply gone dead.

He prayed it was the only thing dead.

***

After tucking Zach into bed, checking his property over twice from the outside, locking every door and window, and setting the security alarm, Clouse settled into the couch, picking up the third diary which he had stopped reading around the halfway mark. A tall reading lamp was already turned on behind him, one of the few fixtures in the living room not stained by his babysitter's blood. Clouse found it difficult getting comfortable within his own house, even with the blinds and curtains drawn shut, and the security system armed.

He was about to start reading when Jane walked into the room, sitting atop one of his thighs, looking down to him.

"How do you feel?" she asked.

"Ecstatic that my boy is back, if that's what you mean."

"But why is he back? Why would the killer just turn him loose like that?"

Clouse thought a moment, setting the book down.

"Because he's proven his point. He can get to me no matter how much we hide, or how many security systems we have."

He moved so his wife could sit beside him on the couch.

"Are we moving again?"

"No. I'm tired of running, Jane. I've got to finish this no matter what."

"*We* have to finish it. You keep running off on these crusades by yourself like I'm not willing to help you."

"I don't want you or the kids to get hurt."

"But you're willing to risk the little brother of your best friend?"

Clouse searched for the correct words.

"You know what I mean. And Randy wanted to go, but he learned pretty quickly that getting involved puts everyone around him at risk."

"So what's next?" Jane inquired. "Any leads to follow?"

"No. But everything is leading back to the hotel. The latest photos were of the hotel in some different spots."

"But you said Mark and Troy checked those places out."

"They were searching for Zach," Clouse corrected. "That's a different kind of search than I intend to conduct."

"Then we're going in the morning?" she insisted.

Clouse thought about it realizing very little harm could come from all of them going down to West Baden. If he was lucky, Zach might remember something useful, even though he hated putting his son in such a position, and right in the very place he was held captive.

"Okay. We can all go."

"Good," Jane said, rising from the couch, taking hold of his hand. "You coming to bed? I think you need to celebrate."

A smile crept across Clouse's lips. He knew what she meant by the devious look in her eyes.

"I do, huh?"

"Oh, definitely. And I have just the thing to wear," she said, pulling on his arm until he rose from the couch.

"Is it revealing and red?"

"*Fire* engine red," she said, pulling him into a kiss. It had been a few weeks since the couple last shared intimate time together.

"Well, I guess I need to check these out," he said, following her up the stairs quietly enough that the kids would not hear.

The diary would have to wait another day.

***

Daniels scrambled from his car beside Hinds' house, dashing to the former security guard's vehicle, finding no one inside. The only glass remaining on the driver's side door where a window once resided was now just an outline of jagged shards.

"Damn my luck," he cursed, knowing the worse of two possibilities had probably occurred.

He walked up to the house's front door, which actually resided on the side, while the driveway continued toward a large, unkempt barn. The doorknob rejected his attempts to get in, so he knocked, seeing no light from inside, and no signs of life. It seemed unrealistic that Hinds would have gone inside and left every light off.

Daniels walked around back, finding the backdoor much the same. A single overhead light in the backyard provided little visibility as the detective turned around. He stepped back into the dead grass, looking for any sign of Hinds.

"Like a moron I don't carry a flashlight," he chastised himself.

His response to the phone call had taken less than five minutes, but he knew that was all it took for Russell Hinds to be a corpse, waiting to fall on him when he least expected it like some cheesy horror movie ending. Without light, or a real idea of where the former security guard might be, Daniels decided his best course of action was to call his department for a patrol unit.

Unfortunately he did not have his cellular phone, so kicking in the door to Hinds' house seemed the only logical alternative.

He was about to do so when a loud creaking noise came from the barn behind him. The noise startled the detective mid-stride. He slowly turned around, expecting to find something horrific staring him down. Instead, he found one of the two swinging doors to the hayloft had come open, squeaking until it crashed against the side of the graying building.

"Aw, shit," Daniels said to himself, starting toward the building, wishing he acted more like a coward sometimes.

Taking a deep breath, the detective crept toward the door, reaching for the holstered gun tucked in the back of his pants. He felt the latch give so he could draw the weapon, clasping it with both hands as he entered the old barn.

Complete darkness surrounded him, except for a few holes in the boards letting in the moonlight. He stood momentarily, hoping his eyes might adjust to the darkness. Quietly, he reached behind him to the wall, hoping to find a light switch. Nothing except splintering wood touched his fingers.

Deciding to open the other door for more light, Daniels kicked his foot back, letting the door swing outward as the yard light offered what little visibility it could. It provided enough for the detective to find his latest lifeless body lying atop a pile of dusty concrete. Daniels lowered his firearm positive he had missed the killer by mere moments.

The head of a stake appeared atop Hinds' chest, the rest buried inside. Little blood surrounded the metal spike because it could not seep through the sealed wound. A large sheet of paper hung from the stake, which Daniels carefully tore off, taking the risk of contaminating the fresh crime scene. He couldn't read the note inside the barn and he wasn't willing to wait one second longer to see what devious words the killer left for him.

Before taking it outside to read it, he examined the body from a distance, seeing Hinds' eyes fully closed, and both hands along his side. A trickle of blood appeared at the corner of the man's lip. Daniels wondered how a man larger in stature than himself could be killed in such an easy manner. He would not be easy to overpower, and driving a metal stake into someone's chest was not typically an instantaneous process.

Death would have been sudden if a spike was driven into his chest, but his position looked almost too peaceful, as though the killer had taken time to alter the body's position.

Daniels shook his head, taking the note outside beneath the yard light. He looked it over, finding ten names scribbled along the far left column. As he read them, a familiar tingle ran through his back, realizing they were ten names from the past.

The year before to be exact.

"Oh, shit. The list."

A list of ten names had haunted both Clouse and himself the year before, particularly since both men were inscribed upon it. One by one, the people on the list were murdered, but Ryan Andrews never got to complete the plan. It appeared someone else wanted to see its completion as Daniels read the new wording below the names.

"The list isn't finished yet. It will be, very soon."

Daniels put a hand to his forehead, letting his hand with the paper fall to his side. His need to find the killer now had personal motivation.

Highly personal.

Chapter 18

Clouse awoke the next morning before everyone else in his family. He spent the first few minutes of his day shirtless, dressed in sweatpants, surveying the spacious yard around him from the cold wooden planks of his front porch.

Hazy skies occasionally spit drizzle toward him and a cold breeze reminded him how foolish it was to stand outside half naked in the cold. He returned to the comfort of his house, pouring a cup of coffee from the finished brew. After adding some cream, he walked into the living room, starting a fire for the sake of comfort to put himself in a reading mood.

He took a seat on the couch, pulled a blanket over most of his body, and opened the third diary to the middle where he'd left off, determined to see if history might assist him.

Clouse had just taken the bookmark out and opened to the correct page when the cordless phone rang in its cradle beside him. He looked to the clock, noting the early seven o'clock hour before picking it up.

"Hello."

"Paul, it's Mark."

"Why such an early call?" Clouse asked, setting the book on the floor.

"I've got lots of trouble."

"What's the matter?"

"I found Russ Hinds dead last night."

"The security guy?"

"Yeah. We found some different stiffs on his property a few days ago. Troy and I had already talked to him."

"So you two are pals now?"

"No," Daniels said in a stern tone. "And don't keep getting me off the subject."

"Sorry."

"Anyway, he calls the station last night wanting me to meet him at his house to retrieve his stuff, but I show up in less than ten minutes and find him dead."

"Dead bodies aren't anything new for us. I take it you found something else?"

"Yeah. There was a list on his body. *The* list."

"Oh, shit."

"That's not all. The killer left a note saying it was time for the list to be finished."

Clouse thought about that statement a moment. He and Daniels were the only survivors from the list the year before, aside from one other person.

"Did you get any clues from the scene?"

"No, and this is where it gets weird. I called in the afternoon detectives from a payphone and when they got there, no body."

"What the hell happened?"

"I don't know. Now Russ Hinds is going to be listed as a missing person at best."

"It's frustrating because he's one step ahead of us and he keeps targeting people we're not expecting."

"And it's pissing me off because every officer on our force thinks I'm a nut. Hell, they're probably going to look at *me* as a suspect pretty soon."

Clouse chuckled a bit.

"And you thought I set you back by showing up."

"It's not funny. I'm taking the next few days off, needless to say."

Daniels informed him further on the Hinds situation and how his own son almost shared Zach's fate, then Clouse told the detective what he had read about, and how Zach had suddenly been returned. The two decided it would be in their best interest to meet and form a plan of action once they were respectively better informed.

"Is there something about our sons he's trying to get across?" Daniels asked. "What's the big idea behind messing with us?"

"I'm not sure. I think it's a message. Maybe he's Ryan Andrews' real father."

"That certainly doesn't help. We have no clue where that asshole came from."

"I'm going to finish these books soon," Clouse said. "Maybe I can get some hints from them."

"And I plan to rack my brain until I find something in one of these cases that gives me some answers. I know there's more than just coincidence with this explosion and Tim's death. You want to meet up later?"

"I'll get back with you on that. I'm taking Jane and the kids on a field trip to the hotel sometime today. I've got to look for myself and see if there's anything I'm missing."

"Troy and I didn't see anything," Daniels said as though Clouse implied otherwise.

"I believe you. It's just everything he's left me lately is related to the hotel."

"You haven't been there since last year, have you?"

"No," Clouse said, implying he lacked the desire to visit anytime soon.

"Enjoy your holiday. I'm going to look through the files I swiped from headquarters."

"Swiped?"

"I suspect my career may be on the skids, and that my days as a detective might be numbered with everything going on lately. With some time off and the evidence at my disposal I might be able to piece something together."

"Good luck."

"Same to you. Keep me posted."

Clouse hung up the phone as Jane walked into the living room, ruining any chances he had of reading the diary further. She sat beside him, putting one arm around him, the other on his thigh, her fingers venturing toward the inside.

"And good morning to you, too," he said.

"Are we still taking a trip?" Jane inquired.

"Sure."

"You realize we may have *hours* before the kids wake up. Right?"

"So much time to kill. What do you have in mind?" he asked, putting a finger to her lips.

"Let's go upstairs," Jane said with a flirtatious grin. "I'll show you what I'm talking about."

"For a doctor you sure are acting unprofessionally," Clouse said as she led him toward the stairs by the hand.

Jane turned to him, putting her arms around his thick neck.

"I like to think of it as part of a good physical fitness routine."

Clouse shrugged and followed her up the stairs.

***

Tackett returned to the county building the next morning for another look at the car in the garage, only to find a different car inside. A mechanic worked on the lights and siren of a new squad car, assuring that they were fit for duty.

"Hey, Tom," Tackett called to the veteran mechanic everyone there called their resident grease monkey. "Any idea where that damaged car went?"

"Yeah. The sheriff wanted us to send it off for repairs with the dealership."

Tackett grunted acknowledgment and walked into the station, finding much more activity than the night before.

He passed the sheriff's office, finding the man busy on the phone, staring down at some documents. Pearce seemed despondent on the phone, as though trying to get something done and it could not happen fast enough. To Tackett, the man had seemed awfully nervous lately. He waved his hand, motioning for the person on the other end to hurry their conversation along. Tackett stared a moment, finally moving along before Pearce noticed him.

Tackett had other things in mind.

A moment later, he stepped out back, waving to a few of the deputies passing him on their way inside. He stepped around the corner, cautiously looking around. With no one in sight, he entered the back parking lot, finding the object of his search glimmering in the early morning sun, except for the one burnt area at the front right side.

It hadn't been sent out yet.

During normal business hours the impound lot would not be locked while deputies were on the premises. Tackett strolled toward the car as though he had business with it, and no one would probably question his presence in the lot anyhow.

As he popped the car door open, Tackett knelt down, looking around the seats and through the car for any indications of who might have caused the damage. He felt compelled to discover the identity because it seemed as though someone wanted to bury the information quickly.

Someone who worked with him.

Though it might endanger his career with the county police if he discovered the wrong person, Tackett's natural intuition to investigate pushed him forward.

Except for the car's usual disheveled condition, he found nothing of significance until he reached under the driver's side seat, finding a slip of paper almost to the back, as though it might have fallen out of a folder or packet, left when the rest of the contents were hurriedly pulled out.

A yellow slip of paper, it contained an address at the top and some price totals at the bottom. It was a receipt to a local trophy store known to produce trophies and jerseys for sports teams and departmental functions. It was easily accessible and its staff personable enough that someone would likely remember who bought the items listed.

And it was only a week old, meaning it practically *had* to belong to whoever had used the car.

Tackett walked out of the parking lot with the receipt in hand, forgetting that the overhead camera kept careful watch of everything he had just done. Its contents could be viewed by any number of people within the county building.

People who might not like his aggressive investigation.

Chapter 19

Clouse walked into the hotel with a great deal more intensity than his wife and the children. While the kids stood awestruck by the atrium's immense size, six stories of rooms looming overhead from within the domed building's walls, he looked around for any clues the two detectives might have missed.

"What are you thinking about?" Jane asked as he inspected the statues along the atrium's carpeted floor one by one.

"I'm just looking for anything they might have missed."

All around him stood six stories of wasted beauty. Each wall contained intricately painted details of gold, green, and red paint. A rich floral design covered the walls and continued through the new customized carpet on the floor. He wished it could have reopened on schedule the previous year, but nothing in his life seemed to go right anymore.

Even inheriting millions of dollars seemed like a curse because it bought him no protection from the dangers around him, and his family and friends were as vulnerable as ever. He felt as helpless as a beggar on the street with none of life's luxuries.

"Do you want me to take the kids upstairs for a while?"

"Sure," Clouse replied. "I'll see if I can find anything useful."

She turned to leave.

"Is your phone on?" he asked.

"Yes."

"If you see anything the least bit strange, no matter how insignificant it seems, call me right away, Jane," he said with a tone hardened by his experiences.

"I will. And you be careful too."

"Always," Clouse said before heading toward one of the four doorways that led to the rounded hallway that surrounded the atrium, providing a view both outside to the garden or inside to the spacious atrium, much as the rooms did.

As he made his way through the atrium Clouse felt the cold steel of the gun Daniels had lent him along his back. He made no mention of it to Jane or the kids, but felt a bit safer knowing he was armed.

He walked out to the hallway, remembering some haunting images from the past two years. All the bodies, all the chaos sent images streaming through his mind like some kind of horrific montage. Never knowing who was behind the horror unleashed on the hotel grounds until the end haunted him. Clouse had seen too many people die needlessly to prove a point. People whose families would never recover, or understand.

Clouse walked back to the dining area with a hidden kitchen where chefs once created dishes in a kitchen equal to most fine restaurants. It sat empty now, devoid of any utensils. Those sat in the basement boxed up, ready for use a year ago. The white walls were as clean as possible in a building nearly a century old. One of the few areas not fully restored during the past decade, the kitchen had simply been given a thorough facelift.

Out the back window, he saw what little yard remained between the hotel and the tree line. At one time, picnic tables lined the grass and pavement drive where workers often sat in the shade, eating lunch or taking a break from laborious tasks, their clothes often dusted with a coat of mortar or dirt.

Now nothing except an open yard remained.

He stepped out back, letting the door close behind him with a light thumping sound. His key would unlock any door, easily gaining him access to the hotel, regardless of where he walked. Clouse stepped around the side of the building, looking up to the windows, remembering the sight of the killer two years before. It was a time when everyone thought he had killed his own wife, and no one believed his innocence.

Often the killer taunted him by showing himself only to Clouse before committing his next murder. The vision faded as quickly as it had come, and he moved on. Clouse strolled into the yard, needing a breath of fresh air to clear his head before he went searching for clues. He could not escape the past, but he could park it in the back of his mind temporarily.

He walked the concrete path to the edge of the sunken garden where several sulfur springs once allegedly cured all the guests' woes when they stayed at the hotel and partook of the water. Though it was deemed worthless and foul in taste by modern standards, the spring water had once been a major attraction for the hotel when it opened.

A water fountain stood in the center of the garden, dry as a bone with its blue paint chipping inside from a year of neglect. Instead of the mammoth variety of flowers and plants along the garden, the dying remains of vines and shrubs lingered. It took little time at all for the hotel and its land to slip back into the decayed state the National Preservation Society had found it in a decade before.

Clouse looked around him as he walked along the brick path, comparing the death of the garden to everything he had seen the last two years. Even as a firefighter, nothing had prepared him for the level of the grotesque sights of his slain friends, or the emotional trauma he suffered from their deaths.

As he walked toward the other end of the garden, the Jesuit cemetery came into view. It sat atop a hill beyond one of the old recreation buildings. He saw a number of graying crosses emerge from the ground over the bodies of Catholic priests long since gone. One in particular had given him fits around the time his first wife died.

The grave of Father Ernest.

For a moment, Clouse almost turned and left. He stood at the corner of the building, almost afraid to look around and see if the grave was intact. Taking a deep breath, he turned to leave, hesitating as his body refused his mind's commands. In truth, his conflicted mind simply didn't want to know the truth, yet *had* to know for the sake of countless innocent people.

If he found the grave disturbed in any way, he would nearly lose his mind. Already, Smith's grave had been disturbed, and now the makeshift grave of Ryan Andrews was unearthed on Russell Hinds' property. Everything seemed to be tying in somehow, and Clouse's mind had ventured to every clue, unable to make the connections.

As he dared to look around the corner, he found more than his initial fear plainly before him. There, atop the hill in a grave set aside from the others, he spied Ernest's grave, dirt mounds all around it, with a surprise standing in the middle of the grave itself.

Dressed completely in black, holding a modified scythe with both hands, the killer bore an evil stare at him through the darkness of his costume's hood.

"Oh, God," Clouse said, his hands fumbling behind him for the gun.

***

Tackett walked into Beckett's Trophies with the receipt tucked in his right pocket. The shirt and tie, along with the gun belt strapped around his waist, gave the clerk the immediate impression he was with the police.

"Hey, Earl," the young man called to the back. "They come to git yuh," he yelled, using worse grammar than a self-proclaimed redneck like Tackett ever dreamed of speaking.

He seemed like the type of kid who had quit high school, taking the first decent job that came his way. Youthful freckles still dotted his face, and his smile revealed several spaces between some teeth that indicated he might have missed corrective dental techniques as a kid.

Tackett had removed his badge during breakfast, so he quickly reached into his left pocket to pull it out, clipping it on his duty belt where it belonged. As he looked up, his eyes locked with those of the man he figured was the owner.

A quick look around the store indicated the owner wasn't much for change, considering some of the trophies looked more than a decade old. The few posters lining the walls appeared faded and fraying in their corners around the thumbtacks barely holding them in place. He supposed small businesses needed to clear a profit with lease prices on the rise. Considering the fairly nice location of the shop in a frequented plaza, Tackett figured the owner did the best he could with his circumstances.

Wearing an apron over dirty khaki pants, a man with gray hair and slight oil smudges along his cheeks stood behind the counter. His face seemed weathered, like a man who had put in a lot of overtime lately. Perhaps too much to remember the buyer of the items on the receipt Tackett had found in the car.

"Can I help you, officer?"

"Detective Troy Tackett, Monroe County Police," he replied, shaking hands with the man. "Are you the owner?"

"Earl Beckett. Yes I am."

"Do you remember this order?" Tackett asked, retrieving the receipt from his pocket.

Beckett put on his reading glasses before examining it a moment, looking over the contents of the receipt and the total price. The items were generically listed, like trophy, plaque, and poster with no further description. He also looked at the date, which triggered nothing further in his memory.

"There's been so much business lately with fall sports ending," he complained. "Let me think a moment."

"I might be able to narrow it down for you. Has anyone from the sheriff's office been in here lately?"

"Well, I can't think of *anyone* in uniform here at all lately."

"Last weekend, driving a department car maybe?" Tackett prodded.

"Well, the sheriff was in here," Beckett finally remembered. "He was dressed in plain clothes and in a hurry to get to a meeting, he said."

"Was this last Saturday like the receipt indicates?"

"Had to be," Beckett said. "I don't do receipts until people pick up their orders."

Tackett looked from the older man to the receipt. Things were suddenly coming a bit clearer to him.

"Thank you," he said to both owner and employee before leaving the store, cursing under his breath at his bad luck.

Chapter 20

Daniels had spent most of his morning reviewing the files he copied from city hall. Things were beginning to make a little more sense, but it was like trying to complete a jigsaw puzzle with important center and corner pieces missing. Without the framework, the rest of the pieces would never fall into place.

Seated in his basement, armed only with the files and a cordless phone, Daniels prepared to commit a full day to finding answers. Only an independent bulb bathed him in yellow light as he adjusted himself on an old love seat.

He picked up the phone, deciding to probe further into a related case.

"Bedford Police," a hardened male dispatcher's voice answered on the other end after two rings.

"This is Detective Mark Daniels with the Bloomington Police," Daniels began, knowing this would be the first of a string of calls he would make before his credibility deserted him. "I need to speak to whoever is in charge of the Niemeyer murder last Saturday."

"Hold on a second," the voice said, softening ever so slightly.

"Unger," a different voice said momentarily, apparently identifying himself. "How can I help you, Mark?"

"Harold? That you?" Daniels asked, remembering a case they had worked together a few years prior.

"Yeah. I hear you're having a rough time of it lately, Mark."

"Worse than you could imagine. I need to know anything you can tell me about the Niemeyer murder last Saturday."

"Personal interest?"

"No. There might be a link to a case I'm working."

"Well, there were six assailants, five of which got away."

"And the one that didn't was a real estate god, right?"

"Yeah. Niemeyer suffered multiple stab wounds throughout his body. He died on the scene within seconds."

Daniels looked through a newspaper clipping. It talked in depth about Niemeyer's death but focused little on the assailants and the lack of evidence issued by police to the press. Either police refused to give out information or there was nothing to give.

"I'd like to know more about the attackers, Harold. Any eyewitness accounts? How were they dressed? Any positive ID's?"

"The only eyewitness account is from the younger brother. Everyone dressed in black robes, and no one else saw anything."

"That's not much help."

"Sorry. That's what's keeping me from putting anyone behind bars. But there was something kind of odd, Mark."

"What's that?"

"Mr. Niemeyer was using an ATM when this whole thing went down. His brother said it was customary before they went out to eat that he withdrew money, and usually paid for the meal. Anyhow, the security camera at that machine taped everything."

"Really?" Daniels asked quickly, hoping for a break.

"Yeah, but the tape to the recording system was inside the same booth and got stolen. We didn't find any clues about who might have done it."

"What bank was it?"

"Let me see," Unger said, sounds of leafing through the files on his desk coming over the line. "It's Bloomington Citizens Commerce, a locally owned and operated chain of banks."

"Run by?" Daniels inquired.

"Well, the chain president is, or was, Daniel Harris."

A realization smacked Daniels upside the head.

Harris was one of the four people killed in the explosion, and Daniels had solved a major part of the problem surrounding his investigation.

"Did that help at all?" Unger asked, breaking his concentration.

"Yeah, it did. Thanks, Harold," Daniels said.

"Care to share what you've got on your end if these cases are related?"

"I'm out of the office a few days," Daniels confessed. "Give the guys a call and they can fax over the files if you want them right away."

"A personal take would be handier."

Daniels figured as much, but he didn't have the time for a play-by-play when his young partner could fill in Unger nearly as well.

"Call Lipscomb. He can get you up to speed."

Though he required more proof, Daniels had a suspicion the four people murdered in the explosion were Niemeyer's killers. The question remained, was the fifth supposed to be a victim, or was he too one of the murderers.

Either way, Daniels knew one thing for certain. He needed to talk with Clouse right away.

***

Clouse stared up at the killer, drawing the Magnum from his backside. As though he was invincible, the darkly clad figure stood unwavering, even at the sight of the gun. Without wasting a moment, Clouse took deliberate aim, closed one eye, and fired directly into the killer's chest, causing him to flail wildly with each shot before finally falling into the grave behind him.

Hesitantly, Clouse started up the hill, knowing it was too easy. There was no chance someone bent on revenge would stand there and take all six bullets to the chest. As he reached the open grave, he kept a safe distance, staring down at the body in the large hole. An empty grave devoid of Ernest's body or a coffin now held the fallen reaper.

Stepping a bit closer, he stared at the black robe, seeing no damage to any of the thin material. Though the killer appeared entirely unscathed by the bullets, Clouse felt compelled to know the identity of who tormented his life.

He put the gun down, reaching for the scythe to secure it before looking beneath the hood to answer the question that haunted him.

Grasping the weapon by its wooden handle, Clouse pressed down, pinning it to the ground before reaching for the killer's hood, certain the bullets would have hit their mark all six times, or close to it.

Almost atop the killer, Clouse saw no wounds, and no blood along the cloth, indicating perhaps the bullets had missed their mark, or never truly fired at all.

"Blanks," he whispered under his breath, too late to escape the killer's wrath as he bolted from the empty grave, clasping Clouse's throat with one hand, holding the scythe with the other.

He released the scythe just long enough to thrust a fist into Clouse's abdomen, sending him rolling down the hill a few feet. As he regained his breath, Clouse looked up to the killer, now emerging from the grave, looming over him like the shadow of death he wanted to portray. The scythe was clutched in his right hand, but this failed to intimidate his target any further.

Clouse charged the killer, knocking them both into the grave, but the black shape regained his senses first, cupping the back of Clouse's head and thrusting his forehead on the hard ground at the edge of the grave. He repeated the process several more times, finally pushing Clouse aside before stepping out of the large hole.

Unwilling to be easily bested, Clouse grabbed the killer's ankle, tripping him. As he fell, the darkly clad figure slashed the scythe around, missing Clouse's head by inches. For a few seconds, the two stared at one another, wondering who dared make the next move first.

Clouse felt blood trickle from his nose and some burning scuff marks along his face from where his skin scraped against the unforgiving soil. He also felt the world around him spinning as though he'd been blindfolded and spun around several times before pinning the tail on the donkey. With his ears ringing, and his equilibrium compromised, Clouse decided he needed to give some punishment rather than receive more.

Before the killer could regain his footing, Clouse dove, tripping him up again, using his cloak against him. The killer kicked him squarely in the side of his face, but only began a momentary escape as Clouse gave chase, catching the killer by the shoulder with his hand, whirling him around into a premeditated punch.

He knew this might be his only chance to end his ordeal on his own terms, to thwart the killer's ultimate plan before it reached a conclusion.

For his efforts, Clouse received a solid punch to the sternum, then a knee in the same area. A fist hit his jaw like an anvil, sending him to the ground long enough for the killer to flee the scene into the trees behind the hotel.

Clouse groaned, regaining his footing slowly, knowing he could not properly pursue the killer with any hope of catching him.

He stumbled a few steps before tumbling to the ground again, looking to the hotel, which looked a mile away in his weakened state.

"Jane," he said, struggling to pull himself forward, even if it was at a snail's pace.

***

Inside the hotel Jane walked with the kids down a flight of stairs leading to the first floor. Even without the lights on, enough sunlight streamed through the windows to give the hotel a lonely feeling, especially with a lack of internal heat. She wondered where her husband might be, because she had found enough time to show the kids all of the hotel's features and more.

When she reached the bottom of the stairs, only the echoes of her footsteps welcomed her and the children. Restless as they were, the kids seemed suddenly on edge, possibly sensing her apprehension.

"Paul?" she called, her voice flowing through the hallways and back to her.

No answer.

She stepped toward one of the atrium doorways, finding no trace of human life, much less her husband. With the kids close behind, she walked into the atrium, which glowed from the morning light, streaming through the glass dome above.

All three stood startled when the sound of a door closing in the distance passed through the grand room.

"Come here," she told the kids who immediately took hold of her hands.

She led them out of the atrium toward the main entrance, expecting to find Clouse somewhere in between, but she found absolutely no one.

"Mommy, I'm scared," Katie said from behind her.

"It's okay. We'll get out of here in a minute."

She led them toward the front door, unsure of exactly who opened a door a moment before. The only thing she knew was that someone else was in the building.

"Paul?" she called, ready to hurry the kids out to the car. Her body tensed from the anxiety of not knowing.

With no answer, she walked toward the light of the glass doors when someone grabbed her from the darkness of the hallway, pulling her close.

Jane jerked herself back from her apparent attacker, finding her husband battered and bloodied from his scuffle.

"Paul?" she asked in shock. "Are you okay?"

"I'm all right," he answered quickly through a bloodied lip. "Have you seen anyone else up here?"

"No. What happened?"

"There's no time. We have to get out of here with the kids *now*."

Feeling pain travel through every vein in his body to every muscle, he opened the door, ushering Jane and the kids outside, careful to lock it behind him before taking them to her car. He had a new mystery to think about concerning the empty graves, but this was the second time he failed to defeat the killer in a physical confrontation, further weakening his mental resilience. There was no doubt this was part of the killer's plan, but he was not destined to find out how on this day.

Chapter 21

Daniels walked into the hospital expecting to find very little about either reason he chose to visit. Using his credentials as an investigator on Susan Jameson's murder, he gained access to her office, a small room on a higher floor containing a not so breathtaking view of the parking garage.

He had to wonder about everything he thought of her while he rehabilitated his legs the year before. Even after a bullet was removed from his back Daniels always wondered why it took so long to regain his footing when his legs felt healthy and everyone said he was ready to walk.

"It's a mental block," he remembered her saying several times. "Somewhere deep down you don't want to walk yet."

"My ass," Daniels muttered as he stepped inside the office, wondering just how many drugs he might have unwittingly taken that altered his mental or physical state.

He wanted to know what her involvement was with that group, and what interest she might have had in hindering his rehabilitation. To think that he spent a year's time, once a week, visiting her when she was part of a murderous clan left him uneasy.

So uneasy, in fact, that he requested his own medical file be brought to him by one of the nurses, again attaching it to the investigation.

As he began looking through her desk, he found little of significance. Strangely, he found a lack of personal items. Most any detective Daniels worked with kept at least one family photo around, and little necessary trinkets like combs, spare keys, or good luck charms. He found nothing that seemed of great personal nature among her belongings.

Perhaps the doctor was more secretive than he imagined. It struck him as odd that she never even made an effort to appear like an everyday person.

He turned on the computer, waiting for it to warm up while a nurse walked in with the file, handing it to him. She seemed a gruff grandmotherly type of woman who had probably seen her share of almost everything at the hospital over the years. She didn't seem particularly thrilled about any patient, including a detective, prying into medical files, even if they were his own.

"Thank you," he said, flipping it open, scanning the contents.

"Anything else?" she asked.

"Yeah," Daniels said, pointing to one of the medications he was listed as taking, but did not particularly remember. "Can you tell me what that is?" he questioned, noticing it was under a different category than the other listed drugs.

"Sure. That's a muscle relaxer we sometimes use on patients who have pulled muscles or tendons. Makes it easier to keep them relaxed."

"How relaxed?"

"If you give them enough, it takes everything they have to sit up."

"Thanks," Daniels said, setting the file down, remembering how close he came to standing on several occasions, only to have his legs give out on him at a crucial moment.

He grumbled to himself momentarily, looking through more of the desk before rolling himself on the chair toward a filing cabinet in the opposite corner. He began looking through a seemingly endless set of files, all looking the same. Each had a name that he assumed belonged to patients, which he confirmed when he came across his own.

"What have we here?" he asked, pulling it out for a look inside.

Most of the papers were documentation, stating how his case was going. In several, he noticed exaggerated narrations of his failed attempts to walk.

"And my potential suicidal tendencies?" he asked aloud, reading a sheet.

He continued reading, realizing his doctor had purposely made him sound far worse than he actually was, both physically and mentally. He looked at the bottom of the sheet noticing several c/c remarks, one of which struck him as very familiar.

Doctor Martin Smith.

"Good God, how deep was she in this shit?" he asked himself, wondering just how far the conspiracy to murder reached, and how far back in time.

Jameson could very well have been involved with Ryan Andrews when he murdered Smith the year before, as well as an entire group. Things were beginning to fall into place, but Daniels felt uncertain who had murdered the group of four conspirators. If he figured that out, he would have the most important answer of all.

***

Tackett made certain the sheriff's car was nowhere in sight when he returned to the police station shortly after eating dinner. By now the afternoon shift was comfortably adjusted to their routine, and he found the man he was looking for seated at a desk reviewing some reports made by his road officers.

"Hey, Jerry, you got a minute?" he asked the afternoon sergeant from the doorway.

"Sure," Alder said. "What do you need, Troy?"

Tackett walked all the way inside the office, closing the door behind him.

Alder gave a curious look as the detective sat across from him.

"You feeling okay lately?" he asked. "You've been acting kind of, well, out of character, Troy."

"It's these murders, you know. I'm not getting very far with them, and it's tough with the families going to the press and all."

Tackett took up a few minutes relating the story of how several families were publicly berating the police. He waited until he had lulled Alder into a sense of trust, putting him at ease. His real reason for coming would have to be snuck in at the end of the conversation, so he needed to soften Alder up some more.

He took a wad of chewing tobacco from the pouch in his back pocket while the sergeant lit a cigarette, settling them both in for a conversation.

"So what else is going on?" Alder asked.

"Not much. Look, I know things have been rough lately, but I got to thinking about doing some public relations when I get some free time. You know, going to local schools and talking to kids," Tackett said before spitting into a used plastic bottle.

"That's good. We haven't had anyone do that since Doyle retired last year."

"Do we have any stuff I could look at? Brochures, handouts, stuff like that?"

"Yeah," Alder said, rising from his chair to lead Tackett into the next room and a closet full of boxes. "A lot of this is Doyle's old stuff. There's department information in there too."

Tackett leafed through the items, finding one of the sheriff's brochures handed out before the election. It gave all of Pearce's credentials, including a bit of what the detective wanted to know.

"Navy SEAL, huh?"

"Yeah," Alder replied. "I guess he did some overseas extraction of prisoners after the war."

"Really?"

"He doesn't talk much about it, but I guess he created diversions while the other guys got prisoners out."

Perhaps explosive diversions, Tackett thought.

"And to think, I grew up on a farm."

"About the most exciting thing I ever did was win the lottery," Alder said.

"And you're still here?"

"When it's split a dozen ways, the money doesn't go that far, especially after taxes."

Tackett nodded.

"I see. You didn't spend it all, did you?"

"Not all of it, but I was young and dumb enough to lose most of it before I knew any better."

Tackett spit in the bottle again, catching a whiff of the juice's minty smell as he took up a few of the materials to verify his bogus claim of departmental public relations. He had the answer he wanted already. Now he wondered if Pearce might have been the explosives setter in Daniels' murder case, or if perhaps he was mixed up with the wrong crowd, fearing for his life.

"Need anything else?" Alder asked.

"No, I'm fine, Jerry. Thanks a bunch."

"Don't mention it. I've got to review those reports. The new guys don't even know how to spell things right, much less draw an accident scene. We're a lawsuit waiting to happen if I don't get them squared away."

"Good luck."

Tackett walked out of the building unsure of what he wanted to do. Pressing the subject with anyone he worked with might get back to Pearce, and without probing around his own workplace he would never get the proof one way or the other of Pearce's involvement in anything.

As he walked to his car Tackett sensed a presence behind him. He looked back to the station, finding someone staring at him through the window where most of the offices were located. There, with unblinking eyes, the sheriff stared at him as though he knew something, or someone, had wronged him.

Tackett was that someone.

Swallowing hard, the detective simply opened his car door and slid inside, ready to take the weekend off and ponder the weighty decision ahead of him.

He had planned to cancel his trip to Ohio where regional rodeo competition was held for the second straight week, but decided the time away might do him some good. There, he could not afford to let his mind wander, or think about anything but the task at hand, or he would wind up flat beneath some bull's hooves.

Tackett planned to call Daniels and exchange information before he left in the morning. Maybe it was time the investigator of the four homicides looked into the sheriff's potential involvement based on an "anonymous" tip.

Chapter 22

Clouse spent most of his day lying in bed recuperating from his wounds. He fell in and out of sleep while Jane wiped his forehead with wet cloths and brought soup for him. Throughout the day, he heard the kids playing outside under her watch, or running upstairs for their toys.

"I'm not sick, you know," he commented when she returned to retrieve his soup bowl and check on him.

"No, but you need rest and good food just the same."

He groaned painfully as he turned over in bed to face her.

"It seems the kids have no lingering trauma," he said, referring to their active play.

"You did a good job of covering up. I guess they bought the bit about you falling down the concrete steps."

Clouse grinned.

"They're naive. Cute, but still naive."

"So, how did it happen?"

"By 'it', you mean how did I get so messed up?"

"I mean, what exactly happened? Did he take you by surprise?"

"Well, no," Clouse said hesitantly.

Jane twisted her face in a quizzical look.

"Then exactly how did you get your new look?"

Clouse explained the situation in moderate detail, leaving his wife further frustrated at his heroics.

"You shot six times?"

"I didn't miss," Clouse insisted. "I'm *not* that bad a shot."

"You were nervous," Jane said. "There's no way you could be accurate on the spur of the moment like that."

"I would not miss all six," he said vehemently. "Something was wrong with the bullets."

"Wrong?"

"Before I crawled my way back to the hotel, I had a second to look around the grave area. There were no slugs anywhere."

"You're not a forensics expert. You missed high and they went into the woods," Jane suggested.

"I'm not buying that."

"Then what are you saying, Paul?"

"That those might not have been real bullets in that gun."

"What?"

"Blanks. I think someone put them in the gun, knowing I was carrying it."

"But Mark gave you that gun. Who else would know what kind of gun it was, and have opportunity to do something like that?"

Only one person came to mind, but his brother had just been butchered by six mysterious suspects, and it seemed unlikely he would be tampering with Clouse's primary means of defense, especially with the way their trip to Tennessee ended.

Still, the killer had breached Clouse's home defenses once before, so access to the gun was not necessarily restricted to a certain few people. And it had sat in his truck a few times while he made trips into the store, a restaurant, or city hall. It would have taken some effort, but a person who knew firearms could have switched the bullets.

Or not.

Either way, Clouse did not want to talk about it until he met with Daniels first.

"Can you grab that book for me?" he asked her, referring to the diary just out of his reach.

"Sure," she said, passing it to him. "Are you learning anything from it?"

"Nothing much. It seems the legend of Father Ernest isn't as stellar as people think."

"No self-induced torching?"

"Not yet. It seems he might have died from something else."

"Too bad," she said, giving him a kiss on the cheek. "I'll leave you alone so you can read."

"And no more soup," Clouse playfully pleaded.

Jane gave a smile and left the room. Before reading, Clouse picked up the phone, tried to reach Daniels and got an answering machine instead. He left a message asking his unofficial partner to come over later, since he was indisposed.

He picked up the book and read several chapters while the house was in a quieter state.

***

It seemed a month or so passed with no incident at the converted hotel. Father Ernest went about his Sunday masses while the rest of church business went along as usual. Father Runnels watched as his senior priest's health began to drastically fail and his faith deteriorated, even in his sermons.

One Sunday morning Ernest failed to show for the usual early breakfast before mass. Fearing the worst, Runnels and another priest went to look for him, unable to find him in his usual spots. He was not in his quarters, nor anywhere on the grounds. They did not want to alert everyone residing at the seminary, but a search of a few hundred rooms would prove difficult with only two people.

"Any ideas?" Runnels asked the other priest.

"Have you seen Henry?"

"Yes, in the atrium reading a book. He wouldn't know where Ernest was anyhow."

"The child never speaks," the priest complained. "He just gestures and points."

Both were about to contemplate their next move when another of the brothers peeked his head in the door, informing them Ernest had shown up for breakfast.

Each gave the other a strange look before hurriedly walking toward the transformed dining room, which appeared more like a military mess hall. Plain, just as the Jesuits wanted it.

A moment later they found Ernest eating an English muffin, lightly buttered, with his crucifix sitting on the table beside him. Strangely, Ernest's recent questions about the validity of his faith had never kept him away from his wooden cross. He sat munching on the muffin as though nothing was any different from the usual Sunday routine.

"Where have you been?" Runnels asked his colleague with genuine concern. "We were worried sick about you, Ernest."

"I went for a walk. I woke up with a headache and more pain than usual, so I took a walk in the woods to clear my head."

"That's not wise, my friend," the other priest said. "If anything happened to you, we'd never find you on time."

"I'm fine," Ernest stated. "In fact, things could be getting better for me."

"Are you finding room for the Lord inside your heart again?" Runnels asked, leaning over toward Ernest, speaking in almost a whisper.

"In a roundabout way," Ernest replied.

He looked almost indifferently around the renovated dining area, apparently still sickened that its lush carpet and decorative overhead lights were replaced with bare floors, white walls, and plain, exposed light bulbs.

While the next few minutes passed, everyone began finishing their breakfast, ready to attend mass. Ernest and Runnels had nearly finished when one of the younger brothers dashed into the room among the handful of late eaters.

He spied Runnels at the table, rushing over with a concerned look.

"Father, we found Brother Tom in the basement." He leaned down to whisper. "Dead."

"Oh, my," Runnels said, rising from his seat. He looked to Ernest, who wore a look of equal concern.

"What is it?"

"It may be nothing," Runnels said, not wanting to alarm anyone just yet. He needed to justify the claim with his own eyes before sharing the terrible news. Besides, he did not want to say anything that might further deteriorate Ernest's condition.

Runnels walked down the hallway behind young Richard, heading toward the basement. He feared the worst because Richard seemed positive his fellow Jesuit was dead. When he reached the bottom stair, he discovered exactly why Richard reached his conclusion so assuredly.

Even from a distance, he could see Thomas' body lying in a distorted position, his neck bent to one side. Behind his body stood a stepladder erected beneath a light fixture. It appeared to be a terrible accident where Thomas had been changing one of the bulbs in a row of light fixtures leading to the basement's deeper storage area.

Runnels made the sign of the cross where he stood, then turned to young Richard.

"Go upstairs and tell the others to attend mass as usual."

"Should I tell them?"

"No. I'll handle the arrangements and call the police. Such a terrible accident," he proclaimed as Richard darted up the stairs.

He walked over to the body, bending over to feel Thomas' skin, finding it cool, though still containing warmth. Thomas had not died long ago. The trickle of blood at his lip had not even fully dried.

"Such a waste," Runnels said to himself. "Terrible. Just terrible."

Runnels would spend the rest of his day talking to police and the coroner, preparing funeral arrangements, and assigning several of his Jesuits to dig the grave that would house Thomas Harding's body.

The first of a few dozen such graves.

Chapter 23

Clouse closed the third diary at its completion, ready to move on to the fourth and final book but the sound of the doorbell kept him from starting it. He slowly dragged himself from the bed and down the stairs to find Jane standing at the edge of the living room, Daniels standing behind her with an uneasy grin crossing his face.

"Man, you did get messed up," the detective said.

"You and I need to talk, buddy," Clouse said, painfully making his way down the few remaining stairs.

"Can I get you something?" Jane offered the visiting detective.

"No, thank you. I can't stay long."

Daniels made his way into a chair across from Clouse, unable to keep from staring at Clouse's wounds. It was apparent he understood the serious nature of his friend's brush with the killer, but could not keep from grinning for some reason.

"I came as soon as I got your message," Daniels stated. "I checked my voice mail from the office."

"You can quit laughing at my expense anytime," Clouse informed him. "It's not like you have a great track record against past killers yourself."

"Yeah, but my battles were never straight-up fights."

Clouse shrugged.

"I don't know. He was physically powerful and deliberate, like he had studied how to beat the shit out of me."

"Based on what we know, he's been planning this a long time. And now I think the four people killed in the explosion might be the result of the same guy."

"How so?"

"Just some very strange coincidences. Like Dr. Jameson being one of the victims, and the banker who was killed. It seems awfully strange that the videotape of Tim Niemeyer's murder from that ATM came up missing when that bank was from the chain that he managed."

"So we're looking at a conspiracy gone wrong?"

"Or a complete setup from the beginning."

Both sat silently a moment.

"I shot the killer six times, Mark," Clouse said, itching to discuss the topic of his attack.

"*Shot* him?"

"The gun you gave me. I shot him six times and he never got hit."

"What are you trying to say, Paul?"

Clouse sat a moment, trying to think of how he wanted to shape his words.

"I think someone switched the bullets to blanks, or perhaps, they came that way."

Daniels slowly nodded, biting his lower lip. Any jovial nature he brought with him disappeared instantaneously when he realized he was being accused in a roundabout way of switching the ammunition.

"There's no way I would leave blanks in my guns. There's no reason I would ever possess blanks to begin with. I don't film movies or put on live shows for public enjoyment. Therefore, I would never put blanks in my guns, especially if I were going to loan a firearm to you."

"I believe you, but it means someone has full access to me, and quite possibly you."

"So now what?"

Clouse shook his head.

"I don't know. There are only so many people it can be, Mark."

"I'm not getting any closer to finding out who Ryan Andrews' father was."

"They never did DNA testing?"

"What good would it do if they had no idea who the parents were?"

Clouse gave a hopeless look.

"Could our guy have been wearing a vest?" Daniels asked from nowhere.

"No," Clouse said. "He didn't flinch in the least. And I aimed for the head twice."

"And you're sure you didn't miss?"

Clouse sighed aloud.

"You and Jane need to run a clinic on my aim. I was too close to miss all six, nervous or not."

Daniels stood to stretch a moment.

"Must be tough to have all this and not be able to enjoy it," he noted.

"It's a bummer," Clouse replied in short.

"You're no better off than I am, I suppose."

Clouse had little time for small talk, especially since Daniels was always the one who carried a businesslike nature everywhere he went.

"Any new ideas?" Daniels asked, finally settling back into character.

"We've covered almost everything. I can't think of any angles we haven't touched on. But I'm a little concerned about this unearthing of bodies."

"Which ones?"

"First Dr. Smith's body gets dug up, no trace of it, then we find Ryan Andrews' body, and now Father Ernest's body is missing again," Clouse said, speaking in terms of two years before when Ernest's corpse was unearthed in part of the attempt to frame him for his wife's murder.

"What do you make of it?"

Clouse shifted uneasily.

"There's a message there, like with the photos. He's doing something in order, almost chronological in nature."

"Then what's next?"

"Next?" Clouse asked. "I think he's taking us back to the hotel. That's where everything started, and where he's leading us. The pictures, the personal appearance, taking Zach there. Whatever he has planned, the hotel will have something to do with it."

"We can't just sit back defensively, can we?"

"Not anymore. I'm just looking for a chance to trip him up. If we can figure out what he's up to next, we can stop him."

"I don't like this," Daniels said.

Clouse understood.

Cops never liked being in a position without control. They thrived, even lived, on being in charge of their situations and scenes. Both men had adapted to being teased by the killers over the past two years, and both were accustomed to putting their lives in some form of danger. On both occasions, however, they had figured out who the killer was in time to spare just a few lives.

Not this time.

Clouse had no control over the situation, and no way to tell who might be killed next. Although, he figured, the killer was not on a rampage like before. He killed very deliberately, and it seemed, only when people got in his way. Both Niemeyer and Clouse's babysitter had been messages, but everyone beyond that seemed to have only committed the crime of being in the wrong place at the wrong time.

"It seems like we're just missing one little clue that would bust this thing wide open," Daniels observed as he stood to go.

"I think you're right about our killer blowing up those people," Clouse said. "But if he wasn't the fifth person at the scene, we have a killer and a potential victim out there."

"Or maybe just a murderer."

"If we knew what he was up to, we'd know who might be in his way, and we might know who's next on his list," Clouse deduced. "And we need to know that person's identity to stop him."

Chapter 24

Tackett drove toward the Ohio border at a rate of speed higher than usual the next morning. His attempts to find Daniels had failed, but he left sufficient information for Daniels to reach him, including his cell phone number.

In his custom striped truck, he stood out among other vehicles. A large truck with dual exhaust, a diesel engine, and enough horsepower to pull fully loaded trailers, Tackett thought his truck could do no wrong.

Today the truck had it easy, since he was towing nothing behind it. His saddle and gear rested in the bed, ready for aggressive use later that afternoon. Dressed in his old boots, a washed but slightly faded shirt, and a black flak vest, similar to what police used, he kept his eyes on the road, moving them only for a second to spit into his empty soda bottle every so often.

He had recently purchased the vest to protect him during bull rides, and to wear while he broke in his horses, but the vest itself was not broken in. Parts of it still dug into his side and his back. Considering how thick he was around the chest, it was nearly impossible to get a perfect fit on such a thick protective vest.

Its Kevlar certainly protected him, but it granted little mercy in the way of comfort.

During his trips to Celina, Ohio, Tackett discovered the better stops when it came to eating or restroom breaks. He saw one of his favorite convenience stores in the distance, partly because it housed a restroom on one side, which provided a quick fill-up, and a quick in-and-out to the restroom without even having to step inside. He always brought his credit card for time efficiency by paying at the pump, often relieving himself before heading down the road.

He felt a sensational urge to stop as the two cups of coffee he drank that morning waged war inside his bladder.

Tackett pulled the truck over to the first available pump, drawing any number of stares as he stepped from the truck in his boots, opting not to remove his black cowboy hat. He looked the part of a bull rider in the middle of a highway rest area town. The detective did not fit in with the families on their way to vacation spots, or the businessmen grabbing some coffee before their meeting in the next town, but he certainly did get noticed.

While he allowed the pump to fill his truck, Tackett stepped over to the men's restroom, finding the two urinals and the stall unoccupied. He did not bother locking the door behind him, and immediately unzipped his pants once he stepped inside the stall.

All around him the stench of urine floated through the air. A complete lack of windows in the restroom provided poor ventilation, and occasionally when he stopped the room would not be thoroughly cleaned, smelling terrible on those occasions. Usually the sound of the faucet dripping carried through the dim room.

As he relieved himself, staring at the graffiti along the ceiling, he wondered just how marred a restroom would have to be before the short Korean owner gave it a fresh coat of paint and an overhaul.

Then again, cleaning it would probably inspire new colorful artwork.

Over the sound of his business Tackett heard someone step into the room and close the door, leaving the sound of a concise echo. Then the lock latched.

He zipped up, listening for any other sounds in the room before he stepped from the stall. He heard nothing, so he carefully swung the door open, looking ahead as he set one foot outside, finding no one there.

The sinks ahead were set to the left, but he could see the fronts of them, and there was no one standing there. Tackett wondered if someone might have just stepped in and left in the same instant, but he swore he heard the lock latch. A tiny utility closet occupied the other side of the entrance, but its door appeared closed and he hadn't heard a second door open.

Tackett walked to the door, pulling on the knob to realize it would not budge. His eyes followed the doorknob up to the latch, where he found it locked. A thought occurred to him that there would be no way someone could fully lock the door and escape. There were no windows, and no place to hide.

No place except the utility closet beside him.

He whirled to find the killer already leaping toward him, knife thrust out in front.

Tackett managed to clasp the shape's arms at the wrist, using his own momentum against him as he threw him against the metal door, creating a crash that would scare the life out of anyone nearby.

Knowing his own luck, Tackett knew no one would hear the struggle.

Tackett threw a knee upward, catching the killer in the abdomen, rather than the intended groin. He then let a fist fly across the killer's face beneath the hood, providing an opening for his attacker to slash his arm with the knife. The detective drew away, backing toward the stall as bloody droplets fell from his arm.

Without warning, the killer charged him, but Tackett turned, sending them both into the concrete wall with incredible impact. Tackett's head hit the wall while the killer had the wind knocked audibly from his lungs. Both regained their senses enough to see the knife hit the ground and bounce outside the stall, far enough that whichever one of them exited the stall first had the best chance of grasping it.

Tackett clasped the killer's costume by the shoulders, pushing him back toward the toilet. Realizing he was about to hit the stool, and possibly lose balance, the killer grabbed Tackett by the vest, hurling him against the wall. Refusing to let the killer escape the stall first, he grabbed at the costume, tearing part of it at the bottom, failing to slow the killer's escape.

Knowing he would be beaten to the knife, Tackett reached to his ankle for the small revolver he kept holstered around his left boot. He had nearly grasped the weapon when the killer charged him. Completely off balance, Tackett was easy prey as the shape threw him against the wall, hitting the back of his head against the unforgiving concrete.

As the detective slumped to the floor, barely conscious, the killer held the knife's handle, wiping the blade with a gloved hand before saddling himself atop the detective's torso. He centered himself along Tackett's sternum, pinning him down with his knees atop the detective's arms.

With his wind knocked from him, the last clear thing Tackett saw was a piece of paper he recognized as leaving in Daniels' mailbox, telling all about the sheriff and his possible involvement in Niemeyer's murder. He placed it there since he left so early in the morning, not wanting to disturb his fellow detective at the crack of dawn.

Tackett's vision blurred slightly as the killer shook his head negatively, as though to scold the detective for such a poor decision. Through masked eyes, he watched until he saw some recognition on Tackett's part of what was about to happen. When Tackett saw the knife rise above the killer's shoulders, clasped in both hands, he knew with both his arms pinned he was helpless to do anything but watch as the knife plummeted toward his heart.

Even with his power, Tackett could not move, much less thwart the killer's attempt at ending his life. He felt his body stiffen as the knife pierced his skin, penetrating muscle tissue and drawing blood. His breaths came hard and he gasped for life as the killer left the blade stuck below his shoulder and took leave of the restroom, satisfied with his logical decision to use the knife over the scythe in such a cramped situation.

Tackett saw sunlight stream through the open door as the killer left, taking off his mask and costume before rounding the corner. His breathing came in heaves and the detective felt his consciousness, and his life hang in the balance. The piercing sting of the knife had become a numb sensation as blood bubbled to the surface of his shirt, staining his new vest. He felt a lump in his throat, perhaps swelling, or maybe just his tongue falling back.

One hand touched the knife, fingering it before tracing the warm stream down to the red pool near his shoulder, scooping up some of the crimson liquid. The hand rolled over as if to show Tackett the situation was as mortal as he thought. He did not recall commanding his hand to do any of that, and his body seemed to be separating from his mind.

His breathing became audible the more he struggled for air. He felt his legs twitch a bit and his eyelids grow heavy. Nothing mattered to him now except ending the struggle, finding the peace that awaited him when his eyes closed. He felt the light leave his eyes as someone's arm touched his own.

"Oh my God! Call an ambulance!" he barely heard as his eyes rolled back in his head and the world around him no longer mattered.

***

Daniels kissed his wife goodbye at the front door when she left for work in the morning. Although he hated to let her go by herself, he needed to stay with the kids, and their family needed some means of support. If his personal days expired, he would have to use sick days or go without pay in one form or another.

He watched Cindy's car pull away, then noticed the mailbox beside the door with its flap open.

"That's odd," he said, closing it before stepping inside.

He returned to the house, hoping the kids were still in bed. He checked, and both were asleep. Daniels loved having kids young enough to stay home. The day would come when they were old enough to attend school, and he dreaded it, but in the meantime, he savored the time at home with them.

Daniels put on a tough front at work. He told fellow officers he wanted his wife to stay home with the kids so he could provide. They bought it, never suspecting how much he loved spending time at home with them. And though he never told Cindy, he was especially thrilled to have his son. If the couple had been blessed with a second daughter, he might have persuaded his wife to try for a third child, but things worked out for the best, and they decided to stop at two.

After checking on the kids he walked to the refrigerator to see what scraps he could mix together for breakfast. Often he created fried omelets from leftover potatoes, bacon, sausage, and eggs. Granted, they were far from healthy, but it beat cold cereal or oatmeal in his opinion.

He pulled the potatoes from the fridge, examining them for green mold before giving them the smell test. Like any normal male, he gave things, including clothes sometimes, smell tests. Usually Cindy confiscated any of his clothes lying around and washed them to prevent him from recycling dirty laundry.

As he set the container down, he saw a note magnetized to the fridge. Apparently, Cindy had left it the night before when he was collecting evidence around the city. It said he had two messages saved in his voice mail.

He picked up the phone, dialing the voice mail access number, then entering his numeric password. After it announced he had two saved messages, he pressed the number one button and listened.

"Detective Daniels, this is Kenny at the state police lab. I pieced together some interesting things from that videotape you recovered at the explosion. And we managed to read some of the paper scraps after using some recovery techniques on them.

"I can't make much sense of them, but maybe you can come down here and check them out at your convenience. Sorry to call you at home, but the detectives said you were on leave for a few days. Thank you."

Daniels deleted the message, ready to check out the results the moment his life allowed him to. Cindy would be home in the afternoon, so he would call and, hopefully, arrange to have Kenny meet him later. In the meantime, the next message began.

"Mark, uh, this is Troy Tackett. I'm leaving for Celina in the morning and, uh, well, I'm leaving some information in your mailbox. It's about the sheriff. I can't get involved, but I want you to check him out. Well, you'll read it and see what I mean. Give me a call if you have any questions." Tackett then provided his cellular phone number. "Thanks. Bye."

A puzzled look came across Daniels' face as he saved the message again. He wondered what on earth Tackett meant, and even more so, where the paper had gone. Since the box had been open, he had no doubt it was there, but who would have taken it?

"Shit," he said, suspecting danger awaited Tackett if someone knew about the note.

He dialed the number to Tackett's phone, letting it ring three times before it transferred to voice mail. Despondent, Daniels could never have known the phone was stuffed in a filing cabinet in the basement of a hospital two hours away from him. He would try several more times to no avail throughout the day, and wonder exactly where his fellow detective might be, and if he was safe and sound.

Chapter 25

After making Cindy promise to stay home with the kids and open the door for no one, Daniels ventured to Indianapolis for a talk with Kenny Shalen, the Indianapolis State Police forensics analyst who contacted him. He had called ahead to ensure the technician would be working, and spoke with him personally. It sounded as though some of the material might be of help to the investigation.

He pulled into the lot, finding the Laboratory Division of the Indiana State Police housed in a small area of the Post Road headquarters. Several spaces in front of the post were marked visitor, so he chose one and made his way through the front door of the building.

Daniels only made it through the first set of doors before he found the second set locked. He had just missed the business hours by half an hour, meaning it would be necessary to push the buzzer beside him. Though he could see the corporal manning the phones and the front door, and vice versa, the man still asked him to identify himself before pushing the button for the magnetic lock to release.

Once the detective stated his business, and who he had come to see, the corporal let him inside and verified his credentials.

Daniels had never actually stepped foot inside the post before, and took to looking around at the portraits of former post commanders and those who had died in the line of duty while waiting for the technician.

"Shalen said he'd be just a minute," the corporal said, openly a bit more at ease with Daniels, since he knew for certain why the detective was there.

"Thanks," Daniels replied before using the drinking fountain.

All around him, chairs sat along the walls in case people waited to see officers for reports, and during the interview sessions of recruit testing. All state police recruits had their interviews at that post, and it looked intimidating to someone who had never worked in such a formal organization before. From what Daniels knew, they were as close to militaristic as a police force in Indiana could be.

Momentarily, Shalen stepped from one of the doors leading around the communications room dressed in a plain blue uniform covered by a dirtied apron. It seemed to have a combination of old stains, including blood and dirt spots, which could not be banished through washing alone.

He appeared young in age, with a quick smile, gleaming eyes, and looks most men would give a body part to have. Apparently, he opted to hide his features all day in a laboratory where half a dozen people might see him during a shift.

School smarts, Daniels thought. All school smarts.

"Detective Daniels?"

"You must be Kenny," the detective replied.

"Follow me and I'll show you what I dug up."

Daniels followed him through several hallways with serpentine turns to a room containing a single door with just enough glass for an informal peek inside. As the two stepped inside, Daniels felt as though he had returned to his old high school biology room.

Black slate countertops shielded against chemical agents from soaking into the wood they protected. Tests tubes inside framed holders lay on various counters and desks while sealed jars filled with formaldehyde and body organs lined shelves toward the back of the room. In several areas, manuals and charts were placed for Shalen and other technicians to use when necessary. The room contained no windows, giving it a damp, musty feel, even though it was maintained at levels higher than most naval ships.

"This is home," Shalen said as they walked between the island tables. "Well, figuratively speaking, anyway."

"Sure," Daniels said, though picturing the technician as having little other life outside the lab. He wore no wedding band, and had given Daniels no inclination of a busy social life in their conversations.

"Are you getting any closer on your investigation?"

"A couple things have popped up," the detective said. "I guess you could say I'm working a few different angles."

"Everything I found is back here," Shalen said, leading the way toward an attached back room with some audio and video equipment.

Along the wall, several enlarged photos were clipped to a magnetic strip. He examined them as Shalen described the process.

"I've got a machine we constructed from a VCR that allows us to view the images like a photo negative and print them at will," he said as Daniels viewed the images one at a time, taken from various areas of the security tape.

One displayed nothing except the background of the ATM, but the other four showed various intervals of the attack on Tim Niemeyer. One in particular showed all six members of the group thrusting their blades simultaneously into their unsuspecting victim. Though the quality of the tape had distorted the image's sharpness, Daniels noticed one of the attackers had allowed his hood to slip, showing his face, and its aggressive, sadistic expression.

"Is there any way to get that in closer, maybe clean it up?" he asked Shalen, pointing to the face.

"I figured you might ask that, and I've already worked with it," the technician said, walking over to a drawer. "This was the best I could do," he said, pulling out another image.

The image appeared pixelated, but enough shape in the eyes and mouth was evident for Daniels to identify him. The man's hair was ruffled and covered with perspiration, indicating he was probably nervous about committing such an act, as any rational person might be.

"Do you recognize him?" Shalen asked.

"Yeah," Daniels said, remembering the four photos plastered across the news identifying the explosion victims. "It's Kevin Pritchett, a mortician in the Bloomington area. He was one of the four bomb victims."

"Sounds like you've got quite a case on your hands."

"This really helps," Daniels said, knowing he held concrete proof linking the four victims to Niemeyer's murder. "Thanks."

"Oh, I'm not done yet," Shalen said. "We also managed to save a few pieces of some of the documents we found in a leather briefcase."

"Anything that made sense?"

"Well, the one sheet looked to be an ownership document of some sort," he said, pulling the fresh copy and the fragile original, now bagged and identified, from a separate drawer.

Daniels let his eyes wander up and down the new copy as several words struck him.

"Beverly Hilton," he muttered. "Property," he said, finding several other words associated with ownership of land. The date indicated the time in which the widow purchased her resort from a family in Southern Indiana.

A resort that burned to the ground many years before the first murders began surrounding the West Baden Springs Hotel and Paul Clouse.

On land, Tim Niemeyer tended for the widow.

"Are these mine to keep?" Daniels asked the technician.

"Sure. I've got copies, and the physical evidence. If you like, I'll see if I can get anything more out of them."

"Please do."

Daniels thumbed through the remaining sheets, finding nothing except medical documentation, leading him to think the briefcase had been Susan Jameson's. He would read them with more scrutiny later.

"Thanks again," he said, shaking the technician's hand.

"A pleasure," Shalen said. "Let me know if I can be of help again," he said, handing Daniels one of his cards.

"Will do," the detective said, ready to take his findings home.

***

Clouse had spent most of the afternoon hours reading after enduring a few hours of playtime with the kids. Keeping up with their energy level compounded the aches and pains suffered at the hands of the killer, slowing his recovery in the process. He soon discovered as boring as the first three diaries had been, the fourth provided enough drama and intrigue to more than make up for its predecessors.

As he read along, he could visualize everything Father Runnels said through his own experiences at the hotel, seeing it both in its lavish decor and the plainer era of the Jesuits. That was the way he first found it, several years before, when he joined the restoration team and Kieffer Construction as a designer.

With the kids both watching television in the next room, Clouse settled in at the kitchen table with a beer instead of soup. After swallowing a few pain relievers, he opened the book to learn the epic ending of what had since become legend in Orange County.

***

Over the next month, the seminary suffered two more fatal accidents, and strangely, Father Ernest's health seemed to return. He credited a miracle to the turn of events in his life, but seemed to grow less interested with the daily routine of the church and the lives of the people around him as time passed.

At times, he almost treated them like they were pets, there for his pleasure or tolerance. One day Father Runnels approached him about his attitude behind the converted hotel at one of several tables reserved for eating meals in the beauty of the outdoors during the summer hours.

They were alone this particular morning.

"Ernest, I'm a bit concerned about the way you've been acting recently."

"How so, Joseph?"

"You're acting as though you no longer care if you're associated with our work here. I mean, you conduct your sermons and masses the same as always, but you keep to yourself, don't talk to anyone, and when you're asked to help with something you always decline with some sort of convenient excuse."

"I can't help that I'm busy, Joseph," Ernest said, cracking a smile.

Runnels would not buy it.

"We've had three funerals the last two months," he said. "First Tom, then Samuel, and Benjamin last week," he said, referring to the brother who first showed Ernest around the grounds when he arrived. "You haven't seemed overly shaken by any of their deaths."

Ernest seemed annoyed.

"Perhaps I can keep my emotions in check, Joseph. Something you seem to have difficulty doing lately."

"You can't play this off on me, Ernest. Ever since these events began, you seem to be recovering a bit more each day. And if I didn't know any better, I would say you appear to be regaining your youth. It's uncanny how you find energy and spirit in these times considering the condition you were diagnosed with. Even the age lines in your face seem to have diminished. Tell me, Ernest. Tell me what you're hiding."

"I have *nothing* to hide," the priest said, rising angrily from the table. "My good fortune should not be tied in with your tragedies," he said, isolating himself from the group verbally once again. "You'll have to look elsewhere to seek out the source of your problems."

As Ernest made haste inside the converted hotel, Runnels looked up to see young Henry staring down from a second story window, as though keeping an eye on his former mentor.

Now a young teenager, the boy had still never spoken, and Ernest's neglect of him continued, though now it seemed more protective than out of a dying wish to be isolated. Henry didn't seem ashamed or worried that Runnels spotted him. His expression to the senior priest looked despondent or sullen, as though his worries were not for himself. The two made eye contact only for a second or two before the boy slowly moved away from the window.

Runnels sighed under his breath, looked to the sky, and noticed ominous gray clouds forming overhead. It was to be a stormy midsummer day, and he had no intention of getting drenched by remaining outside.

Later that afternoon the storm of the year rolled through, quickly flooding the grounds around the hotel, leaving miniature ponds in the sunken garden and spacious lawn. It ruined the hard work Ernest and several volunteers had put forth early in the spring.

As Runnels watched the view from a third story chapel, he listened to the dreadful thunder that seemed to threaten the existence of the grand structure. Lightning speared the ground less than a mile from him with a sense of foreboding and warning not to leave the sanctity and protection of the converted holy grounds.

Footsteps in a hurried pace sounded behind the priest and he turned to find one of the younger pastors standing at the door, out of breath.

"What is it, Daniel?" he asked the younger man.

"It's Father Ernest. He went outside and refused to come back when we called to him. He went off to the woods yelling for us to leave him alone."

Runnels stood a moment in thought. This was not entirely uncharacteristic for Ernest, though it seemed rather foolhardy.

"Did he have that godforsaken cross with him?"

A perplexed look crossed Daniel's face.

"I think he did, sir. Why?"

"Never mind, Daniel. When the storm lets up, gather a small party of the brothers and search for him."

"Yes, Father," the brother said before scurrying off to carry out his task.

An hour later, the storm reached its decline and a team of four went out to look for Ernest. Two of the four had seen him head into the woods when he left.

Despite low visibility and a greater chance of danger from the elements, they took the same path.

When they returned a few hours later, Ernest was not among their numbers.

"No sign of him?" Runnels asked Daniel.

"No. We reached the edge of town and stopped."

"That's for the best," Runnels said. "We don't need West Baden residents thinking we're lunatics running around in the rain. Our public relations have never been overly solid."

"And Ernest won't help if he gets spotted like a drowned rat."

"Certainly not. There will be consequences for the father if there was no good reason for his leaving."

No consequences really came when Ernest returned and said he thought he heard a cry for help in the woods and got disoriented. No one doubted his account except Father Runnels, especially when a young boy from town came up missing two days later.

For the first time, it truly dawned on Runnels that his senior pastor might be involved somehow with the deaths around the seminary, and now the disappearance of the boy. It seemed strange the boy's baseball mitt and bike were found at the edge of a road, but no trace of the child himself could be found.

Even more bizarre, the disappearance happened during the thunderstorm when the boy was undoubtedly hurrying toward his home.

Runnels etched his feelings into the diary, and his suspicions grew when Ernest began donning a cloak in addition to his regular attire that, in the priest's written words, gave him the appearance of the grim reaper. His statement was based on what the director had seen in works of art during his lifetime.

He made the vow as he wrote to monitor Ernest much more closely, and that he felt Henry knew more than he was letting on, though the boy would never truly be able to tell what he knew anyhow.

Either way, Runnels felt Ernest had done something terrible, though he hid his opinion from any public view, especially the police who didn't bother the brothers with anything. Even entrusting his suspicions with any of the brethren would tarnish the reputation of the church, and possibly put his own life needlessly in danger.

***

Clouse closed the book, noticing he neared the end. His eyes felt heavy in what little afternoon light streamed through the window blinds. The sky outside cast a dark gray upon the countryside, as though it might let loose with sleet or snow at any moment. It felt too cold for rain, though it might have been ironic for it to do so, considering what he had just read.

He stood to make himself some coffee, wondering what he could do next about finding the killer. Then again, perhaps his best course of action lay atop the kitchen table beside him.

Clouse would soon know if the diary answered any buried questions.

Chapter 26

Daniels drove back toward Bloomington, passing the last Martinsville stoplight as he dialed a number on his cell phone. With the link established between the four explosion victims and Niemeyer's murder he wanted to set to work on Tackett's lead about Sheriff Pearce. Only one thing stood in his way.

The inability to contact Tackett.

Since leaving the lab he had tried unsuccessfully four times to reach the detective, getting switched over to voice mail each time.

This time the phone rang three times before someone answered.

"Hello?" the voice asked somewhat desperately, as though he had been waiting for a call.

"Hi. I'm trying to reach Troy Tackett," Daniels said, knowing the voice was unfamiliar, and the phone number correct.

"I'm a resident at Carson Memorial Hospital in Ohio," the man said. "There's been an accident. Are you a relative?"

"No, a friend. What happened to him?"

For a moment, silence crossed the line as though the resident was unsure whether to reveal the nature of Tackett's injuries to anyone or not.

"We've been unable to reach any of his family. Most of his phone's stored numbers are for his coworkers. Do you know any of his relatives?"

"No," Daniels said sternly. "But I am a fellow police officer. Can you tell me what happened?"

A few seconds of silence.

"He was stabbed."

"Stabbed? Is he alive?" Daniels asked quickly, feeling a familiar chill tingle through his back.

"Yes, but he's in critical condition. We're not sure if he'll pull through."

"Have you told anyone else?"

"We contacted the police station where he works. The sheriff said he would come up and handle it personally."

"Ah, shit," Daniels said, thinking about what Tackett had left on his answering machine. "Can you give me directions to your hospital and a time estimation of how long it will take to get there?" he asked, looking for the first exit that would begin taking him east on his map. Several existed between Martinsville and Bloomington.

"I can, but the sheriff already-"

"I don't care what the sheriff said. Do not let *anyone* see Troy until I get there," Daniels ordered. "This is a matter of life and death. Now get me those directions."

***

Within a few hours Daniels had phoned his wife, then Clouse, to inform them in brief what was going on and where he was going in case anything happened to him.

He reached the third floor of the hospital after questioning a nurse downstairs, then looked for someone who looked like they knew the regular routine on the third floor. Daniels found a small nursing station when he spied someone out of place walking down the hall ahead of him.

Dressed in a brown uniform that looked distinctly like the county police anywhere in the state of Indiana, the man was heading further down the hall, twirling what looked to be one of the older wooden batons in his left hand. Daniels ignored the station for the moment to pursue the officer, wondering why the sheriff would show up just to stroll down a hallway.

As he drew closer, Daniels thumbed the firearm's holster at his side, suspecting it might not be Bobby Pearce with each step closer.

"Can I help you?" the security officer asked when he heard hurried footsteps behind him, turning just slowly enough that Daniels could remove his thumb from the holster without being noticed.

"The man who was stabbed. Which room is he in?" he asked, pulling his wallet with his police credentials inside.

"Room 312, but I think the sheriff already came to-"

"Damn," Daniels said, bolting the other way.

He had passed 312 on his way down the hall, but paid little attention to what any of the rooms might have harbored inside.

As he reached the room, he drew his firearm, quickly turning the knob and launching himself shoulder-first against the door inside the room. Holding his firearm high, he startled the nurse who stood beside the fallen detective.

"Sorry," Daniels quickly apologized to the nurse as the security officer reached the doorway, wondering what the hell he had missed. "Has anyone else been here tonight?"

"The sheriff stopped by earlier," the nurse replied between breaths, still taken by Daniels' entrance. "He seemed satisfied his officer was being watched around the clock and said he would check back later."

Daniels could not help but take a moment to examine Tackett, covered with tubes running into his arms and up his nose. He looked at peace, but the wound beneath his garments was held together by manmade threads. When he thought about it, Daniels was barely reassured that Tackett might ever make a full recovery both physically and mentally.

"Did he say where he would be?" Daniels asked, returning to the matter at hand.

"There aren't too many places in this town *to* be," the security guard said. "The motel or the diner down the way would be my best guesses."

"Good," Daniels said. He looked to the security guard. "Do not let *anyone*, especially the sheriff, be alone with this man for a second. We don't know who did this to him, and everyone is a suspect. Understand?"

The guard nodded.

"Not for one second," the guard repeated.

Daniels started to leave, but held up a moment.

"Did they say what happened to him?"

"Just that he was found in a convenience store bathroom with blood everywhere. They said the vest he was wearing probably deflected the blade just enough to keep it from penetrating his heart. Damn lucky, he was."

"Well, he might not be yet," Daniels said, hoping his hunch about Pearce proved correct. He started down the hall, talking to himself. "But that depends on me, I suppose."

Within minutes, Daniels found himself darting down the stairs, then desperately searching every driveway between the hospital and the hotel or diner, looking for any type of car the sheriff might be driving. He knew only the makes and models of the past two years would do for any respectable sheriff, so he targeted only those, especially ones equipped with subdued blue and red lights.

He found an unmarked white car sitting at the diner that fit his profile. As he drove closer, he saw Pearce, dressed in street clothes, eating at a corner booth, impatiently passing the time.

"Picking your shot, aren't you, Bobby?" Daniels grumbled as he parked his own car.

Though he felt uncertain why Pearce would want to harm or so closely monitor his detective, Daniels knew Tackett must have possessed evidence against the sheriff or he would never have called. Someone also knew Tackett had left information in his mailbox, and no doubt stole it. If nothing else, Daniels planned to have a chat with the sheriff to put what remained of Tackett's life in the clear.

Soon enough he had his wish. He watched as the sheriff paid for his meal, then stepped gingerly into the cold night air. Daniels felt a knot rise in his stomach, debating whether or not to confront Pearce there in the parking lot or follow him wherever he went.

Not wishing to cause a scene, he chose the latter.

His body grew tenser with each passing minute as he followed Pearce toward the hospital, contemplating the sheriff's intent. Daniels thought about any number of things, including his own mortality in confronting an equally trained officer of the law. He seldom took time to think about the dangers associated with his job, simply remaining vigilant to ensure he made it home to his wife and children every night.

Tonight he focused on the unsaid danger, already knowing he was willing to take the necessary steps to ensure Tackett's safety.

When it came down to it he knew what had to be done, and an overwhelming sense of civic duty always pushed him to take the risk. Experience taught him how to judge right versus wrong in people, and he suspected Pearce meant absolutely no good when he traveled to Ohio.

As Pearce parked his car in the overhead parking lot, Daniels chose a spot between the sheriff and the hospital's back entrance. He swallowed hard, felt his firearm pressing against his side, and opened the car door.

Daniels stepped from the car and stood silently, his eyes staring holes through the sheriff until Pearce turned to see him there. For a moment, he could see Pearce struggle to identify him before a sense of realization came across his face.

A greater sense of realization, almost to the point of complete fear, formed on Pearce's countenance, which the man immediately fought to contain. Daniels sensed the man wanted to run, but there was really nowhere to go, and no explainable reason to bolt from Daniels.

"What brings you out here?" Pearce finally worked up the nerve to ask, stepping cautiously toward the detective.

"Probably the same thing as you," Daniels said, playing it cool, but professional. He would not act chummy with the sheriff because he wanted Pearce to overreact, to make a mistake. Maybe not here, but somewhere, and soon.

"You heard about Troy?" Pearce asked.

"Yeah. I called his cell phone and someone here answered."

"So you just drove from Bloomington straight here to see for yourself?" the sheriff asked with a nervous chuckle.

"You could say that," Daniels replied, carefully stepping away from his own vehicle. "I wanted to make sure Troy's best interests were being protected."

"Well, he's okay, if that's what you want to know," Pearce said, as though that might satisfy Daniels enough to shoo him away.

"That's good. Want to go up and see him together?" Daniels asked with a prompting thumb toward the hospital entrance.

"No, that's okay, Mark," Pearce replied, finally remembering the detective's first name. Elected officials, especially sheriffs, loved using a first name basis with everyone they encountered. It was habit. "You go ahead and I'll check on him later. I hear the hospital food isn't so bad here."

"Yeah, I doubt it would *kill* you or anything," Daniels replied with an almost mocking grin, pushing his own luck a bit.

"God forbid. Just about any food can do us in nowadays," Pearce commented, trying to step away. "I'll catch you later, Mark."

"Take care, Bobby," the detective said, trying to keep an even playing field.

Daniels decided to return to the third floor for a talk with the security guard, to ensure Tackett survived the night.

Then a better idea crossed his mind.

Chapter 27

Clouse sat in front of a large fire in his living room, finally feeling somewhat better after his recent beating at the hotel. He worried about Daniels' trip to Ohio, and even more about Tackett. He knew from experience no one involved with the search for the killer would ever be safe, but the killer was being deliberate enough to follow people out of state, or close to it, to carry out his plan.

"Are you worried about Troy?" Jane asked, sitting on the couch beside him.

"Yeah, but it's so much more than that."

"What do you mean?" she asked, putting an arm around him.

"Like this goes back to the beginning. It's as though the hotel's problems go back further than me working there, or Dr. Smith owning it."

Jane looked at him strangely.

"What has you thinking that?"

"I don't know. But these photos the killer sends me, and the way he carried out this plan of his. He's had this planned for some time."

"You can't control the schemes of a madman, Paul."

"And I can't predict them quick enough to save my friends, either."

"There's nothing else you can do. Being here and keeping us safe is the best option."

Clouse scoffed aloud.

"I don't know if I can even do that. He's beaten the tar out me twice, and I'm not a small man, Jane."

She kissed his forehead where one of the bruises blackened atop his skin.

"I like fixing you up, though."

"That's a relief. I don't know what I'd do without you around."

"I hope you never have to find out."

"Me neither," he said, taking hold of her hand gently. "Are the kids getting ready for bed?"

"They are."

Clouse rose from the couch.

"I'm going to tuck Zach in."

After climbing the stairs, he knelt beside his son's bed, thankful to have him back.

"You tired, kiddo?"

"Not really."

"One of these days we'll have to let you stay up later."

"Why can't I now?"

"Because you need your rest," Clouse said, brushing Zach's hair back from his forehead. "Someday you'll understand how important a good night's sleep is."

"Is the bad man going to leave us alone now?"

Clouse thought about the question a moment, knowing how quickly the minds of children raced to different subjects.

"I don't know, Zach. Maybe the police will catch him soon."

"I hope so. I hate being inside so much, Dad."

"Me too," Clouse chuckled. "Good night, Zach," Clouse said, planting a light kiss on his son's forehead.

"Good night, Dad."

Clouse walked downstairs wondering just who, if anyone, could catch the killer. How many more friends would he have to lose before the murderer's appetite for death was satisfied?

He walked downstairs, hoping to read more of the diary, but Jane had prepared a late candlelight dinner by the looks of the dining room.

Every light was turned off, the only illumination coming from the candles atop their rounded table.

"What's this?" he asked, surprised to see several silver coverings over dishes of food.

"You've been under a lot of stress lately. It's time you did something to relax," Jane said, almost as though it was an order.

"Well, if you insist," he said, pulling a chair out for her.

"Oh, no," she replied, motioning for him to seat himself. "It's my turn to spoil you."

Clouse truly smiled for the first time in days. The diary could wait until morning.

***

Pearce had watched from the end of the hall as visitation hours ended and Daniels was forced to leave. He witnessed Daniels arguing with the security guard down the hall.

"I would prefer to stay with him through the night to make sure he'll be okay," Daniels argued. "Whoever did this to him might still be out there."

"Look, I'll see if local police can post a guard on him. In the meantime, we'll stay with him," the guard said.

Perfect, Pearce thought, grinning from ear to ear. Hospital security would never dedicate one man to a patient, and if they did, their guards usually took numerous breaks. Either way, Pearce planned on carrying out his plan that night, before Tackett potentially regained consciousness and talked.

"Do not leave him alone under any circumstances," Daniels warned the guard.

"I won't. When the midnight shift gets here, I'll make sure someone stays with him the entire time."

"All right. I'll be back in the morning," Daniels said before heading toward the elevator.

Pearce spied long enough to see Daniels board the elevator, and the guard's return to the room. The sheriff looked for a spot on the floor to camp out and watch for activity in room 312. He picked a vacant patient room a few doors down the hall, and on the opposite side of Tackett's room. From there, he could crack the door and listen or watch as he wished.

For half an hour, nothing happened.

Pearce grew a bit nervous, considering he was there after hours with at least three security officers he knew about. His position would mean little so far outside of his jurisdiction if he were caught hiding inside a hospital room.

His body grew rigid when he spied a second security officer walk up to the room and knock. The two officers engaged in conversation for a moment as he watched.

"Everything okay?" the second officer asked.

"Yeah. Nothing's happening. I think that detective is making shit up," the original officer said almost casually. "This guy was attacked by a mugger, pure and simple."

"I don't know. They said nothing was stolen. He was just stabbed and left for dead."

"Ah, whatever," Tackett's guard said. "Hey, can you get me something to drink?"

"Want a soda?" the second guard asked, thumbing toward the machine down the hall.

"Water's fine. There's no pitcher in here though."

Looking across the hall, the second guard looked for a room where he might pilfer water and a larger container.

"That room doesn't have any patients," the first guard said as Pearce quietly shut the door, looking desperately for someplace to hide in case they came looking.

Sure enough, the second guard entered a moment later, looking for a pitcher to fill with water. He found one to the side of the second bed, and decided to fill it in the bathroom, just barely missing Pearce, who hid behind the partly drawn shower curtain.

A fully closed curtain might have attracted his attention.

Once the guard filled the water, he left, giving Pearce an opportunity to breathe easy for the time being.

A few minutes later, he made his way to the door again, noticing both men standing at the doorway. The first guard pulled a pack of cigarettes from his uniform pocket, pulling one from the pack.

"I've got to step out for a few minutes. Can you watch our boy?"

"I would, buddy, but I've gotta do rounds with the pharmacy closing downstairs. Go outside for a few minutes. No one's going to mess with him," the second guard said, looking into the room at Tackett.

"The sergeant would kill me if he found out."

"He doesn't have to know. And he was skeptical about us guarding this guy anyway."

"He was, wasn't he?"

"Yeah. Don't worry about it." He slapped his buddy on the shoulder. "Look, I've got to escort the money drop from the pharmacy and get to my rounds."

"Holler at me when you're done," the first guard called as his buddy ducked into the stairwell.

"Sure," came the echoed reply.

A few minutes passed as Pearce observed the guard, desperately wanting to step outside, but fearing the consequences if he was discovered. The sheriff suspected some of his men made similar decisions, fearing his wrath, but he seldom heard about such incidents.

Either they were good at covering their tracks or they were better behaved than he imagined.

"Come on," Pearce urged the guard under his breath.

For a few more minutes the guard paced the hall near the room, looked carefully both ways, and gave a reluctant sigh. He quickly closed the door and headed for the far stairwell, which led to a direct exit. With his keys he would be able to let himself back inside.

Pearce knew this, and knew how quickly the guard might decide to return, so he darted across the hall the moment the door at the end of the hall closed.

He entered Tackett's room, finding the detective as unconscious as ever, lying in the hospital bed. He breathed easily, but looked helpless with so many tubes and wires crossing and overlapping his body.

"Sorry to do this, Troy, my boy," he said, pulling a syringe from his shirt's breast pocket where it had safely remained since his trip from Bloomington.

What it contained was a virtually untraceable medication the sheriff's SWAT team had recovered from a crime scene several months prior. It would put his detective into cardiac arrest and end his life, assuredly this time. He plunged the needle into the top of the saline bag over Tackett's bed, prepared to thumb the liquid into the sack when a click from his left side caused him to freeze.

"I'm no doctor," Daniels said, shifting around the side of the bed to face Pearce, "but I'm venturing a guess that that's not a muscle relaxer you're about to squeeze in there."

Pearce gave a grin, then squeezed the tainted drug in anyway, proving Daniels' theory that it was far too costly to let Tackett live under any circumstances.

"That wasn't very bright," Daniels said.

"On my part it was," Pearce admitted. "If he lives, I die."

"Well, he's going to live, so your days are numbered."

"Not with what I put in there," Pearce said.

Daniels motioned to Pearce to hand over his gun, which was obscured from view. The sheriff complied as the detective motioned to Pearce to hand over the piece bulging at his ankle. Pearce gave a crooked grin, and slowly handed it over as well.

"You're a little too predictable, Bobby," Daniels said. "Whatever you put in there won't reach Troy's bloodstream."

Pearce's face revealed his confusion as a nurse stepped from the bathroom where she and Daniels had been hiding since the second guard walked into the sheriff's hiding place, allowing time for them both to slip in and carry out Daniels' plan.

"When Bill, the guard, closed the door, that was our signal that he would leave," she stated. "I pulled the needle from our patient's vein so the saline would temporarily be cut off."

"Bill should be back any moment after he calls the local authorities," Daniels said. "I hope attempted murder was worth whatever you wanted covered up, Sheriff."

Pearce shook his head in anger.

"You can't understand what you're dealing with."

"I have a pretty good idea. I think Troy found out you were there the night of the explosion, and that you were the sixth conspirator in Tim Niemeyer's death. Between my evidence and whatever he had on you, I have no doubt it will hold up in court. The only question remaining is whether you killed the other four, or you were an intended victim."

"If I had set the bomb, do you think I would have personally driven there at the time it was supposed to detonate?" Pearce said before realizing he had already said too much.

"Tell me something, Bobby. If you know who the killer is, I have to know."

"I can't. I'm already a dead man. The only chance I have now is to disappear," Pearce said in a straightforward manner.

"Tell me who it is," Daniels insisted.

"I can't. I was never told."

"What?" Daniels exclaimed, unable to believe such a claim.

Before he could continue the informal interrogation, the security guard opened the door, allowing Pearce the briefest of distractions before he shoved past the guard, sprinting down the hall toward the far stairwell.

"Dammit!" Daniels cursed, taking chase. With Pearce unarmed, there was little danger of being ambushed.

Daniels caught sight of the sheriff just as the stairwell door closed. He burst through the door and descended the stairs, skipping two or three at a time as he went. As he neared the exit door at the bottom, he considered two separate scenarios.

One, Pearce could simply sprint to the parking lot in the hope of reaching his car before the detective managed to stop him. Two, he could wait outside the door, trip Daniels up, and possibly take the gun the detective had just drawn from its holster.

Or three, a combination of both.

Reaching the door, he cautiously opened it, realizing he had lost precious seconds because Pearce chose simply to run. Daniels pursued him intensely to the parking garage, seeing the sheriff nervously trying to unlock his door as he reached the corner. Unless he fired shots, Daniels was too far away to stop or hinder Pearce's progress.

From the shadows emerged another threat he was too far away to abolish.

"Bobby! Look out!" he screamed at the top of his lungs, too late to prevent the sheriff from being assaulted from behind.

As the darkly-clad figure clasped Pearce's mouth with one hand from behind, the free hand ran a knife across and into the sheriff's throat, ending his life almost instantly after blood spurted from the victim's compromised carotid artery twice. By this time Bill the security guard had joined Daniels' side, but the detective was already beginning to sprint toward the death scene as the killer retreated the opposite way.

Daniels reached the sheriff's corpse, finding Pearce with eyes wide-open, blood oozing from his throat since the heart no longer functioned to pump it out. The look on his face was one of shock and an understanding peace, as though he expected to die, but not at that moment.

"Fuck it," Daniels said, darting in the direction the killer had taken, reaching the edge of the garage, finding no sign of the killer or any escape vehicle.

Once again, the killer had hit and run without a trace.

After a day of new answers and an untimely death, Daniels had mixed feelings as he walked back to the security guard and the body. His best chance to identify the killer had perished, but at least he had an idea of the connection between Niemeyer's murderers and a leader who had destroyed them and their link to himself.

Now he had an idea of where to look, and the knowledge that his and Tackett's cases shared the same suspect.

Chapter 28

Clouse awoke the next morning to a stream of light through the blinds. His hand wandered across the bed to Jane's soft body as she remained asleep. She moaned a bit, rolled over, and took most of the covers with her.

Shaking his head, Clouse rose from bed, threw on some sweatpants, and decided to read the last of the diary while he could.

After a few minutes, he had started coffee and checked his online mail, including several stocks and favorite websites. For a few minutes, life felt normal, and he remembered how much he missed civilization, a routine, and even working as a firefighter. That all happened before he and everyone around him became a madman's target.

And not so long ago.

No sooner had he shut the computer down than his phone rang. He plucked the cordless phone from its charger before clicking the talk button.

"Hello?"

"Paul, it's Mark. I just got back into town."

"How's Troy?"

"Fine, last I saw. I made sure the hospital security stayed close to him, especially after what happened to the sheriff."

"Sheriff?"

Daniels briefly explained Pearce's fate, and Tackett's condition.

"I'm going to hire a private guard for Troy's room," Clouse decided aloud. "I don't want anything happening to him. I already feel responsible."

"He knew as well as I did what investigating these murders meant. And who would have thought someone would follow him into Ohio?"

"Either way, I don't want him left alone."

"I made sure hospital security stayed with him."

Clouse heard a humming background noise from his friend's end of the line.

"Are you driving?"

"Yeah."

"Where are you, Mark?"

"About a mile from your driveway," Daniels said. "I have something we need to take a look at."

"What might that be?"

"Dr. Smith's calling hours. We planted a video camera, remember?"

Clouse recalled their desperation in trying to find the killer from the previous year.

"I remember. I thought you looked at that already."

"I did, but there must be a couple hundred people walking through that room. You need to look at it too."

Clouse rubbed the weariness from his eyes.

"Okay. We'll watch it."

"Good, because I'm at the foot of your driveway."

A few minutes later, the detective sat in Clouse's living room holding the videotape from the calling hours.

"So what's new?" Clouse asked, almost in pretense.

Seldom one for small talk, Daniels dove right in with the heart of his finds.

"For starters, I've looked into a few things. I checked on the numbers and the paper types from the photos you got, and they're from several different locations. In fact, a different location every time."

"Smart, isn't he?"

"Yeah. And there's no telling if they're even from stores within the city."

"That doesn't help. What other developments are there?"

"Whoever the killer is blew up those four people at the edge of town. Troy figured it out and the killer got the sheriff before he could reveal anything that might compromise his identity."

"Did Pearce know who the killer was?"

"No, I don't think so. But the killer was someone who met with some awfully powerful local folks," Daniels figured. "A doctor, a mortician, a bank president, and the coroner to mention a few."

"And a sheriff. Not bad company at all."

"Well," Daniels said, waving the tape. "Let's have a look, shall we?"

Within the first few minutes, Clouse felt overwhelmed by the number of people attending the doctor's funeral. Most of them he had never seen or met before.

"God, Mark. I don't know most of these people."

"That's how I felt. Focus on the people you do know, Paul. They're the ones who would know *you* well enough to orchestrate this whole thing."

Exasperated, Clouse continued to watch, taking up a pad and pen. He wrote down the names of everyone he recognized inside the video, sadly realizing how many of them had moved away or perished in the past year.

"Tim," he muttered to himself gloomily, seeing Niemeyer shake his hand at the funeral. The last of his high school buddies, and now he was gone.

"Sorry," Daniels said. "I know it's not easy."

"No, it's not."

Clouse watched a few more minutes, restlessly rubbing his knees, then his face repeatedly. He wrote down a few more names before pausing the tape.

"Okay, Mark. Let's talk about who it could realistically be."

"All right. It can't be someone at Smith's funeral because he took that photo of Tim."

"But he could have been at the calling hours."

Daniels nodded.

"Probably someone with no job, no attachments," he surmised.

"That would certainly eliminate ourselves and everyone in our families."

"Someone with revenge on their mind, possibly preceding the events of last year."

"Then that would involve a killer seeking revenge for Roger Summers or Dave Landamere," Clouse said. "We've been through that list before, and we got nowhere."

Daniels took out his notepad, jotting a few ideas down before he forgot them.

"Our killer doesn't like either one of us, so who have we got?"

"We've got someone who knows an awful lot about my inheritance from the good doctor," Clouse said. "He's sent me to a theme park and the hotel which Martin Smith owned. He was also kind enough to follow me along on my honeymoon and photograph my babysitter at the fair."

"What's the name of the lawyer you dealt with?"

"Harold Simms, if you're talking about Smith's lawyer."

"He's the one. We should have a talk with him."

"You think he's a murderer?"

"No, but he may know who has access to the information of Smith's holdings, other than yourself."

"Okay," Clouse said, letting the tape continue to play. "It's too bad he didn't have any living relatives, or anyone who could tell us who these people are. There's no telling who might be pissed off, and for what reason."

"I have a feeling we're going to find out soon enough, one way or another."

***

That afternoon, once Daniels had left, Clouse felt a headache unlike any he had felt in years. Two pills later he felt no better, and every thought entering his mind compacted with every other thought or memory, only made the pain worse.

Finding a suitable private detective to bodyguard Tackett relieved him a little bit, but being locked up in his own house with the constant possibility of harm to himself or his family weighed heavily on his conscience.

He had just decided to lie down when a knock came to the front door.

"I'll get it," Jane said from the kitchen where she monitored the kids playing in the backyard.

They were outside with the dogs, which acted very protective of the kids, especially when strangers came around.

"Thank you," Clouse said, plopping down on the couch.

He heard a bit of discussion at the front door before Jane stepped into the living room. Clouse felt little relief with a cushy pillow supporting his head, wondering how many pain relievers it would take to make him normal again. Closing his eyes helped, but he opened them once he realized his wife wasn't simply passing through the living room.

"There's a courier at the front door, Paul," she announced. "He's got an envelope and says he has specific instructions for you to sign for it."

Clouse wondered what type of package required his signature, and his alone.

"It's just an envelope?"

"Yes."

Clouse labored his way from the couch, slowly making his way toward the front door so he could get a good look at the courier and the package he brought.

Indeed, it was an envelope, but stuffed to a rather thick state. He recognized the courier's uniform as one who delivered to nearly any specified area, at any specified time. In fact, he had used the company himself a couple times when set-tling the conditions and legal battles of Smith's will.

"I'm sorry, sir," the courier said, "but the instructions stated specifically that you needed to sign for this," he said, handing Clouse a pad with the invisible sig-nature capture.

"That's fine," Clouse said, signing before he accepted the package. "Thanks."

He wandered back into the living room, tearing one edge of the envelope, pulling out a short stack of papers.

With Jane observing him, he glanced over the papers with a look of disbelief before a mild look of panic crossed his face.

"What is it?"

"It's a personalized letter from the killer," he said, continuing to look through the stack.

"What does it say?"

"Basically, it says all of us have to stay at the hotel the next two nights for a sabbatical that I'm being forced to take the credit for planning."

"Who else is going to be there?"

"It doesn't mention specifics, but he claims over a hundred people have been invited."

"And if we refuse?"

Clouse hesitated a few seconds, giving her a despondent look.

"We die."

"My God. What else does it say?"

"He says I need to play host and act as though I put this whole thing together because all of the invitations were sent with my name and an itinerary."

"And if you don't?"

"He says my loved ones will meet untimely deaths. He goes on to say he's on the list."

"So he'll be there?"

"I assume so. But he failed to let me know exactly who was invited."

Jane looked to make sure the kids were okay in the backyard, and that they would not hear any of the grave conversation.

"So when do we leave?"

"Tomorrow. Everything starts at three in the afternoon."

"We're talking about a Monday afternoon. Do you think people will actually show up?"

"It sounds like they might not have much choice, but more than likely their invitations were mailed to them some time ago. It says everything at this little soiree is funded by me, and this is a celebration of my friends and those who were instrumental in the hotel's reconstruction. Who's going to turn down a three-day holiday?"

Jane frowned.

"No one."

Just as Clouse was about to review the papers once more, the phone rang. He scooped up the cordless receiver from the couch, pressing the talk button.

"Hello."

"Paul, what the hell is this invitation I just got for tomorrow?"

"Hi, Mark. Is yours friendly or threatening?"

"Oh, mine would be of the threatening variety. Unless you consider 'bring your family or I cut them up like lunch meat' to be a subtle form of humor."

"Was it signed?"

"Vaguely. It just said I knew who it was."

"Mine too. Well, at least we won't be alone."

"No, but he's taking complete control of the situation. We're playing right into his game."

Clouse ventured to the window, staring at two children who had barely experienced life, much less been threatened by serial killers.

"Do we really have a choice?"

"No," Daniels said firmly. "I guess we don't."

"Then I'll see you tomorrow."

Clouse hung up the phone, looking to his wife.

"Well, let's pack."

Chapter 29

After breakfast, the next morning Clouse excused himself from the table while Jane cleaned up after the kids and they begged to go outside.

"Go ahead," Jane said, hoping they were temporarily out of danger since the family was following the killer's instructions.

Clouse walked upstairs to make certain everything he wanted was packed. Content that everything was in order, he looked to the end table, taking up the diary. Plopping himself comfortably atop the bed, he opened the book, prepared to read the last of Runnels' experiences.

***

As time passed, Runnels began to see a transformation in Ernest that disturbed him. An originally eccentric Ernest, who once planted flowers and lobbied for keeping the grounds in their original state, showed he had causes in life. Something cared enough about to speak up about.

His cancer had taken away his will to do such things along with his faith in the Lord he had felt so close to all of his life.

Now he was completely different.

Never was there mention of his illness, as though it had dried up and went away with little more than a few visits to physicians. He acted healthier than Runnels had ever seen him, and he often wore a robe with the hood up, as though he were a monk, or reverting back to very traditional Catholic ways.

Once in a while, the brothers would catch a glimpse of Ernest and say how much younger he looked. They proclaimed it a miracle, but Runnels knew better.

Miracles were not something to be ashamed of, or keep hidden. They were works of God meant to awe and inspire common men and women.

During mass, Ernest kept himself as distanced as possible from everyone else. Even the choir consisting of brothers would be seated opposite the priest so no one could get a good look at him. Ernest acted as though he had a deformity when the changes throughout his body seemed to be a drastic improvement over the life the man once lived.

Over time, the priest virtually refused to speak to anyone, and became seen less often throughout the building. Often he lurked the hallways at night when everyone was in bed, or praying somewhere in the vast building.

He always donned the dark robe and carried his crucifix with him, as though his life depended on its attachment to his skin.

Ernest would eat alone, pray alone, read alone, and most of all, take walks to parts unknown without companionship.

For a month, everything seemed normal, or at least close to that status. Rumors and town happenings had quieted down, some of the brothers were able to sit within a table of Ernest and even speak to him. He complained about pains in his chest and abdomen, similar to those he had experienced when the cancer filled his body.

Often the brothers reported seeing Ernest in the garden, or in the halls, clutching his side as though it agonized him. He sat in the far reaches of the hotel's atrium, reading and sometimes moaning to himself.

Runnels observed his senior pastor when opportunity arose, finding that Henry took quite an interest in his former mentor as well. He seldom saw how Runnels carefully monitored both of them, but it seemed Henry's interest was no longer friendly, or in the interest of Ernest's health or a rekindled friendship.

To Runnels, their relationship seemed more like prison guard to convict about to be released prematurely for parole.

Ernest's agony and return to a normal appearance only lasted another week before George, another of the brothers, disappeared.

After this, the senior pastor's behavior changed drastically. He locked himself in his room constantly, refused to carry out his duties during Sunday mass, which now fell to another priest, and he never came out unless he thought everyone else was asleep.

In jest, some of the brothers made the analogy that a reaper haunted the halls.

A few weeks later, another disappearance occurred, and both Ernest and Henry seemed to disappear for the next few days, though they were rumored to be on the grounds.

Runnels could never catch up with either resident, though they were also said to be keeping their distance from one another. At one point, the senior priest considering involving the authorities, but he possessed no convincing evidence that Ernest had perpetrated any sins or broken any laws. The seminary hardly needed the public scrutiny that a police inquiry brought, so he simply harbored his suspicions. Besides, none of the so-called accidents on the grounds were proven to be anything else by the police or county coroner.

Things culminated when Runnels and several other members of the church discovered Ernest locked away in the basement's storage area. Both access doors to the room were boarded up and locked from the inside. From their position behind the solid wooden doors, the brothers could hear Ernest carrying on by himself.

"Please, please forgive me," he moaned for their ears to take in. "I should never have done the things I've done."

"What is he talking about?" one of the brothers beside Runnels asked him.

"I don't know. It sounds almost confessional."

A moment passed before they heard Ernest speak again.

"Oh, Lord, please forgive me." They heard a sloshing of liquid from within the storage area, especially as it hit the floor, but it sounded less dense than water. "No, I can't go out like this. Please let me have one more chance."

To the brothers this sounded like incoherent rambling. Nothing about Ernest could surprise them, but this was extreme, even for him. They listened intently, knowing it was useless to try the door. One of the brothers had already run out to their garden shed in search of tools that might gain them access to the storage room.

Sounds of something banging, then the sound of something splintering against a wall reached their ears. Possibly a chair? More thumping noises continued the next several minutes as the men outside eavesdropped.

"What on earth is he doing?" one asked Runnels.

"I have no idea. He's probably delusional."

A minute passed before they heard a crackling sound from within the confines of the storage room. Soon after, a curious smell, accompanied by puffs of smoke from under the door joined the sounds from within.

"Oh, no," Runnels gasped, figuring correctly what was happening within.

Ernest began screaming in agony from within as fire engulfed his body, and by the time they broke through a moment later, it was too late.

Fully clothed in flame, Ernest whirled around his final time before collapsing to the floor in a heap, his skin still bubbling and charring as the fire consumed him greedily. A grotesque smell of burnt flesh and chemical accelerant filled the air.

"My God," someone said before turning away in horror.

Runnels stared at the body of Ernest, the crucifix still clutched desperately in one hand. He ordered everyone to clear out of the room, which they hesitantly did once the body was extinguished. As steam rose from the charred corpse, he knelt beside it, wrestling the cross from Ernest's rigid hand, peeling some of the charred skin away accidentally.

He looked into a supply closet within the storage room, finding it empty, but the access hatch where items could be transported upstairs to the cafeteria area was unlocked. The crawlspace allowed trays to be lifted with most any item on them, but appeared too small for an adult to crawl through.

From above he could hear the whispers of the shocked brethren. Already it was labeled suicide, and everyone believed his erratic behavior over the past few months to be signs they had somehow ignored.

Not Runnels.

He suspected the wooden crucifix was somehow a force all its own that Ernest believed in.

***

Clouse read how the many attempts by the Jesuit leader to destroy the cross failed. It would not burn, it could not be crushed, and it refused to be chopped or ground up by any sort of blade. In secret, Runnels grew frustrated, telling his woes only to the diary which the hotel's current owner read with great interest.

Runnels wrote less and less often as his health began to fail, probably from the stress of Ernest and the cross, which the priest had ultimately decided was a cursed object, made by human hands, but cursed by the hand of Satan himself.

Clouse had heard of such objects, but to actually hear a Christian priest speak of them stunned him. After all, they were only a fable told on cable television or in literature. They were not supposed to be connected to his life, or the hotel in any way, shape, or form.

He read the last few entries of the diary with particular attention, especially how it ended.

"For my own sake, and the sake of those around me, I have decided to hide this cursed object. I have several places where it can safely be hidden, but I hope to bury it somewhere where no one will ever find it.

"It has cost us too much pain and suffering already, and Ernest's own personal greed, in a twisted way, has cost us the lives of several brothers and our reputation among the public. Already my superiors have requested we begin arrangements to move from this location to somewhere we can start anew.

"What exactly the cross did for him, I do not know, but my understanding is cursed objects give their users something they need or want. Ernest probably ended his suffering, only to learn that the effects were temporary. He trapped himself in a web of murders and lies, betraying the oath he took long before he came here.

"I can only hope I bury the cross deep enough that no man will ever find its evil again. It will remain close to here, so I can be certain we move away from it. It will be with mixed feelings that I leave these grounds in the next year because it has been our home for so long, and we will be starting all over again somewhere else. My hope for the residents here is that they will be able to put the disappearance of the boy and the other tragic events behind them and move on.

"We will certainly move on, and I will finally heal."

Clouse wondered exactly why the diaries had been in the hotel. He figured Runnels would have taken them with him, but perhaps that was not the case, or perhaps they had somehow been recovered and brought back at a later date.

"Are you getting ready?" Jane called as he set the diary aside, feeling little more informed than he had before reading it. He wondered if the cross could somehow have been connected to the jewels Joan Landamere and Ryan Andrews were allegedly looking for the year before when they went on their murderous rampage.

"I'm working on it," Clouse said. "Are the kids packed?"

Though it sounded like everything anyone could possibly want would be provided at this getaway, he planned to stop for some extras at a store. He felt a need to appear calm in front of the kids. For all they knew this was a family outing, but even their young minds probably had doubts.

Clouse knew what he was getting himself into, but backing out only delayed the inevitable. Twice he had survived insurmountable odds in the face of death, but his luck was bound to run out.

"The kids are packed," Jane said. "I'm going to feed the animals before we leave."

"Okay."

Clouse sat himself at the end of the bed, uncertain of what to make of such a bizarre vacation. He would have to pretend he planned it all, and all responsibility would be his, but at least a full list of activities and temporary personnel had been provided.

He put on a long pair of socks, followed by his cowboy boots, finally deciding on an old fire department sweatshirt to wear. Luckily, he owned a tuxedo and the kids had sufficient clothing for a black tie affair.

Unlike the other patrons attending, he had less than a day's notice. He felt sorry for Daniels, but knew the detective would somehow come through.

He wondered exactly what the next few days would have in store for him, and if he could figure out the killer's identity before the festivities went sour.

Chapter 30

With his family and a bundle of luggage behind him, Clouse let himself into the hotel, finding the lobby as gorgeous and peaceful as ever. Surrounded by a balcony above, with a chandelier and rows of bulb lights to illuminate the area, the lobby illuminated an aura of class and luxury from days past.

Clouse stared at the stained glass windows around the doors, embedded in the walls, noticing little had changed. As low lit as the balcony was, the doorway to the atrium revealed even less. Until Clouse stepped inside the grand area, he had no idea what to expect.

"Wow," he was compelled to say. "This is like being on the *Titanic* or something."

In fully restored glory, as decorated as it had ever been, the atrium held an assembled stage, fully stocked bars on opposite ends, and a sea of tables and chairs throughout, except for an area near the stage left for dancing or performance. Overhead, the chandelier stood ready to illuminate the festivities whenever it was called upon, along with multicolored lights mounted in intervals along the rounded atrium above.

Several years back, when Clouse had begun restoration with Kieffer Construction, a charity ball took place. He had attended with his first wife in a setting similar to what he looked upon with his family at the moment.

This time, however, someone had gone to far greater expense, much like hotel owners had in the hotel's heyday. Back then, ownership brought in numerous acts, including circuses and musical plays. This time, fountains stood near each of the four entrance doors, and souvenir booths were located inside the atrium, as well as several rooms along the first floor.

"It's amazing," Jane said as he set the luggage beside him.

"It is," Clouse replied almost absently, his eyes still transfixed upon the decorate atrium. "This would cost a small fortune to assemble."

"And who would have access to those funds?" she asked. "No company would put all of this up without some sort of down payment first."

"I doubt it," Clouse agreed. "Then again, someone could put it all on my tab since I supposedly put all this on. Who would question my funding?" Clouse said with a shrug.

"Do we have a room?" Jane asked, the kids growing agitated behind her. The newness of the hotel was wearing thin on their easily distracted minds.

"Yeah," Clouse replied, pulling a key from his pocket. "We're not taking it though."

He thought about the subtle rules set by the killer, and none of them mentioned sticking with the room they were assigned.

It was a suite, but it could easily be set to the killer's specifications, designed to serve his purposes, such as monitoring their activities or planting some sort of trap. Clouse would not play into the plan any more than necessary.

He knew every inch of the hotel, including the dome roof, the secret rooms inside the storage area, and the buildings across the yard, but Clouse suspected home field advantage would not help him. Someone else knew the hotel well enough to set up an elaborate show that equaled those of the last century when it flourished.

"I'll be right back," he said, stepping back to the lobby area and around the bend in the hallway.

Even though the hotel was technically round, it always felt like it had corners because each area was distinctly separated by a room, entrance or stairs. The first floor in particular had distinct rooms including the dining room, a smoking room, and several areas where mineral springs or services had been offered during the hotel's functional years.

Finding nothing of interest down the hall he returned to the lobby, finding the newly-done reception area to his left as Jane and the kids continued to saunter around the open area. He opened a half door that reached his waist, stepped behind the counter, and exchanged his key for one to another suite. He chose a room on the fifth floor with several windows across from it for a view of either the atrium or the grounds outside with minimal movement.

Ordinarily rooms were across from one another, and offered one view or the other. He chose a specific room for easy access to both.

"Can I help you, sir?" a young man wearing a white and red uniform said, stepping beside the counter. "I'm in charge of signing in the guests."

Clouse introduced himself as the hotel's owner.

"Sorry, Mr. Clouse. I guess you would know best which room you like."

"I suppose I do. How many of you are working here again?" Clouse asked, acting as though he had forgotten the exact number of people he hired.

"The interviewing agency said there would be about twenty of us between security, house cleaning, the bar, and service jobs."

"And you are?"

"Greg Killian. I'm basically in charge of who does what and who stays where."

"Nice to meet you, Greg. If anyone has a key for Room 501, please reassign them to something on the fourth floor," Clouse requested, handing the young manager his initial key. "I'll trust everything will run smoothly for my guests?"

"It will, sir. If you need anything, don't hesitate to call."

Clouse nodded, heading for the atrium.

"Oh, and please don't let anyone stay on the sixth floor," Clouse added.

The sixth floor was where the primary suite was located, and the room the killer had assigned Clouse and his family to. Though it was huge, and luxurious, the suite was too far away from the festivities, and a bit more dangerous than other areas of the hotel because there would only be one sure way in and out of the area, and it required a key on both entrance and exit doors. To Clouse, this seemed hazardous.

A few minutes later they reached the fifth floor, stepped off the elevator, and carried their luggage toward Suite 501. Jane unlocked the door, and the four stepped inside, ready to settle in for whatever came next.

"How long before everyone else gets here?" he asked Jane since she had brought her watch.

"About an hour."

"Good," he said, taking in the view of the room, and some of his own design ideas.

A full kitchen, living area with a hot tub, and king size beds were just the beginning of the room's features. Unlike the regular rooms, the suites shared the same custom hand paint jobs as the atrium. Meticulous detail covered the walls with vibrant colors in the shapes of red roses adorned with rich green stems and golden trim.

"Cool," Zach said, toying with the refrigerator's icemaker.

Jane emptied both grocery sacks into the cabinets and refrigerator, assuring they would have snacks between the lavish meals promised in the program. While everyone unpacked, Clouse took a moment to walk down the hall, inspecting the massage room where exercise equipment, a sauna, and home theater system were set up. Basically it was converted from the massage and therapy room of old to a modern entertainment area.

For a year it had all sat dormant.

Dormant until someone decided it was time to bring it all back to life. In the killer's madness there seemed a bit of reason, of meaningful purpose.

"Who are you?" Clouse wondered aloud, walking out to the rounded hallway. All around him lay the ideas conceived in his mind several years before.

What seemed like an impossible dream had come true, but the road was paved with the harshest of stone. So many lives had needlessly been taken in the course of his work. And to think, it had all started with a simple misunderstanding blended with some crafty manipulation. But that was two years ago, and this was today.

A different story entirely.

Revenge and material wealth in the form of the hotel had been the first motive.

A hunt for hidden family jewels and a varied form of revenge had been the second.

Now someone wanted to complete the story. It seemed like a plot that revolved around the hotel, but this was not directly about the hotel. Something much deeper had to be the motivation. A hatred far more intense than Clouse had ever witnessed fueled the killer's scheme this time around.

"Paul?" Jane called. "Are you ready to go downstairs?"

"Not yet," he said, stepping around the bend, into her view. "Let's hang out with the kids awhile before we greet my new guests."

When Clouse finally did get downstairs, he found a slew of people checking in around the same time. He felt underdressed for greeting guests, even after changing into a polo shirt and khaki pants, but his main objective was to scope out who had been invited and begin piecing together the clues necessary to solve his horrific mystery.

"Recognize anyone?" Jane asked, taking his side. The kids had run into the atrium to play with several new friends. They would be safe since other parents were with them, and a security guard stood close by.

Still, Clouse had no intention of leaving them in there very long, having no idea who the killer might be.

"A few key people in the hotel's reconstruction, and some major contributors. Not exactly people I normally socialize with."

Both spent the next half hour greeting the guests and making small conversation, then Clouse began to recognize people he really did not expect to be at such an event.

First, Brian Kern, the landscape contractor who had done work on the hotel with Clouse showed up with his family. The last remaining survivor from the murders the year prior, Kern had already been forewarned that his life could be in danger again.

Kern's hands always seemed to have a dirty tint to them because he was constantly planting trees and seasonal plants in his line of work. A tall man with brown hair normally somewhat bleached by the sun and a thick mustache, he was as thick and solid as the trees he dug up and planted all year round.

"What possessed you come to this thing?" Clouse asked him, aside from everyone else.

"Because the letter I got said my chances of survival depended on me being here. I would have called the police, but I figured you would be here and knew what to do."

"I'm just playing along, trying to figure out who it might be," Clouse said. "Whoever it is, he said he'd be here."

Kern looked around. The number of people seemed to multiply like rabbits.

"I feel like I should keep us locked in the room the whole time. What are you going to do, Paul?"

"I'm just going to play it cool and make sure I don't get stabbed from behind with a scythe. Just keep someone near you at all times, Brian."

"I will," Kern said with a two-finger salute before heading back to his family.

Clouse would not have to wait long before Daniels and his family walked through the lobby doors.

"Anything pop up yet?" the detective asked Clouse as he walked over to him. Cindy took the kids to visit with Jane a moment. "Dead bodies? Leads? Anything?"

"None of the above. I don't have a clue what we're looking for, but I doubt it's going to come strolling through that door," Clouse said, looking toward the glass doors, which seemed to open every minute or two with the arrival of new guests.

Clouse took a moment to greet several guests who recognized him, but Daniels could tell he was faking the smiles and putting up a front when he spoke so hospitably to the guests. As they moved on, his expression immediately went to that of all business again.

"Let's go outside, Mark."

When they stepped out on the balcony, greeted by a cool, blustery day, the pair spied cars lined up the brick walkway reaching from the road to the hotel itself. Nearly a quarter mile walk, the path held cars on both sides, indicating just how many people would be attending the event.

"This has to be almost everyone," Clouse said, realizing an hour had passed since the figurative floodgates had opened.

"They gave me a key on the second floor," Daniels said.

"You feel comfortable there?"

"I'm not going to feel comfortable *anywhere,* Paul."

"What I meant was that I can get you a room up near us. You can stay with us if you want to. There's plenty of room."

Daniels shrugged.

"We'll see how it goes the first night. Hell, I don't know what to expect from this."

"Me neither. I guess we'll start finding out tonight at the dinner."

"I'll have you know it's no easy thing finding a tux at the last minute."

"But you're resourceful. You cops always get perks us regular folk don't," Clouse joked with some intentional word play.

Daniels grinned.

"I did call in an old favor as a matter of fact."

Clouse looked to the clouds in the sky, threatening snow or something a bit wetter if the temperature stayed around the freezing point. Winter was right around the corner, but the fall season was apparent in view, and even in the smells around the hotel. Clouse detected the scent of burning leaves, and cooked vegetables, like pumpkin or squash. At the foot of each concrete stairway to the hotel, corn stalks and decorative garden plants, including carved pumpkins were set for everyone to see.

Someone did not want the Halloween season to end, even if it had occurred a few weeks prior.

"Go ahead and get checked in, Mark. I'll see you tonight."

"You'll be all right?"

"I'll be fine. I'm going to stay down here and mingle a little bit longer. Maybe I'll see some more people I recognize."

"Good luck," Daniels said before heading inside.

"I'll need more than that," Clouse told himself before opening the glass doors and returning to the disturbing charade inside.

Chapter 31

As he stood at the edge of one of the atrium entrances Clouse took in the sights and sounds around him, trying to avoid looking at the list of activities clutched in his right hand as dusk descended upon the hotel.

He could hear the sounds of the orchestra from inside the atrium, soothing the moods of the numerous guests before the meal was served. A hum of intertwined conversations sounded much like a beehive from where he stood. The smell of food, and of the lingering fall season, entered his nostrils.

"Standing out here isn't going to help you move through that list any faster," Jane noted as she walked up behind him, placing her hands gently on his shoulders.

"But it will keep me from having to deal with it. God, who plans this many things for one evening?"

"Apparently our mystery host has quite a flair for parties."

"And a working knowledge of how to spend money. He would have to know the hotel pretty well to plan these things, Jane. He has events tied to specific rooms."

Jane worked her way around to his front side.

"You know as well as I do how many people have toured this building since they began the restoration process. We're talking over one-hundred-thousand or so."

"True, but we're only looking at a few hundred, tops, here tonight. And that still doesn't help me."

"Dinner's going to be ready soon. Do you want to head in?"

"No," he said, finally looking at the overwhelming list. "I'm going to check on the storytelling room and see what kind of education the kids are getting."

"Don't be long, Paul," Jane warned. "We can't afford to look suspicious if we're being watched."

"I won't," he said, forcing a grin. "If I do end up paying for all this, I'm certainly going to enjoy what little I can from it."

As he walked around the hall, dressed in full tuxedo and shined black shoes, Clouse felt a touch uneasy in pressed pants, as though it restricted him in personality too. He nodded and said a greeting to the few people who passed him in the hallway, but this life was not him. Even though he had inherited a great deal of money, it would never change who he was on the inside, or how he chose to live his life.

He neared the room where the kids sat on the floor, mostly Indian style, listening to a man nearly old enough to be Clouse's grandfather. He spoke with a colorful narrative voice, one that could frighten the hardiest of adults at a campfire.

As though to make the experience as close to a cool, camping evening as possible, the lights were out except for a string of white holiday lights along one wall and several jack-o-lanterns lining the floor of another wall.

Someone had set the gutted pumpkins almost everywhere in the hotel, as though to warn Clouse about the imminent danger ahead.

Traditionally the killers of the past two years had set up rooms with the jack-o-lanterns to confuse their prey before carving into their bodies with a scythe. Clouse thought of several such people, including his first wife, who had met their ends that way.

"It's almost eight o'clock," the old man said as Clouse slumped against a wall outside, keeping out of view. "Time for one more ghost story before we head off to play."

Clouse looked around him before settling in for the story. The last thing he needed people to think was that he was more concerned with the children's activities than the festivities in the atrium.

"A long time ago, there was a colony of priests settled in here at the hotel," the old man began as Clouse rolled his eyes. He knew what the story would be about, but he wondered which twist would be placed on it.

"They lived among the town's people for many years, conducting their school for young priests here at the hotel. They stripped the hotel of all its beauty, and made it plain, just like they were.

"One day a priest named Father Ernest came to lead their church services, but he did not like what they had done to the hotel. He became angry with what his fellow priests had done to such a beautiful building, but no one would listen to him.

"Then one day one of the priests disappeared."

"What happened to him?" one of the children asked with a hard swallow.

"No one knows," the narrator continued. "One by one, several other priests disappeared, and strange things happened in this very hotel. Their bodies were never found, but some say Ernest was the reason they disappeared. They say he was slowly going insane.

"He would dress in dark robes like I'm wearing here tonight, and he donned a hood just as I am now, so that no one could tell who he was."

Pausing momentarily, the man eerily raised the hood over his head, leaving little except his chin showing from the black draping cloth.

"But they knew who he was, and what he had become. He was death itself. He was the Grim Reaper, come to their little community to steal souls and take what he considered unfit life from this hotel."

Clouse shifted in the hallway, realizing some creative license was being used in the telling of this tale. He figured no one except himself knew the entire true story since no one still living had ever read the diaries.

At least he assumed no one had.

"On a night very much like this one, cold and dark, Ernest stalked the halls one, final time. He planned one last mysterious ending for one particular priest. Ernest found a room appropriate for carrying out his deed, and soon after, the priests were beckoned to this room by the odor of something burning behind locked doors."

Looking as ominous as Ernest once had beneath the hood, the narrator's face barely showed through the black cloth as he paused.

"When the priests opened the doors, can you imagine what they found?" he asked, finding nothing but blank stares from the children, waiting in anticipation, some ducking or burying their heads from fright. "They found the remains of Ernest, who had made himself one with the hotel. He took his own life within the confines of the building he loved so much so he could always be with it.

"Some say Ernest's spirit haunts these walls today. You may see him in the halls, the bathroom, the grand atrium." He paused. "Or even your own room upstairs."

Clouse rolled his eyes, just imaging how many parents would be forced to escort their children to every single room in the hotel for fear that an apparition would appear for the sole purpose of frightening them.

He chose to walk away before the epilogue was told, back to the atrium where dinner was likely being served already.

As he looked back to see if the kids were leaving the room, Clouse rounded a portion of the hallway, bumping into someone, scaring the daylights out of him.

"Mark," he said after taking a step back and catching his breath. "Why aren't you with the others?"

"I needed a smoke and wondered where the hell you went," Daniels replied. "I've been finding some interesting people at this little party."

"Such as?"

"Well, I had an interesting conversation with Tug McCabe this afternoon. I also saw your lawyer check in."

"I don't have a lawyer."

Daniels shrugged indifferently.

"Okay, Smith's old lawyer. That Simms guy."

"You're not really surprising me here, Mark. All these people are directly or indirectly involved with the hotel and the affairs surrounding it the past couple years."

"Yeah," Daniels said, reaching into the breast pocket of his tuxedo, "but this isn't."

He pulled out a folded newspaper, handing it to the hotel's owner.

"What's this?" Clouse asked, unfolding it to reveal a tragic accident that occurred at a theme park local to the newspaper.

"After you were summoned to that theme park, I checked into any strange events that might have happened since the park opened. Being new, and state-of-the-art, it only housed a couple mishaps, but one in particular struck a chord and I called the newspaper people to follow up on an archived internet story they printed."

"Man killed in roller coaster accident," Clouse read the headline aloud.

"It goes on to say the rear car of a new coaster somehow derailed, flopped upward on a sharp descent, and crushed the man's skull against a steel track that would normally be a safe distance from any coasters or people passing by."

"So what does that have to do with any of this?"

"Does the name Beverly Hilton mean anything to you?"

Clouse thought only a second.

"Isn't she the one who owned that property Tim was so interested in buying last year?"

"The one and only. Get this, Paul. It was her son whose head became a splintered watermelon a few years ago with that accident."

"You're awfully tactful with your words. I take it your department lets other people inform people of their deceased loved ones?"

"They do, but what I'm interested in here is the fact that her son gets killed, she owns that property, has a connection with your best buddy, and there's already a connection between her burned out resort and this hotel. It could be nothing, or it could tie together and be absolutely everything to do with all this."

"It could," Clouse deduced. "But she's in her eighties or something close to that. She's not going to run around wielding a scythe, chopping people up."

"No, but there's extended family."

"Too bad we don't have time to investigate this angle further."

"We might have a chance. Beverly Hilton is staying here the next two days with all of us. I overheard a conversation with her and some couple who called her by name."

Clouse rubbed his chin in thought.

"We should have a talk with her then. But first, we need to get back to the dinner before someone comes looking for *us*."

Chapter 32

Clouse and Daniels returned to the room full of round tables as the meals were being wheeled to each table. From the smell of the food, it might be a combination of seafood, steak, and poultry.

"This could cost me dearly," Clouse said, shaking his head.

"You can afford it, buddy," Daniels grinned wryly before splitting off toward his table.

He went to sit at his table with Jane and the kids, finding a surprise sitting beside his wife, wearing a concerned look on his face.

"Randy," Clouse said. "What are you doing here?"

"I got a certified letter at my house yesterday stating I needed to be here for this or my family might meet terrible circumstances."

"How did you know who sent it?"

"He knew about the incident at the theme park in detail. I wasn't about to call his bluff."

"All right," Clouse said. "Sit with us and act natural. We might be close to figuring out who's behind this."

"Oh?"

"I'll talk to you about it later."

Dressed like everyone else in the room, Niemeyer fit in, but he acted a bit more nervous and tense than the unsuspecting guests. Clouse would have to keep him settled down, though he could hardly blame the man after losing his brother and having the rest of his family threatened. Considering his potential career choice in law enforcement and his lifestyle, Niemeyer was high strung under ordinary circumstances.

He fingered the table repeatedly until their dinner arrived in covered dishes. Even then, his interest in eating seemed minimal. His fork tapped or twirled in his food for the most part.

"You're here, Randy," Clouse said in a low voice so no one else heard. "No one is going to get hurt."

"Except maybe us," Niemeyer retorted. "I don't like being forced here like this. It's like being a cooped up chicken wondering when Farmer Brown's going to come visit with his axe."

"I know," Clouse said, taking a bite of the stuffed chicken breast on his plate. "But the good news is the killer is staying here with us."

Niemeyer grimaced.

"Out of two-hundred people it'll be easy to spot him," he said with a sarcastic tone.

"It's better than what we had yesterday. At least now we know *where* he is."

Niemeyer shrugged.

"I'm not reassured, if that's what you want."

"Just understand that you're not here alone," Clouse said. "There are a lot of us here with something to lose."

"Sure, but who can I trust?"

Clouse looked to Jane and the kids who tried to maintain a calm demeanor while eating their expensive dinners. His wife gave him a look that implied he should leave Niemeyer alone and keep his cool during the festivities. After all, it was only the first night.

He had already commented on how beautiful Jane looked in her golden gown, lined with shiny, threadlike streamers from her shoulders to just above her knees where the gold ended. Her hair glistened from the spotlights on stage, and for a change, it was completely let down, dangling around her shoulders with fresh curls applied during a perm that morning. Though the timing seemed all wrong for a hairstyle change, Jane decided to act the part of a dignified hostess the best she could.

His expression lightened as he grinned her way, letting her know she was right. He looked to the children who seemed oblivious to their real purpose of staying at the hotel.

Amazingly, they had put up little resistance toward the trip, and he wondered if they had any notion of why they were truly there. Clouse thought he had put on a good show when the threatening letter came, and later when he explained to them that they would be taking a family trip to where the trouble had begun, and where Zach had been taken during the kidnapping.

At any rate, they were already there, and he was that much closer to figuring out who was responsible for the slaying of more of his friends. Clouse had solved it twice before, and both times he was nearly too late to save his own life. This time the lives of almost two hundred other people rested in his hands because he knew why they were really there.

And his time to figure out the truth burned away like the candles centered at each of the round tables.

***

After a night of dining, dancing, and drinking, Harold Simms staggered up the stairs to the fourth floor where he seemed to be one of the few residents around. Nearly everyone else had been given rooms on higher floors, while a few occupied those below him.

A small man in stature, the lawyer lacked both the height and muscle that might have made him a good athlete, or even more of a force in the courtroom. What he lacked in physical traits, Simms made up for in intelligence and a voice that could have easily made it on television or radio.

For less money.

He had made out quite well on Smith's death the year before, and the subsequent transition of funds and property to Paul Clouse. He was more than happy to attend a gala thrown by the new owner, and to celebrate a new beginning for the hotel he had more than a small part in restoring because he handled so much of the legal paperwork.

After all, he hoped to retain Clouse's business.

Simms entered his room, found the closer of the two beds awaiting his arrival, and dropped himself across it, wanting to simply rest and take in the night's events before he considered what to do next.

"I'm feeling good," he announced to himself as he lay there motionless.

A few minutes went by before the lawyer stood up and began undressing himself. Even for someone accustomed to suits and black-tie affairs, he preferred his evenings after the events much more.

He took his tie and shirt off before venturing into the bathroom to start the shower. As it ran and steam filled the hotel room, Simms went about removing his shoes and socks. He opened the closet door, looking for something more comfortable while lounging about in his hotel room once he completed his shower.

Simms felt competent enough to work on some documents before heading to bed. The women and alcohol had not impaired his judgment enough to keep him from all work.

Setting his laptop computer upon the work desk, Simms turned it on before stepping into the bathroom to take his shower. By now, the steam funneled out of the room and clung to the walls, making for a very humid shower.

Ten minutes later, he stepped into the bedroom, ready to open some files on his computer, but he found the screen blank.

"What's this?" he asked, hitting a few keys on the keyboard with no response.

He tapped the power button, but no power kicked on. Simms dropped to his knees, looking at the outlet, finding his laptop completely unplugged, certain that was not how he had left it.

Simms poised himself on one knee, looked across the room, and saw a black figure blocking the room's only means of egress, holding a scythe. Since the doors automatically locked whenever patrons entered the room, the person must have had his own way in. Whether he entered before or after Simms was unknown, and at this point irrelevant.

"Who are you?" the lawyer demanded. "Is this some sort of sick joke?"

Nodding his head in the negative sense, the figure raised the scythe and stalked toward the lawyer, who was still knelt down.

Simms bolted up, heading toward the bathroom. A rather small room, it would provide little protection, and none at all, if the killer broke through the door. Changing his mind, he darted toward the main door, ducking under the killer and his strange weapon of choice. His hand grasped the doorknob but a scythe lodged itself in the center of the door before he could pull it open.

As the killer pried his weapon from the door, Simms scurried behind the bed for shelter, leaving himself an exit across the bed if the killer followed. Indeed, he did follow, but as Simms started across the bed, the killer clasped his ankle, yanking him back. The lawyer struggled to get free, but was tugged across the bed and forcefully stood up by his powerful assailant.

With the power of the killer's hand behind it, Simms' head smashed into the trim beside the glass doors overlooking the atrium. Even if he had been run through the glass, no one was left below to hear the sounds of his suffering at the late hour.

Using incredible force, the killer launched Simms against the wall where the wind was knocked from his lungs and his head dented the virginal paint along the plasterboard. He quickly tried to regain his thoughts and enough sense to escape, but it was too late.

A scythe swung toward his abdomen, and impaled him against the wall with a thud barely audible to the neighbors, who likely figured Simms had found himself some company for the evening.

Slowly looking down at the source of immense pain in his stomach, Simms groaned, reaching for the killer's mask, but the figure stepped back, pulling his weapon with him, allowing the lawyer to slump to the floor and suffer his last few minutes of life alone.

Stepping carefully across the room to avoid tracking any blood, the killer removed his costume before leaving the room, certain no one saw him leave as the door locked behind him. Harold Simms would not be missed during the next day's festivities, and by the time anyone found him, it would be too late to stop his fiendish plan.

Either way, the next day would prove quite entertaining.

Chapter 33

During the next afternoon, a formal lunch was held in the atrium where most of the guests attended, before the option of a tour of the grounds or a locally written play being performed on the stage in the atrium was given. Several gift shops were open, as well as the bar, for those who didn't like the first two choices.

An entertainment station on each floor would keep the kids and electronically-inclined adults occupied if none of the other options looked good. As it was, Clouse, Daniels, and both of their wives ate a light lunch of sandwiches and small salads. Though lunch was light, the desserts looked heavenly, except for the calorie count.

Most of the children, including their own, were enjoying a scavenger hunt within the confines of the old bowling alley and recreation building. It was redone on the outside, but the interior was gutted, merely holding raw building materials. This gave the children places to hide and enjoy themselves within a supervised, enclosed space.

"This is going to cost me too," Clouse muttered, looking over the color menu displaying almost a dozen dessert dishes from a local chef.

"Quit complaining," Daniels said. "You don't even know if you're flipping the bill for this yet."

"It may not matter. And I've got bigger concerns than the bills. I would love to know just why the killer brought us here. So far it's been more like a vacation than a death threat."

"I don't know about a vacation," the detective said. "My idea of a vacation is a week at the lakes, enjoying nature, fishing, and sleeping under the stars."

"And using an outhouse?" Jane questioned.

"Comes with the territory," Daniels responded. "But if that's what it takes, so be it."

Daniels suddenly perked up as someone entered the room.

"That's Mrs. Hilton," he said, eyes fixed upon the older woman who was escorted by a man young enough to be her grandson. "It's time she and I had a little chat," he said, rising from his seat.

"Go easy," Clouse warned. "I don't need people suspecting anything around here is wrong if they aren't tied in with our killer."

"Tact is my middle name," Daniels said plainly before walking off.

"Actually it's Edward," Cindy corrected for the benefit of the two people still sitting with her.

Clouse grinned.

"He's one-of-a-kind."

"And more. It's hard living with such a devoted cynic."

"Oh, I can imagine," Jane said, glancing toward Clouse.

"What?" he asked defensively. "I'm nowhere near as bad. To Mark the whole world can be suspected of something."

Cindy nodded agreement.

"And it seems you have a little trouble finding the good in people lately, too."

"Only when my family is threatened."

Cindy looked at her plate, pushed it aside, and stood to leave.

"Since we're without children for the afternoon I think I'm going to enjoy one of those nice hot tubs upstairs, then maybe take in a movie."

"Enjoy," Clouse said. "Maybe I can talk Mark into joining you. He could use a little relaxation."

"Please do," Cindy said before heading for the closest atrium arch.

He doubted she would find an open hot tub because several guests had sounded anxious to try the devices. If she was around other people, Clouse felt fine about letting her go upstairs. Besides, she was never an intended target of the killer the past few years.

Clouse and his wife finished their plates a moment before Daniels returned. He seated himself with a perplexed look across his face.

"Well?" they both asked him.

"I don't know. It's kind of weird how she ended up suing Dr. Smith over the loss of her son, even though they were acquaintances, and then her big resort burns down shortly after that. A resort she claimed she was going to sell anyway."

"And you think she's gone whacko at eighty-years-old and started hacking people up?" Clouse deduced.

"No. Don't be ridiculous. I think there's some bad blood between her and Smith, and maybe one of her family members killed him last year as retaliation. Hell, she could be related to Ryan Andrews for all we know."

Clouse shrugged.

"Possibly. I think one of us should have a chat with Harold Simms to see what the real story is. And I'm concerned about so many of our old acquaintances showing up here. I may start asking to see some of their invitation letters."

"Don't be hasty," Daniels said. "Talk to McCabe. He shows up yesterday, talks to me a few minutes, and I haven't seen him since. The Tug McCabe I met is very much a socialite."

"Okay. I'll track him down and see what he's doing."

"And where is my wife?"

"She went upstairs to try one of the hot tubs," Jane said.

Daniels stood from his chair so fast it fell backwards to the floor.

"And you let her?"

The couple looked at one another.

"She just left a few minutes ago," Clouse said. "Surely she wouldn't be a target-"

"My ass," Daniels said, bolting from the atrium toward the closest elevator.

***

Upstairs, Cindy had already dressed down to a bathing suit for her time in the water. She marched down the hall and soon found herself in the water relaxation room at the end of the hall. Strangely, the handful of people who wandered the spa area, apparently ready for rest and relaxation when she arrived had now departed. A skylight illuminated the area very well when she stepped inside, finding a stand with towels and the new hot tub ready for use. Several ordinary tubs and steam machines were also available, and Cindy felt certain an appointment for each would be necessary if the hotel ever opened for business.

Filled with new tile across each wall, and the floor, the room looked like a case of athlete's foot waiting to happen.

She felt the water in the hot tub, assured it was plentifully warm. Cindy slowly climbed in, flipping a switch on the wall behind her to activate the bubbling action of the tub. As the bubbles rose from beneath, tickling her bare skin as they went, she heard them reach the top and make a popping sound as they burst like a pot of boiling water.

Though the hotel had once provided guests with all sorts of luxury, she liked the newer version much better. New ideas mixed with traditional know-how had created a blend of luxury only the rich could usually afford.

As she settled into the tub, immersing herself in the pool of ecstasy, Cindy heard a noise from the hallway beyond the new double doors of the room. She looked, but saw nothing out there. For a moment, she returned to the warmth of the pool, trying to assure herself her mind was playing tricks on her, but the noise of a door closing down the hall startled her.

She turned to look once again, but only the shadow of someone walking toward her down the hall was visible along the floor because of the skylight. A little shriek escaped her lungs before she could control herself and see that the man had come down to try out some of the devices.

"Sorry," he said before moving to the opposite side of the room, exploring his options.

With a towel draped across his shoulder, wearing only swimming trunks, he stood in front of an odd machine that looked like something carried over from the hotel's traditional days.

"I didn't mean to be so paranoid," Cindy apologized. "This place is so big it sometimes gives me the creeps."

"It's okay.

"Do you know what this is?" he asked her curiously, pointing to the old device.

"I'm no expert, but I believe that's one of those old steam massage machines. They usually blow steam on you from every direction."

He opened it, revealing small nozzles lined across the inner walls. A look behind the machine revealed hose connections, along with power.

It would still work.

"Sweet," he said to himself, turning it on. "Thank you," he told her just as Daniels barged into the room, fully clothed, and openly unhappy about something.

"Mark," Cindy said with a flirtatious smile, obviously not expecting him upstairs so soon. "Want to jump in? It's more comfortable than I thought it would be."

His expression did not lighten.

"You shouldn't be down here alone," he said so the man across the room could not hear. "It's not safe to go running around by yourself."

"Then join me."

"I can't. There are people I have to talk to."

"Fine. I'll take my chances then."

"Cindy, we're not having this argument. Stay with me a little while longer and we'll do something tonight."

She simply stared at him, unable to believe he could be so overly concerned with her safety. It wasn't as though she had snuck off to the basement or walked the wooded grounds behind the hotel by herself. Any number of people were coming and going through the spa area, and her husband wasn't exactly the life of the party thus far. When he refused to move or lighten his expression, she lifted herself from the water and swung her legs back over the tub in compliance.

"Fine. But you owe me some time to ourselves later."

"I promise," Daniels said, looking at her with a little more love than he had allowed himself to display lately. "Later."

As the couple left, Brian Kern climbed into the steam massage machine, pulling the two flaps shut behind him. Only his head emerged from a centered hole in the machine. The rest of his body fit inside, engulfed by the soothing steam flowing along his skin, lulling him into a state of rest and relaxation he had not felt in years.

He knew there was no way he should be alone in the middle of the afternoon relaxing in a massage machine for no reason at all, but the time of day alone gave Kern a level of comfort.

Perhaps a false sense.

A few minutes later he found himself nearly as comfortable as Cindy had been, and he shut his eyes, letting several sweet memories of his work on the grounds intertwine. Countless hours of hard work, he put into the building as the landscape contractor. Though his strength was creating walkways, planting trees and flowers, and accurately placing statues and benches in backyards, Kern was no flake.

Kern fit in with the construction workers when he worked on renovation projects. He also spent time coaching basketball, which he had played through high school and college himself, nearly making it professionally.

Several knee injuries and a desire to live a more conventional life in Indiana kept him close to home. Now a wife and three kids kept him busy, and counted himself blessed to have survived the killings from the year before when he was placed on a list with several other men who met terrible endings.

He had worked with Clouse several years on the hotel, and the two men spoke briefly during the incidents of the year before. Despite the danger in coming to the hotel, Kern felt certain Clouse had everything under control.

Enough so, that he relaxed inside the massage machine.

He failed to notice when the double doors shut because his mind was so engrossed with his body's relaxation.

Not until someone stuck a broomstick handle through the handles of the machine's doors did Kern open his eyes, and when he did, a horrific reality faced him down.

"Hey!" he exclaimed, seeing a cloaked figure above him. "What are you doing?"

Kern could only watch helplessly as the figure's hand edged toward the heat control, turning it up to a dangerous level.

"Oh, please, don't do that," Kern pleaded as he pushed against the doors of the machine, but their sturdy build kept him trapped inside.

They were built in an era when things were built to last, long before even he was born.

Before he left, the killer tore off a piece of duct tape, placing it over Kern's mouth to prevent the contractor from calling for help as he died from enough heat to steam roast him inside the machine. The steam rose in temperature from the killer's tinkering as Kern's muffled cries barely sounded above the hum of the device.

As he carefully stepped from the room, the killer checked both ways down the hallway before closing the doors and removing his disguise. From there, he would head downstairs to mix in with the crowd so no one would ever know the difference.

Chapter 34

Downstairs, the afternoon passed as gingerly as a Southern day on the front porch. People mingled, took their time, enjoyed the hotel's elegant beauty, and walked outside to enjoy the remains of the gardens on one of the last warm days of the year.

Clouse looked at the situation as very similar to the *Titanic*'s maiden voyage. Surrounded by imported beauty, the guests were oblivious to the danger and potential death around them. He wondered just how much longer it would take for the ship to sink.

Until he saw Tug McCabe walk in, Clouse had been contemplating a hundred different things he could do rather than stand around pretending to be a gracious host.

"How's the state trooper business?" he asked the investigator who had transferred posts after the murders the year before. He had come very close to becoming a victim himself.

"It's better these days," the husky police officer answered. "How's the millionaire business?"

"It has its drawbacks." Clouse acted as though he was counting them on his fingers. "Let's see. Psychotic killers hunt you and your family down, relatives you never knew are suddenly calling you up, and you're confined to living a secluded life away from everyone you ever knew for both security and financial reasons. Really, though, it's not that bad."

"Sounds it."

"And you? Do you regret moving to the other end of the state?"

"Sometimes. I don't miss the ex-wives, but it's tough being away from the rest of my family. Still, I might have found number four."

Clouse smirked. He was on his second wife by default, and McCabe had gone through three already, despite their age proximity.

"Didn't bring her along?"

"No. I didn't know if it would be safe, and she had family visiting this week anyway."

McCabe took in a complete view of the atrium, acting more calm than Clouse figured he actually felt.

"I love the way this place looks. We never really had time to enjoy it before."

"That's true," Clouse said. "Usually the floor was covered in blood or I'd be chasing a blade-wielding nutcase through here."

Clouse's cellular phone rang at his side before the two could further their conversation.

"Hello?"

"Paul, it's Mark. I need you upstairs at my room right away."

"Just me?"

"Yeah. We've got a situation."

After excusing himself, Clouse made it upstairs within a few minutes to find Daniels leaning against his room's doorway. The detective had a grim look across his face as he motioned to his friend to follow him down the hall.

"What have we got?" Clouse asked.

"I'm not quite sure."

When they reached the water relaxation room they found the steam massage machine tipped over in an awkward position on the floor with its hoses and electrical units ripped from their restraints on the wall. Near the top of the machine, a small pool of blood settled atop the tile floor, and the doors were broken outward with parts from a broom handle resting nearby.

Still, there was no body.

"Anyone else see this?" Clouse asked.

"No. Cindy asked me to look for one of her rings down here and this is what I found."

"Any idea who was inside?"

"I think it was that Brian Kern you worked with. He was toying around with the machine, Cindy said."

"Just great. Any water trail or anything to follow?"

"Not really. It reaches the hallway and stops. The carpet might have already soaked it in, or maybe he never actually walked out."

"Brian was a big guy. He could have torn that from the wall, but I don't know why he wouldn't have looked for help."

Daniels looked at the machine.

"We need to put this back up," Clouse said.

"This could be a crime scene," Daniels argued.

"And there could be a lot more crime scenes if we let everyone know what's *really* going on here."

The detective thought a moment, looking down the hallway as the sound of a closing door echoed from the end of the hall.

"Fine," he said, reluctantly helping Clouse set the machine back on its feet and watching for any hallway travelers as his friend mopped up the blood with a nearby rag.

It went completely against his nature to cover up what could be a crime scene, particularly one that was not documented, but he understood the inherent danger if he did otherwise.

"Are you happy?" he asked Clouse as they stood at the threshold of the room, looking inside. The room looked perfectly natural again.

"Happy would be a bit extreme. Satisfied, perhaps."

Clouse looked at the floor with a sense of gloom showing in his face.

"What's the matter?"

"I can't believe the son-of-a-bitch would go after Brian like that," Clouse said slowly, with a numb realization striking him. "Why won't he face us in the open, Mark?"

"Because it's a game, Paul. And that's no fun."

"Fun?" Clouse questioned, an enraged sneer replacing his confusion. "I'll show him a different sort of fun."

He stomped off down the hall, leaving Daniels to question just which gear his friend's mind had switched into.

After a quick trip to his room to retrieve his leather jacket, Clouse found himself on the grounds a moment later, trying to keep a distance from other guests while searching for ideas on where the killer might be traveling on foot, or even storing any dead bodies he collected.

Keeping an eye on all of the guests would prove impossible, and with just he, Daniels, and their wives knowing the entire truth, there would be no help in monitoring guest activity. Hotel security was minimal, and considering who actually bought and paid for them, Clouse wanted no part in bringing them into the fold.

Frustration ate at him, but he felt compelled to avoid sitting back while guests disappeared around him or dropped like flies. He found himself behind the cafeteria area where trucks used a ramp to unload deliveries of all sorts. From there, a person could wander up a dilapidated trail to the spot where the old church once stood. With the church torn down in 1932, the area was now enshrouded within the stone foundation with the statue of a Jesuit saint overlooking the area.

Clouse decided to walk toward the converted bowling alley, taking the brick walkway behind the sunken garden. Though not nearly as scenic, it provided safe harbor from questions and conversations he didn't feel much like partaking in at the moment.

As he passed one of the old springs, now decorated with stained glass that would swing open in the summer to let the sweetest of breezes pass through, he thought he saw a pair of eyes staring through one of the clear areas of one window. The eyes burned a hole through him, with a darkness he had rarely seen.

Clouse turned away for only a second, but when he glanced back, he saw no eyes, no one inside the spring at all.

He spun around fully, walking backwards as he stared into the spring, expecting to see someone ducking out of the only entrance. Visibility through the building was easy since so much of it was glass, but Clouse saw no shadows, and no movement.

Shrugging it off, he turned around, heading for the storage building where he saw the kids playing inside through the large front window. A grin crossed his face against his will when he saw Zach and Katie playing inside, though he quickly wiped it away when he remembered his purpose for crossing the garden area.

Clouse passed the building, looking straight ahead to the cemetery on the hill above him. It was there Ernest was buried; it was there Ernest was dug up, and it was there that certain bodies had been hidden two years before when Clouse's own brother-in-law and boss set him up in a death trap less scary than the setting preceding it.

He stood there momentarily, staring up at the mound of dirt surrounding the empty grave. Most of it had been replaced, but tufts remained around the site.

"Damn them," Clouse muttered. "If it wasn't for them, none of this vicious circle would still be going today."

"If not for who?" a voice behind him asked.

"Now you're following me?" Clouse asked, turning to see Daniels.

"No. I managed to sneak up on you the five minutes you sat here daydreaming about those graves and talking to yourself."

Clouse started up the hill with Daniels in tow.

"I was just thinking about how this all started, Mark. *Now* look at it. We've got revenge for revenge for more revenge here."

"You sure about that?" Daniels asked as they stood over the grave, covered by loose dirt.

"I don't know what I'm sure of. This just seems a little more personal than before. I mean this guy has photos, sends me halfway across the country, and sets up all of this bullshit. This goes a little beyond the regular personal level."

Daniels stared down for a minute.

"You thinking there's something inside here?"

"It's been done before."

"Are you suggesting a midnight dig?"

"No. Even if we found something we couldn't risk telling anyone."

"Why not? It's the last night here. Everyone leaves tomorrow."

"But whatever our killer has in mind is going to come out tonight. He didn't get us all here just to let us leave peacefully and refreshed tomorrow morning," Clouse said.

"No, he didn't. Let's say we get back and find out just what he has in store for us?"

"Okay."

As the two began walking back to the hotel, Clouse thought he saw shadows around the old bowling alley, but dismissed it as the children playing until they reached the corner of the building. He realized all of the kids were inside and no doors were open.

"I keep seeing shadows, and people in buildings, Mark. Tell me I'm not losing it, please."

"You might not be, but I'm going to if Brian Kern's wife keeps coming up to me, begging me to find her husband."

"What did you tell her?"

"I told her my good buddy Paul Clouse hired hotel security for such things, and that she needed to talk to them, or you."

Clouse shot his friend an unfriendly look.

"There might still be time for me to hire the killer and turn him on you."

"Lighten up. I told her Brian was probably just goofing off in the garden or something, since he loves that landscape stuff."

"And?"

"She had already looked there."

"And?"

"I told her he was probably exploring the place, and that guys just do that stuff."

"But you and I know better," Clouse commented.

"Yeah. You wouldn't catch me examining architecture."

"I meant about Kern's whereabouts," Clouse said, slapping Daniels' arm with the back of his hand.

Rubbing the newly sore spot, Daniels sighed aloud.

"Look, we don't know for sure what happened up there."

"Oh? We find blood on the floor and evidence that someone was locked up in the piping hot steam massager, and we have no clue? Reality check, Mark, it doesn't look good since your wife said Brian Kern was the last person she saw in that room."

"Okay, so maybe our killer got to him, or maybe things got a little kinky with his girlfriend on the side. Either way we don't know and we should not care because we're next if we don't get inside and figure this out."

As the two approached the hotel's main stairs, they took in the view of six stories above them, all brick and concrete, and all very dangerous in more ways than one. Behind them, the sun began its descent, transforming daytime to dusk once more.

Perhaps for the hotel's last time.

"Well, here goes," Clouse said, leading the way up the stairs.

Chapter 35

Daniels stood among a few other patrons outside as he lit a cigarette on the veranda, spending a few moments away from the thoughts of death and bloodshed the hotel provided. Strangely, he could not confirm any of either such phenomena on this trip.

He could only assume.

Since tonight was an informal night, he had packed the tuxedo and dressed in more familiar attire. Judging by the appearance of the people around him, everyone had their own notion of how to appear on such a night, so it was a mixed bag.

As the detective looked at the stars overhead, listening loosely to the conversations around him, a lady dressed in a vintage, full dress from several decades before strolled up behind him, standing there until he took notice. Certainly not Victorian, the dress appeared to be something from the years when rock music was born. Still white and clean, the dress struck Daniels as something likely worn at the hotel during its numerous eras before he was born.

Though she appeared easily old enough to be his mother, her poise gave him the indication she might be someone of importance, or at least believe fully in her own worth. A certain twinkle in her eye gave the impression she would age gracefully and defy death until the last possible moment.

"Can I help you?" he asked as she stood behind him.

"Are you the detective who found the guilty parties last year? Some people inside pointed you out to me."

She spoke with a childlike curiosity, but Daniels could tell her intent was gravely more serious than a child's. Her appearance and the way she conducted herself let Daniels know she wasn't the typical person he dealt with on a daily basis. Perhaps wearing such an old dress was her way of throwing back to the past, or perhaps shrugging off the important person she once was by dressing in such period attire for the party inside.

Either way, her wits and intelligence had obviously not blemished with her age, and he could read her as someone who was secretly sizing him up simultaneously.

"I take it you're not wanting an autograph," Daniels said with a grin, flicking away his cigarette.

"No. I heard you were looking for any pertinent information about the Landamere family after last year's events."

"I said so for the newspaper, yes. We were trying to figure out more about her accomplice though, than we were about Mrs. Landamere."

"My name is Mary Witherspoon," the lady introduced herself. "And," Mary said as she began circling Daniels, "many years ago I was Joan Landamere's next door neighbor."

"Oh?"

"Oh, yes," she answered emphatically. "My husband was a promising surgeon at the time, and we were able to afford a rather nice estate.

"Much like my husband, it seemed Mr. Landamere was away quite often on business. Occasionally Joan and I would do girl things. You know, we would flirt with men in public, shop, travel. All the sort of things we were permitted to do those days without our husbands finding out."

"So you were out quite a bit," Daniels inferred.

"Yes, until Joan began feeling sick one day. She was out quite often by herself, and my understanding was she had several male suitors, though she never brought any home with her. Anyway, she took ill and began to spend more and more time by herself. She never wanted to go out, and eventually she stopped inviting me over altogether.

"Well, I understood she was going through some phase, and not feeling so well, so I stayed away for some time. Then, one day I noticed she was gardening in that lavish backyard of hers."

"Wait a second," Daniels interrupted. "You're telling me they had the same house back then, that they owned just last year?"

"Yes. I believe they rented it out while they were away. They never sold their estate, even when they moved away, as though they planned on returning one day. So, anyway, I went over to Joan's to see how the poor girl was doing. I made my way to the gate, and noticed something odd about her figure that made me change my mind. At that moment, I understood why she no longer wanted me over, but I had no idea why she would want to keep it."

"Keep what?" Daniels inquired, suspecting what she was getting at.

The woman looked at him as though he were a dog incapable of learning a new trick.

"The baby, of course. She was pregnant, detective."

"Good God," Daniels said to himself. "How long ago would you say this was?" he inquired.

"They moved away shortly after Mr. Landamere returned, and we moved the year after that." She figured in her head. "I would dare to say about twenty-two years ago."

Daniels looked at her, thought about it, and felt a realization that sent a tingle through his entire body.

"Thank you," he said, starting toward the hotel to find Clouse, not requiring elaboration on the details mentioned early in their conversation. "You may have helped me more than you know."

"You're welcome," she said, feeling better now that she had gossiped a bit, just like the old days. She snapped her fingers suddenly. "*Damn.* I didn't even get his name for a dance later. I *am* losing my touch."

***

Though the second evening was not formal, it involved at least as many events as the first night had. Clouse was putting on a dress shirt minus the tie when Jane returned from taking the kids to the daycare providers downstairs. Again, they would probably have more fun than the adults.

"Zach was talking about a story one of the elders told last night," she commented.

"I heard some of it. Not exactly what I would read him for bedtime."

"Kids these days learn things at a younger age. I doubt it will leave emotional scars with everything he's been through."

"It scared the shit out him, Jane," Clouse said, trying to comb his hair after walking in the bathroom. "He's only six."

Jane decided against wearing a dress, opting for slacks and a blouse. This would be the informal night with lots of dancing, drinking, and stories. Ordinarily

Clouse would enjoy a night like this. The type of night his first wife and he would enjoy together. Angie loved the spotlight and mingling with people, partly because it helped her software business flourish, and partly because it gave her chances to show off her husband and his career as an architecture designer.

She tended to ignore his main career as a firefighter, probably afraid it would dampen the opinion others held of herself and Clouse. He loved both of his occupations, but always felt more pride in being a public servant.

Jane never put such pressures on him, and he never let it bother him that she brought home more income than he did before the inheritance. He loved that she was so giving of herself and her time, sometimes for little or no pay before, during, and after a large sum of money entered their lives.

As Jane finished getting dressed, Clouse stepped to the open door-sized window for a look over the atrium. Only a decorative railing reaching just below his waistline kept him from potentially falling out of the window. Below, people were already dancing and laughing the night away. He wished he could share in their ignorant bliss, but truly he could not.

Not on this night.

He looked up to the sixth floor where his suite would have been, finding the lights turned on outside the room.

"Goddamn it," he said.

"What is it?" Jane called.

"Everyone knows I like those sixth floor lights turned off," Clouse complained. "That's the way Dr. Smith wanted it, and that's how I want it."

"Why don't we run up there and turn them off?" Jane inquired. "It's only one floor up."

He hesitated a moment, then shrugged.

"Sure."

A few minutes later the couple took the back stairs up to the suite, reaching the first set of double doors, which opened into a long lobby area in front of the room. With fine China and portraits of the hotel, it was an elegant room in its own right, but the real magic lay behind the brown double doors leading into the largest suite in the hotel.

Clouse dimmed the lights until they were off, but Jane squeezed his arm.

"Can we go inside? Just for a minute?"

"Why do you want to go inside?"

"We hardly ever get to visit this place, Paul. While we're here, I would love to see the suite we pass up week after week to sit at home."

Clouse raised the lights.

"Okay. Wait here and I'll check it out first. If someone had a key to get in this lobby, they might have access to the suite too."

He unlocked the door, having enough trouble that Jane began to pull out her set of keys, but he finally let himself in, never noticing the opposite set of double doors on the other end of the lobby were quietly being unlocked.

As Clouse ventured further into the room to inspect it, he ventured past the kitchen, and into the first bedroom, trying the lights. He flipped the switch a few times to no avail, and saw a strange light around the corner where the bathroom was set. The light flickered a strange orange color and he knew, even before he dared look, what that meant.

When he rounded the corner and saw the jack-o-lantern staring back at him, he knew the game had started again, and the advantage was not his.

"Jane!" he called. "Come in here! Quick!"

***

The killer, dressed completely in black, and faceless as always, barged into the lobby, forcing a shriek from Jane. She froze in terror as the killer charged toward her, clasping a knife. When he stopped to handcuff the door shut to prevent Clouse from interfering with his dirty work, Jane found opportunity to dig the keys from her pocketbook and run toward the opposite door.

"Jane!" she heard her husband yell through the locked doors as he tugged against the handcuff restraints lined across the door handles. "What the hell's going on?"

She screamed as she let herself out of the room, running for the closest cover the sixth floor could offer. Clouse continued pounding on the door and tugging at the handles to no avail, then turned, looking for an alternative way to escape the room, or get the doors open.

Jane darted down dark hallways, barely furnished, since most were just various entertainment rooms, until she reached a passage into the main hallway where any number of rooms awaited her. It felt like being in a funhouse with doors on every side of her as she ran for cover or escape. Occasionally she would stop to try one of the knobs, but none were unlocked.

Every time she paused, the killer seemed to draw a bit closer. She screamed for help with no replies. Suddenly she remembered her husband requesting no one stay on the top floor.

"Oh, dammit!" she said at the last attempted door.

She made it to the elevator, pushing the button, but there was no telling which floor it was sitting on, since the crew had not put indicators in. Unwilling to take a chance, and with the killer closing in with a purposeful march, she darted toward the stairs, taking their winding spiral path downward as the cloaked figure pursued. Jane's unwitting move ensured she never reached the safety of the crowds below, but rather, fell into his perfectly planned trap.

Reaching the bottom stair, Jane found herself confronted with a distant run to one of the atrium entrances, or the nearby cafeteria area. Though it would be vacated at the moment, the cafeteria would give her assured access to the outdoors where she would be free to run to the front of the building in either of two directions, or take a path of escape further back if necessary.

As she heard the steps of the killer making the last flight of stairs, she darted for the back area, pushing her way into the dining room, and through the large cafeteria in back. The dining room held one exit to the back, but she decided to hide behind some appliances in the cafeteria to wait to see what the killer did.

Horrified, she watched as he made his way into the cafeteria, holding a knife in his right hand, looking desperately in every direction. She felt certain he did not believe she had made it out the back, and if he knew the hotel at all, he knew that particular backdoor closed slowly.

And he was never that far behind her.

Her body tensed as she watched him explore the cafeteria further, and even step to the opposite side where food supplies were stored in bulk. Between two sets of shelves, ducked behind a stack of canned vegetables, Jane peered through a small hole between boxes, and she watched as he scurried from the room in an apparent desperate attempt to find her.

Leaving the cover of the boxes, Jane looked along the countertops for something to help her defend herself. A paring knife was the only weapon available, but she swiped it up and headed out from the cafeteria defensively, only to be surprised when the killer lunged at her from the opposite side of the doorway, missing as he tested the carpet's durability with his face.

With a shriek, Jane threw open the backdoor, ran along the loading dock, then found a choice at the end of the plank.

She could run along the pavement in either direction toward the front of the hotel, but her chances of outrunning him were already proven to be slim, or she could take one of two ways around the wooded grounds leading up to where the cathedral had once stood. Being in excellent physical shape, she decided to take the treacherous spiraling concrete walkway upward.

Long since decayed and crumbling, the steps were overgrown with moss and weeds, but they were just awkward enough that someone less familiar with the grounds than her would have trouble navigating their way to the top.

Once in the open area she would still be surrounded by darkness and the cool night, but she could decide her best course of action without compromising her life.

She stumbled several times in her hurry to the top, but managed to reach the open area where the bald head of the St. Ignatius statue looked straight ahead, over her, oblivious to her plight. She made her way to the statue, carefully looking around, hearing nothing. It wasn't until Jane brushed against the cold concrete that a hand clasped her own, and the glimmer of a blade caught her eye as the killer stepped from around the statue.

In a terrified panic, she wondered how he could have beaten her to the top. As she struggled to break his grasp, Jane's blouse tore loose from his fingers and she was hurled head-first into the statue, rendering her unconscious, and unaware of her own fate.

***

Using a few of the tools he found in the kitchen, Clouse had managed to remove the knobs from the doors before making it down the stairs to the second floor. He found no signs of Jane or the killer, and fortunately, no blood stains.

He reached the edge of one of the interior rooms using his key, and looked over the festivities below, cursing them because they were a smokescreen for the disaster awaiting Clouse, and possibly everyone below.

Music carried through the entire hotel like one big amplifier, and Clouse felt the vibrations of the bass as he placed his hand against the glass, looking for any sign that Jane might have made it to safety amongst the crowd below.

A hand against Clouse's shoulder startled him, and as he jumped back a step, he found quite possibly the only friend he had left standing behind him.

"Mark, what are you doing up here?"

"I saw a glimpse of someone running around up here," Daniels answered. "I came up and found this room open. What the hell is going on?"

"It's the killer. He locked me in the suite upstairs and took off after Jane. I don't know where they went."

"Aw, fuck," the detective cursed. "We've got to find one, or both, quick."

Clouse took a deep breath, refusing to believe any harm had come to his wife.

"Okay. I'll check the downstairs, and around the grounds. You make a sweep of each floor. Check each door and work your way up."

Daniels nodded.

"If I find that asshole, I'm shooting first, interrogating his corpse later."

Clouse gave a nod before heading out the door to the downstairs.

Daniels waited a few seconds after his friend left to decide how he wanted to handle the search. Behind Clouse, the door had closed halfway, and without the benefit of lights on inside the room, Daniels decided to catch it before he was enshrouded in darkness.

Instead, he caught a glimpse of his objective walking by as he swung the door open.

For one instant, Daniels stared at the cloaked figure, and it was obvious from the hesitation that the killer was equally surprised. Though only one set was visible, both of their eyes widened intently with the sudden, unforeseen prospect of a confrontation. The notion lasted only a second as the killer drew a knife overhead to continue his work by making the detective his next victim.

Too busy reaching to stop the knife to draw his pistol, Daniels clasped the killer's arm as they both went flying into the room, hitting the ground with enough impact that the knife eluded both of them and spun into the darkness.

Now the advantage belonged to Daniels, if he could reach the firearm tucked away inside his jacket, snugly nestled into a shoulder holster. Apparently aware of this, the killer kept both of the detective's arms away from his body, then worked in a few body punches. Daniels felt the wind burst from his lungs, but he fought back with a palm strike to the mask beneath the hood, stunning the killer momentarily.

As he regained his footing and reached for his weapon, Daniels allowed the figure to football tackle him straight into a wall, striking his spine where he had been shot two years prior. Though the pain of hitting the wall was not intense enough to pull more than a brief grunt from him, Daniels felt certain he had felt a portion of his back give way.

A bullet had stripped him of his ability to walk for nearly a year because it damaged vertebrae near his spine, and his back would never be as healthy again. It seemed as though his adversary knew this critical information.

Before he could contemplate how to defend himself, Daniels took a knee to the groin, but shoved the killer off before more damage could be done.

With only the light from the hallway streaming in, the killer blended in with the darkness as Daniels released the latch on the shoulder holster, letting the nine-millimeter slide into his hand. Suddenly, however, the room seemed eerily quiet, and he could not detect where the killer was hiding, if he was in the room at all.

Standing perfectly still, his back still planted against the wall, Daniels' eyes shifted nervously back and forth, wondering where the killer might be, and more importantly, if he was armed.

His eyes struggled to adapt to the low light, and Daniels caught a glimpse of the knife thrusting its way toward his abdomen. During his reaction of spinning the pistol toward his assailant, the blade caught the top of his right wrist, cutting through his flesh and a few small blood vessels before he swatted it away with his free hand as the firearm fell to the floor.

Wasting no time, the killer swung Daniels to the wall beside the glass doors, which overlooked the atrium, again hitting his back against them. The figure took hold of the detective's head, thrusting it back against the window three consecutive times, creating a spider web in the glass.

Each room contained one double-glass-door fixture, which would swing open to overlook the grand atrium. Only rooms on the fourth and sixth floors contained the balconies which allowed guests to stand above the atrium while the remaining rooms simply held guests inside with the decorative railings along the mammoth windows.

Daniels realized as the killer swung the doors open, what he had in mind. He convinced himself at that moment he would not allow himself to be thrown over without taking the killer with him.

As the killer grabbed Daniels by the jacket, the detective locked arms with the dark figure, blood still oozing from the fresh wound along his arm. Daniels locked one leg behind his assailant in such a way that it tripped up the mysterious figure, sending them both over the decorative gate, plummeting toward the atrium floor below.

From a normal second story fall, both would probably have survived, mostly intact, but a round table below ensured a closer and possibly softer landing. Both crashed through the middle of the table, breaking most of the dishes and vases in the process, as the table snapped into two pieces. If the fall itself hadn't drawn the attention of the guests, the thunderous noise from the impact certainly would.

Instantly to his feet, the killer looked for a weapon to finish off the subdued detective, but thought better of it as all eyes were upon him, and the crowd had already begun to swarm around them. As Daniels lie writhing in pain from the impact on his back, the cloaked figure forced his way through several guests and out the closest atrium door, planning to make a cameo appearance without a disguise so no one could assume he was responsible for the mayhem.

"Oh my God! Are you okay?" one lady asked Daniels.

"Of course I'm not!" he yelled. "I just got stabbed and fell from a balcony."

Clouse made it to the edge of the crowd, shaking his head. His search for Jane had revealed nothing, and now Daniels had fallen prey to the killer. He felt certain his wife was now the killer's captive, meant to be used as collateral to ensure he didn't call the police or leave the premises.

"This has to end tonight," he told himself, determined to stay until he knew who was responsible for wrecking his life, and the lives of everyone he cared about.

Chapter 36

After announcing that a prank had gone horribly wrong, Clouse dismissed the rest of the guests for the remainder of the weekend and told them he would make it up to them at a later date. Most seemed reluctant to believe his last-minute excuse for cutting the festivities short, but after seeing the condition of Mark Daniels, few dared argue.

As a few families walked down the main stairs from the hotel toward their vehicles, Clouse walked along the cot, which would carry his friend to the Paoli hospital, where his back and other body parts would be checked thoroughly.

Daniels appeared fine as they wheeled him carefully down the concrete steps. He was awake and alert, apparently feeling little pain from the tumble.

"How's the back?" Clouse asked, walking beside the stretcher.

"It's okay. I can feel my toes if that's what you mean."

"Good. Don't you even think about coming back here tonight."

"Of course I'm coming back, Paul. We've got to find Jane."

Clouse shook his head.

"No. He's got her. And now he's got me right where he wants me."

"What about the kids? Cindy can take them if you want."

Clouse had last seen her trying to manage her own two children, getting them ready for the ride to the hospital.

"No. You two have your hands full. If he wants the kids he's going to find them, but I don't think that's what he wants. At any rate, they're staying here with me."

Daniels grimaced.

"You're signing your own death warrant if you stay, Paul. Get out of here, go home, call the police. Hell, buy your own island or something. Just don't end it this way."

Clouse tapped on his friend's forearm lightly, as though it might be the last time they saw one another, alive at least.

"I've got to, Mark," he said, breaking off toward the hotel. "Just remember one thing," he called back. "I owe you my life, and now I'm going to give yours back to you."

Daniels started to say something, but changed his mind as the paramedics loaded him into the ambulance. He seemed to wonder if Clouse had something overly drastic in mind.

As the ambulance drove away, and people passed him along the stairs, it felt like his life passed in slow motion. He was on his way to the gravest confrontation of his life, and it meant the difference in the lives of everyone around him.

He wandered through the hotel, feeling a sense of urgency as guests passed him. Some were hurried to leave, others reluctant. His concern for Jane grew as he questioned whether his hunch was accurate. For all he knew, she could have been murdered, but he put the worst of his thoughts aside and made his way up to the suite.

Inside, Zach and Katie waited for him.

"Kids," he said, kneeling down. "I need you to promise me you won't answer the door for anyone but me when I leave."

"Where are you going?" Zach asked quickly.

"I have to go see someone, son. You and Katie will be alone for a little while. I left you guys some food in the cabinet, and there's lots of stuff on television."

"Where's Mom?" Katie questioned.

"I have to go find her, Katie. She's with the person I have to meet."

"Can we go home when you get back?"

"Yes. We'll go home."

As Clouse made his way to the elevator, he wondered if they would all make it home. He questioned whether he and Jane would be reunited. Most of all, he had to know who was responsible for all of the chaos in his life.

***

An hour later, all of the guests had finally left. Clouse spent much of the hour pacing the floors of the hotel, looking for any sign of Jane or the killer, finding nothing except departing families and further despair.

Trapped by his thoughts and worries, Clouse had forgotten to monitor which guests actually left the hotel, and to lock the doors to ensure no stragglers returned. As it was, everything was unlocked, and he had no idea what to expect.

Clouse walked along the third floor aimlessly, thinking about his wife, his kids, and how he could avoid getting everyone killed when he stopped at a triple glass panel in the hallway that overlooked the atrium below.

There, in the center, he could see the killer plainly among the colored floodlights from above and the sea of tables in every direction. For a moment, Clouse's eyes locked onto the cloaked form and the eyes behind the hood and mask. When Clouse bolted from the area the killer seemed to look in amazement to see where his prey had run off to, but Clouse soon reappeared in the adjacent room. Throwing open the double doors that led to the balcony, he seemed to regain his composure in the killer's view.

"What the hell do you want from me?" Clouse demanded. "What is it going to take to end all of this?"

Looking up, the killer stared before pointing to the suite on the sixth floor where Clouse had avoided going all night since Jane's abduction.

He stared up, finding the lights turned on, and a body of some sort hanging in the center of the room. From his vantage point, he could not tell who it might be, but he felt certain the person wasn't among the living.

"Damn him," Clouse said, looking down to the atrium.

Nothing except tables and the temporary stage could be seen.

"Ah, shit!" he said to himself, taking off for the nearest set of stairs. The elevator would take too long, and he was opposite the sixth floor suite anyway.

He shoved his way into the nearest stairwell and bolted up the stairs before stopping short of the fourth floor. Taking a moment to think, Clouse realized he was playing right into the killer's plan, just as he had before. He wanted to rush up there and see if his wife was okay, or even there, but he realized the killer was not just going to let him have his way.

Clouse decided to visit his room one last time before heading upstairs, but when he came to the suite's door, it was already ajar, and no kids were inside.

Every muscle in his body tensed, and Clouse felt his temperature rise. He wanted to kill the man responsible, he wanted to save Jane and avenge Daniels, and he wanted to know who had taken his last high school friend away from him.

"Motherfucker," Clouse cursed to himself, pounding the wall with his fist. He looked toward the beds and remembered the gun Daniels had loaned him was beneath one of them.

Darting to the bed, he pulled the case out from underneath, took out the gun, and began loading it. Feeling a bit warm and restricted, Clouse began to take off his jacket until an idea of a different sort struck him.

"I'll teach you to kidnap my kid and put me through all this bullshit," he muttered as he set the gun on the bed and began looking around the room for some other necessities before heading upstairs.

If it was meant to be the final confrontation with the man who had ruined the remains of his life, Clouse intended for it to be memorable, win or lose.

Chapter 37

Five minutes after visiting his room Clouse unlocked the door to the suite's lobby, sliding carefully past the one door as he stared at the corpse hanging in the center of the room. Slowly rotating toward him, he could hear the creak of the noose until the face of the body came into view.

"Brian," Clouse muttered upon confirmation of Kern's body.

Every piece of exposed skin was shriveled and red like a lobster. Kern had indeed been cooked alive inside the steam massager, and the lighter coloration around his mouth revealed no one had been able to hear his pleas for help because his mouth was taped shut.

Now his eyes were closed forever, too.

He dangled there, hands limp at his sides. Only the swimming trunks he had worn were still covering his body. Even Kern, slightly taller and as physically adept as Clouse himself, had been overpowered. The hotel's owner wondered what it would take to stop this predator.

A grim desperation covered Clouse's thoughts of everyone coming out alive. Even if his plan worked, there was no telling what booby-traps the killer might have left for him.

He reached for the keys in his pocket, fumbling them for a moment as he found the correct one for the suite. Taking a deep breath, Clouse let himself in, feeling something brush against his boot as he did so.

Clouse flipped the switch for the lights, but nothing happened. Forced to open the double doors for light, he discovered all the light bulbs had been removed. He also discovered Harold Simms' body sprawled across the floor at the threshold. The pale front and purple hue of his backside indicated Simms had not been murdered within the past few hours, and Clouse did not recall seeing the lawyer at all throughout the day.

He felt the revolver press against his back where he had placed it, and the urge to reach for it overwhelmed him, but he decided to press on and discover what other horrors awaited him in the suite.

Enough light entered the room that he could see the family room and the conference table, but the two bedrooms on opposite sides and the kitchen could not be seen with such weak light. Clouse quickly felt his way into the kitchen area to search the cupboards for the flashlight he had placed in there the year before with the intention that he and Jane might stay a night or two. He believed the new wiring might leave the hotel prone to power outages, so he wanted to be prepared.

He made his way to the closer bedroom, finding it and the inner bathroom devoid of life, or dead bodies. Clouse had little time to admire the beauty of the marble floor and walls inside the restroom, but he would have preferred to remain there a while longer and avoid the inevitable task of searching for signs of life. He wanted to find his wife and children alive, knowing the opposite discovery would remove any remaining will to live from him.

Still, he worked up the courage to cross the living area and examine the other bedroom, not noticing the main doors had closed somewhat since his entrance.

Clouse shined his flashlight beam across the second bedroom's floor, finding a motionless body beside the bed, hands tied behind the back, but no gag or additional restraints.

Kneeling beside the person, Clouse shined the light while feeling along the face and head to see who it might be. He felt blood along the scalp, shined his light across his hand and verified the fact, and pointed the beam into the face of the person.

"Randy," he said, realizing it was Niemeyer's younger brother.

His prodding hands had not stirred the younger man, and from the looks of the situation, he would be unconscious for some time. Clouse verified a pulse, thankful Niemeyer was alive before he moved toward the bathroom, hearing muffled cries as he did so.

"Jane!" he exclaimed in a hushed voice so no nearby serial killers would hear him. "Thank God you're alive," he said, removing her gag.

"Paul, be careful," she said immediately. "He's still around here."

"I know," he said, beginning to remove her bonds.

Beside her, a prone Katie was also bound and gagged.

Clouse paused a moment as he heard the front doors slam shut and no sound after that. His body felt numb with the realization that the killer was present, and the chances of escape had just deteriorated immensely.

"I'll be right back," Clouse said, leaving Jane to try and remove the rest of her bonds. He started toward the door of the bedroom, finding a jack-o-lantern set upon the conference table. It illuminated the area just enough to display the killer knelt down beside his possible next victim, holding a knife to Zach's throat.

"Welcome home, Paul," the voice said from beneath the hood, obviously lowered an octave or two for purposes of disguising it.

"What do you want, you sick fuck?" Clouse asked. "Let my boy go."

"First, I want you to throw that gun over here," the killer said.

Clouse hesitated, giving a purposely blank look.

"I saw you load it. Throw it over here now!"

Clouse pulled it out, hesitated a moment, and finally tossed it over to the killer's feet. He stood up, staring at the killer as a broken man, his only line of defense now gone.

"Very good," the killer said, lightly shoving an unrestrained Zach toward his father.

Clouse caught him, giving him a quick hug before defensively pulling him to his side.

"Put him in the room with the others," the killer ordered.

Clouse obeyed, urging Zach into the room, despite his son's protests.

"It'll be okay, son," he said.

"And shut the door," the killer commanded.

Clouse did so.

"None of them have seen my face, so maybe I'll let them live. After all, it's you who murdered my son and destroyed *my* life, so it's you who should pay, isn't it, Paul?"

Clouse stared at the costume a moment, sizing up the man inside it. He wondered who on earth could be beneath the black cloak. The candle inside the gutted pumpkin flickered, giving him a more of an eerie presence than normal. Given the fact he wielded a knife, and had just picked up the revolver from the floor, he seemed even more threatening.

"Still don't get it, do you?" the killer asked. "Who could possibly have knocked up Joan Landamere twenty-two years ago and given her a son while her hubby was away in Paris?" the killer asked rhetorically.

Clouse waited, growing a bit impatient, despite the threat of weapons.

"So, who the hell are you?"

"Someone you know entirely too well, Paul," the killer said, pulling down the hood, and taking off the mask beneath, revealing thick, black hair and a countenance almost as young as Clouse's own. "Or do you know me at all?" he asked, finally using his regular voice.

Clouse stared a moment at the features of the man. Though difficult to see in the low light, he began to picture the man with wrinkled skin, more of a hunched walk, and no desire to harm people whatsoever.

It seemed impossible, and Clouse felt afraid to utter the answer, afraid he was wrong, and even more fearful he was correct.

"Dr. Smith?"

Chapter 38

"How did it feel to have all that wealth and find yourself helpless when it came to finding your son?" the man across from Clouse asked. "That's exactly how I felt last year when I tried to save mine."

"How the hell can you be alive?" Clouse questioned aloud. "And how can you possibly look so damn young?"

"Oh, we have so much to talk about, my boy," Smith said, a smile laced with insanity crossing his face as he waved the gun and the knife about. "I'd offer you a seat, but I don't want you taking any *unnecessary* risks. You'll just have to stand while I explain everything to you."

"How?" Clouse asked plainly. "How can you be alive? How can you have shaved years off your life? How the fuck can you justify killing off almost everyone I care about? I thought I knew you, doc. What happened to the man who cared so much for this hotel, and about the people who worked for him?"

Smith simply bobbed his head in annoyance while Clouse spoke. It was obvious he was ready to simply explain himself, carry out his plan, and be done with all of it.

"Listen to you. Do you think I just did this for fun? And do you really think it's all just about you? Quit being so selfish, Paul, and shut up. You'll get all the answers you want, and then some."

Smith paced the room a bit, thinking about where to start.

"You want to know why I've been busy terminating some of your dearest friends? We'll start there.

"See, Paul, about twenty-two years ago when David Landamere was gallivanting around the world building his treasures, he was leaving his young wife home alone, and quite lonely she was. You know Joan and David never had a very secure marriage. Everyone around here knew it was a marriage of convenience, and that they each slept with whomever they wanted, whenever they wanted.

"Back in those days, though, I was already on my way to becoming a successful doctor, and the one thing I wanted my wife could never give me. Joan could not resist me, or my money when I offered to fill those lonely nights with, well, passion. And when Joan found out she was pregnant, she became desperate, fearing what would happen if David ever found out.

"I asked her to keep the baby, you see. I would personally take charge of her pregnancy outside of the hospital, and when Ryan was born, I also did the delivery. Everything was kept secret because Joan remained hidden in her estate for a year while David was overseas. He never knew the better.

"And when Ryan was born, I was overjoyed, but knew I could not keep him. At least not yet. I was still married, and there was no explaining such an incident to my wife without her demanding a divorce of me. See, Paul, I bided my time, waiting for my wife to die of, well, *natural* causes."

Clouse recalled his wife's passing several years back when the doctor first purchased the hotel. It seemed a rather sudden death as he recalled, though Smith said she had suffered slowly for some time.

"My son was worth the wait. *Well* worth the wait. You know how important sons are, don't you, Paul?"

Clouse stood stoically, unable to even nod in reply. The entire story numbed him to the point that he could only listen.

"At any rate, Ryan was born. We enjoyed him a few days and decided to part with him before we grew too emotionally attached. I wrapped him up in a basket and left him in front of the emergency room where he was soon picked up. After that, I kept a close eye on his adoption and his growth. The Andrews family gave him a good home, but the time came when I knew he was ready to meet his real father and take his place with me. Dave and Joan moved to St. Louis when he returned, and another potential menace was removed from my life."

"But they came back," Clouse noted. "And you set them on their killing spree?"

Smith held up a foreboding finger.

"That's not quite how it worked. When they returned, I gave David the job as the project manager to keep Joan happy and quiet. Joan had hinted that she might blackmail me for part of my estate, possibly with David's blessing."

"Blackmail? Publicly?"

"No. Worse. She planned to tell my wife. So, tragically, my wife had to leave this world."

Clouse shook his head in disbelief. He was beginning to see just how much of this entire three-year ordeal stemmed back to the one man he believed he could trust. A man who was supposed to be dead and buried.

"So now things were in the clear, Martin. Why turn David into a killer?"

"Oh, I didn't set David to his terrible deeds. He and Joan had a plan to take over the hotel, and find the alleged jewels on their own."

"But there were no jewels?"

"Not in the sense they were led to think. I was on my way to collecting artifacts for the hotel's restoration and I had a feeling David was intercepting some of them. That's why I set up an elaborate story and had them start on a wild goose chase."

Clouse looked to the floor, then back at the doctor.

"So what exactly were *you* looking for?"

"I had my own reason for hunting down old relics, but I couldn't do it alone. It was time to locate Ryan and tell him everything he was missing in life. It seems my son understood he was destined for something greater and he was more than happy to help me establish my Coven. He underwent a rite of passage by joining a powerful, and wealthy community. Ryan was my eyes and ears when he established the Coven.

"He was more than happy to help me in my search by pocketing the sheriff, a local banker, a real estate tycoon, the doctor to help slow your friend's rehabilitation, the local coroner, and a mortician."

"To cover up your death," Clouse deduced.

"Oh, and that wasn't easy, either. I was lucky Ryan kept you too busy to watch me plummet to my death. You never did see me fall, did you?"

"I saw you fall over the edge."

Smith grinned.

"But you never watched my daring stunt as I hooked myself on a rope at the last second and quickly scaled my way down. With my previous age and deteriorating condition, that was no easy feat. Rather dangerous if I say so myself. If I had missed, I would have died. If the release trigger that retracted the rope failed, you would have seen and suspected."

"A shame," Clouse said sarcastically.

"In a manner of speaking, yes. Perhaps then, you would never have murdered my son. Can you possibly understand what it's like to pick your son up at the side of the road, bleeding from his intestines? To operate on him for three agonizing hours only to have him die in your arms? Damn you, Paul, I could have made you understand by killing your precious Zach. And I still could if I wanted to."

"But it's not Zach you want, it's me," Clouse said, protective to the last in his attempt to reinforce Smith's reasoning that he was the responsible party.

"Maybe, maybe not. I could make you suffer like you did me."

"And you're not taking into account that you sent your son to kill me, my wife, and the only friend I have left in this world?" Clouse asked.

"My intent was never to kill all of you. The whole idea about using Zach to fetch the jewels was Joan's. I had nothing to do with that."

Clouse felt he had missed something.

"So you were working with Joan Landamere?"

"No, no," Smith said in an annoyed tone. "I let Ryan work with her because she heard of the Coven somehow and with David dead, wanted revenge on you and your friend Daniels. I figured she might be of use in helping me locate my item, so I had Ryan pair with her under the pretense he was seeking wealth and power, willing to do anything to obtain it.

"Because I never asked the Coven to kill for me, until Tim Niemeyer that is, Joan worked strictly with Ryan and the late Stephen, whom I understand you met. Everything was going smoothly until you murdered my son."

"You still haven't told me what it is you're after, doc."

"Maybe you aren't as intelligent as I figured you were. You read Father Runnels' diaries, didn't you?"

Clouse nodded.

"And you haven't put it together?"

Clouse simply stood and stared, a perplexed look crossing his face.

"Very well. I'll fill in the blanks."

"Please do."

"As you probably read, Ernest held a particular cross very near and dear to his heart. Have you ever heard of cursed objects, Paul?"

"I've *heard* of them. They're supposed to have a special purpose and give their users something they want, but there's always a price to the user's desire. I've always thought they were fable, something you see in the movies."

"Well, they're real, and Ernest's cross is one of those objects, or rather the gem embedded inside it is cursed. It wasn't until I was diagnosed with terminal cancer several years ago that I thought it necessary to seek out such an object. You see, the cross will heal all wounds and restore youthful nature for a price."

Clouse's eyes shifted as he thought back to the diary.

"You have to kill to satisfy it."

"Exactly. And that's how I've grown younger and more powerful right before you. Twice you've confronted me and both times, I've left you lying on the ground. I could never have wielded such power before."

"Was it worth it? I mean using your son only to have him die so you could survive?"

Smith sneered.

"You know that was never the idea. Everything was working perfectly. Ryan never knew Joan was his mother. I had described his mother as a wicked, tormenting woman who had died years before. He had no idea who she really was, and he agreed to kill her when we had finished with our search for the cross."

"Almost a perfect scam," Clouse conceded. "But you haven't explained exactly how you knew about the cross's power. Did you infer it from the diaries?"

"I never read the diaries," Smith revealed.

"Then how did you know?"

"I *lived* it, Paul," he said as though it were common knowledge. "I really can't believe you haven't put it all together yet."

Clouse's eyes widened with realization.

"*You* were Henry?"

"Martin Henry Smith is the name I eventually took. I truly befriended Ernest until I found out exactly what evil was behind his mask of deception. It was then that I had to destroy him before he harmed anyone else, so I locked him in the basement storage area, coated him with gasoline, and set him on fire. I escaped up the shaft and no one knew the difference.

"Eventually the priesthood sent me to college, and the Ernest legend was born after I became a bit tipsy at some fraternity parties and told a twisted version of the truth. It's amazing how much those stories carry through the years."

"My God," Clouse stammered. "So you killed Ernest with the best of intent and ended up just like him years later?"

"I suppose in a way, yes. Ironic how we both acquired similar fatal diseases, isn't it?"

"So why kill off your Coven?"

"It was inevitable. They blundered the only murder I sent them on, and it was only a matter of time before someone figured them out and traced them back to me."

"And why so much trouble over finding the cross? Why couldn't you have just located it without buying the hotel and setting up Joan and David?"

"Actually, both were quite necessary. I had no idea whether Runnels had hidden the cross on hotel property or the Hilton resort, and I had no idea what information David had already stolen from me, so I used them both to track down what I needed. I had no idea they would create such a maniacal plan, but I didn't care as long as they got me what I wanted.

"Runnels traveled to the resort occasionally, so it was conceivable he hid it there. That's the reason it burned several years ago. With the building gone, and the lot basically vacated, we were free to search the grounds and the tunnels beneath undetected, but we ran into a problem."

"And you needed a child to memorize the tunnels and get the cross for you because no adult could fit through the smallest parts."

"But he didn't. Your little bastard only found its former box and a partially burned map indicating where it had been moved to. It took me another two months after my son's death to locate the cross and plan my new life. In the meantime I kept a close eye on you and everyone important to you, right down to your babysitter."

Clouse stepped back, shaking his head.

"So all of this is about you and a search for this cross to save your own skin. I can't believe the last three miserable years of my life, my wife's death, losing everyone I loved and cared about, is all because you murdered them and stepped aside to let Dave and Joan Landamere kill in your name. I wish I had never gone to work at this place, and now I'm stuck with it."

"Not for long."

Smith let a grin slip across his lips as he patted the jack-o-lantern beside him.

"You know, I must say you were an innocent victim of circumstance. David developed quite a plan in tricking your brother-in-law to don this costume. I guess everything has come full circle. Hasn't it?"

"I suppose it has. And to think, you could have stopped all of this at any time. I have you to thank for every single murder that's happened the last three years because you were too damn selfish to just look for that fucking cross yourself."

"You have your version, I have mine. And when this is all over, I will reclaim my inheritance, my hotel, and my life. And you will just be a sore memory burned in the archives of my mind."

"It'll have to be in your mind, because you certainly don't have a soul."

Smith grinned, looked down to his knife, and pointed the gun at Clouse's head. The hotel's new owner stared at the barrel, waiting for Smith's next move, swallowing hard.

"The best part will be killing the rest of your clan and using their blood to continue my life," Smith revealed. "I'll especially take my time with your son, so he can understand what kind of suffering my Ryan endured."

"Fuck you!" Clouse said, taking a step forward.

"No, fuck you," Smith said, firing a shot toward Clouse's head.

Smith watched as the man's head whipped back, a stream of red mist emerging from his forehead. Clouse hit the ground with a heavy thud, his body lying motionless afterward.

He smiled with the satisfaction that his arch nemesis, the killer of his son, lie dead. He headed toward the room, taking enough time to bend over and examine Clouse's body, smearing some blood from the man's forehead along his fingertips. Feeling a crusty edge of skin in the blood, he grunted to himself before standing to finish his work in the other room.

The fun was just beginning.

Chapter 39

Smith barged into the other room just as Jane pulled the bonds from her wrists and Niemeyer began stirring woozily. Something hard and metallic had struck his head from behind, and he had no idea who was the responsible culprit.

His answer loomed above him, holding a knife, which glimmered in the faint light from outside the window blinds.

"You first, Mr. Niemeyer," Smith said, beginning to lean over for a better angle at the bound man's throat. "I killed your brother purely out of revenge, but your death will have a far greater purpose than you will ever comprehend."

"Fuck you, asshole," Niemeyer said, his words as pained as the throbbing in his head. "You obviously needed help with that one," he added, lifting both legs and squarely kicking Smith in the groin, sending him hurling back to one wall where the wind was knocked from him.

"Bastard," Smith sneered, lurking forward again to finish off the helpless Niemeyer.

Jane, now fully out of her restraints, tripped up the would-be killer with one foot. He had failed to notice her in the bathroom with Katie and Zach, his attention fully on his most capable victim. Now they had his full attention as he stood, tracing the knife with his thumb and forefinger, a haunting, evil look in his eyes.

He managed to take only one step toward them before a man's yell came from behind him and a force as large as himself tackled him into the adjacent wall. Jane saw her opportunity to scurry the kids out of the room as the man struggled with Smith for the knife. She stopped short of the door, peering through the darkness to see who it might be, but could not identify either shape in such low light.

She followed the kids in a direct path to the front door, kicking her husband's limp arm as she did so, not even realizing he lay in the center of the living area. Her first priority was the children and their safety.

In the midst of the struggle, Niemeyer managed to wriggle his way toward the door in the hope of finding a way to undo his bonds and help. As he neared the door, the two combative men fell over the bed and into him, knocking his already ailing cranium against the door, rendering him unconscious again.

"You don't give up easily, do you, detective?" Smith asked Daniels as they locked arms in an effort to gain control of the knife.

"I knew I should have blown your ass away from behind," Daniels said between labored breaths as he exerted every ounce of strength he could to wrestle the knife away from Smith. "I was afraid I might not get a clean shot at your head."

"I certainly didn't miss with your friend, and when the opportunity presents itself, I'll be happy to leave a hole in your cranium too," Smith said before throwing his elbow into Daniels' cheek. "Or maybe I'll just carve one instead."

"Don't bet on it," Daniels replied before launching his knee into the doctor's open groin area, protected only by a thin nylon cloak.

As Smith writhed in pain, Daniels sprinted into the other room where Smith had left the gun lying on the floor. He scooped it up, aiming it at the doctor as he entered the room, knife in hand, ready to bargain for his life if necessary.

Before he could utter a word, Daniels fired the gun into the chest of the attempted immortal, leaving a spatter of red where the slug found its mark.

Smith looked down at his chest, a look of shock crossing his face.

The shock did not come from the fact he was dying, but rather that there was extremely little pain from the impact. He reached down to swipe the blood away, realizing there was no blood at all.

In fact, there was no hole in his chest whatsoever.

"It's a splattering paint shell," Clouse said, rising to his feet, wiping the realistic paint away from his forehead. "They use them in movies, and if you search hard enough and spend the money, you can use them in your own firearm."

"But this one has real bullets," Daniels said, pulling a nine-millimeter from behind him where it had remained tucked into his belt.

"And they hurt from close distances," Clouse noted to Daniels, rubbing the sore spot along his forehead.

"Very clever," Smith said, maintaining his position near the door. "But you must consider caution with a firearm," he said, reaching behind him, "when a person has hostages," he finished, pulling Niemeyer to a seated position, placing the knife near the unconscious man's throat. "Wouldn't you say?"

"We're not letting you leave, doc," Clouse said.

"No, but you are going to throw that gun over here."

"Not a chance," Daniels said. "I'm not giving you a weapon to murder *me* with."

"Oh, yes you are, or there will be more blood on your hands," Smith retorted.

"All right then," Daniels said, removing the clip and the one bullet remaining in the chamber before tossing the gun to Smith. "Now you have the gun."

Smith sneered as Clouse held his hand out and Daniels dumped the bullets into it. The hotel's current owner then pocketed the ammunition with the slightest of grins crossing his face.

"Let's do this right, doc," he said. "Just you and I to the end. You knock me out a third time, you get the bullets and plug a hole in me. But be warned, I will beat you from one end of this hotel to the other for everything you've done to me."

"Very well," Smith said, "but we lock the other two in here and finish this in the hotel, as though it were our gladiator arena," he added with a dramatic wave of his arm.

"Fine. Toss me your cuffs, Mark."

Daniels complied, and Clouse allowed the doctor to step outside and cuff the door before the two stared each other down. Clouse could read the doctor's expression, but not his mind. Knowing he had enough fortune left from what he had withdrawn prior to his falsified death, Smith could flee the country and make a new life regardless. He stood only a moment, then took off, running for the nearby stairwell.

"No you don't!" Clouse yelled, giving chase, tackling Smith halfway down the spiraling staircase, sending them both tumbling downward to the fifth floor, the knife leaving the doctor's grasp, falling through the rails to the bottom floor.

The two wrestled along the landing momentarily until Smith struck his adversary with a right fist to the jaw that floored Clouse long enough for another escape attempt. He only made it to the next stairwell before he was hit from the side and rammed against a jutting corner, his spine impacting against the unforgiving corner.

Taking advantage of the injury, Clouse punched Smith squarely, twice in the jaw and several times in the stomach, weakening him while he could. Each time he felt the wind forced from Smith's lungs he drew more power and punched just a bit harder.

After all, there were a lot of people to avenge.

And to save.

Clouse still found it impossible to believe Smith had orchestrated his own death, and was basically accountable for everything the past three years. Almost three-dozen lives could be attributed to Smith's negligence and selfishness, and the time for retribution was at hand.

No matter the cost.

As he grabbed Smith by the collar and dragged him toward one of the doors left open from a tenant's departure, Clouse heard a gunshot ring out above him. He knew Daniels had recovered the revolver and used some of his own bullets to reload it and blast the handcuffs away to free himself.

It would be a matter of time before he could reach the area where the struggle now ensued, and Clouse hoped he would not be too late.

Smith felt his back bend along the top of the stairwell as Clouse pushed his torso over the top, leaning the doctor dangerously outward for a spill four stories below. Unwilling to simply be pushed over, or have his back injured any further, Smith punched for Clouse's throat, catching just enough of it to free himself and begin another escape toward the bottom of the hotel.

Clouse steadied himself against the wall, gasping for air a few seconds before following Smith's trail down the spiraling staircase. He saw the rejuvenated doctor the entire run down, but when they reached the bottom floor Smith opted to dart through the atrium, rather than try for the front door.

"You're not losing me, doc," Clouse warned, pursuing until he was able to draw close enough to dive at his adversary.

The leap resulted in him catching Smith's ankle and holding on, flooring the doctor with a tremendous thud as both landed on the tile near the atrium's edge. Both regained their footing quickly and Clouse blocked two quick punches thrown by the murderer, ducking a third, which landed Smith's hand into a statue behind Clouse.

A distinct snap was heard as Smith's fist impacted the concrete, and he knew at least one bone in his wrist was broken. Another kill with the aid of the cross would heal his new wound, and rejuvenate his youth in one fell swoop.

His hopes of murdering Clouse as planned sank with the fracturing of his wrist. Smith's only hope would be to escape and hide for some time, then return when his enemies least expected it, to finish his work.

"You might as well give it up," Clouse said as they stared each other down. "I'll be damned if I let you leave my sight again."

"You've already damned yourself and everyone around you," Smith sneered. He pulled the wooden cross from behind him, holding it like a knife. "This will make certain the blood leaking from your body after I kill you won't go to waste. It will be my greatest triumph."

"Did you use your own son's blood, doc?" Clouse taunted him. "Wouldn't want it to go to waste, would you?"

"You-" Smith began to say with an infuriated look before simply charging Clouse, tackling him to the floor before laying into the man's face with his good hand, now rolled into a fist.

Clouse managed to kick the doctor off of him, allowing Smith to think better of the situation. He scooped up his cross and darted toward the closest exit from the atrium. He appeared to have made it when Daniels stepped from behind the open arch, pointing a gun at the doctor's head.

"Seems you have some unfinished business here," the detective informed him.

"Please," Smith pleaded. "I have lots of leftover cash. I can make you rich."

"So can he," Daniels said, pulling another firearm from his side, tossing it to Clouse who sauntered toward him. It was the Magnum he had loaned him before, now loaded with real bullets.

Jane, the kids, and Niemeyer had walked in another entrance, approaching Clouse as Daniels monitored Smith with the gun. Clouse had a moment to think about exactly what he wanted to do, and when his son walked up, taking hold of his hand, he knelt down beside him.

"Are you okay, Zach?"

The boy nodded.

"I don't know what I would do if I ever lost you."

"Me too, Dad."

Zach squeezed his hand, and at that moment, Clouse knew exactly what he had to do.

Too many possibilities lingered in his mind about what Smith might ultimately do. He could run, hide, skip bail if he was placed in jail, or he could escape justice altogether with his funds and reclaim the fortune he had left Clouse under somewhat false pretenses.

He knew what needed to be done.

"Mark, can you take everyone outside and call the authorities? I'll finish up with the good doctor."

Daniels nodded, apparently suspecting what Clouse had in mind. In fact, the detective wanted no other ending after three years of torment. The only true way to put the entire conflict to rest was to lay Smith to rest.

As the detective led the others outside, Clouse paced a moment, wondering exactly how to kill in cold blood. Unlike Smith, he was usually incapable of such an act, but he noticed Smith's eyes darting toward the group, as though he knew it was his last chance to escape once they left.

Or to act upon his plan.

Using only a split second, Smith reached for the cross and hurled it toward Clouse in a swift underhand movement, like a fast pitch in girls' softball. Clouse managed to fire the weapon, winging Smith in the shoulder, before the cross's hard wood cracked him alongside the forehead, knocking him to the floor.

Smith wasted little time in recuperating and dashed toward the fallen weapon, but Clouse managed to trip him as he ran past, allowing him to mount Smith's chest and fire a series of punches toward the doctor's face as retribution for a few minutes earlier.

Throwing his hands up in self-defense, Smith tried to block the melee, but this only allowed Clouse to take hold of his hair and thrust the back of his head into the unforgiving concrete below, taking Smith to the brink of unconsciousness.

Seeing the doctor's eyes begin to roll back, Clouse picked up the cross, tossed it away from both of them, and walked toward the fallen revolver. He had just bent over to pick it up when he realized Smith was charging him, and it was already too late to swing the gun around, so he fired a round into the floor, dropping the weapon as he was leveled to the ground by the weight of his adversary.

Both rolled around the floor, struggling for control, each sensing the loss of energy and momentum during their battle. As they regained their footing, Clouse threw a hard right punch that sent Smith spiraling toward the next open arch in the atrium before he collapsed upon the floor. Weary, but standing, Clouse stumbled toward the open arch, looking at the base of the winding staircase when

Smith found the energy to charge him once more as he bent over to look at something familiar.

Smith's eyes widened with the realization of a mortal wound puncturing his body when Clouse raised his right hand, thrusting the knife dropped early in their struggle into his abdomen, creating a gaping slit. The fresh gash no hope of survival without immediate medical assistance due to internal and conventional bleeding.

As Clouse stood, he watched Smith writhe in pain momentarily, the blood leaking from his insides as it stained the once beautiful tile floor at the edge of the atrium. He had no evil looks for Clouse at this point. Groping for the cross too far from his reach, Smith seemed to realize his mortality, and how the last three years of perpetrating and orchestrating gruesome murders were about to catch up with him.

"Hope you enjoy hell," Clouse said under his breath.

Groaning his last breath, the doctor expired a few minutes later, sprawled painfully across the floor. Standing over him, unable to believe the agony in his life was finally over, Clouse sighed an exasperated breath.

Daniels rushed in the opposite end of the grand room, looking somewhat perplexed at the sight of Clouse standing over a stabbed Smith.

"I thought you were just going to shoot him."

"I was," Clouse said, walking toward his friend. "But I guess that would have been too easy."

"And we don't like it easy, do we?" Daniels said, forcing a grin as the two met halfway and shook hands, giving a quick hug, as though they were military buddies surviving a war together.

In many ways, they had.

Epilogue

While all of the kids dashed from the minivan toward the wooden dock seated between the chalet and Lake Monroe, the adults took a bit more time unloading suitcases and coolers from the vehicle.

It was late spring, six months after the traumatic events at the hotel. Clouse and Daniels had agreed to take some time off from their working lives to take their families camping at some land Clouse had purchased in the off-season. After tearing down the existing cabin, he had hired a company to build a custom chalet along the lake where they loved to go boating during the warm months.

Most of the past two days had been spent at the theme park Clouse now owned, and the kids loved the rides and the behind-the-scenes tour of the facility before it opened on the second day. Even so, they were anxious to be home again.

In the end, everything had worked out perfectly.

Clouse kept his estate, and the money, but donated heavily to local charities, and started several of his own. He owned property around the country, and opened a few businesses he and Jane had always thought about running.

"Who cares if we make money?" he asked his wife when they opened.

Simply living their dream and employing hundreds of people was reward enough for the couple to feel reasonably certain they could manage businesses if they brought in the right people.

Tackett survived his attack, returned to work within a few months, and received a promotion in the newly revamped county police department.

Clouse financially aided Brian Kern's wife, along with several other surviving family members of friends he lost. He could never bring his friends back, and though he knew he was in no way directly responsible for any of their deaths, a hint of guilt always rested in the back of his mind like dust on a shelf.

Randy Niemeyer had finished his degree in law enforcement and began pursuing jobs where he would be able to do investigations, especially homicide. His brother's death seemed to haunt him, but in such a way that he understood how families felt. He planned to better help victims who lost loved ones cope while bringing killers to justice.

When Clouse had a new building constructed for his business with Jane, he ordered a certain metal chest, containing a certain wooden cross, to be buried ten feet beneath the concrete bed of the building. He watched every step of the process until the chest was most definitely in an unrecoverable state.

Police never quite understood how Smith could have still been alive, but with help from Daniels, Clouse was able to reconstruct the doctor's evil plan, leaving out the supernatural occurrences of course, and explain most of why Smith had done the things he did. In no way had the will been altered, so Clouse kept his inheritance, even if he had killed his benefactor.

After the incidents of the past three years and the discovery of their origin, Clouse researched the crucifix and found similar items existed, possibly closer to home than he imagined. In time, he decided, he would take steps in recovering the items to avoid them falling into the wrong hands, causing the pain he knew from experience.

Though he doubted he would personally search for such items, Clouse could afford to hire people loyal enough to trust, and ambitious enough to continuously search, no matter how frivolous the results might seem at times.

Overall, life seemed as good as could be expected, but Clouse felt a void in his life knowing Ken Kaiser, Tim Niemeyer, and his first wife, Angie, were taken from him. He knew he wouldn't be seeing them again after their brutal, unwarranted murders.

"Not in this life anyway," he said, looking up to the sunny sky above toward the heavens.

"What?" Jane asked, holding his hand as they walked toward the dock where the kids were already wading their feet in the warm water.

"Nothing."

Daniels set down a cooler outside of his vehicle taking Cindy's side as they walked toward his friends. Watching the kids with a grin, he knew they would never be in the same amount of danger Smith had placed them in.

"Can't wait to see the place," Daniels commented as they walked down a set of wooden steps that eventually led to the dock, or branched off to resorts on either side of them.

Clouse reached into the pocket of his shorts, pulling out a set of keys.

"Feel free," he said, handing them to his friend. "It's all yours."

Daniels turned to head toward the door, then realized what Clouse had said, or rather, meant.

"What do you mean, all mine, exactly?"

"I mean I had this place built for you two," Clouse replied, both he and Jane smiling as Daniels and Cindy exchanged shocked looks.

Behind them stood a two-story chalet equipped with everything a luxury home could hold, and it overlooked one of the best areas of the lake, secluded away from every other cabin on the lake, aside from one.

"Yeah, that one's ours," Clouse said, looking to the cabin next door, nearly identical in structure.

"You're kidding," Daniels said, letting out a bit of an exasperated laugh. He had no idea what to say or do. "We really can't-"

"Sure you can," Jane said. "They're both already built. We wanted to do something special for you two."

"You always said your dream vacation was camping on the lake," Clouse said to Daniels. "Now you can do it anytime you want."

Daniels struggled for the words to thank his friend, but Zach ran up and saved him the trouble, grabbing his father's hand.

"Can you tell us ghost stories tonight, Dad? Around the fire?"

"Sure, Zach. I think Mark wants to show you how to fish later, too."

"Cool!" Zach said, giving Daniels a toothy smile before rushing back to tell the other kids.

"I can't thank you enough," Daniels said. "*We* can't thank you enough," he quickly corrected, his arm tightly wrapped around his wife's shoulder.

Clouse turned to look at the kids and the beautiful lake behind them.

"I've been thinking a lot lately," he said. "And the two things I've realized are that money doesn't buy true happiness, and it doesn't replace the things you've lost in your life. The ones you truly care about."

"Everything happens for a reason, doesn't it?" Jane questioned, taking hold of his forearm, realizing she was not a replacement for his first wife, but in many ways had provided a healthier lifestyle for him, and stuck around through the bad times.

"Amen to that," Clouse said, giving her a quick kiss.

All four looked into the sky behind the lake as the sun began to set with a red glow, glistening along the trickling waves of the lake. Finally, a peaceful, relaxing dusk was upon them, and they could rest easier, taking the road to recovery one day at a time.